EMPIRES AND KINGDOMS

REBELLION and DECEIT

David Eugene Andrews

Glenhaven Press

Laguna Hills, California

Dedication

This book is dedicated to my older brother, Bill Andrews, who helped proofread the manuscript of Rebellion and Deceit.

Table of Contents

Table of Contents iv

Prologue 1

Chapter 1 — *Sipahi* Horsemen 6

Chapter 2 — Demands at the Divan 14

Chapter 3 — Imperial Harem 21

Chapter 4 — Dutch *Odalisque* Dilara 32

Chapter 5 — Duke of Mercoeur 42

Chapter 6 — Second Spanish Armada 45

Chapter 7 — Triple Alliance 55

Chapter 8 — Secret Negotiations 61

Chapter 9 — War Horses at Ostend 70

Chapter 10 — Ancient Customs & Privileges 79

Chapter 11 — Sir Francis Vere 86

Chapter 12 — Fast March to Turnhout.. 93

Chapter 13 — Red Lentil Soup 100

Chapter 14 — Eunuchs and Viziers 107

Chapter 15 — Enemies of the Eunuchs 115

Chapter 16 — Warning at Turnhout Castle 125

Chapter 17 — Hasten to the Heath 133

Chapter 18 — Battle of Tielenheide 141

Chapter 19 — Thirty-Eight Captured Flags.. 150

Chapter 20 — We Gather Together 155

Chapter 21 — Forty *Ich-Oglans* 163

Chapter 22 — *Sanjak* of Pécs 172

Chapter 23 — Necessity and Despair 181

Chapter 24 — Weep Over the Graves 194

Chapter 25 — Bands of Lusty Men 199

Chapter 26 — *Marquise* Gabrielle d'Estrées 205

Chapter 27 — Spilt Nuts and Apples 218

Chapter 28 — Thunderbolt Marshall *de* Biron 227

Chapter 29 — Abandoned by his Friends 238

Chapter 30 — Chief Gardener Ferhad *Agha* 248

Chapter 31 — Garden Organ and Palace Poem 256

Chapter 32 — Shut inside Kutahya 263

Chapter 33 — Pozega Spoils 272

Chapter 34 — *Stamboul* Slave Market 276

Chapter 35 — Candle Workshop 282
Chapter 36 — Green Fountain 288
Chapter 37 — Captain Francisco *del* Arco.................................. 295
Chapter 38 — Velvet Siege Begins 302
Chapter 39 — Talks Abruptly End 309
Chapter 40 — Maximilien *de* Bethune 317
Chapter 41 — Building a Platform 328
Chapter 42 — Arrival of the King's Mistress 335
Chapter 43 — Unmatched Fury 341
Chapter 44 — Victory or Death 346
Chapter 45 — Mining and Sapping 354
Chapter 46 — Mussels and Oysters 359
Chapter 47 — Styrian Border Raids 362
Chapter 48 — Beautiful Bursa 370
Chapter 49 — Bribes and Corruption 380
Chapter 50 — Admiral, Count, & Cardinal 384
Chapter 51 — More Dangerous Thoughts 394
Chapter 52 — Cardinal's Relief Army Advances 400
Chapter 53 — Henry IV Encounters the Cardinal 406
Chapter 54 — Right of Conquest 412
Chapter 55 — Aisha Reacts and Filia Departs 418
Chapter 56 — Winter Quarters of the Ottoman Sultan..................... 420
Chapter 57 — Dance and Music Room 424
Chapter 58 — Clockmaker's Letter 436
Chapter 59 — Rebellion Reaches Bursa 442
Chapter 60 — Safiye *Valide Sultana's* Court 449
Chapter 61 — Castle of the Seven Towers 453
Chapter 62 — Grand Mufti Sun'Ullah *Effendi*............................. 458
Chapter 63 — Not for Justice, but Necessity 464
Chapter 64 — Inside her Palace.. 475
Glossary 477
      Glossary of Terms 477
      Glossary of People 485
      Glossary of Place 494
Acknowledgements 499
About the Author 499

EMPIRES AND KINGDOMS

Rebellion
and
Deceit

Prologue

Which ere long he [Grand Vizier Yemisci Hasan Pasha] would present her [Aisha, Sister of the Sultan], whose ransoms should adorn her with the glory of his conquests.
Captain John Smith

Salon, Ibrahim *Pasha* Palace, Stamboul, Rajab, AH 1011 (Dec. *AD* 1602)

FRENCH TRANSLATOR FILIZ finished sipping her coffee and placed her tiny cup on the low table. "The runaway carriage must have frightened King Henry's mistress."

"Gabrielle could have been killed!" Aisha *Sultana*, sitting cross-legged on the cushioned platform, echoed her friend's sentiments.

"If the wheels of the second carriage had not miraculously fallen off, Gabrielle d'Estrées would have died, thrown over the cliff," Captain John Smith agreed. "Both she and her unborn child most certainly would have perished."

The young widow, Aisha, questioned her English slave, "So Gabrielle gave birth?"

Filiz translated the Turkish into French.

"*Oui*, to a girl in Rouen," John, speaking French, replied. "King Henry IV declared their daughter legitimate. He had Catherine-Henriette *de* Bourbon baptized at the Abbey of St. Ouen in Rouen. All of the important clergy of France participated, but the Cardinal of Florence waited in Paris until after the ceremony. This Papal Legate would not go to the ceremony, since King Henry had not legally married Gabrielle."

"I understand, religion has its rules." The young widow, Aisha, like her brother Sultan Mehmet III, was born within the Imperial Harem of the New Palace. Though her father, Sultan Murad III, had not officially married their mother, Safiye, Aisha, like all royal children born into the Imperial Harem, was considered legitimate. While her father was alive, her mother was known as *Bash Kadin or* Chief Lady, since her eldest son, being the firstborn of the Sultan, would inherit the throne. Her mother, however, had not legally married her father, as tradition and law forbade it. Islamic religious advisors spoke most adamantly against the practice.

Aisha told her French translator, Filiz, "Authorities did not want my great-grandfather, Suleiman *the Magnificent,* to marry Hürrem *Haseki Sultana.*" Aisha remembered the story of how Hürrem *Haseki Sultana,* a favorite of Suleiman *the Magnificent,* wanted to build a mosque in her own name. That was something a *kadin* was forbidden to do. All concubines and *kadins* were considered to be slaves of the Sultan. Because they had birthed the sultan's children, *kadins* had their own apartments inside the Imperial Harem. Notably, though, the mosque complex could only be constructed in the Sultan's name.

Known as Roxelana, reflecting her Ukrainian birthplace, Hürrem persuaded the Sultan to declare her free woman. As soon as he did, Roxelana, a *kadin* because she birthed the Sultan's child, refused to sleep with him unless he legally married her. When Suleiman relented and married Roxelana, her son became heir to the throne, usurping the right of the Sultan's firstborn. Turmoil in the Imperial Harem ended only after her rival and her son were sent far away, to Manisa, beyond Bursa in Anatolia. Hürrem kept the title of *haseki,* since she was the Mother of the Prince.

"The Cardinal of Florence did not delay his journey for very long," Captain John Smith said, "for the Cardinal soon arrived in Rouen, staying at the plush *Hotel de* Bourtheoulde."

"The storm that struck the Second Spanish Armada?" Aisha asked. "So many sailors died."

"More Spanish soldiers and sailors died in their winter quarters at Ferrol than in the turbulent storm."

Aisha shook her head at the folly. "But the rich Spanish King went bankrupt?"

"King Philip II blamed it on Spanish gold spent in the Lowlands. He did not like having his most talented men entering banking instead of serving him at his Court."

"*Capitano,* you decided not to go to Scotland?"

"My purse was almost empty, so I chose to stay in France. Captain Joseph Duxbury recruited me to fight alongside him."

"Aisha!"

Harsher than normal, the tone of her mother's voice startled the noblewoman. Somehow, she had not seen her cross the garden. Similar to a brood circling about a mother hen, her maid servants circled the *Valide*

Sultana at the door. When *Capitano* John Smith rose, the eyes of Aisha's younger sister, Fatima, the wife of Khalil *Pasha*, the former governor of Constantinople, widened.

"Mother!" Aisha exclaimed. "We didn't expect you back so soon."

"I can see." Her mother raised her hands and showed her palms.

Her mother's indignant expression spoke volumes.

Aisha gestured to her slave. "The *Capitano* told Filiz and me how he went to Paris and Rouen. He received ten shillings from his father's estate and traveled freely."

"Ten shillings? That certainly does not sound like much."

"It is not."

"Perhaps the slave is just trying to protect the wealth of his family." Her mother peered directly at John. "What does he know about France, anyway? The slave is from Bohemia. *Yemisci* Hasan *Pasha* told us. The slave probably lies, too."

"John is no liar," Aisha insisted. "He's English."

"Though I like Queen Elizabeth, most English are pirates and liars. Besides, if the 'Bohemian' slave is not rich, then he should be working. Do you think we run a charity?"

Queen Elizabeth had given Saifye *Valide Sultana* a fancy white carriage. She also gave the sultan a magnificent organ.

"Not until your New Mosque is built."

Construction on the mosque overlooking the Golden Horn had been suspended.

Filiz reached for her *hijab*. "Perhaps I should leave?"

Her mother nudged her younger daughter, Fatima, forward to help her.

"No need, sister." Aisha escorted the French translator to the door. "Thank you again for all your help, Filiz."

Her mother stepped aside. "Do come back again."

Before the door closed, her mother clapped her hands. "Overseer!"

The muscular Black eunuch quickly appeared. "Yes, Safiye *Valide Sultana*?"

"Take the Bohemian slave to his quarters!"

As the overseer of the harem of the Palace of Ibrahim *Pasha* escorted John through the garden, the young widow stepped towards the Vaulted Chamber, her apartment. The Palace had been named for the Grand Vizier of Suleiman *the Magnificent*, who had built it, and not for *Damat* Ibrahim *Pasha*, Aisha's late husband.

"Aisha, where are you going?" Her mother gestured to the sofa. "Now sit down."

"The day has been long." Aisha feigned a tired voice.

"We must find out who will pay the ransom for your slave."

"Do you not believe I am trying?" Aisha attempted to make herself comfortable.

Her mother moved closer. "We cannot keep feeding your slave forever."

"John must have received a reward from someone."

"Unless he stole the clothes he wears."

"John's no thief; he has been recruited."

"Recruited?"

"Captain Duxbury recruited him. How else could he have met *Yemisci* Hasan *Pasha*?"

Yemisci meant 'Fruiterer,' a name given to the Grand Vizier because of the skills he learned as a youth while tending the fruit trees in the imperial gardens. Called *Pasha* or leader, *Yemisci* Hasan *Pasha* had been promoted to *Beylerbey* or Governor of Governors before he became Grand Vizier. Before the Ottoman army retired for the winter, the Grand Vizier had led nearly of 100,000 *sipahis* and *janissaries* in their fight against the Holy Roman Empire in southeastern Europe.

"So, you do believe the Grand Vizier?"

"I must. You arranged for *Yemisci* to marry me." Aisha had become a widow less than a year earlier, when the previous Grand Vizier passed away.

"Yes, he did pay the *kabin* of four thousand ducats, but if the Bohemian slave is rich, when are you going to receive the ransom money?" Similar to a dowry, but paid by the groom or his family, the *kabin* formalized an Ottoman marriage contract.

"As soon as I find out where it is," Aisha said. "Before he declared bankruptcy, King Philip II of Spain complained his gold and silver ended up in his enemy's hands in Holland."

"Holland?"

"John mentioned to Filiz that he might go to Holland. The Dutch have become rich traders."

"Yes, I have heard that, but when will you get the money?"

"Stop your worrying, Mother."

Vaulted Chamber, Palace of Ibrahim *Pasha*

THE HEAD MAIDSERVANT of Aisha's Vaulted Chamber delivered the letter. "Your overseer says it's from the Grand Vizier. The messenger from Belgrade arrived after dark."

"From my betrothed?" The Sister of the Sultan brought the letter next to the candelabra and scanned the writing. "The Grand Vizier promises to send me more captains."

With a twinkle in her eye, her servant smiled. "Like Captain John Smith?"

Aisha refused to respond. "He still insists I keep the ransoms for myself."

"*Yemisci* Hasan *Pasha* must not know."

"And you will not tell him about John."

"Are you worried?"

"About the Grand Vizier? Since the armies of the Holy Roman Empire have retired for the winter, I am certain the Grand Vizier is safe, at least until spring."

The full moon illuminated the palace chimneys rising above the domed kitchens. Her servant reached up and drew the long drapes of the vaulted chamber.

Leaning back on her pillows, Aisha reflected on the stories John had told her that day. She loved hearing about France, but John was no longer a youth. Captain Joseph Duxbury had recruited her English slave to train him to become a soldier.

Nothing could deter Aisha. *I must discover the truth.*

Chapter 1 — *Sipahi* Horsemen

Atmeidan, Stamboul, Ottoman Empire, Rajab AH 1011 (Dec. AD 1602)

"MAKE WAY! AISHA, Sister of the Sultan!" The crier ran ahead of Aisha's carriage as it departed the First Courtyard of her stately abode. "Make way! Make way!"

Two oxen pulled the covered *araba* and exited the main gate of the Palace of Ibrahim *Pasha,* turning up the *Atmeidan,* the ancient Hippodrome of Constantinople. When she felt a bump, Aisha pulled back the draped curtains. Several escorts ran alongside. She opened them further and showed countless horsemen to Beatrice, the Venetian sister of Gazanfer *Agha,* the Chief White Eunuch. "So many *sipahis.*"

Similar to the knights in Christendom, these well-armed Turkish horsemen served as Ottoman cavalry during the fighting season. They carried long lances, bows and arrows, and curved swords.

The Venetian matron, seated next to Aisha on the cushioned seat, leaned forward. "My husband Ali told me that more *sipahis* have returned from the frontier."

Campfires dotted the largest open space in *Stamboul*—500 paces long and 400 paces wide. Though the Greek and Roman chariot races depicted on one side of the stone base of the Obelisk of Theodosius had long ceased, games on horseback were often held after Friday prayers. Beyond a second tall obelisk and an Oriental Plane tree to her right, the *sphendone*, the rounded-end portion of the former stadium, remained intact. Between the two obelisks, a third statue had serpents wrapped around a pole. The mouths of their three heads opened upward, warding off the snakes that once plagued the former capital of the Byzantine Empire.

Other portions of the ancient stadium no longer stood. Stones from the dismantled stands of the Hippodrome provided the foundation of her palace, as well as the Palace of the *Kaimakam,* the governor of the largest city in Europe. Large stones for other palaces arrived by ship over the Sea of Marmara from the ruins of ancient Troy in Anatolia, Asia Minor.

"*Sipahis* from Belgrade?" Aisha asked. "Did they bring any word about *Yemisci* Hasan *Pasha?*"

"Nothing new from your betrothed," Beatrice responded. Her husband, the *Agha* of the *Janissaries,* had negotiated the marriage contract between Aisha and the new Grand Vizier, second only to the Ottoman Sultan in power. "The Khan of the Crimean Tartars will winter in Hungary. With such strong allies, the Grand Vizier will be safe."

"But the *sipahis*?" Aisha recognized the dress of the riders encamped on the other side of the obelisks lining the stadium's spine. "Why have not they returned to Anatolia?"

"Perhaps the *Celali* rebellion." Beatrice referred to the name of a deceased leader of an earlier rebellion.

"If only we had peace."

"Like when your brother was circumcised?"

"The festivities here lasted for days," Aisha said. "When I was a young girl, I watched with my mother behind that latticed balcony, while my father, Sultan Murad III, viewed the happenings from the palace balcony by the Second Courtyard. Dignitaries and ambassadors observed the festivities from newly built wooden stands, three stories tall."

"There were parades?" Beatrice had immigrated from Venice years after the festivities.

"On the third day, the *sultanas* arrived, accompanied by large works of shaped sugar, built on wagons and pulled by fifteen horses—eight dressed in red damask and seven in silver. Other delightful works of confectionery included nine large elephants and twenty-one camels, both single and double-humped."

"Sounds delightful."

"Plays and shows took place in that section over there." Aisha pointed to a small circle of ruins, remnants of an outdoor Greek theatre.

"And your brother?"

"After he was circumcised, he was sent away to be Governor of Magnesia in Anatolia."

"Beyond Bursa and Mount Olympus?"

The snowcapped mountain in Asia Minor could be seen on a very clear day.

"Both my brother and I were born in Magnesia. Before my father became Sultan, he had been appointed governor of Magnesia, too."

Her carriage sped towards the New Palace, the *Seraglio* of her brother, Sultan Mehmet III, the most powerful monarch on earth. Commonly referred to as the *Sublime Porte*, the New Palace was the seat of power for the entire Ottoman Empire, an empire that stretched from Bosnia and Hungary to Baghdad and Mecca, from Yemen and Egypt to Algiers and its tributary, the Kingdom of Morocco.

The carriage turned after it reached the *Hagia Sophia*, a huge domed building at the far end of the Hippodrome. Nearly 1300 years earlier, the Byzantine Emperor Justinian had built the main Christian Church of

Constantinople high on the first of the seven hills of the city that Emperor Constantine once called the New Rome.

"When Emperor Justinian saw the *Hagia Sophia,* he pronounced, 'Solomon, I have surpassed thee'," Beatrice said.

"He was talking about the Temple of Solomon in Jerusalem?"

"Yes, a few decades after the crucifixion of Jesus Christ, the pagan Romans attacked Jerusalem and carried many items away from the rich temple to Rome."

After Mehmet the Conqueror captured the city 150 years earlier, the Turks transformed the *Hagia Sophia* into the Great Mosque of *Stamboul.* Almost every Friday, Aisha's brother, Sultan Mehmet III, crossed the roadway from the New Palace to visit it.

Morning prayer had long passed, but a muezzin would soon climb one of the four tall minarets and issue the call for the second prayer of the day. For now, the large mosque and the mausoleum built next to it seemed quiet. Her father, who died of natural causes, was interred there, along with nineteen half-brothers. Immediately after her brother acceded to the Ottoman throne, they were circumcised and killed. No matter how young, rivals would not be permitted to challenge Sultan Mehmet III's earthly authority.

The broad roadway next to the *Hagia Sophia* grew crowded. A mosaic mix of not only Greeks and Turks, but also Arabs and Moors from North Africa caused the carriage to slow beneath the New Palace walls.

Those walls, forming a triangle and extending for several miles, encompassed the New Palace at the most pleasant part of the city, the tip of a peninsula. One side of the triangle faced the city, now crowded with nearly one million people, but the other two sides faced water. The north wall faced the Golden Horn, the deep harbor that separated *Stamboul* from Galata. On the distant hill, the Galata Tower rose above compounds housing foreign ambassadors from Venice, France, and England. The third wall faced the Sea of Marmara beyond the crest of the hill rising straight ahead. That sea, named for an island where marble was mined, connected the Bosphorus and the Dardanelles, the two straits leading to the Black and Aegean Seas, and separating Europe from Asia. In short, *Stamboul* stood at the crossroads of the world.

The carriage angled around a covered wagon used by *Janissaries*— the loyal foot soldiers of the Sultan—during their night watch.

The street grew even more crowded with merchants from Egypt, Armenia, and Albania. All stepped aside when *sipahi* officers trotted forward. Imperial gatekeepers waved the leaders and their escorts forward.

"Merchants who want to see the Sultan?" Beatrice asked.

"Many want to sell goods," Aisha said, "but others seek justice."

"From your brother?"

"Or the *Kaimakam* and the Council at the Divan."

With the absence of the Grand Vizier in Belgrade, the *Kaimakam* chaired the ruling council.

Imperial Gate, New [Topkapi] Palace, *Stamboul*, Ottoman Empire

THE CARRIAGE SLOWED outside the Imperial Gate. Aisha reached and opened the shutters on the left side. She sat back when she saw the large niche built into the wall. The Sister of the Sultan recognized the severed head placed inside. It belonged to a White Eunuch and still had its eyes wide open. Next to the nook, a triangular scroll recognized the criminal in bold writing. It read: *To be a warning to those who would be warned.*

"Do you know what he did?" Aisha asked.

"I heard that the eunuch was caught trimming bushes in the lower gardens."

"That is no crime," Aisha responded.

"But the Black eunuchs yelled *'Hevlet'*."

"To announce my brother was escorting one of his concubines?" Aisha asked. "So this White eunuch was a gardener?"

"No longer. He did not hear, or did not heed the warning."

"Truly, he must not have heard." Aisha reread the scroll.

On the other side of the gate, a second mitered niche held another skull. A second scroll detailed his crime.

Fifty gardeners were assigned to guard the Imperial Gate. Some of them carried bows and arrows, others bore firearms. One of them, carrying a scimitar at his side, stopped the carriage. "State your business."

"Do you not recognize the carriage?" The driver pointed to an old *Janissary* and the Black eunuchs. "I bring the Sister of the Sultan to the Imperial Harem."

"Do they know you are coming?"

Aisha, who recognized the turbaned leader of the gatekeepers, opened the shutters further. "*Kupuji-Bashi* Hasan!"

As soon as the *kapuji-bashi* saw the Sister of the Sultan, he waved. "Let them go by!"

The gatekeepers occupying the arched entryway stepped aside, and as the carriage moved forward, Beatrice leaned toward Aisha. "They should not have stopped you."

Aisha tilted her head and raised her hands. "No." She told the head gatekeeper as they passed him, "You've trained your men well."

As the carriage entered the Courtyard of the *Janissaries*, daylight brightened the white turban of a bearded official. The *Bostangi Bashi*, or Chief Gardener, brought his small horse alongside the carriage. The Chief Gardener had charge of not only the palace gardeners, but also the palace guards. "Sister of the Sultan, did you experience a problem?"

"No, Ferhad *Agha*," Aisha replied. "Your new gatekeepers performed their duties."

"I instructed them to be extra careful."

"Careful?"

"Just rumors. I am sure it is nothing." He glanced at a group of *sipahi* riders watering their horses. "Let me escort you to the Gate of Greeting."

The number of horses surprised Aisha, since only *pashas* and other great men were allowed to ride into the palace.

Beatrice lowered her veil. "Have you seen my brother?" Although she had accepted Islam after she had arrived in *Stamboul*, many believed she remained a Christian in her heart.

"I did not recognize you, Fatima Hatun." The Chief Gardener called Beatrice by the name of the youngest daughter of the Prophet Mohammed—given to her when she moved to the city. "Your brother Gazanfer remains with the Sultan, but your husband Ali and the Deputy Grand Vizier, Hasan *the Clockmaker*, stay in the Divan."

Courtyard of the *Janissaries*, New [Topkapi] Palace, *Stamboul*

THE CARRIAGE LUMBERED slowly into the Courtyard of the *Janissaries*—a large, irregular-shaped plaza. Beyond the road to their right stood the hospital serving all of the New Palace, except the Imperial Harem. Guards stood at the front door, next to the White eunuch who ran the facility.

"My brother told me new *Janissary* cadets are assigned to the hospital," Beatrice said. "But I am always amazed at how young they look."

The *janissary* cadets, called *acemi oglan*, wore robes and hats shaped like long cones.

"The novice boys in this courtyard do not go to war," Aisha informed Beatrice. When the carriage stopped, she leaned out the window. "What is the delay?"

"Two ox-drawn carts," her driver responded.

Two wagons filled with firewood had crossed their path. On the near side of the hospital, more oxen struggled up the hill. Arriving from both east and west, ships and galleys had brought the fuel across the Sea of Marmara to the royal docks below. Though now anchored in calm seas, as soon as they had finished unloading, pilots would take their vessels to their next destination. Some would sail a short distance to the Golden Horn, the protected harbor on the other side of the New Palace, but others would travel across the Mediterranean to other Ottoman lands.

"So much wood." Beatrice pointed across the wide courtyard to the stacks beyond the armory, the former Church of St. Irene.

"I hope it is not as cold as the last two winters," Aisha replied in Italian.

The first wagon reached the woodpile, and servants began immediately to unload it, adding the firewood to the huge stack, already piled yards high.

"At least there should be enough wood for the kitchens."

"*Si*, Beatrice."

The firewood would heat the countless rooms of the palace, as well as fire the multiple ovens in the nine kitchens lining the right side of the next courtyard.

Beyond the wood stack, riders dismounted in front of full stables. Above the stables, a long gallery stored more armaments.

"More *sipahis*?" Aisha asked as the carriage resumed its journey. It rolled slowly straight ahead, toward the Gate of Greeting, less than one hundred yards away. Two cylindrical towers, topped by upside-down cones, framed this second gate. Sharp iron spikes extended above the battlements between the two parapet towers. "The last time I was here, a skull of a *pasha* was attached to one."

"Not all heads are taken to the niches by the Imperial Gate?" Beatrice asked.

"No, only the heads of lower-ranking officials are placed outside."

Beatrice pointed to several *sipahis* watching horses by the horse fountain. "Something must be amiss."

Aisha recognized one *sipahi* officer standing by his steed. "That *sipahi* is a friend of my betrothed, the Grand Vizier."

"He appears unhappy."

Aisha heard drums and looked back toward the Imperial Gate. An *orta* or battalion of *Janissaries* marched behind their officers.

"You are right, Beatrice. He appears disgruntled. Something must be going on." Aisha gestured to the famous *Janissary* Tree, where justice could be rendered from sturdy branches. "More than one rebellion began by that tree." The tree stood near the executioner's fountain.

"How?"

"*Janissary* companies overturned their cooking cauldrons. The last time it happened, they were upset with their pay, but today?" The carriage reached the Gate of Greeting. Like the Imperial Gate, fifty gardeners kept guard at that Gate, enforcing the rules. No one could enter without a purpose, and no one, except the Sultan himself, could ride on horseback into the next courtyard. All were required to follow protocol.

Janissaries Carrying a Kettle

"What is the delay?" Aisha asked. She needed to find a Dutch translator in order to find out whether her English Slave told her the truth. The *odalisque* Dilara inside the Imperial Harem was her best hope, but the morning was elapsing quickly.

"*Sipahi* leaders meet with the Deputy Grand Vizier, Hasan *the Clockmaker*, at the *Divan*." The gatekeeper stepped back, letting Aisha and her escorts enter without delay.

Chapter 2 — Demands at the Divan

There remained at Constantinople [Stamboul] some odas [battalions/regiments] of Janissaries and a more considerable body of Sipahis [Turkish Horsemen]. These last were for the most part deprived of their timars [lands] by the troubles. They beset continually the door of the Kaimakam Saatçi [Hasan the Clockmaker], who acted for the Grand Vizier [Yemisci Hasan Pasha or Hasan the Fruiterer].
<u>*History of the Turkish or Ottoman Empire, Vol. II*</u> *by Vincent Mignot*
Translated from French by A. Hawkins, Esq.

The Seraglio [New Palace or Topkapi Palace] is rather a collection of palaces and apartments added to one another, according to the caprice of several emperors [Sultans], than one single palace: It is justly call'd the Great, since perhaps 'tis the largest in the Universe, and it lodges him who is call'd by way of excellence the Grand Seignior, Emperor of Emperors, King of Kings, Distributor of Kingdoms and Principalities, and Lord of the White[Mediterranean], Black and Red Seas, & etc . . . Nothing can be richer than the materials of it . . . It is cover'd with Lead . . .
<u>*Travels Through Europe and Asia, Vol. I*</u>
by Aubry de la Motraye

Divan, New Palace, *Stamboul*, Ottoman Empire *AH* 1011 (Dec. *AD* 1602)

"REBELS DESTROYED many of the *timars* in Anatolia!" Katib Jemazi, turbaned leader of the *Sipahi* delegation, stood before the *Kaimakam* and the Divan, the ruling Council of the Ottoman Empire.

With the Grand Vizier absent, commanding Ottoman forces in distant Belgrade, *Saatçi* Hasan *Pasha*, in his stead, chaired the Divan, named for the open building on the left-hand side of the well-groomed courtyard. Numerous columns supported the building's low roof. The Sultan, if he so chose, could listen unseen from a nearby, latticed window. A rail separated the petitioners from the council, sitting beneath its golden ceiling.

"You need not raise your voice." *Kaimakam* Hasan stayed seated. His moniker *Saatçi* meant *Clockmaker*. When he was young, he had been trained to repair timepieces. Two judges with full grey beards sat next to him: the *Cazi* of Rumelia, the province of Turkey in Europe, sat to his right; the *Cazi* of Anatolia, Asia Minor, sat to his left. The *Agha* of the *Janissaries* and the lesser viziers of the Divan also listened to the demands. "We can hear."

Justice Tower above the Divan and the Second Courtyard of the New Palace, early 1800s

"Our demands must be met. The *sipahis* must be compensated for the loss of their *timars*."

"We have sent Khosru *Pasha* to be the *Beylerbey*, the Governor-General of Diyarbakir Province," Hasan *the Clockmaker* said. "With the armies of Aleppo and Sivas, this new general will achieve victory."

"Like those sent before? How can the new eunuch general win?" The *sipahi* leader lifted his palms. "The rebel ransacks everything that stands in his way. The *sipahis* receive no monies from their *timars*."

"Hasan *the Fool* puts all to fire and sword, and makes havoc wherever he goes," a second leader added. "How can our men return to their *timars*?" In exchange for their service when the Sultan called them to war, the *sipahis* held title to these landholdings. Unlike feudal lands in Christendom, *timars* could not be inherited. "They fulfilled their duties and fought against the Holy Roman Empire, but their estates are now gone."

"Ankara surrendered without a fight." Hasan *the Clockmaker* gestured to a *defterdar*, a treasurer standing behind him. "Do you not know that the rebels stole the tribute due to us?"

"How could our men fight the rebels?" Katib Jezami asked. "The *sipahis* left their estates at the beginning of the season."

"To war against the Holy Roman Empire with the Grand Vizier on the European frontier." Ever since Hasan *the Fruiterer* had departed

Stamboul to command all Ottoman forces in Europe a year and a half earlier, *Kaimakam* Hasan *the Clockmaker* had chaired the Divan.

"The *Janissaries* of Aleppo and Damascus should have fought the rebels." The *sipahi* leader pointed to Ali *Agha*, the head of the *Janissaries* and brother-in-law to the Chief White Eunuch. "The *sipahis* must be paid. The Treasury should be opened."

"That cannot be done," *Kaimakam* Hasan *the Clockmaker* insisted. "The *defterdars* can pay only the Imperial Cavalry—those riders are directly assigned to the Sultan."

"All *sipahis* must be compensated," Katib Jemazi insisted.

The *Kaimakam* glanced at two *defterdars*, both assigned to the imperial treasury. At one time, the treasury was housed in the Castle of Seven Towers, guarding the western gate of the city, but it was now kept inside the New Palace. "Your concerns will be considered."

"Gazanfer *Agha* is responsible," Katib Jezami said. "If the Chief White Eunuch cannot open the treasury, then the Chief Black Eunuch must open the mosques."

"To pay the *sipahis* from the imperial mosques? That is unheard of! " The *Kaimakam* glanced at several members of the *ulema*—the religious council, who mingled beneath the golden ceiling, on thick carpets strewn in perfect order. The spiritual leader of all Islam, who held the title of Grand Mufti, did not attend. Hasan *the Clockmaker* turned in the direction of the Imperial Harem. "Osman *Kizlar Agha* will never consent to that."

"Ask the Grand Mufti!" The *sipahi* leaders glared at Hasan *the Clockmaker* and backed out of the Divan."We will return," he paused, "tomorrow."

The *sipahi* leaders exited the Divan and trooped down the stone walkway, angling back toward the Gateway of Greeting.

Back at the horse fountain in the Courtyard of the *Janissaries*, Katib Jemazi met Poiraz Osman *Bey*, a *sipahi* leader who had recently returned from the European frontier. "Will you join us at the feast?"

"Tonight?" Poiraz Osman *Bey* asked.

Katib Jemazi quieted when he noticed the Chief Gardener approaching on horseback.

"The Divan is over?" the Chief Gardener asked.

"Yes, but nothing was resolved." Katib Jemazi knew anyone not satisfied with the decision rendered by the Council could appeal to the Sultan. In practice, however, few risked their lives. Instead, they accepted whatever justice the Divan meted out. "We must tell the *sipahis* on the *At-meidan*."

~ ~ ~

THE CHIEF GARDENER rode alongside the carriage of Aisha, Sister of the Sultan. "No delays!" Seated atop his small horse, he waved the carriage forward. "I shall see you later." It surged through the Gate of Greeting and veered left, toward the Carriage Gate of the Imperial Harem.

Aisha leaned out the window. "Halt! Stop the carriage!"

As soon as the driver obeyed her command, a Black eunuch opened her door.

"What is it?" Beatrice asked, in her native Italian.

"Your brother, Gazanfer *Agha*." Aisha pointed to the beardless man in a large white turban. The little man with immense power stood at the far end of the Courtyard of the Divan, at the Gate of Justice, Majesty, and Felicity. Beyond that gate—called the *Sublime Porte*—the Sultan confirmed or overturned the most important decisions of the Council. Both weak and strong could appeal to him on matters of life and death.

Still veiled, Aisha and Beatrice exited the carriage. More impressive than the Courtyard of the *Janissaries*, columned arcades characterized both the near and far ends of the first formal courtyard of the New Palace. Paved pathways crossed the courtyard in four directions. In one area, *Janissary* cadets stood in formation behind their captain. Two very long feathers, arching from the top of the captain's turban, nearly touched the ground.

The Sultan alone could ride into this courtyard, and his thirty horses comprised the most magnificent in the whole of the Ottoman Empire. The galleries above the stables did not hold armaments, but jeweled harnesses and lavish saddles.

Throughout the courtyard, tall cypresses lined the walkways through the well-kept lawns. A handful of tamed gazelles even grazed nearby. A diagonal path led to the Divan, further up the left side. The Tower of Justice rose above that building, still swarming with turbaned viziers and court officials.

Along the walkway leading right, porters with large baskets on their backs carried wood to the nine separate kitchens. Smoke rose from the chimneys of the connected buildings. Dissipated slowly by shifting winds, the white wisps drifted against blue, midday skies.

Beatrice nudged Aisha. "Ever since I arrived here ten years ago, I've always been impressed with the kitchens."

"*Certo*," Aisha spoke Italian in hushed tones, "the imperial chefs prepare the best dishes in the world."

The first, large kitchen prepared the Sultan's fare, while the second one prepared dishes for the Sultan's Mother in honor of her fruitfulness. Chefs in the kitchen in the middle, with thick plumes of smoke now rising, prepared food for those in the Divan, who now exited the open building.

"Several weeks ago, the kitchens served a savory feast in honor of the new Venetian ambassador," Aisha said.

"I heard it was delicious."

"Is that your husband?" Aisha pointed to a man taking fast strides. The sleeves of his robe sported rich, silk patterns. A small plume of feathers flopped out of his turban.

"Yes, Ali meets with my brother, Gazanfer, at the Gate of Felicity."

Beatrice's brother, the Chief White Eunuch and closest advisor to the Sultan, had his apartment beyond that gate, directly ahead. That courtyard also held the Throne Room, rarely seen. Normally, only White eunuchs and special guests were allowed into the next courtyard. Weeks earlier, after the feast, the new Venetian ambassadors were escorted between guards holding each of their arms. Forced down on bended knees, the ambassadors delivered gifts and kissed the robe of Aisha's brother, Sultan Mehmet III.

The breeze grew stronger as the two women quickened their pace. As the tips of the tall cypresses swayed, shedding dried needles near their feet, they slowed their strides. A line of servants traversed the courtyard in front of them. They carried produce in their wide aprons from the fifth kitchen on the right to the Divan on the left.

Gate of Justice, Majesty and Felicity, New Palace

BY THE TIME the two women reached the arcades of the Gate of Justice, Majesty and Felicity, Beatrice's brother had already exchanged words with her husband. Ali began his career as a scribe, but after Gazanfer *Agha* arranged for his sister marry him, Ali rose step by step. Eventually, he became *Agha* of the Janissaries, the powerful foot soldiers loyal to the Sultan. Aisha's betrothed, Hasan *the Fruiterer*, once held that same position. With the support of her mother, her betrothed became *Kaimakam* and later, the Grand Vizier.

"Greetings, Sister!" Gazanfer *Agha* said warmly. When he became the *kapi-agasi* or the Chief White Eunuch, he had kept his former position as *oda bashi*, the head of the Sultan's Privy Chamber, an office he inherited after his older brother had died young. Confidantes of Sultan Murad III, the two Venetian brothers agreed to undergo the cut and become eunuchs. When Murad acceded to the Ottoman throne, Gazanfer advanced into the inner palace, where only eunuchs were allowed. "And Aisha, I did not expect to see you today."

"Beatrice agreed to accompany me to the Imperial Harem."

Hidden beyond the next courtyard, the Imperial Harem housed more than 300 concubines, as well as the mothers of her brother's children.

"To visit the Sultan's Mother?" Gazanfer *Agha* remained very close to the Sultan's Mother. Even after her brother became Sultan, he retained both titles he had held during her father's lifetime.

"And mine, too."

The quarters of Safiye *Valide Sultana* were the most magnificent of the whole palace, the best in *Stamboul*. These apartments overlooked Seraglio Point, the tip of the peninsula, where the Golden Horn meets the Sea of Marmara. Fishing vessels departed early every day, returning later in the morning or early afternoon with their holds full. When the winds shifted, large sailing vessels plied the waters. Some sailed east toward the Black Sea and Asia, others sailed west toward the White Sea, also known as the Mediterranean.

"The *sipahi* officers did not appear happy." Beatrice asked her husband and brother, "Is this something we should be concerned about?"

Gazanfer *Agha* checked with her husband, Ali *Agha*. "Do not worry, Sister. I am sure it is nothing."

"Good," Aisha turned back toward the Divan. "The day goes by so fast, and I must find the *odalisque* Dilara from Holland." A corridor behind the Divan led to the Queen's Gate and the Imperial Harem, where even White eunuchs were not allowed.

"Please give your mother my regards," Beatrice said. "I shall talk to her later."

"You are not joining me in the Imperial Harem?" Aisha asked.

Beatrice glanced at her husband. "No, Ali and I must talk, but here is the gift I promised you."

Still veiled, yet more determined than ever, Aisha decided not to use the Queen's Gate, the main entrance to the Imperial Harem behind the Divan. Instead, the Sister of the Sultan hurried straight ahead through the

Gate of Justice, Majesty, and Felicity. She strolled past the Throne Room of her brother. Aisha headed directly across the Third Courtyard, toward a building housing the most precious jewels of the Empire.

Aisha clutched the fine gift from Beatrice in her hand, but did not want to keep it for herself. The beautiful noblewoman hoped the Chief Black Eunuch would love it.

Chapter 3 — Imperial Harem

Travels Through Europe and Asia, Vol. I
by Aubry de la Motraye

Secret Gate, Imperial Harem, New Palace, *AH* 1011 (Late Dec., *AD* 1602)

NOT FAR FROM a thick iron grate that separated the Third and Fourth Courtyards, Aisha turned her skeleton key and unlocked the door. She stepped into the dark passageway—the secret entrance to the Imperial Harem. But shiny scimitars blocked her path. Tall and strong, two Black eunuchs stepped into the light. Inside the small stairway leading to the Fourth Courtyard, they kept a vigilant guard.

"We were not told of your visit." The eunuchs sheathed their curved swords.

Aisha pushed her way between them. "I must find *Valide Sultana* Safiye."

At the other end of the stairway, two shorter eunuchs—no less deadly than the two giants—appeared. They, too, sported scimitars, ready for use against any man with wandering eyes. They also displayed second weapons, sheathed daggers tucked into wide sashes, wrapped snugly about their waists.

Though just as deadly, the dagger Aisha kept safely hidden beneath her garments was more ornate. "I must find *Valide Sultana* Safiye."

"Your mother holds court in her apartment." The two shorter eunuchs stepped back, and Aisha proceeded across the Fourth Courtyard.

A dozen young *odalisques* stopped kicking their small ball. "Aisha!"

Aisha smiled and waved. "I wish I could stay and play." She had not partaken of the sport for many years and continued through the next building, a hallway that connected the apartments of one of the Sultan's Favorites to the Main Dormitory—the home of nearly three hundred *odalisques*, the most beautiful virgins in the Ottoman Empire.

Tulip Garden, Imperial Harem, New Palace

AISHA SLOWED HER stride at the tulip garden, where every year the harem held a small festival. In the spring, multi-colored tulips—tended by other Black eunuchs—blossomed, but that was months away. With winter approaching, the bulbs remained dormant underground. Weeping willows and mulberry trees cast long shadows on the far side, but Aisha knew the fragrant scent of lilacs and jasmine would someday return.

When a tall, dark figure approached, Aisha stopped and turned. Aisha recognized the Chief Black Eunuch, taller than the other Black eunuchs, moving toward her. "Peace be unto you, *Kizlar Agha* Osman!"

"Peace be unto you, too," the Chief Black Eunuch responded.

Kizlar Agha meant Master of Girls, but the Chief Black Eunuch was also one of the most powerful men in the whole empire. Ranking below the Sultan and the Grand Vizier, the *Kizlar Agha* held the title of *pasha*, a general. When he traveled, the three horsetails in his standard signaled his authority: most *pashas* only had two, the source of the common saying, 'a *pasha* of two tails.'

"Thank you."

"I heard you were in the Palace."

"So quickly?"

Aisha was not surprised, for rumors spread faster inside the New Palace than wild flowers in the spring.

"Your carriage is already inside." Beneath his flowing robe, the Chief Black Eunuch wore a floral gown. "Your mother will be expecting you soon."

"Yes, I shall see her shortly, but first I need to find Dilara."

"The Dutch *odalisque*?"

"Fatima Hatun reminded me she was here." Aisha used the Turkish name of the Venetian sister of Gazanfer *Agha*. No *odalisque* could leave the harem, but nothing could stop Aisha from learning more about *Capitano* John Smith. She needed to know how her English slave met her betrothed. *Would it be possible to take Dilara to her own palace?*

Aisha pulled the corner of the silk from her bag. "I thought you might be interested in the latest Venetian fabric."

"May God give you a blessing." *Kizlar Agha* Osman's eyes widened, and he accepted the gift. "Gold silk?" He let the fabric slip through his fingers. "I will find Dilara at once."

As a young Black eunuch hurried toward the Main Dormitory, he passed a short Jewish woman, who stepped into the garden. "Aisha, what an unexpected pleasure."

"*Kira* Chacun?" The Chief Black Eunuch lurched forward. "We did not expect you until later."

The richly dressed Jewish woman wore neither hijab nor veil. "I brought my new assistant." She slipped her hand into her pocket and attempted to hand him several coins. "For your trouble."

The Black Eunuch glanced at Aisha. "No, I would not want to get you into the trouble that *Kira* Esperanza faced."

Esperanza Malchi had been the *kira* of the harem for more than a decade, but the *sipahis* became jealous of her wealth. Only a few years earlier, they accused her of selling *timars* for money, instead of distributing the fiefs to their fellow horsemen who had proved their valor in battle. *Kira* Esperanza was killed, her limbs nailed to the doors of Turks accused of accepting bribes.

"You are right, I shall be more discreet."

"I will tell you a secret, *Kira* Chacun." The Chief Black Eunuch leaned closer. "As you know, the Sultan sees his mother almost every morning."

"Yes, to take her advice."

"But he did not always do so," the Chief Black Eunuch said. "About seven years ago, *Valide Sultana* Safiye did not want him to go to battle in Hungary."

"What did she do?" the young assistant asked.

"She sent the most beautiful *odalisque* in the harem to persuade her son to stay, but the Sultan could not be persuaded, so he took out his dagger and killed the girl in the garden."

"Mehmet III killed her?"

"The new Sultan acceded to the cries of the *Janissaries* and led the Ottoman Army into battle." The Chief Black Eunuch added, "The new

Sultan almost died, but obtained the title of *ghazi* or warrior. Since his victory in Hungary, he has not returned to the Long War, and the Sultan's Mother wants to keep him happy in the harem."

"And me?" *Kira* Chacun said.

"Perhaps you can help."

"My assistant can teach the *odalisques* this newest needlework." She opened her bag filled with cloth and needles. "That is why I brought these."

"Very well. Was your assistant searched?"

"We know the rules: all guests must be searched." More than one man, disguised beneath a burqa, had attempted to enter the harem. "Your able eunuchs searched her and found nothing."

"Very well." The Chief Black Eunuch bowed. "Aisha, I must take my leave. Your mother requires my presence."

Kira Chacun turned back to Aisha. "Perhaps you will join me and visit Ahmet?"

"Is something wrong?" Aisha asked.

"Your nephew is ill."

Apartment of the Second Consort, Imperial Harem

AISHA AND *KIRA* Chacun walked to the doorway of the Apartment of the Second Consort, facing the Tulip Garden. Handan *Sultana*, the Mother of Ahmet, the Sultan's second-eldest son, met them in person. "*Kira* Chacun, I'm so glad you could make it."

"I came as quickly as I could," the Jewish matron said.

"And Aisha—"

"I trust I am not intruding." Aisha worried about her nephew. Over the previous decade, illness had taken the lives of more than one of the Sultan's sons. "Is it serious?"

"I hope not, but the doctors from the palace hospital could do nothing."

Doctors brought through the Queen's Gate could not always help. Any doctor brought into the Imperial Harem had to be blindfolded. Even if he were a White eunuch, that blindfold could never be removed. Always guarded by attentive Black eunuchs, the physician could only examine the hands and arms by touch, by feeling the skin of his patient without even a peek.

"Come with me." Handun *Sultana* led *Kira* Chacun and Aisha into the next room, where Ahmet rested on his bed.

The *Kira* sat down next to him and helped him sit up. She reached down and pulled a wineskin out of her bag. "Drink this." She lifted up the wineskin, and the boy, about 12 or 13 years of age, sipped from it.

"Is that wine?" Handan *Sultana* whispered.

The *Kira* glanced up.

"Perhaps some things should remain unsaid." Aisha knew Muslims were not allowed to drink alcohol. After the *janissaries* had rioted, her brother blamed it on drinking and closed all drinking places in the city. Even the foreign embassies of Venice and France had trouble securing the wine they were allowed to use.

"I shall never say a word. The doctors have not been able to help."

"You once belonged to a doctor, didn't you?" Aisha asked.

"Yes," Handan *Sultana* said. "I was taken from Bosnia and given to a doctor from Rumelia Province. That doctor, who circumcised the Sultan, gave me to your brother."

"I just reminisced about those festivities with the sister of the Chief White Eunuch."

"After your brother was circumcised, I went with his harem to Magnesia in Anatolia."

Kira Chacun laid Ahmet's head back on the pillow. "Now rest."

Apartment of the *Haseki Sultana*, Imperial Harem

AISHA HURRIED TOWARD the furthest end of the Palace, the prettiest place in all of *Stamboul.* The city walls extended west, all the way to the Byzantine Castle of Seven Towers. It once held the treasures of the empire, but now held important prisoners awaiting trial, or others who had committed crimes not worthy of death. Beyond the gardens and woods, strong seawalls protected the New Palace. Cadets kept watch both day and night inside the stone towers. Interspersed at regular intervals, these tower bastions overlooked the long wall and the sea beyond.

Standing in front of the Apartment of the *Haseki Sultana*, Halime *Sultana* scolded her son. The mother of the Sultan's eldest son, Mahmud, did not appear happy, but her lecture abruptly ended when she glimpsed Aisha approaching.

Years earlier, when she and her brother were just children, Aisha lived with her mother, Safiye, in the Apartment of the Sultan's Favorite. At that time, her Venetian grandmother, *Nur Banu*, occupied the larger Apartment of *Valide Sultana* next door. Related to the Albanian House of *Basso* or Basta, the maiden name of her mother, *Nur Banu*, had travelled by boat across the Adriatic to visit her father, the Governor of Corfu. On the way to that Venetian island, Turkish corsairs captured the Venetian girl at the age of twelve, presented her, and brought her into Selim's harem.

Both the *Valide Sultana* and his favorite maintained their own courts, and both had views of the Sea of Marmara. Beyond choppy seas, the shores of Asia Minor, known as Anatolia, could be clearly seen.

Halime *Sultana*, the mother of the presumed successor to the Ottoman throne, stepped in front of her son. "Aisha, what a pleasant surprise. Are you here for a visit?"

"No, I planned to visit my mother," Aisha responded. "Is something wrong?"

"With my son? No, I was talking to Mahmud about a request we plan to make."

"I wish I could talk, but I do not want to be late."

"We shall see you soon in her hall."

As Aisha rounded the corner of her mother's apartment, she stopped at a terrace. Below, she spied Seraglio Point, the tip of the peninsula where the Golden Horn jutted out into the waters connecting the Black and Mediterranean Seas. The gate by the tip was called *Top-Kapi*, for the cannons protected that gate from any sea attack. Though the winter sun streamed from above, a cold north wind kicked up and chilled her to the bone. Aisha scurried inside to warm herself. Several of the more than 50 servants assigned to the Apartment of the *Valide Sultana* immediately greeted her. One of them, who, like the others, stayed both night and day in that apartment, put a shawl over her shoulders and escorted her to a stoked stove.

Chamber of the Sultan's Mother, Imperial Harem

"CROWN OF VEILED Heads," the Chief Black Eunuch addressed the Sultan's Mother in the tall square chamber overlooking her privy garden, the center of her apartment. The plush room faced the Privy Garden of *Valide Sultana* and the interior part of the Imperial Harem with its three long halls.

"Speak, *Kizlar Agha* Osman." *Valide Sultana* Safiye motioned with her left arm.

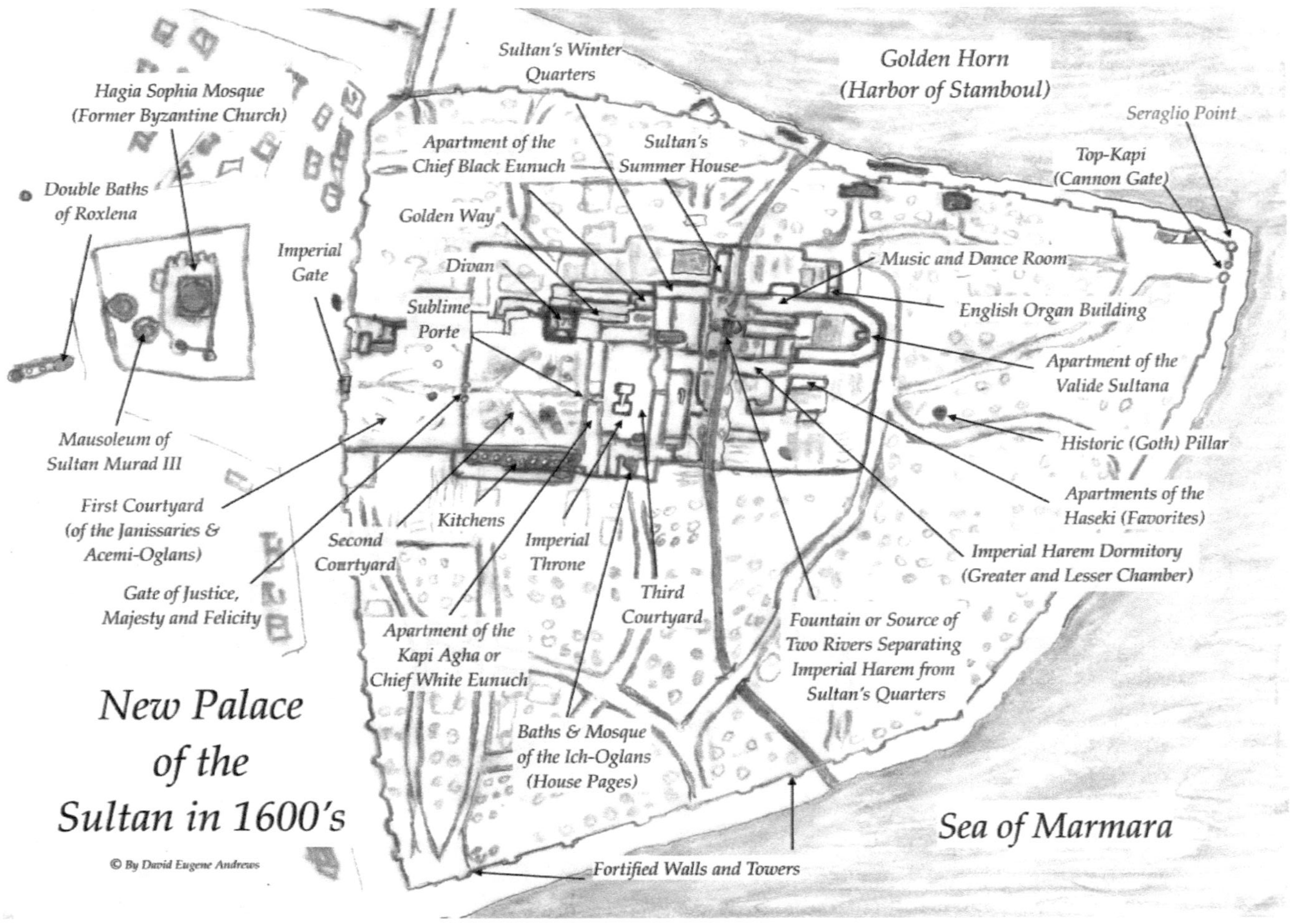

Hagia Sophia Mosque (Former Byzantine Church)
Sultan's Winter Quarters
Golden Horn (Harbor of Stamboul)
Seraglio Point
Double Baths of Roxlena
Apartment of the Chief Black Eunuch
Sultan's Summer House
Top-Kapi (Cannon Gate)
Golden Way
Music and Dance Room
Imperial Gate
Divan
English Organ Building
Sublime Porte
Apartment of the Valide Sultana
Historic (Goth) Pillar
Mausoleum of Sultan Murad III
Apartments of the Haseki (Favorites)
First Courtyard (of the Janissaries & Acemi-Oglans)
Kitchens
Imperial Harem Dormitory (Greater and Lesser Chamber)
Gate of Justice, Majesty and Felicity
Second Courtyard
Imperial Throne
Third Courtyard
Fountain or Source of Two Rivers Separating Imperial Harem from Sultan's Quarters
Apartment of the Kapi Agha or Chief White Eunuch
Baths & Mosque of the Ich-Oglans (House Pages)
Fortified Walls and Towers
Sea of Marmara
New Palace
of the
Sultan in 1600's
© By David Eugene Andrews

"New techniques of needlework are being taught to the youngest *odalisques* in the work hall." He referred to the Work Hall, the second of three long halls.

"I would like to see them tomorrow. Is there something else?"

Kizlar Agha Osman stepped closer to the throne, while her daughter Aisha remained unseen behind a latticed screen. Like the throne of her son in the Third Courtyard, the Sultan's Mother had her chair on a raised platform. Though her son held council on special occasions, Valide Sultana directed the daily affairs of the Empire from the inner harem, conferring with the Chief Black Eunuch, who told her everything. Her mother held court every morning. Outside the entrance to this Chamber, Abdul Rezak *Agha,* the Black Eunuch assigned to the Sultan's Mother, caught her eye. Aisha motioned for him to wait before announcing her presence. *Kira* Chacun had remained with Ahmet and his mother in the Apartment of the Second Consort.

"The Council in the Divan just completed their meeting," *Kizlar Agha* Osman said. "Both *sipahi* horsemen and the *janissary* foot soldiers demanded change."

"Change?"

"Officers are unhappy with the war in Hungary and the rebellion in Anatolia."

"But we sent the eunuch Khosru *Pasha* to be commander at Diyarbakir."

"Great praise is due to his Majesty, the Sultan."

"But?" the Sultan's Mother asked.

"Everything remains as before."

"Report back, if anything changes."

"Yes, Safiye *Valide Sultana.*" The Chief Black Eunuch bowed.

"Go, tell my son. I have something for him."

"As you wish."

As the Chief Black Eunuch exited towards her son's apartment, the Sultan's Mother turned toward the entrance. "Abdul Rezak *Agha,* what is the commotion?"

"Your daughter Aisha has arrived," the second most powerful eunuch inside the Imperial Harem replied.

Aisha stepped into the room, brightened by candles and lanterns. On one side of the room, her mother sat upon a golden sofa, framed in gilt. Blue-tiled walls reached toward the high ceiling.

"You were delayed?" Her mother shook her head. After her grandmother died, her mother advised her grandfather, and when he died, she advised her brother. Her name, Safiye, meant pure.

"It was so cold outside," Aisha said. "I stopped and warmed myself by a hearth."

Her mother motioned Aisha forward, adding in Italian, the *lingua franca* of the harem. "Come, sit by me."

"*Si, Madre.*"

Aisha had learned Italian from her Venetian grandmother, the favorite of her Grandfather, Sultan Selim II. She later gave birth to the future Sultan Murad III and became known as *Nur Banu*, 'woman of splendor'. When Aisha's father, Murad, acceded to the Ottoman throne, *Nur Banu* became the *Valide Sultana*, the richest and most powerful woman in the whole world. When *Nur Banu* died, Aisha inherited all of her exquisite jewelry.

Aisha sat down, cross-legged on a cushioned pillow, something she had done since she was little. "Mother, I have a request."

"Have we found out where in Bohemia the family of your slave lives?" Her mother, just over fifty years old, wore an elegant dress. Her hat rose a foot above her head, and matching tassels draped down to her waist.

"No, not yet."

"Well, how can we collect the ransom?"

"That is why I came here today."

"For money?"

"No, Mother, for an interpreter."

Safiye *Valide Sultana* turned to her Black eunuch. "Abdul Rezak *Agha*, who speaks Bohemian?"

"We have several *odalisques*. And the one Hasan *the Fruiterer* sent to us speaks Bulgarian."

"Are any of them old?"

"Mother, I do not need someone who speaks Bohemian. I need someone who knows Dutch."

"Dutch?"

"Yes, the Captain is going to Holland." Aisha quieted when she recognized a loud tapping sound.

Her brother, the Ottoman Sultan, approached—his silver slippers tapped louder with each step. As the tapping slowed, Abdul Rezak *Agha* quickly ushered several of the younger *odalisques* in the opposite direction—out of the room. After their initial introductions to the Sultan, the *odalisques* must be trained. Only after several years of training did the Sultan's Mother present the girl again. Before that time, her brother did not want to surprise any of the three hundred *odalisques* of the harem unannounced.

"Son, please sit by Aisha and me."

Though Mehmet III was only in his thirties, his black beard already had streaks of gray.

Aisha scooted several feet away, and her brother, who had gained much weight since ascending to the throne, stepped onto the raised platform and plopped down in a sturdy chair. "I will get some exercise this afternoon."

"Shooting arrows?" Aisha asked.

"Yes, in the yards."

As the Sultan and their mother conversed, *Kizlar Agha* Osman, the Chief Black Eunuch, escorted the Sultan's eldest son and his mother into the room.

Mahmud, the sixteen-year-old youth, who had not yet been circumcised, bowed. "Honored father."

"You may speak."

"When will you send me to govern a province?"

Imperial Harem, New Palace, Stamboul, circa 1680

"In due time," Sultan Mehmet III said.

"You were a governor at my age."

The Sultan glanced at his mother and told his son. "You must wait."

Showing the obeisance required of a son, yet obviously disappointed at the answer, Mahmud bowed. "It was an honor to see you this morning, Grandmother." He bowed again and backed away, exiting

30

the throne room along with his mother, the *Haseki* Sultana Halime. They left by the same door through which they came.

"Perhaps it is time for Mahmud to get circumcised," the Sultan said.

"We should wait until Aisha marries Hasan *the Fruiterer*."

"The Grand Vizier is in Belgrade," Aisha said.

"Yes, we know." Sultan Mehmet III pushed himself up from his chair. "I think it is time for my second meal."

"We shall have your kitchen deliver it immediately." The Chief Black Eunuch motioned for a dwarf to deliver the message to his kitchen and escorted the Sultan back to his quarters.

The tapping of the silver slippers finally faded, and Aisha asked the *Valide Sultana*, "Mother, I have a request."

"Speak."

"About the Dutch *odalisque*, Dilara?"

"Go on."

"I wish to bring her to my palace for a visit."

"How can we guard her?" the Chief Black Eunuch, responsible for all women in the harem, interjected. "That cannot be done."

The Sultan's Mother motioned for quiet. "That is a most unusual request."

"Nothing will happen," Aisha said.

Her mother considered her request. "*Kislar Agha* Osman, take my daughter to Dilara."

The Chief Black Eunuch gracefully bowed. "As you wish."

Aisha hooded her head and, escorted by the tall eunuch, stepped outside. On the other side of the Privy Garden of the *Valide Sultana*, three long buildings extended back toward the Third Courtyard. *Kislar Agha* Osman and Aisha veered toward the tall, wooden hall. The Dormitory of Women housed three hundred *odalisques*.

Chapter 4 — Dutch *Odalisque* Dilara

The Sultan goes often upon this Lake in a Brigantine, being followed by some jesters and Mutes, who minister occasion of delight, some by pleasant encounters, the other by their ridiculous faces and gestures, and sometimes tumbling them into the water to give him occasion of laughter: He himself is pleased to lay ambushes for them, to make them fall by the Platform into the Lake . . .

Those [women] of the Serrail [Sarai or 'palace' in Persian], which make the greatest show by the luster of the graces are most commonly strangers taken in the war, or ravished by force: But bred up with an incredible care, to make them learn civility, to play of some instruments of music, to sing, and to work with their needles, most decent for maids of quality: these good parts, added to their natural perfection, make them the more commendable: they are for the most part Christians; but their disaster, causing the beauty of their bodies to serve . . .

General History of the Serrail by Michel Baudier
Translated from the French by E. Grimestone

Greater Chamber, Dormitory, Imperial Harem, New Palace, *AD* 1602

BEAUTIFUL *ODALISQUES* SWARMED around Aisha, the Sister of the Sultan, in the Greater Chamber of the Dormitory for Women.

"Aisha seeks Dilara," the Chief Black Eunuch told the *Kadun Kahia*.

"The *odalisque* from Holland? I was not told," the Mother of Maids responded.

"An oversight, I apologize." The eunuch looked around. "But where is she?"

"Dilara stays in her room." *Kadun Kahia* pointed to the second-floor balcony.

"*Kizlar Agha* Osman, thank you for helping me," Aisha said, "I am sure you have important matters to attend to."

"Yes, I do." The Chief Black Eunuch bowed. "I must join Gazanfer *Agha* and your brother. They dine in the Third Courtyard." He hurried past the fountain of green marble. Above, at the ceiling, a circular cupola glistened gold and blue azure.

Though many stared, Aisha did not let any of the women follow her up the wide staircase and onto the second floor. The large dormitory, split into the Greater and Lesser Chambers, was roughly three hundred feet long and forty-five feet wide. The interior of the three-story building opened to the ceiling. Outer rooms faced the outside, while long balconies faced the middle. Older *odalisques* peered down from the third-floor balcony.

One young girl with long black hair greeted Aisha with a smile. "We rarely receive visitors."

"You are so beautiful." Aisha continued her walk down the second-floor balcony.

A *kadun*, tall and thin, asked, "What brings you here?"

"I must find an *odalisque*," Aisha responded. "They told me Dilara stays here."

Kizlar Agha (Chief Black Eunuch) & Odalisque

They walked together down the hall. "This is her room."

The room, like all of those in both chambers of the dormitory, had ten beds—five on each side. It also had a bed in the middle that belonged to the *kadun*, an older matron assigned to monitor the behavior of the younger women. Lamps, though dimmed, stayed lit all night long. The matron listened to the conversations of the *odalisques* and reported them to the *Kadun Kahia*, ensuring everything was kept in strict order. Some *odalisques* would be admonished, but others would be groomed to be presented to the Sultan. Still others might join the court of the Sultan's Mother or one of her son's Favorites.

The *kadun* or matron welcomed Aisha into the empty room. "Dilara takes lessons in needlepoint in the Work Hall."

"Is that her coat?" Aisha asked.

"Yes, but—"

"We might go for a walk." Aisha picked up the garment and went down the wide stairs at the end of the hall, not far from the furnace room of the harem baths.

Baths, Imperial Harem, New Palace, *Stamboul*

"YOUR BROTHER CHOSE a new *odalisque* earlier this morning." The *Kadun Kahia* pointed to a few *odalisques* inside the disrobing room, the first of three main rooms in the large *hamam*, the bath between the Main Dormitory and the Work Hall. Aisha knew the ritual well. After her brother selected the beautiful girl, that *odalisque* would be pampered all day in the Imperial Harem bath. Fountains constructed of white marble lined the walls. Gurgling water from hot and cold taps filled the sitting pools. Aisha kept on her raised patten shoes and peeked inside to see the one her brother had chosen. Though jealousy often surfaced as each *odalisque* vied for the Sultan's affection, the one selected this day was given the respect due her.

Twenty young beauties surrounded that *odalisque* in the middle room. An African maid, meanwhile, took a brush and scrubbed the shoulders of the chosen one. After the young woman's skin was washed at one of the fountains, the *odalisques* would sit in the hot room and talk, telling the chosen *odalisque* the great privileges she would receive. After being perfumed and clothed in the cold room, she would be taken to the Sultan's bedchambers that night. If she conceived and gave birth, her son might become Sultan, the ruler of the Ottoman Empire. Many *odalisques*, though, secretly cherished girls, for the Sultan's sons—other than the eldest, the successor to the Ottoman throne—often perished. Both Aisha's brother and father had killed their closest rivals: each had all of his own half-brothers beheaded. Aisha lost nineteen half-brothers when Mehmet acceded to the Ottoman throne, but her thoughts quickly turned to finding Dilara.

"We should hurry to the needlepoint class before the women have their meal." Aisha, escorted by the *Kadun Kahia*, exited the harem baths.

Work Hall, Imperial Harem

PLUSH PERSIAN CARPETS covered the floors leading into the Work Hall. Odalisques gathered to learn needlepoint and other useful skills. The assistant to the Jewish *kira* taught the latest patterns and techniques to a circle of ten young women. After the *odalisques* completed their small garments, the Jewish *Kira* would often buy the works.

To find a worthy husband and avoid dying as an old maid, older *odalisques* would sometimes sell the very gifts the Sultan had given them. The Sultan would be very upset if he found out, but some *odalisques,* who had no knowledge of the outside world, were desperate to acquire wealth. But they sold those exquisite gifts very cheaply. The Jewish *kiras* were always willing to help and would sell them on the outside.

Kira Chadun, having ended her visit to the second consort, arrived from the opposite end of the hall. "I wanted to check on my assistant."

A young Greek girl, about the age of Aisha's nephew, spoke up, "Is Prince Ahmed feeling better?"

"Prince Ahmed sleeps soundly," the Jewish *kira* said. "You are new here?"

"I still must be trained." The Greek girl put down her needlework.

"I thought I was going to find Dilara here." Aisha asked, "Where is she?"

"Dilara finished her handkerchief a while ago," the assistant said. "She went to the Music and Dance Hall to help teach the newest *odalisques.*"

Aisha and the *Kadun Kahia* walked on the carpets reaching the third hall, just as long as the Dormitory and the Work Hall. Nearly fifty *odalisques* practiced music—either singing or stringed instruments. Towards the center of the Music and Dance Hall, an enclosed porch with high windows, covered by latticed screens, extended out to their right. Terraced gardens overlooking Seraglio Point and the Golden Horn surrounded the vestibule on three sides. As soon as Aisha and the *Kadun Kahia* stepped into the large room, the music and dancing ended abruptly.

Music and Dance Hall, Imperial Harem, New Palace, *Stamboul*

THE *KADUN KAHIA* escorted Aisha to the young teacher. "I believe this is whom you seek."

"Ah, Dilara?" Aisha recognized the Dutch odalisque. "Beatrice reminded me that you would be here."

"I remember the day I arrived in the Harem." Dilara returned the warm greeting. with a pleasing smile. "You were so kind to me, but that was years ago."

"Do not remind me of my age." Aisha laughed. "I almost forgot, I was young."

"And you had already married *Damat* Ibrahim *Pasha*."

"Yes, but he is gone."

Dilara brought the Sister of the Sultan into the center of the dancers. "Would you like to see the Bulgarian girl your betrothed sent to the harem?"

"*Yemisci* Hasan *Pasha* never told me." Aisha motioned for the newest *odalisque* to begin. As the dancer with long hair and longer legs twirled, Aisha commented, "I see she has much talent."

"Yes, not at all clumsy," the *Kadun Kahia* said with a proud smile. "She has made much progress since raising her finger."

Aisha knew that when a new *odalisque* was brought into the Imperial Harem at a tender age, any hope she held of returning to her father and her family vanished. For the families of the *odalisques*, it was a disaster, for they would never see their daughters or their sisters again. For the new *odalisques*, the reality began to sink in, and some accepted their fate quicker than others. Like Aisha's mother had so many years before, the *odalisque* realized she would never return home.

All *odalisques* relinquished their Christian faith. With the solemnity of an oath in an Italian court of law, each raised her index finger and, in Arabic, stated the *shahada*, the first pillar of Islam: "There is no God but Allah, and Muhammad is his Prophet."

Each and every *odalisque* staying in the Imperial Harem had professed the same, and, likewise, as Sultan Murad III's eldest daughter, Aisha had accepted her fate. A sultana or female member of the Royal household, Aisha held vast privileges, but she also had a kind heart, often stopping to give alms. She truly cared for those who suffered, whether poor and destitute or simply injured. Most of all, she cared for her English slave, *Capitano Giovanni*. Captain John Smith had largely recovered from the wounds he had suffered, but nothing could stop her from finding out the truth, not even her mother. She needed to know how he met her betrothed. As a young man, Smith had traveled to Rouen, where Captain Joseph Duxbury recruited the English lad to join him and fight against the Spanish in both France and Holland.

After the Bulgarian girl finished her exhibition, the Sister of the Sultan took the Dutch *odalisque* to the side. "Dilara, I must have a word with you."

"Yes, most certainly." Dilara dismissed the younger *odalisques*. "I believe we have completed the lesson."

"Young ladies, come with me." *Kahia Kadin* said goodbye to Aisha and Dilara and escorted the remaining *odalisques* away.

Aisha then motioned for Dilara to sit down on the cushioned sofa by the window overlooking the outer gardens. "Remind me, how did you learn Dutch?"

"More than ten years ago, I sailed on a merchant ship with my father, the captain."

"What happened?"

"Though Dutch, we flew under the French flag. Barbary pirates attacked us."

"Were you scared?" Aisha asked.

"It happened so fast. They took over the deck." Dilara breathed deep. "My father fought, but did not survive."

"They sent you here, to the Imperial Harem?"

"The corsairs sold me at auction to the Eunuch *Beylerbey* in Algiers, who sent me here with one hundred other virgins."

"Yes, I remember that gift. The eunuch was reinstated. And you?

"I cannot return to Holland," Dilara said. "The life here is all I know."

"But you still know Dutch?" Aisha asked.

"How could I forget?"

Aisha leaned closer. "I need your help translating."

"You do?" Dilara asked.

"Yes, I received an English slave named Captain John Smith."

"I don't understand. You say that he is English?"

"Yes, but he says he speaks Dutch."

"And you need my help?"

"I must know if the *capitano* tells the truth." Aisha asked, "Will you help me?"

"But to leave the harem? What about the Sultan?"

Without the Sultan's expressed permission, an *odalisque* would normally never be allowed to leave the Imperial Harem.

"No one will question me," the Sister of the Sultan said. "Now put on your coat. It is cold outside."

Dilara looked around. Only two Black eunuchs lingered by the door.

"All is arranged, no need for concern. My brother eats his meal inside the Third Courtyard with the Chief White and Chief Black Eunuchs."

Aisha and Dilara wrapped heavy *hijabs* about their heads. They draped their coats over their shoulders and exited the vestibule of the Music and Dance Hall. When they stepped onto the terrace gardens, Aisha asked her new translator, "You learned Dutch at home? In Holland?"

"My father sometimes took me to the bourse in Amsterdam. He allowed me to sit in the corner when the merchants docked. I learned everything by listening."

The harbor below was filled with galley and merchant ships, but only a few had full sails. They skirted the outside part of the Summer Quarters of the Sultan. Pillars supported the building that extended furthest out toward the harbor. The structure rose several stories high.

"I usually do not go this way," Dilara said. "The Sultan would not be happy to see me leave."

"Do not worry."

The two women rounded the Sultan's summer quarters and reached a large terrace courtyard. On the other side, the winter quarters of the Sultan were built slightly lower. Both summer and winter quarters, built perpendicular to one another, overlooked the Great Basin, an open reservoir large enough for a small boat. The Great Basin fed the many fountains of the hillside gardens leading down to the Golden Horn, the harbor of *Stamboul*. At the bottom of the hill, on the other side of the fortified walls fronting the busy harbor, the Sultan stored his barges inside long sheds.

Aisha's father used to toss dwarfs from his boat into the basin or from his barges in the harbor. None of the little men drowned, but when the old one, who had befriended young Aisha, got hurt, he confessed, *Falling into the water stung.* She did not tell anyone, for she would rather keep things peaceful within the palace.

When Aisha's brother acceded to power, he did not like that amusement. Along with most of his father's *odalisques*, Sultan Mehmet III sent the small people away to the Old *Seraglio*, the old palace in the center of the city. Most of the older women would remain there for the remainder of their lives. A few of the aging *odalisques* might obtain a marriage to a great *pasha* and take a few slaves and their favorite dwarfs with them.

38

Beyond the far side of the basin, next to the quarters of the Chief Black Eunuch, a long building housed more than one thousand Black eunuchs, mutes, and dwarves.

Golden Way, Imperial Harem

ON THE OPPOSITE side of the courtyard, not far from the main palace mosque, Aisha and Dilara walked along the Golden Way, the covered hallway that the Sultan used when he visited the *Divan*. When Aisha's brother first came to power, he occasionally listened to the council proceedings from a hidden room near Justice Tower, but for the last several years, he rarely rendered judgment. Staying secluded in the Imperial Harem, Sultan Mehmet III conversed with the Chief White Eunuch, the Chief Black Eunuch, and with his mother instead.

Aisha and Dilara soon reached the Queen's Gate—named not for the *Haseki Sultana* or the Sultan's favorite, but for the *Valide Sultana*, the Sultan's Mother. Instead of exiting the main entrance to the Imperial Harem behind the Divan, Aisha and Dilara stayed inside, passing through a room occupied by twenty or thirty Black eunuchs. These eunuchs, as well as nearly one thousand more living inside, enforced the writing inscribed above the Queen's gate, words Aisha had read many times. The verses from the *Qur'an* admonished what everyone knew: no man would dare enter the harem—only the Sultan or his young sons could.

Less than a minute later, Aisha, Dilara, and her growing number of escorts reached a line of carriages stationed by the Carriage Gate.

Dilara exclaimed, "Such a pretty carriage!"

The Black *eunuch* gestured for Dilara to be silent.

"Pretty enough for a princess," Aisha said. The fancy white carriage with two large rear wheels stood between the Divan and the stables. "Queen Elizabeth of England gave this carriage to my mother." Servants brushed the two white horses. Other servants polished the carriage body parked at the end of the pathway outside. "And Mother said I could use it today."

Not wishing to be seen, since Aisha knew that Turkish horsemen did not like horses used like beasts, like oxen pulling carts, the two women discreetly entered the white carriage. The eunuchs closed the door and with the latticed windows shut tight, Dilara lowered her veil. "Aisha, your shoes are so pretty."

"Perhaps, my shoemaker will fit you a pair."

"Can you tell me more about your slave?" Dilara asked.

"While visiting France, Captain Joseph Duxbury recruited him to be a soldier to fight Cardinal Albert of Austria in France and the Netherlands. When you see John, find out all you can."

"I shall."

The white carriage lurched forward.

Salon, Palace of Ibrahim *Pasha*, *Stamboul*, *AH* 1011 (Late Dec. *AD* 1602)

AISHA ESCORTED DILARA to the well-lit Salon rising in the center of her garden courtyard, the Third Courtyard of the Palace of Ibrahim *Pasha*. As the two women entered her reception room, Aisha realized she could find almost anything in *Stamboul*, even a Dutch translator. "Dilara, I want you to find out all you can about the *capitano* and how he became a soldier." She motioned for her to sit down on the sofa beneath the tall window. "I must find out if my English slave really knows Dutch."

"I'll find the truth," Dilara promised. Her eyes widened when Captain John Smith, escorted by two Black eunuchs, entered the room.

Aisha dismissed her guards and smiled at her bearded slave. "*Capitano*."

John, dressed in his officer's uniform, smiled back and greeted her in Italian. "*Buon giorno!*"

"*Buon giorno, Giovanni!*" Aisha replied, saying 'John' in Italian. "We brought Dilara, the Dutch translator, back from the *New Palace*."

The *odalisque* from the Imperial Harem curtsied in the European manner. "*Goede middag.*"

"*Goede middag.*" John raised an eyebrow. "*Spreek u Engels?*"

"*Nee,*" Dilara answered. "Did you learn Dutch in Holland?"

"I learned Dutch while helping *Stadholder* Maurice and the *Republiek der Zeven Verenigde Nederlanden.*"

"The Republic of the Seven United Netherlands." Dilara translated what John had said into Turkish.

"How did you learn Dutch?" John asked.

"My father traded for spices from the Indies," Dilara said.

"Like the seasonings traded at the Egyptian Bazaar?" Aisha asked after hearing the translation.

"Yes." Her Dutch translator turned back to John. "Sometimes, Dutch merchants sailing in the Mediterranean would stop and buy them at Alexandria. The Ottoman Empire controls the trade through the Red Sea and Egypt." Dilara paused. "So you were recruited to become a soldier in the Netherlands?"

"And in France, under the banner of Captain Joseph Duxbury." John added, "After the English and Dutch sacked Cadiz in southern Spain during the summer of 1596, the Spanish King ordered his fleet to attack England and help the Catholics in Ireland. King Philip II wanted to take revenge vengeance against Queen Elizabeth for destroying his relief fleet worth millions. Nearly ten years after the Spanish Armada advanced to the Channel, he ordered the formation of a Second Spanish Armada.

"While King Philip II of Spain prepared his fleet, his most loyal ally in France, the Catholic Duke of Mercoeur, faced his own troubles with King Henry IV of France. The French King wanted Brittany, but the Duke of Mercoeur resisted. The Duke could not accept the fact that King Henry IV had partaken of the Mass and had become a Roman Catholic."

Chapter 5 — Duke of Mercoeur

Illustrious and Most Excellent Lord [Phillipe Emmanuel de Lorraine, Duke of Mercoeur]

I saw an order of Your Excellency that leaves me astonished that Your Excellency (being who he is) knows that there is a Most Christian King in France (Henry IV), since His Holiness [Pope Clement VIII] gave him absolution, treats him as such, and I am a Legate to him. His Holiness wants all to hold it [the forgiveness of the king's past sins], so that this also will be admitted in the province [Bretagne/Brittany] of Your Excellency's government . . .

Most excellent and illustrious lord, I kiss the hands of Your Excellency,

Cardinal de Florence [Allesandro de Medici], Legate [of Pope Clement VII]
Paris, Last day of September 1596
Translated from French by D.E.A.

Chateau des Ducs de Bretagne, Nantes, France, October *AD* 1596

THE DUCHESS ENTERED the large suite of her husband, the Duke of Mercoeur. Inside the *Chateau des Ducs de Bretagne*, the Chateau of the Dukes of Brittany. Philippe Emmanuel de Lorraine looked up from a letter he held in both hands and smiled at the sight of his wife, Marie. "Our daughter?"

"Francoise is fast asleep." Marie de Luxembourg pointed to his hand. "A letter?"

"*Oui*, from Paris." The Duke of Mercoeur set the parchment on a table. After embracing his wife, he stepped back. "The Cardinal of Florence says His Holiness has granted King Henry absolution. He insists that our government here accept it, too."

After partaking of the Catholic Mass, King Henry IV entered the gates of Paris. Later, he sent his proxy to Rome, where Pope Clement VIII had accepted King Henry's conversion from the Reformed Christian Faith propagated by Jean Calvin and the French Huguenots.

"Can we?" Marie of Luxembourg, a descendant of the Dukes of Brittany, held the title of Duchess of Penthièvre.

"The Pope wants the war between France and Spain to cease, but we must ensure that the true Roman Catholic religion remains in Brittany."

"But how?" the Duchess asked. "King Philip II has withdrawn almost all of the Spanish garrison at Blavet."

"The truce between the French King and us will extend until January. We can replace the Spanish *tercio* with three thousand of our own men."

"But their pay?" Marie asked.

"The monies must come from Spain."

"*Sire!*" A guard appeared.

The Duke turned to the doorway. "*Oui?*"

"The envoy from King Philip II."

"Show him in."

The guard back away, and the Spanish envoy entered, bowed to the Duke, and kissed the hand of the Duchess.

"Good to see you again." The Duchess of Penthièvre glanced at her husband. "Our daughter will soon awaken from her nap."

Philipe Emmanel de Lorraine, Duke of Mercoeur

The envoy let go of her hand. "Francoise is almost four, is she not?"

"How nice of you to remember." She picked up her scarf. "Her birthday's next month."

Marie gracefully ambled across the marble floor, and as soon as she exited the suite, the Duke of Mercoeur motioned for the envoy to sit down. "Any response from Madrid?" The Duke pulled his chair closer.

"To your request for monies?" The Spanish envoy gestured 'no' with his hand. "None, so far."

"How can I fight the King of France alone?" Even though the Marshall of France, Jean VI d'Aumont, had succumbed to a musket wound he received while reconnoitering the *Chateau de* Comper, the Duke had to abandon that important castle a year earlier. "I cannot hold Brittany forever for *Infanta* Isabella." He referred to the daughter of King Philip II and Elizabeth of Valois, who was the daughter of the French King Henry II.

"There's no confirmation that this year's silver fleet has arrived. King Philip II is also short of funds. Many of the chief merchants in Seville teeter near bankruptcy."

"I know they lost much when Sir Walter Raleigh and the English sank the Indies supply fleet in the harbor of Cadiz. But the King?"

"His Most Catholic Majesty still wants to land ten thousand soldiers to support the Earl of Tyrone in Ireland. Nearly one hundred ships and galleys have been mobilized at Lisbon."

"It is so late in the year." The Duke sighed as he gazed out the arched windows of the Chateau. Thin clouds streaked high over Brittany. "And if winds keep the *Adelantado Mayor* of Castile from reaching Ireland?" The Duke knew the *Adelantado* had been appointed admiral of the second Spanish armada.

"The Spanish fleet has orders to land at Milford Haven in Wales, to seek support from Welsh Catholics."

"The English must suspect an impending attack."

"It is no secret that King Philip wants to take vengeance on the Queen of England. Along with my concurrence, I forwarded your suggestion that the *Adelantado* should winter the Spanish Armada here in Brittany."

"I trust the King responds soon." The Duke peered down into the tufa courtyard. Near one of the guard towers, several of his seasoned officers drilled his pikemen. Most had fought alongside him when he defeated French forces under the Duke of Montpensier at the Battle of Craon four years earlier. If King Philip did not send aid, the Duke might be forced to make peace with King Henry IV. "In the meantime, I must continue the truce with the French monarch."

On the opposite side of the courtyard, the Duchess led their daughter out of the Ducal residence by the hand. The Duke caught the eye of his confidante. He trusted his wife very much. If King Philip II did not send his fleet to Brittany, King Henry IV might offer the Duke of Mercoeur other positions—such as Admiral of Brittany, or perhaps Admiral of France.

Chapter 6 — Second Spanish Armada

The King [Philip II of Spain] has sent orders that the Armada is to sail at once, even though provisions are not ready. The Adelantado [Mayor of Castile] summoned all the captains and pilots to give their opinion on oath. On this the Adelantado drew up a memorial, which was signed by them all, and forwarded to the King, who, however, repeated his orders in a more imperative form. This obstinacy of His Majesty in sending out the fleet at this bad season makes people believe that it is to be directed at the Queen of England, in revenge for the insult she put upon him [at Cadiz in the summer of 1596] in the very heart of Spain.

Agustino Nani, Venetian Ambassador in Spain

Madrid, 3rd November 1596

***Palacio de los Austrias*, San Lorenzo de El Escorial, Spain, Sept. *AD* 1596**

KING PHILIP II of Spain steadied himself on his cane. "It is settled: our *Gran Armada* shall sail to Ireland."

"I'll return to Lisbon and oversee final preparations. Nearly one hundred ships will be readied." Martin *de* Padilla *y* Manrique, the Adelantado Mayor of Castile, gathered his papers at the *Palacio de los Austrias* at San Lorenzo de El Escorial. "Along with the two thousand soldiers from Blavet in Brittany, the six Apostles in the Bay of Biscay at Santander will be brought to Vigo."

"And the Dutch merchantmen we captured after Cadiz?" King Philip II asked. Following the English and Dutch sack of that important southern port, the monarch of both Spain and Portugal had finally returned from Toledo to the stark palace court outside Madrid.

"Sent to Lisbon and converted to fighting vessels," the Adelantado replied. "Italian soldiers from Genoa and Naples are expected. Seville and Andalusia are raising companies of men, too, but we need more monies for the carpenters and engineers."

"This year's Silver Fleet has not yet arrived from Havana," King Philip II said. "Press the workmen into service. The defense of our Kingdom and our estates requires it."

"*Si*, your Majesty." The Adelantado stepped to the door.

"I will accompany you to the courtyard." The King motioned for his daughter, *Infanta* Isabella, to help. Daughters of the kings of Spain and Portugal held the title of *infanta* rather than princess.

When they reached the courtyard, and the Adelantado mounted his horse, the gates opened. Before he could depart, a fast messenger entered and quickly dismounted.

"What is it?" the King asked.

The messenger bowed and handed the King a letter. "The Silver Fleet has landed at Sanlucar!"

Sanlucar stood at the mouth of the Guadalquivir River in southern Spain.

"Every ship?"

"Only one is missing, but they brought back twelve million in silver and gold."

"And our share?"

Infanta Isabella leaned closer to her father. "Four or five million."

"*Excellente!*" The King turned to the Adelantado. "Finalize the preparations."

Palace, San Lorenzo de El Escorial, Spain, Thursday, 24th Oct. *AD* 1596

A MONTH LATER, *Infanta* Isabella straightened the papers on her father's desk. As soon as King Philip II entered the room, his trustworthy daughter reported the news she had heard at Mass that morning, "Prayers for the armada's success have been said daily throughout Spain."

"In Toledo and Seville?"

"Everywhere," *Infanta* Isabella replied. "Many even chant a new psalm called '*Contra Paganos*'."

"We shall succeed against that dreaded pagan Queen of England —"

"Once and for all," the *Infanta* interrupted.

"The English Jesuit Robert Persons has translated the treatise into Latin."

"I hope Pope Clement VIII accepts it," the *Infanta* said.

"His Holiness must accept it. When Queen Elizabeth dies, you are entitled to the throne of England, but it may not be easy to secure that island kingdom."

"*Si*, Father," the *Infanta* agreed. "King Henry IV has sworn an oath with the Queen's Ambassador at Rouen."

"They have even invited our seven rebellious provinces of the Netherlands to join them." The King then added, "Your cousin, Albert of Austria, may be threatened."

A guard opened the door. "Your Highness, the ministers are waiting."

"Send them in."

Both Foreign Minister Juan *de* Idiaquez *y* Olazábal and Domestic Minister Cristobal *de* Moura bowed as they entered the King's presence. *Don* Cristobal *de* Moura waved a letter. "We have news from the Adelantado."

"What does the Count of Santa Gadea say? Are his preparations complete?" the King asked. "Has the fleet sailed?"

"The preparations are complete," the minister replied, "but your Armada has not sailed. The Adelantado Mayor of Castile encloses a petition."

"A petition?" King Philip II questioned.

"Yes." Cristobal *de* Moura handed the petition to Isabella, who handed it to the King. "Because of the lateness of the season, all of the captains and pilots of the fleet have signed."

"What do you mean?" The King grew agitated. He waved the document. "What does it say?"

"Because the risk of storms is so great, they fear your Armada would be shipwrecked."

"The attack on Cadiz must not stand!" The Spanish monarch rose. "I will have no further delays!" He pounded on the desk. "The *gran* Armada must sail!"

"To Ireland, to help the Irish Catholics?" Cristobal *de* Moura asked.

"No," the King said, "to Brittany."

"But the Irish? Dozens of priests are ready to sail."

"We need to help the Duke of Mercoeur."

"But the port of Blavet in southern Brittany is shallow and not large; it cannot handle the six Apostles."

The six Apostles, the largest ships in the Spanish fleet, had deep drafts. Besides caravels, numerous galleys joined the fleet.

"We will attack King Henry at the port of Brest. I want to divert his attention from Cardinal Albert and Flanders, but under no circumstance shall the Armada sail into the channel or go beyond Calais."

"We do not want a repeat of what happened eight years ago," *Don* Juan *de* Idiaquez added. "In the first Armada, we lost more ships in the storm than in the battle."

King Philip signed the revised orders. He handed the letter, sealed with wax, to a waiting messenger.

After the ministers departed, the *Infanta* approached the King. "Father, do you need to rest?"

"I do not need rest!" The king's countenance grimaced, his body stiffened. "Passing gravel is so painful."

Lisbon, Portugal, 25ᵗʰ October *AD* 1596

ONBOARD THE FLAGSHIP of the invincible Armada, the Adelantado broke the royal seal and read the latest orders from King Philip II.

"What is it?" the general of the land army asked.

"New orders. King Philip II insists we sail immediately." The Adelantado of Castile surveyed Lisbon harbor, where more than half of the fleet of ninety-eight ships and support vessels remained anchored. Along with more than thirty Jesuit priests, the finest of the Portuguese nobility had already boarded. Galleys from Naples and ships from Seville had delivered armaments, cannons, and supplies. Nearly a dozen support vessels from Sanlucar would sail with them.

"The sea has finally calmed, but it's so late in the year."

Scattered clouds, remnants of the latest storm, drifted to the east.

"The King is adamant. He insists we go before winter."

"To Ireland?"

"No, to Brest," the Adelantado replied.

"At the tip of Brittany? But what shall become of the priests and their families?"

"I know. But we must obey his Most Catholic Majesty." The Adelantado looked at his Council. "Load what you can. We sail in the morning to Vigo to meet the rest of the fleet."

Cape Finisterre, Galicia, Northwest Spain, Evening, 27 October *AD* 1596

"BATTEN DOWN THE hatches!" the Adelantado of Castile ordered.

"Aye! Adelantado. A nasty storm." The helmsman gripped the wheel and relayed the command.

The Adelantado's stomach rose with each wave and sank just as quickly. When gale-force winds buffeted the flagship of King Philip's Second Invincible Armada, he ordered, "Furl the mainsail!" He did not want it ripped to shreds.

Ahead, skirting the fast-approaching weather, several ships cleared Cape Finisterre. They sailed north to open seas. Behind, scores of other ships tossed. Many floundered in the terrible tempest at the tip of the rocky cape.

"The transports from the Bay of Biscay?" the Adelantado asked.

"The ones with soldiers from Blavet?" the helmsman asked. "They haven't cleared Baiona."

The ancient town of Baiona stood at the entrance of the Bay of Vigo in Galicia, the province bordering the Atlantic at the northwest corner of the Iberian Peninsula.

"At least they are protected at Vigo." The Adelantado told the helmsman, "We must make it beyond those reefs."

The helmsman tacked close to the wind, but a strong gust whipped the ship. Tossed side to side, it rose over the raging waves. Water splashed over the bow.

The sky darkened further, and bells rang louder.

"All hands on deck! All hands on deck!"

The storm intensified with gusts whipping the side.

Closer to shore, a small transport hit a reef. Its bow pointed toward the sky. Lightning brightened the heavens. Waves pounded and the ship's ribs groaned below. Another wave crashed against the castle. Wood splintered, chunks of timber floated in the water.

Sailors tossed excess baggage over the rail. Others grabbed the lines. Some waved their arms and screamed, "*Misericordia! Misericordia!*" The devout were ready to die.

"We can do no more. Save the ship!"

"Aye, Aye!" The mate motioned to the sailors, who retrieved the mizzen sail, but it ripped, tearing lengthwise.

The sea churned and percolated. Foam and froth blew across the deck with each rise of the tide. Through the night and into the next day, the powerful storm continued its onslaught. The dark skies finally broke the next afternoon.

Sailors manned the pumps below, while carpenters patched countless leaks. Most of the seasoned sailors had weathered the storm. But the land soldiers on board did not fare so well; most had become sick and remained pale from their initiation.

A sailor high above in the crow's nest pointed to shore. "Ferrol!"

The Adelantado's ship limped past Coruna and into the port of Ferrol on the far side of the *ria* or bay.

Second Spanish Armada Wrecked — Coasts of Portugal and Spain - Autumn 1596

Ferrol, Galicia, Northwest Spain

TRANSPORTS FROM VIGO carrying soldiers from Blavet arrived two days later. In the harbor of Ferrol, the Adelantado of Castile welcomed the commander of the Biscay squadron onto his badly damaged ship. "How bad?" the admiral of the fleet asked.

"We saw the remnants of a dozen ships on the reefs of Cape Finisterre." The squadron commander peered around the bay. "Only forty ships and galleys here?"

"We may have lost more than fifty, including the ones carrying the Portuguese nobility and many Jesuits."

"And the supply ships? The sailors?" the squadron commander asked.

"At least two thousand dead," the army general said.

"We must retire here for the winter." the Adelantado peered to shore. "Find housing on land."

"The town is not large," the general said. "I will write the King."

"Very well." The Adelantado watched the weakened men disembark.

Palacio de los Austrias, **San Lorenzo de El Escorial, Early Nov. 1596**

IN EARLY NOVEMBER, *Infanta* Isabella gazed at the skies above the mountains outside the palace at San Lorenzo de El Escorial. High clouds streaked eastward. King Philip II and his daughter had already received word that the new armada had sailed from Lisbon on the 25th of October.

"Word from your Admiral, the Adelantado Mayor of Castile," *Infanta* Isabella told her father.

Foreign Minister Juan *de* Idiaquez and Domestic Minister Cristobal *de* Moura joined the king and the *Infanta* in his study.

"What does the Count of Santa Gadea say?" the King asked.

Isabella scanned the paper before summarizing the message to her father.

"What is it?"

"On the twenty-seventh, the Armada met a violent storm off Cape Finisterre."

"A storm? Why do the heavens wail against me? We lost so many ships in the first Armada. And now?" King Philip II asked. "Is it bad?"

The *Infanta* read and relayed the general's report. "Thirty ships are missing. Eighteen took to the open sea, but at least twelve ships and two thousand infantry have been lost."

"Sunk in the sudden storm?"

"The Adelantado believes so."

"And the rest of the Armada?"

"The Count of Santa Gadea has taken refuge at the port of *el* Ferrol."

The King indicated his disapproval and turned to Foreign Minister Juan *de* Idiaquez. "Send word to my nephew Albert in Brussels. If I cannot get revenge on Queen Elizabeth for her attack on Cadiz, perhaps the Cardinal can."

"We will need more monies."

~ ~ ~

TWO DAYS LATER, King Philip II met with a delegation from Seville and Castile. "We need more revenues."

"Beyond the millions we've already given?" the leader of the delegation asked.

"At least three million more."

"We gave and gave. We have no more."

"We must protect Christendom, the Catholic religion, our kingdom, and our domains."

"You have your estates."

"They're mortgaged to other bankers and financiers. You must lend me more," the King declared.

"Twenty-eight million over twenty years is not enough?"

"I insist. The kingdom needs it."

"Your Highness, we protest the one and one-half million in Bills of Exchange drawn on Cardinal Albert's account."

"No more credit? You risk losing our Lowlands!"

The delegation from Seville bowed and quickly departed.

The King turned to his ministers. "We have no choice."

"Devalue the currency?" Domestic Minister Moura asked.

"No. We must repudiate all of our debts." The King pondered for a few seconds. "Too many talented people have abandoned agriculture and mechanical work and have gone into banking and trade instead. The silver and gold from the Indies have ended up in rebel hands through trade. To protect Christendom, our kingdom, and our domains, we must reclaim all revenues to our estates."

"But our creditors will go bankrupt!"

"We have no other means to help ourselves. It is their fault. Those same merchants refuse more bills of exchange." The Spanish King declared, "Issue the proclamation: we repudiate all debts. All other payments from our estates are null and void."

Le Havre de Grace, France, Autumn *AD* 1596

"SO THE RICHEST nation in history has gone bankrupt?" Captain Joseph Duxbury asked the French merchantman. Two young English recruits and John, the teenage youth from Lincolnshire. gathered round.

"In Genoa, more than a million in interest has been lost. Merchants from Lyon to Antwerp cannot pay their bills. I suspect the Frankfurt exchange will face dire consequences."

"So the Spanish fleet was lost?" John Smith asked. "Are you certain?"

"A fast truth," the French merchant declared. "The Spanish merchant from Bilboa saw the letters from the General himself."

Seawater slammed against the ragged rocks at *Le Havre de Grace*. John Smith peered toward the Western horizon. The cold wind and salty spray stung his face. Whitecaps broke over choppy waters. Gray clouds portended more rain.

"That's the ship to Scotland." Captain Joseph Duxbury pointed to a vessel anchored in the tidal harbor.

"I can go to Scotland later." John checked to make certain that the papers David Hume of Godscroft had given him in Paris stayed dry. "I am ready to begin my life as a soldier."

"Do you know how to fight?" Captain Joseph Duxbury asked.

"I practiced with a sword a few times."

"I can teach you more."

"And I learned a little bit in Orleans, where I served Lord Willoughby's sons."

"The brave Lord Willoughby?"

"Yes, the Lord who knighted Francis Vere."

"Yes, I heard. Lord Willoughby prevented Spanish barges from leaving the Low Countries," Captain Duxbury said.

John knew the story that happened eight years earlier. "The Catholic allies couldn't assist the first Spanish Armada to invade England."

"The Spanish king, Philip II, still claims control of all of the Low Countries for Spain. He has sent his nephew, Cardinal Albert of Austria, to bring the Seven States of the United Netherlands back into submission."

The quest for Dutch independence began several decades earlier. Of the seventeen original provinces in the lowlands, only ten remained loyal to the king of Spain. The *Republiek der Zeven Verenigde Nederlanden* formally declared its independence.

"But Queen Elizabeth and King Henry IV have formed an offensive and defensive alliance," John said. "And Holland and Zeeland?"

"The Seven United Provinces have been under her Majesty's protection, but now the King of France has sent the Duke of Bouillon to make them a full partner in the alliance. King Henry IV insisted that the term 'States' be added to the agreement and overcame the objections of both the English nobility and the Queen. She wanted to keep the free Dutch provinces under her protection." Captain Duxbury added, "John, I will teach you how to fight and how to ride."

White caps lapped against the walls of *Le Havre de Grace.* John did not take long to answer. "Yes."

"Very well, English recruit," Captain Duxbury said. "Are you ready?"

Young John Smith, now sixteen years old, snapped to attention and saluted. "I will fight for you."

Chapter 7 — Triple Alliance

Around this time the 2,000 English [soldiers], so long promised, came into France to join with the 4,000 Swiss and other troops of the King [Henry IV]. They would preserve and keep the time throughout the winter until the war [against Spain and Cardinal Albert] began anew.

Journal, Anthony Duyck, 27 November 1596
Translated from Dutch by D.E.A.

Salon, Palace of Ibrahim *Pasha*, AH 1011 (Late December AD 1602)

AISHA ESCORTED DILARA to the well-lit Salon built in the center of her garden courtyard, the Third Courtyard of the Palace of Ibrahim *Pasha*. As the two women entered her reception room, Aisha realized she could find almost anything in *Stamboul*, even a Dutch translator. "Dilara, I want you to find out all you can about the *capitano* and how he became a soldier." She motioned for her to sit down on the sofa beneath a window framed by textured drapes. "I must find out if my English slave really knows Dutch."

"I'll find the truth," Dilara's eyes widened when Captain John Smith, escorted by two Black eunuchs, entered the room.

Aisha dismissed her guards and smiled at her bearded slave. "*Capitano.*"

John, dressed in his officer's uniform, smiled back and greeted her in Italian. "*Buon giorno!*"

"*Buon giorno, Giovanni!*" Aisha replied, saying 'John' in Italian. "We brought Dilara, the Dutch translator, back from the *New Palace*."

The *odalisque* from the Imperial Harem curtsied in the European manner. "*Goede middag.*"

"*Goede middag.*" John raised an eyebrow. "*Spreek u Engels?*"

"*Nee,*" Dilara answered. "Did you learn Dutch in Holland?"

"I learned Dutch while helping *Stadtholder* Maurice and the *Republiek der Zeven Verenigde Nederlanden.*"

"The Republic of the Seven United Netherlands." Dilara translated what John had said into Turkish.

"How did you learn Dutch?" John asked.

"My father traded for spices from the Indies," Dilara said.

"Like the seasonings traded at the Egyptian Bazaar?" Aisha asked after hearing the translation.

"Yes." Her Dutch translator turned back to John. "Sometimes Dutch merchants sailing in the Mediterranean would stop and buy them at Alexandria. The Ottoman Empire controls the trade through the Red Sea and Egypt." Dilara paused before asking, "You were recruited to become a soldier in the Netherlands?"

"And in France, under the banner of Captain Joseph Duxbury." John added, "After the English and Dutch sacked Cadiz in the summer of 1596, the Spanish King ordered his fleet to attack England and Ireland. King Philip II sought to exact revenge against Queen Elizabeth for having destroyed his fleet in that southern Spanish port. Nearly ten years after he sent the Spanish Armada, he ordered a Second Spanish Armada to sail, but like the first time, he did not succeed. That autumn, a storm ravaged his fleet off the coast of Spain. Around that same time, Captain Duxbury recruited me at Rouen, in France. I agreed to join him on the coast, at *Le Havre de Grace.*"

"To serve in France?"

"And also in Holland. As allies, we served under *Stadtholder* Maurice, the son of William of Orange-Nassau. Several decades earlier, Prince William had started the War for Dutch Independence. They fought against the harsh oppression of the Spaniards."

"But where is Orange and Nassau?" Aisha asked.

"Orange is in southern France, but the County of Nassau is in the German-speaking territories of the Middle Rhine River Valley. In late 1596, the Seven United Provinces of the Netherlands joined the recent alliance between England and France."

"A triple alliance?"

"Yes, a triple alliance," John answered. "Queen Elizabeth agreed to send two thousand English soldiers to help her 'brother,' King Henry IV of France."

"And you?"

"Six years ago, I began to train with other English recruits along the border of Normandy and Picardy."

CAPTAIN JOSEPH DUXBURY brought young John Smith from *Le Havre de Grace* at the mouth of the river Seine to join the two thousand other English soldiers sent by Queen Elizabeth to aid her ally King Henry IV in northern France. The two English regiments trained at Aumale, a small town nestled in the rolling countryside northeast of Rouen, along the border of Normandy and Picardy.

"We have learned how to use the sword, the pike, and the battle axe." "This morning, we will practice shooting the arquebus." Duxbury held up a three-foot firearm in front of fifty of his men. The captain demonstrated the proper technique for using the matchlock firearm — shorter than a musket yet longer than a pistol. He waved his newest recruit forward. "John Smith, come here."

"Yes, Captain!" John, following his Captain's lead, practiced firing the arquebus. He loaded the black powder, the musket ball, and practiced numerous times. Using a slow-burning rope wrapped around his thigh, he lit the short arquebus match cord attached to the serpentine lock. He aimed the weapon and squeezed the trigger. The match pan flashed, the bullet fired.

After a few hours of practice, Captain Duxbury again lined up his company inside the small chateau. "We will now practice with the sword."

"But we already know," one recruit retorted

"You will practice again. Hold your sword like this."

The soldiers raised their swords. They practiced fighting against each other, charging and blocking blows.

"Stop!" Captain Duxbury raised his hand. "John, get ready. Everyone else watch!"

Captain John Duxbury drew his sword and charged at John. The new recruit raised his sword and blocked the hard blow. He countered with a broad swing. The two swords clashed. Duxbury attacked again. John blocked it. On the third attack, Duxbury disarmed the young soldier from Lincolnshire. "You make progress."

"You beat me again." John picked up his weapon. He glanced at his fellow recruits. "We want to fight Cardinal Albert."

"Our chance to fight the Spanish in Artois or Hainaut will come soon enough. King Henry IV still wants to recapture Calais from Cardinal Albert."

Albert had captured the port of Calais a year earlier.

"How long must we drill?" a recruit asked.

"Until your skills are perfected." Duxbury commanded, "Company, line up! Retrieve your pikes!"

John and the other recruits grabbed their long pikes. Holding their pikes upright, the fifty new recruits stood shoulder to shoulder, in rows of five. Veterans watched from the edge of the small square.

"Advance the pike!" Duxbury pointed to the gate of the chateau. "March as though the enemy is on the other side of a breach!"

John and the other soldiers lowered the sharp tips of the pike.

"Men, we are a fighting unit. Keep together! Close those ranks."

The English soldiers marched steadily toward the open gate.

"In battle, if the first row falters, the second row pushes forward. Whether a breach or a gate, you must capture it."

When the company rushed through the gate, Colonel Thomas Baskerville gestured his approval. "Captain, your men improve every day."

Captain Duxbury motioned for his men to fall in line. "They are eager to fight."

"I have just arrived from Rouen." Colonel Baskerville pulled his horse around. "The French are not yet ready."

"The Assembly of Notables?" Captain Duxbury asked.

"The nobles have not yet agreed on the means to pay the army."

"But at least our men are paid."

"Yes, for now the Queen pays our wages, but the nobles must find more money. After six months, King Henry IV is obliged to pay."

"They cannot agree?"

"The Papal Legate has arrived in Rouen, and many of the French nobles want to negotiate with Cardinal Albert for peace." The Colonel gestured to several wagons arriving from Rouen behind him. "But now I need your help."

"Colonel?"

"King Henry IV wants these munitions taken to Amiens. Your company can provide the guard in case the Duke of Aumale attacks."

Captain Duxbury saluted and turned. "Men! You heard the Colonel. Get your gear. Mount up!"

John and the rest of the company rushed and retrieved their gear. Within minutes, they mounted their horses and exited. They rode alongside the wagons—some filled with gunpowder and others loaded with cannonballs.

Hours later, John peered north across the Somme River and spied a group of horsemen heading away from Amiens. "The Duke of Aumale?"

"No sign of the Duke," Captain Duxbury said. "Those soldiers are the Swiss allies of the French."

"Is the Duke of Aumale, French?" John asked.

"At the start of the French Wars of Religion, the Duke, Charles of Guise, joined the Catholic League and fought against King Henry. The Duke had command of all of the Catholic forces in Picardy, including Amiens." Duxbury pointed down the road, where tall walls surrounded the river town, the most important city in Picardy.

"The walls look much stronger than those at Aumale," John said.

"They are," Duxbury agreed. "But when the king offered Amiens a garrison, the city declined."

"Declined a Royal garrison?"

"When the capital of Picardy surrendered to King Henry IV several years ago, they insisted. They included it in the stipulation."

***Porte de la Hotoie*, Amiens, Picardy, France, Late December, *AD* 1596**

DUXBURY AND SMITH accompanied the wagons through the *Porte de la Hotoie*. As soon as they reached the Cathedral, the English recruit stopped and looked up. The single spire and nave seemed even higher than when he had spied it at a distance, outside the town. Near the side door of the cathedral, a large man wearing religious garb stood and watched the procession of wagons pass by until it reached the town square.

"So many supplies." John counted forty cannons. "But no Royal soldiers?"

"I will ask," Duxbury said.

The wagons stopped in front of the Governor of the town. After exchanging greetings, Captain Duxbury asked Count St. Pol, "I heard King Henry recently reiterated his desire to place a garrison inside your town."

"No garrison needed." The Governor motioned for his men to unload the wagons. "My men are strong enough to face Cardinal Albert, if he or the Duke of Aumale dares to attack."

"But their loyalty?"

"Their loyalty, like mine, cannot be questioned." The Governor of the town added, "Besides, these armaments are not for defense. King Henry wants to retake Calais."

"So the ammunition?"

"With these additional wagons, we have enough to arm all of the allies for a spring offensive."

"Including the Dutch?" Duxbury asked.

"The Seven United Provinces of the Netherlands formally approved the treaty between Queen Elizabeth and King Henry at the end of October."

"The triple alliance is strong?"

"King Henry must still give his final approval for the entry of the *Republiek der Zeven Verenigde Nederlanden* into the alliance. When he does, the Dutch will provide him with four thousand troops."

"We have heard rumors that the King seeks peace."

"Yes, secret negotiations."

John wondered whether he would ever get to fight.

Chapter 8 — Secret Negotiations

Albert, who was most willing to be nominated to be King of the Romans, sent the Admiral of Aragon to the Emperor [Rudolph II]. . . The Emperor asked the Admiral of Aragon if he could recommend an experienced soldier, who the ministers of Flanders value and who could guide the army in Hungary. The Admiral, after approval of the Archduke [Cardinal Albert] recommended Giorgio Basta.

<u>History of Philip II, King of Spain</u> by Cabrera de Cordoba
Translated from Spanish by D.E.A.

Inner Courtyard, Coudenberg Palace, Brussels, Summer, *AD* 1596

ALBERT OF AUSTRIA, the Governor of the Lowlands, stood in the courtyard of the hilltop palace of Coudenberg inside Brussels. Arriving through the principal gate, the carriage of the Admiral of Aragon, Francisco *de* Mendoza, approached Albert, the former Cardinal of Toledo. Since reaching the capital of the obedient Provinces in February, the Admiral had faithfully served Cardinal Albert as his High Steward, his Chief of Household.

The carriage circled around the rectangular courtyard, passing a small, hexagon-shaped fountain structure. The carriage slowed as it passed the main building holding both the living quarters and offices of the newly appointed governor. With its arched walkways and dormer windows, this three-story structure spanned the whole length of the courtyard. Its outer side overlooked the tiltyard where knights jousted. Vast parklands, suitable for hunts and chases, surrounded this palace of the Dukes of Brabant, and later those of Burgundy. The Dutch word Coudenberg meant 'cold hill.'

After the requisite, formal exchange of greetings, Cardinal Albert told the Admiral of Aragon, "King Philip II agrees that you should go to see all of the Catholic Electors in Germany."

Three ecclesiastical, Catholic archbishops and four secular Prince-Electors chose the King of the Romans.

"If Emperor Rudolph II dies without an heir, the Elector of Palatinate could become the new Holy Roman Emperor."

Emperor Rudolph II had established his throne in Prague in the Kingdom of Bohemia.

"It would be a disaster if all of Germany became Protestant. That is why you need to persuade the electors and my brother that I should be made the Holy Roman Emperor."

"Will not your brother be displeased that you—instead of he—will marry *Infanta* Isabella Clara Eugenia?"

"Rudolph's engagement to *Infanta* Isabella was broken off years ago, and he married another."

"Yes, but that marriage failed." The Admiral of Aragon had inherited his own title via his wife, who had passed away early in their marriage. With his wavy hair and full beard turning gray, Francisco de Mendoza also had a receding hairline. Now almost fifty years old, the Admiral was about a dozen years older than the Cardinal. "Will Rudolph agree to step down? He has said that he would not mind having the Reich end with him."

"As my High Steward, I trust your judgment. Attempt to convince Rudolph to resign and support me to be the new King of the Romans."

"I like that sound. But will not the Electors object?"

"Tell them it would not be the first time an Emperor has been deposed."

"But what of your two other older brothers?"

"King Philip II considers neither Mathias nor Maximilian to be suitable candidates."

"Not Catholic enough?"

"Yes, according to His Most Catholic Majesty in Spain. Something must be done. It cannot be destined that my brother Rudolph will be the last King of the Romans."

A servant opened the carriage door. The Admiral stepped toward it, but turned back. "Is there something more?"

Cardinal Albert handed him a letter. "Besides telling the House of Austria about my marriage to his daughter, King Philip II would like you to arrange the details of the marriage between Prince Philip of Spain and Margaret of Austria."

"Your confidence is not misplaced. I am certain Archduke Charles II of Styria would have been pleased to have his pious daughter marry the future King of Spain. His widow will be most pleased." Styria with its capital at Graz, southeast of Vienna, Austria, also kept a border with Hungary to its east. The Admiral stepped into his carriage and closed the door. "Any word from the town of Hulst?"

"Giorgio Basta reconnoiters the fortifications. Count Maurice of Nassau-Orange built his reputation when he captured Hulst, and I intend to reverse it."

"The cost of Spanish lives may be high."

"My soldiers' lives belong to God; their bodies belong to the King."

"General Basta arrives now." The Admiral pointed to the far principal gate.

Accompanied by his small guard, the able Albanian general quickly dismounted. "Hulst can be won."

"I wish I could listen to your full report, but my mission for the King must not be delayed." The Admiral of Aragon motioned to his driver. "I must take my leave, but I shall write often."

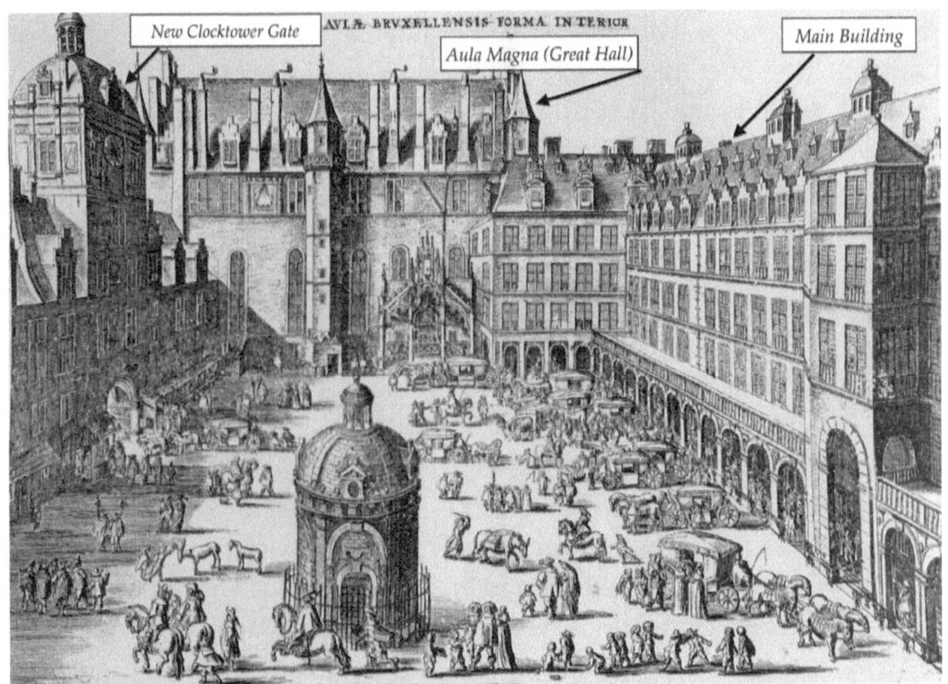

New Fountain & Inner Courtyard - Coudenberg Palace, 1600s

Aula Magna, **Coudenberg Palace, Brussels, November *AD* 1596**

MONTHS LATER, INSIDE *Aula Magna*, the large hall of Coudenberg Palace, an attendant dusted the benches. When she walked toward the door, the new governor of the Seventeen Provinces of the Lowlands stopped her. "You are not disturbing me. Finish your work."

"As you wish." The attendant retrieved her dusting cloth, lifted the soft cushions, and wiped the hard benches. She replaced the cushions where delegates from the obedient provinces would sit and finished her work in the hall. Massive tapestries depicting hunts and other nature scenes adorned the walls.

Cardinal Albert reflected on the events that transpired since his arrival in Brussels in February. Marshall Savigne *de* Rosne led the Catholic army and captured the French port of Calais on the Channel opposite Dover. During the summer, Rosne marched north and besieged Hulst. While implementing the plans of Giorgio Basta, thousands of Spanish soldiers died, and an enemy cannonball killed the Marshall. Nonetheless, Hulst capitulated in August before a final assault.

The death of Marshall *de* Rosne weighed heavily on his mind, but greater problems confronted the Cardinal. King Henry IV of France had concluded an offensive and defensive alliance with Queen Elizabeth of England. Moreover, the French King had sent emissaries to The Hague in Holland, as well as to the courts of Northern Europe.

Prince Philip William of Orange, whose own large palace or *hof* stood nearby, entered the chambers where the States-General met. "Am I disturbing you?"

"No." Albert, now seated on the throne once occupied by Charles V, waved the Catholic Prince, the older half-brother of Count Maurice, forward. "I was just thinking about the alliance between France and England."

"At the end of October, the Seven Rebellious Provinces approved the alliance at The Hague," Prince Philip William said. "And King Henry has sent ambassadors to the Protestant electors of the Holy Roman Empire. He wants the kings of both Sweden and Denmark to join him."

"Any word about the Second Spanish Armada?" Albert asked.

"Not yet. Hopefully, the fleet will aid the Duke of Mercoeur in Brittany and distract King Henry."

As they conversed, the chamber door swung open. A messenger entered, bowed, and handed Albert a letter. "From Spain."

The Cardinal read the shocking news and sank back into his chair.

"What is it?" Philip William asked.

Albert's able general, Giorgio Basta, and other officers entered the room. President Jean Richardot, the head of his Privy Council, joined the others, including heads of the five *serments* or oaths of Brussels. Among these loyal *serments* was the famous *Serment de Saint Georges*. Like the other *serments*, this guild pledged and maintained its loyalty to the Dukes of Brabant.

"A violent storm met the Second Spanish Armada off Cape Finisterre on the twenty-seventh of October. Most of the ships were destroyed; others went missing. Thousands of sailors and soldiers died." Albert recognized the shock on the faces of his advisors. "Neither the Duke of Mercoeur in Brittany nor Hugh O'Neil in Ireland will receive any relief."

"Will no aid come to the lowlands?" President Richardot, like many other noblemen and women, sported a wide, ruff collar.

"None." Albert, no longer dressed in his traditional ecclesiastical attire. Instead, he donned a ruff collar thicker than Jean Richardot's. "Bring me *Seignior La* Balvena."

"The gentleman of Count de la Fera?" An attendant answered.

"Yes," Albert said. "We need to communicate directly with King Henry IV."

As the first messenger and the attendant exited, a second messenger arrived. He waved a letter—sealed parchment. "From your older brother."

"News from the Holy Roman Emperor Rudolph II?" Cardinal Albert wondered whether Rudolph would resign in his favor.

"No, your other brother, Archduke Maximilian of Austria."

Cardinal Albert knew Maximilian commanded the armies of the Holy Roman Empire. "Maximilian faced Sultan Mehmet III in Hungary?" He broke the seal.

"Yes, along with Sigismund Bathory, the Prince of Transylvania," the messenger said. "They confronted about 100,000 *sipahis*, *janissaries*, and Tartars at Mezo-Keresztes outside Eger in upper Hungary."

Albert could tell the news was not good. The Cardinal read the expression on the messenger's face like he had read words written on the scroll himself. "How bad?"

"Very bad. Sultan Mehmet III and the Ottoman Turks routed the Emperor's army at Keresztes."

"How?"

"Maximilian had the distinct advantage of a strong position in a secure mountain, but Prince Bathory urged him to attack, so they crossed the water. The army attacked the Sultan's camp, killed thousands, and even reached the Sultan's tent. Archduke Maximilian's army began to pillage and plunder, but too soon."

"What do you mean?"

"We learned from a captured Turkish officer that the Sultan's tutor urged him to stand firm. Hasan *Pasha* attacked from one side, while Cigalazade Yusuf Sinan *Pasha* and the brother of the Khan of the Crimean Tartars attacked from the other side. They routed Maximilian's army, taking many prisoners."

"No!" Albert could not believe his ears. "And my brother?"

"Maximilian escaped, but the Turks and the Tartars killed between 35,000 and 36,000 Christians."

"That many?" The news shocked Albert. He sank further into his chair. "Where is my brother now?"

"The army fled to the mountains. Your brother Maximilian returned to Vienna, while Sigismund Bathory retired to his princedom in Transylvania."

Within the hour, *Seignor* Balvena entered the Council Chambers. "Find out from King Henry what it will take for him to agree to peace," Albert said.

"Yes, your Highness." Balvena bowed and stepped back.

"Use discretion."

"As always."

Balvena departed from Brussels to head for Rouen in Normandy.

Aula Magna, Coudenberg Palace, Brussels, December *AD* 1596

ABOUT A MONTH later, Cardinal Albert conversed with Giorgio Basta inside the *Aula Magna*, the large reception room inside Coudenberg Palace, where Emperor Charles V once ruled both the Holy Roman Empire and the Kingdom of Spain. It was said the sun never set on his empire: it reached much of the New World, including both Peru and New Spain. "I received another letter from the Admiral of Aragon. He attempts to form a new Christian alliance against the Turks."

"When you become the new Emperor, will you still govern the Lowlands?" Basta had deep-set eyes and a full, black beard.

"When the Pope finally gives his approval for me to marry, *Infanta* Isabella will receive the Lowlands as part of her dowry." Cardinal Albert needed a formal Papal dispensaton in order to marry his first cousin.

"You are well able to rule both the Empire and the Lowlands," Giorgio Basta said.

"Yes, but being elected Emperor is more difficult than we imagined, since the emperor is normally the King of Bohemia, as well as the King of Hungary."

"And those two kingdoms are inherited?"

"Even if my oldest brother abdicates those thrones, my other two brothers are next in line." The Cardinal looked directly at the Albanian cavalryman. "But that is not why I called you here today."

"It is not?" Basta asked.

"In the weeks since the rout in Hungary, Emperor Rudolph asked the Admiral whether there was a general whom the ministers in Flanders could recommend to lead the armies in Hungary."

"Perhaps the Count of Varax, who led the artillery assault on Calais?"

"No. The Admiral recommended you. I most heartily agree."

"I am most honored by your confidence . . ."

The door opened, and an aide entered. "Excuse the interruption, but *la* Balvena has returned from his second trip to Rouen."

"Send him in." Albert of Austria sat back down in his chair and acknowledged the *Seignior.* "What does the King of France say?"

"Henry IV is anxious for peace," *Seignior* Balvena replied. "His Most Christian Majesty wants you to know that he sincerely regrets the defeat at the Battle of Mezo-Keresztes in Hungary."

"And?"

"King Henry IV told me that if he had been in Hungary, he would have either been victorious or would have perished in the attempt."

"I have no doubt about that."

Albert of Austria

The Cardinal knew his foe.

"King Henry IV wants peace with you, so that *'presto!'* he can go to Hungary with his brave nobles, with his infantry, and plenty of Swiss."

"Presto?"

"King Henry IV's exact word." *Seignior* Balvena added, "His Most Christian Majesty trusts you are a man of your word."

"The King knows my soul. I would much desire to obtain peace with France, but the rebellious Dutch must be subdued." The Cardinal dismissed his agent. "Deliver a blue suit of armor to King Henry."

"The latest fashion." Balvena bowed, took backward steps towards the door, and bowed again. "As you wish."

With Balvena's exit from the Chambers, Cardinal Albert brought in his General of the Artillery, the Count of Varax, and Nicolo Basta. Like his cousin Giorgio Basta, Nicolo had faithfully served the Catholic cause in the Seventeen Provinces of the Netherlands for many years.

"Nicolo, your cousin has agreed to command the Holy Roman Empire's army in Hungary. You will now be my new Commander of the Cavalry." Cardinal Albert turned to the brother of the Marquis of Varambon. "Count Varax, what is our plan for the northern army?"

"We will rendezvous at Turnhout in Brabant," the Count responded. "We have 4,000 infantry, including the Italian *Tercio* of Trevico, the German regiment, and the Walloons of Colonel La Barlotte."

"And five squadrons of cavalry," Nicolo Basta said.

"Once all of us reach the rendezvous point, we can march north," the Count added.

"We will do our best to pay the army," the Cardinal said. "Even though the Spanish financiers refused King Philip's request to lend more coin and even returned my Bills of Exchange."

"Your request for supplies?"

"Unfilled." The Cardinal elaborated, "I am attempting to secure more monies from the House of Fuggers in Germany to help finance our cause. I want your army in the north to face the Dutch rebels, and also one in the south."

"To face the French?"

"Only if our efforts for peace do not succeed."

Cardinal Albert, accompanied by Giorgio Basta, escorted the Count of Varax and Nicolo Basta out into the courtyard, where a light, cold rain fell.

68

After Nicolo Basta said farewell to his cousin, the new cavalry commander mounted his horse.

"The seven rebellious provinces must be brought into obedience," Cardinal Albert commanded.

"As soon as the weather cooperates." The Count of Varax saluted and mounted his horse, too.

"Yes, by Spring." The two officers and their armed escort rode through the principal gate.

Cardinal Albert turned to Giorgio Basta. "I know the Empire will make use of your service."

"I will gather my belongings and my command staff," Giorgio Basta said. "I will leave for Vienna and Prague in the morning."

After Basta exited the courtyard, the weakening storm dissipated. Winds from the north pushed the clouds away.

While negotiating for peace with France, Cardinal Albert began raising two armies—a large one to face France in the south and a smaller, yet veteran one to deal with the rebels of the north.

Chapter 9 — War Horses at Ostend

Amiens, Picardy, France, Early January *AD* 1597

"HOW DO YOU know so much about the secret negotiations?" Captain Joseph Duxbury asked Francois d'Orleans-Longueville, the Governor of Amiens.

"*Monsieur la* Balvena just departed Amiens with the latest proposals from President Richardot in Brussels," Count St. Pol responded. "He was taking a letter to *Seigneur de* Villeroy in Rouen."

"The King's Foreign Minister?" John Smith asked. "You saw the contents?"

"No, but the Cardinal and the King of Spain want peace."

"But on what terms?" Captain Duxbury asked.

"It remains unsettled, but the Papal Legate is in Rouen and has met with King Henry more than once. Pope Clement VIII wants peace between the Catholic Kings of France and Spain."

"And if peace fails?" Duxbury asked.

The Count gestured to the ramparts surrounding and protecting the city. "Within these walls, we have 15,000 men able to bear arms. We can muster within an hour."

"And us?" Duxbury glanced at his company, comprised mainly of new recruits. Soldiers unhitched a cannon and lined it next to more than three dozen others.

"We appreciate your escort, but if we do not need the King's men, we certainly do not need you." The Count turned his attention to a noblewoman walking across the square. "I have already said too much; I see my wife is here."

"*Excusez moi*, but we should be going." The Countess looked in the direction of the Cathedral.

"Do not be offended, but you English do not partake of the Mass," the Count said. "Lent is only weeks away."

An English messenger rode past the Cathedral. The clergyman who had been watching them had disappeared. "Captain Duxbury?"

"What is it?"

"New orders from Sir Thomas Baskerville."

As his Captain read the letter, John asked, "What does it say?"

"Both English regiments must vacate Aumale and go to St. Valery and Crotoy at the mouth of the Somme." Duxbury folded the order.

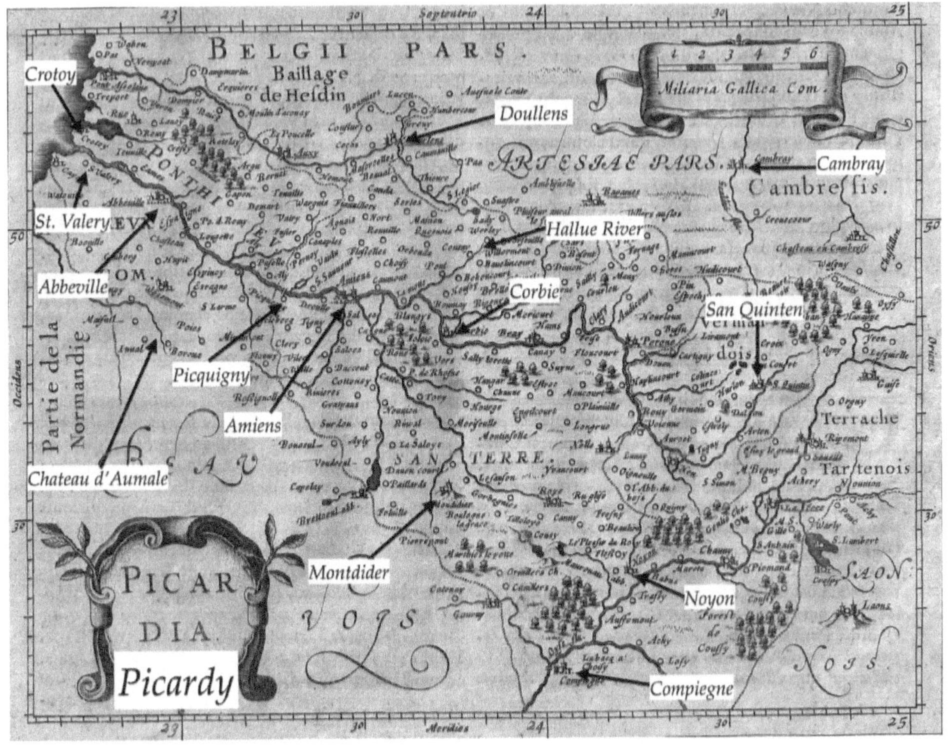

"Further away from the enemy?"

"The enemy still controls Calais on the coast and threatens Boulogne and Montreuil. We will leave as soon as the last of the supplies are unloaded."

"My men can handle the work," the Count said.

"Very well." Captain Duxbury turned to his men. "Mount up."

Gate Montrescu, Amiens, Picardy, France

"HALT!" CAPTAIN DUXBURY ordered. "Changing of the guard!"

Immediately after exiting Amiens proper, John Smith and the rest of the English company stopped in the middle of the small span. A few were on horseback, but most were on foot. The Gate of Montrescu stood directly in front of them. Built like a small square fort, but surrounded by water, the strong gate could withstand any attack.

With the changing of the guard completed, Duxbury led his company forward onto the small island. Passing the guards newly stationed inside the enclosed gatehouse, they began crossing a second, longer span.

"With the forts of Corbie to the East and Longpre to the West." Duxbury pointed upstream and downstream. "The Somme provides a natural defense from any attack from the north."

"So much talk of peace," John said.

"Perhaps a truce, but King Henry will be reluctant to agree to a temporary one. It would only give time for Spain to regroup following King Philip II's refusal to pay his debts."

Hitting the Somme's northern banks, the young recruit noted the large man in a priest's garb watching the happenings. John had first seen him standing by the door of Amiens Cathedral. "Captain?"

"Yes, a priest."

While some marched, small French horses carried some of the English company. They headed west along the right bank of the Somme, opposite Longpre and Picquigny. Looking to the north, John spied two burnt mills. When he caught up with his Captain, he asked, "The mills?"

"The enemy, led by the Duke of Aumale, has burnt all of the mills between Doullens and Amiens. The countryside can no longer support the armies of King Henry."

Outside Abbeville, a walled town on the lower Somme, John recognized the uniforms of the Swiss infantry. "How many Swiss?"

"Several thousand infantry are housed in the suburbs of Abbeville. Even though the King sent them a few pieces of cannon, the town did not want to house the Swiss within their walls." Duxbury stopped his company on the right bank of the Somme. "We must wait for the end of the high tide in order to cross."

When the tide did subside, Duxbury spurred his horse. As the 100 horses galloped through the water, the English recruit caught up with his captain. "The river provides protection!"

"Yes, but if we can cross the Somme, so can the Cardinal."

St. Valery-*sur*-Somme, Coast of France, Mid-January *AD* 1597

WRAPPED BENEATH THIN blankets, an English recruit shivered next to a dying fire. "So cold!" His teeth chattered, and the blanket flutter. Other recruits rubbed their arms.

"We need more wood." John Smith rose and wrapped a wool scarf about his neck. He waved for two other recruits to join him, and they headed for the door. "We will find some."

"Do not enter the abandoned houses," Captain Duxbury cautioned.

"The locals will not be in them."

"They left when the plague hit last summer."

"We can't die of cold."

"The black plague has passed." Duxbury agreed with a nod. "Go, but keep a sharp eye for dead vermin or new infestation."

"We will help you." Another recruit and his friend stood up, and they exited their encampment at St. Valery, where the Somme emptied into the English Channel.

Hours later, John and the others returned with a stack of wood. "I also found some biscuits in one of the houses near the river," John said. "No life anywhere."

"Take your rest," Duxbury ordered. "Tomorrow, we train with the carbine."

After sunrise the next morning, along a country lane outside St. Valery, the English recruit mounted his horse. His armor was strong, his hands ungloved, and it felt good to be out in the countryside. John Smith did not like being confined inside, in close quarters. Several of his fellow recruits had stayed behind, having fallen ill with chills.

Captain Duxbury handed the young English recruit a carbine, a matchlock firearm longer than a pistol. "See the target?"

John held the single-shot carbine upright. "I can strike it."

"Secure your grip."

John obeyed and spurred his horse forward. When his steed reached a gallop, he anchored the butt of the weapon against his shoulder. Passing, the shot smashed the center of the target. He pulled his horse around as the target, fixed to a stake, spun.

John returned to the start of the dirt lane. His captain nodded his approval.

Another recruit said, "Luck."

Duxbury addressed the recruit. "You are next."

The next young recruit mounted his horse, and Duxbury handed him a carbine. "Sight the target?"

With the match in the serpentine lock glowing, the recruit attacked the mark, but missed, even though the carbine was filled with small shot. The second recruit returned to Duxbury. "Much more difficult than it looks."

Captain Joseph Duxbury mounted his horse. As they headed back to Saint Valery, he pointed to a field. "Tomorrow, we will train together as a company." When the company colors snapped in the cold wind, he pivoted. "Hurry up, I will have no sluggards in my company."

Smith dug his heels into his steed to keep pace along the road paralleling the Somme. "I am no sluggard."

"I see." Duxbury led his company into St. Valery. "William, the Duke of Normandy, once sailed with his army from the port of St. Valery."

John knew the story well. "William the Conqueror invaded England and defeated the Anglo-Saxon King Harold at the Battle of Hastings."

Inside the town, Colonel Thomas Baskerville coughed as he greeted them. "Captain Duxbury, we need more horses from Ostend. Take several men, your ship awaits." He pointed to the small vessel anchored at the river's mouth.

Captain Duxbury turned to John. "No time for dinner."

English Channel, Late Evening, 17th January *AD* 1597

PUSHED BY FAIR winds, the ship from St. Valery sailed up the English Channel. With only a small sliver of the new moon shining, the constellations seemed brighter than usual. The sea captain pointed out the pointer stars of the Big Dipper to a sailor. He tacked the vessel, following the brighter North Star through the night. To the east, torches lit up the walls of a harbor. Captain Duxbury told John, "That is Boulogne."

"Where French General Saint Luc keeps guard," John queried.

"Yes, against raids by Spanish forces. They hold several French towns in the countryside surrounding Calais."

At the horizon, the eastern sky lightened as they sailed further up the French coast. Across the straits, the morning sun hit the white cliffs of Dover. Below them, a French vessel tacked south. The sea captain from Saint Valery tacked east. The Spanish flag flew above the walls of Calais.

"Even though Marshall *de* Rosne captured Calais a year ago, a cannonball killed him during the siege of Hulst last summer."

"Who commands the army of Cardinal Albert now?" John asked.

"The Count of Varax. He was the General of Artillery when the French garrison at Calais surrendered. King Henry wants Calais back, but Queen Elizabeth also wants to occupy it. Her Majesty told the French King that if England could keep Calais as a cautionary town, she would conquer it herself."

"For how long?"

"Until French debts are paid in full."

The ship sailed into the German Sea, also known as the North Sea. With prevailing westerlies keeping his sails full, the sea captain peered at a sailor in the crow's nest above. He cupped his mouth and raised his voice, "Keep a sharp eye!"

"Aye, Captain! No sign of Spanish galleys."

The ship sailed past the pirates' lair, Dunkirk, and the winds soon eased.

"We have reached the coast of Flanders," Captain Duxbury said. "Over there is the waterway leading to Nieuwpoort."

On the other side of the little river, the sandy beach widened. Rolling dunes, some fairly high, continued for miles.

"How much further?" John asked.

"Ostend is the next port."

Ostend, Flanders, Mid-January *AD* 1597

FRENCH SAILORS SECURED the mainsail, and the small ship entered the crowded harbor. As his company disembarked, Captain Duxbury asked the Harbor Master, "Why so much commotion?"

"You must ask the Governor himself."

The docks buzzed with activity. Other English soldiers led horses onto one ship and loaded supplies onto another.

"Where is he?"

"Sir Norreys is at Saint Peter's Church." The Harbor Master pointed to some stairs.

When they reached the top, John saw a round steeple several blocks away. After crossing Market Square, they found the English Governor in the cemetery, standing above a gravesite.

"Ashes to ashes, dust to dust," the English minister, reading from the Geneva bible, concluded the funeral service. "Thou art dust, and to dust shalt thou return."

The Governor tossed dirt on the coffin and turned.

"Governor?" Captain Duxbury saluted. "Who was he?"

"A young soldier."

"How did he die?" John asked.

"An accident. But he served the cause of Dutch freedom."

"Sir Thomas Baskerville sent us to pick up larger war horses and bring them back to France," Duxbury said.

"You cannot take any."

"We must. My orders." Duxbury presented them to Sir Edward Norreys.

"And I have mine. The States General at the Hague have ordered me to send three companies to Geertruidenberg."

"But we need horses in France. Calais must be recaptured."

"We know Cardinal Albert has difficulties in Calais."

"How so?" Duxbury asked

"The Spanish crown repudiated its debts. Their soldiers have not been paid. The garrison at Calais mutinied, but the officers were able to squelch it."

"How?" John asked.

"Three of the mutineers were hanged."

"Then you agree we can take the horses?" Duxbury asked.

"No. Sir Robert Sydney insists the war horses go to Geertruidenberg. They must arrive there on the twenty-second. There may be some fighting."

"Action?" John quickly asked. "What kind?"

"The messenger did not say. He waited until the French Ambassador Buzenval departed the Hague to go to Zeeland and return to France," Sir Norreys explained. "The horses must go and be in

Geertruidenberg in three days. Sir Francis Vere and Sir Robert Sydney have confirmed."

"Where our horses go, we go, too," Captain Duxbury said.

"Will we ride across Flanders?" John peered out at the Flemish countryside. Far beyond the walls of Ostend, Spanish riders patrolled.

"The enemy is too strong."

"What about Colonel Baskerville?" John asked.

"He told us to bring back horses. I will not return to France without them."

Harbor, Ostend, Flanders, Monday, 20th January *AD* 1597

THE NEXT MORNING, the ships, one after another, exited the harbor of Ostend. Three-foot companies, about 300 Englishmen, were aboard. Duxbury and Smith boarded the ship with the unsettled horses. They set sail north for Geertruidenberg and away from France.

John took out the papers of introduction to the court of King James VI in Scotland.

"Master David Hume gave you those in Paris?"

"Yes." John put them back inside his cloak.

"If one day you become a courtier in the King's court," Captain Duxbury told John, "you must know that officers must sometimes take the initiative."

The ship sailed up the Flemish coast. They passed the entrance to Sluis. The main island in Zeeland came into sight. When the ship tacked east, up a wide waterway flowing into the German Sea, the town of Flushing appeared over the port bow.

"We call Flushing a cautionary town—because England governs it," Duxbury explained. "The Queen is entitled to the town's revenues in lieu of the monies she lent to the Seven United Provinces."

Off Coast of Flushing [Vlissingen], Zeeland, 20th January *AD* 1597

DUTCH AND ZEELAND ships joined the vessels from Ostend. John Smith and Captain Duxbury watched English soldiers flood their decks.

A Dutch officer approached. "Sir Robert Sydney brings men, too. He acted on the request from His Excellency and Sir Francis Vere."

"Sir Vere returns to Holland?" Duxbury asked.

"At the beginning of January."

"Did not he lead one of the three English regiments at the sack of Cadiz?" John remembered hearing the account in London.

"Yes, last summer. Sir Walter Raleigh led the sea assault on the Four Apostles, the large Spanish ships protecting the Indies Merchant Fleet. The Earl of Essex held overall command of the English and Dutch forces on land. Colonel Vere conceived the plan to capture the town, and Sir Thomas Wingfield flawlessly executed it."

John remembered hearing the story of the death of the uncle of his close friend, Robert Bertie. "Before a Spanish musketeer killed Wingfield in Cadiz's market square."

Sailing past Fort Rammekens and the port of Middelburg, other ships joined the growing fleet.

"But that is not the only news," the Dutchman said.

"You arrived from the Hague?" John asked.

"*Ja, wij zagen* Sir Francis Vere *daar*."

John began to learn Dutch. "You saw Sir Vere there?"

"*Ja, Twee weken geleden.*"

"Two weeks ago?"

"*Ja.*"

Salon, Palace of Ibrahim *Pasha*, *Stamboul*, *AH* 1011 (Late Dec. *AD* 1602)

"YOU LEARNED DUTCH?" Aisha asked inside the Salon of her palace.

"*Je leerde Nederlandse taal?*" The pretty Dutch *odalisque* translated Aisha's words into her native language.

"I began to learn to speak it about six years ago, *Signorina* Ch'Aratza Tragabig-Zanda." John mispronounced Aisha's name and title, the Sister of the Sultan.

Dilara translated his words, so Aisha could understand.

"Do you think he speaks the truth?" Aisha asked in Turkish.

"I have just met your slave," Dilara said. "It is far too early for me to judge."

After servants brought out light pastries on silver trays, Aisha smoothed the folds of her silk gown and reseated herself. Sitting on the cushions adjacent to John, she urged him, "Continue, tell me more."

"In the early winter of 1597, Sir Francis Vere rode through the watery countryside of Holland, heading towards *Den* Hague."

Chapter 10 - Ancient Customs & Privileges

As 'tis apparent to all, that a Prince is constituted by God to be Ruler of a People, to defend them from Oppression and Violence, as a Shepherd his sheep; and whereas God did not create the People slaves to their Prince, to obey his commands, whether right or wrong, but rather the Prince for the sake of the Subjects (without which he could be no Prince) to govern them according to Equity, to love and support them as a Father his Children, or a Shepherd his Flock, and even at the Hazard of Life to defend and preserve them. And when he does not behave thus, but on the contrary oppresses them, seeking Opportunities to infringe upon their ancient Customs and Privileges, exacting from them slavish compliance, then he is no longer a Prince, but a Tyrant, and the subjects are to consider him in no other view.

So having no Hope of Reconciliation, and finding no other Remedy, we have, agreeable to [the] Law of Nature, in our own Defense, and for maintaining the Rights, Privileges, and Liberties of our Countrymen, Wives and Children, and latest Posterity from being enslaved by the Spaniards, been constrained to renounce Allegiance to the King of Spain, and pursue such Methods appear to us most likely to secure our ancient Liberties and Privileges.
The Act of Abjuration, 26th July 1581, The Hague (Translated by John Somers)
Passed by the States General of the Seven United Provinces

Den Hague, South Holland, Seven United Provinces, 3rd January AD 1597

SIR FRANCIS VERE and his entourage rode along a muddy road toward The Hague, the seat of government for the Republic of the Seven United Netherlands. After spending the autumn in England, the able English commander crossed the North Sea at the beginning of January to return to and serve with England's most faithful ally. At almost forty years old, the English commander had a long nose. Streaks of gray ran through his dark beard.

As they drew nearer to *Den* Hague, the long arms of a windmill turned directly ahead. Almost touching the ground, its narrow blades groaned and creaked with every gust of wind. Built next to a dike, the windmill pumped excess water from a soggy field into a canal, already swollen by days of rain. Along the edges of the field, where stacks of once-golden hay dotted the ground, dozens of cows grazed, seemingly oblivious to the returning visitors from England. The breeze whipped the colors of Vere's flag. He held fast to his family's motto: *Vero, nihil verius.* The Latin words meant 'Nothing is truer than the truth.'

Among Vere's veteran entourage were several who had joined the expedition to Cadiz, Spain. All had previously served in Holland and the Netherlands.

"Sir Vere, how did Holland become such a faithful ally of the Queen?" one young nobleman asked.

"Fifteen years ago, Holland and Zeeland and the other provinces of the northern Lowlands signed a declaration called *Plakkaat van Verlatinge,*" Sir Vere replied.

"What does that mean?"

"Placard of Desertion, but it is really an Act of Abjuration."

"A declaration of independence?"

"Of sorts," Sir Vere said. "Because of the tyranny imposed by King Philip II, the Dutch declared themselves free from Spanish rule. The King of Spain not only opposed their Reformed Christian beliefs, but also curbed ancient liberties and privileges. In 1581, the States General met at The Hague and petitioned Queen Elizabeth. She placed the provinces under her protection and sent the Earl of Leicester to govern the Lowlands."

"But is not the Netherlands independent now?"

Sir Vere assented, nodding in agreement. "About ten years ago, in 1587, the Seven United Provinces declared themselves an independent republic."

"Like ancient Athens?"

"Yes, but King Philip II has not relinquished his claim. And last summer, King Henry IV of France and Queen Elizabeth invited the Seven United Provinces to join their alliance."

"I see," the young nobleman said.

As they rode toward the next field, Dutch horsemen practiced using long pistols and carbines instead of lances. Sir Vere recognized the able Captain General overseeing the training.

Maurice of Nassau-Orange stopped the exercise and galloped to the returning Englishman. "Welcome back, Sir Vere."

"It feels good to be back in Holland," Sir Vere said. "Your horsemen?"

"We are reforming the cavalry."

"I see, in the French manner, with carbines." Sir Vere watched the first line of horsemen attack. They stopped before a stack of hay, discharged their firearms, and peeled around in order. They lined up again at the back of the company. In like manner, the second line of horsemen discharged their carbines at the target and peeled about in single file. At the rear of the company of fifty horsemen, they reloaded their weapons. "But the horsemen?" Sir Vere asked. "Do they object, Your Excellency?"

"No," Captain General Maurice said. "Along with giving them carbines, we raised their daily pay."

While they headed to The Hague, Sir Vere recognized the experienced Dutch Cavalry Commander, Philip of Hohenlohe, riding east.

"Hohenlohe says he will visit the princes of Germany," Maurice said.

"Do you believe him?" Sir Francis Vere asked.

"Not entirely, for he desires to fight the Ottoman Turks in Hungary."

***Binnenhof*, The Hague, South Holland**

CAPTAIN GENERAL MAURICE and Sir Francis Vere, along with their escorts, entered the Binnenhof, the seat of government for the Seven United Provinces. When they reached a square fronting a large pond, Sir Vere stopped and told the new recruit, "The Count of Holland founded The Hague as a place to hunt. He built a lodge by this pond."

The recruit pointed to a group of young citizens harmonized in front of barren trees lining the far side of the water. "What are they singing?"

"*Het Wilhemhus*," Maurice replied. "A song about the life of my father, William the Silent, as well as the struggle for religious liberty."

The young men and women rehearsed the melody once more. "*Die tyranny verdrijven, die my mijn hert doorwondt.*"

"What do the lyrics mean?" the new recruit asked.

"Defeat the tyranny, which pierces my heart."

***Ridderzaal, Binnenhoff, Den* Hague, 3rd January *AD* 1597**

GUARDS SALUTED HIS Excellency Maurice and Colonel Vere at the entrance of the *Binnenhof*. On this inner square of The Hague, in front of the *Ridderzaal*, they dismounted. Two parapet towers, circular structures with conical tops, rose in front of the A-framed building known as Knights Hall.

The Dutch Advocate Johan van Olden-Barnevelt greeted them on the steps. "Welcome back, Sir Vere."

"*Dank u*," Vere replied.

The bearded Advocate glanced at several *stadholders*, the representatives of the several provinces. "I speak for the States General. We are very glad your Queen has renewed your command."

"We have much work to do. Queen Elizabeth wants to dislodge Cardinal Albert's men from Calais."

"But that town belongs to France."

"And her Majesty?"

"Queen Elizabeth believes the States should feel privileged that they have been allowed to join the alliance with King Henry IV."

Ridderzaal at the Binnenhof, The Hague

"We know that the Dutch have been under her protection," the Advocate said.

"Yes, but after the States General assisted the Queen in the action at Cadiz, your ambassadors no longer have to enter into the Queen's presence on bended knee."

"Even if we agree to help with a siege of Calais on the English Channel, the French may not be ready."

"Not ready?"

The Advocate gestured to a French nobleman. "The French Ambassador Paul Choart *de* Buzenval can explain."

LESS THAN A fortnight later, in the middle of the month, Sir Francis Vere approached Ambassador Buzenval during a banquet honoring the Frenchman. "Queen Elizabeth believes that regaining Calais is of utmost urgency."

"As I told you before, our nobles in Rouen have grave doubts whether a siege of Calais would be successful."

"But Cardinal Albert captured the city."

"It would take an army of at least twenty thousand. The enemy could do great damage in other quarters."

"The Queen will certainly be disappointed, and the Dutch have promised to aid the cause."

"I will relay your concerns to His Most Christian Majesty, King Henry IV, but I cannot promise that you will be satisfied."

Unhappy with the ambassador's response, Sir Francis Vere returned to his seat next to *Stadholder* Maurice. He ate some Gouda cheese and wanted to season his meat with pepper, but there was none. Trade with Lisbon, whose merchants controlled the spice trade to the East Indies, had become even more sporadic after the Sack of Cadiz. King Philip ruled both Spain and Portugal and imprisoned the Dutch merchants.

The Dutch Advocate Olden-Barnveldt rose and quieted the assemblage. The sound dissipated in the rafters above.

"It is most fitting that we hold a banquet in this hall, where we passed the Act of Abjuration from the Spanish tyrant." The Advocate gestured to the far side of the room. Two sets of five benches faced each other. "We held a large banquet for Prince William of Nassau-Orange, the Captain General of the Dutch forces and the father of *Stadholder* Maurice." The Advocate peered at Maurice of Nassau-Orange.

"I trust I can be as good a Captain General as my father," Maurice of Nassau-Orange said.

As servants brought out the dessert of Dutch apple pie, Sir Francis Vere leaned toward *Stadholder* Maurice. "You have already proven your worth."

The Advocate continued, "Just over two months ago, I signed the agreement with England and France to resist the ambitious designs of the Spanish tyrant. Tonight we honor Ambassador Buzenval, the representative of His Most Christian Majesty, King Henry IV."

The guests applauded, and the French Ambassador rose. "Tomorrow, when I return to France, I will do everything I can to gain King Henry's final approval of the Triple Alliance. I believe the objections have been overcome. Nothing can break the friendship amongst England, France, and the Seven United Provinces of the Netherlands."

After the banquet finished, the French Ambassador departed Knight's Hall and the *Binnenhof*.

Captain General Maurice signaled for the commander of one of his cavalry units, Marcellus Bax, to approach. "Yesterday morning, Bax arrived and gave me a report."

"I heard of the rumors." Sir Francis Vere had commanded the Queen's forces in the Lowlands after Lord Willoughby returned to England.

"*Ja!*" Bax chimed in agreement. "They are true. We have found the Cardinal's men encamped at Turnhout in Brabant."

"How many of the enemy?" Sir Francis Vere asked.

"About four thousand, including the formidable *tercio* of *Marquis* Trevico of Naples," Captain General Maurice said.

"The *Marquis* has returned to Italy and has left his Sergeant Major in charge," Marcellus Bax said. "The Count of Varax has overall command, with the Albanian Nicolo Basta in charge of 300 cavalrymen."

"And fortifications?" Sir Francis Vere asked.

"There is no fort at Turnhout," *Stadholder* Maurice said.

"Only a tower," Bax added.

"In the open?" Sir Francis Vere asked. "The enemy does but tempt us to beat him."

"I agree," *Stadholder* Maurice said. "I have already drawn the first patents." He motioned to a messenger and handed him some letters. "Take these to the English Governors in Flushing and Ostend. We will rendezvous at Geertruidenberg in exactly one week. We must have the utmost secrecy. Do not mention the reason."

The messenger wrapped the message in a pouch. After mounting his fast steed on the far side of the inner courtyard, he spurred it. He soon disappeared into the dark, nearly moonless night.

Prisenhof, Delft, South Holland, 20th January *AD* 1597

FIVE DAYS AFTER messengers had departed The Hague, Sir Francis Vere had already begun to prepare for the upcoming excursion to

84

Geertruidenberg. At the town of Delft, southeast of The Hague, Sir Vere asked a young English nobleman, "Do you see that building?"

"The convent," the young rider responded.

"At one time, it was, but a tragedy happened here about thirteen years ago. William the Silent was assassinated by a Spanish agent. Maurice of Nassau-Orange was only sixteen years old when his father died inside this hall."

"So young to lose a father." The recruit shook his head. "Why was William called Silent? Was he quiet?"

"No. Prince William just refused to argue about his Christian faith," Vere explained. "Later, his son Maurice became the *stadholder* of Holland and Zeeland. When the Earl of Leicester returned to England, Maurice became Captain General of the Republic."

Walking past *Oulde Kerk* and along the canal of *Oulde Delft*, the Englishmen arrived at the Dutch arsenal. Topping the redbrick building and former chapel, the weathervane indicated the prevailing westerlies. One by one, soldiers received muskets, pikes, and swords. The Dutch officer distributed carbines and heavy armor to the horsemen. Other munitions, including gunpowder, were loaded onto wagons.

With his men now fully outfitted for battle, Vere lined them up in formation at the market square. Musketeers and pikemen marched past the *Neiuwe Kerk* with its tall spire and through *Ootpoort,* a gate with two circular towers. The company exited the East Gate, and a cavalry trumpet sounded. English riders joined the footmen.

His colors flying, Sir Francis Vere motioned forward. "We catch ships at Rotterdam!"

Chapter 11 — Sir Francis Vere

God send [us, so] we do not, like the [proverbial] cart, in which one of the horses ever stick[s] in some slough or other, and [the team of horses] never draw[s] with their whole strength together.

Sir Robert Sydney to Lord Henry Howard
Flushing[Vlissingen], Zeeland, The Lowlands, 19 January 1597

Willemstad, North Brabant, Netherlands, Tuesday, 21ˢᵗ January *AD* 1597

THE SHIP FROM Ostend tacked between two more islands in Zeeland. When it veered again, John Smith turned to the Dutch messenger. "You delivered the orders?"

"To Sir Robert Sydney," the Dutchman replied. "The Governor of Flushing brings three hundred men. And two days ago, I sailed from Rotterdam and delivered similar orders to the garrison at Bergen op Zoom." The Dutchman pointed over starboard. Flowing from Northern Brabant, the Scheldt River emptied into the estuary. "Captain General Maurice wants the hundreds of horsemen from that fortified town to meet him at Geertruidenberg, too."

"I remember hearing about how Lord Willoughby defended that town when the Duke of Parma besieged it almost ten years ago," John said.

"You know Lord Willoughby?"

"My father worked as a yeoman for him, and I am friends with his two sons, Robert and Peregrine Bertie. They told me how their father put forth a strong defense in 1588."

"The Duke of Parma might have succeeded in capturing the town," the Dutch messenger said, "if Maurice had not brought a relief army to break the siege."

"*Ja*," John said. "And afterwards Lord Willoughby knighted Francis Vere for his valor on the battlefield."

An hour later, prevailing westerlies pushed the ship from Ostend through the widening waterway. John Smith peered over the bow. "I spy no galleys."

"Spanish galleys from Sluis pose little threat this far inland," Captain Joseph Duxbury said, "Few venture up the *Hollandsch Diep*."

"And none make it past the guns of Willemstad," the Dutch messenger pointed to the fortifications off the starboard side. Cannons protruded from the fortified city named for Prince William, the father of His Excellency, Maurice of Nassau.

Biesbosch, **The Netherlands, Wednesday, 22nd January** *AD* **1597**

THE WATERWAY OPENED when the ship reached the *Bies Bos*, a large inland lake fed by branches of the Rhine and Meuse rivers. The lake provided a natural barrier between Northern Brabant and South Holland to the north.

"So many ships," John said.

"Close to a hundred," the messenger added. "Count Maurice ordered fifty companies of foot to meet him at Geertruidenberg today."

"Captain General Maurice will be there?"

"He sails from Dordrecht." The messenger pointed out the vessel flying the orange, white, and blue colors representing Nassau-Orange. "Sir Francis Vere and the munitions will be at Geertruidenberg, too."

The vessel from Ostend hugged the southern edge of the *Bies Bos* waterway, John peered over the port bow. Streams of light broke through the clouds. Illuminated by bright light, a lone, white-tailed eagle soared above the wet woodlands known the *Biesbosch*.

The English recruit glanced at the other soldiers, some of whom took care of horses. "We were wondering about the plan."

"I have heard rumors," the messenger said, "but Captain General Maurice did not specify his reasons in the summons. He only insisted that everyone gather at Geertruidenberg today."

Captain Duxbury and John Smith strolled back across the deck of the double-masted ship. Over the starboard bow, triangular bastions extended beyond the fortified walls of Geertruidenberg.

John checked the legs of one of the horses.

"How's he doing?" Captain Joseph Duxbury asked his young recruit, barely seventeen years of age.

John Smith straightened his stance. "Ready for battle."

"SIR FRANCIS VERE, the harbor is full." The helmsman pointed to the fortified town. Soldiers disembarked from roughly twenty ships anchored in the small harbor on the town's western edge.

Colonel Vere did not hesitate. "Unload on the far side, up the Donge River."

Sir Francis Vere

"You know the terrain?" the helmsman asked.

"I fought here four years ago," Sir Francis Vere said. "When His Excellency Count Maurice besieged Geertruidenberg, Dutch ships blocked the harbor entrance. With the aid of Count Hohenlohe, Captain General Maurice captured this town, the gateway to Holland."

"Did not Count Hohenlohe travel to Germany?" a younger English officer asked.

"Count Philip van Hohenlohe departed *Den* Hague several weeks ago."

The ship sailed past the walls of Geertruidenberg and up the tributary of the *Bies Bos*. It dropped anchor on the far shore, and, as soon as the planks were lowered, the horses were led down the narrow ramp.

As the foot soldiers came ashore, Colonel Vere commanded, "Keep moving!"

As soon as they had disembarked, the ship weighed anchor and another vessel took its place. The new ship began to unload more supplies, horses, and men along the river's shore, when Colonel Vere recognized Joseph Duxbury. "Captain Duxbury?"

"We brought more horses from Ostend." Captain Duxbury gestured to the armored horses led by his young recruits. Few had full beards.

Within a few hours, dozens of companies, including one from Zutphen commanded by Captain Johan van Rensselaer, congregated on the fallow fields outside the fortified town.

Sir Robert Sidney, the English Governor of Flushing, or Vlissingen, in Zeeland, found Sir Frances Vere. Robert's older brother, Sir Philip Sidney, had perished at the Siege of Zutphen a decade earlier.

"You received the summons?" Colonel Francis Vere asked.

"Three days ago, I wrote to the Queen's secretary and brought three hundred men." Sidney's soldiers assembled in the same area as Captain Duxbury and the other men from Ostend. "I told him that I hoped God would let our companies work together and not like a cart where one horse becomes stuck in a muddy channel, while other horses pull ahead. The cart hems and haws."

"We must work together," Sir Francis Vere agreed.

The able Captain Nicholas Parker brought several companies of English horsemen to the English section. "My horsemen are ready, but what is our goal?"

"Captain General Maurice will tell us as soon as the rest of the army gathers."

Count George Everard of Solms, along with many companies of Hollanders and Zeelanders, appeared. Raised in the County of Solms outside Frankfurt, the German Count had volunteered his able services for many years. The Scots under Sir Alexander Murray also came in force. Within several hours, scores of ships had unloaded. The encampment south of Geertruidenberg expanded, ever larger.

Colonel Vere and the other officers waited for instructions from His Excellency Maurice of Nassau-Orange, Captain General of the Republic. From the southwest, another English company of foot soldiers marched toward the camp. Sir Francis Vere recognized the colors of the company assigned to the garrison at Breda. His younger brother, Captain Horace Vere, rode at its head.

When his brother dismounted, Colonel Francis Vere warmly greeted him. "I am pleased you made it."

"We received the orders yesterday." Captain Horace Vere saluted the other officers. Captain Joseph Duxbury stood at the edge of the circle.

"Did you encounter anyone?" Captain General Maurice asked.

"No enemy scouts."

"And the Governor of Breda?"

Breda had been captured seven years earlier, when seventy soldiers hidden beneath planks in a boatload of peat. Like the Trojan horse at Troy, the boat entered the strong town with enemy soldiers pulling the boat. That night, the seventy overpowered the guard tower, opening the gate to *Stadholder* Maurice, Count Hohenlohe, and Sir Francis Vere.

"He brings four cannons and arrives here now." Captain Horace Vere pointed to horses and wagons. Large horses pulled two half-cannons through the muddy slough. Behind them, other horses pulled two field pieces, small cannons. Six companies of the Netherlanders, both musketeers and pikemen, marched behind them.

When the Governor of Breda dismounted, Maurice asked him, "Your horsemen?"

"My captains have been informed. They were waiting for several patrols to return."

"Have you heard from Bergen op Zoom?"

"Nothing from their garrison, your Excellency."

Sir Frances Vere remembered the day, years earlier, when Lord Peregrine Willoughby, the old English fighter from Lincolnshire, had knighted him at Bergen op Zoom. "We could use their strong cavalry."

"And those of Count Hohenlohe." Captain General Maurice glanced in the opposite direction, to the northeast.

"I thought he was going to the Duchy of Cleves," Sir Francis Vere said.

"Hohenlohe was waiting for more escorts near the border with Germany. A week ago, I asked the Count to come to Gorninchem and await further instructions."

Sir Vere peered down the empty road to the northeast: not a soul appeared.

"Bring my officers here." Captain General Maurice motioned to messengers. "As most of you know, we learned that the Count of Varax is at Turnhout in Brabant."

"Are you going to besiege them?" Sir Robert Sydney asked. "No one in Christendom is better than you, when executing a siege."

"There will be no siege at Turnhout. Though its castle is surrounded by water, it is an open town."

"In the open?" the Count of Solms asked. "Since our war for independence began nearly thirty years ago, the Spanish Army in Flanders has never lost in an open field."

"Where is the rest of the cavalry?" Captain Horace Vere asked.

The English and Scottish horsemen were there, but only a few companies assigned to Marcellus Bax had arrived.

"Some are accompanying Count Hohenlohe to Germany," Commander Bax said.

"Before I departed the Hague, Advocate Olden-Barnevelt and I informed all members of the States General," Captain General Maurice said. "They approved the action at *Ridderzaal* and asked me to keep them apprised of the adventure."

"The adventure to Turnhout?" Captain Horace Vere asked.

"The rumors are true. We are going to confront the enemy army at Turnhout. The States General also insisted that I not expose my life to peril."

"I told the Advocate, 'they tempt us much,'" Sir Frances Vere said.

The moon, not quite one-quarter full, rose over the army of the Republic. From around the camp, the captains and colonels assembled.

"Brave men, come closer!" His Excellency Maurice urged. "For thirty years, the Spanish have defeated us in battle after battle, just because we wanted to worship freely. The Duke of Alba ordered the assassination of my father, William the Silent. He was loyal to the King of Spain, but the King's governors usurped our ancient rights and privileges. In the name of religion, they killed thousands of our countrymen, calling them 'heretics,' torturing many, and burning their bodies.

"Tomorrow, we march to Turnhout. I do not need to tell you that we will face their best, the most experienced men Spain can muster." The Captain General turned to a trusted officer. "Marcellus Bax, explain the plan."

The able officer stepped forward. "Turnhout is about twenty-five miles away. Cardinal Albert has named his General of Artillery, the Count of Varax, as his General-in-Chief. We do not know where Varax plans to attack, but we can be certain that they will do great mischief. We must prevent that. The Albanian Commander Nicolo Basta leads their cavalry, but the strength of their army consists of four thousand seasoned soldiers."

"Have we confirmed who they are?" Captain Horace Vere asked.

"The German regiment of the Count of Sultz, the Walloons of Achicourt and La Barlotte, and the famous Neapolitans of the *Marquis* of Trevico."

"But did not the intercepted letter from Cardinal Albert to King Philip say the *Marquis* was in Italy?"

"Yes, along with Alfonso d'Avalos, but their regiments are here."

"We intend to take advantage of any weakness," His Excellency Maurice said. "With secrecy and speed, we will prevail."

"Will we wait for more horsemen?" Captain Nicholas Parker asked.

His Excellency Maurice pondered for a second before deciding. "We march at dawn."

Dutch and English soldiers had gathered quickly and in force, five thousand strong men.

Chapter 12 — Fast March to Turnhout

"In youth I was instructed, taught, and fostered
In true religion, for the which my blood I often shed,
Maintaining it against all tyrant's cruelty,
And the most bloody Wolf of Rome, and all his subtlety.
From Spanish yoke I set Holland at liberty,
And Zeeland, with the Provinces that now united be:

"And hoped them long time in peace for to maintain,
If suddenly a murderer had not me strangely slain.
But my most valiant son, the worthy Prince Maurice,
Supplying their defect therein, took on him my office:
And my posterity shall them always defend,
And cross the purpose of their foes, whatever they pretend."
"William of Nassau, Prince of Orange, Earl of Nassau"
Poem by Edward Grimestone, <u>A General History of the Netherlands</u>

Geertruidenberg, North Brabant, Thursday, 23rd January *AD* 1597

THE SKY LIGHTENED, and Sir Francis Vere roused his English fighters. "Break camp!"

Throughout the vast encampment, English recruits and veteran soldiers rubbed their eyes and gathered their weapons. Fires blazed anew, pushing back the fog and haze; meanwhile, soldiers warmed their hands.

"Three days of victuals!" Colonel Francis Vere gestured to the supply wagons stationed on the other side of the fires.

Pikemen and musketeers soon lined up in front of quartermasters distributing dried meat. While a few soldiers stuffed hearty portions into their mouths, others saved the dried meat and placed the hard biscuits into their knapsacks.

English horsemen, meanwhile, prepared for the march by checking their firearms and swords. They saddled their horses and fed them grain.

After eating their morning victuals, the horsemen put on the rest of their heavy armor and mounted their rides.

As the sun broke over the horizon, *Stadholder* Maurice told Colonel Francis Vere, "Colonel Charles *van der* Noot will take the Vanguard today."

In twin columns, the army with the Vanguard in front began its march. Further back, Captain Nicolaes *van der* Aa commanded Captain General Maurice's personal guard. Some of his guards were armed with muskets, others with arquebuses—firearms with two-foot barrels. As the first regiment marched south, Captain Vere ordered his men to line up in formation.

"Colonel Vere will command the *Battalia*." Captain General Maurice spoke of the center regiments of the army.

"Yes, Your Excellency." Sir Francis Vere, on horseback, assigned his eight companies of English footmen to Sir Robert Sydney and the remaining English companies to Captain Henry Docwra.

English captains ordered, "Shoulder your muskets!"

The English musketeers raised their twenty-pound muskets over their left shoulders. The musket mouths faced upward, so if it accidentally misfired, it would not injure their fellow soldiers. Small touch-boxes, placed in bandoliers, held individual charges of powder. This bandolier belt extended from the shoulder to the opposite hip. They also carried round bullets and extra powder in pouches or horns. In their right hands, they carried the long fork, which steadied the muzzle when it would be aimed and fired. Between the two smallest fingers of their left hands, they secured a very slow-burning rope. Lit at both ends, this match would charge the powder when the captains ordered their men to give fire.

Pikemen raised their long pikes with sharpened tips upright. The companies of pikemen, like the musketeers, carried swords as well.

"I will march with Captain Henry Docwra." Captain Horace Vere led his company of footmen and joined the seven other companies of the next English regiment.

Behind those two English regiments, Colonel Alexander Murray led two regiments of Scotsmen. Some Scots, wearing wool, could be identified by the distinctive plaid patterns of their respective Highland clans. More than a dozen other companies of Hollander, Zeelanders, and other Netherlanders comprised the last three regiments of the Rearguard. In total, the army had fifty companies of footmen.

The Governor of Breda commanded the artillery. Along with two half-cannons and two field-pieces, horses pulled eight wagons filled with ammunition and supplies. Aided by three English horse companies under Captain Nicholas Parker, the cavalry commanded by Marcellus Bax protected the flanks.

With the army in good order, Captain General Maurice passed Colonel Vere. "We must catch the enemy at Turnhout."

Captains relayed the order, "March!"

Accompanied by the horseman holding his colors, the Captain General galloped to the front of the advancing Vanguard. Colonel Vere, determined to keep pace, yelled, "Push on, men!"

The Dutch army, along with its close allies, marched steadily south.

Oosterhout, North Brabant

LESS THAN TWO hours later, after reaching the small town of Oosterhout, a small cloud of dust rose in the west. A couple of hundred cavalrymen, organized in several companies, trotted towards the advancing army.

"The enemy?" the officer holding Vere's colors asked.

"No," Colonel Francis Vere responded. "The cavalry of Breda." Vere recognized a second group of riders, as numerous as the first. "And Bergen op Zoom."

"They made it," his flag holder, a seasoned veteran, said.

"Not an hour too soon."

The new riders rode to the front to intercept Captain General Maurice, who halted the army. Colonel Vere spurred forward to confer.

"I knew you would join us," Captain General Maurice told the newly arrived captains from Breda.

"Our men returned from patrol," one Breda captain said.

"Any sign of—"

Captain General Maurice stopped mid-sentence.

All eyes in the Vanguard turned in the opposite direction. All heard the unmistakable thunder of heavy cavalry.

Marcellus Bax pulled his horse around. "The Cardinal?"

"No." Colonel Vere recognized the horseman with light hair and a pointed beard. "Count Hohenlohe." Quickly approaching from the east, the newest companies drew near.

"But I thought Hohenlohe went to Germany to fight the Turks?" the Captain from Breda asked.

"I wrote for him to go to Gorinchem," Captain General Maurice informed. "He must have received my second message."

More than a hundred riders, armed with carbines and swords, reached the Vanguard.

Philip of Hohenlohe saluted Captain General Maurice. "I have brought companies from Nijmegen and Zutphen."

"You augment our cause."

"I served your father. I will serve you."

"Very well, we shall put aside our differences." The Captain General told the middle-aged Dutch officer, "You are my most able horseman. Take command of the cavalry."

With the addition of the riders of Breda and Bergen op Zoom, the number of heavy cavalrymen had grown to 850 riders, divided into fifteen cornets.

Philip, Count of Hohenlohe, Cavalry Commander

Unlike the mixed cavalry companies Vere had seen before he left the

Netherlands to fight the Spanish at Cadiz, Sir Francis Vere saw no lances. The lancer companies of the Republic had been transformed into ones carrying carbines and long pistols. Every cavalryman and *curraisier*, dressed in full armor, mounted their horses, also fully armored.

"No time to waste," Captain General Maurice motioned. "Forward."

Count Hohenlohe organized the horse into four troops. He gave command of the riders of Breda to *du* Bois, and the riders of Bergen op Zoom to Bax. Louis Lauren had command of the Nijmegen riders, while Parker kept command of the three English cornets.

The trumpets of Captain General Maurice sounded. The army resumed its march through leafless forests and open meadows.

Rarely stopping to rest, the army marched steadily south. By early afternoon, they had trekked more than ten miles, but still less than halfway to Turnhout. Fields remained fallow for it was still the dead of winter.

Captain Horace Vere spurred his horse and reached his older brother. "In all my years of fighting, I've never seen an army more determined than this assembly of free men."

"Nor have I."

Ravels, North Brabant, Late Evening, 23rd January *AD* 1597

BY NIGHTFALL, ALLIED forces had trudged more than twenty miles. The Vanguard stopped at Ravels, less than three miles from Turnhout. Sir Francis Vere had not heard a single word of complaint. He found Captain General Maurice. "Any sign of the enemy?"

"No, just a few farmers."

The army settled into sections. The soldiers ate meat and biscuits. Around midnight, the four cannons and the last of the eighty wagons arrived at the camp.

Colonel Vere told the men in the English section, "Rest." He walked to Captain General Maurice and Marcellus Bax, already deliberating on their next action.

"The Count of Varax must know of our position," Sir Vere warned. "If the Spanish army attacks, they can swarm down on us."

"We have sent our scouts," Captain General Maurice countered.

Minutes later, one of the scouts returned. "The Spanish army still embeds itself at Turnhout."

"Excellent," Captain General Maurice said.

"How far?" Sir Vere asked.

"Turnhout is less than a league away," the scout responded.

"An hour's march."

"Or less." Captain General Maurice nodded.

"The stream of Neethe separates Ravels from Turnhout," the scout elaborated. "A stone bridge across the swollen stream is unguarded."

Captain General Maurice turned to Bax. "Secure the bridge."

"If they attack us?"

"You must defend the bridge. Protect it at all costs."

"We will, against all hazards."

"If you are attacked, signal us. I will come posthaste."

"The English will second," Colonel Francis Vere interjected, "with the rest of the army."

"I'll set up sentries." Marcellus Bax immediately mounted and led the four Cornets from Bergen op Zoom down the dark road to Turnhout. Two hundred horsemen disappeared into the night to secure the bridge.

~ ~ ~

LEANING AGAINST A tree trunk, young John Smith raised his collar high. Like several other recruits in Captain Joseph Duxbury's company, he planned on sleeping sitting up. Most soldiers slept on the ground. Many footmen in the fifty companies covered themselves with blankets, but others wrapped themselves in heavy wool coats.

Most English horsemen retired near their horses, corralled in makeshift pens. The war horses from Ostend were tied to bushes or low-hanging branches.

Unable to fall asleep, John Smith wearily watched officers withdraw into a barn. By the time the quarter moon had set behind the trees, Colonel Vere had joined them.

Maurice of Nassau-Orange, however, stayed up. He picked up straw and started several small fires. He added fuel to several other fires, brightening his camp.

An hour or two later, the sound of hooves awakened the English recruit from his short, deep sleep. John Smith rubbed his eyes and peered across the dimly lit encampment. A horseman from Breda had returned, and Colonel Vere came out of the barn.

The Northern Brabant horseman dismounted tund reported, "We have secured the bridge."

"Any sign of the enemy?" Captain General Maurice asked.

"No, but the night is so still," the scout reported, "we could hear the voices of the enemy at Turnhout."

"Will you sleep?" Sir Francis Vere asked.

"Not tonight, but you should get your rest."

"Your Excellency?"

"Colonel, tomorrow, you shall lead the Vanguard."

The veteran English commander walked past his banner, firmly planted in the ground, and entered the barn.

Well past midnight, young John Smith doubted he would slumber long.

Chapter 13 — Red Lentil Soup

The Sultana Valide [Safiye] gave the dignity of Grand Vizier to her protege the Kaimakam, Hasan the Fruiterer[Yesmci Hasan Pasha]. The Sultan [Mehmet III] made Hasan a present of the tents, the horses, the camels, the mules, the arms of [the previous Grand Vizier [Damat] Ibrahim [Pasha]. He promised him even his wife, the Sultana Aisha, in marriage after the due lapse of the months of widowhood.
History of Turkey, Vol. III, Book 23 by Aubry de Lamartine
Translated from the French

The meat and poultry were eaten with the fingers; each individual fishing up, or breaking away, what pleased her eye; and several of them tearing a portion asunder, and handing one of the pieces to me as a courtesy, with which, be it remarked, par parenthèse, I should joyfully have dispensed.
The City of the Sultan and Domestic Manners of the Turk
By Julie Pardoe

Salon, Palace of Ibrahim *Pasha*, Rajab *AH* 1011 (Late December *AD* 1602)

AISHA ATTENTIVELY LISTENED to the *odalisque* Dilara translate John's words from Dutch into Turkish.

"*Slagvaardig?*" the Dutch *odalisque* asked.

John signaled his agreement. "Yes, ready for battle."

Out of the corner of her eye, movement at the salon's entrance caught the attention of the Sister of the Sultan. "What is it?"

"Lady Aisha." Her servant bowed at the doorway. "Will we be serving the red lentil soup now?"

"Yes." Aisha waved her servant forward. "While it is hot."

The servant and several assistants, carefully carrying ceramic bowls, gently set them down on a low table in front of her guests. The hint of mint topping the red lentil soup wafted throughout the large room. "Still hot." She served the freshly baked flat bread on matching plates.

Aisha knew John must have been hungry, but her newest slave waited for her to taste it first. *John must be a gentleman at heart*, she thought. "Have some soup." She waited for John to taste it. "What do you think?"

John finished another spoonful. "Mint?"

Dilara translated John's question from Dutch into Turkish.

"Do you like it?" Aisha asked.

"Very much so." John reached for and broke off a piece of flatbread. "My appetite must be returning, and this is tastier than the victuals we ate outside Turnhout. But I must be honest, we did not care."

"How so?"

"We were satisfied with our provisions, for our cause was just. The tyranny of King Philip II against the Netherlands needed to cease."

"And you marched so far?" Aisha sipped her soup. "Twenty miles in a single day?"

"From Geertruidenberg to Turnhout in Brabant, but it did not seem that long."

"You were young?" Aisha asked in Italian.

"*Certo*, an English recruit, almost six years ago."

Six years earlier, the *janissaries* had persuaded Aisha's brother, Sultan Mehmet III, to take personal command of all Ottoman forces. Over the objections of their mother, Safiye *Valide Sultana*, he went to the European frontier and barely escaped with his life.

After the Sultan returned victorious to *Stamboul*, Aisha's husband, Grand Vizier *Damat* Ibrahim *Pasha*, took personal command of the army. He was called *Damat* or bridegroom, because he had married into the royal family. Meanwhile, here in *Stamboul*, *Yemisci* Hasan *Pasha* became the *Kaimakam*. Standing in place of the Grand Vizier, he governed the empire. His name *Yemsici* meant 'Fruiterer,' for when the White eunuchs first began to train him, Hasan tended and trimmed fruit trees. When he was promoted, he gained the title of *Pasha*.

Four years later, Aisha's aging husband, *Damat* Ibrahim *Pasha*, died outside Belgrade. After appointing Hasan *the Fruiterer* as his new Grand Vizier, the Sultan gave him everything that Ibrahim owned—tents, horses, camels, and arms. Sultan Mehmet III even promised Aisha to him. The new widow would become the new Grand Vizier's wife, but the marriage could not happen quickly: the time for mourning would have to pass. Though Hasan *the Fruiterer* did not want to leave *Stamboul*, the Sultan had sent him north to lead his army and reverse Ottoman losses.

"Aisha?" Dilara asked.

The Sister of the Sultan put down her spoon. "This soup is delicious."

The Dutch translator leaned closer. "What is it?"

"I still do not know how my betrothed met the *Capitano.*"

"Where is the Grand Vizier?"

"In Belgrade."

Kale-Megdan, Citadel of Belgrade, *Rajab AH* 1011 (December *AD* 1602)

ATOP THE WALLS of *Kale-Megdan,* the citadel of Belgrade, the Grand Vizier peered west across the Sava, a tributary of the Danube. A black sea of Tartar warriors rode slowly away from Belgrade towards the Hungarian plain. Tens of thousands strong, these Tartar warriors had trekked nearly a thousand miles from Crimea, south of Ukraine and Russia, but they arrived late in the fighting season. They blamed their delay on threats from Cossacks roaming the Dnieper and Don Rivers. Khan *Ghazi* Giray II had to ensure everything was in order at Bakhchisaray, his capital on the Crimean Peninsula.

Kale-Megdan Citadel above Lower Town - Belgrade on the Danube

Renowned for their use of the bow and arrow, these fierce warriors had few equals on the battlefield. When they reached the Danube River valley, the Ottoman Empire's greatest ally struck fear in the hearts of their enemies. With the imminent onset of winter, the Grand Vizier had appointed several cities in Hungary to be their temporary quarters.

"Who returns so soon?" Mohammed *Pasha* pointed to Tartar riders trotting back to the riverbanks. The hilltop fortress of Zuben commanded the heights above the confluence of the Sava with the Danube.

102

"The Khan sends a delegation?" Grand Vizier Hasan *the Fruiterer* counted more than twenty riders. He considered the Khan to be the greatest leader that the Tartars of Crimea had ever known. These Tartars were descendants of one of the four Mongol tribes of Genghis Khan. The Crimean Tartars had converted to Islam nearly 200 years earlier.

"Perhaps his two sons."

"It must be important."

The Tartar delegation dismounted and loaded their horses onto flat-bottom boats. Minutes later, after the pilots ferried them across the Sava, the delegation arrived in the courtyard of the citadel. The two sons of the Khan stepped forward. The eldest son, *Kalga* Toktamish Giray, carried a rolled piece of parchment in his hand.

"You came back so soon," the Grand Vizier said.

"We were not that far." *Kalga* Toktamish handed the scroll to the Grand Vizier. "My father wished to thank you again for your hospitality with a short poem."

Earlier during the week, the Grand Vizier had hosted a large banquet in honor of the Khan. He felt he had to reciprocate the banquet the Khan had held for him.

"You did not travel this far only to deliver a poem," the Grand Vizier protested.
"Is there a problem with the quarters I have assigned?"

"No, my father will certainly be pleased with his accommodations, just as he was here."

After glancing at his treasurer, Etmekji Zadeh, whose palace the Khan had been allowed to use while he stayed in Belgrade, the Grand Vizier asked, "What is it then, *Kalga* Toktamish?"

"My brother and I wish your favor," *Kalga* Toktamish Giray said. Second in command of all of the Crimean Tartars, his title *Kalga* meant 'He remains'. If the Khan were to die, either in battle or from natural causes, the *Kalga* would remain and assume power, at least until a new leader of the Crimean Khanate was selected. The *Sublime Porte* of the Ottoman Empire in *Stamboul* would confirm that selection.

"Favor?" The Grand Vizier led the two brothers back up the citadel walls.

"We wish to raid the borderlands," *Kalga* Toktamish said.

"The borders of Austria?" The Grand Vizier peered to the west.

"And Styria."

"In reward for your service, you are allowed to spoil enemy lands."

The Crimean Tartars would traditionally kill anyone who resisted and capture the rest. As they had done in Wallachia, they would drive the men, women, and children back to the slave markets and sell them to the highest bidder. The remaining unsold women would be sent back to Crimea and kept for the Tartar warriors themselves. Any male offspring the women produced would be raised in the Tartar way. Living in yurts, their movable huts, the boys would be trained to ride the horse and fight with pride.

"If winter delays?" the younger brother, *Nur-eddin* Sefer Giray, asked. Third in command of the Crimean Khanate, Sefer's title *Nur-eddin* meant 'Light of the faith'.

"As long as you are ready for next spring's campaign." The Grand Vizier had assigned Pécs in Hungary to be the winter quarters for their father, Khan *Ghazi* Giray II. "But I do have one request."

"What is that?" *Nur-eddin* Sefer asked.

"That you send any enemy captain of quality directly to me."

"You mean like the rich 'Bohemian' officer you bought at Axiopolis. You sent him to your betrothed, Aisha?"

"You heard?" The Grand Vizier peered down the wide Danube in the direction of Axiopolis. That ancient Roman border town stood closer to the mouth of the longest river in Europe, before it emptied into the Black Sea.

"At the banquet last night," *Nur-eddin* Sefer answered.

"My father, His Royal Highness, appreciates the honor you bestowed upon him," *Kalga* Toktamish Giray noted. As direct descendants of the ancient Mongol leader, the Girays claimed royal lineage. "We shall make certain that you receive all the best prisoners."

The Grand Vizier did not doubt that the Khan's two sons would fulfill their promise. Within weeks, he would obtain new rich captives he could send to his betrothed, Aisha.

The two sons of the Khan returned to their escorts, who remained gathered in the citadel's courtyard. After being ferried back across the Sava, the Tartar delegation remounted their short Tartar horses. They trotted over the trampled remains of harvested fields and caught up with the last of the Crimean-Tartar army, more than 50,000 men strong. They headed northwest towards the Great Hungarian Plain. Besides Pécs, the place assigned to their father, portions of the large Tartar army would stay at Mohacs, Szigetvar, and other fortified towns beyond the Drava, the next upstream tributary of the Danube.

The Tartar riders disappeared toward the western horizon, and the Grand Vizier turned his attention to the Danube River Valley. Frosted branches and fallow fields meant autumn crops had been harvested. On the river itself, boats normally carried goods and grains to Belgrade.

Directly below, after the Sava emptied into the Danube, the waterwheels of the mills anchored offshore churned slowly. Their steady, rhythmic claps could be heard throughout the fortified city, especially during the quiet of the night. Though the mills turned, the amount of grain crushed and separated had diminished. The Long War between the Ottoman Empire and the Holy Roman Empire had already lasted almost a decade.

Six years earlier, Sultan Mehmet III had led Ottoman forces to victory at the Battle of Keresztes, up the Tisza River Valley on the other side of the Danube. After the subsequent capture of the castle of Eger in northern Hungary, the Sultan, having gained the title of *ghazi*, or warrior, retired to *Stamboul.* Mehmet III never returned to the European frontier, but instead ordered his Grand Vizier to lead the Ottoman army.

Two years earlier, after the previous Grand Vizier *Damat* Ibrahim *Pasha* had died, Hasan *the Fruiterer*, with the support of the Sultan's Mother and the Chief White Eunuch, was appointed to take his place. When the new Grand Vizier entered Belgrade, the headquarters of Ottoman power in Europe, he discovered that Szekesfehervar was under siege by the Duke of Mercoeur and the armies of the Holy Roman Empire. Before the Grand Vizier could garner the forces necessary to relieve the siege, Szekesfehervar had fallen. Less than a year later, however, Ottoman fortunes had reversed. By the end of summer, Szekesfehervar, the ancient Royal Capital of Hungary, had been recaptured.

The Grand Vizier gestured in the direction of Buda and Pest, cities on opposite sides of the Danube. "Mohammed *Pasha*, you led the Ottoman forces to victory and ended the siege of Buda."

"In late autumn, the armies of the Holy Roman Empire became anxious when they heard the Crimean-Tartar army had arrived in Wallachia," Mohammed *Pasha* said, "but they were delayed."

"And not by their raids," the Grand Vizier said.

"When the Khan and his sons first arrived in Wallachia, they captured hundreds of men, women, and children."

"Less than two months ago, scouts reported that a Christian army of around 12,000 men had crossed through the passes from Transylvania into Wallachia," The Grand Vizier pointed at the Carpathian Mountains on the other side of the Danube.

"Last night, at the banquet held in his honor, the Khan told us how the battle unfolded," Mohammed *Pasha* said. "Major portions of the Khan's fast-moving army had just arrived from Crimea when they and a contingent of *Janissaries* led by your Lieutenant, Mustafa *Agha*, caught up with the Christian army north of Târgoviște in Wallachia."

"The battle lasted the whole day, and the Tartar losses were terribly large," the Grand Vizier said. "Thousands upon thousands of warriors lost their lives."

"But their warrior army is still strong."

"Yes, more Tartar reserves joined us after the battle. Even though I have sent most of the *sipahis* and the *janissaries* back to *Stamboul*, we hold onto our gains."

"The enemy will not risk its army in the dead of winter."

"Yes, but winter is not yet here." *Yemisci* Hasan *Pasha* and his guests descended the stairs into the sunny courtyard. "Tonight, after dinner, I must write to my future wife." He caught the scent of mint and saw servants bringing trays with bowls of steaming soup and stacks of pita bread.

"What are they serving?" the Tartar son asked.

"Red lentil soup."

Chapter 14 — Eunuchs and Viziers

By chance I called to my dragoman [interpreter] and asked him the cause of their running away; then he said the Grand Seignior [Sultan Mehmet III] and his concubines were coming, we must be gone in [on] pain of death; but they [did] run all away and left me behind, and before I got out of the house they were run over the green [and] quit out at the gate, and I run as fast as my legs would carry me after, and four Negroes or Black Moors came running towards me with their scimitars drawn; if they could have catched me they would have hewed me all in pieces with their scimitars.

When I came to the wicket or gate, there stood a great number of acemi-oglans, praying that I might escape the hands of those running wolves . . . Now as I was running for my life, I did see a little of a brave show, which was the Grand Seignior himself on horseback, many of his concubines, some riding and some on foot, and brave fellows in their kind, that were gelded men [eunuchs], and keepers of the concubines; Negroes that were as black as jet, but very brave; by their sides great scimitars; the sabers seemed to be all gold

. . .

"Dallam's Travels with an Organ [from Queen Elizabeth] to the Grand Seigneur"
From Master Thomas Dallam, <u>Diary</u>, Mid-October 1599

Archery Range, Sultan's Quarters, New Palace, *Rajab AH* 1011 (*AD* 1602)

SULTAN MEHMET III relaxed his fingers and released the bowstring. The arrow flew towards the target, a round ball on top of a tall, wooden pole. When it hit the target, the world's most powerful monarch waved to his best friend and confidant, the Chief White Eunuch. "Gazanfer *Agha*, come here!"

Exiting the columned promenade of the Sultan's summer quarters, Gazanfer *Agha* walked onto the Sultan's archery range, placed within the vast gardens of the New Palace. Cypress trees, fountains, and kiosks filled the slopes leading down to the tip of the peninsula, where the Golden Horn met the straits separating Europe from Asia.

"Excellent shot!" Gazanfer *Agha* knew his master loved to exercise with the bow, as well as his sword.

The Sultan, who liked to show his strength by using his sharp scimitar to break iron rings, pulled back his bowstring. The arrow flew high again, but this time it missed the target. "Enough exercise for this day."

"Will you rest in the kiosk and watch the ships?" Gazanfer *Agha* pointed to the building in the midst of the garden. A pleasant path extended down to the seagate called Topkapi, meaning Cannon Gate. Though built for the protection of the palace, its cannons only fired when returning the salutes of foreign ships entering the harbor. Other cannons captured from Ottoman campaigns in Europe rested unmounted on the beach.

"Perhaps after my meal," the Sultan said.

"You must be famished," Gazanfer *Agha* said.

"Yes, I am late for my second one."

Sultan Mehmet III normally ate six meals a day and, after the *Divan* finished, sometimes listened to the *Kaimakam's* report on the morning's most important decisions. Gazanfer *Agha* momentarily considered relaying the *sipahi* demands from the morning session, but as *Kapi-Agha*, he decided against it. His title meant 'Keeper of the Gate' and agreed with the Sultan's Mother, who did not desire to upset the Sultan with the unwelcome news of the rebels' progress in Asia Minor. "I was going to check on the progress of your new book of poems this afternoon."

"Yes, I love those you have already shared." The Sultan handed off his bow to a younger eunuch, who placed it on a rack.

"I shall leave after your meal," Gazanfer *Agha* said.

"Do not stay long. You know how much I enjoy your company."

About fifty years of age, the Chief White Eunuch had already outlived many other eunuchs, who did not survive to old age. Afraid they would be unable to feed their starving children, poor parents living in the Kingdom of Golkonda and other lands around South Asia often sold their young to merchants at the first sign of famine. While young girls would be groomed to become maids or concubines, the merchants would simply castrate the young boys, cutting off the scrotum. Though nearly half of the boys might die during the procedure performed on them between the ages of nine and twelve, the surviving eunuchs would be raised to meet the demand of rich households. Those trained, beardless eunuchs would safeguard the women's quarters throughout the East.

Many of those boys who survived the cut would be taught the pillars of Islam and sold to other traders. They might transport these young

White eunuchs overland to the Great Mughal Akbar's Empire in northern India, or by caravan to Persia. Others, sent across the Indian Ocean, might eventually serve in the apartments of the Sultan. These White eunuchs strictly enforced the rules among the thousand *ich-oglans* in the Third Courtyard outside the Imperial Harem. The eunuchs would not hesitate to have them bastinadoed, using canes to punish the bare soles of the feet of those boys who strayed.

Unlike most White eunuchs, Gazanfer and his brother had agreed to become eunuchs when they were almost twenty years old, in order to enter the inner sanctums of the New Palace. Largely as a delayed reaction to the procedure, his brother later died, but Gazanfer *Agha* survived. He added his brother's position as *Oda-Bashi* or Chief of the Privy Chamber to his own. The *Lion*, as Gazanfer was known, faithfully served three Sultans—Selim II, his son Murad III, and his grandson Mehmet III—one after another in succession.

Kapi Agha (Chief White Eunuch in 1788)

The discreet advisor to the Sultan expected to live many more years.

The Sultan and the Chief White Eunuch strolled on marble walkways, past the columned arcade of the Sultan's summer quarters. Pipes echoed from the large pool. Its waters fed the fountains of the lower gardens. Gazanfer *Agha* glanced back at the two-story kiosk built in the midst of the garden. Another larger kiosk, also overlooking the waters, housed the pipe organ that Queen Elizabeth of England delivered as a present to the Sultan three years earlier. "Shall I send for the Chief Black Eunuch? Perhaps he can send for one of your favorites."

Unlike the White eunuchs brought from the Kingdom of Golkonda, young Black boys were more severely castrated, with cuts clear to the belly.

Brought from the interior parts of Africa down the Nile into Egypt, the *Beylerbey* of Cairo would train many Black eunuchs and select those to be sent to the New Palace, to serve as guards and tutors inside the Imperial Harem.

In the warmth of the afternoon, Black eunuchs would sound a warning cry, and the White eunuchs and young cadets tending the gardens, avoiding death, would flee. Sometimes the Sultan would arrive on horseback, and the younger women on ponies. During other afternoons, he would stroll with one of his Favorites and her train of women. In either case, only Black eunuchs were allowed to see him with his Favorites or his *odalisques*, the beautiful virgins of the harem.

"No, but I would like to see the *Valide Sultana*," Sultan Mehmet III said.

The *Agha* used sign language to relay the request to a mute, a favored Black eunuch, who was also deaf in both ears.

Imperial Harem, New Palace, *Stamboul, Rajab AH* 1011 (Dec. *AD* 1602)

COMFORTABLY SITTING CROSS-LEGGED on the sofa, Safiye *Valide Sultana*, the sixty-year-old Mother of the Sultan, motioned for the Chief Black Eunuch to approach. "The *Divan*?"

"The council eats its noontime meal. *Kaimakam* Hasan *the Clockmaker* will soon render the more difficult decisions."

"All except the ones the *sipahis* demanded."

"They want to be compensated for the loss of their *timars* in Anatolia."

"The rebel *Scrivano* and his brother Hasan *the Fool* stole them, not us!"

"They know that, but the *sipahis* will not listen."

The Sultan's Mother gestured 'no' by clicking her tongue, lifting her chin, and raising her eyebrows. "*Kislar Agha* Osman, what about the imperial mosques?"

The Chief Black Eunuch motioned to the Treasurer, another Black eunuch who bowed and reported, "Monies from the mosques of rebel-controlled towns have not been sent. The kitchens of our mosques, especially Suleiman mosque, feed the people fleeing the turmoil in Asia Minor." Suleiman mosque overlooked the Golden Horn, the harbor of *Stamboul*.

"Refugees from Ankara?"

110

"Those inflows have slowed," the Chief Black Eunuch said. "And monies from Ankara have not been sent. The city fought against our newest general and forced him out."

"For what reason?"

"Earlier in the summer, Ankara paid a ransom to Hasan *the Fool* and the rebels. The city refused to accept the punishment our eunuch general Khosru *Pasha* decided to inflict."

"But Ankara must submit," the Sultan's Mother said as a Black mute entered the room and signed with his hands that her son wanted to see her. She turned back to the Chief Black Eunuch. "Before you go to the *Divan*, stop and tell my son I shall see him in the Dance and Music Hall."

"As you wish." The Chief Black Eunuch bowed and retrieved from his long robe the key to the door between the Imperial Harem and the Sultan's chambers. Her son, the Sultan, possessed the only other one.

Divan, Second Courtyard, New Palace

SERVANTS RETRIEVED NAPKINS from the laps of the members of the Divan. The Chief White Eunuch, standing next to the Chief Black Eunuch in the shadows behind one of the columns, watched the Imperial Council of the Ottoman Empire finish their midday meal. The simple fare had lasted exactly one-half hour and included white bread, the best in all of *Stamboul*, baked in the ovens of the fifth, the middle of nine kitchens. Two hundred officers oversaw the culinary work of more than 500 cooks of the New Palace. All reported to the Chief White Eunuch.

Besides the middle kitchen, two other imperial kitchens baked white bread. Harvested from fields outside Bursa in Anatolia, the white wheat was shipped directly to mills facing the harbor. Porters carried the sacks of grain on their backs and delivered them directly to the Second Courtyard of the New Palace. Only the three domed kitchens assigned to the Sultan, the *sultanas*, and the Divan received that milled wheat. The other six kitchens used coarser grain harvested from fields in Tartaria, Egypt, or other parts of the empire.

As the Chief White Eunuch watched Hasan *the Addicted* inhale smoke from a water pipe, he heard a clock chime from the hall behind. The *Kaimakam*, Hasan *the Clockmaker*, must have heard it, too, for he returned to his seat in the center of the long benches, directly beneath a latticed window. In the room above them, the Sultan, remaining unseen, could hear and observe the matters of state—the proceedings of his Divan.

Whereas Fourth Vizier Hasan *the Addicted* received his name from his smoking habits, Hasan *the Clockmaker* obtained his moniker from the training he received as a youth. Like all cadets housed near the kitchens on the far side of the courtyard, the *Kaimakam* received training in an occupation that agreed with his talent and temperament.

The Grand Vizier would normally chair the meeting of the Divan and announce its decisions, but he remained in Belgrade as *serdar*, commander of the Ottoman forces. The Long War against the Christian armies of the Holy Roman Empire had already lasted seven years. Unless matters changed, the imminent onslaught of winter guaranteed the Grand Vizier would not return from the European frontier any time soon.

Following the Friday sabbath, the *Kaimakam,* who stood in the place of the Grand Vizier, chaired the council meetings every Saturday through Tuesday, the first four days of the week. Under this open pavilion, the Judge of Rumelia sat down in the highest place of honor, directly to his left. The Judge of Anatolia sat next to him. Other viziers—the 'burden-bearers' of the Sultan—occupied their seats on either side, ready to listen to the *Kaimakam.*

The latticed window above the council, meanwhile, remained closed. The Chief White Eunuch knew the room behind the wooden shutters was empty. Sultan Mehmet III was not in that room, but inside his quarters, between the Chief Black Eunuch's quarters and the Imperial Harem.

One by one, the *Kaimakam* announced the most difficult decisions of the day. Decades earlier, when Sultan Selim II ruled the Ottoman Empire, the Chief White Eunuch often stood by his side. If the Sultan disagreed with the decision, he would violently shake the shutters. The council would then revise its decision. Selim's son, Sultan Murad III, rarely looked down from the window, retiring to the Imperial Harem instead. Ever since returning from his campaign to Hungary in the first year of his reign, Sultan Mehmet III had done the same. His mother, Safiye *Valide Sultana,* and Gazanfer *Agha* oversaw the day-to-day affairs of the empire.

The capital case brought to the Divan that morning was decided, and the last charges against the accused were dropped. The *Kaimakam* announced, "You are free to go."

The defendant grabbed his head and bowed low. "Thank you! Thank you!"

"Go." The *Kaimakam* turned to the council and dismissed them. "We will return tomorrow, at dawn."

The treasurers and scribes returned to their various offices. The *Chiaus Pasha* with his silver staff had already sent out ten of his *chiauses*. Those ushers or messengers would deliver the edicts and verdicts that the Divan had earlier rendered. Each usher carried a Turkish mace on his mounted journey. Whether near to *Stamboul* or far away, everyone in the vast empire had to obey. Other officers attending the Divan joined the throng of people exiting through the Gate of Greeting and the Courtyard of the Janissaries.

The Chief White Eunuch and the Chief Black Eunuch, Osman *Agha,* approached the *Kaimakam.* "The *sipahis?"*

"We listened to the complaints," Hasan *the Clockmaker* said, "but they left earlier."

"Only the petition of the *sipahis* remains undecided?"

"No decision could be rendered," the *kamiakam* added. "It could not be decided today."

"Is it true?" The Chief White Eunuch raised his fur-lined sleeves.

"Yes," Hasan *the Clockmaker* said. "The returning *sipahis* want monies."

"From the Treasury?"

"Or the mosques?"

"From the imperial mosques?" the Chief Black Eunuch repeated the shocking demand.

"They are upset," the Fourth Vizier interjected. Hasan *the Addicted* had returned to his *nargile,* the Turkish water pipe, refilled with fresh tobacco. Smoke rolled from the amber mouthpiece.

"But they were paid," the Chief White Eunuch said. "On the European frontier, before they returned."

"Some lost their homes," the *kaimakam* said. "Their *timurs* were burned outside Ankara."

"We sent a new eunuch general to Anatolia. His *janissaries* have stored up arms and ammunition in Bursa."

"The Sultan should be told."

"The Sultan's Mother does not want to upset her son," the Chief White Eunuch said.

"But the insolence of the soldiery," *Kaimakam* Hasan *the Clockmaker* countered. "A report should be given."

"The fighting season in Europe is over, but our general has not finished his campaign in Anatolia."

"The fighting season is not over?"

"Do not tell the Sultan."

Hasan *the Clockmaker* hesitated and pondered. "You must give me that order in writing."

Gazanfer *Agha* turned to his assistant, a younger White eunuch. "A pen." The Chief White Eunuch sat down at a table and drafted a short letter before handing it to the Fourth Vizier. "When you give your report, ask the Sultan to sign his *tugra*."

"What is it?" the Fourth Vizier asked. Hasan *the Addicted*, the hero of Kanizsa, had been promoted after he withstood the enemy. A hard frost forced the Austrians to lift their siege of that important Hungarian border town.

"An order to the *Kaimakam*, telling him not to bother his Majesty with details of the rebellion."

"You will not present it yourself?"

"The Sultan has asked me to retrieve a poem from my madrasa." Gazanfer *Agha* handed the paper to the Fourth Vizier. "Take it to the Sultan now; he is expecting you."

The Chief Black Eunuch escorted Hasan *the Addicted* through the gate leading to the Golden Way, the guarded passageway behind the Divan.

Chapter 15 — Enemies of the Eunuchs

The [Grand] Mufti is the principal head of the Mahometan Religion or Oracle of all doubtful questions in the [Islamic] Law, and is a person of great esteem and reverence amongst the Turks; his election is solely in the Grand Seignior (Sultan), who chooses a man to that office always for his Learning in the Law, and eminent for his virtues and strictness of life & his Authority is so great amongst them, that when he passes judgment or determination in any point, the Grand Seignior himself will in no wise contradict or oppose it.
<u>History of the Present State of the Ottoman Empire, Book II</u>
By Sir Paul Ricaut, Late Consul at Smyrna, London, 1686

"When I [Poiraz Osman Bey] came to Constantinople, I perceived the sipahis going on with their mischievous purposes, but at first declined taking any share in them. Katib Jezami and the others came running about me; and when I tried to escape them, they followed me urging me to join them . . . "You're making yourself singular,' they said."
Poiraz Osman Bey to Grand Vizier Hasan the Fruiterer
Annals of the Turkish Empire by Mustafa Naima
Translated from Turkish by Charles Frasier

Column of Constantine, Second Hill, *Rajab AH* 1011 (Dec. *AD* 1602)

MIDDAY PRAYERS ENDED and faithful Muslims spilled out of the small mosque and onto the crowded square. Some headed in the direction of the Grand Bazaar, joining Armenian and Jewish merchants who frequented that covered marketplace. Nearby, a smaller market sold slaves. A few more of the devout prayers sauntered towards the large bathhouse on the eastern side of the square—not far from where the old Roman Senate building once fronted the Forum of Constantine. Turkish women, fully covered, avoided contact with several Greek clergy and streamed toward the other entrance of the *haman*. The double-domed bathhouse had been built a decade earlier.

Poiraz Osman *Bey*, recently returned from the European frontier, found Katib Jezami and another *sipahi* leader in the shadow of the Column of Constantine. The turbaned *sipahi* governor, somewhat reluctant to meet with the disgruntled *sipahi* leaders, left his horse at a nearby stable. He came to the appointed rendezvous location and listened to their report.

"The morning Divan?"

"Too many people. We should not talk here." Katib Jezami motioned to a few boys playing at the foot of the column. "Come here."

Two boys cautiously approached. "What do you want, sir?"

"Your parents?"

"At the kitchen." The older boy pointed to the mosque complex. "Waiting for food."

"You are not from here?"

"No, from Anatolia. We escaped from Ankara last summer."

"Your father, too?" Osman *Bey* asked.

"He wants to work in the Grand Bazaar."

Katib Jezami pointed to the tall column wrapped with bands of iron. "Can you climb it?"

"I don't know, it seems so high," the older boy said.

The younger, slimmer boy volunteered, "I can!"

"Good!" Katib Jezami handed the boy a coin. "Climb it!"

Originally bound at the joints with wreaths of brass, the marble column once stood higher. Placed in the center of an open forum, a statue of the founder of Constantinople once topped the column. Later, lightning struck and dislodged its highest sections. The lifelike statue toppled; the column was scorched. Byzantine emperors later replaced the statue with a cross, but when Sultan Mehmet II conquered the city, the Ottomans removed the Christian symbol. The forum and the Roman Senate building had long since disappeared, and a mosque complex in honor of an eunuch was built on its western side. In the very center of the square, only the burnt column remained. It had stood at the top of the Second Hill of *Stamboul* for more than a thousand years.

Katib Jezami handed a coin to the older boy. "Watch him."

Hand over hand, the limber boy grabbed iron bands. As he climbed higher and higher, throngs of people stopped and watched. Young children stopped their mothers. Older men around the edge stared at the boy making his way up the marble column.

As the crowds gathered round and watched the boy climb, the *sipahi* leader took Poiraz Osman to his disgruntled compatriots at the edge of the square. "I've brought Osman *Bey*."

Hasan Khalifel looked directly at the recently returned *sipahi* leader. "I am glad you could join us."

"I have still not decided."

"Osman *Bey*, your hesitancy will do you no good."

The climber distracted the crowds, and the *sipahi* leaders slipped away from the square. Making sure no one followed them, they scurried down a narrow side street.

Coffeeshop, *Stamboul, Rajab AH* 1011 (December *AD* 1602)

AFTER WAVING THE *sipahi* leaders into his empty coffeehouse, the owner shut the door behind them. He led them to the back and ushered them behind a curtain in a cushioned den.

Guzelce Mahmud *Pasha*, wearing a large turban, stood up, "I am so glad you could join us, Poiraz Osman Bey. Have a seat."

By the time Guzelce and the remaining *sipahis* settled themselves, the owner came back with strong coffee. He served them the black brew in tiny cups.

"The *Kaimakam* would not satisfy our demands," Hasan Khalifel reported.

Two of the other leaders dragged tobacco smoke through flexible tubes. The *nargile,* or Turkish water pipe, percolated.

Interior of a Turkish Cafe—Nargile, Coffee, Fountain, circa 1840

"We should proceed with our plans." Katib Jezami turned to Poiraz Osman *Bey*. "You must join us. Sun'Ullah *Effendi,* most of the viziers, and even the military judges are with us."

"I came to listen, nothing more."

"If Sultan Mehmet III does not address our demands, we must consider replacing him."

"Overthrow the dynasty?" Poiraz Osman *Bey* asked. "How? With whom?"

"We must consider three," Guzelce Mahmud *Pasha* said. "The Tartar Khan could replace the Sultan."

"But *Ghazi* Giray II is with the Grand Vizier in Belgrade." The *sipahi Bey* remembered how the Grand Vizier had dismissed him and his men at the end of the fighting season.

"Yes, and both the Grand Vizier and the Khan are allies of the Sultan's Mother," Katib Jemazi said. "That will not do, unless the Khan is replaced by another."

"Such as his nephew?"

"Perhaps, but if the sultan's son could take over?" Guzelce Mahmud *Pasha* asked.

"Prince Mahmud is young," Poiraz Osman *Bey* said. "And to replace a living Ottoman? Has that ever been done?"

"I do not know," Katib Jemazi said.

"The *janissaries* like him and they can be persuaded to join us," Hasan Khalifel said, "but not with the present *Agha* of the *Janissaries.*"

"You are right," Katib Jemazi agreed. "Ali *Agha* is married to the sister of the Chief White Eunuch."

"And he negotiated the marriage contract of the Grand Vizier and Aisha." Poiraz Osman *Bey* asked, "And who is the third?"

"Sun'Ullah *Effendi,*" Guzelce Mahmud *Pasha* said.

"The former Grand Mufti?" Poiraz Osman *Bey* asked. "To be elevated to the Caliph, the Successor to Mohammed the Prophet?"

"Possibly," Hasan Khalifel said. "His deputy invites us to a feast."

"I have heard enough." Poiraz Osman *Bey* rose and set down the cup; the bottom third remained filled with grounds. "I should go."

"So soon?"

Poiraz Osman *Bey* squeezed by the curtain and opened the door.

"Wait! You must join us," Katib Jezami insisted. "The Grand Vizier remains in Belgrade, and you are here."

"I must go." Poiraz Osman *Bey* exited the coffeehouse.

"Osman *Bey*!" Katib Jezami and the other *sipahi* leaders followed him outside, down the narrow street. By the time they caught up with him, they were nearly outside a plain-walled compound, the horse stables. "Poiraz Osman *Bey*, you must join us for the banquet."

"I do not feel comfortable."

"Do not make yourself singular! The banquet is tonight."

Inner Courtyard, Gazanfer *Agha* Complex, *Rajab AH* 1011 (Dec. *AD* 1602)

THE CHIEF WHITE Eunuch waited by the inner gate of his *madrasa*, the first religious school in *Stamboul* established by someone outside the Sultan's immediate family. On one side of the small courtyard, the headmaster of Gazanfer *Agha* Complex completed his lesson. "Recite the *shahada*," he told his bearded students.

"There is no God but Allah," the seated students voiced the first pillar of Islam in Arabic. "And Mohammed is his prophet."

"Favored students," the headmaster said, "we stop today's lesson to welcome our benefactor, who helped rebuild the Arabian birthplace of Mohammed the Prophet."

The students lined up and kissed the hem of the Chief Eunuch's robe.

"Your headmaster informs me of your progress in studying the *hadiths* or traditions," Chief White Eunuch Gazanfer *Agha* said. "I am certain Sultan Mehmet III will be pleased to hear of your progress in following the orthodox way." He turned to his brother-in-law. "You remember Ali, *Agha* of the *Janissaries*."

"Yes," the headmaster said. "And they know Ali means lion."

Ali *Agha* wore a tall hat, signifying his important position as *Agha* of the *Janissaries*, the powerful foot soldiers of the Sultan.

"And Gazanfer means lion, too," the oldest student said.

"Not everyone who serves the Sultan has to be named lion," Gazanfer *Agha* turned to the twenty-year-old man beside him. "I have brought along my nephew. "

Ali *Agha* informed them, "My wife's youngest son arrived only two years ago—"

"So treat him kindly," Gazanfer *Agha* interrupted. "He learns Turkish at the New Palace, so I would appreciate any help you may be able to give him." The Chief White Eunuch did not mention how his nephew had been taken and brought to *Stamboul*.

"That is all for now." The headmaster dismissed the students. A few gathered around Gazanfer's nephew, but others returned to the dozen classrooms, each marked by a chimney and a small dome. Low, plain walls surrounded the whole *madrasa*.

A larger dome topped the small mosque at the far end of the courtyard. The Valens Aqueduct, towering above and behind it, spanned the valley between the Third and Fourth Hills. The ancient aqueduct, built by the Roman Emperor Valens more than one thousand years earlier, supplied water to an underground cistern by the *Eski Serai*, the Old Palace. After it fell into disrepair, Suleiman *the Magnificent* rebuilt the aqueduct that now supplied more cisterns and the countless fountains of *Stamboul*.

"The new poem?" Ali *Agha* asked. After the Chief White Eunuch had arranged for Ali to marry his Venetian sister Beatrice, he received promotions—rising step by step, from head of the Sultan's horse to *Agha* of the *Janissaries*.

"The writer finished the poem yesterday." The headmaster led the Chief White Eunuch, his nephew, and his brother-in-law into one of the domed rooms.

Gazanfer *Agha* recognized the three men. "Stay seated, do not let me interrupt your work." The Chief White Eunuch knew Sultan Mehmet III preferred short stories with moral endings. Both the Sultan's father and grandfather, Sultan Murad III and Selim II, had broader interests in history. They also enjoyed poems written in the Persian tongue.

While the three men worked, Gazanfer *Agha* opened another book. "Nephew, this is the <u>Book of Festivals</u>. Sultan Murad III wanted the festivities surrounding the circumcision of his son Mehmet to exceed those given by Sultan Suleiman *the Magnificent*."

"And the book?"

Valens Aqueduct in Stamboul/Constantinople, circa 1839

"It shows it all." Gazanfer *Agha* opened it up in the middle. "This picture shows a coffeeshop on wheels that was paraded on the *Atmeidan*." He spoke of the Hippodrome in front of the Palace of Ibrahim *Pasha*. "During the festivities, the patrons

120

argued inside, causing Sultan Murad III to laugh so hard that the coffee sellers soon enjoyed a reprieve."

"The coffeeshops had a bad reputation?" the nephew asked.

"Very much so, even worse than they do today."

"The ink is almost dry." The scribe handed the completed poem to Ali *Agha*. "I hope the Sultan likes it."

"I am certain the Sultan will enjoy this," Ali *Agha* said, "but what of the Book of Poems?"

"Almost complete," the headmaster of the *madrasa* said. "The illustrator is more than halfway done."

"And the binding?" The Chief White Eunuch looked at the third man, still seated.

"Even now, I prepare the binding. It will be ready by spring."

"I hope the Sultan likes that poem better than the new story told to his father," the headmaster said.

"You know of Murad III's storyteller?" Gazanfer *Agha* asked. "The stories he presented?"

"Who has not heard of that encounter?" the headmaster asked. "The storyteller worked hard on writing new stories, but when he recited them, Murad III was very displeased."

"The Sultan had heard all of the stories before," Gazanfer *Agha* said. "Another man had memorized them and told the sultan."

"So the storyteller did not receive the monies for his efforts?" the scribe asked.

"Not the large sum he expected," Gazanfer *Agha* said.

"He received a mere pittance?" the scribe asked.

"I do my master's bidding."

"I trust this poem will be more pleasing." The headmaster handed over the writing. "One last thing before you leave."

"What is it?" Gazanfer *Agha* waited a moment. "Speak."

"We have heard rumors."

"Rumors?"

"From the religious council. Some in the *ulema* wish to bring back Sun'Ullah *Effendi* as *Sheikh ul-Islam*."

"As Grand Mufti of all Islam? Only the Sultan can do that." Gazanfer *Agha* took the scroll, quickly exiting his *madrasa* with his nephew and brother-in-law.

GAZANFER *AGHA* AND his brother-in-law rode on horseback, side by side, toward the Palace of the *Agha* of the *Janissaries*. The wide building overlooked the middle part of the inner harbor. Other White eunuchs, both aides and guards, accompanied the two *aghas*, while a small group of *janissaries* marched on foot.

"You rarely leave the presence of the Sultan," Ali *Agha* said. "Must you return to the New Palace soon?"

"The Sultan plans to spend the afternoon with *Haseki* Halime."

"The mother of Prince Mahmud? Many of the young *janissaries* like him."

Ahead, to their left stood the Infirmary of the *Janissaries*, where foot soldiers wounded in Wallachia a month earlier were still recovering. Ahead, to their right stood Suleiman *Camii*, the most magnificent mosque in *Stamboul*. The architect Sinan had built the large structure with its four minarets for Suleiman *the Magnificent*. The tombs of Suleiman and his wife Roxelana were on the far side.

A leader of a *Janissary* patrol, inspecting the streets, intercepted and stopped the entourage. His men, like always within the city, did not carry muskets, only long sticks.

"Problems?" Ali *Agha* asked.

"Opium brought from Anatolia was smoked in several of the coffee shops. Coffeeshop patrons lie dazed in the street."

"Past noon? Tell the coffeeshop owners, the streets must be clean." Ali *Agha* pointed ahead. "More refugees from Anatolia?"

"Waiting at the *imaret* for food. More families arrive each day."

"I will tell the Chief Black Eunuch when I get back to the New Palace that the kitchens are full."

Passing by the outside of the courtyard of Suleiman Mosque and the tomb of Sinan, the party reached the gate of the Palace of the *Agha* of the *Janissaries*.

"It is much later than I expected," Gazanfer *Agha* said. "The Sultan will be expecting me before he eats his next meal."

"You will stop by and see your sister?"

"Yes, my nephew wants to see his mother before returning to the New Palace."

Palace of the Sister of the Chief White Eunuch, *Stamboul*

THE CHIEF WHITE Eunuch stopped and dismounted inside the fair palace of his Venetian sister. Over the years, Gazanfer *Agha* had learned to be discreet in handling affairs, both domestic and foreign, particularly with the Republic of Venice.

A decade earlier, before his sister Beatrice had arrived from her failed second marriage, Gazanfer had attempted to replace a *sanjak* disliked by the Republic. Following the death of Nur Banu, the mother of Murad III, the Sultan's favorite, Safiye, gained influence. *Haseki* Safiye, the mother of Murad's firstborn son, heard about the effort to replace the Ottoman governor and admonished both Gazanfer and the Venetians for interfering in internal affairs.

Ever since, the Chief White Eunuch became more circumspect in his actions, but his efforts had been rewarded. Now favored by Safiye *Valide Sultana,* he was able to secure this goodly palace for his sister. In addition to the guards assigned for her protection, Gazanfer *Agha* had given his sister one hundred slaves. A dozen of those slaves flocked around the Venetian matron as she crossed the main courtyard. Beatrice motioned for them to stay by the main building before she addressed her brother, "*Fratello,* you brought my son."

"*Si,* my dear sister."

Her youngest stepped forward. "*Madre,* he took me to his *madrasa.*"

"We needed to retrieve the new poem for the Sultan," Gazanfer *Agha* said.

"Another one for the collection?" Beatrice asked.

"Yes, the one your husband suggested."

More than a decade earlier, Gazanfer's mother had settled in *Stamboul.* On the day her daughter Beatrice arrived from Venice, her mother died. Fleeing her second marriage, Beatrice stayed in *Stamboul* and converted to Islam. Her brother, Gazanfer *Agha,* arranged for her to marry Ali, and over the past ten years, he made certain his brother-in-law prospered.

Beatrice leaned closer to her brother. "Can my son visit me this evening?"

When Beatrice first came to *Stamboul,* both of her sons stayed in Venice, but when the youngest visited an island, Gazanfer had arranged for him to be taken. Under the Chief White Eunuch's watch, her youngest son stayed with him inside the New Palace. His persuasive attempts to bring her eldest son to *Stamboul*, however, had not succeeded. That son from her first marriage remained in Venice.

"I am certain that can be arranged, but my nephew must return to the New Palace before nightfall."

"I heard Aisha escorted a Dutch *odalisque* out of the harem," Beatrice said.

"Yes, to interview her new slave," Gazanfer *Agha* said, "but *Kizlar Agha* Osman informed the Sultan."

"*Il Gran Signore* did not object?" Beatrice referred to the Sultan in Italian as the Grand Lord.

"That Aisha took the Dutch *odalisque* back to her palace?" the Chief White Eunuch asked. "No, he loves his sister as much as I love you."

"Thank you for your kind words, brother. Can you stay for a meal?"

"I wish I could, but the Sultan finishes his walk in the garden, and I must return to the New Palace and deliver the poem." The Chief White Eunuch, surrounded by other White eunuchs, mounted his small horse. "*Il Gran Signore* waits for me."

The palace gates swung open.

"Make way!"

Chapter 16 — Warning at Turnhout Castle

At the gathering of the commanders, limited to Nicolo Basta, Juan de Guzman [With the aging Alonso de Mondragon being absent], [Sergeant-Major] Jeronimo Dentice, and the colonels of the regiments of the several nations, a warning was declared: the enemy came marching, resolved to fight . . .

Guerras de Flandes by Carlos Coloma
Translated from Spanish by D.E.A.

Salon, Palace of Ibrahim *Pasha, Stamboul*, Late December *AD* 1602

CAPITANO JOHN SMITH finished his bowl of red lentil soup and set down his spoon. Aisha asked her handsome slave, "Would you like some more?"

"Soup?" John lifted the bowl. "It is so delicious."

A waiting servant served him another bowl, so Aisha told John, "You must continue."

Dilara, the lovely Dutch odalisque, relayed the request.

"All of the new recruits kept ready," John resumed speaking Dutch. "And reports of our arrival reached the Count of Varax and Colonel Claude *la* Barlotte, one of his commanders."

Once more, Dilara translated John's words into Turkish. Aisha motioned for her guards, two tall Black eunuchs, to step outside. Her favorite female attendants sat down, leaning closer.

Castle, Turnhout, Brabant, The Lowlands, 24th January *AD* 1597

TORCHES LINED THE drawbridge and pushed back the darkness enveloping the village of Turnhout. Earlier in the evening, the commander of the cavalry, Nicolo Basta, had sent out scouts from the company commanded by Juan *de* Guzman. The Count of Varax needed to confirm rumors of a large enemy army approaching rapidly from the north. The Catholic army had arrived weeks earlier in order to reduce the burden placed on fortified towns, such as Antwerp. Secondly, the army was poised to disrupt the succors and sustenance provided to towns and cities controlled by the Protestant rebels.

Shortly after midnight, the scouts returned and quickly dismounted. When Claude *la* Barlotte, the Colonel of one of the two Walloon regiments, saw the scouts report to Nicolo Basta, he knew the news was not good. The able Colonel accompanied Basta and the scouts across the bridge leading into the castle.

Lit by flickering candles, the upper windows of the stone edifice overlooked the village square. Its smooth walls rose three stories above a dark moat. After walking through a passageway and across the large courtyard, they found Karl Ludwig, the Count of Varax, conversing with the rest of his command staff.

"The rumors the farmer told us are true," Nicolo Basta said.

"Is it General Maurice of Nassau?" Varax asked.

"Resolved to fight, Maurice brought his army." Barlotte turned back to the scout.

"Veteran leaders, including the Count of Hohenlohe and Sir Francis Vere," the scout informed. "I saw their flags at Ravels."

"Only a league away?" Varax asked.

"Less than two hours' march," Colonel Claude *la* Barlotte added.

"So many? So soon?" The Count turned to his officers. "We must decide our course of action."

"We should go and meet them," Colonel *la* Barlotte volunteered.

"We should stand our ground around the castle," said Sergeant Major Jeronimo Dentice, the assigned commander of the regiment of the Marquis of Trevico. "They cannot dislodge us here and we can hold out until Cardinal Albert sends reinforcements."

"We are in the open." The German Count of Sultz stepped forward. "We need to retreat to Herentals. It is less than a day's march away and we can deploy behind its fortified walls."

"How many in the enemy army?" the Count of Varax asked.

"I counted fifteen cornets," the scout said, "Around eight hundred fifty horsemen."

"And foot companies?"

"Fifty flags, nearly five thousand men."

"The pikemen and musketeers of the Italian *tercio* are strong," Sergeant Major Dentice said. "We can deploy our battalions in the market place and make a strong stand."

"But we have few trenches," the Count of Sultz protested.

"We should deploy toward the bridge leading to Ravels," Colonel *la* Barlotte argued.

"We must dig in."

While the discussion continued, a new scout entered the room. The Count of Varax turned to the door. "What is it?"

"The enemy cavalry has captured the bridge over the creek."

The Count recoiled in disbelief. "We won't be able to meet them."

"The enemy has also brought cannon."

"Cannon?" The Count of Varax peered at his officers. "We have no walls and cannot afford to wait for reinforcements. We must retreat." He gestured to Sergeant Major Dentice. "Escort the baggage to Herentals."

"The *tercio* of the Marquis *de* Trevico?"

The marquis had returned to Italy, but his regiment stayed in Brabant.

"They will form the Rearguard and I will march with them." The Count of Varax commanded, "I insist on an orderly retreat."

Colonel Claude *la* Barlotte and the rest of the officers exited the castle. Juan *de* Guzman took the two scouts back to the campsite of the cavalry company of Alonso *de* Mondrago. In lieu of that aging leader's absence, Guzman held command. The other officers, likewise, returned to their regiments to organize the rushed retreat.

~ ~ ~

THREE HOURS LATER, Sergeant Major Jeronimo Dentice, accompanied by a cornet of cavalry, led a train of wagons past the church out of the town.

As soon as they were gone, the Count of Sultz mounted his horse. His standard bearer and young Lieutenant Ernst, the illegitimate son of the Count of Mansfeld, rode next to him. His German regiment of nearly one thousand men marched south towards a wooden bridge.

As soon as the Vanguard departed, the first regiment of the Walloons under Colonel Achicourt, including Charles Bonaventure *de* Longueval, the Count of Busquoy, departed.

Colonel *la* Barlotte organized the twelve companies in the second regiment of Walloons. After he counted the dozen standards in front of him, he turned back. The Count of Varax mounted his horse to lead the rearguard, the regiment of the *Marquis* of Trevico.

Just south of Turnhout, after Colonel Claude *la* Barlotte's regiment had passed over the bridge, the Count of Varax motioned to his workmen. "Dismantle the bridge."

Even as the Rearguard was passing above, the workmen used levers, taking away the side rails and pulling apart planks below. At the same time, the remaining four companies of horsemen under Nicolo Basta crossed upstream.

The Count told other soldiers at that shallow point, "Chop down the trees." He ordered several dozen musketeers to keep guard while the workmen finished.

With the night disappearing, the Walloon regiment marched down the treelined lane, the Count of Varax reached the front of the rearguard and told Colonel *la* Barlotte, "We've escaped the trap."

Ravels, Brabant, the Lowlands, Daybreak, January 24, *AD* 1597

"RISE!" SIR FRANCIS Vere nudged Duxbury's slumbering recruit, leaning against the tree. "Ready my horse."

"Yes, Sir!" John Smith adjusted his boots and grabbed his sword. The recruit rushed to the horse. Captain Joseph Duxbury exited the barn.

Vere scanned the awakening encampment at Ravels. During the night the mist had thickened, but that did not dampen Vere's determination. They needed to attack the enemy at Turnhout before they escaped. Straw fires flared higher beneath brightening skies.

After securing his heavy breastplate, Sir Francis Vere strolled to his saddled horse and tightened the girth beneath its belly. Its nostrils flared. Its breath whitened the damp air.

Vere grabbed the reins and mounted. The horse raised its head and neighed.

"Easy!" Sir Francis Vere patted its neck and intercepted Sir Robert Sydney. He told the Governor of Flushing, "Rouse your men. We have the Vanguard."

Sydney relayed the command to his captains exiting the barn. Colonel Francis Vere's younger brother, Captain Horace Vere, and the other captains hastened to their companies.

Within minutes, the English foot soldiers devoured their morning victuals of dried meat. They readied their weapons, long pikes and muskets. With their captains, they assembled into company formation.

Behind the Vanguard, the Scottish companies of Colonel Alexander Murray readied to march in the *Battalia*. Large horses pulled the four cannons up the center road. In the Rearguard, the Dutch and Zeelander foot soldiers of the Count of Solms and Lord Charles van der Noot prepared for battle.

Captain General Maurice rode to Colonel Vere and gestured to the east. "The day is breaking."

"We are ready." Colonel Francis Vere turned and yelled, "Cavalry!"

With arquebuses and carbines slung over their shoulders, the riders quickly mounted. Organized into companies of roughly fifty horsemen, they all wore heavy armor, thick enough to withstand musket shots.

The horse captains, each accompanied by a long cornet attached to a banner, led the heavy cavalry to the front of Vere's Vanguard of twenty-one hundred men. The sixteen hundred English and five hundred Dutch were poised to battle the waiting enemy.

The mass of men marched toward the River Neethe and the bridge that separated the village of Ravels from Turnhout.

Bridge of River Neethe, Turnhout, Brabant, 24th January *AD* 1597

WITHIN AN HOUR, the Vanguard reached the stone bridge that Marcellus Bax and his two hundred horsemen had guarded all night. The river Neethe flowed high and fast from earlier rains.

Captain General Maurice asked Bax, "Commander, any sign of the enemy?"

"No sign of attack,"Marcellus Bax reported, "but we heard enemy voices throughout the night."

"Send out scouts."

"I'll take my men."

Captain General Maurice assented and Marcellus Bax turned to the captains from Bergen op Zoom. "Ride with me."

Those horsemen rode toward Turnhout, less than an English mile away.

While those few companies reconnoitered, Sir Francis Vere led his horsemen across the bridge. He organized the horsemen into battle formation. "Be prepared for any surprise, in case the Count of Varax attacks."

Behind the horsemen, the foot soldiers crossed the bridge. They, too, moved into battle formation. Musketeers flanked the sides and pikemen with their upright three-pronged spikes marched in the middle.

Meanwhile, as the sun hit the top of the trees, horses pulled the artillery pieces across the bridge. The center *Battalia* regiment of Murray and the Rearguard of Solms and *van der* Noot moved forward.

Minutes later, several scouts, riding hard, returned.

"The enemy has escaped," one scout said. "The Count of Varax sent his baggage to Herentals in the middle of the night."

"And his army?" Captain General Maurice asked.

"His Rearguard is in sight."

Captain General Maurice turned and ordered. "Colonel Hohenlohe, your cavalry!"

"*Ja*, your Excellency." Colonel Hohenlohe led his cornets of cavalry forward.

Sir Francis Vere turned to his captains in the Vanguard. "March as fast as you can."

Sir Francis Vere spurred his horse to the front of his company of horsemen.

North of Turnhout, Brabant, The Lowlands, 24th January *AD* 1597

JUST OUTSIDE TURNHOUT, Captain General Maurice and Colonel Francis Vere intercepted Commander Marcellus Bax. Several horsemen entered the open village, but kept out of musket range of the gray castle on the other side of the central market square. The roof on one side of the castle was slanted. Its sheer walls rose several stories above a surrounding moat. On the far side of the castle, a church steeple glistened in the morning sun.

"A small garrison defends the castle." Commander Marcellus Bax presented a townsman.

"You completely surprised Count Varax. He planned to make a stand," the townsman reported, "until he heard you brought artillery. After midnight, the Count ordered the baggage loaded and two hours later the train went away. Before daybreak his four regiments marched toward Herentals."

"A half day's journey away," Commander Marcellus Bax said.

"Which way?" Captain General Maurice asked.

The townsman pointed south. "Over the footbridge."

The cavalry circumvented the castle, rode past the church, and neared the banks of the River Aa.

Footbridge over Aa River, South of Turnhout, Brabant, January *AD* 1597

THE LEADERS OF the army stopped just out of firing range. Enemy musketeers protected workers dismantling the sole footbridge over the swollen stream. On the other side, the Neapolitan regiment of the *Marquis de* Trevico slowly marched away, south down the narrow road to Herentals.

The workers hurried with their levers and axes. Only two planks remained.

Captain General Maurice brought his horse around. "Officers!" His cornet sounded the call to assemble.

The commanders of the foot regiments, as well as the horse companies, spurred their horses. As soon as they had dismounted and gathered around him, Captain General Maurice asked, "Shall we pursue?"

"It's too late, they've escaped." The Count of Solms gestured to the soldiers still marching from the north. "Most of our foot have not exited Turnhout."

"An ambush," Sir Robert Sydney argued. "The Count of Varax conceals his forces."

"It's a trap." Veteran cavalry Commander Hohenlohe nodded. "They've already crossed the river. If they reach the Heath of Tielen, they'll deploy in battle squares and annihilate us when we exit the lane. They're Cardinal Albert's best; they've never lost."

"It's too difficult to pass," the Count of Solms added. "We'll have no chance to put our army into order."

"The horses cannot cross." The Count of Hohenlohe pointed upstream.

Wagon tracks and hundreds of hoof prints led down to a wide crossing. Heavy branches blocked the entrance. On the far side of the Aa, the obstacles appeared greater. Several fallen trees impeded passage. High water lapped against a muddy morass of twigs and boughs.

"They've escaped."

All in the War Council nodded in agreement, except two. Captain General Maurice glanced at Marcellus Bax.

"We've come too far," Commander Marcellus Bax said. The commander had brought word of the enemy to the States General at the Hague earlier in January.

"Your reputation," Sir Francis Vere echoed.

"And ours," Commander Marcellus Bax said. "We must pursue."

"We can't wait and let them escape."

"We marched all day. It would be a disgrace, a shame."

A high-pitched creak halted the discussion. Workers leveraged the loosened plank and slid it into the river. One plank remained.

"I can delay the enemy until the rest of the army catches up," Sir Francis Vere insisted.

The first Dutch company attached to the Vanguard reached them.

Captain General Maurice nodded to Sir Francis Vere. "Take my Personal Guard."

Sir Francis Vere pointed to the plank. "Captain Nicolaes *van der Aa!*"

"Musketeers!"

Chapter 17 — Hasten to the Heath

Some of our musketeers coming up, they were beaten thence, having before, much to their advantage, broken the bridge in such sort that our foot men could pass but two and two. Their army retired in very good order in maintaining continual "eskarmouches" [skirmishes] with ours, until they attained to a large heath [Tielenheide], where Sir Francis Vere, our Colonel, with Sir Robert Sydney and some other on horseback . . .
Captain John Chamberlain to the Earl of Essex, 30th January 1597

His Excellency, seeing how long the foot soldiers were taking, resolved to send all of the Cavalry to the fight . . . And the foot soldiers hastened as much as they could . . .
<u>Der Nederlandsche Oorlogen</u> by Pieter Christiaensz Bor
Translated from Dutch by D.E.A.

They might well have bidden us farewell, because our foot could not have come up [in] time . . .
Sir Robert Sydney to the Earl of Essex
Letter from the Lowlands, January 1597

Footbridge over Aa River, Outside Turnhout, Brabant, 24th Jan. *AD* 1597

DUTCH MUSKETEERS MARCHED in good order toward the broken footbridge. About fifty yards from the river, Captain Nicolaes *van der* Aa stopped his men. When the first dozen formed a straight line, the workers dismantling the bridge dropped their tools. They ran and dove for cover. One last worker kicked part of the guard rail into the water. It floated away.

The musketeers steadied their barrels on four-foot rests, lit small ropes, and aimed.

"Fire!" Captain *van der* Aa commanded.

Muskets flashed. Clouds of black smoke rose. The hindmost enemy worker keeled into the water.

While the first line of musketeers reloaded, the second line advanced, stopped, and readied their long guns on their U-shaped rests.

From the far banks, enemy musketeers fired. Clouds of black smoke rose above green bushes.

Too late to duck, bullets whizzed by Sir Francis Vere. He brought his horse around and saw Marcellus Bax lead eight or more of his riders toward the water, downstream from the bridge.

Closer to the water, more enemy musket shots rang out. Bax's horse stumbled and fell. Before he hit the ground, Bax jumped away, escaping injury. He stood above his horse, breathing deeply.

Seeing its blood ooze to the ground, Sir Francis Vere knew the dying steed would not survive.

Marcellus Bax motioned for another horse and quickly remounted. He resumed his advance and bolted toward the river.

Sir Francis Vere gathered a handful of horsemen, including Captain Joseph Duxbury and his new recruit John Smith. He halted when he reached Captain Nicolaes *van der* Aa. "I need a few musketeers."

Captain Nicolaes *van der* Aa obeyed the order. "You five!"

"Double up, behind my horsemen," Sir Francis Vere commanded.

John, Captain Duxbury, and the other horsemen extended their hands.

"Keep your powder dry!" Sir Francis Vere spurred his horse toward the water. His horsemen followed.

At the water's edge, the English colonel urged his steed to jump a fallen tree. Its front legs cleared the obstacle, but its hind legs did not. Vere heard bones crack. It stumbled into the water, throwing him forward.

The splash annoyed him, but Vere swam the final yard. He pulled himself up on the far bank. He motioned for his six horsemen to hurry. Though the water reached their saddles in the shallowest part of the stream, the musketeers held their muskets high and dry. As soon as the riders reached the bank, the six musketeers dismounted.

"Follow me!" Sir Francis Vere led them up the embankment. He wanted to flank the bridge and stepped into a small clearing.

Muskets flashed. A bullet grazed his shin.

"Ambush!"

His six musketeers raised their weapons, aimed, and fired. His five horsemen circled the skirt of the clearing and charged.

Within minutes, they had flushed out the defenders, who scurried along the edge of the woodlands. Along with the enemy workers, they fled to join the retreating army.

From the opposite bank, Sir Robert Sydney pointed to Vere's horse, floundering in the water. "Sir Vere?"

"It broke its leg." Sir Francis Vere grimaced and ordered, "Put it down!"

A musket shot rang out. The horse floated downriver beneath the single plank.

"Bring him another!" Sir Robert Sydney ordered. A horseman grabbed the reins of an auburn horse. The two horses plunged into the swollen stream. A few other English horsemen followed him.

Above them, Captain General Maurice reached the horse passage and motioned. "We need this cleared! This side first."

Sir Sidney, with the two horses, circumvented the trees blocking the exit. The auburn horse with white lower legs shook off excess water. Sydney delivered it to Vere.

Meanwhile, Marcellus Bax arrived from the downstream side. "We dislodged the remaining guards. They didn't want to die."

From the opposite direction, the first Dutch musketeers edged across the plank. Captain *van der* Aa reached Colonel Vere. "Your leg?"

"Merely a scratch." Sir Francis Vere wrapped a white cloth around his shin. He tied it snug and slowed the bloodflow.

"My eighty musketeers have all crossed," Captain Nicolaes *van der* Aa informed.

Sir Francis Vere mounted his new horse and pointed. "To the woods!"

Captain Nicolaes *van der* Aa blazed a path for his eighty musketeers. With their muskets resting on their right shoulders, the men hurried in single file. All carried their musket rests in their left hands. Some used them like walking sticks on the uneven ground.

About one hundred twenty more Dutch musketeers crossed the broken bridge. As each squad crossed, Colonel Vere directed them to catch up with Captain Aa. He glanced back across the river and recognized his younger brother Horace at the head of an English foot company, waiting to cross the sole plank.

Behind the English Vanguard, on the road from Turnhout, several thousand additional foot soldiers of the Republican Army and their Scottish allies marched toward the plank.

Between tall beech trees, the enemy army retreated.

Sir Francis Vere wondered, *Would the army of Cardinal Albert escape before the foot soldiers could cross?*

Road to Tielen, North Brabant, Early Morning, 24th January *AD* 1597

COLONEL VERE COMMANDED Sir Robert Sydney, "Don't lose sight of them."

"Horsemen!" Sir Robert Sydney took the dozen English riders, including Duxbury and Smith, with him. Together with Marcellus Bax and the Dutch horsemen, they trotted after the enemy.

Sir Francis Vere spurred his horse through the woods bordering the road to Tielen. Within minutes, he caught up with Captain Nicolaes *van der* Aa. "We need to flank their slogging army."

"Ahead!" Aa directed his men to a small rise overlooking the road.

Well hidden in among scrub oak and brush, the first squad of musketeers readied their weapons.

Each musketeer poured powder down the long barrel and, using a long rod, packed it. Taking a round bullet from a small sack, each rolled it down the same barrel and jammed the rod a second time. Next, each musketeer took a slow-burning cord tied loosely to his thigh and lit the end of the small match cord above the priming pan and the trigger. Very proficient, the musketeers had loaded their weapons within two minutes.

The musketeers steadied their long guns on the musket rests and aimed.

The flank of the Italian *tercio* marched only a few dozen yards away.

"At your command," Captain Nicolaes *van der* Aa said.

"Fire!" Sir Francis Vere ordered.

Twenty musketeers obeyed. The volley felled several enemy soldiers.

The enemy army slowed. Horses were repositioned. Enemy musketeers aimed into the woods. As the Count of Varax deployed soldiers to guard his extended flank, Captain Nicolaes *van der* Aa led his other musketeers ahead.

Sir Francis Vere found the Dutch captains of the remaining companies. "Move forward. Harass the enemy."

With the musketeers in good order, Vere returned to the narrow road, behind the horsemen of Sir Robert Sydney and Marcellus Bax. Ahead, in tight formation, these few horsemen spanned the whole width of the lane.

With their colors flying, Marcellus Bax and Sydney kept pace with the retreating army in plain view.

136

"They cannot see our true strength," Sir Sydney told Vere.

"We can't let them attack the musketeers in the woods," Sir Francis Vere said.

"We won't let them," Commander Marcellus Bax agreed.

Sir Francis Vere returned to the musketeers. They fired from behind tall trees and low brush. The musketeers rotated ahead, hiding their strength and keeping their volleys strong. Minutes turned to hours. They advanced and reloaded again.

Meanwhile, Bax and Sydney dallied with the enemy army, many thousands strong. Periodically, John Smith, Captain Duxbury, and twenty or thirty other horsemen charged the Rearguard of the *Marquis de* Trevico. They attempted to parlay their weak position into something much stronger.

The enemy countered the faux threat. Their plodding retreat slowed, allowing the rest of the Republican Army to close the gap.

The Count of Varax deployed his Italian musketeers. As soon as the Neapolitans readied their weapons, the Dutch and English horsemen retreated beyond firing range.

After an hour, Vere returned to Sydney and Bax. He told one of the riders. "Tell Captain General Maurice to hurry."

The messenger galloped towards Turnhout.

A little more than half an hour later, he returned to Vere, "The first English foot companies have crossed the river."

"The cavalry?"

"Four cornets from Breda forded the stream."

Sir Francis Vere immediately sent another horseman. "Tell His Excellency the Heath of Tielen is less than two miles ahead. If the Count of Varax traverses it, he will escape to Herentals."

While the two hundred musketeers entertained the enemy, Sydney and Bax charged again. With each faux attack, the enemy slowed.

"What if they turn and pursue?" one rider asked.

"Then their army won't escape," Sir Vere replied. "As long as the rest of our army advances."

The messenger returned. "The foot soldiers cannot cross in time."

"The cavalry?"

"Captain General Maurice sends the Count of Hohelohe."

Sir Francis Vere sent another messenger. "Tell his Excellency that if he sends forward all of his horse, he might secure a fair victory. If he does not, the enemy will soon escape safely away."

The messenger galloped hard.

After harassing the enemy for three hours with only two hundred musketeers and thirty horsemen, Sir Francis Vere peered back. *No sign of help.*

Heath of Tielen (Tielenheide), Brabant, Late Morn., 24ᵗʰ January *AD* 1597

THE STRAIGHT PASSAGEWAY opened up into the wide Heath of Tielen. On the left side, woods and brush fronted the open field. On the right side of the heath, the high river Aa still paralleled the way to Herentals.

"Battle formation!" Colonel Claude *la* Barlotte yelled.

With company banners waving and pikes held high, the one thousand men in his Walloon regiment gathered into a large square. Like the infantrymen in the other regiments, they wore only cloth mesh for protection. Company colors flew among the field of sharp pikes.

Ahead, two more squares marched along the left-hand side of the heath. Karl Ludwig, Count of Sultz. led the German Vanguard. His young Lieutenant Ernst, the son of the Count of Mansfeld, held his standard. Behind them, Colonel Achincourt led the first Walloon regiment. From his own Walloon Regiment, Colonel Claude *la* Barlotte viewed the Neapolitan Rearguard of the *Marquis de* Trevico, where the Count of Varax, the General of the whole army, rode high on his horse.

When General Varax exited the lane, his Rearguard moved into battle formation. Company by company, the pikemen lined up in the center. Musketeers marched along on the flanks.

From his left, Dutch musketeers skirmished with intermittent fire.

At the sound of more musket fire, Colonel Claude *la* Barlotte told his able flag bearer, "They've harassed us for hours. When we reach the next lane, the harassment shall cease."

Less than a mile ahead of the four Catholic regiments, the baggage train, protected by Sergeant Major Dentice and a company of cavalry, had mostly exited the heath. Unlike the woodlands from Turnhout, the woodlands ahead were darker and wetter. "We have our cavalry." Colonel Claude *la* Barlotte gestured to the left flank of the retreating army. Led by the Albanian Nicolo Basta, four companies of lancers and arquebuses on horseback provided a buffer against the enemy hidden in the woods.

Sporadic musket fire continued. The four regiments trudged toward the narrow exit.

~ ~ ~

WHEN MUSKET BLASTS subsided, Sir Francis Vere heard another, more welcoming sound—pounding hoofs of advancing cavalry.

"Count Hohenlohe!" Vere recognized the riders from northern Brabant, the Count of Solms, and the leader of the heavy cavalry. "Captain General Maurice?"

"He will be here as soon as the rest of the cavalry crosses."

Ahead, the enemy Rearguard formed into a large square. The other three enemy squares moved farther away.

"I'll take the flank," the Count of Hohelohe said.

Sir Francis Vere signaled his approval.

The Count of Hohenlohe led the four cornets from Breda to the large expanse to the right of the four thousand enemy soldiers. Accompanied by the Count of Solms with four more cornets from Brabant, Hohenlohe kept out of musket range. Further to the right, alders lined both banks of the River Aa.

To counter this threat, the enemy cavalry moved to the right-hand side of their retreating army.

To gain a view of the whole field, Sir Francis Vere rode to a high point near the trees where Captain *van der* Aa's musketeers remained hidden.

Accompanied by some horsemen, the last of the enemy baggage exited the southern end of Tielenheide. The German Vanguard led the retreating army toward the narrow lane, less than a mile away.

Sir Francis Vere found Sir Robert Sydney. "The baggage train has already escaped. Beyond this open heath lies the narrow path. Tell Count Hohenlohe the Vanguard must be stopped before it reaches the exit!"

"And you?"

"I must find His Excellency." Sir Francis Vere turned his auburn horse around. "We must bring up all of the horse!"

Sir Francis Vere galloped past four more companies of horse; the strong cornets of Bergen op Zoom trotted faster toward the Heath of Tielen.

~ ~ ~

IN A SHORT period of time on the narrow road to Turnhout, Colonel Francis Vere found the Captain General Maurice. "If we do not attack now, the Count of Varax will escape."

His Excellency gestured to a Scottish officer. "Captain Edmonds, take your three companies and go with Sir Vere."

"And you?"

"I will hasten with Captain Parker." Maurice gestured three horse companies skirting past the hard-marching English Vanguard. "The cornets from Nijmegen will soon be here."

Sir Francis Vere turned his horse. Captain Edmonds and his Scottish companies accompanied the English Colonel back to the Heath of Tielen, where Dutch musketeers still fired from the woods.

As soon as Marcellus Bax returned from the last faux skirmish with the Rearguard, Vere told him, "His Excellency hastens!"

"Time for me to go." Marcellus Bax spurred his horse toward his own horse company. The riders from Bergen op Zoom kept pace with the enemy Rearguard, staying to their right out of musket range.

Arriving back from Hohenlohe and his eight cornets waiting in the middle of the Heath, Sir Robert Sydney galloped past Bax and reached Sir Francis Vere. "I pointed out the German Vanguard exiting."

"Less than a musket shot away?"

"The Count resolves to fight—"

Sir Francis Vere turned and signaled. "Trumpeter!"

Charge!

The cornets of Solms and Hohenlohe echoed the call.

Charge! Charge!

Chapter 18 — Battle of Tielenheide

By order of . . . Maurice, the Cornets of Breda engaged the enemy. The Spanish Cavalry, showing little proof of resistance, drove before their Vanguard forthwith, as if they wanted to gain some advantage . . .

Historie van de Oorlgen by Emanuel van Meteren
Translated from Dutch by D.E.A.

When even then our English troops had attained the Heath [of Tielen] in two battalions, the one consisting of the companies from Flushing, Ostend and the Brielle, the other of eight of our regiment, which view so amazed the enemy, thinking all the army had been at hand that even then they lost their spirit . . .

Captain John Chamberlain to the Earl of Essex, 30th January 1597

And in the space of one quarter of an hour neither pike nor ensign standing of them, nor no defense made, but by running away, or crying 'Misericordia!'

Sir Robert Sydney to the Earl of Essex
Letter from the Lowlands, January 1597

Walloon Regiment, Heath of Tielen, Brabant, Noon, 24th Jan. *AD* 1597

DISTANT TRUMPETS BLASTED and garnered the full attention of Colonel Claude *la* Barlotte, who commanded the third of the four Catholic foot regiments. The able Colonel had more than a thousand men under his command. Beyond the three companies of Spanish horse who protected his right flank, eight cornets of enemy horse had turned directly towards them.

Wearing metal helmets and dressed in dull armor, the horsemen from Breda in Brabant trotted ever closer, ever faster.

"Captains!" Colonel Claude *la* Barlotte yelled. "Prepare! They charge!"

The dozen company flags rising above the pikes of his Walloon regiment shifted, but Colonel Claude *la* Barlotte knew this battle would be different. In most open field battles, when armies faced each other, enemy horsemen with long lances would charge and attempt to break the squares.

If the lancers penetrated the front lines, the foot soldiers would follow, killing the common soldiers, unless they surrendered. They would surround the officers, and especially the general. Any captured captain or colonel would be held for ransom, with the general worth the most.

Unlike previous encounters with the Brabant horsemen of Breda, this time the enemy carried no lances, only carbines and swords. Moreover, the foot soldiers of *Stadholder* Maurice had not arrived on the Heath of Tielen. The veteran Walloon Colonel was not worried.

Several hundred horsemen, lancers, and arquebusiers on horseback protected the right flank of the Catholic army. The four regiments of the Count of Varax totaled more than four thousand men. Marching south along the left side of Tielenheide, the foot soldiers outnumbered the enemy horse by more than five to one.

Enemy trumpets sounded. *Charge!*

Closer, the trumpets sounded again. The Brabant horsemen veered away from directly attacking the two Walloon squares. They circled behind the last company of Spanish horse. As they began to trot, many reached for their weapons.

Charge!

The Brabant cornets sounded louder. In each company, riders rode in lines four to six men wide, in rows six to ten men deep. Galloping harder, their heavy cavalry raised their carbines and approached the regiment of Colonel Claude *la* Barlotte.

Outnumbered, the light Spanish horse hurried past Barlotte. When they peered back, fear spread across their faces. With panic in their eyes, the Spanish refused to engage the Brabant horsemen.

The Counts of Hohelohe and Solms did not let up, but pursued the Spanish, pushing them past the flank of Barlotte's regiment and the nine companies in the square of the other Walloon regiment of Colonel Achicourt.

Hundreds of horses—the pursued and the pursuer—galloped alongside the German Vanguard. At the narrow exit leading to Herentals, Cavalry Commander Nicolo Basta waved his arms. The three Spanish horse companies did not stop, but bolted down the dark passageway, past the horsemen of Juan *de* Guzman and Basta, who stood with dozens of Spanish lancers.

Colonel Claude *la* Barlotte knew that any advantage the Spanish horse had given the army had disappeared, too.

When Brabant trumpets sounded a different refrain, the German Vanguard still slogged toward the exit, less than 50 yards away.

Brabant trumpets blasted a second time. *Halt!*

Hohenlohe's horsemen obeyed. They cut off their pursuit and pulled their horses around. Lowering their carbines, they once more closed ranks—this time before the German and Austrian Vanguard.

The eight companies faced the head of the retreating army. The thirteen-foot companies of the Count of Sultz, a veteran regiment totaling more than 1,000 men, could only escape by dislodging the Brabant horsemen.

Northern Entrance, Heath of Tielen, Noontime, 24ᵗʰ January *AD* 1597

TRAILING THE CATHOLIC army at the northern entrance of the Heath, Sir Francis Vere eyed the vast expanse. Dozens of flags flew amongst a field of tall pikes and long muskets along the left-hand side of the field of battle. Four enemy squares advanced toward the southern end, where the Counts of Hohenlohe and Solms had chased the enemy horse away. Their horsemen were poised to attack.

Much closer, Marcellus Bax and the four cornets of Bergen op Zoom trotted slowly. They mirrored the steady movements of the fifteen companies of the Italian Rearguard. To Vere's left, the Scotsman Edmonds with his four cornets of horse moved into attack position. Further to their left, one Dutch company of musketeers exited the woods and followed the *tercio* of the Marquis *de* Trevico.

Behind Vere's and Sydney's twenty English horsemen, Captain General Maurice brought the last of his eight-hundred-fifty cavalrymen. Captain Nicholas Parker, with three cornets from Nijmegen, galloped down the road from Turnhout. Further away, foot soldiers hastened. The first of the English foot came into sight.

"Ready your carbines!" Sir Francis Vere yelled.

Dressed in full battle armor, these horsemen, including Captain Joseph Duxbury and his new recruit John Smith, had made more than a dozen false charges over the previous three hours. Once more, they poured black powder into their priming pans. They took the slow-burning ropes, loosely tied to their thighs, and lit the short cords above the trigger. With their matches lit, his men raised their carbines, the long pistols.

Sir Francis Vere lowered his visor and raised his sword.

Next to him, his flagman raised his cornet to his lips.

Vere signaled.

Charge!

The loud clarion resounded across the wide heath.

The cornets of the Count of Hohenlohe and the Count of Solms echoed the call.

Charge!

Far ahead, the Brabant horsemen raised their carbines. The eight companies charged the Vanguard. Seconds later, gunshots sounded from afar.

Much closer, the horsemen of Vere and Sydney galloped toward the center of the Rearguard. Unlike the dozen false charges during the previous three hours, this charge on the famous soldiers of Naples proved real and true.

From the woods, Dutch musketeers assisted, sustaining their intermittent volleys upon the left wing of Italian musketeers.

Along with those of Vere and Sydney, the cornets of Edmonds and his four companies sounded. Vere spurred his horse. His horsemen charged.

While Italian captains prepared their pikemen for the assault, the first line of Neapolitan musketeers aimed and fired. A few Scottish horsemen fell, but the rest of the cavalry advanced.

Vere would not stop, and neither would Edmonds.

Both cornets sounded again. *Charge!*

The heavy cavalry squadrons galloped straight toward the Italian regiment. Both Scots and English lowered and aimed their weapons. The horses surged forward, reaching battle speed.

The second line of Neapolitan musketeers readied, aimed, and discharged their muskets. Bullets flew. One hit Vere in the chest, but it did not penetrate the thick metal. A second bullet, however, hit his horse. It weakened below him, then slumped and collapsed.

Sir Francis Vere avoided being pinned when he landed, but blood spurted from the belly of his auburn horse.

Angry at the sight, Colonel Vere renewed his vow to win. He waved his cavalry unit forward. As they rode past him and his fallen horse, they kicked up loose dirt. Vere did not care about the mud on his visor and armor. With renewed vigor, his few horsemen charged the Italians, whose captains countered, encouraging their famous soldiers to stand strong.

Both wings of enemy musketeers reloaded. The right wing of Italian musketeers readied their weapons. They raised their muskets; a few aimed at Vere.

At that moment, Marcellus Bax and the heavily armed cuirassiers of Bergen op Zoom swooped across the Heath. Those four companies thundered toward the Italian right flank.

Less than twenty feet from the Italian musketeers, the cavalry halted. The first line of horsemen aimed their carbines and discharged them at point-blank range. Dozens of musketeers, clothed only in cloth mesh, fell.

The first line of horses peeled both left and right, alternating one after another. The second line advanced and, within seconds, discharged their weapons, killing many more musketeers. As the third line advanced, the first riders rejoined their companies at the rear of their squadron. They reloaded the carbines with powder and shot. Meanwhile, the fourth line advanced in perfected revolving fire. Many more enemy soldiers died. The rout intensified.

Scores of musketeers fell back into the center of the Square, pressing the pikemen, now unable to receive any charge.

John Smith returned to Sir Francis Vere. "My weapon jammed." John dismounted. "Take my horse."

"I must return to the fight." Sir Francis Vere mounted his third horse of the day.

The onslaught of persistent gunfire filled the field. When a nearby Scotsman fell, Captain Duxbury retrieved the riderless horse for his new recruit.

At the southern end of the Heath of Tielen, the Count of Hohenlohe continued his attack. The enemy Vanguard reduced their resistance. German musketeers on the wings fell back into their Pike. Many fled to the woods, while others sought safety in the Walloon regiment behind them.

At the center of the Heath of Tielen, Captain General Maurice mirrored the movements of the Walloon *Battalia* with his reserve horse. Carbines and arquebuses at their side, Captain Nicolas Parker's horsemen, along with the three cornets of Nijmegen, faced the right flank of the two Walloon regiments.

At the Rearguard, like wildfire through a dry field, fear spread across the faces of the Italian footmen.

Colonel Vere turned to find the cause. Behind him, the English foot spilled through the entrance of the Heath. They quickly moved into battle formation.

Sir Vere recognized the banner of his younger brother. It flew above one of those first foot companies. Captain Horace Vere had finally caught up with the fleeing army, an army chased since dawn. A company of English musketeers advanced. When they reached Vere's fallen horse, they aimed and fired.

Though their officers attempted to keep order, the Italians appeared stunned and shocked at the sight of the English foot. The Italian musketeers faltered. Dozens of musketeers in the left wing scattered and headed to the woods. Other Neapolitan musketeers fell back into the forest of pikes.

More bullets penetrated the enemy's protective mesh. Carbines flashed with each shot. The smell of black gunpowder tinged the air. The slaughter continued. Hundreds of the enemy died instantly. The heavy cavalry pulled their swords, trampling forward over fallen soldiers and reaching the pikemen.

Remounted on another horse, John Smith slew one pikeman and a second.

An Italian pikeman swooped his hooked pike and pulled a nearby horseman off his ride. As soon as the Italian stabbed the English soldier, shots rang out from the woods. A Dutch musketeer shot the Italian dead.

"Misericordia!" Neapolitan soldiers with anguished wounds cried out loud.

"They don't want to suffer," Captain Joseph Duxbury told Captain Horace Vere.

"They're ready to see their Maker."

"Misericordia!" An Italian handed his dagger to an English musketeer. The Englishman immediately used it on him, ending his pain. Another wounded enemy soldier avoided a slow and painful death.

"Misericordia!" More wounded Catholic soldiers cried loudly

Again and again, Dutch and English soldiers obliged, heeding the cry for mercy. Shots rang out. More weapons were discharged into enemy chests. Other Italians died by the sword. The slaughter continued, unabated.

Italians fled to the Walloon regiment of Colonel Claude *la* Barlotte, squeezed along the left edge of the Heath.

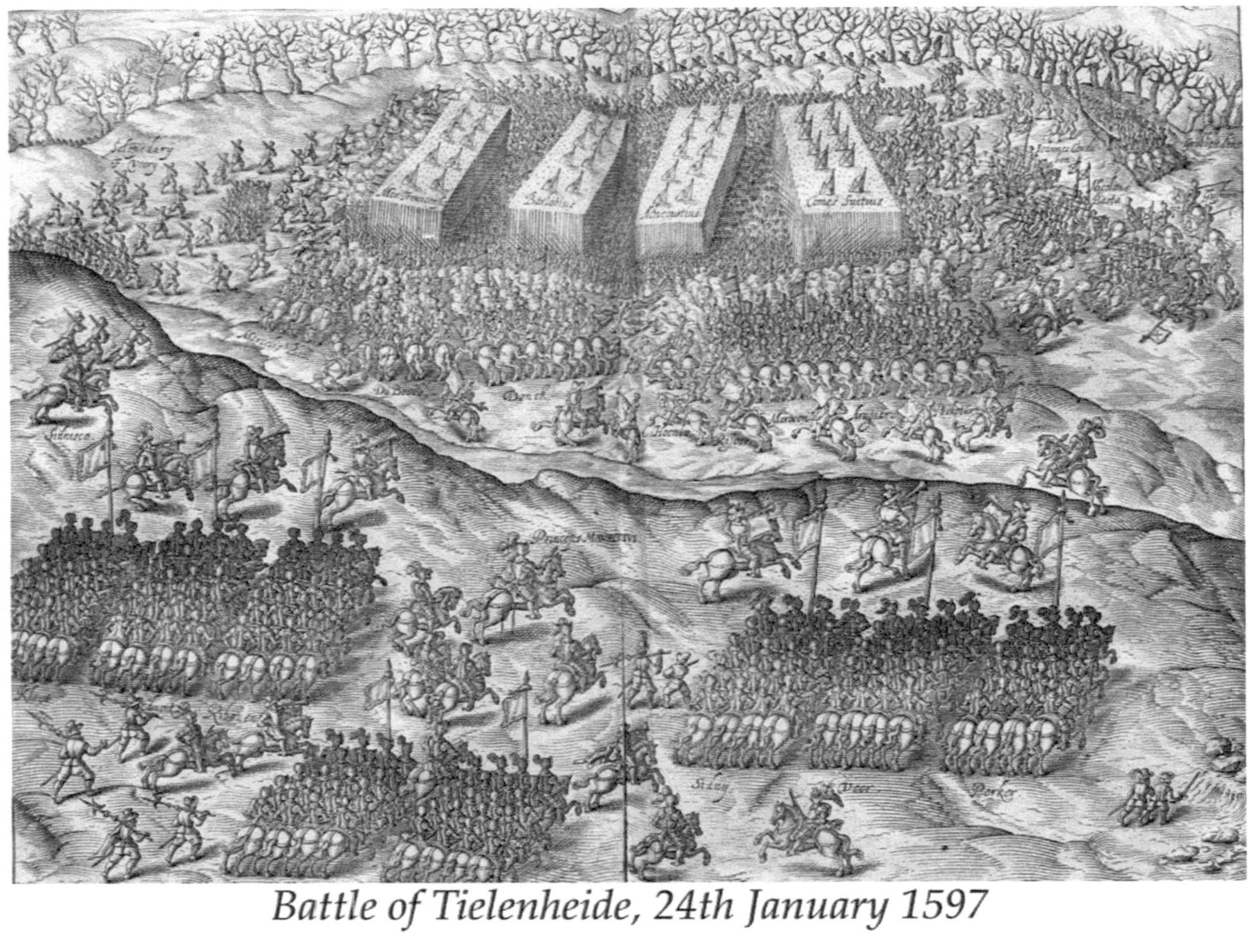

Battle of Tielenheide, 24th January 1597

To their right, in the middle of the Heath, the cornet of Captain General Maurice blared. *Charge!*

Captain Parker's horses lunged forward. All four horse companies held in reserve attacked the *Battalia*—the two Walloon regiments of Baron d'Achicourt and Colonel *la* Barlotte. As each line of the reserve fired their carbines, more Walloon soldiers fell.

Wave after wave, the reserve horsemen repeated the incessant fire. With that onslaught, the Walloon pikemen and musketeers dropped their weapons and scattered to nearby woods.

Other horsemen rounded up and captured fleeing combatants. As they scurried to the bushes at the edge of the heath, Scottish, English, and Dutch horsemen caught them by twos and tens.

Sir Francis Vere looked down. His bandage had loosened, but he stood above a slain enemy officer. "Who was he?"

"The Count of Varax," an Italian prisoner answered. "A musket shot killed him."

"Put the general on a wagon. Show him the respect he deserves." Vere grimaced. A young musketeer must have unknowingly killed the enemy officer. Vere would have preferred to hold him for ransom.

Middle of Tielenheide, Early Afternoon, 24th January *AD* 1597

ALONG THE EASTERN side of the Heath of Tielen, Colonel Claude *la* Barlotte could no longer maintain the battle order of his Square. When Captain General Maurice sent the reserve cavalry, Barlotte's pikemen and musketeers fled to the woods. Like the German Vanguard and the Neapolitan Rearguard before, both Walloon Squares collapsed. The three cornets from Nijmegen and the one from England continued their attack.

Unable to maintain the fight, Colonel Caude la Barlotte fled. Before he could exit, English horsemen surrounded him. As he raised his hands, a squad of Brabant horsemen, some carrying spoils from the baggage train, reentered the Heath. When those riders skirted toward the river, forty Spanish lancers reentered the Heath. The Spanish cavalry had returned, but they did not follow the fleeing Brabant horsemen. Instead, they charged the center.

Sitting atop his stallion, Captain General Maurice directed the action through his trumpeter. The Spanish lancers rode hard toward the Captain General. Above the confusion of the battle, his trumpeter sounded a warning cry.

148

The English captain turned and viewed the threat. He motioned for several of the horsemen guarding Colonel Claude *la* Barlotte to assist. While several Dutch riders engaged the Spanish lancers, the English captain galloped toward the threatened commander.

At the same time, the first two English foot companies advanced toward Maurice, marching double time. When the English pike reached him, they angled their pikes forward. In steady steps, they advanced toward the Spanish Lancers.

Maurice of Nassau-Orange at Battle of Tielenheide - January 24, 1597

~ ~ ~

ONE OF CLAUDE *la* Barlotte's captains returned and slew one of the weakened guard. His men drove two other horsemen away.

Colonel Claude *la* Barlotte urged his horse forward and escaped. Likewise, the Spanish Lancers spurred their horses and exited. When Colonel *la* Barlotte reached the plundered baggage train, he found Sergeant Major Jeronimo Dentice being held prisoner. His Walloon lancers charged the enemy guard and freed him. With the Brabant cavalry advancing down the narrow lane, the two freed prisoners abandoned the baggage and escaped, trotting toward the Herentals Fort.

Colonel Claude *la* Barlotte did not want to tell Cardinal Albert of Austria in Brussels the horrendous news: in fewer than thirty minutes, the Count of Varax had suffered a humiliating defeat. *How could the Colonel explain the terrible chastening?*

Chapter 19 — Thirty-Eight Captured Flags

I have gotten 38 colors and one standard [coronet]. I return thanks to God for this good success and the rather as I think her Majesty [Queen Elizabeth] will receive singular contentment from it, and that it will prove of service to her affairs. This, Monsieur [Essex], is what I have to present you with for the New Year.
Letter from Maurice of Nassau to the Earl of Essex
The Hague, 29 January 1597

At first they refused to yield, but next morning, after the cannon had played three tyre [times] upon them . . .
Captain Henry Dockwray Letter to the Earl of Essex
The Hague, Seven United Provinces of the Netherlands, 30th January 1597 [New Style]

Tielenheide, Brabant, The Lowlands, 24th January *AD* 1597

"THANK YOU GOD for the victory!"

The voice of His Excellency, Captain General Maurice, echoed across *Tielenheide*, the Heath of Tielen.

An afternoon breeze kicked up dried leaves on the battlefield, littered with hundreds of dead and dying bodies. From one end of the heath to the other, the swirling foliage lodged against fallen soldiers—Italians, Walloons, and Germans.

The cool breeze hit his young face. "We won from the beginning." John Smith sheathed his sword.

"It did not last long." Captain Joseph Duxbury pointed to enemy prisoners. English and Scottish captains traipsed across the field, bringing them by tens and twenties to Colonel Vere. The English commander still stood near the body of the enemy general.

"Bring me the general's standard," Sir Francis Vere commanded.

When Captain Duxbury nodded, John quickly obeyed.

"We'll deliver it and the General's corpse to His Excellency."

Two soldiers lifted the body of the Count of Varax onto a horse.

By the time the Englishmen reached Captain General Maurice, other Dutch and English captains brought more captured flags.

"How many standards?" Maurice asked.

"Thirty-eight," the Count of Hohenlohe said.

Victorious soldiers, who gathered around the Captain General, displayed the enemy standards.

One captain of horsemen, who had reentered Tielenheide, raised high a captured cornet. "And a cornet of the cavalry squadron that had protected the baggage train." The captain assigned to Parker's company delivered the cornet of Mondragon to the Captain General and gestured to several wagons returning from the road to Herentals. All were filled with abandoned weapons and supplies. "But Sergeant Major Jeronimo Dentice escaped through the bogs."

"Escaped? How?"

The general did not appear happy.

"Spanish horsemen counterattacked."

Maurice van Nassau-Orange displayed his regret. "And the other colonels?"

"All, including Claude *la* Barlotte, escaped," Commander Marcellus Bax said. "But we did capture the son of the Count of Mansfeld, who served under the Count of Sultz." He pointed to Ernst, the young German.

"How many men did we lose?"

"Eighteen or twenty Dutchmen," Marcellus Bax reported.

"About ten Englishmen." Sir Francis Vere added, "What do you want to do with the body of the Count of Varax?"

"Take it back to Turnhout. The castle still holds out."

"And the enemy dead? There must be more than 2,000."

Captain General Maurice gestured to local farmers emerging from the woods. "Pay those farmers to bury them."

With nearly five prisoners in tow, the army fell back into order. Leaving the dead behind, they exited the heath and marched back to Turnhout.

~ ~ ~

BY NIGHTFALL, THE victorious army of the Republic of the Seven United Provinces of the Netherlands had reached the open village. Along with their English and Scottish allies, the army surrounded the moated castle.

A Dutch trumpeter summoned the enemy governor. "Will you surrender?"

"No, we will wait for relief."

"You'll have no relief. You have until morning." His Excellency commanded, "Position the cannons. We attack at dawn."

Turnhout Castle, Brabant, 25th January *AD* 1597

THE FOLLOWING MORNING, Captain General Maurice stood before the simple castle. He repeated the previous night's demand, "You must surrender!"

Two half cannons and two field pieces pointed at the lowered gate. Behind them, thousands of Dutch and English pikemen stood in formation, ready to storm the isolated castle when a breach was made.

"The castle won't surrender," a Zeeland officer reported. "But they have only forty men inside."

"Don't they know that the Count of Varax can't come to their aid?" John Smith asked. "He and twenty-four hundred of his men died yesterday."

"Fire!" Maurice ordered.

Four artillery pieces blasted the stone edifice.

"Fire! Fire!"

The flying debris from the third round settled into rubble. A messenger appeared at the castle gate.

"Cease fire!"

The messenger crossed the moat. "The governor wishes to negotiate."

"Negotiate?" Maurice asked.

"You're not going to execute us, are you?"

"If you don't surrender, I will attack." Maurice questioned, "But why would you think I would execute you?"

"Cardinal Albert ordered that if we took any prisoners, we should immediately put them to the sword."

"Is this true? No quarter will be given to my men?" The honorable Maurice turned to his officers and pointed to the five hundred prisoners. "Guard the prisoners closely, make sure none escape!" Maurice peered at the messenger. "I assume the governor is an honorable man. What does he propose?"

"He will depart the castle, but wishes to take his baggage."

"And the castle?"

"It will be yours without further defense."

"Tell your governor I agree to the terms."

Within the hour, the Governor of Turnhout vacated the castle. After crossing the moat, he stopped with his baggage.

"You may take the body of the Count of Varax with you, but I need you to take a message to Cardinal Albert." Maurice handed the Governor a letter. "I must know whether the Cardinal ordered that 'no quarter' be given to my soldiers. I will release none of the prisoners until I know. I want a reply!"

The governor took the note. His expression turned solemn as he exited Turnhout and headed down the road to Tielenheide, Herentals, and Brussels.

"I would prefer to ransom these prisoners and their 16 captains." Captain General Maurice's voice trailed off. "But if the Cardinal does not change his orders . . ."

Later that day, several farmers brought wagons filled with pikes and muskets into the church. "Taken from the fallen Italians."

"And the dead?"

"More than two thousand two hundred. We are still burying them where they died."

"Very well." Captain General Maurice turned to one of his captains. "You will guard the castle."

"And the rest of the army?" Sir Vere asked.

"Everyone will return to their own garrison."

In the middle of the afternoon, the army trekked north, reaching the village of Clume by nightfall.

Geertruidenberg, Brabant, 27th January *AD* 1597

MOST SHIPS REMAINED anchored in the *Bies Bos*, the waterway of Geertruidenberg when the victorious army returned to the original rendezvous point.

"Thank you for your brave work," Captain General Maurice told Sir Francis Vere and Sir Robert Sydney. "You may return to your garrisons. I have enough guards for the prisoners."

"I will accompany my brother's company to Breda and check on the fortifications," Sir Francis Vere said.

"Colonel Vere?" Captain Duxbury asked.

"After I return to the Hague, the Queen may have need of me at sea."

"The companies from Ostend?"

"I will meet them at the Hague."

"And our horses?"

"Go to the Hague. I will decide there."

While Sir Francis Vere followed the riders of Breda to the west, the Nijmegen riders rode to the northeast. When Sir Robert Sydney with his men embarked on the boats back to Flushing, Maurice asked Count Hohenlohe, "Any word from Cardinal Albert?"

"Not yet," the Count of Hohenlohe peered down the road toward Turnhout. "Wait." He gestured to a galloping rider. "Perhaps he brings us news."

The messenger dismounted. "No word from the Governor General, Cardinal Albert of Austria."

"If the Cardinal does not rescind his order to give 'no quarter,' I must consider whether or not these five hundred prisoners should live." After Maurice penned another letter, he handed it to the messenger. "Take this to the Cardinal. Tell him, I give him twenty days. If he does not ransom them, the prisoners will be hanged or drowned." His Excellency insisted the captives remain well-guarded.

"What about the thirty-eight colors and the cornet?" Captain Joseph Duxbury asked when the messenger left.

"We'll present them at The Hague."

While the Dutch companies embarked onto their vessels, John Smith led the horses from Ostend back onto the same ship they had arrived on less than a week earlier. This time, however, the ship did not sail beneath the cannons of Willemstad and through the Holland *Diep*.

Duxbury, Smith, and the horses sailed across the *Bies Bos* instead. At Rotterdam, the companies and horses from Ostend disembarked.

Excitement charged the air in town after town. As the victorious army marched through South Holland, men, women, and children waved their arms in joy. Some children in wooden shoes even marched alongside the English companies on the road to The Hague.

"Where will we stay?" John asked.

"At the English garrison in Leiden, north of the Hague."

Chapter 20 — We Gather Together

"We gather together to count the Lord's blessings;
He hastens and chastens His will to make known.
The wicked oppressing now ceases from distressing. Sing praises to His Name;
He forgets not His own.
                    Adrianus Valerius, "We Gather Together"
Set to Dutch Folk Tune, 1597, Translated from Dutch by Theodore Baker

The Burcht, Leiden, South Holland, Winter *AD* 1597

THE ENGLISH MARCH across South Holland ended, but the trek had swelled John's thirst, so when he spied a well inside the Burcht, the old castle of Leiden, he hurried straight towards it. With his steed in tow, he reached the well and found a lone Dutch woman standing next to it. The sprightly lady, wearing traditional wooden shoes, turned and smiled. She offered the young English recruit a ladle, brimmed with water.
John Smith drank his fill. *"Dank u wel."*

"No need to be so polite," the woman answered. "The English are true friends."

"And my horse?" John asked.

"Bring me that bucket."

As soon as the horse drank its fill, Captain Duxbury called from the castle walls.   "John, come here!"

"Dank u wel," John told the woman, again.

"No need to be so polite!"

"You'll have to forgive me." John returned the cup. "That's the way I was brought up."

"And we say what we mean," the Dutch woman responded. "Our 'yes' means 'yes' and our 'no' means 'no'."

John tied his horse to a rail and passed by a Dutch cook tending a kettle over a fire. His nose caught a whiff, a scent of something good. "What are you cooking?"

"We call it *Hutspot,*" the Dutch cook said.

John ascended to the top of the walls and found his captain.

"Dinner must be ready," Captain Joseph Duxbury said.

"The cook said it was *Hutspot.*"

"We call it hotchpotch."

"Hotchpotch?" John asked, "What's that?'

"Almost twenty-five years ago," Captain Joseph Duxbury explained, "the citizens of Leiden resisted Spanish soldiers for more than four months. The townspeople were starving, and the Spaniards were well-entrenched." He pointed to the surrounding countryside. The circular castle itself had been built on a hill, at the confluence of two branches of the Rhine. A moat surrounded the town. "But William the Silent came up with a plan."

"What plan?"

Captain Joseph Duxbury pointed to the lowlands beyond the walls of Leiden. "Do you see how the polder lands lie so low?"

"Yes." John attempted to guess at the plan.

"Dutch soldiers broke the dykes and flooded the polders. Their admiral ordered his flat-bottom boats to attack the Spanish forts. When the Dutch ships reached the city walls, the Spanish abandoned their positions. They left a big pot of *hutspot* that the Dutch quickly devoured."

"What's in it?"

"Stew made with potatoes."

"From America?"

"Yes, Spanish explorers brought back white potatoes from Peru."

"Ready!" the cook yelled.

"Go ahead!" Captain Joseph Duxbury said.

The English recruit descended from the walls and drew closer to the fire. He joined other English soldiers gathered around the large pot, but the cook told the men, "No, sit down at the tables. My nieces will serve you."

The lively girls brought the bowls, filled to the brim.

"What is that?" John pointed to the cream-colored vegetable.

"Parsnips."

The concoction of meat, potatoes, parsnips, carrots, and onions smelled delicious, and he laughed. "I can see why the Dutch like it so much."

"As the old English proverb says," Captain Joseph Duxbury said.

"What's that?"

"Hunger is the best sauce."

Pieterskerk, Leiden, South Holland

EARLY SUNDAY MORNING, the English soldiers of the garrison attended a service at *Pieterskerk*, the Gothic Church of Leiden. Wearing traditional raiment, the English chaplain read from the Bible:

"Then the King of Egypt called for the midwives, and said unto them, 'Why have ye done thus, and preserved alive the men-children?'

"And the midwives answered Pharaoh, 'Because the Hebrew women are not as the women of Egypt: for they are lively, and are delivered ere ye midwife come at them.'"

"After this," the chaplain said, "God prospered the midwives and the people, but Pharaoh charged that every man-child born be cast into the river."

Young John Smith, sitting of the front row, mouthed, *Moses?*

"Yes, when the mother of Moses could no longer hide her son, she put him in a basket. When the daughter of Pharaoh found the baby in the river, he cried. She had compassion on him and raised Moses as her own, inside the house of Pharaoh. Forty years later, the Prophet Moses had to flee. Moses later led his people out of Egypt and through the parted sea, and set the Hebrews free."

John remembered hearing the story as a child in Lincolnshire, England.

"But that is not what I wish to talk about today." The preacher held up his Bible. "This English version of the Bible was published in Geneva. A little more than fifty years ago, Mary became the Queen of England and began persecuting the Protestants. The Catholic queen put many to death, but some scholars fled England and escaped to Geneva, where they joined the French Reformer John Calvin. Joining other scholars, they located the copies of the original manuscripts in both Hebrew and Greek. For the first time, these scholars translated both the

Old and New Testaments into the Bible, publishing it in Geneva in 1560.

"We are very thankful for the victory God granted us at Tielenheide by Turnhout." The preacher looked directly at the soldiers from Captain Duxbury's company. "For just as God prospered the Hebrew midwives, he prospers the United Netherlands." The chaplain turned the Geneva Bible toward the congregation. "Nearly fifty years ago, before the War for Dutch independence began, the translators made side notes in the Bible. Speaking of the midwives, it states here: 'Their disobedience herein was lawful, but their dissembling evil.'"

John was somewhat perplexed and mouthed, *'lawful?'*

"Yes, it was lawful for the midwives to disobey the King of Egypt in order to save the baby boys as they were born. And I might add that it is right for us Englishmen to help the Dutch in their War for Independence. When the King of Spain, through his governors, kills Dutchmen who believe the Bible, it is lawful to fight against them and their oppression." The preacher paused. "But let me add a warning . . ."

The soldiers, the recruits, and the others in the congregation listened attentively.

"After the lively Hebrew women gave birth, the Pharaoh ordered every male child killed, drowned in the river. As the note states . . ." The chaplain showed the page from the Book of Exodus. "'When tyrants cannot prevail by craft, they burst forth into open rage.' When news of your victory on the Heath of Tielen reaches the King of Spain, you can be certain that you will hear from him again." He shut the Bible. "Godspeed to all of you. Amen."

John and the rest of the company knelt at the front rail. From the minister of the Church of England, they received the bread and wine, representing the body and blood of Jesus Christ.

University of Leiden, Leiden, South Holland

CAPTAIN JOSEPH DUXBURY and his young recruit crossed a small bridge over one of Leiden's canals the next morning.

"Colonel Francis Vere wanted to find His Excellency Maurice's younger brother."

"His brother?" John asked.

"Yes, Frederik Henry studies at the University of Leiden, the first in Holland."

"Sir Francis Vere is over there." John pointed to the English Colonel talking to several students by a two-story building. When they reached the group, Colonel Vere explained, "Frederik Henry, the attack at Tielenheide began when your brother ordered the cornets of Breda to engage the enemy."

"The victory?" Frederik Henry asked.

"Complete."

"I would like to fight."

"For now, your brother Maurice wants you to study," a teacher said.

"Yes, I know." Frederik Henry and his friends went inside the building.

"Captain Duxbury?" Colonel Vere inquired. "Officers will convene in one hour."

"I will not be late."

As Colonel Vere headed back to Burcht Castle, Captain Duxbury turned back to John, "Frederik Henry's father built this university after Leiden survived the Spanish siege of 1574. Prince William of Nassau-Orange offered the citizens of Leiden a choice."

"How so?"

"Prince William told them that because of their heroism, they could either be exempt from taxes, or he would build them a university."

"Most towns would gladly avoid taxes." John asked, "But Leiden chose this university?"

"That Prince William built. And even though he was assassinated, now his youngest son attends it. Many other famous students have studied here, and the university also has a medical school and a garden. Let me show you."

A Dutch teacher led them to the botanical gardens.

Hortus Botanicus, Leiden, South Holland, Winter _AD_ 1597

"ORIGINALLY, MEDICAL SCHOOLS planted gardens of herbs and roots in order to find plants that would soothe and heal," the teacher said, "but not every plant was found useful."

"What do you mean?" John asked.

"Take this bulb. The French Ambassador sent one like it from Constantinople, but as far as we know, it did not have a medicinal purpose."

John held the small bulb. "Good for food?"

"No, but when you bury it and wait out the winter, it blooms in the spring." The gardener opened a book. "Like this." The page showed a red tulip.

"Colorful," John said.

"Some blooms are single colors, yellow or red, but others have streaks. About five years ago, Charles *de* l'Ecluse brought these Turkish bulbs here." The gardener pointed to an older man. "He wrote a book about plants in Spain and Portugal, and this one I use to identify the flowers."

"But the books say Carolus Clusius," John said.

"That is his Latin name."

Den Hague, South Holland, 4th February *AD* 1597

AT THE HAGUE, the excitement surrounding the victory had not diminished. John walked on the lakeshore near the Binnenhof about a week after arriving in South Holland. On a sunny winter morning, Dutch citizens congregated in small groups.

Pleased that his Dutch had improved, John approached a Dutch citizen. "Why the celebration?"

"Weren't you there?" The Dutchman grabbed his arms with both hands. "We're so grateful for your help."

A second Dutch burgher reached out. "You were at Turnhout?"

"*Ja.*"

"Perhaps the tyranny will finally end?" the first suggested.

"The Cardinal's army wasn't simply defeated," the second citizen added, "it was vanquished."

"I'm just a soldier, following my captain's orders." John gestured to Captain Duxbury, who conversed with some Dutch officers. "Besides the dead, other soldiers surrendered. Captain General Maurice has threatened to kill them if the Cardinal doesn't pay the ransom."

"Didn't you hear?" the first citizen asked.

"What?"

"The Cardinal will pay. He levies a new tax on the subjects of Brabant," the burgher replied. "The Cardinal wrote that he never commanded his soldiers to give 'no quarter' to our soldiers.

"So His Excellency Maurice will release the prisoners?"

"*Ja.*"

John wondered if he would fight any of them again.

"But Maurice is an honorable general, and his reputation increases," the Dutchman added.

"During and after the Battle of Tielenheide." John turned. "Singing?"

Wearing wooden shoes, two young women joined two men by the water's edge.

"New words to an old Dutch tune." The Dutchman led John closer to the quartet.

"What's it called?" John asked.

"*Wilt heden nu treden.*"

"We gather together?"

"Yes, a new song thanking the Lord for the victory at Tielenheide."

The two Dutch girls smiled at John. They began the song anew. "*Wilt heden nu treden voor God den Heere.*"

John learned the words as they sang the tune again:

"We gather together to ask the Lord's blessing; He chastens and hastens His will to make known. The wicked oppressing now ceases from distressing. Sing praises to His Name; He forgets not His own.

Beside us to guide us, our God with us joining, Ordaining, maintaining His kingdom divine; So from the beginning the fight we were winning; Thou, Lord, were at our side, all glory be Thine!   We all do extol Thee, Thou Leader triumphant, And pray that Thou still our Defender will be. Let Thy congregation escape tribulation; Thy Name be ever praised! O Lord, make us free!

Next to the lake, more of the citizens joined in the contagious song. By the time the group got to the last stanza, John joined in, too, "Thy name be ever praised, Lord make us free!"

An officer approached Duxbury and informed, "Your presence is requested at *Ridderzaal.*"

Ridderzaal, **The Hague, 4th February** *AD* **1597**

CAPTAIN DUXBURY AND John departed the lakefront. After crossing the inner courtyard, they met Sir Francis Vere at the two-story building with its steep roof.

Inside *Ridderzaal*, Smith stared up at the high rafters and recognized a yellow flag with a large X in the middle. "So many?"

"All of the flags captured on Tielenheide were brought here."

Thirty-eight flags hung from the ceiling.

Maurice of Nassau-Orange & Captured Flags at Ridderzaal

"With the Cardinal's army defeated, they won't be able to mount a campaign in the spring," a Dutch member of the States Council predicted. "And at long last, the King Henry IV has sealed his approval of the treaty."

"The Republic of the Seven United Netherlands has formally joined the offensive and defensive alliance of France and England," Captain Joseph Duxbury said.

"I have orders to go to sea," Sir Vere told Captain Duxbury. "King Henry IV will be well-pleased when he hears of the victory and the strength of the Triple Alliance."

"And us?"

"English horsemen from Leiden will accompany you back to France."

Chapter 21 — Forty *Ich-Oglans*

Those who are most promising, and who have the better physique, are intended for the service of the Grand Seigneur [the Sultan] and for the employment of what touches his person:
We call them Ich-Oglans, which means Youth of the Interior.
<u>Voyage de Levant Fait (per the Commandment of the King in the Year 1621)</u>
Translated from French by D.E.A.

The Ich-Oglans are young men, bred up in the Seraglio [New Palace], not only to serve about the Prince [Sultan], but to fill, in time, the first posts of the [Ottoman] Empire. . . The eunuchs are very cruel, and being vex'd at their own miserable condition, discharge their anger upon those who have suffer'd in the same kind . . .
From Pitton de Tournefort to Count de Pontchartrain
A Voyage into the Levant, Vol. II, Translated from French

They took me one day to the mufti's deputy, who invited me to a splendid feast; I assembled that day with the rebels . . ."
Poiraz Osman Bey to Grand Vizier Hasan the Fruiterer
Annals of the Turkish Empire by Mustafa Naima
Translated from the Turkish by Charles Frasier

Salon, Palace of Ibrahim *Pasha*, Rajab *AH* 1011 (Late December *AD* 1602)

"WE GATHER TOGETHER." Dilara finished translating *'Wilt heden nu treden'* into Turkish.

Aisha dabbed the green remnants of mint from her lips. She handed the soft napkin to her servant, turned, and smiled at her slave. "*Capitano?*"

"A Dutch song of thanksgiving," Captain John Smith had finished the last of his broth. "And thank you for the tasty soup."

"How could only eight hundred fifty horsemen devastate an experienced army of five thousand?" Aisha wondered. "The English lost so few men?"

"The Dutch lost only a few men more at the Battle of Tielenheide in Brabant."

"And the enemy flags from Turnhout? All thirty-eight hang in Knight's Hall at The Hague?"

"From beams spanning higher than the ceiling here in your Salon." John lifted his empty bowl. "Thank you again for your red lentil soup, so delicious."

Happy John loved her soup so much, Aisha reflected on the day. After bringing Dilara from the Imperial Harem, she found mint in the kitchen and gave it to her chef. He used it to top the red lentil soup, adding the perfect amount of flavor, but now the shadows grew long. The setting sun beamed through the high windows of her Salon.

Aisha told her slave, "You must wait." She grabbed Dilara by the hand. "The afternoon is gone, and I need to return you to the Imperial Harem before my mother becomes upset."

"I wish I could stay longer." Dilara smiled at John. "*Vaarwel.*"

"*Vaarwel.*"

Aisha stopped at the door and glanced back at John, who remained seated, cross-legged on the floor. "Do you think John tells the truth?"

"I know for a long time the English and Dutch have been allies against the Spanish. Dutch merchants to the Levant fly under the English flag. If John did not fight at the Battle of Tielenheide, he must be close friends of those who did." Dilara looked directly at Aisha. "Your English slave may indeed be telling the truth."

"I think I believe him." Aisha hesitated. "But why would Hasan *the Fruiterer* . . ." Her voice trailed off. "Dilara, I must bring you and Filiz back soon."

"The French translator? You need her again?"

"Yes, I do." Aisha had first brought Filiz to her palace when John told the story of how he went to Orleans to find the eldest son of Lord Willoughby. The Sister of the Sultan told the Overseer. "Take my slave back to his quarters."

"As you wish, Lady Aisha." The Overseer bowed and scowled at the slave.

"But treat him kindly."

The Overseer did not appear pleased.

"If you insist."

"I do. My guest shall receive no harm."

"Your guest?" The overseer bowed again. "As you wish."

As he escorted John by the elbow out the far door, Aisha motioned to the servant girls, all staring. "Servants!"

"Yes, my Lady," the young servants chimed in unison.

"Everything must be cleaned before I return."

"Yes, Lady Aisha."

The young widow escorted Dilara across the garden courtyard. She told the Black eunuch driver of her waiting carriage, "Take Dilara directly back through the Carriage Gate of the Imperial Harem. Do not open the door for anyone but *Kizlar Agha* Osman."

Gate of Justice, Majesty, & Felicity, 2nd Courtyard (Far End), New Palace

PULLED BY TWO oxen, the Araba carriage belonging to Aisha, Sister of the Sultan, slowly crossed the courtyard before disappearing behind the Divan.

"*Kizlar Agha* Osman, the Dutch *odalisque* must be returning." The Chief White Eunuch stood in front of the Gate of Felicity, the *Sublime Porte,* the entrance to the Third Courtyard. As *Kapi Agha* or Keeper of the Gate, no official—no matter how great his rank—was allowed to see the Sultan without Gazanfer's expressed permission.

"In time for the evening prayers," the Chief Black Eunuch answered. Only after the enclosed coach passed through Carriage Gate would his Black eunuch guards open its sealed curtains and doors. He pointed to the Gate of Greeting with its two parapet towers at the opposite end of the courtyard. "Your nephew returns."

"Good, I was beginning to worry." Hours earlier, the Chief White Eunuch had left the young Venetian man of twenty at the palace assigned to and kept by his mother, Beatrice. Gazanfer *Aghu* was happy his nephew did not abuse the liberty given him earlier that afternoon. He did not want the other cadets schooled in the Third Courtyard to become jealous.

"Tomorrow, I must hear the petitions relating to the endowments." Osman *Agha* carried on the tradition begun by the previous Chief Black Eunuch, who had served for sixteen years under Sultan Murad III. Both eunuchs held weekly meetings in the Audience Gateway behind the Divan.

"Yes, of Mecca and Medina."

"It is not too early to plan the pilgrimage. With Hasan *the Fool* leading the rebellion in Anatolia, the faithful must sail to Alexandria, in Egypt," the Chief Black Eunuch said. "You must excuse me, I told the

Sultan's Mother I would escort Dilara directly back to the dormitory. Remember, do not tell anyone."

"I have learned to be discreet." The Chief White Eunuch did not want a scandal surrounding an *odalisque* leaving the Imperial Harem any more than the Chief Black Eunuch did. The Chief Black Eunuch crossed the Second Courtyard, walking past the four chambers of the Treasury before disappearing behind the Divan.

When his nephew reached him, the Chief White Eunuch told him, "Good, you are in time for evening prayers."

"How much more time will I stay in the Second Chamber?"

"Until you learn everything you need to know." The Chief White Eunuch escorted his nephew through the Gate of Felicity and into the Third Courtyard. "You progressed well in the first chamber." Several other White eunuchs walked with them.

"I have learned to read and write Turkish."

"Yes, and you've learned the prayers in Arabic." The Chief White Eunuch looked at the first chamber, where the newest arrivals of the *devshirme* had already begun their training. He recognized the two young Bulgarian boys the Grand Vizier had sent days earlier. Like the other four hundred boys in the first chamber or school, they had all been circumcised after saying the *shahadah*, the first pillar of Islam. Holding down their heads, the boys silently crossed their hands across their chests. Instead of staying in the first or little chamber for six years, his nephew, being slightly older, had advanced to the Second Chamber in less than two.

At the Second Chamber, his nephew continued learning Arabic, but he also began reading Persian and Tartarian—the Turkish language used many words from those two languages. The *ich-oglans* or 'Interior Youth'— especially those in the Third and Fourth Chambers—had access to books. The large library contained many.

"Your instructor said you are learning to use the bow."

"I hit the target several times this morning."

Besides studying the better use of language, the four hundred boys in the Second Chamber learned to wrestle and to use weapons. The White eunuchs always kept a close watch on the students. Any deviation or idleness would be punished.

A White eunuch in front of the Second Chamber used a bastinado to bludgeon the bottom of a boy's foot. "You belong to the Sultan. You must obey." The eunuch again hit the boy's foot with the stick. "No more whistling."

The Chief White Eunuch did not doubt the punishment was justified. He also knew the stern White eunuchs kept watch by lamplight throughout the night. The *ich-oglans* slept in rooms with forty other boys, not unlike the *odalisques* of the Imperial Harem beyond the walls to their right, who slept in rooms of fifteen. He turned back to his nephew. "Everything is arranged. When you graduate from the Second Chamber and into the Third, you will learn a trade."

Many of those in the Third Chamber began their personal service to the Sultan, including tasks such as folding his clothes perfectly, caring for his hawks, or servicing his table. Only forty boys graduated from the Third Chamber into the Fourth Chamber. From those forty *ich-oglans*, the Sultan chose who would serve him directly. Their pay doubled, and their attire improved. No longer dressed in common cloth, they wore silk and gold.

Ich-Oglan (Interior Youth) and Writing Master, circa 1788

Clean-shaven, like the younger youth, a lock of hair hung down by each ear. None, however, were allowed to look directly at the Sultan. They kept their heads down, or faced punishment: beating or worse.

The call for evening prayer rang out, and one thousand *ich-oglans* from the four chambers quickly and quietly lined up. The Chief White Eunuch hastened to join Sultan Mehmet III at the Imperial Mosque directly ahead with its two minarets.

THE SULTAN PLOPPED down on the sofa to eat his fifth meal of the day. Evening prayers at the Imperial Mosque had ended, and a steward spread out a cloth made of hides from Bulgaria in front of him. He motioned to the chief steward, who accepted the first dish from one of his subordinates at the door. He first brought out the *mezes*, then the other dishes, one by one. Freshly prepared in the Sultan's kitchen, stewards ran between that kitchen on the other side of the Second Courtyard and this room, his normal eating place.

Everything was set in perfect order. His attendants surrounded him, but his favorites and his concubines never joined him. His women were not allowed to partake in his meals, since he had not paid monies to them as part of the *kabin*, the marriage contract requiring Muslim men pay monies to their brides or their families. Though Sultans occasionally married their favorites, his mother, Safiye, never ate with his father, Sultan Murad III. Sultan Mehmet III, likewise, did not eat with any of his *hasekis*, including the mother of his eldest son, Prince Mahmud.

As soon as the Sultan finished his appetizers, he motioned for the Chief Steward to take the dish away.

"Are you pleased, your majesty?" the Chief Steward asked.

The other stewards did not look directly at the Sultan, but kept their heads down and their arms folded. His sword bearer and the bearer of his wash basin stood to the side. The Chief White Eunuch, always nearby, kept the Sultan company.

"Much so." The Sultan finished one plate and gestured to the Chief Steward to pick it up and take it away. The sultan feasted on mutton, one of his favorite meats. Like before, when he finished the dish, the Chief Steward took the half-empty platter away, handing it to a waiting steward at the door. He would run it back to the kitchen, where the cooks and confectioners assigned to the Sultan worked.

Those novice youths, who wore rounded caps shaped like crystallized sugar loaves from Cyprus, toiled in the kitchens, or in the stables, or in the gardens. Other *acemi oglans* rowed the sultan's caiques when he went out on the water or cut wood used in the kitchen or the stoves that warmed each room. The stronger and more skilled *acemi oglans*—the tribute boys of the *devshirme* taken from Christian Bulgaria, Greece, or Hungary—would become *janissaries*, the most loyal of the Sultan's soldiers.

The Sultan continued to feast. He enjoyed eating the best culinary creations—the most delectable in the world.

Sun'Ullah *Effendi's* Deputy's Home, *Rajab AH* 1011 (Dec. *AD* 1602)

LINGERING ECHOES OF the day's final call to prayer had long ended. A waxing moon rose above the main streets of the crowded city of *Stamboul* and a religious leader, a deputy of Sun'ullah *Effendi,* welcomed his turbaned guests through a side door of his two-story home. His mentor, Sun'Ullah *Effendi,*wpreviously held the title of *Sheikh-ul-Islam*, the highest religious authority in the Ottoman Empire. Before he lost his position, he had spoken against the influence of the Sultan's Mother and other women of the Imperial Harem on the government. This night, the former Grand Mufti deemed it inappropriate to attend the splendid feast.

The *sipahi* leaders had dismounted, and as the deputy's servants led their horses around the corner, the *sipahis* met Guzelce Mahmud *Pasha* and entered the house.

"I know it is crowded, but make yourself comfortable," the Deputy said. Select members of the *ulema*, the religious council, flanked both sides. As soon as the *sipahi* leaders sat down, cross-legged on the thick Persian carpets, he motioned for his servants to serve coffee.

Guzelce Mahmud *Pasha* addressed the *sipahis,* "Did Poiraz Osman *Bey* agree to join us?" Earlier in the day, the other *sipahi* leaders had followed and chased Osman *Bey* out of the coffee house, but Guzelce *Pasha* had stayed behind.

"Osman *Bey* remains unconvinced, but I expect him shortly," Katib Jemazi, the *sipahi* leader, said.

"Is it because of loyalty to the Grand Vizier, or perhaps the Jewish *kira*?" Guzelce asked.

"I told him things have changed over the past two years, since the controversy of the *kira*, Esperanza Malchi—"

"Sun'Ullah *Effendi* could not issue the *fatwa* against the Jewish merchant woman," the Deputy interrupted. "Whether Jew or Christian, he must protect the lives of the *dhimmi* living in our midst. And especially if the non-Muslims are people of the Book."

Khalil *Pasha*, then Governor of *Stamboul*, had delivered the *kira* to the *sipahis*, several of whom were in the room. Khalil would never attend this type of meeting because he was married to Fatima, the younger sister Sultan Mehmet III and Aisha. After the Sultan's Mother heard how dogs chewed up the *kira's* body in the middle of the *Atmeidan,* and her limbs had been nailed to the doors of her alleged accomplices, the Sultan removed his brother-in-law from his office.

"We should have killed the Chief White Eunuch while we had the opportunity," a *sipahi* leader said. "Gazanfer *Agha* confiscated the taxes assigned to us."

"All that is past," the Deputy of Sun'Ullah *Effendi* said, "yet now the whole empire is in chaos."

"Things have worsened. Refugees escaping the rebellion in Anatolia overflow *Stamboul.* The onset of winter may make things worse."

"The rebel *Deli* Hasan *Pasha* consolidates his power," one *sipahi* leader said.

"It has been arranged," the Deputy said. "The Council has appointed Guzelce Mahmud *Pasha* to lead Ottoman forces in Anatolia and subdue *Deli* Hasan and the *Celali* rebels."

"We did not divulge to Osman *Bey* our plan to rid the Empire of Gazanfer *Agha and* Osman *Kizlar Agha,*" Katib Jezami said.

"The Chief White and Black Eunuchs run the Ottoman Empire for the Sultan's Mother and must be held to account," the Deputy of Sun'Ullah *Effendi* said.

"It was Gazanfer *Agha* himself who insisted that the eunuch Khosru *Agha* lead the Ottoman army in Anatolia," the *sipahi* leader Hasan Khalifeh said. "Six or seven times, he chose men to suppress *Deli* Hasan and the rebels. The latest attempt by the eunuch Khosru *Pasha* failed, too. That mistake must not be repeated."

"We did replace Khosru *Agha* with one of our own." The deputy looked at Guzelce Mahmud *Pasha,* the new commander.

"I am still organizing the paid horsemen of the Palace and the *janissaries,*" Guzelce Mahmud *Pasha* said. "With your help, I will recover what is lost, but the *Agha* of the *Janissaries* resists my efforts."

"Ali *Agha* has just come back from the frontier," Katib Jezami said, "and is too loyal to the Grand Vizier."

"Perhaps another *Agha* of the *Janissaries* should be appointed."

"A military judge and more viziers have joined us." The Deputy looked at Abdul-Miamin Mustafa *Effendi.* This well-respected *Cazi* of Rumelia, one of two military judges who sat in the Divan, gestured his agreement.

"But it may take more money," Guzelce Mahmud *Pasha* added.

"Sun'Ullah *Effendi* has agreed to send his nephew to Ankara." The Deputy gestured to Chelebi Kazi, the young man sitting to his left.

"I will leave in the morning." The nephew of the former Grand Mufti sipped his drink and eyed the door.

Guzelce Mahmud *Pasha* rose to his feet. "Poiraz Osman *Bey!*" He extended his arm, welcoming the *sipahi* from Belgrade. "You have arrived in time for the feast."

The smell of freshly cooked dishes filled the room.

"Yes, yes. Servants!" the Deputy said. "Feed our newest guest, Osman *Bey,* first."

Chapter 22 — *Sanjak* of Pécs

Karah Omar Agha of Petchevi [Pécs] relates the following story: "When we were in pursuit of the infidels, flying before us, we sometimes came up to 10 or 15 of them sitting and warming themselves before fires, which they had made; but, when they saw us approaching, they started up upon the legs, took off their hats, and made obeisance to us. The fact is we were weary of cutting and slashing the poor wretches, and therefore did not think it manly to kill men, who were vanquished and suffering like those just now mentioned. The like of these creatures we passed, and went on slaughtering and hewing down all such as still had the hardihood of arms."

Karah Omar Agha was rewarded for his services in this campaign [Kanizsa, AD 1601] with the Sanjak of Petchevi [Pécs or Bes-Kelise, meaning Five Churches] . . . The Khan [Ghazi Giray II] departed for Petchevi [Pécs], and his men were distributed in the above-mentioned towns and villages.

<u>Annals of the Turkish Empire, Vol. I</u> by Mustafa Naima
Translated from the Turkish by Charles Fraser

Suleiman Bridge, Oslijek, Drava River, Hungary, *AH* 1011 (AD 1602)

WOOD PLANKS RESOUNDED. Tartar hooves pounded on Suleiman Bridge, spanning the Drava River in Ottoman Hungary. The two sons of Khan *Ghazi* Giray II caught up with their father and the Crimean-Tartar army on the elevated pathway, the gateway to Buda and the European frontier. In the misty air of the Hungarian plain, Tartar warriors, tens of thousands strong, trotted their short horses over the weathered edifice. They neared their winter quarters in the *Vilayet* of Buda, southwestern Hungary.

This wooden wonder not only spanned the rising tributary, but also angled over colorful marshes—the faded red, orange, and brown of late autumn. Winter had not yet set in, and with the heavy mist, no enemy could easily burn this important structure, twenty feet wide and five miles long. Roughly seventy-five years earlier, about five years after his victory at Belgrade, Suleiman *the Magnificent* commissioned more than twenty-five thousand men to build this bridge, about twenty miles upriver from where the Drava flowed into the Danube. Guard towers, interspersed every four hundred paces, protected the weathered bridge from bandits the Turks called *Hajduks*, free-spirited Hungarian raiders. *Janissary* guards above scanned the swamps, but their eyes mainly focused on the Khan and his Tartar army, streaming back as far as the eye could see.

His eldest son, *Kalga* Toktamish, told the Khan, "When we returned to Belgrade, the Grand Vizier mentioned he was worried Pécs may not be able to supply all our needs. He forwarded a letter to the *Sanjak* of Pozega. Here's a letter for you, too."

Before leaving Belgrade, Grand Vizier *Hasan the Fruiterer* had hosted a splendid feast. He had previously written the *Sanjak* of Pécs and other Ottoman governors. He requested their assistance in welcoming the Ottoman Empire's most important ally.

"Toktamish, you and your brother can take your men to Pozega, but first we will ride to Pécs together." *Ghazi* Giray II kept his horse steady at the head of the Tartar army. Riding next to him, a strong warrior held his standard—a white mare's tail marked with streamers of green taffeta.

The morning mist began to burn off. The Crimean-Tartar Khan told his younger son, "Nearly four hundred years ago, our ancestor Batu Khan first set his sights on Hungary. After Cuman refugees from central Asia sought shelter in Hungary, the grandson of Genghis Khan pursued them. Batu Khan brought armies through Poland, through Transylvania, and up the Danube, not far from the route we followed. Batu Khan defeated the Hungarian King Bela IV at the Battle of Mohi."

"Where?" the younger son, *Nur-eddin* Sefer Giray, asked.

"On the other side of the Danube in the spring of 1421." The Khan pointed to the northeast. "Towards the headwaters of the Tisza River in Northeastern Hungary, not far from Eger, the castle that Sultan Mehmet III captured six years ago."

"Our ancestors did not stay?"

"No, the Great Khan died the next year, so Batu Khan and the leaders of the other hordes were summoned back to Tartaria in central Asia. By the time the Mongols and Tartars returned to Hungary sixty years later, many more towns had fortified castles."

A *janissary* captain met the Tartar leaders as they exited the bridge. "My company will march with you to Pécs."

"This is my eldest son, *Kalga* Toktamish," Khan *Ghazi* Giray II said.

"General *Bey-Ogli*." The captain used the Turkish title meaning 'the leader's son'.

"What is this place called?"

"Darda. We built this new fort here to protect Suleiman Bridge from the *Hajduks*."

Baranya *Palanka*, *Villayet* of Buda, Ottoman Hungary

THE TARTAR WARRIORS continued their trek and several hours later reached the front of a rebuilt *palanka*, an Ottoman fort reinforced with mortar. The square palisade had rounded corners, and a tower rose above its main gate.

"Three years ago this spring, infidels from Kanizsa attacked and completely destroyed this *palanka* of Baranyavar." The *Janissary* captain pointed out burnt timbers. "Hasan *the Addicted*, the former *Agha* of the *Janissaries* who was *Sanjak* of Pécs at that time, gathered his men, but the enemy fled over the Drava and burned the bridge."

"The infidels escaped?" the Khan asked.

"No, Hasan *the Addicted* commandeered boats. His men crossed the Drava and pursued the raiders, finally overcoming them. He killed many, while others drowned in the swamps. The remainder he captured and brought to Belgrade. Grand Vizier *Damat* Ibrahim *Pasha* questioned the prisoners about Kanizsa."

"He did not plan to attack Kanizsa?"

174

"No, for that year's campaign, the Grand Vizier had planned to attack Esztergom, a strong fortress upriver from Buda on the Danube."

"Because Buda was threatened?"

"Yes, but with the bridge destroyed, he made other plans: to attack and lay siege to Kanizsa, a very strong fort beyond Pécs and Szigetvar." The *janissary* pointed west, up the Drava River Valley.

Plains of Mohacs, *Villayet* of Buda, Ottoman Hungary

TRAVELING SEVERAL MORE miles, further in the direction of Buda, they reached the plains of Mohacs.

"When did the Ottomans ally with France?" the Khan's son asked.

"A little over seventy-five years ago. After King Francis I of France was defeated by Emperor Charles V of the Holy Roman Empire, he was imprisoned in Pavia in *AD* 1525. Once freed, the King of France sent an embassy to *Stamboul* and suggested an alliance with the Ottoman Empire against Charles V."

"Did the Ottoman Sultan accept?" the Khan's son asked.

"Yes, in his letter to King Francis I, Sultan Suleiman told him, 'Night and day, our horses are saddled, and our sabers are girt'," Khan *Ghazi* Giray II said. "So the next summer, Sultan Suleiman brought his army of one hundred thousand men and three hundred cannon over the newly built bridge to Mohacs."

"Here?"

"Yes, here on the plains south of Mohacs, Sultan Suleiman met King Louis II of Hungary and Bohemia in battle. The Sultan gained a great victory. When King Louis II departed the field at dusk, his horse fell into a swamp. Weighed down by his armor, the Hungarian King drowned."

As a cold rain fell, the Khan told one of his commanders, "You will winter here."

As that leader and his closest men entered the fortified town, several thousand Tartars began setting up their yurts outside its walls.

Khan *Ghazi* Giray II, his two sons, and the bulk of the Tartar army turned west, advancing across the plains, toward Pécs.

Pécs, *Vilayet* of Buda, Ottoman Hungary

NOISY WATERWHEELS TURNED at mills below the snow-dusted hills of Pécs, the city of five churches. Through light snow, the Crimean Khan noted vineyards planted on the lower mountainside, not far from a parish church, a convent, and a monastery. The swollen creek flowed along the eastern edge of the city and across the fruitful plains, emptying into the Drava, several miles away.

Recent rains slowed their trek from Belgrade, roughly 150 miles distant. It slowed further with the season's first snow. Flurries whitened the land. A thin layer covered both the fallow ground and the cattle grazing in the nearby meadow.

The Khan dismissed his ten-thousand-strong personal guard. Securing hides to simple wood frames, they set up their yurts, circular tents. Dozens of tents soon dotted the fallow fields, the *timars* and the larger *ziamets* of Pécs. Though the Tartars in their wars sought captives to sell, they were not allowed to pillage Ottoman lands.

While some Tartar warriors led their horses to drink from the stream, other warriors hacked down trees, building spits and open fires.

"It is your turn," one commander told a young warrior. Besides the horse they normally rode, each warrior had brought along two or three extra horses, not only for fresh rides, but also for food. Even though cattle were near, the Tartar warriors preferred horsemeat to cow beef.

"Wait!" the Khan intervened. "That mare is pregnant!"

"Kill no mares." The officer stopped his young warrior and turned to another. "Where's your horse?"

"Over there."

"Your turn!"

With the campfire roaring and the spit ready, that warrior unsheathed his sword. He snuck up from the side and severed the small stallion's head.

While some warriors finished setting up camp, others warmed their hands around campfires. They waited for the horse to be cooked; the spits were turned.

Satisfied that the camp was set, the Khan spied a white mare as he crossed the stream. Desiring to drink warm milk, he told his slave, "Bring that mare."

The Khan, his sons, and the officers crossed the moat and stopped at the eastern gate of the walled town. The *Sanjak* of Pécs greeted his Royal Highness.

"I noticed the vineyards outside of town." The Khan pointed to the hills.

"The Christians use them in their rituals, but no wine is allowed inside Pécs."

"Wine is evil."

"Earlier this year, an innkeeper in *Stamboul* was tortured for serving wine," the *Sanjak* of Pécs related.

"And his customers?"

"Most of the Turks caught drinking were condemned to the galleys."

"A deserving punishment."

The *Sanjak* of Pécs brought the Khan and his sons toward the center of town. "At one time, Pécs was the richest bishopric in Hungary. In Latin, it was called *Quinque Ecclesias* because of the five churches, but the Archbishop of Pécs did not want to see the town destroyed."

"So he surrendered?" the Khan asked.

"To Sultan Suleiman."

Crescents rose above the five churches inside the town. They had all been turned into mosques. They retained the name Pécs; *Bes-Kelise* means 'five churches' in Turkish.

They stopped in the bazaar at the center of town, where the Khan told one of his leaders. "Tomorrow, take your men and go to Szigetvar."

"That fortress town fell to the Ottomans about thirty-five years ago, " the *Sanjak* of Pécs informed, "the day after Sultan Suleiman *the Lawgiver* died of natural causes."

The Khan's eldest son, called *Bey-Ogli*, peered at the cloudy skies. "The snow?"

"It is light. You should be in Pozega by nightfall." The Khan turned to the western gate. "Some of our army will winter in Koppan."

"Further away?" the *Sanjak* of Pécs asked.

"Closer to Kanizsa and the enemy."

"We will join together in the spring." The Khan accompanied the *Sanjak* over another moat and entered the Bishop's Castle, in the northwest corner of the town. Anchored by four stone bastions, the castle housed the Cathedral of St. Peter and Paul and a bishop's palace, where the *Sanjak* of Pécs now lodged in place of the former Archbishop. The former University of Pécs, the first in Hungary, had been turned into a *medrese*, where mullahs taught both the *Qur'an* and the *hadiths*, the prophetic traditions.

They sat down on rugs in a room warmed by a roaring fire. One of his men served the Khan warm milk from the mare.

"Following our victory at Kanizsa, the Grand Vizier confirmed me as *Sanjak* of Pécs for my efforts."

"What happened?" the Khan asked.

"Two years ago, Grand Vizier *Damat* Ibrahim *Pasha* besieged Kanizsa. While the enemy waited for relief, a prisoner lit a match and set fire to their gunpowder, and also destroyed a tower. Without relief and powder, they surrendered to the Grand Vizier."

"His last victory before he died?"

"Yes, *Damat* Ibrahim *Pasha*, who was married to Aisha, Sister of the Sultan, will be remembered as the Conqueror of Kanizsa. Before he died the summer before last, he appointed *Tiryaki* Hasan *Pasha* as *Sanjak* of Kanizsa."

The Khan knew *Tiryaki* Hasan meant Hasan *the Addicted*, a nickname given to the former *Agha* of the *Janissaries* because he smoked so much. "The enemy returned?"

"In force," the *Sanjak* of Pécs said. "After the enemy broke our siege of the castle of Ober-Limbaugh, Archduke Ferdinand gathered a large army at Varazdin. After the Archduke began his siege of Kanizsa, his brother Mathias joined him. A second army had conquered the ancient capital of Hungary, Szekesfehervar."

"A long siege?"

"Yes, by tens of thousands of soldiers of the Holy Roman Empire, but before the siege started, Hasan *the Addicted* deceived the enemy into believing he had no cannon. They moved their camp close to the walls, and when supply wagons arrived, the enemy, believing the Turks would use them to vacate, let them into town."

"So, Hasan *the Addicted* tricked the enemy?"

"Yes, but then the siege intensified. It lasted more than two months and then, a little more than a year ago, the noonday skies darkened."

"A storm?" Khan *Ghazi* Giray II asked.

"Wind and rain. By midnight, the rain had turned to snow, and by morning, a blizzard. For three days and three nights, it continued. The snow reached to a man's waist."

"And you?"

"As soon as the storm cleared, the cold quickly froze the waters surrounding Kanizsa. I took three hundred chosen men and attacked their trenches. The enemy fled, and we captured their cannon. Archduke Ferdinand, entrenched on the road to Szigetvar, attempted to rally his men.

We pursued the enemy and cut off their heads. For each head they brought back, our brave soldiers were rewarded with gold."

"So you routed the enemy?"

"We slew thousands, but it was so cold that sometimes we came up to 10 or 15 frozen infidels, warming themselves. The enemy soldiers stood up, took off their hats, and bowed to us. We did not kill them, but let them live and chased others, still fighting. By the time the rout was over, we laid more than 30,000 heads at the *Pasha's* feet."

"And the Archduke Ferdinand?"

"We fired a cannon at his tent, and the enemy general fled," the *Sanjak* said. "Ferdinand escaped with his life. Inside his tent, we found his throne, bedecked with gold and silver, inlaid with diamonds in each leg. He also had a dozen chairs on each side of his throne, each covered with velvet and garnished with pearls."

"And where was Hasan *the Fruiterer?*" Khan *Ghazi* Giray II wondered.

"Though we deceived the enemy into believing that his vast army was on its way, the Grand Vizier never reached us. Hasan *the Fruiterer* stopped at Szigetvar before the storm hit. When the storm lifted, some of his troops attacked his tent with rocks. Though order was restored, three days later, two divisions deserted him because of the cold. The first division crossed the bridge over the Drava, but when that second division reached it, many drowned."

"Drowned?"

"Thick ice collapsed the bridge."

"And *Tiryaki* Hasan *Pasha?*" Khan *Ghazi* Giray II asked.

"When the Grand Vizier informed the Sultan, he sent a letter congratulating Hasan *the Addicted* and promoting the former *Agha* of the *Janissaries* to be his Fourth Vizier. He sits at the Divan in *Stamboul.* The *Padishah* Mehmet III also confirmed my appointment as *Sanjak* of Pécs."

"What of the booty and the spoils?"

"Though the *janissaries* who first captured the Archduke's tent were given those first spoils, it took two months for us to collect the supplies abandoned by the enemy."

"I saw cannon at Belgrade."

"We brought forty-two cannons to Kanizsa, but did not need them all, so we sent the rest to Belgrade and to the Grand Vizier." The *sanjak* stood up. "Are the losses you suffered outside Târgoviște in Wallachia troubling you?"

"No," Khan *Ghazi* Giray II hesitated. "But my three brothers cause me worry. Salamet, Mohammed, and Shahin *Giray* joined the *Celali* rebellion in Anatolia."

"So far away."

"Yes, but if the rebel Hasan *the Fool* captures *Stamboul,* he will declare himself the new Caliph and appoint Salamet as the new Khan of the Crimean-Tartars."

Chapter 23 — Necessity and Despair

For the Scrivano [Abdul-Helim, called Kara-Yazici or the Black Scribe] was no sooner dead, but that a younger brother [Deli Hasan or Hasan the Fool] of his, no less warlike and courageous than himself (to the great contentment of the rebellious) stepped up in his place, fiercely prosecuting the wars his brother had before him taken in hand . . .

Their army was exceeding great, every man joining himself unto the first forces, which were in good estate, being not as yet by any greater power repressed, and rich with the spoils they had taken. These men had besieged Ankara, a great and strong town in Asia, and seemed resolutely set down for the carrying thereof. Whereof the citizens being afraid, and out of hope of relief, came to parley, offering unto them a sum of money to redeem themselves and their city . . .

Shortly after, the new captains of Sultan Mehmet [III] arrived there also . . . who would needs make it treason, and put to death the citizens, for having given such money as is aforesaid unto the rebels, though it were done for the preservation of their lives . . .

These poor citizens with this so cruel a resolution dismayed, and out of all hope of finding favor at such merciless mens hand, resolved now to hazard all, and so upon the sudden taking up arms, stood upon their own defense. Hereupon arose a great a cruel fight betwixt these soldiers and the citizens, both the subjects of one prince, and the one side armed with pride and covetousness, and the other with necessity and despair . . .
<u>General History of the Turks, Second Edition</u> *by Richard Knolles*

Citadel, Ankara, Asia Minor, *AH* 1011 (December *AD* 1602)

ATOP THE STONE walls of the citadel of Ankara, the rebel leader Hasan *the Fool* peered down at his army. The citadel commanded the heights and also the valley, famous for the fine fabric spun from its Angora goats. Outside the walls of the lower town, the rebel army set up its encampment.

"We paid you two hundred thousand Sultanates," the Governor of Ankara said.

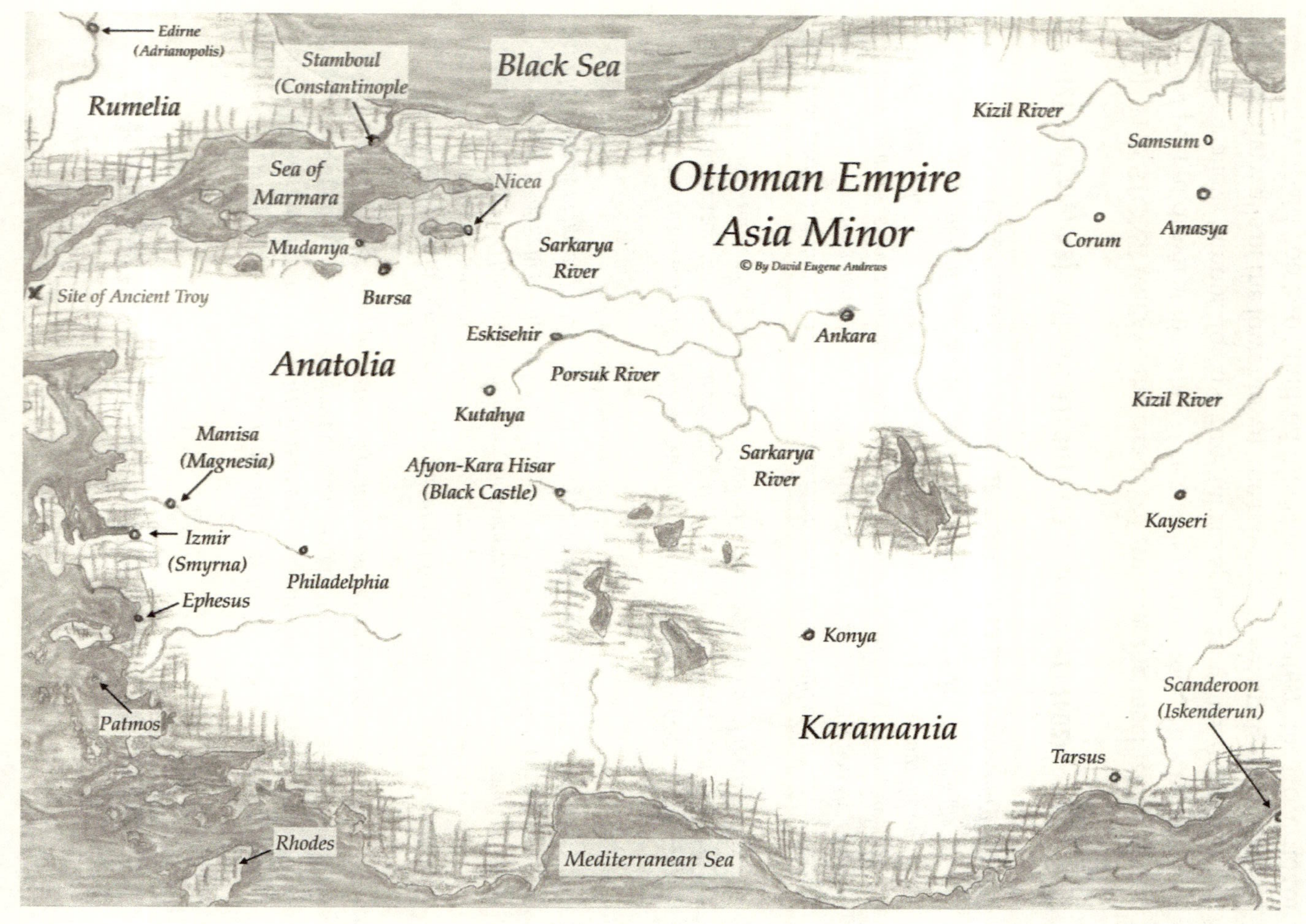

Edirne
(Adrianopolis)
Black Sea
Stamboul
(Constantinople)
Rumelia
Kizil River
Samsum
Sea of
Marmara
Nicea
Ottoman Empire
Asia Minor
© By David Eugene Andrews
Corum
Amasya
Mudanya
Sarkarya
River
Site of Ancient Troy
Bursa
Eskisehir
Ankara
Anatolia
Porsuk River
Kizil River
Kutahya
Manisa
(Magnesia)
Afyon-Kara Hisar
(Black Castle)
Sarkarya
River
Izmir
(Smyrna)
Kayseri
Ephesus
Philadelphia
Konya
Scanderoon
(Iskenderun)
Patmos
Karamania
Tarsus
Rhodes
Mediterranean Sea
182

Though far from the sea, the name Ankara meant 'anchor' in both Latin and Greek, reflecting its importance as the trade center for Anatolia, or Asia Minor. Others claimed the name Ankara came from '*angūr*,' the Persian word for 'grapes.' No one questioned the fruitfulness of this important valley in central Asia Minor.

"And we received another one hundred thousand from the surrounding countryside." Hasan *the Fool* recalled the negotiations with the rebel leader and the payment, sacks of coins. With the help of the three brothers of the Tartar Khan, he would have sacked Ankara during the early summer, but the citizens of Ankara came out and parleyed before his final assault. "We caused you no more mischief, and so we went away."

"But after you departed, we had to fight anyway," the Governor of Ankara said.

"Not against us." Hasan *the Fool* glanced at the three Tartar brothers standing next to him. Other rebel leaders stood nearby.

"No, but when the new eunuch general Khosru *Pasha* arrived, he told us he would punish us."

"For what?" Hasan *the Fool* asked.

"For paying you the three hundred thousand ransom," the Governor of Ankara said. "The Sultan's appointees claimed we were disloyal—they called it treason."

"Those soldiers would have sacked Ankara and put us to death," a second Ankara leader said, "but I think the eunuch general and his army truly coveted all we still owned."

"We had to defend ourselves and save our lives. We took up arms, slew many, and overcame the Sultan's army." The governor pointed to pockmarks in the citadel walls. "The remaining soldiers fled out of the city."

"Will you join the rebellion?" Hasan *the Fool* gestured to his army, tens of thousands strong.

Since the time of the Flood, the Turks had wandered in central Asia. Before this tribe arrived in Asia Minor, the Gauls, Persians, Greeks, and Romans ruled Ankara in succesion. Many vines once covered the hillsides, so some claimed the name Ankara derived from '*engur*,' the Persian word for 'grape.' Moving fast like a leopard, Alexander the Great conquered the Persians, and at his death, his kingdom was divided—instead of his family—among his four generals.

One of Alexander's generals ruled Ankara and Asia Minor, but he was conquered by Seleucus, the general from Syria, who ruled this northern kingdom. As prophesied in the book of Daniel, this kingdom was attacked by the southern kingdom, by Ptolemy from Egypt. As accurately foretold in Chapter 11, a marriage of a northern king to a daughter of the southern king led to peace, but the betrayal of Berenice renewed hostilities. Her brother attacked from the South. Later, the Romans robbed and supplanted the Greeks and Macedonians. After the fall of the Roman Empire, Ankara became part of the Byzantine Empire, centered in Constantinople. Centuries later, shortly after the founding of the Ottoman Empire, the Prince of Kutahya arrived from his mountaintop castle in western Anatolia. He conquered Ankara for Sultan Orhan.

In the centuries since the Turks conquered Anatolia, the Ottomans had lost Ankara only once. A famous Tartar warrior named Timur *the Lame*, sometimes called 'Tamerlane,' conquered Ankara when Sultan Bayezid foolishly went out hunting and was captured. His army found itself cut off from a small river, their sole source of water. So, they were forced to retire. Several years later, Tamerlane died, and the Ottomans reclaimed the city and the citadel.

"Not for now." The Governor of Ankara looked at his other leaders, still armed with swords and daggers. "But we will not forbid those who might wish to join you."

"Have we heard anything more about the eunuch Khosru *Pasha*?" Salamet Giray, the estranged brother of the Crimean-Tartar Khan, *Ghazi Giray II*, asked. Upon the recommendation of the Chief White Eunuch, Gazanfer *Agha*, Sultan Mehmet III appointed Khosru *Pasha* to be his commander in Diyarbakir Province earlier in the year.

Hasan *the Fool* glanced to the east. "The troops of Aleppo, Maras, and Sivas are all with him. If the new Governor-General and his *Janissaries* march this way, we must be prepared for a big battle."

"Our warriors are ready." Salamet Giray, along with his two brothers, gazed down at yurts housing thousands of their warriors. A few warriors exercised their short Tartarian horses.

"Especially if Hafiz Ahmed *Pasha*, the Governor General of Kutahya, also attacks from the west."

As the sun began to set over the valley, the successor to his brother *Scrivano*'s army noticed guards bringing a man up the narrow streets from the lower town.

"Do you know who that is?" Salamet Giray asked.

"I believe it is the nephew of the former Grand Mufti," Hasan *the Fool* said. "Two years ago, before the rebellion began anew, that nephew obtained a pardon for my brother from the Sultan and secured the *Sanjak* of Corum for him."

By the time the governor, the three Tartar brothers, and the rebel leader descended the stairs, the mufti's nephew had entered the main gate. In the center of the paved courtyard, the nephew placed his hand on his chest and bowed. He lifted the hem of the leader's overcoat, leaned down, and kissed it. "Greetings, *Deli* Hasan."

"Chelebi Kazi, I see you have returned," Hasan *the Fool* said.

"I helped your brother Abdul-Helim, and I can be of service to you, too."

"Join us after evening prayers," the Governor of Ankara said.

Reception Room, Upper Castle, Ankara

STOKED FIRES WARMED the large reception room of the upper castle. The whole leadership of the rebellion, including Salamet Giray and his two Tartar brothers, sat down on the mats and rugs covering the floor. Servants carried in low tables, soon crowded with platters filled with simple dishes, mainly mutton and rice. Long napkins were placed across their laps, and everyone feasted.

Onto a raised section of the room, three musicians entered. Playing strings, a flute, and a drum, they strummed a melancholy song.

"How did the rebellion begin?" Salamet Giray leaned toward Hasan *the Fool*.

"Years ago, my brother, Abdul-Helim, who had been appointed the *Beylerbey* or Governor-General of Ethiopia, was dismissed. We were originally from Anatolia, but he ended up in Syria, working for the *sanjak* of Aleppo, not in his Divan or council, but as a scribe. He kept the account of all of Aleppo's corn, whether bought or sold."

"So Aleppo is where he became known as *Kara-Yazici?*"

"Yes. In Aleppo, my brother, who had black hair like me, became known as *Scrivano*, the Black Scribe. However, he became restless and did not stay long, retiring to the country," Hasan *the Fool* said. "My brother told me Allah promised him he would do great things and become King."

"We became *segbans*, private soldiers," an old *segban*, who had fought with *Scrivano*, spoke up. "*Scrivano* became our leader and was very liberal. When we defended Aliduli, the territory between Syria and Mesopotamia, he gave all he had gained to his soldiers."

"When the *Porte* sent a new *sanjak* to replace the local governor at Jaffa in the Holy Lands, my brother offered his services a second time, bringing 300 arquebusiers with him." Hasan *the Fool* pointed to an arquebus, a firearm much shorter than a musket, but longer than a pistol.

The old *segban* lifted the arquebus. "Whether on horseback or on foot, when we used our arquebuses and fired in unison at short range, we devastated our enemies, wiping out their line of attackers, stopping and killing them as they trekked."

"With these men and their firearms," Hasan *the Fool* said, "my brother successfully defended the governor, and his fame spread."

"The *Sanjak* of Aleppo, however, noticed his former scribe threatening his territory, so he gathered an army to destroy him," the old *segban* warrior said. "The *sanjak* attacked *Scrivano*, but we defeated him and departed in glory."

"How did Hussein *Pasha* join *Scrivano*?" Salamet Giray asked.

"Hussein *Pasha*, the Ottoman governor of Karaman, the largest province of southern Anatolia, found himself in debt. He stole coins from the Ottoman *defterdars* or treasurers and even plundered his own towns. The Vizier Mehmed *Pasha*, who was the son of the former Grand Vizier Koca Sinan *Pasha*, sent the eunuch governor of Damascus to subdue him. Seeing he could not fight such a large force, Hussein *Pasha* abandoned his territory, traveled east, and found *Scrivano* at Urfa on the Euphrates River. My brother welcomed his newest ally at the Castle of Urfa, where they united their growing army."

"There is a fountain at Urfa, isn't there?" Salamet Giray asked.

"Yes, full of fish. The Jews, Armenians, and Turks all agree that the fountain was Jacob's well. Jacob found beautiful Rachel there, but to marry her, his Uncle Laban forced him to serve him for seven years. At the end of his time of servitude, his uncle tricked Jacob into marrying his eldest daughter, the veiled Leah. Jacob had to serve his uncle another seven years far him finally to take Rachel as his bride."

"So, like the union between Jacob and his uncle Laban, the union between *Scrivano* and Hussein *Pasha* did not last?" Salamet Giray asked.

"*Scrivano* established his government at Urfa, but the *Sublime Porte* in *Stamboul* sent the Vizier Mehmed *Pasha* himself to fight us."

"Go on."

"The Vizier landed at Scanderoon, the port for Aleppo in Iconium, and soon gathered sixty thousand men from as far away as Damascus. The new Ottoman general brought twenty pieces of artillery from Aleppo and besieged the Castle of Urfa."

"But for two months, he did not succeed," the old *segban* fighter said. "Many of the Vizier's men did not want to fight against *Scrivano*, their friend, but against Hussein *Pasha*, who had burned and looted Karaman, so they began to leave. At the beginning of that winter, the Vizier General proposed to *Scrivano* a way to end the siege, and he agreed. Hussein *Pasha* was delivered to the Vizier and sent in chains to *Stamboul*."

"Where he was put to death," Chelebi Kazi, the nephew of the former Grand Mufti, informed. "His hands and feet were cut off in the Divan of the New Palace. After being put on a horse and displayed up and down the streets of *Stamboul*, Hussein *Pasha* was impaled at the Woodgate in *Stamboul* for all to see."

"What did the Vizier Mehmed *Pasha* do?" Salamet Giray asked.

"He dispersed his army back to Aleppo and Damascus and retired for the winter at Caraemit, not far from Diyarbakir, the castle on the Tigris River."

"Did *Scrivano* stay in Urfa?"

"No," Hasan *the Fool* said. "With their castle in ruins, the citizens of Urfa paid my brother fifty thousand sequins to leave. *Scrivano* also accepted the vizier's offer to become *Sanjak* of Amasya in Cappadocia."

"On our way from Crimea in Tartaria and Circassia, we passed through Amasya," Salamet Giray said. "Didn't the original *Celali* rebellion begin in Amasya?"

"Yes, more than eighty years ago, *Sheikh* Celal first rebelled against the Ottoman dynasty at Amasya. Even though the *Sublime Porte* in *Stamboul* attempted to label *Scrivano* a *Celali* rebel, my brother did not claim to be one. On the contrary, *Scrivano* charged the Ottoman general sent by the Sultan as the real oppressor. That general oppressed the people, and so he was the 'real' *Celali* rebel."

The Mufti's nephew interjected, "Knowing this, my uncle Sun'Ullah *Effendi* persuaded the Sultan to make *Scrivano* a *sanjak*."

"But *Scrivano* did not stay in Amasya?" Salamet Giray asked.

"No," the *segban* leader said. "*Scrivano* did not fear any power, but he did not feel safe at Amasya and retired to the country, finally placing himself between two mountains above Sivas."

"Is that where the Vizier Mehmed found him?"

"Yes, when the Vizier returned, *Scrivano* ambushed and wounded him in the left arm. The Vizier soon recovered and returned, but *Scrivano* struck him again, killing his horse and wounding the vizier in his thigh. More than a thousand *janissaries* were killed, and we could have taken the Vizier prisoner, but *Scrivano* decided to let him go."

"That's when the Vizier Mehmed, the son of Koca Sinan *Pasha*, returned to Caraemit, the city built with jet-black stone. While the Vizier took time to let his two wounds heal, the *Sanjak* of Sivas traveled to *Stamboul*," Chelebi Kazi said. "He convinced the *Porte* that the tyranny of Vizier Mehmed caused the rebellion to grow, so the *Kaimakam* recalled the Vizier back to *Stamboul*. I used monies that *Scrivano* gave me and convinced them to appoint *Scrivano* as *Sanjak* of Corum."

"Another town near Amasya? So *Scrivano* became a *sanjak* a second time?"

"Yes, but the peace did not last," Hasan *the Fool* said. "About two years ago, *Scrivano* again retired to a mountain called *Yildiz*, above Sivas and Tokat."   "We call it *Yildiz* or Star Mountain, because it is so high," the old *segban* leader said. "Very fruitful with plentiful water above, it has only a few narrow ravines leading to the top. If anyone decided to attack us, we could sally down the paths and slaughter them."

"The *Porte* then sent a new general, the eldest son of the famous Grand Vizier Sokollu Mehmed *Pasha*, to fight him and me. After he arrived at Caraemit, the new general sent his Lieutenant *Haji* Ibrahim and his army to find my brother. In the middle of autumn, *Haji* Ibrahim took forces from nearby Kayseri. His vanguard found my brother's baggage train on its way up into the mountains above Sivas."

"The guards fled, so *Scrivano* lost everything," the *segban* leader said. "It had taken us months to collect what was lost in that one day. Not only did we lose twenty-two pieces of cannon, but many of our men scattered, returning to their families in Aleppo and Tripoli in Lebanon. Only *Scrivano* and a few thousand of us remained. We retired further north, to Samsun. The people of the port of ancient Pontus on the Southern Coast of the Black Sea welcomed us."

"But an illness overcame my brother and ended his life."

"After *Scrivano* died, we did not want the Ottomans to find his body and burn it," the *segban* leader said. "We dismembered his body, cutting off his legs and arms— everything, each part of his body was buried separately."

After the somber song ended, a graceful figure appeared, dancing to a more fluid beat.

"I see your court has grown." The mufti's nephew pointed to sets of beautiful eyes peering from behind a divider.

"Some of the women belonged to the court of my brother, but many more belonged to a *sultana*, the wife of the new *Vizier* General sent to scourge us."

"After they heard of your attack on the *sultana*, those in *Stamboul* called you *Deli*."

"Perhaps they think I am reckless or crazy, but they do not understand," Hasan *the Fool* answered. "It does not matter what people call me, that vizier had great greed."

"But how did you capture the women?" the youngest Tartar brother asked.

"We were on our way to join my brother in the mountains. Then we heard of a caravan heading to the Governor-General, who had been sent to chasten us."

"You mean the son of the famous Sokollu Mehmed *Pasha*?"

"Yes, the son of the former Grand Vizier Sokollu *Pasha*, whose wife was the sister of Sultan Murad III. He served under three different sultans. A little more than two decades ago, Grand Vizier Sokollu died on the European frontier. His son became the Ottoman *Beylerbey* of Damascus. During the war against the Persians, he achieved a victory."

"And since then?"

"He returned to *Stamboul*, but about two years ago, the *Porte* in *Stamboul* appointed his son as *Beylerbey*, not of Damascus but of Diyarbakir. About 60 years of age, Sokollu's son was sent to subdue *Scrivano* and me. When he arrived in Diyarkakir, that province centered between the Euphrates and the Tigris Rivers, the new *Beylerbey* sent for his wife."

"I knew of her—a *sultana*." The mufti's nephew referred to a member of the Royal family.

"The *sultana*, along with her harem and her escorts, almost made it to her husband at Caraemit, before Diyarbakir. "

"You found them?"

"At their encampment, only two days from Caraemit," Hasan *the Fool* said. "We easily overpowered her guards and collected five million in gold and burned the rest, including her tent, worth eighty thousand."

"But her court?"

"We did not take her whole harem," Hasan *the Fool* laughed. "We sent three or four old women to the Vizier at Caraemit."

"The son of Sokollu must have been angry."

"Yes. We retired with the Sultana's harem and carried all of the gold to our haven in the mountains, but soon learned the vizier had followed us. He stopped at Tokat."

"Did you attack?" Chelebi Kazi asked.

"We conquered the suburbs of Tokat and plundered its famous gardens, filled not with natural flowers, but real jewels, including emeralds."

"And those sparkling jewels now adorn our saddles and reins," the *segban* leader added.

"What of the son of Sokollu?' the nephew of the mufti asked.

"He had been most greedy. He even kept most of the money for himself, instead of paying his soldiers."

"The corruption of the Sultan was rampant. We paid for more soldiers to join us," Hasan *the Fool* said.

"My brothers and I also joined you, " Salamet Giray added.

"Though we could not conquer the castle of Tokat, an informant told us that the son of Sokollu strolled along the top of its walls every morning," Hasan *the Fool* said. "When the Vizier stopped at his normal resting place, an Arquebusier used his firearm and shot and killed the son of Sokollu."

The song ended, and when the tall Circassian dancer drew closer, Hasan *the Fool* dismissed her with a wave of the hand. "I do not feel like any more entertainment."

"What is wrong?" the Governor of Ankara asked.

"The Eunuch Khosru *Pasha* is not that far away."

Marketplace, Lower Town, Ankara

THE REBEL GENERAL Hasan wore the winged feathers that caused many to call him *Deli* or 'fool.' He rode towards the walled marketplace built beyond the fortified walls of the lower town the next morning. Unlike many other towns that had opposed their progress, the Main Marketplace of Ankara remained untouched. The rebels had neither burned nor destroyed their houses, whether inside the lower and middle town, or outside the fortified walls and the surrounding countryside. The two-story khans that serviced the caravans plying Anatolia still stood.

A pair of riders, armed with arquebuses and lances, brought their horses around. "Will we go back and seek out the eunuch general?"

"Let the new Governor-General of Diyarbakir come to us. The longer they march, the more tired his soldiers will be."

"And if it rains?"

"Even better. We will stay here as long as necessary."

Leaving the men, Hasan *the Fool* and Chelebi Kazi entered the main gate of the enclosed Marketplace and dismounted in front of a booth. A worker picked up a lock of white mohair from a small mound. He stretched the strand, spun it into a yarn, and began to weave it into a *sof* or *camlet*.

At the next booth, the shelves that normally held the fabric, whether plain or dyed, were empty. Two merchants argued with each other.

"Where is my *sof*?" a prospective buyer charged.

"You are late."

"I could not come until now. It took me some time to find the money."

"But the best of the *sof* is gone, already loaded on the caravan to Bursa and *Stamboul*." The merchant pointed to the caravan leaving the khan outside the gate. Ankara merchants never shipped out the sheared long locks, but only cloth.

"You must wait until more is woven."

The prospective buyer rushed toward Hasan *the Fool*, bowed down, and lifted the hem of his garment. He kissed it and raised his eyes. "You must judge."

Hasan *the Fool* pointed to a table further away along one wall. "Let the *cazi* settle these small disputes."

"But *Caliph* Hasan?" The buyer used the term for "successor." Hasan's brother *Scrivano* had verified their lineage, tracing it all the way back to the tribe of the Prophet Mohammed.

"I do not have time for such things."

As the two merchants returned to their bickering, Chelebi Kazi asked, "What shall I tell my uncle?"

"If he becomes Grand Mufti again, we will await his ruling," Hasan *the Fool* said.

"It may take money."

"As we discussed last night, I will give you ten percent of what I collected —thirty thousand."

"Much can be done." The nephew waved to several of his men, who had accompanied him from *Stamboul*.

They led their horses to a tent outside the marketplace, where the *defterdar*, or treasurer, handed him and his men thirty large bags—each bulging with coin.

"Will you go directly to *Stamboul*?" Hasan *the Fool* asked.

"We will catch the caravan."

As soon as Chelebi Kazi and his escorts caught up with the caravan heading west, Hasan *the Fool* remounted his steed and rode to the Tartar encampment across the white bridge on the other side of the stream.

Salamet Giray exited his yurt, a rounded tent, and soon brought out his nursing wife and several sons.

"Chelebi Kazi has departed for *Stamboul*. When I claim my rightful place, I shall make you Khan of the Crimean Tartars."

After *Ghazi* Giray II had been restored to the Tartar throne, Salamet had been made his *Kalga*, the presumed successor to the Crimean Khanate. Salamet, however, had been dismissed, replaced by Toktamish, *Ghazi* Giray II's eldest son.

"The throne should be mine," Salamet Giray said.

"It will be." His two brothers, Shahin and Mohammed Giray, stepped forward.

Hasan *the Fool* turned back to Salamet. "Your boys are growing."

"The goats' milk of this place must agree with them." Salamet Giray pointed to a mixed herd of sheep and goats grazing in front of an Armenian Christian church. "But we could use more."

"Shepherds have already brought their flocks and herds down from high pastures."

Cattle and Sheep outside Ankara, Asia Minor, AD 1838

As the shepherd divided his herd into two, leading his sheep to his right, and leaving the goats behind to his left, Hasan *the Fool* rode towards him. "I need your goats. My friends want milk."

"We made our tax."

"Do you dare argue?"

"No, I have worked hard, and winter fast approaches."

"Their coats are thick, and the weavers need mohair." Unconcerned that it might butt or bite, the rebel leader dismounted and wrestled the white goat with its soft, long locks. He took out his knife.

"They should not be sheared until the spring. The goats will freeze."

"You are right." Hasan *the Fool* cut a lock of hair, remounted his steed, and brought it around. "Take them all!" He told his guards. "After they are milked and sheared, slay them. My men will like roasted goat meat."

As they herded the goats back to the Tartar encampment to be milked, a messenger approached, riding hard from the east. "The troops of Aleppo and Sivas have gone home."

"They abandoned their General Khosru *Pasha*?" Hasan *the Fool* asked.

"The Ottoman eunuch has retired to Diyarbakir."

Hasan *the Fool* turned to Salamet Giray. "Tomorrow we ride."

"East, back to Diyarbakir?"

"No, west, to Kutahya."

"We will be ready."

"At daybreak."

Chapter 24 — Weep over the Graves

Moreover, I did see the Great Turk [Sultan Mehmet III] when he entered this church [Hagia Sophia] and howsoever it lie close to the Gate of his Palace [Topkapi], yet he came riding upon a horse richly trapped, with many troops of his chief horsemen, standing with the courts of his Palace, and from the Court Gate to the Church door, between which troops on both sides, he passed as between walls of brass, with great pomp. And when a Chiaus [usher] (or pensioner), being on horseback, did see me close by the Emperor's side, he rushed upon me to strike with his mace, saying, "What doth this Christian dog so near the person of our Great Lord?"

But the Janissary, whom our [English] Ambassador had given me for a Guide and Protector, repelled him from doing me any wrong, and many Janissaries (according to their manner) coming to help him, the Chiaus was glad to let me alone, and they bade me bold to stand still, though I were the second or third person from the Emperor.

Fynes Morrison, <u>Itinerary</u> in AD 1597

When she [Aisha, Sister of the Sultan] . . . weep over the graves . . .

<u>Travels</u> by Captain John Smith

Mausoleum of Murad III, *Hagia Sophia*, *Rajab AH* 1011 (Dec. *AD* 1602)

BENEATH THE DOMED mausoleum of her father, Aisha and her sister Fatima stood next to their mother, Safiye, the *Valide Sultana*. After their father's death, it took four years to build the octagonal mausoleum on the grounds of the *Hagia Sophia*, the main imperial mosque of the city. Every Friday, her brother, like his father before him, travelled the short distance from the New Palace to the *Hagia Sophia* to attend the weekly services.

Beautiful red Iznik tiles with mosaic patterns adorned the rounded ceiling of the mausoleum. Underneath the dome, white calligraphy on a wide band of blue tiles encircled the whole room. Two sets of windows, one above the other, normally let in plenty of light, but on this dreary morning, the lamps extending from the ceiling were lit. Circular columns supported the dome, and below the band of blue Iznik tiles, a third set of windows illumined the alcoves on the main floor.

Her mother, whose given name, Safiye, meant "the pure," faced the direction of Mecca. "We pray for Murad's salvation and ours." She waited a minute longer before stepping back from the green crypt of her departed husband. "I loved your father so much. I was presented to him when I was only thirteen."

Aisha knew the story well. Born of and taken from Christian parents, her mother was from Rez, a small village nestled in the Mountains of Dukagjini in Albania. Sometime after her conversion to Islam, she became the Favorite of her father, remaining so for more than 20 years. Her grandmother *Nur Banu*, the daughter of a Venetian nobleman, became jealous, so she expanded the number of women in the harem to reduce her mother's influence. During his whole reign, Sultan Murad III rarely, if ever, left greater *Stamboul*.

After *Nur Banu's* death, her grandmother's body was laid to rest in Selim II's mausoleum next door. Since then, her mother had no true rival. Except for the time her brother led the Ottoman army to Hungary, her mother's influence continued to grow, unabated.

Baptistry and Mausoleums of Hagia Sophia

Quiet and subdued, Aisha, following her mother, circled the outside of the room, for the main floor was full. When Aisha's father acceded to the Ottoman throne, Sultan Murad III had five of his brothers—all potential rivals—strangled. Their bodies rested in the Mausoleum of Selim II, Aisha's grandfather, next door. Sultan Mehmet III maintained the Ottoman tradition. The floor not only held the large tomb of Aisha's father, but also many smaller coffins. All corpses faced the same direction—Mecca.

Like a cold winter rain, sadness swept over Aisha. She stopped and stared at the 19 green crypts and remembered the day when her brother acceded to the throne. Mehmet III had their 19 younger brothers—each delivered from a different concubine—brought into his presence, one by one. After each kissed his hand, he had each of them circumcised. Following the advice of the muftis and the *ulema* or religious council, Sultan Mehmet III handed handkerchiefs to the palace mutes. These mutes strangled each of their half-brothers, one after one.

Upon their deaths, their crypts were kept inside a tent, but when the mausoleum was finished, their bodies were laid to rest by their father's sarcophagus.

"It is time for us to leave," her mother said, so Aisha and Fatima followed the *Valide Sultana* out into the courtyard. In front of them stood the much larger domed *Hagia Sophia,* the former Byzantine church transformed into an imperial mosque.

"Aisha, will you be joining Fatima and me in the Imperial Harem?" her mother asked. They stood beneath one of the mosque's four minarets.

"I am feeling a little tired." Aisha glanced at her younger sister, the wife of Khalil *Pasha,* a former Governor of *Stamboul.* "I would prefer to return to my palace." The Palace of Ibrahim *Pasha* stood at the opposite end of the nearby Hippodrome.

"Very well, but you must come to the baths tomorrow."

"I will if I can, but Filiz will be visiting me in the morning."

"Your French friend?"

"She helps me."

"It should not take that long to find out where the family of your slave lives."

"Yes, Mother." Aisha did not want to continue the conversation.

A Black eunuch opened the doors of the fancy White Carriage that Queen Elizabeth had shipped to her mother several years earlier. The short ride to the New Palace across the crowded street would not take long.

"Aisha!" A woman held her infant close to her breast and begged.

The Sister of the Sultan walked up to the forlorn woman and gave her a coin. "For you and your child. Go, buy something to eat."

Salon, Palace of Ibrahim *Pasha, Rajab AH* 1011 (December *AD* 1602)

THE FOLLOWING MORNING, Aisha greeted her friend at the door of her bright Salon. "Filiz, thank you so much for coming."

"I know I am early." The French translator surveyed the room. "Your mother?"

"I saw her yesterday at my father's grave."

"Your mother visits quite often."

"She always insists on doing what is proper."

"I trust you do not mind that I brought a few of my attendants," Filiz said.

"No, no." Aisha motioned for the attendants to sit down on the cushions. "Make yourselves comfortable."

"Is that a new jacket?" Filiz asked.

"So observant of you to notice." Aisha extended her sleeve.

"Silk?" Her friend touched the fabric. "So smooth."

"Please be seated, Filiz. I shall be back very soon."

In the garden courtyard, Aisha found her Chief Overseer on the other side of the barren apple tree. Fallen leaves covered the ground. "Bring my slave to me."

"Right away, Lady Aisha." Her dependable Black eunuch bowed.

A thin column of white smoke rose from the chimney as Aisha took time to enter the kitchen. "The lamb?"

"Marinated all night long," the chef said.

"Good, I want *shish kebab* for my guests."

"Very well, we'll have it ready just after noon."

"*Excellente*," Aisha said. "In the meantime, tea and pastries will do."

Aisha returned to the garden and noted several Black eunuchs escorting her slave. They waited for Aisha to enter her Salon first, but she then turned back to the Overseer. "You may untie him."

"Are you certain?" The Overseer hesitated before undoing the leather bands. John tipped his head to Aisha. "*Buongiorno*." He said good morning in Italian.

"You remember, Filiz?" Aisha asked.

"*Bon jour*, Filiz."

Aisha told John in Italian, "Have a seat, *capitano*." She dismissed the overseer to wait outside. Servants soon arrived with warm pastries and hot tea. "You returned to France?"

"*Si, signorina.*"

Aisha did not tell him she was a widow, not a 'miss'. She leaned back to listen to the *Capitano* speak French.

The English recruit glanced at the French translator and began his story anew. "Sir Francis Vere gave us more horses in Holland, so in the winter, almost six years ago, a few Dutch soldiers, Captain Duxbury, and I sailed back to France."

Chapter 25 — Bands of Lusty Men

Since our march to this place and our sudden change from fire to no fire at all, our bands are weakened with the number fallen sick, so that mustering last week past upon some passports given, thereby to make a check to the Queen [Elizabeth], I found them decreased not above 57, and sick 300 and odd, all their apparel worn out, the bareness whereof in this wild, cold, and wasted country being a principal cause of their sickness.

Yet are there some eight or nine bands full of lusty men and very strong . . ..
Captain William Lylle to the Earl of Essex
St. Valery, France, Late February 1597

Market Square, St. Valery-sur-Somme, France, February *AD* 1597

AT THE DOCKS of St. Valery, a fishing town at the mouth of the Somme River, John Smith calmed a sprightly horse. Other recruits corralled the remaining fifty horses, enough to supply a whole cornet and all brought from Ostend. A handful of Dutch soldiers, having disembarked with the English company, accompanied Captain Joseph Duxbury to the middle of the fortified town.

"I need to talk to Sir Thomas Baskerville in private," Captain Duxbury told John. Weeks earlier, the English General had requested Duxbury to bring back horses from Ostend, a coastal town in Flanders.

"No need for that!" Sir Baskerville, the commander of the two thousand English soldiers in France, crossed Market Square. "You've been gone too long."

"Didn't you receive my message?" Captain Joseph Duxbury asked. "The Governor of Ostend insisted the horses go to Turnhout."

"You should have returned."

"We could not come back empty-handed." Captain Joseph Duxbury gestured to the horses. "Besides, the action at Turnhout and Tielenheide delayed us."

"We heard about His Excellency's victory. The rout on the Heath of Tielen has encouraged everyone, but our ranks here are diminished."

"It's much colder than when we left."

Another gust blew from the north. The winter sun provided little warmth. Ice glistened in the crevices of the town's stone wall. The round towers on either side of the gate cast long shadows.

"Many of the companies are weaker," Sir Thomas Baskerville said. "About fifty men have died. More than three hundred are sick. I have asked Queen Elizabeth to send more men and bring our strength back to two thousand."

"The number promised in the treaty with King Henry IV," Captain Joseph Duxbury added. "Has his Majesty contributed?"

"To our pay?" Sir Thomas Baskerville paused. "No. Until the Assembly of Notables approves new imposts, I am not hopeful."

"My men's weekly pay?"

"Each private receives a little more than three shillings."

"Instead of four?"

Sir Thomas Baskerville agreed, "Captain Duxbury, show me your horses."

"All are strong." While they walked toward the newly arrived horses, Duxbury turned to John. "Find out how the rest of the company is doing."

"I'll find the men." John motioned for a Dutchman to follow him. They walked down a narrow street. "That house."

Icicles lined its thatched roof.

John tugged open the wooden door. As he entered the doorway, he ducked. Drops of icy water fell onto his neck. He shivered. Inside the dark room, he stood back up. The icy coldness trickled down his spine.

"Close the door!"

John recognized the voice of the English preacher assigned to St. Valery. The small fire flared and illuminated the preacher's profile. A black kettle steamed near the hearth.

"Can't you see these men are sick?"

As soon as the Dutchman entered, John pulled on the lopsided door. Closing it was not as easy as opening it. The brisk cold wind was strong. The hinges stuck, so John tugged harder and pulled it shut. His eyes slowly adjusted to the darkness.

Packed like fish in a hold of a ship, sick soldiers covered the dirt floor. Lying side by side and head to toe, the soldiers squirmed under thinning blankets. A few wheezed. Some moaned, others coughed.

By the glow of the fire, the English preacher touched a soldier. "The Lord gives strength to the weary."

"Have you seen my friend?" John asked.

"Over there." The preacher pointed to the mud wall. "Take him some broth."

After dipping a cup into the kettle, John helped his friend sit up. "Drink this."

"You're back?" his friend asked.

"We brought horses," John said.

"Horses?" The soldier finished his broth. "I'd like see."

"The fresh air might do him good," the preacher said.

When John, the Dutchman, and the other recruit went back outside, they found Captain Duxbury.

"Mount up!" Captain Joseph Duxbury said. "We go on patrol."

"Can I go, too?" the sick soldier asked.

"Are you well enough?"

"I want to ride."

Along with the handful of Dutch soldiers, Duxbury led his horse company of 50 men up the banks of the Somme.

~ ~ ~

OVER THE NEXT several weeks, the company grew stronger. Bands of lusty men trained and patrolled, and trained and patrolled again.

Citadel, Montreuil-sur-Mer, France, 11ᵗʰ March AD 1597

IN EARLY MARCH of the year 1597, Captain Duxbury's company of horse scouted the countryside and terrain north of the Somme. John Smith complained to his captain, "We never see any action."

"The French at Boulogne and Montreuil stand between the enemy and us."

When they rode through a field, John commented, "I see so few cows."

"The Spanish and Walloons stole most of them last autumn."

"But now?"

"The French General *Seigneur de* Saint Luc has counterattacked and stopped most of the raids. Saint Luc's actions, however, have garnered Cardinal Albert's attention."

"How so?"

"The Cardinal has sent fifteen hundred Spaniards into Calais, the town that the late Count of Varax helped to capture last spring." Duxbury motioned north, towards the French coast.

The English company rode across a stream and up a hill. Fortified walls surrounded the French town of Montreuil.

Once Duxbury's company was inside the walls, the French General, Francois d'Espinay, *Seigneur de* Saint Luc, signaled for the English captain to halt. "I did not request any English."

"You wrote Sir Baskerville that you might need our help," Duxbury said. "Sir Baskerville wanted us to patrol."

"Not this far north." The French Catholic General had deep-set eyes. A few veterans stood near the black-bearded general. Most French soldiers in the square seemed as young as Smith.

"We needed to hear firsthand," Captain Joseph Duxbury said.

"The Walloons began to mutiny in Calais, so Spanish soldiers replaced them. We heard many have died because of the plague, but despite these problems, the Cardinal has added munitions and supplies at St. Omer."

"The King of France has his arsenal at Amiens," Captain Joseph Duxbury said.

"I counted forty cannons," John interjected.

"Yes, the King's arsenal is strong," *Seigneur* de Luc said. "Besides the cannons and plenty of munitions, the King stores tons of wheat, plus enough French francs to pay an army for weeks."

"Can I ask about your medallion?" Duxbury pointed at the general's chest. *Seigneur de* Saint Luc wore the large pendant around his neck. A white dove descended in the middle of a gold Maltese cross. With eight points, the cross was framed in white.

"Only knights inducted into the Order of the Holy Spirit can wear this medallion." The French General explained about the highest order of knights in France, before asking Duxbury, "You brought Dutch with you, too?"

"A small contingent assigned to me. The Dutch have promised to aid King Henry IV with four thousand men."

"His Most Christian Majesty has ratified the treaty with the Dutch Republic."

"Now it is a triple alliance-France, England, and Holland." Captain Joseph Duxbury added, "We needed to know the road here."

"You have seen it."

Duxbury turned to his men, "We ride back to the Somme River, to see the Swiss at Abbeville."

"I'll show you the way," a soldier dressed in the Swiss style said.

"You are Swiss?" Captain Joseph Duxbury asked.

"Yes, I've delivered a message to the French general."

With few words, they exited Montreuil.

Along the road to Abbeville, one of the Dutch soldiers commented, "The French do not seem too enamored with either you or us."

"The Catholics do not always appreciate Protestant help," Captain Joseph Duxbury said, "but until the French improve their finances, we are their strongest allies."

"Has the Assembly of Notables in Rouen accomplished anything?" John asked.

"All they do is talk. They've yet to come up with a plan to reform the finances, but don't worry. The King appreciates the help the Queen gives."

"And the help we give, too," the Swiss messenger added.

Abbeville, France, Tuesday, 11ᵗʰ March *AD* 1597

FOLLOWING THE SWISS guide, Duxbury led his horse company down a narrow path.

When the path opened up, John rode alongside the new Swiss acquaintance. "Tell me about the Swiss."

In the field ahead, a company of Swiss infantry marched in formation.

"Ever since Constable Montmorency hired many of us as mercenaries, the Swiss have provided the King with some of his most loyal support."

"Where is the King?"

"Haven't you heard? His Most Christian Majesty has returned to Paris."

"I've been to Paris." John checked his pouch. He still carried letters of introduction from a Scottish nobleman, David Hume of Godscroft, to the court of Scottish King James VI in Edinburgh.

Duxbury's cavalry company approached several Swiss officers watching their men.

After introductions, one of the Swiss officers informed Duxbury and John, "Two of us were personal guards for King Henry IV. He arrived back at the Louvre about a month ago with his mistress, Gabrielle d'Estrées, *Madame la Marquise de* Monceaux."

Chapter 26 — *Marquise* Gabrielle d'Estrées

The preparations that were making for war did not prevent their [them from] enjoying at Paris all the amusements that winter commonly brings along with it. The gentleness of the government secured the tranquility of the public, who tasted all the sweets of it, without any of that alloy which so long a time had embittered all their pleasures. Gallantry, shows, [and] plays took up the time of the courtiers; and the King [Henry IV], who liked these diversions through taste, permitted them through policy.
Maximilien de Béthune, Baron de Rosny [Later, Duke of Sully]
Translated from French by Charlotte Lennox

He [King Henry IV] made up a masquerade of sorcerers and went to see all the company of Paris. He went to President Saint-Andres and [Sebastien] Zamet's, and all sorts of other places, always having at his side the Marchioness [Gabrielle d'Estrées, Madame la Marquise de Monceaux], who unmasked him and kissed him whenever he entered."
Pierre de l'Estoile,
Translated from French by le Petit Homme Rouge

La Porte Neuve, Paris, France, February *AD* 1597

WINTER COLDNESS BROUGHT an early end to the royal excursion to the French countryside. The French monarch, along with his mistress Gabrielle d'Estrées, sat opposite three ministers inside the royal carriage. Outside the opened windows, mounted Swiss guards kept pace with the slow-moving coach. It approached the gate closest to the Palace *de* Tuileries where the King's sister, Catherine *de* Bourbon, resided. Built near the Louvre, the top floor of the long building overlooked the fortified walls.

As the royal carriage approached the outer gate of Paris, King Henry IV decided to broach the subject of his marriage to Gabrielle with one of his closest advisors, Nicolas *de* Harlay. "*Seigneur de* Sancy, have you given it any more thought?"

A year earlier, the King had requested Sancy's help to secure a divorce from Queen Marguerite *de* Valois, who was known as *La Reine* Margot. Sancy refused to go to Rome to present the petition to Pope

Clement VIII, so Gabrielle became convinced that he despised her. She relayed her suspicions to the King.

"The courtiers often talk about your wish to remarry." The cool wind did not seem to bother the rich Frenchman. Slightly over fifty years of age, he owned a thirty-five-carat diamond that some called the *Beau Sancy*, a stone that the King greatly admired. Sancy had purchased the pear-shaped diamond in Constantinople when he was the French Ambassador to the Ottoman Sultan.

Besides that jewel, Sancy also owned a second, even larger diamond: at fifty-five carats, it was known simply as *'le Sancy.'* A former member of the Reformed Religion, the nobleman had avoided death by converting to Roman Catholicism during the St. Bartholomew's Day Massacre, twenty-five years earlier. "Especially since you bestowed upon your mistress the title of *la Marquise de* Monceaux."

"She deserves the title." Sancy adjusted his hat, concealing even more of his receding hairline.

Dressed warmly with a blanket over her lap, Gabrielle said, "*Seigneur* Sancy, let me ask you a question. If the Pope grants the King a divorce, and the King and I marry, can our son Cesar become a legitimate heir to the throne?"

"*Madame, Non!* In France, the bastards of the kings are always the sons of harlots."

Her eyes instantly teared up. Gabrielle pulled down her veil.

The King frowned, but spoke not a word. His Majesty reflected on *Seigneur* de Sancy's harsh words. Though the King and Gabrielle's son Cesar had been conceived and born while she was married to *Monsieur* Liancourt, her marriage had been annulled. Although the King had

Mistress Gabrielle d'Estrees

decreed his son Cesar to be legitimate, that did not seem to matter to Sancy, and neither did Gabrielle's rising nobility.

After the King had purchased the *Chateau de* Monceaux from the creditors of the late Catherine *de* Medici, he gave it to his mistress. Last autumn, he raised Monceaux to a Marquisate and bestowed upon Gabrielle the right to be called *Marquise*. After Gabrielle's arrival at Rouen in October, countless callers addressed the former *Madame de* Liancourt by her new title, *Madame la Marquise de* Monceaux. Clearly, Sancy was not impressed with Gabrielle's rising status.

The King appreciated the support Sancy had given him throughout his reign. In the early years of the civil wars, Sancy had hired three thousand Swiss mercenaries, using monies from his personal estate. The King, who had appointed Sancy to be his Superintendent of Finance, relieved the rich nobleman of that position the previous summer.

The only sounds were the turning of wheels, the creaking of wood, and the jingle jangle of harnesses. The royal carriage proceeded past the gardens and palace of the Tuileries and through Neuve gate beneath the *Tour de Bois.*

King Henry IV of France and of Navarre

Approaching the Louvre, the King glanced past the wing where, for nearly twenty-five years, Catherine *de* Medici, using the maidens of her court, influenced the affairs of the kingdom. Further upriver, the *Pont aux Meuniers* no longer spanned the Seine. Only the stone bases of former arches remained. Large water wheels no longer turned. The mills and houses built atop the Bridge of Millers had disappeared. Two or three days before Christmas, on the day of Saint Thomas, early winter rains had swept away the bridge, the mills, the houses, and the lives of three hundred men, women, and children.

The carriage turned and entered the square courtyard of the Louvre in sustained silence. The Swiss guard opened the door. As the King and his mistress exited, neither spoke. The three other passengers also departed without a word.

No one had dared to break the silence.

Hotel de Zamet, Paris, France, Mid-February, *AD* 1597

SEVERAL EVENINGS LATER, King Henry IV and Gabrielle d'Estrées rode in their carriage, heading towards the third masquerade of the evening. Not far from the *Hotel de Ville* and the *Bastille*, they approached the *Hotel de* Zamet, the home of the important Italian financier.

"Do you remember the opening of the Assembly of Notables in Rouen last November?" Gabrielle asked.

"Yes, and we still need a reform of the finances."

"In your speech, you said, 'Unlike other kings, you put yourself in the hands of Notables'."

"Oh yes," said the King. "And after my speech, I brought you out from behind the curtain. When I asked your opinion, you said you objected."

Gabrielle smiled and responded, "But you said, '*Ventre-saint-gris!* I submit, but I have my sword at my side.'"

"That I did, and I still wear my sword at my side." The King donned his mask and recalled the one time he did not have his sword at his side.

Two hours before dawn, on Saint Bartholomew's Day in 1572, the King of Navarre and his cousin, the Prince of Conde, were awakened inside the Louvre. Forbidden to carry their swords, they were transported between menacing guards lining the courtyard archways, passing the corpses of several Huguenot gentlemen who served them. The two cousins did not know whether they would survive the hour.

When taken to the King of France, Charles IX declared, "Revere me as the image of God, and cease to be enemies of the image of my mother. If you do not attend Mass, I will consider you guilty of treason against divine and human majesty."

Agreeing to attend Mass, the lives of the two cousins were spared, but they were closely watched and kept under guard. Henry's page, Maximilien *de* Bethune, who was not quite twelve years of age at the time, joined the King of Navarre at the Louvre. His Huguenot father, who had escaped Paris and fled to the Huguenot stronghold of La Rochelle, wrote and urged his son to follow Henry's example, so the boy, too, regularly attended Mass. About two years later, the Prince of Conde, donning a disguise, fled from his captors at Amiens in Picardy to Germany, where he immediately began raising a Protestant army.

When the physically frail King Charles IX died of natural causes on Pentecost Sunday in 1574, his younger brother, Henry *de* Valois, returned from Poland and Lithuania, abdicating the throne where he had recently been elected king. He traveled via Venice, where a courtesan named Veronica Franco entertained him. The favorite of his mother, Catherine de Medici, Henry arrived in Paris in September. Reputed to have a bevy of beauties surrounding him, he was married the day after he was crowned King Henry III in Reims. He immediately broke the three-month truce with the Huguenots.

Catherine's youngest son, *Monsieur* Francis *de* Valois, became disaffected from his older brother, the new monarch. In September of 1575, Francis escaped from her watchful eyes and established his court at Dreux, raising an army of malcontents.

King Henry of Navarre, meanwhile, was being ensnared by *mademoiselles* Carnavalet and Charlotte *de* Sauve, two women under the influence of the long, white arms of the Queen Mother. In February of 1575, while hunting near Senlis, north of Paris, the King of Navarre, along with his page Maximilien *de* Bethune, finally escaped on horseback. Thirty of his party made their way to Alençon, where soon, the Prince of Conde and *Monsieur* Francis joined him. At nearby Tours on the Loire, Henry of Navarre, once more, began to openly practice his Calvinist faith. Despite the slaughter of so many Huguenots three years earlier, King Henry of Navarre found himself at the head of an army of 50,000.

New overtures of peace from the Queen Mother ended this new War of Religion; it abruptly halted. Like the Peace of Saint-Germain-en-Laye, negotiated six years earlier, great promises were made. Before he was murdered in Paris at the very start of the massacre in 1572, Admiral Gaspard *de* Coligny had received his promised wife, 100,000 crowns, and the nominal command of the French armies. Four years later, in 1576, the Peace of Monsieur, with its sixty-three articles, brought *Monsieur* Francis back into his mother's sheepfold. The treaty granted him money and territory and prestige. He held the title of Duke of Anjou—a territory once claimed by the Plantagenet kings of England. Then separated from

Monsieur Francis, the King of Navarre retired to La Rochelle. But within months the War of Religion began once more. Yet when Francis, holding the titles of Duke of Anjou and Alençon, died of malaria in 1584, Henry of Navarre became the presumptive heir to the French throne.

The coach came to a stop in front of the *Hotel de* Zamet. Swiss guards opened the carriage door and the King alighted. Even though he wore a wizard's mask, he also kept his sword.

With his mistress masked and walking a step ahead of the French King, the door to the *Hotel de* Zamet opened. The large foyer was crowded with courtiers and women whose eyes flashed behind their own handheld masks.

Heads turned when the King and his beautiful mistress entered the reception room.

"Is that *Madame de la Marquise*?" one noblewoman with a black mask asked.

"If that is Gabrielle, then—"

The music and the conversation stopped.

The affable French king stepped through the door. He thoroughly enjoyed the dancing and the festivities. Twenty years earlier, in 1578, Catherine *de* Medici, the Queen Mother of France, ostensibly wishing to balance the influence of the strict Catholic Guises, brought her daughter Marguerite and thirty-three maidens-in-waiting to Nerac in Gascony. Following the lead of King Henry, the Calvinist strictness of the court of Navarre greatly relaxed. Known as the *l'escadron volant* or 'flying squadron,' these pretty and witty maidens from Paris covered their breasts in the heat of spring and autumn some of the time.

Galliard Dance Steps, 1588

In the afternoon they mingled with Henry's courtiers along avenues of laurels and cypresses—strolling together in a park opposite the chateau, on the left bank of the River Baise. During most evenings for many months, the squadron, powdering their long hair with perfume and wearing dresses with narrow waists, taught the gallants how to dance. After learning smooth ballets and galliard steps, both courts laughed and watched performances of Italian comedies. Exchanging pleasantries on many passing nights, all desired to charm and supplant each other.

Lasting through the winter and into the following summer, negotiations for a new treaty granting some rights to the Huguenots concluded. Once signed in 1579, the Treaty of Nerac, like the two treaties before it, did not last long. King Henry of Navarre saw through the deceptions first conceived by Catherine *de* Medici in her wing of the Louvre, and later weaved by her minions at Coutras and Nerac in southern France. Enamored of beauty and charm, courtiers revealed secrets. A nearby Huguenot castle fell, and the French Wars of Religion began anew for the seventh time.

His own Queen Margot returned to Paris where her brother, King Henry III of France, still reigned. But later, she became her brother's prisoner at the Chateau *d'*Usson in Auvergne. Even after the king's death in 1589, the Queen, once admired for her pearly white bosom, had remained in the south of France. She had held her own court there for over a decade.

"Quelle surprise!" Sebastien Zamet stepped to the center of the room.

"I would like to present His Most Christian Majesty." Gabrielle unmasked the King and kissed him.

The astonished guests, many of whom held colorful and ornate masks themselves, applauded.

"So unexpected." One attendee nudged her partner.

"What an honor," added another.

The guests bowed and curtsied; the music and dancing resumed.

Courtiers, nobles, and the women seemed pleased and greeted the affectionate couple one by one. When the King and his mistress sat down, Sebastien Zamet stood before the couple, smiling and bowing many times.

Tuileries Palace, Paris

THE FRENCH MONARCH and *Madame la Marquise* visited the King's sister at the Tuileries a few days later. The Palace, built for Catherine *de* Medici, the Queen Consort of Henry II and mother of Margot, was only a short distance from the Louvre. Several stories tall, the main building had a large entryway. The King and Gabrielle climbed the wide staircase.

Tuileries Palace, circa 1840

"Some in Paris are upset about your sister," Gabrielle said.

"Yes, I have heard, but nothing I can do or say will make her change from the Reformed Faith of our mother," the King told Gabrielle. Catherine had attended Mass following the Saint Bartholomew's Day Massacre, but after Count, along with young Maximilien *de* Bethune, brought her back from Paris to Tours, she attended a Calvinist sermon. Because of her renewed adherence to the Reformed Christian Faith, Catherine *de* Bourbon had not attended the baptism of Henry and Gabrielle's daughter. Gabrielle had given birth to their daughter at the Abbey of St. Ouen in Rouen the previous November.

"And today is certainly not the day to attempt to convert her."

"Yes, you are right. My sister is ill."

Strolling down the hall, the King noticed Catherine de Parthenay, the Dowager Princess of Rohan and her thirteen-year-old daughter, Anne *de* Rohan, descending the stairs. The King's sister had suggested her seventeen-year-old son, Henry II de Rohan, marry Marguerite, the infant daughter of Rachel *de* Cochefilet and Maximilien *de* Bethune, Baron *de* Rosny, as soon as Marguerite reached the age of consent in about a decade. Both the Dowager Princess and Marguerite's mother, Rachel, approved Catherine *de* Bourbon's suggestion of this union between two Huguenot families. But King Henry IV strongly objected—he had neither been informed of nor granted his prior approval.

Continuing down the long hall, the King and his Mistress entered the large bedchambers. Attendants lined the walls, and the King raised his hand. "Sister, no need to rise." He had forbidden his sister to marry the Count of Soissons, a man she had long loved. Though a blood relative, the Count's loyalty to the crown had been rightly questioned.

"How nice of you to visit." Catherine *de* Bourbon sat up. Her attendant puffed a pillow behind her. "How is my Goddaughter doing?"

"Catherine-Henriette is very alert and grows each day," Gabrielle said. "You must see her."

"As soon as I recover."

"How about some music?" The King motioned to the lute player standing at the door. "I know you like the Psalms."

"Just like our mother."

With great skill, the musician played the lute. Others, in the manner of the Reformed Faith, began to sing psalms.

The King joined in the singing, but Gabrielle eased closer to him and placed her hand over his mouth. He

Catherine de Bourbon, Duchess du Bar

questioned her with his eyes, and she glanced to the far side of the room. Several Catholic noblemen had stopped talking.

Gabrielle was right, the King realized. *It was best not to start a scandal.* The King decided not to sing psalms in the Reformed manner. Many Catholics, both inside Paris and outside, especially in the Kingdom of Spain, questioned Henry's commitment to the Catholic faith. At the behest of Gabrielle, before his army attacked Paris, King Henry IV partook of the Mass. Less than four years earlier, after hearing about Henry's conversion, Paris opened its gates.

After his mistress removed her hand, Henry whispered, "Very well."

When the others finished singing, *Madame* Catherine told her brother, "I hope you enjoy the baptism of the Constable's son."

"I am certain we will," the King said. "The Papal Legate, Alexander de Medici, will preside over the ceremony."

"Are the rumors true that Catherine-Henriette is destined to marry the boy?"

Gabrielle glanced at the King and smiled at *Madame* Catherine. "The Constable of Montmorency's son?"

The King smiled back. "It is a thought." He turned to his sister. "But we look forward to the Baptism."

"I hope the Legate is able to convince the Pope to grant the divorce and allow you two to marry," Catherine said.

"We truly appreciate your love and support," Gabrielle said.

On the way back to the Louvre, Gabrielle informed the King, "Margot wrote to me and claims she needs money to live."

"I have always supported her." The King did not mention the poor state of his finances, largely caused by the endless wars of religion.

"And now?"

"Perhaps Queen Margot can petition the Pope directly and request His Holiness to grant the divorce." The King knew he could never be reconciled to Margot. Her mother, Catherine de Medici, either hatched or approved the plot to kill Henry's close friends, members of the Reformed Religion, whom she called Huguenots, meaning 'vow-fellows.' Twenty-five years earlier, his friends had followed the young Henry to attend the wedding ceremonies held in front of the Cathedrale de Notre Dame. Henry's Calvinist mother, Queen Jeanne d'Albret, could not attend, for she had died two months earlier. Some Calvinists suspected she had been poisoned, since she wore perfumed gloves presented by a Florentine member of the Queen Mother before turning ill.

Less than a week after the wedding, and with many of his friends of the Reformed Faith still in Paris, Margot's brother, King Charles IX, purportedly told his followers, "Kill them all!" Though Margot protected her husband, Henry, during the St. Bartholomew's Day Massacre, the marriage was strained. For more than fifteen years, Queen Margot had remained in seclusion and under guard at the mountaintop *Chateau d'Usson* in southern France.

Rue de Infants Rouges, Paris, 5th March *AD* 1597

INSIDE A SMALL church near the Temple, King Henry IV held the infant son of Constable Montmorency, the highest military officer in all of France. The Papal Legate, Alexander de Medici, presided over the short ceremony. When the Cardinal of Florence motioned, the French King handed over the young boy.

The Papal Legate dipped his hand into the basin and sprinkled water on the boy's head. "I baptize you in the name of the Father, the Son, and the Holy Spirit."

The King would have preferred the Legate had baptized his daughter at the Cathedral of Saint Ouen in Rouen the previous November, but Papal propriety prohibited it. A French Cardinal, loyal to the King, performed the baptismal rites on their second child instead.

After the ceremony, while Gabrielle's aunt conversed with the Constable and his wife, the King asked the Legate, "Will you be attending the feast at the *Hotel de* Montmorency?"

"No, I am afraid I will not. But I will be staying longer in Paris than previously planned."

"That is good news."

"As long as there is hope that peace between France and Spain can come to pass, Pope Clement VIII believes I will be of greater service here than in Rome."

"We have talked about a truce, and my ministers are negotiating with Cardinal Albert of Austria in Brussels about how long it should last."

"And I have written the Duke of Mercoeur in Brittany about accepting you as a true Catholic." The Italian Legate stepped towards his carriage. "For now, I must bid you adieu."

As soon as the Legate departed, Gabrielle, dressed in green, stepped into the sun. Her headdress, adorned with diamonds, sparkled in the light. The King reached up and fussed with her hair. "You do not have enough jewels."

"What do you mean? I have twelve."

"*Oui, Oui.* I see, I can count." He beamed and peered into her eyes. "Instead of twelve, *Madame la Marquise*, you should have fifteen."

Hotel *de* Montmorency, Paris, 5th March *AD* 1597

AT THE BAPTISMAL dinner at the *Hotel de* Montmorency, everyone found their seat. Though it was the time of Lent, the Constable motioned servants to bring in the main dish. The first one brought a very large platter with a huge, well-garnished sturgeon, freshly caught, rushed to Paris from the coast.

"How marvelous," the King said.

The next servant brought in a second platter with another sturgeon, as large as the first. Fruit galore, bowls overflowing the rim, were set in the middle of each table.

"Paris has never seen such magnificent fare." The King added, "And the fruit? So much."

"With your permission, your Majesty," the Constable said.

"Yes, yes, eat, eat."

The courtiers, including the youngest, Henri II *de* Rohan, and the other guests ate their fill. The King smiled when he bit into a soft pear.

Gabrielle squeezed a little more lemon on her sturgeon. "I love the tartness." When she bit into the wedge, the Italian Zamet shook his head.

During the meal, the musicians played, and afterwards, the guests all danced, in keeping with the custom of the season.

Tuileries Palace, Paris, 11th March *AD* 1597

"TONIGHT SHOULD BE the best dance of the whole season," Gabrielle told the King.

"Yes, my sister feels better. She has planned it all. A dance ballet will be held, and twelve noblemen will attend."

"Including the Baron *de* Rosny?"

"*Oui,*" the king responded.

"But that's not the real object, is it?"

"You are right. One of the most beautiful ladies of the court needs a husband. Most of the old men want to be gallant."

"All twelve of them?" Gabrielle asked.

"All but one. Maximilien *de* Béthune, Baron *de* Rosny, had to be convinced."

"Yes, he is happily married." After his first wife died, Rosny married for a second time.

"I know you want to marry, too, but these things take time."

"Especially, when some, like Sancy, are opposed to it." Gabrielle asked, "And Rosny?"

"Rosny does an excellent job at the Council of Finance. He found more royal rents hidden from Sancy by Zamet and the other financiers."

Inside the hall, *Madame* Catherine de Bourbon greeted her brother and the *Madame la Marquise*. Catherine always enjoyed parties. After Baron *de* Rosny learned to fight, she brought him to the Chateau *de* Pau in Bearn, the capital of the Kingdom of Navarre. The sister of King Henry introduced the young man, then age seventeen or eighteen, to the ways of a courtier. She even taught him how to dance.

The ballet dancing and performance lasted for hours. Baron *de* Rosny danced only with his wife.

When the King and his mistress returned to the Louvre Palace, he did not go to his corner *Chambre du Roi*, but to the room immediately adjacent to it. He told his guard, "It is very late. I prefer not to be awakened."

"*Oui*, Sire," the Swiss guard answered outside his bed chamber.

"But if any important packages arrive during the night, do not fail to awaken me." King Henry IV donned his night garments and climbed into his canopied bed.

His head barely touched the pillow, and his Most Christian Majesty fell into a very deep sleep.

Chapter 27 — Spilt Nuts

At about eight in the morning of the eleventh of this month, five or six of the advance guard entered the gate, carrying sacks of nuts and apples, as though they were peasants from the neighboring villages going to market. They sat down inside the gate, feigning to be tired, and waited till the wagon and the other men came up. . . They came onto the bridge and stopped in such a position that half of it was under the arch of the gate, where the portcullis would fall, and the other half still on the bridge. . . The men with the sacks then, as though by accident, spilt their nuts and apples, and the guard naturally rushed after them . . .

Piero Duodo, Venetian Ambassador in France
Dispatch to the Doge and Senate, Translated from Italian
Paris, France, 22nd March 1597

Council Chambers, Brussels, Belgium, Late February *AD* 1597

INSIDE HIS ORNATE Council Chambers in Brussels, Albert of Austria, the former Viceroy of Portugal and Archbishop of Toledo, and currently King Philip II's Governor-General of the Seventeen Provinces of the Netherlands, convened his council. President Richardot of the Privy Council, as well as the Catholic Prince William of Orange, attended. Cardinal Albert told the members, "A truce for four or five years would be advantageous. It would allow us time to put our finances in order."

"France will only agree to a truce of four or five weeks," President Jean Richardot said.

"So a truce cannot be obtained?"

"Not yet, but the French Ministers affirm that the French nobles assembled in Rouen prefer peace."

"We must persuade King Henry, so we can direct all of our resources to subduing the seven rebellious provinces."

"Maurice of Nassau has sent back the body of the Count of Varax from Turnhout," one member reported.

"Our general should not have lost the Battle of Tielenheide," Cardinal Albert said.

"According to your directions, his body was buried in a private ceremony," President Richardot said.

"And the captains responsible for the disgrace?"

"Imprisoned."

Cardinal Albert signaled his approval.

"Ransom monies have been raised to pay for the prisoners held by the Dutch," President Richardot said. "But many other troops still need to be paid."

"King Philip II knows our predicament." Cardinal Albert had often written to the Spanish monarch. "But even when we offer to pay higher interest rates, the Fuggers have refused to lend us more."

Like the Italian financiers in Genoa, the Fugger bankers in Germany had suffered losses when King Philip declared all of his debts void the previous December.

A general stepped forward. "We need to replace the German and Italian troops lost on the Heath of Tielen."

"I have requested the Admiral of Aragon to see my older brother in Prague."

"Holy Roman Emperor Rudolph II will send replacements for the German troops?" the General asked.

"Perhaps in late Spring or Summer."

While the Cardinal wondered if he would receive any good news, a messenger appeared at the door. "Cardinal Albert?"

"What is it?"

"Governor Hernán Tello *de* Porto-carrero of Doullens has arrived."

"Send the Governor Tello in."

Shorter than everyone else in the room, Governor Hernán Tello entered the chambers and bowed.

"What have you learned?" Cardinal Albert asked.

Spanish Sergeant

"My sergeant, Francisco *del* Arco, has surveyed capital of Picardy. Entering several times, he pretended to be the Confessor of the Bishop of Amiens. The citizens of Amiens have enlarged their arsenal with forty cannons, many caskets of gunpowder, countless bullets, and storehouses full of wheat." Governor Hernán Tello *de* Portocarrero scanned the room. "But Amiens can be taken."

"Taken? But how?"

"I have a plan," the enterprising Hernán Tello *de* Portocarrero explained. Adding more details, he delivered his impassioned conclusion:

"How great will be our good fortune, how great our glory, if we, coming in with the rest of our men, can purchase such a city for our king, which is the chiefest of Picardy, and one of the most esteemed of all France? How great will the present plunder be for all of you? And how much greater rewards are we hereafter to expect from our King Philip II? But this action will prove particularly glorious to us, the commanders, who, making this success memorable to perpetuity, shall thereby likewise eternalize our own names.

"Amiens is within three short days' journeys of Paris; the country open, without either rivers, woods, or any other obstacles. Amiens may then be made so great a magazine of arms, and may admit of so numerous a garrison, as may rather be termed an army than a garrison; and how easily may we then march even to the gates of Paris? Infest all the adjacent countryside? And every day add to our acquisitions in Picardy?

"So, as King Henry of France will at last have good reason to repent his having chosen rather to make war than peace with our King. I confess, as there cannot be a purchase of greater importance, so must we expect to meet with all possible difficulties therein. I know what the nature of a surprisal is, and how great the difference is between the framing it in our fancies, and the effecting of it. I know that Amiens is a great city, full of a warlike people, and who will speedily make in, either to keep us from making ourselves masters of the gate, or to take it from us, when we shall have gotten it.

"But I would we had got it, as the careless keeping of it, may make; us hope we shall; as for the rest, it will be our parts, by the vigor of our bodies, and the valor of our arms, not only to maintain the entrance but to advance further into the inhabited places, and at last to make full conquest of the city. I speak my hopes; let us then courageously pursue our march, and let each of us discover the design unto our soldiers, and enflame them thereunto. I, for my part, will rather act than command. And whether I shall live or die, how can I live or die more gloriously?"

Citadel of Doullens, Border of Picardy and Artois, 10ᵗʰ March *AD* 1597

ON THE TENTH of March 1597, Governor Hernán Tello *de* Portocarrero exited the Eastern gates of the Citadel of Doullens at Dusk. Spanning many acres and protected by strong bastions, the citadel housed an able garrison of soldiers. Since the Spanish captured the town two years earlier, the citadel's high walls had been reinforced to withstand any French counterassault.

Hernán Tello *de* Portocarrero did not want to let French sympathizers know its weakened state, so the Governor secretly led several of his strongest companies. Marching out after nightfall, they arrived at the rendezvous point at Orville, several miles east of Doullens, up the Authie River.

Orville, Picardy, France, 10ᵗʰ March *AD* 1597

SEVERAL SPANISH COMPANIES of *Don* Alonso *de* Mendoza, as well as German and Walloon companies, had already arrived. Among the Walloons were several companies that had earlier mutinied in Calais due to a lack of pay. Four hundred Irish, led by Captain Edward Bostock of Stanley's regiment, reached the small village at the appointed time, bringing the total number of foot soldiers to 2,200 men.

Several horse companies also approached. The Governor of Doullens appointed a Neapolitan named Girolamo Caraffa, the *Marquis* of Montenegro, to lead the five hundred horsemen forward.

"Where are we going?" a Spanish captain asked.

"I will tell you on the way," Governor Tello responded.

In the darkness, the army crossed the Authie in silence. In good order, the Spanish army marched south. The last quarter of the moon provided the only light.

As the night grew colder and the journey longer, crusty ice crunched below marching feet.

For hours, the Spanish army headed steadily south. Before sunrise, they had covered vast ground, about twenty miles. The cavalry of the Marquis *de* Montenegro took possession of the Abbey of St. Joseph and handed it over to the infantry with hardly a sound.

THE VANGUARD, CONSISTING of a Spanish and a Walloon company, occupied the Abbey of Mary Magdalene. The Abbey stood about five hundred paces before the Gate of Montrescu, and within cannon shot of the foremost bastions of Amiens. The bulk of the army hid in the vineyards, while the captains gathered under the strong arches of the Abbey.

"We are going to attack Amiens?" one captain asked.

"We will win it by surprise," Governor Hernán Tello said. The winter sun had yet to rise.

"With so few men?"

"Cardinal Albert has approved the plan."

"It can't be done, Governor," another captain protested.

"You just want to marry that rich widow," another added.

"You know?" the Governor retorted.

"We heard the story."

Governor Hernán Tello *de* Portocarrero realized the officers knew he wanted to marry the rich French widow. She had told the Governor she would not marry him as long as his town of Doullens was Spanish and her city of Amiens remained in French hands. Either both towns would become French, or both Spanish. Until the war between Spain and France ended, the widow would not consent.

"I have been inside Amiens." Sergeant Francisco *del* Arco stepped forward. He told the gathering of officers, "Their guard is weak, especially in the morning during Lent." The days leading up to the celebration of Christ's Resurrection Easter were often characterized by fasting.

The Governor glanced at his commanders. "No one possesses the valor of you, my experienced captains."

"But we have arrived so late," the first captain persisted.

"The bravery of our valiant soldiers cannot be matched." Governor Hernán Tello gestured to Sergeant *del* Arco. His sergeant towered over him.

"But it is almost dawn," the Walloon captain said.

"We will prevail."

"I agree." The Spanish captain, whose company marched in the Vanguard, stepped forward. "We place our success and our hope in the hands of God, who gives victory to whom He pleases."

"Captain," Governor Tello pointed forward. "Hide your men in the bushes." The Governor turned to the Walloon captain. "Have your one hundred soldiers also hide until the gate opens."

The Walloon captain climbed to the top of a tree.

Built like a square fort, the northern gate of Amiens faced the road toward Doullens. Slanted walls extended from both sides. A little after seven o'clock the iron gate was raised. After the initial rush of citizens entering and leaving the city had slowed, the Walloon captain signaled from the tree. Tello nodded to Sergeant *del* Arco. Fourteen soldiers would attempt to secure the *Porte de* Montrescu. The short governor sent them forward.

Gate of Montrescu, Amiens, Picardy, Morning, 11th March *AD* 1597

DRESSED IN COUNTRY attire, Sergeant Francisco *del* Arco strolled down the road. Three other soldiers in similar clothes walked with him toward the Gate of Montrescu. Beneath their cloaks, they carried pistols and daggers, and over their shoulders, sacks of walnuts and apples.

Trailing behind Sergeant *del* Arco, three horses pulled forward a wagon with four men aboard. Filled with wood and covered with hay, the wagon halted when its driver, a Burgundian captain, pulled the reins. Following the wagon, another six soldiers likewise dressed in peasant attire, waited for the plot to unfold. Those last six also remained beyond the sight of the guards of Amiens.

With the portcullis raised, Sergeant Francisco *del* Arco and the first three soldiers entered the fortified gate. Several guards warmed their hands by a fire.

His three compatriots set down their heavy sacks of nuts and apples. Breathing heavily, they sat down next to them.

"You can't stop here." The sergeant of the guard held a long halberd, a weapon combining a spear with sharp ax blades.

"We've walked so far." Though a Spaniard from Aragon, Sergeant *del* Arco spoke excellent French. "We just need to catch our breath."

Another guard added wood to the a small fire.

"You must move, I said."

"We will, we will," Sergeant *del* Arco said. "In just a few moments."

"We should do as he says." The soldier with the sack of apples slowly rose.

"You do not mind if I warm my hands." Sergeant *del* Arco rubbed his arms and shivered. He needed to bide his time, so the wagons and the other two groups of soldiers could reach him.

The French sergeant allowed *del* Arco to move by the fire.

As the soldier with the apples sat back down, an old peasant entered the gate. "Sergeant, you should be alert. A Spanish army passed over the Authie River last night."

"You saw them?" the Frenchman asked.

"I heard."

"We should tell Count de Sol." One of the guards stepped toward the bridge over the Seine in the direction of the city proper.

"The Governor is at the Cathedral. The services have just begun."

"This must be a joke," the French Corporal said. "The Spanish would not dare move against Amiens and our strong militia."

"You are right." The French guard returned to the fire.

Several moments later, the wagon filled with wood and covered with hay entered the gate. It stopped under the portcullis, where the gate meets the bridge.

From his vantage point by the fire, *del* Arco could see the last six Spanish soldiers approaching. One of them carried a long pole.

Following the guard's directions, the first three peasants rose. When one of them attempted to lift his sack over his shoulders, he accidentally spilled the nuts. They scattered on the ground.

"Fool, pick them up!" the French sergeant yelled.

"Fool!" The second peasant shoved the first.

"Don't call me a fool!"

A small scuffle ensued. The sack of apples opened.

"Pick up the nuts!"

Two guards rushed to help. Two other French guards, warming their hands by the fire, laughed at the small melee, but the chuckles did not last long.

The Burgundian captain of the wagon lifted the pin holding the harness. The three horses tied to the wagon were cut loose. The wagon, lodged under the portcullis, could not move.

The peasant scrambled for the nuts on the ground, accidentally kicking one further away.

"Pick them up!" the guard yelled again.

The last of the fourteen soldiers dressed as peasants entered the Gate as those three horses wandered through the apples.

The French sergeant looked around. "Where is that strong country fellow?"

"Me voici!" Sergeant *del* Arco grabbed the halberd and wrestled it out of the guard's hands. He pulled out his pistol and mortally shot the guard, whose body slumped down onto the cold, damp ground.

In a similar fashion, the three other peasants killed the guards who had rushed to help pick up the nuts.

Rising from beneath the long planks, four soldiers revealed their weapons. They swarmed the guards rising near the fire.

The French guard above slashed the rope and lowered the gate. The portcullis slammed onto the wagon. Vertical bars hit the ground, stopping passage. Several bars, however, did not go through. They became stuck atop the wagon of planks. Crawling quickly, soldiers squeezed through the discarded hay. They had just enough room.

With the alarm, as soon as the first shots were fired, the Walloon, Spanish, and Irish captains rushed forward with their companies of foot soldiers. They swept beneath the portcullis two by two. The city's militia, meanwhile, rushed to the counterscarp, the outer wall rising above the

Surprise at Amiens by Deceit, 11th March 1597

ditches, but the confrontation with the attackers did not last long. The three hundred soldiers of the Cardinal's Army dislodged those city defenders.

With the Gate of Montrescu now raised, the Spanish cavalry followed in force. The riders rode into the main square, and within an hour, the rest of his army came to the assistance of the peasant soldiers, who still occupied the gate.

Governor Tello and the last of the twenty-two-hundred-foot soldiers marched into the center of town. They captured all of the armaments and occupied the main intersections before the city's five-thousand-man militia could respond.

"The governor of Amiens?" Governor Tello asked.

"We wounded Count St. Pol," Sergeant *del* Arco said, "but he escaped out of the Gate of Beauvais. The French guard closed the gate behind him because the Count bribed him with five hundred crowns. Other noblemen fled out the other gates, but many could not escape."

"Are the gates secure?"

"Now."

Street by street, the Spanish and Walloon soldiers told the citizens, "Stay in your home."

Tello told his officers, "Shoot anyone who resists."

"And our soldiers?" one officer asked.

"Assign three or four houses for each of your soldiers to pillage. They can keep the plunder themselves."

"The weapons of the militia?"

"The townsmen must give them up."

"And if they hide their muskets?"

"Shoot them on sight."

At the home of the Governor of Amiens, Tello found the wife of Count St. Pol. "Do not worry, we will not harm you."

"What will you do with me?" the wife asked.

"As soon as your husband pays the ransom, you'll be set free."

Chapter 28 - Thunderbolt Marshall *de* Biron

The people there [Paris] are wonderful[ly] discontented herein, insomuch as in the streets, they cried, "Drown the whore, hurl her over the bridge!"

The Marshall [de] Biron being come down thither with three thousand horse and divers regiment of foot, yet ours [the English] were the first advanced and the bravest there and best commended of all that speak of the army: these troops keep the town [Amiens] guarded that nothing can [come] in or [go] out.

Captain William Lylle to the Earl of Essex
St. Valery, France [19 March 1597]

The Marshall de Biron, who is "The Thunderbolt" of this Kingdom, is pressing Amiens night and day, and means to attempt an escalade, if the opportunity presents itself. He has cut to pieces 300 men who were marching on Amiens.

Piero Duodo, Venetian Ambassador to France
Paris, 22nd March 1597 (Translated from Italian)

Abbeville, Picardy, France, 11th March *AD* 1597

CAPTAIN JOSEPH DUXBURY and his young recruit John Smith watched the Swiss infantry finish their fighting exercises outside Abbeville, about thirty miles downriver from the capital of Picardy. After they forded the Somme and entered the fortified town, Duxbury's company dismounted to refresh themselves inside its strong walls.

"Has anything important ever happened in this small town?" John asked.

"A royal marriage once happened here," the Swiss guard said. "When Mary Tudor turned 18 years of age, she married King Louis XII."

"The King of France? Here in Abbeville?"

"Yes, and Anne Boleyn attended her wedding as her Maid of Honor. But the French monarch died only two months later into his third marriage."

"Killed?"

"No, natural causes." The Swiss laughed. "They say overexertion, trying to have a son. King Louis XII was more than thirty years older than his redheaded wife."

"And afterwards?"

"Mary secretly married Charles Brandon, the First Duke of Suffolk, in France," Captain Duxbury said. "Because Mary Tudor did not tell her brother, King Henry VIII, and receive his permission beforehand, her second marriage became scandalous."

John heard the sound of a dozen horses and turned toward the riders. "Is not that the Governor of Amiens?"

"Yes, but Count St. Pol rides without his boots." Captain Duxbury approached the group of twelve. As soon as the Count and his small escort dismounted, he asked, "What is wrong?"

"Amiens has fallen."

"Fallen? How?"

"Spanish soldiers disguised as peasants spilt a sack of nuts and overpowered the French guards."

The news stunned Duxbury, John, and the other soldiers. All knew the war with Spain had come to them. Paris had become a frontier town; the open fields north of the capital were threatened.

"Get horses ready." Count St. Pol moved to the door of the Swiss commander. "Hand me a pen." He quickly wrote a note. "I must inform His Most Christian Majesty." King Henry IV stayed the Louvre Palace."

A rider departed and galloped out to the river town, toward Paris.

The Count scribed two notes and sealed them. Not waiting for the wax to fully harden, he handed them to two messengers. "I need aid and immediate assistance from General Saint Luc at Montreuil and Sir Thomas Baskerville at Saint Valery."

"We will go to Amiens," Captain Duxbury said.

"Do what you can," the displaced Governor of Amiens said.

Duxbury turned to John and the other horsemen in his company. "Mount up, men!"

His colors at his side, his men fully armored, Duxbury motioned forward. "To Amiens!"

Amiens, Picardy, 12th March *AD* 1597

THE DAY AFTER the fall, Captain Duxbury led his company of horsemen through the barren countryside north of Amiens. Wagons, overflowing with goods, travelled on the road away from the Gates of Montrescu and toward Doullens. A small band of light Spanish cavalry rode alongside them.

With seamless motion, Duxbury unsheathed his sword. He raised it above his head. "Take it back!"

The fearless English soldiers on horseback charged the wagons, hurrying to escape. Several Spanish riders were killed, but an officer at the front escaped.

"Who was that soldier?" Captain Duxbury asked a prisoner.

"Sergeant Francisco del Arco," the captured Spaniard said. "Governor Hernán Tello *de* Portocarrero sends him to Cardinal Albert in Brussels.

~ ~ ~

SEVERAL DAYS LATER, when French riders rode from Corbie in the east, John asked, "The King's horsemen?"

"No, Charles *de* Gontaut, *Duc de* Biron and Marshall of France," Captain Duxbury said. "Like a thunderbolt, the Marshall cut down three hundred riders attempting to enter Amiens last week."

Passing the Abbey of Mary Magdalene, Marshall Biron approached Amiens from the north. To test the defenses of new Spanish Governor, the French riders rode within musket shot of the Gate of Montrescu. When they edged closer, Spanish lancers, led by Marquis of Montenegro stormed out of the gate, pushing the probing Frenchmen back.

Captain Duxbury told his men, "Retaking Amiens may not be easy."

"Every gate is well-defended," Marshall Biron agreed.

"We must tell the King."

"His Majesty wants us to meet him at Picquigny."

"Thunderbolt" Charles de Gontaut, Duc de Biron

The Marshall stationed two companies at the Abbey of Mary Magdalene and then rode northwest.

When they were out of sight of Amiens, they turned back toward the Somme River and Picquigny.

Porte de la **Barbarane, Chateau** *de* **Picquigny, Picardy, 23rd Mar.** *AD* **1597**

THE GENERAL OF the English army in Picardy, Sir Thomas Baskerville, led his regiment from St. Valery through the riverfront town of Picquigny. Sir John Aldrich, along with companies from his regiment from Crotoy, a town opposite St. Valery at the mouth of the Somme, joined Baskerville and the other English forces. Together, they marched up towards the castle.

Built on a hill overlooking the town and the Somme, the Chateau of Picquigny had thick stone walls. French guards watched from two high walls leading to the lower gate of the Chateau, the *Porte de Garde*. Several companies of Dutch foot soldiers followed the English regiments.

"Dutch soldiers?" John asked.

"Newly arrived from Holland, Zeeland, and Ostend," Captain Duxbury said. "Part of the Triple Alliance."

"I recognize some of them."

A month earlier, some of those Dutch foot soldiers had marched to Turnhout in Brabant. Most arrived too late to participate in the Battle of Tielenheide. By the time the footmen reached the heath, the battle was over. English and Dutch cavalry had already vanquished the Count of Varax and his army.

The English and Dutch soldiers joined the encampment in the open fields outside the *Porte de la Barbarane* and the main building of the Chateau. "And King Henry IV?"

"He arrives now." Duxbury pointed to the procession cresting the hill.

Royal horsemen trotted, as the flags of Kingdoms of France and Navarre waved. Behind those heavily armored riders, more of the King's personal guard, both musketeers and pikemen, marched in double time.

The fully armored King, wearing feathers in his hat, rode through the midst of the small encampment and through the Gate of Barbarane. French guards stood at attention as he entered the gate. It rose four stories, higher than the adjoining castle walls and the steeple of the nearby chapel.

Accompanied by a French officer, Sir John Aldrich told Captain Joseph Duxbury, "The King wants his officers to join him inside."

Captain Duxbury ordered John, "Accompany me."

"The King arrived quickly," John said as they walked through the gate manned by French guards.

"Amiens fell less than two weeks ago," the Frenchman said.

"How did the King find out?" John asked while they waited for more officers to arrive in the courtyard.

"After the King attended a party at the Tuileries, a fast messenger sent by Count St. Pol arrived at the Louvre. It was in the middle of the night," the Frenchman continued the story. "When a messenger entered my chamber, I left my wife, Rachel, and our infant daughter, Marguerite, and hurried to the Louvre."

King's Bed Chamber, Louvre Palace, Paris, 12th March *AD* 1597

AWAKENED MINUTES EARLIER from the deepest of sleep, King Henry IV paced with his arms folded. In the darkest hour of the night, His Most Christian Majesty, still dressed in his bedclothes, was greatly troubled. The bad news could not be worse: Amiens had fallen; the whole arsenal lost. *Such deceit!*

Held to end the state of war between France and Spain, the recent truce talks had turned into a nightmare. Amiens, the key to the Kingdom, had been conquered. No other city stood between the capital and the armies of Cardinal Albert and the Spanish-controlled Lowlands.

While his courtiers stood in the corners and leaned against the walls of his chambers in complete silence, the King's mistress wept by his bed.

The King lowered his head and quickened his pace to and fro, circling back and forth again, until his closest advisor, Maximilien *de* Béthune, the Baron de Rosny, entered his chambers.

The King raised his head and walked to the door. He met Rosny and squeezed his hand. "Ah, my friend. What a misfortune! Amiens is taken."

The King related to Rosny what he knew about how Amiens had fallen.

"Your person is well," Baron Rosny said. "And I have just finalized the means by which Amiens can be returned. Several other places Cardinal Albert has taken will be restored to France."

"Is this true?" the King of France and of Navarre asked.

"Without much difficulty."

The King raised his eyes. "This blow is from heaven. Because those poor people refused a small garrison I desired to give them, they are lost."

He paused and peered about the room. "I have sufficiently played the part of the King of France." He picked up his sword. "'Tis time I assume the character of the King of Navarre!" Before Henry ruled France, he had inherited the small Kingdom of Navarre from his Huguenot mother, Jeanne d'Albert. He turned to Gabrielle, still weeping. *"Madame la Marquise,* we must quit our finery, mount our horse, and wage one more war."

Gabrielle took her kerchief and dabbed the wetness from her rosy cheeks and teary eyes.

King Henry IV told his commander. "Awaken the King's horsemen. Summon my loyal regiment of Navarre. We ride at dawn."

Less than two hours later, all of the King's horsemen had gathered in the courtyard of the Louvre. As the King mounted his steed, Gabrielle d'Estrées took off her necklace. "I shall be the first to aid you."

"Your necklace?" King Henry IV asked.

"As well as diamonds and jewels. I will sell them all for you."

"You love France as much as I. Give the money to Rosny. He will know what to do."

Accompanied by his horsemen and his personal guard, the King rode out of the Louvre and Paris on that late winter morning, spending one night at Pontoise before arriving at Beauvais.

In Paris, meanwhile, crowds gathered by the plaza in front of Notre Dame Cathedral, as well as on both banks of the Seine. They blamed Gabrielle, the King's mistress, for the loss of Amiens, the sole cause that the wrath of God had fallen on them. One mob even marched over the *Pont au Change* and chanted, "Drown the whore! Throw her over the bridge!"

Courtyard, Chateau *de* Picquigny, Picardy, 23rd March *AD* 1597

AS SOON AS the Frenchman finished his story, several French noblemen entered the main building. The English officers followed, and Captain Duxbury told John, "Stay close to me." The last to enter, they stayed by the door of the large room.

King Henry IV rose to his feet. "I strengthened the defenses of both Beauvais and Montdidier and visited Corbie to the East." The King turned to the Marshall de Biron, "Give me your report."

"We have been able to intercept supplies destined for Amiens, but each of the gates is protected."

"Can we attack Amiens?"

"We have too few cannons."

"And men?"

"Only two French regiments. Those of Picardy led by General St. Luc from Montreuil, and the one you lead."

"Of Navarre." The King did not doubt the valor of his most loyal troops. "I have written many letters to my friends all over France. I hope those who meet in Saumur come soon."

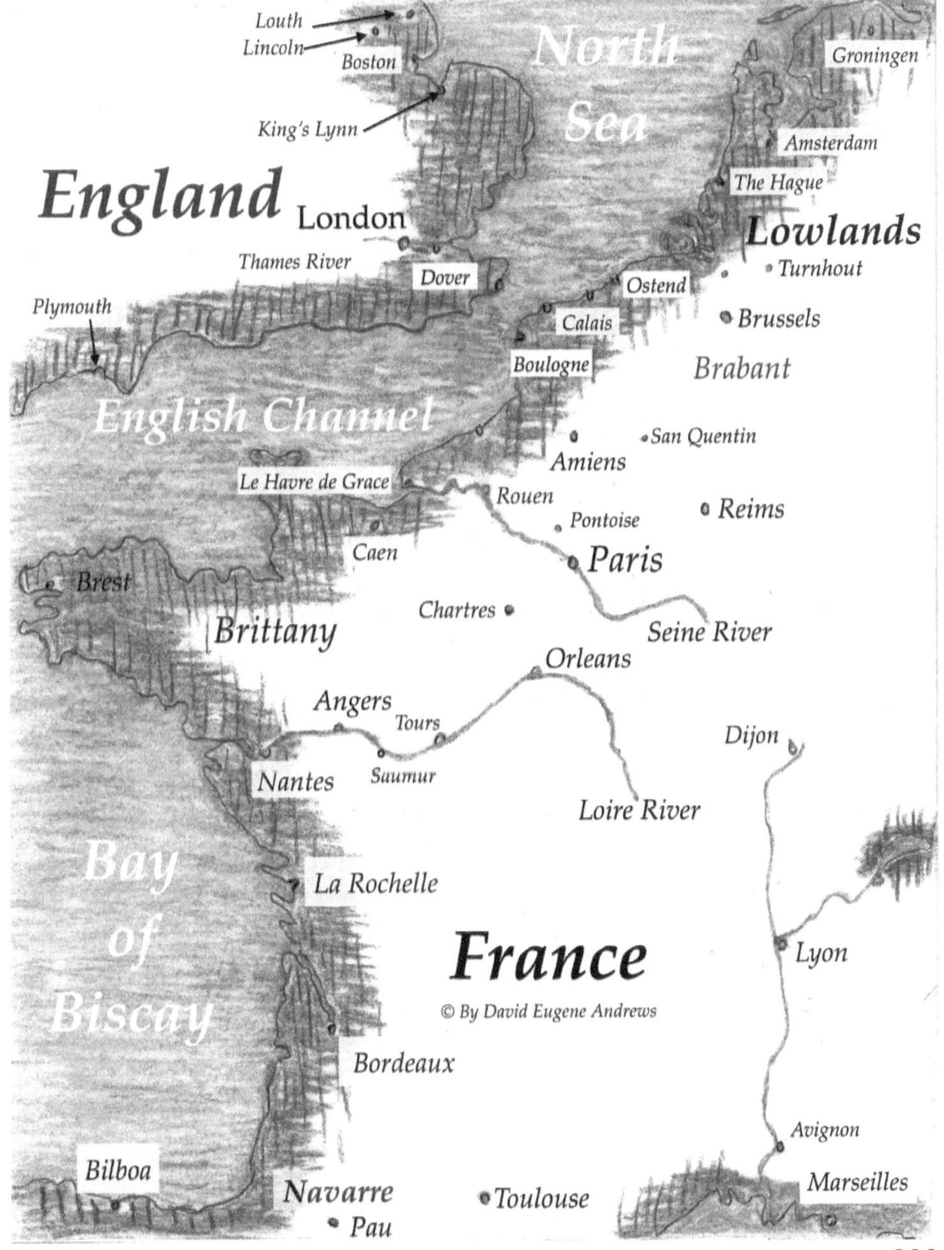

"Money is also lacking," the Marshall said.

"Gabrielle has sold her jewelry and sent me 50,000 crowns. It will pay expenses. But I agree, we need more."

"What if we capture a town and hold it for ransom?" the Marshal asked.

"Doullens?"

"Perhaps, the Cardinal would not expect it." The King turned to Marshall *de* Biron. "Where do you suggest we rendezvous?"

"At Vignacourt."

By the next morning, the King's army of five thousand men had crossed the Somme River. Joining with five hundred horsemen, they marched up the valley northeast of Amiens.

Royal Camp, Vignacourt, Picardy, 25th March *AD* 1597

THE NEXT DAY, the King gathered the French and English officers in front of his tent. Though Cardinal Albert had destroyed most of the storehouses of grain, the small river provided fresh water for both horses and men. Soldiers cut down trees with axes.

"Marshall *de* Biron, you will lead the regiment."

"And the English?" Sir Thomas Baskerville rasped.

"The Duke of Epernon will command the other regiment, including the rest of the French, your English regiment, and the Dutch."

"Can they fight?" the Duke asked. A former member of the Catholic League, the Duke, had submitted to the King only recently. Confronted at Marseille in Southern France by the Prince of Joinville, the Duke had relinquished claims to the government of Provence the previous year.

"My men are able." Sir Baskerville held overall command of English forces in France. Sir Arthur Savage served as his Lieutenant Colonel.

"Your companies are weak."

"Some died during the cold winter." Sir Baskerville attempted to hold back a cough. "But my twelve hundred English fighters are strong."

"And the Dutch? They are not even Catholic."

"The States General are allies," the King said.

"The ladders are ready." The Marshall pointed to carpenters readying the steps.

"For Doullens?" Sir Baskerville asked.

"No, for Arras in Artois."

234

Arras, County of Artois, Seventeen Provinces, 26th March *AD* 1597

AFTER MARCHING ABOUT twenty miles and crossing the Authie River, the two regiments reached the outskirts of Arras in the province of Artois, loyal to Brussels. Awaiting final orders, John Smith dismounted and sat next to a Dutch soldier.

"In some ways, the war for our independence began here," the Dutch soldier said.

"What do you mean?" John asked.

"After Don John of Austria defeated the Ottoman fleet at Lepanto, King Philip II appointed his half-brother to be the Governor General of the Seventeen Provinces of the Lowlands. Here in Arras, Don John convened an assembly that stated only the Catholic Religion would be allowed in any of the 17 Provinces. It was called the Union of Atrecht."

"Atrecht?"

"Dutch for Arras."

"But you are not Catholic?"

"No, we don't pray to dead saints, but directly to Jesus and God. We follow the teachings of Martin Luther and John Calvin," the Dutch soldier said. "In response to the Union of Atrecht, Prince William of Orange-Nassau and the Seven Provinces of the North held a meeting in Utrecht. In Holland, Zeeland, Utrecht, and four other provinces united to form the Union of Utrecht."

"The Seven United Provinces of the Netherlands?"

"Eventually, it moved its capital to Den Hague."

"Company!" Captain Joseph Duxbury commanded. "Line up!"

The company reassembled and prepared to storm the bridge. The ladders were kept ready, in reserve.

The Duke of Epernon signaled. The soldiers captured the first gate and the drawbridge.

"The Marshall?"

"The French will attack the far side."

Moving quickly and quietly, soldiers rushed the gate and crossed the bridge. Fear swept over the faces of the guards.

When Duxbury and John rushed toward the second gate, the guards dropped the portcullis.

"Bring up the petards!" the Duke ordered.

Gunners moved two small cannons into place.

"Fire!" the Duke yelled.

The French gunners discharged the petards, but the shots did not reach their intended targets. The cannonballs shot through the openings, exploding with minimal damage. They fired again, but caused only minimal damage.

"I hope the Marshall is more successful than we are." Captain Joseph Duxbury took his men out of musket range.

Gunfire sounded from the far side. The Marshall Biron scaled the walls and gained entry into the city.

Inside the citadel, the defenders held off French soldiers attempting to storm the gate in order to let Epernon's regiment inside.

"Will it open?" John asked.

Walloon soldiers rushed and fought off the few French fighters.

"I recognize the officer." The Dutch soldier pointed to a man with wavy dark hair. "It's Charles Bonaventure de Longueval, the Count of Bucquoy."

"In Arras?" Captain Duxbury said. "Cardinal Albert must have sent reinforcements."

Minutes later, the French soldiers fled the city, leaving many of their ladders behind.

Hours after darkness fell, after crossing the Authie River and carrying back the unused ladders, the French army reached the King at Vignacourt.

French Camp, Vignacourt, Picardy, France, 26th March *AD* 1597

THE DAY AFTER Marshall de Biron's failed attempt to capture Arras, King Henry IV convened his War Council.

"We fought our way to the main square, but the young Count of Bucquoy fought back," Marshall de Biron reported.

"The English failed us," the Catholic Duke of Eperonon said. "They should have captured the gate."

"Your cannons were too small to blast through," Sir Thomas Baskerville said. "A breach could not be made and the ladders were not ready."

"They will be next time," the Marshall said.

"We must consider the alternative," the Duke suggested.

"What's that?" the King asked.

"We must negotiate a truce, a peace with Spain."

"The Queen can help," Sir Baskerville interjected.

"We must not give up Calais," the Duke of Epernon said. "What good is it if the Queen possesses it instead of the Cardinal?"

After the meeting ended, Baskerville conferred with and confided in his captains at the English and Dutch section of the camp. "We have no friend but the Marshall."

"Biron speaks kindly of the Queen," Captain Duxbury said. "But the Duke of Epernon?"

Sir Thomas Baskerville grimaced and shook his head. "The Duke expelled the French Calvinists out of Metz and demolished their fine church."

Chapter 29 — Abandoned by His Friends

"Ah! I am assailed by so many needs. I know not which saint I should devote myself to, in order to leave this unhappy passage. All those of the [Reformed] Religion continue to demand things that I cannot give them, without dissolving the unity of my other subjects. . . .

My sorrow and pain increases so much I will no longer die of boredom!"
King Henry IV to Count de Schomberg at Chateau de Saumur
Vignacourt, Picardy, 31st March 1597
Translated from French by D.E.A.

The loss of Amiens has reversed all of my designs. Beginning in the month of April, I was going to assail the enemy . . .

This very great heartbreak deepens, because of the resistance of my friends to come to me
. . .

King Henry IV to the Earl of Essex
Vignacourt, Picardy, France 3rd April 1597
Translated from French by D.E.A.

Chateau de Saumur, Saumur on the Loire, France, Late March *AD* 1597

SPRING REACHED *CHATEAU de Saumur* in the scenic valley of the Loire River. Though the trees were still barren from the cold winter, a few birds chirped their morning song in late March. Alighting from branches attempting to bud, they took flight. Darting back and forth, they sped above peach trees not yet blossoming. They circled around parapet towers, circular turrets with conical caps that rose above the castle walls.

Monsieur Claude *de la* Tremoille accompanied a representative of the Duke *de* Bouillon across the castle's courtyard. Just over forty years of age, *Monsieur la* Tremoille was one of the most powerful Calvinists in France. Both adhered to the Reform doctrines of the Frenchman John Calvin, who had written <u>The Institutes of the Christian Religion</u> decades

238

earlier. The brown-bearded nobleman took off his hat at the steps of the main building.

Philippe *de* Mornay, the Governor of Saumur, greeted the two men. "Our meeting is about to begin." His brown beard came to a point inches below his chin.

Though the King had authorized the new assembly on his estates at Vendome near Orleans, the conference did not remain there. It moved further away from Catholic Paris to the safer location of Saumur.

Château de Saumur on the Loire River, France, circa 1845

Governor *Seigneur du* Plessis-Marley led the two men inside. *Seigneurs du* Plessis-Marley and *la* Tremoille took their seats at the front of the assembly.

The President of the Assembly reconvened the meeting. "Before the King's representative returns, is there any business you want to discuss?"

"Will the Duke of Mercoeur agree to make a treaty with us?" one delegate asked.

"If we let that last member of the Catholic League keep Brittany, we can keep all of our territories," another delegate said.

"Will the Duke of Mercoeur agree?"

"The Spanish garrison in Blavet has not been paid and may mutiny," the delegate said. "Mercoeur will agree to a truce."

"We need a leader," the first delegate said.

"Perhaps Henri *de la* Tour d'Auvergne, the Duke of Bouillon?"

"The Duke of Bouillon could be persuaded," his representative said.

"But what about King Henry?" another delegate asked. "Will his Majesty cede part of France?"

"Certainly not." The representative of King Henry IV stood at the door. He held up a letter and handed it to the secretary.

When the assembly quieted down, the secretary read aloud the king's request for aid.

"How can we help him?" *Seigneur du* Plessis asked. Not quite fifty years old, the important Protestant nobleman added, "We need assurances that our churches will be protected from the Catholic parliaments."

Philippe de Mornay, Seigneur du Plessis-Marly, Governor of Saumur

"Those assurances have not been granted." Claude *de la* Tremoille stood up. "Our assembly in Loudun ended last year with nothing, nothing but empty promises."

"We should obey the summons," another delegate said. "He is our King."

"We cannot help the king until he issues a new edict protecting the Reformed faith," *Seigneur du* Plessis said.

"What has the king done for us?" *Monsieur la* Tremoille asked. "Our churches are not protected, and we cannot worship in freedom. We risk arrest in Paris, in Rouen, and in many other cities. The Edict issued by King Henry III at Beaulieu twenty years ago does not help us. We have loyally supported Henry de Bourbon, but this new war is between Spanish and French Catholics. We gain nothing by putting our lives in danger."

"The King must issue an irrevocable edict. We deserve the same religious rights as the Catholics. Our tithes must go to the Reformed church, not Rome. We have an inalienable right to worship Jesus and the Father."

240

Royal Camp, Vignacourt, Picardy, 31st March *AD* 1597

THE KING AGAIN convened a War Council at his camp at Vignacourt, north of the Somme River, on the last day of March, 1597. In front of the King's large tent, a messenger reported to the Dutch, English, and French officers in attendance. "Yesterday, at Amiens, Girolamo Caraffa, the *Marquis* de Montenegro, tested our forward position, but four hundred French horsemen pushed him back before abruptly stopping the pursuit."

"My colonel stopped?" Marshall de Biron asked.

"Not a second too soon. Hidden behind bushes between the Abbey of Mary Magdalene and the Gate of Montrescu, Spanish infantry were waiting to ambush our counterattack."

As the messenger spoke, a second messenger arrived and dismounted near one of the fires. Waving a letter, he bowed. "Your Majesty, from the President of the Reformed Religion Assembly in Saumur."

"*Excellent,*" King Henry IV said. "We can use their help." He motioned for his secretary to read the letter.

The King's secretary began reading. "Give us a law under which we may be able to honor."

"And if I do?" King Henry IV asked.

The secretary continued, "It says, 'We will boldly answer to those of the Catholic faith. We will prove to be your most loyal subjects.'"

The stunned King waved for his secretary to stop. "Ever since I began my reign in Navarre, those soldiers have fought beside me." The perplexed sovereign paused. "Why do they abandon me in this time of my greatest need?"

After his War Council ended, the King told Sir Baskerville and the other English officers, "I cannot issue an edict now. My other subjects will not agree, and the parliaments in Paris, Rouen, and elsewhere will not register it. To push my Catholic subjects now? Many would run to the arms of my Spanish enemies." The bewildered monarch raised his eyes to heaven. "I know not which saint to pray to." He grimaced and scanned the members. "Will no one else come to my aid?"

"You must ask our queen," Sir Thomas Baskerville said.

Captain Duxbury and the other English officers uniformly assented.

"I must tell my sister the Queen the truth. My heart breaks because my friends do not come to me."

"And Calais?"

"If Queen Elizabeth captures it from the Cardinal, I will let her keep it as a cautionary town until we can pay her what France owes."

Doullens, Border of Picardy and Artois, Early April *AD* 1597

ONLY A FEW days later, in early April, 'Thunderbolt' Marshall *de* Biron again led the French army north. French infantrymen carried the same ladders they had failed to use a week earlier at Arras.

"Captain, will we attack Arras again?" John Smith asked.

"No, Doullens," Captain Duxbury said, "and this time the ladders will be ready."

"Unlike Arras."

Sir John Aldrich rode alongside Duxbury. "Marshall de Biron should have ordered a general assault. If he did, Arras could have been captured and ransomed, and the army paid."

"Wasn't Hernán Tello *de* Portocarrero the Governor of Doullens?" John asked.

"Yes, before he captured Amiens," Captain Duxbury spurred his horse forward.

The whole army followed the Authie River down to Doullens. It quickly surrounded the citadel.

Two hours before dawn, Marshall *de* Biron ordered the attack, and his French soldiers rushed to the walls. Spanish musketeers fired at the French. As the French leaned their ladders against the walls and started to climb, John pointed. "Our ladders are too short."

"The walls are higher than Arras," Captain Duxbury said.

Standing on the highest rung, the French soldiers strived to reach the top. They could not cross over.

Within minutes, the Marshall ordered, "Retire!"

His trumpets sounded retreat. Within an hour, the French army began its trek back to Amiens. As the English rearguard followed Marshall de Biron away from the Authie River, John peered northeast.

In the distance on the road from Arras, an enemy regiment of foot soldiers approached Doullens.

"Walloons?" John asked.

"Of the Count of Bucquoy," Captain Duxbury said. "The horsemen of Juan *de* Guzman protect his flanks."

Royal Camp, Vignacourt, Picardy, 3rd April *AD* 1597

WHEN THE FRENCH army reached the camp at Vignacourt, Marshall *de* Biron, with both his French and English officers, gathered in front of the King's tent.

Biron told the King the news. "Besides the Count of Bucquoy and his regiment of Walloons, Cardinal Albert sent Juan de Guzman with five companies of horse."

The dejected monarch could not believe what his ear heard. His countenance saddened. "Every effort to strike back at the Cardinal has failed."

"The other diversions have failed, too," an officer informed the *ad hoc* council.

"With so few cannons, we can besiege neither Doullens nor Arras," Marshall *de* Biron said.

"I have asked for thirty cannons. The Duke of Mayenne alone has promised six." The King pondered. "But with our enemy at Doullens, we must begin our siege of Amiens. Relief must not reach the occupiers."

Querrieu, Picardy, Early April *AD* 1597

AFTER BREAKING CAMP the next morning, King Henry IV led his army to the Hallue River valley. After marching several miles, the army reached the town of Querrieu, where a bridge spanned the river.

Several French companies marched southeast toward the fortified town of Corbie, but the bulk of the army followed the King southwest towards the capital of Picardy.

"We must begin our siege here, on the northern side of Amiens," the King said.

"To prevent relief from the Cardinal, our horse will be headquartered at the castle of Camon." Biron assigned several hundred French horsemen to the small castle, only two miles upriver from Amiens.

At the smaller Castle of Riviere, also on the Somme, the Marshall assigned several English companies to stand guard.

At the Abbey of Mary Magdalene in front of the Gate of Montrescu, the King directed, "We must build a strong fort at the Hermitage at this Abbey."

"We will never give up the Hermitage," Marshall de Biron said.

IN THE PRESENCE of the King, a little more than a mile downriver from Amiens, at the village of *Longpre-les-Amiens*, Marshall *de* Biron, told Sir Baskerville, "We need to build a half-moon and a pontoon bridge."

"Like Camon?"

"Relief must be stopped, both above and below the city."

"The King looks in pain," John Smith said.

"They say he suffers from gravel," Captain Duxbury informed his men.

"His doctors?"

"They'll start treatment for passing stones and begin the purge by bleeding the bad blood."

The King with his guard retired to the *Chateau de* Picquigny, further downriver.

Sir Baskerville told the English soldiers, "Someday, the Cardinal will attempt to break our siege of Amiens. If he does not break through at the Hermitage to reach the Gate of Montrescu, he must find another place to cross."

"At *Longpre-les-Amiens*?"

"This place is one of the easiest spots to cross the Somme." Sir Baskerville pointed to the south side of the river. "If the Cardinal enters the suburbs around the Abbey of St. John, he can throw relief into Amiens."

"You heard the General. The siege of Amiens starts here." Captain Duxbury pointed. "English soldiers, start digging."

The English horsemen dismounted and joined the companies of infantry. Alternating between spade and shovel, John Smith dug.

"We want a strong fort to protect this passage." Colonel Aldrich pointed to small boats tied side by side.

A few French soldiers crossed the river. Closer to Amiens, beautiful villas, gardens, and mansions surrounded the Abbey of St. John.

Longpres-les-Amiens, Picardy, 7ᵗʰ April *AD* 1597

ENGLISH CAPTAINS DISTRIBUTED the weekly pay to their men a couple of days later.

"It's not all we were promised," one soldier grumbled.

"Several captains have expended all of their credit," Captain Duxbury said.

English captains, always recruited from the ranks of the nobility, took personal responsibility for paying their men.

"Our general found a money changer in Saint Valery and pawned his silver plate and other items," the quartermaster added. "Because the French nobles have not approved the finance plan."

"What do you mean?" Captain Duxbury asked.

"Nobles in Paris refuse to lend any money, except in exchange for judgeships."

"They want to buy judgeships?"

"Yes, but the Constable, acting in the King's absence, rightly refuses."

"And the King?" John asked.

"The King plays the role of constable, here in Picardy."

John knew his captain referred to the highest military officer in France.

"But the King is short of bullets, cannons, and powder," Duxbury said. The French called the lead musket ball a *'boulette,'* meaning small ball.

John peered east, towards Amiens. "Unlike Governor Tello."

The Spanish governor retained dozens of cannons inside the walled city.

A fast horseman approached from the north. "The Cardinal sends a relief army!" He galloped toward Picquigny.

"Fall in, men!" Captain Duxbury said.

John mounted his horse.

Less than an hour later, the King rode at the head of his horsemen. The King held his reins with his right arm. His left arm was bandaged.

"Was the King wounded?" John asked.

"No," Captain Duxbury answered. "Lame from the bleeding."

The English companies followed him across barren fields. As the army advanced north, Marshall *de* Biron and the French regiments joined the growing force.

Biron sent scouts ahead.

After several hours, the scouts returned.

"The reports are false," the scout said. "The enemy cannot be found."

The King grimaced and held his arm. "Marshall *de* Biron, you must defend the Kingdom until my regimen is completed. I will stay several days at Beauvais." He paused. "I must return to Paris; the army must be paid."

Most English and French soldiers gestured their agreement.

Captain Duxbury, John Smith, and the other English soldiers returned to enlarge the fort at *Longpres-les-Amiens*.

While the fort took the shape of a half-moon, the King crossed the Somme, retrieved his belongings at Picquigny, and traveled south.

***Longpres-les-Amiens*, Picardy, Early April *AD* 1597**

THE FOLLOWING DAY, a French nobleman arrived. He crossed the pontoon bridge. "The *Madame la Marquise* nurses the King at Beauvais."

"She is not in Paris?" John asked.

"Gabrielle escaped Paris because her life was threatened," the Frenchman responded. "After the King departed for Picardy, many blamed Gabrielle for the disaster in Amiens; some even wanted her killed."

"They blamed Gabrielle?" John asked.

"Not all. Some priests blamed the other woman for 'lighting the wrath of heaven.'"

"What other woman?"

"The King's sister, Catherine *de* Bourbon."

"What did she do?"

"Madame Catherine held services for the Reformed Religion in the Tuileries Palace."

"I am not surprised," Captain Duxbury said.

"Not surprised?" John asked.

"Ever since Adam blamed Eve for giving him the forbidden fruit, some men have blamed women for their own shortfalls."

"Which woman do you blame for the fall of Amiens?" the Frenchman asked.

Captain Duxbury did not hesitate. "Neither."

The Frenchman continued, "In the King's absence, Gabrielle attended meetings in the Palace of the Archbishop."

John remembered seeing it when he was with the Scotsman David Hume of Godscroft the previous year. "Next to Notre Dame Cathedral?"

"*Oui*." The Frenchman told what he learned.

Palace of the Archbishop, Notre Dame Cathedral, Paris, Spring *AD* 1597

COURTIERS, FINANCIERS, AND nobles gathered inside the Palace of the Archbishop of Paris. The Constable finished his opening remarks. "The

246

Papal Legate Allesandro de Medicis has written to Cardinal Albert asking him why he attacked Amiens while simultaneously negotiating a truce between King Philip II and King Henry IV."

"Do you have more to add?" the Archbishop asked.

"We should allow *Madame la Marquise* de Monceaux to speak."

The Mistress of the King stepped into the center of the gathering. "You must help the King with both men and money."

The aging Constable stayed seated. "The financiers have money."

"The Assembly of Notables in Rouen is responsible for finding the solution," the Italian financier Zamet suggested.

"We could levy subsidies by admitting Jews into some of the great towns," a nobleman proposed.

"Jews?" another asked. "We cannot allow Jews back into France!"

"The Pope allows them in Rome."

"I have sold all of my diamonds and sent 50,000 crowns to the King," Gabrielle said. "Can you not match my gift?"

"The King could sell offices of justice."

"Sell justice?" Constable Montmorency displayed his displeasure.

"For the right price—"

"The Council of Finance should decide on the means to raise taxes."

"The people are so poor. How can they pay more?"

As the debate continued, tears flowed down Gabrielle's cheeks. "You must help."

"We will meet tomorrow." The Archbishop dismissed the council.

~ ~ ~

AFTER GABRIELLE d'ESTREES climbed into her carriage, the driver exited the quarters and drove it across the large square in front of Notre Dame Cathedral.

As they exited the square, a small mob moved toward her carriage. Her driver snapped his whip, and the carriage quickly veered away, toward *Pont du Change*.

Catholic partisans pursued the escaping carriage on foot. Repeating earlier chants, they shouted louder and louder. "Drown the whore! Hurl her over the bridge!"

Chapter 30 — Chief Gardener Ferhad *Agha*

And here I cannot but upon this occasion recount unto you a matter most worthy to be recorded in history, that happened in the lifetime of the last Emperor Murad III at Constantinople. And thus it was. That one of those youths, which are brought up in the Royal Seraglio [New/Topkapi Palace], having leisure & conveniency to read the Holy Bible, and thereupon by the meditation and working of the Grace of God, being brought to the knowledge of his error wherein he lived, caused himself to be carried into the presence of the Great Turk [Murad III], and there with a Christian courage and boldness told him, that if he would preserve his soul from the eternal fire and damnation, he must surely cease from following the impious superstition of Mohammed, and humble himself under the obedience of the True Law of Jesus Christ, the Savior and Redeemer of the whole world.

But he was for the same, as though he committed a most heinous and grievous offense, condemned publicly to be spitted alive upon a stake, where he iterated and repeated the same words to all the people, with such effectual terms and inflamed with the fiery spirits of the Holy Ghost, that many of the beholders feeling themselves inwards enkindled therewith, did burst forth in commiseration of his death, into very disdainful and despiteful speeches against Murad: and if the tumult had not been appeased at the first, by the Praetorian bands, certainly there had followed thereupon a most dangerous and perilous sedition.

The Ottoman of Lazaro Soranzo
Translated out of the Italian into English by Abraham Hartwell

Salon, Palace of Ibrahim *Pasha*, *Rajab* AH 1011 (Late Dec., *AD* 1602)

"DISGUISED SOLDIERS SPILLED nuts and deceived the French guards?" Aisha asked.

"And baskets of apples, too" her English slave added. "Like the Greeks, who hid inside the Trojan Horse at Troy, Spanish soldiers hid beneath the wood at Amiens and attacked the guards."

Aisha remembered hearing about Troy from her father, who immersed himself in history. Called 'Truva' in Turkish, the ruins were located in Asia Minor, south of the Dardanelles in northwest Anatolia. Ottoman craftsmen used stones from those ruins to build palaces in *Stamboul*. "Parisians yelled 'kill the whore'? They wanted to hurl Gabrielle over the bridge?"

Aisha's friend Filiz continued translating her questions from Turkish into French.

"Even though King Henry IV's mistress sold her diamonds for 50,000 crowns to recover Amiens," young *Capitano* John Smith responded, "Catholic partisans threatened to drown her."

"The Parisians tried to kill her, but did she escape?" Aisha asked

"*Oui*, Gabrielle d'Estrées eventually joined the French King at Amiens, but her troubles did not end there."

"No?"

"After the King's mistress arrived at his camp, Marshall *de* Biron voiced his opinion aloud. 'Just as the presence of Venus animated the valor of Mars, Gabrielle animates the bravery of King Henry.'"

"I know Venus is the goddess of love, but Mars?" Aisha asked.

"The Greek god of war."

"The Marshall?" Aisha thought aloud. "So outspoken?"

"Yes, the 'Thunderbolt' Marshall of France did not hold his tongue."

Aisha motioned for her English slave to stop.

Her servant stood at the door. "Lady Aisha, your *shish kebab* is marinated."

"My friends, you will excuse me." Aisha rose and sauntered straightway to the kitchen. The lamb appeared moist, the fire ready, she told the chef. "Skewer it. Don't let it touch the grill."

"Never."

After the cook placed the first skewers above the charcoal, Aisha returned across the garden. Servants carrying silver trays filled with the appetizers followed her. She told Filiz and John. "The *shish kebab* should be ready in minutes."

Aisha extended her hands, and one of the servant girls immediately stepped forward with a porcelain vase. She poured water over them. Another servant girl captured the excess water in a basin, and a third handed her a cotton towel. After Filiz finished washing her hands, Aisha told John, "You wash, too."

Before they had finished the assortment of *meze*, consisting of white cheese and melon, the head servant stepped forward. "Shall I bring in the next course?"

"Yes, yes, bring it in," Aisha urged.

The servants brought in more plates and a platter.

"The feast at the *Hotel de Montmorency* sounded delicious," Aisha said. "The two sturgeon?"

"It must be like the fish served in the New Palace," Filiz said.

"It makes me hungry just thinking about it."

The servants soon brought in the third course. The aroma of the sizzling *shish kebab* filled the room.

"It smells delicious." Filiz dabbed her lips with a napkin.

John picked up the skewer of roasted lamb. "What's this called?"

"*Shish kebab.*"

"*Shish kebab?*" John repeated the Turkish words.

"*Shish* means skewer," Filiz said. "*Kebab* means roasted. The lamb must be fully roasted, since Muslims are forbidden to eat blood."

"And this?" John pointed to a side dish.

"*Cacik*, made with yogurt and chopped cucumber, spiced with a dash of mint."

"*Yogurt?*"

Filiz translated the word into French. "*Yogurt* means 'thicken'."

After the servants offered flat *pide* bread to the guests, John ate the *shish kebab*. "Delicious."

"My own recipe," Aisha said. "I marinated it in olive oil seasoned with lemon juice."

"So tender."

"But not so sweet?" Aisha smiled as John appeared to savor every bite.

"Tender and tasty."

Glad he enjoyed it, Aisha watched John and her lovely friend eat their fill.

"Aisha, this is as good as anything served in the sultan's kitchen—" Filiz peered out the window. "Time has gotten away."

"Yes, the hours have flown." Aisha dabbed her lips. "Filiz, would you mind returning in a few days?"

"To continue the story? No, you are my friend."

"I shall send my carriage for you."

The French translator put on her jacket. "John, I must bid you adieu."

As Filiz wrapped her shawl about her shoulder, John rose. *"Au revoir."*

"Au Revoir."

"Capitano, our conversation will resume when Filiz returns." Aisha escorted her friend and her attendants out of her Salon and into the garden. She motioned to the Overseer guarding the door. "You may take the slave back to his quarters."

The Black eunuch grunted and beckoned John. "Come with me."

Third Courtyard, New Palace, *Stamboul*

WHITE EUNUCHS WAITED outside the apartment of Gazanfer *Agha*, the *Capi Agha* or Keeper of the Gate. The Chief White Eunuch maintained his apartment immediately adjacent to the Gate of Justice, Majesty, and Felicity—the *Sublime Porte*. He alone decided who entered the Third Courtyard and the inner palace. He knew that in the morning, the Sultan enjoyed going to his library.

Taking his closest aide, the Chief White Eunuch joined his loyal entourage, ready to address every need and attentive to every whim. They began to cross the Third Courtyard. Impeccably maintained and normally silent, this marble courtyard had fountains, as well as pavilions and chambers.

The *ich-oglans,* who resided in common rooms, had already begun their morning routines in their four schools. Those rejected as *ich-oglans* or interior youths would join the ranks of the *acemi-oglan.* Donning tall, pointed hats, the *acemi-oglan* would, after learning a trade, become *janissaries,* the foot-soldiers of the empire.

The forty *ich-oglans* selected for the Fourth School advanced to the highest ranks of the Ottoman Empire. White eunuchs tested the young men, ensuring no lingering influence from their Christian parents remained. The chosen of the chosen, no one questioned their loyalty. Dressed in satin and gold, they wore robes as colorful as the one Jacob gave to his youngest son Joseph.

The Chief White Eunuch took only a few steps before he halted his entourage in front of the Throne Room, where the Sultan granted audiences to foreign ambassadors or listened to reports and petitions from important *pashas.* Gazanfer *Agha* turned to one of his closest aides. "Bring the poem I picked up at my madrasa. I wanted to present it to the Sultan this morning."

"I know where it is. I saw it on the bookshelf by your desk." The trusted White eunuch hurried back to the apartment.

Gazanfer *Agha* glanced inside the Throne Room, the separate building with its gold and azure ceiling. Covered in red cloth and inlaid with mother-of-pearl, the Ottoman throne stood beneath an overhanging canopy erected at the start of Mehmet III's reign. Only a few weeks earlier, with the French Ambassador but not the English ambassador in attendance, the New Palace hosted a banquet of twenty-five courses for the outgoing and incoming Venetian ambassadors, who presented gifts. Escorted by the arm between pairs of eunuch guards, the two Venetian ambassadors entered the Throne Room and approached the Sultan on bended knee. They kissed the Sultan's robe before exiting the same way they had entered, never turning their backs.

A much earlier incident from the time of Sultan Murad III flashed across Gazanfer's mind. One of the forty *ich-oglans* who had advanced to the Fourth *oda* or school gained full access to the palace library. The young man, having read the Holy Bible, the scriptures of the Old and New Testaments, persuaded Gazanfer *Agha* to bring him into the sultan's presence. The young man spoke boldly to Sultan Murad III:

If you want to preserve your soul from eternal fire and damnation, you must surely cease from following the superstitions of Mohammed. You must humble yourself under the obedience of the True Law of Jesus Christ, the Savior and Redeemer of the whole world.

Eunuch guards seized the young man and would have immediately beheaded him, but the Sultan decided to make a public display instead. The next day, he brought him to the front of the Gate of Felicity. A great crowd gathered in the Second Courtyard, and the young man, standing in front of that fair porch, spoke as boldly as he had to the Sultan. The anguished Sultan covered his ears and motioned his judgment.

The young man, who was spitted alive on the stake, died, but the turmoil grew louder and louder. Many in the crowd had been convicted of their sins and repented. The people openly spoke against the Sultan's cruelty and may have rioted. The palace guards, the *peichs* or footmen, and the *acemi-oglan*—the novice youths who would later become *janissaries*—forcibly dispersed the crowds.

"Capi Agha, I found the poem." The White eunuch who had been sent to the apartment returned, but the Chief White Eunuch refused the scroll.

"Keep it. You can present the poem to the Sultan at his library." The Chief White Eunuch led his cohorts across the paved courtyard, past the small mosque serving the inner palace, and into a smaller, side courtyard. To their right stood the entrance to the Imperial Harem, where White eunuchs were not allowed—only women and Black eunuchs. To their left stood the two-story apartments of the Chief Black Eunuch, and straight ahead was the Sultan's Winter Quarters.

Unlike his predecessors, the Chief White Eunuch also retained his previous position as *Oda Bashi* or Chief of the Privy Chamber. Within the hierarchy of the inner palace, no one had ever been more powerful than Gazanfer *Agha.* To maintain both positions, he had learned to be discreet in matters of state as well as personal affairs.

"Capi Agha." The Chief Black Eunuch intercepted the Chief White Eunuch.

"What is it, *Kizlar Agha Osman?"*

"The Sultan decided to take a short, morning walk."

"Is he alone?"

"None of the women are with him."

"I will find him." The Chief White Eunuch turned to his aide. "Wait for us in the Sultan's Library." He turned back to the Chief Black Eunuch. "Tell Safiye *Valide Sultana,* I shall present the newest poem to her son."

"Yes, her morning audience is about to start." Osman *Kizlar Agha* used his key, opened the door, and entered the Imperial Harem.

Outside Porticos, Sultan's Summer Quarters, New [Topkapi] Palace

THE CHIEF WHITE Eunuch, meanwhile, walked through the Sultan's Winter Quarters and beneath the porticos of the Summer Palace. He spied the *Bostanji Bashi* mounted on his horse near a fountain fed by the large pool. Ferhad *Agha* oversaw all of the palace guards, as well as the novice youth working in the gardens and tending the fountains. After he directed his *acemi-oglan* to trim the trees and rake up dead leaves covering the walkway leading down to Topkapi Gate, he spurred his small horse up the hill, past a marble pillar, the ancient Column of the Goths, commemorating the Roman victory over their enemies.

"*Bostanji Bashi* Ferhad," Gazanfer *Agha* said. *Bostan-ji* meant 'Gardener,' while *Bashi* meant 'Chief.'

"You must be looking for the Sultan," Ferhad *Agha* replied. "I will escort you to the kiosk."

The standalone kiosk overlooked the Golden Horn and the Sea of Marmara. Merchant ships and galleys plied the waters--some toward the Black Sea and some to the White or Mediterranean Sea. Beyond the water, the rocky shores and rolling hills of Asia Minor seemed touchable.

"I saw that the last of the glass in the Throne Room has been replaced," Gazanfer mentioned. After the two Venetian Ambassadors met Sultan Mehmet III, the Venetian merchant ship *Martinella*, anchored in the harbor, had fired a salute. Shockwaves from its cannons shook the Throne Room, breaking panes of glass and causing the plaster to fall. The *acemi oglan* rushed to the scene and confronted the Venetian ambassadors, demanding they turn over *Martinella's* captain, so he could be properly punished.

"After I interceded with the ambassadors, the Venetians promised to pay for the repairs." *Bostanji Bashi* Ferhad *Agha* said.

Bostangi Bashi (Chief Gardener)

"Yes, the repairs were finished quickly," Gazanfer said.

"The glaziers and the plasterers completed their tasks."

"Even better than before. And you? Did you receive compensation?"

"Yes, the Venetians delivered the Italian sporting dogs they had promised." Ferhad *Agha* had suggested such a present might assuage the damage. "I have not yet had the opportunity to use them." He pointed down one of the paths where several *acemi oglans* trained the dogs and turned back to Gazanfer *Agha*. "But what is wrong?"

"The thought crossed my mind of what happened the previous time the glass broke."

"You mean at the kiosk?" The *Bostanji Bashi* gestured in the direction of the lower gardens. Not far from the well-manned gate at the tip of the peninsula, Mehmet III's father often enjoyed

254

a panoramic view of the Golden Horn and the Sea of Marmara.

"I was thinking about the time nearly eight years ago, when Sultan Murad III sat in that kiosk and listened to his band playing music," Gazanfer *Agha* said. "When two Egyptian galleys fired a salute, the shockwaves, like those from the Venetian cannons, shattered glass. Sultan Murad III uttered, 'In my younger days, a whole fleet could fire a salute and not cause any damage.'"

"I remember the story. Broken pieces from the kiosk's ceiling lay all about him."

"The distressed sultan realized his reign had come to an end. He said, 'I see the fate of the kiosk as a reflection of my own life.' Sultan Murad III died that very night." Gazanfer whispered, "I hope the shattered glass from the Venetian ship does not portend the end of the reign of my current master any time soon."

"Or anyone else close to him." The *Bostanji Bashi* looked down at Gazanfer *Agha*.

"Remember, do not speak of the *Celali* Rebellion in Anatolia to the Sultan."

"I shall not." Chief Gardener Ferhad *Agha* dismounted outside a gate leading to an enclosed courtyard. Younger gardeners harvested clusters of grapes; others tended vines climbing wood trellises and stone walls.

The two walked by a pleasant pond, well-stocked with tropical fish outside the adjoining pavilion. Gazanfer *Agha* knew deep tones from a pipe organ would soon emanate without anyone touching the keys. Connected to a clock, it would play at the same time every day. The same month that Queen Elizabeth of England had delivered a white carriage to Safiye *Valide Sultana*, she also gifted this fancy organ to Sultan Mehmet III.

Chapter 31 Garden Organ & Palace Poem

The Grand Seigneur [Sultan Mehmet III], being seated in his Chair of Estate, commanded silence. All being quiet, and no noise at all, the present [the organ from Queen Elizabeth of England] began to salute the Grand Seigneur; for when I [Thomas Dallam] left I did allow a quarter of an hour for his coming thither. First, the clock struck 22; then the chime of 16 bells went off, and played a song of four parts. That being done, two personages, which stood upon two corners of the second story, holding two silver trumpets in their hands, did lift them to their heads, and sounded a tantara [a flourish like a Spanish drumbeat]. Then the music went off, and the organ played a song of five parts, twice over. In the top of the organ, being 16 foot high, did stand a holly bush full of black birds and thrushes, which at the end of the music did sing and shake their wings . . .

In the meantime, the Kapi-Agha [Gazanfer Agha], being a wise man, and doubted whether I had so appointed it or no, for he knew it [the organ] would go of itself but four times in 24 hours . . .
Diary of Thomas Dallam, 25th September 1599

Kiosk, Imperial Gardens, New Palace, *Rajab AH* 1011 (Dec. *AD* 1602)

"YOUR MAJESTY." CHIEF White Eunuch Gazanfer *Agha* bowed at the entrance of the double pavilion. The back of a sixteen-foot high organ abutted the common wall made of stone. Two rows of marble columns also supported the tall ceiling. "*Kizlar Agha* Osman told me I would find you in the Gardens."

Sultan Mehmet III smiled when he recognized his most trusted servant. "I decided to take a walk." The Sultan brought the amber mouthpiece of his Turkish water pipe to his lips and motioned for Gazanfer to approach him, seated in his chair.

Gazanfer *Agha* eased himself across the Persian carpets and noticed his reflection shining in the polished porphyry. Though the stone wall touched the ceiling, the other three walls did not—only reaching halfway up. If the weather turned stormy or inclement, thick cotton curtains could be lowered from the ceiling, protecting the fancy organ and carpets.

"Come, join me." The Sultan exhaled smoke out of the sides of his mouth and both nostrils. "It has been days since I saw the organ play."

A pleasant breeze dissipated the rising smoke.

"I believe the clock has been fixed." The Chief White Eunuch pointed to a small clock built inside the organ. Though the organ played automatically four times each day, the clock had slowed in recent weeks. "*Kaimakam* Hasan *the Clockmaker* recommended the best clockmaker in *Stamboul,* who adjusted it last week."

The Chief White Eunuch drew closer to the Sultan, even though it was forbidden for anyone to touch him. If anyone—even accidentally—did touch the Ottoman ruler, it would mean certain death. Gazanfer alone was exempted. Elbow to elbow, his robe touched the throne. The Sultan and the eunuch waited in silence as the pendulum swung back and forth. The clock softly ticktocked, ticktocked.

The minute hand sprang forward to the top of the hour. The organ began to play in exactly the same way it had three years earlier, when the Englishman Thomas Dallam had set it up.

The Chief White Eunuch remembered the Sultan's reaction the first time he heard it play. Queen Elizabeth of England had sent the organ to him as a present on the *Hector,* a merchant ship. After spending months— from winter to summer—at sea, it badly needed repair. The cold and heat of the long journey inside the hold had taken its toll. The wood had separated; the glue no longer held it together. Thomas Dallam and three of his English compatriots unloaded it and set it up outside the English ambassador's residence in Galata, across the Golden Horn. After several weeks, the Chief White Eunuch went there and saw that it had been repaired.

At the end of that summer, the Sultan took his caique, or royal barge, to spend a month with his mother at another palace six miles across the water. Mr. Dallam, meanwhile, brought the organ in pieces through Topkapi Gate at the waters' edge, then up the hill, and through the garden. He assembled the organ in this kiosk, the most stately of any pavilion of the New Palace. It took a few more weeks to reset the organ, but before Dallam had a chance to test it, Sultan Mehmet returned from the summer palace. The Sultan disembarked from his golden caique and made his way up through the garden at the beginning of that autumn.

Then, like now, the Sultan sat in his chair, and the clock struck ten. The bells chimed, and miniature trumpets blared. Three years ago, the Sultan waited 15 minutes to hear it again, and when the clock struck and rang but once, Gazanfer *Agha* wisely pulled the pin that Thomas Dallam had shown him. The organ keys again moved by themselves, and the musical sequence played out as before. Immensely happy, the Sultan had pulled out a fistful of gold coins, dropping many into Mister Dallam's cupped hands.

Just like then, the organ finished its rendition. At the end, the black birds and thrushes in the bushes atop the organ sang and flapped their wings.

The Sultan seemed pleased with the performance, and the Chief White Eunuch told him, "There was something I wanted to show you."

"What is it?'

"A surprise, in your library."

Queen's Gate, Second Courtyard, New [Topkapi] Palace, *Stamboul*

OUTSIDE THE QUEEN'S Gate, the Chief Black Eunuch conferred with the *Kaimakam*. Called *Saatçi* Hasan, meaning Hasan *the Clockmaker*, the *Kaimakam* chaired the Divan or Council since the Grand Vizier remained absent in Belgrade. "I relayed the concerns about the growing unrest in *Stamboul*. I told the Sultan's Mother, 'The *sipahis* blame Ali *Agha* for the turmoil in Ankara and Anatolia.'"

"How did Safiye *Valide Sultana* respond?" the *Kaimakam* Hasan *the Clockmaker* asked.

"To their demand that Ali *Agha* be replaced as leader of the *janissaries*?" *Kizlar Agha* Osman asked. Several *janissary* officers congregated near the gate leading to the First Courtyard, but the *Agha* was not with them.

"Yes."

"The *Valide Sultana* said Ali *Agha* could not be blamed for the turmoil, since he spent this past year traveling back and forth to the Danube." The Chief Black Eunuch knew Ali *Agha* had negotiated the marriage of the Grand Vizier to Aisha, Sister of the Sultan. "I told Safiye *Valide Sultana*, 'The *sipahis* do not care. They are adamant and will not relent.'"

"Before we can address the issue, we must find another."

"Perhaps the *Bostangi Bashi*?"

"Ferhad *Agha* was with the Sultan in the garden, but I will mention it to the Chief White Eunuch when I find him." The Chief Black Eunuch was indebted to the Chief White Eunuch for promoting him. The previous Chief Black Eunuch, whose name was inscribed inside the Gate of Audience behind him, died.

Hasan *the Clockmaker* took his seat between two military judges and reconvened the Council of turbaned viziers. Scribes seated at low tables meticulously wrote down the proceedings and drafted the pending orders. *Sipahi* officers and other *pashas* stood near the pillars supporting the open building. Other petitioners waited on the lawn and beneath the porticos surrounding the Second Courtyard.

"Guzelce Mahmud *Pasha*, you may approach."

"In the time since I was appointed to replace Khosru *Pasha* as Ottoman Commander in Anatolia last week, I have made a list of materials I will need to conduct my upcoming campaign."

Hasan *the Clockmaker* perused the list and shared it with the other viziers. "It seems very thorough."

"The task is large, but the sooner supplies can be sent to the storehouses of Bursa in Anatolia, the sooner I can suppress the rebellion by Hasan *the Fool!*"

The *Kaimakam* handed the list to the Treasurer. "Are there funds?"

The treasurer looked at it. "Enough for gunpowder and field cannons."

"Pay for the essentials."

The two military judges and all of the viziers agreed. A scribe, kneeling before his low desk, penned the order.

"That is all for now," *Kaimakam* Hasan *the Clockmaker* said, dismissing the Council. "After our midday meal, I will announce the remaining decisions."

Kizlar Agha Osman stopped inside the Queen's Gate and told the head of his guard, a strong, Black eunuch, "If you see Ali *Agha*, tell him that the Chief White Eunuch awaits him in the Sultan's Library."

Sultan's Library, New Palace

INSIDE HIS DOMED reading room, the library attached to his personal quarters, Sultan Mehmet III settled into his cushioned chair. Two bookcases, each with a handful of illustrated books laid flat on the shelves, including histories of the Ottoman Empire, were read to the princes under the guidance of the Chief Black Eunuch. The Chief White Eunuch noticed the *Kaimakam* approaching and stepped away from one of the tall bookcases. "Is the Council meeting finished?"

"No, but I have orders for the Sultan to approve," Hasan *the Clockmaker* said.

"Orders for what?"

"To resupply Bursa." The *Kaimakam* showed the prepared papers in the doorway.

"Yes, we talked about Guzelce Mahmud *Pasha's* new campaign. The *sipahis* must be appeased," the Chief White Eunuch whispered. "Funds from the Third Treasury can be used." The Chief White Eunuch stepped in front of the bookcase and addressed the Sultan. "Before we get started, the *Kaimakam* has today's orders for you to sign."

"Yes, yes."

The Sultan seemed impatient, so the Chief White Eunuch motioned for one of the four White eunuchs standing next to the other bookcase to retrieve the *Tughra,* the imperial seal engraved with Mehmet's fancy signature. The drawer was opened, and the Chief White Eunuch handed it to the Sultan. As soon as the Sultan stamped the decree, the Chief White Eunuch gave the papers to the *Kaimakam,* who, always facing the Sultan, stepped backwards until he moved out of sight.

Hoping his brother-in-law would arrive, the Chief White Eunuch delayed revealing the surprise. Nearly a decade earlier, after his sister Beatrice had arrived from Venice to escape a bad second marriage, Gazanfer *Agha* arranged for her to marry his protege, Ali *Agha*. He wanted Ali to deliver the poem he had received from the Headmaster of his madrasa by the Valens Aqueduct.

Court jesters, meanwhile, distracted the Sultan on the other side of the circular fountain. The Chief White Eunuch stood with his hands folded next to a bookcase. Stacked flat on the shelves, the books included many that Gazanfer *Agha* had personally commissioned—translations of stories from Arabic and Persian. The courts of Selim II and Murad III often wrote verses in Persian, but Sultan Mehmet III preferred simpler tales written in Turkish. The translated books contained illustrated stories of chivalry and love, as well as a Persian tale of a grocer and a mouse.

The jesters and dwarfs finished their routine and started a second one when the Chief White Eunuch spied his brother-in-law standing in the doorway. "Ali *Agha,* I hoped you would arrive. You suggested the collection of short stories and poems."

The Sultan stopped the routine. "Where is my surprise?"

"I will let Ali *Agha* present it," Gazanfer *Agha* said.

Ali *Agha* bowed and approached the Sultan's chair. He kissed the hem of the Sultan's long robe before stepping back. "We have a poem we want to share with you."

"A poem?"

"Yes, one penned by the Headmaster of Gazanfer *Agha* Complex." Ali *Agha* asked, "Would you like for one of us to read it?"

Deaf mutes along one wall used sign language and repeated the question silently to one another.

"Let me see." The Sultan took the scroll. Next to him, a midget with a serious countenance leaned out from behind the throne. Standing as tall as he could, the dwarf peered over the Sultan's elbow. The Sultan finished reading the first page and smiled. "This starts well."

"Without Ali's help, the poem would not have been written." The Chief White Eunuch retrieved the scroll. "He commissioned it, so I thought he should have the privilege of presenting it. If you would like, the official reader can recite the poem."

"That would please me immensely."

As the Chief White Eunuch returned to his formal position. He stood perfectly still and folded his hands in front of him. The other White eunuchs mimicked their master. Even the dwarfs and jesters on the other side of the round fountain kept perfectly quiet.

The official had a good voice and read the whole poem, a simple tale dedicated to the Sultan himself. When he finished, the room remained quiet for a long time. All waited for the Sultan to render his final judgement.

"This pleases me immensely," Sultan Mehmet III said.

"Excellent," the Chief White Eunuch said. "That is the last piece for the new Collection of Poems."

"I cannot wait," Sultan Mehmet III said.

Ali *Agha* bowed. "The only items that remain to be done are the illustrations."

"Excellent, I look forward to its completion. When will I be able to see the whole book?"

"The illustrators take much time to make it right. The collection should be ready to be bound in perhaps a year."

"Keep me abreast of the progress." The Sultan rose from his throne. "I believe it is time for my next meal."

"It shall be prepared at once." The Chief White Eunuch bowed and sent one of the White eunuchs by the other bookcase to tell the cooks in the Sultan's kitchen. He knew the Sultan would be hungry, so he had arranged for the delivery of the appetizers.

The Sultan, meanwhile, turned to the court reader, "Please find the *Book of Festival* or read me the translation of those Persian tales again."

"The *Book of Festivals*."

As the reader opened the illustrated book of the events surrounding the Sultan's circumcision, runners from the kitchen stood at the door. They relayed the *mezes* or appetizers for the Sultan's next meal.

While the Sultan nibbled from his golden platter and everyone else listened to and viewed the illustrations from the *Book of Festivals*, Gazanfer *Agha* caught up with his brother-in-law exiting through the door.

In the small courtyard of the palace mosque, Gazanfer broke the news. "I thought you should know. There are rumors the *sipahis* want to take your title."

"As *Agha* of the *Janissaries*?"

"Yes, but do not worry. You need not curry the Sultan's favor. He loves me."

Chapter 32 — Shut inside Kutahya

For carrots and cabbages Kutahya beats the world . . . The carrots are three times the size of our best; and I know not by what number to multiply in order to express the superiority of their flavor. The cabbages are still more remarkable . . .

Although we soon found that the boys were lively enough, the people of Kutahya do not enjoy the reputation of being quick and clever. Halil thought them all very slow and stupid, for he could hardly get an answer from any of them, or any intelligible direction to the shops in the bazaars, or any kind of information. He fairly lost his patience—a difficult thing for Halil to lose—"What!" said he, "are there no men here?" "Men!" said a roguish Greek: "art thou looking for men? Dost not know that not men but cabbage grow at Kutahya? It is easy to see that thou art a stranger, and comest from afar off."
Turkey and Its Destiny, Vol. I by Charles MacFarlane, Esq.

Rebel Camp, Porsuk River, Anatolia, Eve, Rajab *AH* 1011 (Dec. *AD* 1602)

AT THE RIVER'S edge, Hasan the *Fool* finalized his plans to attack the important Ottoman fortress of Kutahya, further up the Porsuk River, a tributary of the Sakarya, one of the main rivers of Anatolia. The Sakarya flowed north before emptying into the Black Sea. Led by *Deli* Hasan *Pasha*, the rebel army, forty thousand strong, had journeyed from Ankara, a little more than one hundred fifty miles to the east. After passing Eskisehir, meaning old city, the rebel army continued its journey southwest up the narrowing Porsuk River valley.

The *janissaries* of Aleppo and Damascus might have impeded the rebels' progress, but earlier in the year, when the *janissary* leader from Damascus had visited Aleppo, he was murdered. The *janissaries* from Damascus marched to Aleppo. They wanted to exact justice from the five officers inside Aleppo, who were most responsible. When those five were not delivered, the *janissaries* from Damascus besieged Aleppo throughout the spring. After intervention from *Stamboul*, the besiegers retired to their own quarters in Damascus. They had not been seen in the field since the summer.

Hasan knew his nickname, *Deli*, meant 'Fool,' but the former Governor of Baghdad did not consider himself one. He wanted his fighters fully ready. Their trek had been easy and swift, but they would need to be fully rested for the upcoming fight. He assigned sections for each company in the encampment. His rebel fighters included Kurds, Turkomans, as well as *firaris*, the so-called runaways of Mezo-Kerezstes.

Turkish "Deli" or "Fool" Rider

All leaned their lances against nearby trees. Their saddles would become their pillows. Each brought his own provisions—biscuits, dried flesh, and rice.

The camp also included three large sections of Crimean-Tartars, who had already lit their campfires. Several small Tartar horses had already been slaughtered and gutted. Campfires crackled, and spits next to them turned slowly.

"Tell us, how did your brother *Scrivano* start the rebellion?" the eldest of the three Tartar brothers asked.

"When Sultan Murad III still reigned in *Stamboul*, he appointed a former *cavus* or sergeant to be *Sanjak* of Safed," *Deli* Hasan *Pasha* said.

"Safed?" the youngest Tartar brother asked.

"Located in what the Jews call the Land of Naphtali, north of the Sea of Galilee. Shem, the son of Noah, founded this ancient town. The *Sanjak* of Safed hired my brother, Abdul-Halim, to protect the nearby trade routes. My brother commanded a *segban* of three hundred musketeers."

"What happened?"

"Safed is part of the territory governed by the *Beylerbey* of Damascus. When the Sultan appointed someone new to rule Safed, my brother *Scrivano* persuaded his patron to fight the *Beylerbey* of Damascus."

The section of the camp assigned to those three hundred paid mercenaries, the *segban* loyal to his brother, stood nearby.

"Did *Kara Yazici* win?"

Kara Yazici meant 'Black Scribe' in Turkish and *Scrivano Nero* in Italian.

"No, we were forced to flee," the *segban* leader said. "But he soon offered our services to the Druse in Lebanon facing similar circumstances. Later, we relocated to the eastern part of Asia Minor. Safiye *Valide Sultana* wanted more taxes to fund her 'New Mosque.' The capital became richer, while the provinces became poorer."

Like the earlier *Celali* rebellions, oppressive taxation by the Sultan caused much dissatisfaction.

"After my brother declared himself an independent prince at Urfa, Sultan Mehmet III sent the *Beylerbey* of Karaman to suppress him." *Deli* Hasan *Pasha* pointed southeast, in the direction of the large province, the *Vilayet* of Karaman.

"But that *Beylerbey* did not succeed?"

"No, to the contrary. Instead of fighting my brother, this *Beylerbey* of Karaman changed sides and joined forces with us. About that time, my brother traced our lineage back to the Prophet Mohammed. He declared himself to be the new Caliph, the Successor to the Prophet. This Ottoman governor became his new Grand Vizier."

Rebel Leader Kara Yazici (Scrivano, or Black Scribe)

"But this *Beylerbey* of Karaman decided to reconcile with the *Sublime Porte*," the *segban* leader said. "He was recalled to *Stamboul*."

"An unfortunate choice for him," *Deli* Hasan *Pasha* added.

"Yes, the *Beylerbey* of Karaman lost both his hands and feet at the *Divan* before he was impaled on Woodgate."

"But your brother kept Karaman, and the rebellion grew."

"Over the past two years, other disgruntled townsmen and peasants joined the rebellion to avoid paying higher taxes levied to support the European war against the Holy Roman Empire. More and more men joined our cause." *Deli* Hasan *Pasha* looked at his officers. "Erzurum, Sivas, and the other towns of Asia Minor now fight with us against the tyranny of *Stamboul*."

"And when your brother *Scrivano* succumbed to death last winter, you took charge," the Tartar commander said.

"We have had much success." Hasan *the Fool* acknowledged the commanders. "I have captured Ankara and overthrown Ottoman power in Asia. Besides Karaman, these dominions undivided now belong to me." He looked north in the direction of the Black Sea. "Salamet Giray, when we take *Stamboul*, you shall become *Khan* of the Crimean Tartars."

"Tomorrow, we will fight hard for you," the three Tartar brothers all agreed.

Hasan *the Fool* turned to the leader of the *firaris*, the runaways of Mezo-Kerezstes. That battle in Hungary took place in October 1596. "What is the real reason you joined my brother?" He wanted to know the true motives of those thousands of disaffected *sipahis*.

"We do not like the Sultan," the leader of the runaways answered. "Six years ago, we joined Sultan Mehmet III and his Grand Vizier *Damat* Ibrahim *Pasha*. After Ottoman forces captured an important castle in northern Hungary, Sultan Mehmet III gained the title of 'Conqueror of Eger.'"

"How did the battle unfold?" *Deli* Hasan *Pasha* asked.

"In the fields of Mezo-Kerezstes in northern Hungary, Archduke Maximillian and the armies of the Holy Roman Empire finally arrived. Soon, Prince Sigismund Bathory of Transylvania and Michael *the Brave* from Wallachia joined him. When they charged us, they pushed our Asiatic cavalry us off the field—all the way past the Sultan's tent."

"The Sultan wanted to run, too?"

"Yes, Sultan Mehmet III was afraid and wanted to retreat. He sat atop his camel and watched from a distance as the enemy started to plunder his abandoned riches. Only the reserve riders of Cigala Zade Sinan *Pasha* remained with him, but when the Sultan's tutor pointed to the green Standard of the Prophet, he persuaded the Sultan to stay."

"What happened?" *Deli* Hasan *Pasha* accepted a bowl of rice from a cook.

"The infidels thought they had won, but the cooks and the stable hands still in the camp began to fight with their knives. When Cigala Sinan *Pasha* heard the commotion, he sent in the reserves. The battle quickly turned."

"Many Tartar warriors pursued the enemy, even to their gates," Salamet Giray added.

"Tens of thousands of the enemy were killed," the runaway leader said, "and afterwards, Sultan Mehmet III promoted Cigala Zade Sinan *Pasha* as his Grand Vizier."

"In place of *Damat* Ibrahim *Pasha*?" *Deli* Hasan *Pasha* asked. "That was not good for you."

"No. After the victory, Cigala Zade Sinan *Pasha*, blaming us for the early stages of the battle, calling us 'runaways.' The new Grand Vizier pursued us and captured many of our compatriots."

"Their punishment?"

"Beheading."

"The rest of us escaped to Anatolia," another runaway leader added, "and joined the army of your brother."

"Cigala Zadeh Sinan *Pasha* did not like how *Ghazi* Giray II led the Crimean-Tartars, so he appointed Fetih Giray as the new Crimean-Tartar Khan," Salamet Giray said.

"But Fetih did not remain Khan?"

"No, for soon the Sultan's Mother, Safiye *Valide Sultana*, had her son-in-law, *Damat* Ibrahim *Pasha,* reinstated as Grand Vizier. He sent an emissary and once more confirmed *Ghazi* Giray II as Khan of the Crimean Tartars."

"After Fetih Giray was executed, it was unsafe for us to stay in Crimea," Salamet Giray said, "so we joined your brother *Scrivano*, too." He and his two younger brothers had brought thousands of disaffected Tartar warriors with them.

~ ~ ~

THE NEXT MORNING, *Deli* Hasan *Pasha* put large wings on his shoulders. Like the winged Hussars of Poland, he believed the sight and sound of flapping feathers would confuse and confound his enemies. He attached a second, smaller set to his upper arms and sat astride his Syrian horse. His army, having finished their breakfast, rolled up their blankets, gathered their weapons and mounted their horses, too.

The three half-brothers of *Ghazi* Giray II, likewise, bestrode their shorter Tartar horses. One of their commanders used a knife and cut the vein of the horse's leg. Mixing the warm blood with the mare's milk, he drank the mixture. Wiping his mouth with the back of his hand, the Crimean-Tartar mounted his steed, primed for battle.

Upper Fortress, Kutahya, NW Anatolia, *Rajab AH* 1011 (Dec. *AD* 1602)

OUTNUMBERED AND OUTMANNED, the Ottoman *Beg* or Governor urged his horse up the steep hill. Hafiz Ahmed *Pasha* glanced back. His army of foot and horse trailed behind him. Behind them, miles to the east, a cloud of dust rose above the vast, flat plains. He could see it with his own eyes—the reports from his scouts were true. The whole rebel army of *Deli* Hasan *Pasha* had departed Ankara, two hundred miles away. Tens of thousands strong and all on horseback, the rebel army had grown. They trotted towards him, ever closer. Their kettle drums pounded.

The Governor knew his men were no match against the seasoned rebels in the open field. If the *Beglerbeg* of Anatolia were here, the Ottoman loyalists could confront the rebels. Earlier in the year, this Governor of Governors had recruited thousands of *sipahi* horsemen in Asia Minor and led them to join the Grand Vizier at the European frontier. Yet the *Beglerbeg* of Anatolia and the *sipahis* had not returned from the prolonged fighting season against the Holy Roman Empire in Hungary.

The Governor of Kutahya escaped through the gates to the hilltop castle, the Upper Fortress. "To the walls!"

Janissaries emptied their barracks and rushed up the stairs. Stationing themselves along the stone battlements, they primed their weapons and readied their muskets. Their barrels extended beyond the crenelated walls and many of the castle's twenty-four towers.

"Cannoneers!" The Governor pointed to round towers anchoring the corners of the large fortress. Behind the castle, a steep ravine protected the castle from assault, but the road from town was flatter. He had only one hope of survival. "Reinforce the walls."

As the rest of his army of footmen and horse made their way up the hill and through the gate, the Governor hurried into his quarters. "Scribe!"

"Yes, sire."

"No time for formalities. Write down the message, 'Our position is dire.'"

The scribe pulled the pen and ink from its case. On the parchment, he penned the short letter. As soon as the turbaned governor finished dictating his message and made his mark, he picked up the scroll and

268

handed it to his messenger. "Tell the governor of Bursa that *Deli* Hasan and the rebels are approaching. Kutayha needs reinforcements."

Kütahya , Anatolia (Asia Minor), Ottoman Empire, circa 1835

"As you command." The messenger bowed and rushed out the door to mount a waiting Arabian, the governor's fastest horse.

As the final remnants of the governor's loyal Ottoman troops entered, the mounted messenger trotted his horse out of the fortress and down the hillside. A few of the more prominent citizens of Kutahya made it inside before the heavy gates closed.

"What about my neighbors?" one of the leaders asked.

"We do not have provisions for everyone." The governor dismissed the citizen. Farms around the town below produced carrots and grew cabbage. The cisterns inside provided ample water, but the fortress storehouses were not full.

The governor went up to the walls. Not far from the Porsuk, a tributary of the Sakarya River and flowing northeast from the town, the relentless advance of the rebel army continued across the flat plain. "The eunuch general was supposed to fight them."

At the beginning of the fighting season, Gazanfer *Agha* had sent General Khosru *Pasha*, an eunuch like himself, to quell the unrest.

"He was no more successful than the previous ones," an officer reported. "The troops of Aleppo abandoned him, and the rest of his troops retired. They said it was winter."

"But *Deli* Hasan *Pasha* did not follow the eunuch general? To attack him in Diyarbakir?"

"No, the brother of *Scrivano* instead turned west, towards us."

"The rumors about looting the Garden of Paradise in Tokat must be true."

"Yes, before *Scrivano* died, he plundered that artificial garden," a *janissary* captain said. "His fighters placed the rubies and other precious stones on their shields."

Deli Hasan *Pasha,* wearing his winged attire, had taken up the fight: his jeweled rebel armor sparkled in a plethora of colors. In the afternoon sun, enemy riders moved up the hills and lined the horizon. In the valley floor, one division was darker than the rest. The three estranged brothers of the Tartar Khan had brought their warriors from Crimea, all dressed in black sheepskin.

The Governor moved to the north wall and watched the townspeople scurry below. Their houses cluttered the hillside all the way down to the river. "They did not expect *Deli* Hasan to attack here, either."

"All are in fear," the *janissary* captain said. A lower fortress had been built to protect the water supply and the artisans, who provided ceramic cups, bowls, and plates to *Stamboul.*

Kutahya was a very important place, a one-time capital of Anatolia, where princes learned to rule. A former Grand Mufti and many scholars came from Kutahya. Fifty years earlier, Suleiman *the Magnificent* had appointed his son Selim as governor. Before he inherited the throne, Sultan Selim II had governed this part of Anatolia from this hilltop fortress. It was also here that the Chief White Eunuch, Gazanfer *Agha,* and his older brother had served Prince Selim.

When Selim II came to *Stamboul,* he brought the two brothers, but they could only serve in the inner parts of the New Palace if they agreed to be castrated. The older Venetian brother died within several years, but Gazanfer *Agha* survived and thrived. Though Selim II was known for his drinking excesses and even called "the Sot," the Chief White Eunuch flourished, not only during Selim II's reign, but also during his son's and grandson's. Some scholars and poets from Kutahya served in Gazanfer's madrasa.

Below the walls of the upper castle, workers in numerous ceramic shops shuttered their doors. Most of the artisans were descendants of tile makers from Tabriz, brought from that town after Selim I captured it during earlier wars against the Persian Empire. The walls of the town and the larger compounds were low, deterrents to robbers and thieves, but not to armies.

Many townspeople fled into their wooden homes, but others loaded their ox-drawn carts with their movables. As the pounding kettle drums grew louder, they rushed away through the narrow streets, past the minarets of the mosques.

Further away, up the narrowing Porsuk River Valley, the messenger slowed his Arabian in the middle of a clearing. Scores of refugees fled towards the wooded mountains, but the lone rider passed them and resumed his gallop northwest, towards Bursa, the first capital of the Ottoman Empire.

From the opposite direction, musket fire rang out.

Chapter 33 — Pozega Spoils

If he find there is no enemy to oppose him, he [Crimean-Tartar Khan] advises how far they shall invade: commanding every man (upon pain of his life) to kill all the obvious Rustics; but not to hurt any women, or children.

Ten or fifteen thousand he commonly places where he finds most convenient for his standing camp; the rest of his army he divides in several troops, bearing ten or twelve miles square before them, and ever within three or four days return to their camp, putting all to fire and sword, but that they carry with them back to their Camp; and in this scattering manner he will invade a Country, and be gone with his prey, with an incredible expedition.

Travels by Captain John Smith

Were now in the latter end of December [AD 1602] come into Hungary; the Khan [Ghazi Giray II] himself with 40,000 to Quinque Ecclesiae [Five Churches or Pécs], and his sons [Toktamish and Sefer Giray] and with 20,000 more into Pozega (a fertile country lying between the great rivers Sava and Drava): where they spoiled as well the Turks as the other poor Christians, pretending all the frontier country with the whole command thereof to be given unto them by the Turkish Emperor [Sultan Mehmet III] in reward of their service.

General History of the Turks by Richard Knolles

Pozega, Slavonia [Serbia/Hungary], Late December, *AD* 1602

DOZENS OF TARTAR warriors surrounded the homestead and dragged out two old inhabitants from their house.

"Where are the men?" *Kalga* Toktamish Giray, speaking Turkish, asked.

The couple shrugged as if they did not understand. They cowered in fear, and Toktamish motioned for his dismounted warriors to sweep behind the house, to search the barn.

Minutes later, his men returned with a few goats and sheep.

"Is this all?" Toktamish asked.

"Why steal from me?" the old man asked.

"You do speak Turkish?"

"We sent grain to the *Sanjak* of Pozega."

The old woman tensed up and began to cry.

"The Sultan gave us the whole land, a reward for our service." Tokmatish remounted his horse. "Lieutenant, take the wagon, too."

"What about the couple?"

"Leave them. They're worth nothing as slaves."

His warriors took an old ox and hitched it to the wagon.

"Nothing more in the barn," the Lieutenant said.

"Burn it!"

Tokmatish and his warriors returned to the main road, where other bands loyal to the Khan's eldest son joined him. To his left, smoke rose from countless farmsteads dotting the wooded hillsides and the plains below. His warriors placed younger captives and women onto the wagons, but older boys and young men were chained together, tied one to another. Prisoners and warriors, carts and wagons trudged toward Pozega, the main seat in this Turkish-controlled land, the Slavonian plain between the Sava and Drava rivers. These two right tributaries of the Danube marked the borders of Hungary to the north and Bosnia to the south.

Pozega, Slavonia, circa 1692

The winter flurries of the week before had departed, and the snow completely melted. Before Toktamish and his younger brother had left Pécs, their father, Khan *Ghazi* Giray II, appointed Pozega to be their winter quarters. Its hilltop castle rose in the center of town across the stream.

Not far from the stream and its mills, *Kalga* Toktamish Giray met his brother, *Nur-eddin* Sefer Giray, at their standing camp. From the opposite direction, his warriors brought more prisoners. Thousands of yurts—framed huts covered with skin—had already been set up. While some worked on setting up more yurts, other groups of warriors sat in circles around fires. While keeping warm, they waited for their evening meal, slowly stewing in large black cauldrons.

Only after their warriors finished would their prisoners eat. Lightly guarded and seated together just outside the camp, the prisoners would eat the leftovers.

The *Sanjak* of Pozega, coming down from his castle and crossing the stream, confronted Toktamish and Sefer, "You raid everywhere and take everything."

"The Sultan gave the frontiers to us, for our service."

"We are entitled," the younger brother added.

"*Sanjak!*" one of the prisoners yelled.

A Tartar guard threatened the man.

"You can't sell him into slavery," the *Sanjak* of Pozega said. "I know him. He's Muslim."

"You can redeem him."

"I will pay no ransom," the *Sanjak* of Pozega said.

Toktamish told his younger brother and his guard, "Let him go."

Still upset, the *Sanjak* of Pozega returned across the stream and up to his hilltop castle. As dusk fell, two Turkish riders exited the town. One took the winding road north, through the hills towards the Drava and Pécs. As an owl hooted, the other rode southeast—down the valley on the road leading to Belgrade.

Kale-Megdan, **Citadel of Belgrade,** *Rajab AH* **1011 (December,** *AD* **1602)**

GRAND VIZIER HASAN *the Fruiterer* prepared for Friday prayers and washed his hands at the Fountain of Mehmed *Pasha* Sokollu. Cool water flowed from the walls of the square fountain—named for former Grand Vizier Sokollu, who hailed from Bosnia and built it 25 years earlier. The current Grand Vizier stepped back, took a towel from his servant, and dried his hands beneath a skinny sapling. Planted at the corner of the fountain, the tree would provide shade in the summer, but today it stood leafless, a testimony that winter would soon arrive. The Grand Vizier hoped it would not be as cold as the previous year.

After prayers inside the small mosque, the Grand Vizier crossed the stone courtyard of the Citadel of Belgrade. Belgrade, standing roughly halfway down the long Danube River, had become an t Ottoman anchor decades earlier. High above, along the walls, enemy cannons, confiscated from Christians at the recent sieges at Kanizsa and brought down the Drava River, protected the fortress. Emblazoned beside the Arms of the Holy Roman Emperor, the brass pieces displayed the Christian dates of 1596, 1598, and 1600. The clopping sound of a horse entering the gate behind him caught his attention. The Grand Vizier stopped and turned.

"Grand Vizier!" A messenger quickly dismounted, holding a letter in his hand.

"What is it?"

The messenger approached through the midst of the entourage and bowed. He lifted the hem of the Grand Vizier's garment and kissed his robe. "The *Sanjak* of Pozega sent me. The Crimean Tartars have looted the farms."

"I did not give permission for that."

"The two sons of the Crimean Khan said they can raid and spoil everywhere."

"Pozega is not the frontier. Those are Turkish lands. I assigned those *timars* to the *sipahis.*"

"*Kalga* Toktamish and *Nur-eddin* Sefer do not listen to you *sanjak.*"

"Take your rest." Grand Vizier Hasan *the Fruiterer* dismissed the messenger. He and his entourage returned to his quarters, where he ordered his scribe to pen the complaint. After applying the seal, the Grand Vizier handed it to an officer. "Deliver it to my friend, Khan *Ghazi* Giray II in Pécs. His sons may raid the frontiers beyond Kanizsa, but not Pozega."

The officer backed away. Accompanied by several guards, the officer galloped out of the courtyard.

"Those raids must stop," Grand Vizier Hasan *the Fruiterer* said.

"Shall we tell the *Sublime Porte* in *Stamboul?*" a trusted aide asked.

"No need to upset the Sultan, or his mother."

Chapter 34 — *Stamboul* Slave Market

Besides the [Old] Bedesten [Ic or Innermost Part of the Grand Bazaar], there is another, less-environed, with a wall and supported by sixteen small pillars [New or Sandal Bedesten]; in the enclosure where of they sell linen cloth and silks, but without it is the detestable market where they sell men and women: on the one side they buy slaves, which are already instructed to serve or to practice some trade; and on the other, those which know not anything.

These places represent better than the former, the fearful image of the Turkish tyranny: It binds them to slavery which the God of the World hath created free: The Merchants visit such merchandises, and such as have an intent to buy, do first see the persons of either sex naked: they handle the parts of their bodies, to observe if they be found, and they uncover that which Nature herself hath labored to hide . . .

<u>*The History of the Serrail and of the Court of the Grand Seigneur, Book I*</u>
By Michel Baudier; Translated from the French by Edward Grimestone

Queen's Chamber, New Palace, *Stamboul*, 24th December *AD* 1602

HER WINDOWS RATTLED and the Mother of the Sultan stopped mid-sentence. Seated on her throne inside her opulent chamber, she listened. A second cannon sounded over the water and the windows rattled again. "Two?"

"Yes, Safiye *Valide Sultana.*" The Chief Black Eunuch, dressed in his long robe, stood by her side. "Two *odalisques* were caught last night, together in the Lesser Chamber."

"*In flagrante delicto?*" The Venetian sister of the Chief White Eunuch asked. Unable to visit her busy brother, Gazanfer *Agha*, Beatrice had entered the Imperial Harem to see the Sultan's Mother about procuring candles for the Venetian ambassador.

"Any doubt?" The Sultan's Mother had earlier seen the two young women together in the baths.

"Of their lust for each other?" *Kizlar Agha* Osman replied. "None. The *kadun* in the chamber heard noise. In the middle of the night, she caught them in the foul act by candlelight."

The *Valide Sultana* and everyone else knew of the consequences of unseemly behavior. The *kadun*, the older matron assigned to the chamber of fifteen *odalisques* would have informed the *Kadun Kahia*, the Mother of Maids, who called for the Black eunuch guards. Those eunuchs would have taken the two *odalisques* to a private gate in the harbor walls.

Placed aboard a small *caique* and stuffed inside separate sacks, the two culprits would have been rowed away from the shore. Beyond the fishing nets, executioners would have dumped the weighted sacks, tightly bound at the top, into the middle of the channel.

At daybreak, seaside cannons announced the number of *odalisques* tossed overboard. Over the previous weeks, the cannons had fired more often than usual. The Imperial Harem was not quite full. The Sultan's Mother needed to rectify the shortfall.

"Many young women have entered the slave market this week," the Chief Black Eunuch announced.

"From Africa or Europe?"

"Some from Algiers, but many white slaves were captured in the Ukraine, or Moldavia, or Wallachia by the Crimean Tartars."

"The Crimean-Khan brought his warriors to help the Grand Vizier." The Sultan's Mother decided, "This time, I shall select the virgins myself. Ready my carriage."

"The horses are harnessed."

Underground Vault, *Sandal Bedesten, Stamboul*

THE GUARD LIFTED his lamp as the *Kaimakam* of *Stamboul* and the *Agha* of the *Janissaries* halted mid-stride. It had been months since they had inspected this hideous part of the slave market, the darkened recesses below the *Sandal Bedesten*. In these underground vaults, the most onerous slaves were kept until they were ready to be sold.

A former scribe in the Third Courtyard of the New Palace, Ali *Agha* did not particularly like this aspect of his responsibilities. He had forgotten about the rancid stench; the smell of urine was strong. Slaves relieved themselves in small holes dug in the back of their cells. Many had not bathed in weeks.

Kaimakam Hasan *the Clockmaker* lifted the lamp and illuminated a dark corner of the underground vault. "The last time I was here, I ordered this debris to be cleaned."

Two long rats scurried out of the mound of rubbish and disappeared through a crevice in the wall.

"That was before I took over the duties," the Inspector of the slave market countered. He had paid a hundred purses into the Imperial Treasury for the privilege of his position. Seated at the iron gate, he collected monies for every slave sold, whether male or female.

The officials drew closer to the group of slaves, the worst of the worst: some appeared weak, but others strong; some were trained, others not. Both black and white slaves were housed together; ethnicity mattered little.

"Why is this slave chained?" The *Kaimakam* pointed at a slave with hollow eyes.

"Fought with another," the Slave Inspector said. "He had to be punished."

"And that one?" the *Kaimakam* pointed to a stronger one, who grimaced his white teeth.

"Rise!" The guard snapped his whip and yelled at the chained slave. His back had fresh welts; his ragged shirt had fresh tears.

"An example for the rambunctious ones," the Inspector said. "Every slave in this section has been a troublemaker. Slaves like him must learn their place."

"But we cannot let them die," Ali *Agha* said. "Their owners would want compensation."

Within *Stamboul*, the number of slave merchants totaled about two thousand. Many of these rich owners stayed in the nearby Khan reserved for their trade.

The Inspector led the *Kaimakam* and the *Agha* of the *Janissaries* to the center of the underground vault. Male slaves were crowded into cells on either side, but those in the center waited for barbers.

"These are the newest ones from the European frontier." The Inspector pointed to slaves seated in the center vault. Several barbers with large scissors cut their long hair close to their scalp and trimmed their beards just as short. If any of the Christians converted to Islam, they would be sent to the other type of barber, who would circumcise them. The recovery from that cut took several days. Those new converts would never be set free—all would remain slaves.

278

A guard bounded down the stairs. "Inspector, the Sultan's Mother is at the Gate."

"You must excuse me, *Kaimakam.* I cannot make her wait."

"Ali *Agha,* your wife Beatrice is with her," the guard said.

"Here?"

"We will continue our inspection upstairs," *Kaimakam* Hasan *the Clockmaker* said.

Iron Gate, *Sandal Bedesten, Stamboul*

SAFIYE *VALIDE SULTANA* pulled back the curtains of her white carriage as it stopped at the outer gate of the *New Bedesten.* Though more than one hundred years old, the main building with its cupolas and pillars was called new, because it was built a decade after the *Old Bedesten,* a mere one hundred paces away. She looked at Beatrice and spoke in Italian, "The slave trade is much more regular than in the days after Sultan Mehmet II conquered Constantinople."

"What happened?" Beatrice asked. At the invitation of her powerful Eunuch brother, she had followed her mother from Venice only a decade earlier.

"At that time, the slaves were sold on the street, but the Sultan saw an accident."

"An accident?" Beatrice asked.

"A female slave was nursing her child. She stood to get out of the way of a horse, but the chains around her legs rattled."

"What happened?"

"The loud noise frightened the horse. The rider lost control and the horse rose onto its rear legs. Its front hoofs landed on the woman, killing her and injuring her child. Sultan Mehmet II was troubled, so, moved with compassion, he started the slave market. He ordered all slaves to be sold in markets, behind low walls."

"Safiye *Valide Sultana.*" The Inspector of New *Bedesten* stepped through the iron gate. "What an honor to have you visit us today. Are you interested in some *sandal* cloth for the harem?"

Comprised of both silk and cotton, the striped *sandal* cloth was sold in the center of the covered bazaar. Sixteen small pillars supported domed enclosures. On shelves, expensive silks from Bursa and fine linen fabrics were stacked high. Its traders were renowned for living according to the famous verse in the *Qur'an: El-kasib Habib-ullah,* meaning *'The merchant is*

God's favorite.' At the doors, watchmen carried halberds and swords, while outside criers and brokers cornered potential customers.

"No, Inspector, I wish to see the newest slaves."

The slave buyers sat in small booths, at tables positioned near the low, outer wall of the *New Bedesten*. The slave sellers towed their slaves, one or two at a time, behind them. They stopped in front of each table, and if any buyer was interested in a slave, he would examine her carefully. He would inspect her teeth and her hair, her arms and legs, and her hands, searching for any defect. If she proved acceptable, the slave would be bought; if not, the seller would proceed to the next table.

After taking the Sultan's Mother and Beatrice into his office, the Inspector motioned for a slave seller. "Perhaps that one." The seller led an African woman into the office. Normally sold on the far side of the building, these untrained slaves, often half-naked, came from the interior parts of Africa. Brought to *Stamboul* via Cairo, Tunis, or Algiers, those slaves handled the menial work; the healthier ones were worth more.

"I do not need one to work in the baths," the Sultan's Mother said.

"She's not trained, but she is healthy."

The woman's worth would increase after she was trained. She would garner a higher price if resold.

"I keep all of my slaves." The Sultan's Mother turned and spied a group of female slaves by the outer walls, seated in a circle on the ground. On this side of the *New Bedesten*, the female slaves were more costly. Some had been trained in the arts, such as needlework, musical instruments, or dancing. If any of these slaves were resold, they would sell for less. More than likely, these female slaves would have had some character defect, perhaps too obstinate or too difficult to manage.

The Sultan's Mother had spent years perfecting her ability to select appropriate beauties. It displeased her to admit it, but she had learned the art of selecting women from the mother of Murad III, the father of her children. *Nur Banu* had become jealous of how much her son Murad loved Safiye, so she vastly increased the size of the Imperial Harem to more than three hundred *odalisques*. The price of female slaves here in *Stamboul* soared. After Murad died and her son acceded to the Ottoman throne, Safiye had been unable to persuade her son to stay in *Stamboul*. Eight years earlier, Mehmet III led the Ottoman army into battle in northern Hungary, but her son was almost killed. After his brush with death and his victorious return, Mehmet III showed no inclination to return and fight.

The Sultan's Mother pointed to the prettiest beauty seated on the blanket. "I like her demeanor."

"Docile?" the Chief Black Eunuch asked.

"Yes, but she has lively eyes." Safiye, who wanted to ensure her son remained satisfied at the palace, knew the kind of women he preferred. "Make sure she is a virgin."

"You need not say." The Inspector nodded to the slave merchant, who motioned for the girl to stand up. He took the girl by the wrist and gently led her to the office for the approval of the Sultan's Mother. "The matron over there has examined all of the new girls. None has ever been touched."

The Sultan's Mother lifted the girl's chin. "Yes, she will do." She pointed to another being led to a far booth. "And how about her?"

One half an hour later, the Sultan's Mother had finished her selection, and the *Kaimakam* and Ali *Agha* approached. "You do not usually come to the market."

"No, but I had heard about the beauty of the new slaves, and we have room in the Imperial Harem." She glanced at the Inspector before turning back to the *Kaimakam*. "Your inspection? Is everything in order?" Much of the monies that the Inspector had paid for the privilege of his office had trickled into her coffers. The double tithe paid for each slave sold flowed into the imperial treasury.

"Yes, everything is in perfect order. We will next inspect the fur market." He gestured to the street leading to the furriers and fur hat makers. Those furs came from the Caucasus Mountains or from Muscovy, across the Black Sea.

"To see if they are selling black fox?"

Only her son, the Sultan, and the Grand Vizier could wear the rare black fox.

"Yes, but winter approaches."

"Yes." The Sultan's Mother looked at the Chief Black Eunuch. "The women in the harem might appreciate the warmth of Siberian sables." She continued, "Ali *Agha*, I must return to the palace, but can you escort your wife to my daughter Aisha at her Candle Workshop?"

"We planned to also inspect the *Old Bedes*—" Ali *Agha* looked at Hasan *the Clockmaker*. "Perhaps the *Kaimakam* can complete the task without my assistance."

Chapter 35 — Candle Workshop

<u>Narrative of Travels in Europe, Asia, and Africa in 17th Century, Vol. I, Part 2</u> by Evliya Efendi
Translated from the Turkish by Joseph Von Hammer

Odun Kapi [Timber Gate], Harbor of *Stamboul*, Christmas Eve, *AD* 1602

HUNCHED-OVER PORTERS, BURDENED with heavy loads of sticks, plodded through *Odun Kapi*, Timber Gate. They carried winter fuel, destined to be delivered to the larger khans dotting the city, or to private homes lining the narrow streets. Further up the hill, a stone tower rose above the crowded neighborhood. Erected following a series of devastating fires, its watchers manned the tower continuously, both day and night. At the first sight of flames, they would sound an alarm. If the fire spread, workers would rush to the area, tearing down all houses in the fire's path.

Aisha waited for Beatrice, the sister of the Chief White Eunuch, just outside the gate. Wood was stacked high between the fortified walls and the harbor shoreline. Merchants standing in front of the stacks not only sold the sticks to warm homes, but also lumber to build houses.

The fortified walls facing the shore extended east, past Prison Gate and the Fish Market, reaching the New Palace of her brother, the Sultan. To the west, the harbor walls touched the ancient land walls of Constantinople. Further away, the Golden Horn narrowed at the foot of wooded hillsides. Aqueducts from Belgrade Forest, the source of the city's fresh water supply, fed underground cisterns and countless fountains, including the Green Fountain Aisha had constructed for her favorite shoemaker.

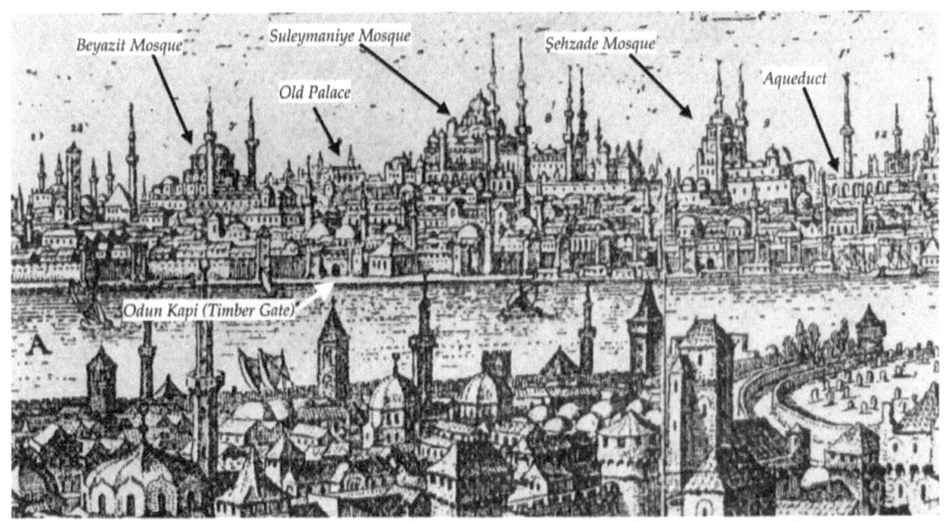

Golden Horn Harbor in Stamboul, Ottoman Turkey, circa 1635

On the opposite bank of the harbor, Galata Tower overlooked the neighborhood that once housed Genoese merchants. Following Sultan Mehmet II's conquest of *Stamboul,* Venetians were relocated from their assigned neighborhood behind the Timber Gate to Galata. They displaced the Genoese, who had waged war against the Ottomans. Now that suburb housed both the Venetian and French embassies.

"Where is Beatrice?" Aisha asked her maidservant. "I need to get back to my palace."

"To continue your conversation?"

"Yes, with John."

Aisha, peering down the shoreline toward the busy Fish Market, recognized Beatrice's husband Ali with his tall hat. As the *Agha* of the *Janissaries* moved past Prison Gate, named for the prison behind the wall, Aisha saw his wife, too. "Beatrice!"

"Thank you for meeting me," Beatrice said. "I was delayed at the *New Bedesten* with your mother, but my husband was kind enough to escort me."

"Ali *Agha,* thank you for bringing her here."

Two more porters walked by, but instead of lugging sticks, they carried honeycombs.

The women and the *Agha* followed the porters into Timber Gate. Aisha's candle workshop occupied both sides of the large stone structure. The aroma of honey filled the air.

"I wish I could stay, but I must meet with my captains." The *Agha* of the *Janissaries* conducted business in his own palace near Suleiman Mosque, up the hill above Timber Gate. "I see my wife is in good hands."

As soon as Ali *Agha* departed, Aisha asked Beatrice, "Is something wrong? Your husband seems upset."

Agha of the Janissaries and Kadi-Asker (Military Judge)

"I do not know for certain, but the *sipahis* demanded that the Imperial Council appoint a new leader for the *Janissaries*."

"Ali would have to give up his palace?"

With the help of the Chief White Eunuch, Ali had continually advanced in both position and prestige over the past decade. After she decided to stay in the Ottoman capital, instead of returning to her failed second marriage in Venice, Beatrice converted to Islam and agreed to marry Ali *Agha*. "Yes, if the viziers insist."

"But he has done so much for me," Aisha said. Recently returning to *Stamboul*, Ali *Agha* had negotiated the marriage contract, called the *kabin*, and delivered the terms to her betrothed, Hasan *the Fruiterer* in Belgrade.

"At least I have my palace." Beatrice stayed in a large palace assigned to her brother, Gazanfer *Agha*.

Many weeks had passed since Aisha had entered Timber Gate and visited her workshop. Her father, Sultan Murad III, had authorized a *vakif, or* charitable foundation, by imperial decree. Years later, that amply endowed foundation, through an *Agha* and an Inspector, managed her workshop of one hundred men. Those two trusted men ensured its proceeds were distributed solely for Aisha's benefit.

284

Unlike the tallow wax made from animal fat, the candle wax in her candle workshop smelled sweet. The shop supplied the candles for her brother's palace, the imperial mosques, and all of the important viziers. Only authorized candle merchants could sell her candles—each marked with the imperial seal. No one dared to forge that seal, a crime punishable by death. And if any merchant mixed tallow inside the wax, the punishment might prove just as harsh.

"Aisha, Sister of the Sultan, we did not expect you today." The Inspector and the *Agha* of the workshop wore large turbans.

"Have you met Fatima?" Aisha used the Islamic name given to Beatrice after she had followed her mother to *Stamboul.* Her mother lived only a year after she had moved from Venice, passing away the day before her daughter's arrival. Aisha motioned the older woman forward.

"Yes, I remember seeing her with her brother, Gazanfer *Agha*, in the New Palace last year," the Inspector said.

"I sometimes find goods for the Venetian *bailo*." Beatrice referred to the Venetian ambassador.

"He needs candles?" The Inspector pointed to brass holders holding long candles. Shorter porcelain holders had mosaic designs. "For the Latin churches?"

"It is Christmas Eve."

In the back of the shop, a worker crumbled honeycombs over a vat on the hot stove. Another stirred the beeswax to keep it from sticking to the side. Yet another worker lifted a smaller vat, already simmering. His helper held a wick, and the worker poured the liquid wax into the first colored jar.

"That smells heavenly," Aisha said.

"These are already cooled." The Inspector brought one from the rack. "We've been able to add oils and scents."

"I like these one." Aisha checked with the Inspector, who nodded his assent. She told her Venetian friend in Italian, "You may take them."

Beatrice hid the beeswax candles, all of the highest quality, beneath a fold of cloth. "In Venice, Christmas was my favorite time of the year." She cautioned Aisha, "Please, do not tell your mother."

Aisha knew that her devout mother would not be happy if the sister of the Chief White Eunuch practiced Christianity, even in secret.

Outside the shop, but still inside Timber Gate, two Greek women dressed in black approached Aisha. "Your candles are the best. We wanted to honor the Greek Patriarch of Constantinople."

"Tonight, for Christmas Eve?" Aisha asked.

"No, we celebrate Christmas in thirteen days."

"Yes, different than Roman Catholics," Beatrice said.

Aisha turned to the Inspector, standing in the doorway of her shop, "Can we help them?"

"The Superintendent of Suleiman Mosque will be here shortly." The Inspector glanced in the direction of the city. "There will not be enough candles for the mosques and viziers."

Aisha addressed the two Greek women, "Please, come visit me at my palace next week."

After the two Greek women exited, Aisha told Beatrice, "I will take you to your ferry by the Fish market."

They took a step toward the carriage when a man running along the shore bolted past it on the other side.

A guard slammed the butt of his stave onto the ground. "Thief!" His stave thumped again. "Seize him!"

A guard atop Timber Gate pointed. "Don't let him escape!"

The thief rushed on the other side of the wood pile and along the shores of the Golden Horn.

"There he goes!"

Guards exited Timber Gate and chased after him, but the thief stole a small boat and shoved off into the inner harbor.

While guards ran below walls facing the inner harbor, other guards commandeered boats.

"What is the commotion?" a voice behind Aisha called out.

Aisha turned around. "A thief, but he will not escape." She saw that the Superintendent of Suleiman Mosque had entered the gate.

"Aisha *Sultana*, I did not expect to see you at your shop."

"The Inspector says you wanted special candles?" Aisha asked. Turkish men and women, unrelated to each other, normally did not converse. But Aisha, the Sister of the Sultan, held prerogatives unavailable to other women.

"Yes, before Friday."

"We will deliver them to you on Thursday morning," the inspector interjected.

"Aisha, have you heard from your betrothed?" the Superintendent asked.

"The Grand Vizier winters in Belgrade."

"Has he sent you more slaves to ransom?"

"You heard?" Aisha asked.

"When you write the Grand Vizier, please give him my regards." He paused. "And to your mother also."

"I shall tell the *Valide Sultana* of your good wishes," Aisha said.

The Superintendent, appearing satisfied, headed back through the gate and into the city, while Aisha, following Beatrice into her carriage, warned her driver, "I cannot be late."

As the carriage moved forward, she told Beatrice, "I must meet Filiz at the Eastern Gate of the Old *Bedesten*."

Glancing back to the middle of the harbor, Aisha saw that the thief had been apprehended. Further ahead, wagons and carts, loaded with spices from Egypt and the Far East, lined the crowded waterfront. The smell of ginger filled the air.

After passing Prison Gate, the carriage slowed by the Fish Market. When it stopped, Beatrice stepped out of the carriage. Aisha told her, "Make certain to visit me soon. I will need your help."

"With your English slave?"

"You speak Italian better than I."

Beatrice finished securing her candles. "I almost forgot."

"What is it?" Aisha asked.

"You wanted to surprise the Dutch *odalisque* Dilara with a pair of shoes. Her *kadun* traced her feet, and when I was at the Imperial Harem, a Black eunuch handed this paper to me."

"Ah, my friend." Aisha asked, "How can I repay you?"

"You already have."

Her waiting *Janissary* escorted Beatrice to a small boat to be ferried across the Golden Horn to deliver the candles to the new Venetian *Bailo.* Aisha told her driver, "I am late. I must meet Filiz below the bird, the Eastern Gate of the Old *Bedesten*."

Fish Gate, Harbor of *Stamboul*

GUARDS WAVED THE carriage through Fish Gate, but it slowed as it passed the uncompleted mosque of her mother, the *Valide Sultana*. The foundation of the New Mosque had been laid, but its construction was suspended; walls reached only knee-high above the ground. The Long War in Europe and the turmoil in Anatolia had cost the treasury much. The bulk of the Jewish neighborhood had been torn down, but workers toiled no longer.

Chapter 36 — Green Fountain

In one of the most frequented spots in Constantinople is the Old [Ic or Inner] Bedesten; it is a great warehouse like a fortress, where the goods of all the military men and viziers are deposited; for this purpose are employed many hundred magazines below ground, with iron gates . . .

On the north side, the Gate of the Booksellers, on the west that of the Cap-makers, on the south that of the Girdle-makers, and on the east that of the Goldsmiths, upon which is figured a formidable bird opening its wings. The meaning of this symbol is to say, "Gain and trade are like a wild bird, which if it's domesticated by courtesy and politeness, may be done so in this Bedesten." This Bedesten has cupolas covered with lead, supported by large stone pillars, and windows with iron shutters.
Narrative of Travels in Europe, Asia, and Africa in 17th Century, Vol. I, Part 2
by Evliya Efendi. Translated from the Turkish by Joseph Von Hammer

And on the north [of the Old Bedesten] the Slipper Bazaar with its fascinations, one slakes his thirst at the [Green] Fountain erected by the daughter [Aisha] of Sultan Murad III for the refreshment of a shoemaker, whose work always gave perfect satisfaction, and most surprising of all, was always done on time.
Constantinople, Vol. II
by Edwin A. Grosvenor

East Gate, Old [Ic] Bedesten, Rajab AH 1011 (Christmas Eve AD 1602)

GREEK MERCHANTS OPENED their wooden chests of precious gems. "Aisha *Sultana*, something special for you?"

Aisha rarely ventured down Jewelers Street, but she decided to exit her carriage and walk the last portion of her way to the Old *Bedesten*.

Her eunuch guard stepped in front of the loud Greek. "The Sister of the Sultan has no interest."

"No interest? Here? In the greatest market of the world?" The Greek closed the chest. Its loose iron hoops rattled.

"I must meet a friend." Aisha calmed the turmoil.

"Ah, a friend?" The Armenian merchant in the next booth spoke, just above a whisper. He unwrapped a white cloth and presented an uncut turquoise stone before her. "Perhaps she would like this gem from Persia?"

Aisha gazed at the stone. "It is pretty, but these things must wait."

Aisha preferred emeralds and diamonds, like the ones she had inherited from her fraternal grandmother, *Nur Banu,* the mother of Sultan Murad III. She sauntered further through the next bazaar, past Jewish merchants selling stringed pearls. At last, Aisha spied Filiz, the French translator, examining gold chains.

"You look lovely today, Aisha *Sultana.*" Filiz stood outside the East Gate of the Old *Bedesten.* "But why did you want to meet me in such a busy place?"

"I wanted to see my shoemaker and thought you would like to come along." Aisha, who wanted to reward the Dutch translator Dilara for her service, carried the paper that Beatrice had given her.

"My husband never brought me here."

"You mean the Old *Bedesten*?"

A bird with open wings marked its entrance.

"Yes, I was brought up in the Imperial Harem, but after the death of your father, Murad III, I was sent to the Old Palace. The Jewish *kira* arranged our marriage."

"Your husband is an important vizier."

"Yes, but he never took me inside the Old *Bedesten.*"

"He probably thought you did not want to see the arms that are there." Aisha could tell that Filiz was interested. Nearby, several young men intercepted potential customers. "We cannot stay long."

"You are so courteous and polite," Filiz joined Aisha, walking toward the East Gate. When her eunuch guards touch their curved sabers, the skinny young men pursuing new customers scattered, disappearing into a growing crowd of onlookers.

"I have always wondered about the meaning of this bird." Filiz gestured to the emblem above the arched gateway. "It is not from the old Constantinople?"

The Superintendent of the Old *Bedesten* appeared in the gateway. "No, this *Old Bedesten* was built after the conquest." He referred to Mehmet the Conqueror, who captured Constantinople 150 years earlier.

"My friend and I wish to go inside," Aisha said.

"Let me escort you."

"So what does this bird signify?" Filiz asked.

"Gain and trade are like a wild bird," the Superintendent explained. "If it is to be domesticated by courtesy and politeness, it may be done in this *Bedesten*."

Of all the marketplaces in *Stamboul*, this *Bedesten* was the most important. Like the Candle Factory, revenues funded a *vakif*, a charitable foundation. Whereas the revenues of the *vakif* of the Candle Factory benefited Aisha, the *vakif* of the *Old Bedesten* paid for the upkeep of the *Hagia Sophia*, the imperial mosque.

Inside the vaulted chamber, the Superintendent continued, "The seventy Turkish merchants inside here are all very honest."

Aisha knew none would dare steal from each other. Pillars supported the large arches. Light from the domes above illuminated the walkways.

The chests were filled with fancy armaments and also with rare gems. When a vizier lost his life by decree or by natural causes, an account of his belongings would be made, and the goods deposited in the Old *Bedesten*. The Superintendent gave an account and reported directly to the Imperial Treasurer.

In the darkened recesses of the labyrinth of streets, Turkish merchants passed the hours, conversing quietly and smoking tobacco. If business proved brisk, they would murmur praises to Allah, but if it were slow, they would murmur 'God wills' and accept their fate.

At night, the windows would be bolted, and the heavy iron gates kept shut. Beneath a tiered, brass chandelier hanging from the ceiling, they stopped to look at a gem. Aisha told Filiz, "We must be going; I cannot be late."

"To see John?" Filiz asked.

Aisha spied the *Kaimakam* and a team of inspectors entering from the South gate. She overheard a shopkeeper worry about the soldiers accompanying Hasan *the Clockmaker*. "I hope the *janissaries* do not riot."

"The Sultan sent monies to the Grand Vizier, who paid the *janissaries* before they returned from the frontier," the other shopkeeper said.

Aisha knew *janissaries* had rioted before, but, unlike her mother, she did not involve herself with the concerns of government. "Thank you, Superintendent. I see you will soon be occupied with business."

Green Fountain, Shoemaker Bazaar

UP AND DOWN the narrow street leading north from the Old *Bedesten* to the Shoemaker Bazaar, smiling eyes greeted the Sister of the Sultan. Aisha and her French friend, Filiz, skirted around the Green Fountain she had built for her favorite shoemaker, whom she had not seen for weeks. Clear water flowed into the rectangular basin of emerald green marble.

Few dared to interfere with Aisha, a close member of the royal family, but as the crowds parted, a young, somewhat disheveled boy approached the two women. "Would you like some slippers?" The boy spoke quickly. "I can lead you to a shop with the best prices in the Slipper Bazaar. It is only one alleyway further."

"Get away, young boy." Her eunuch guard, showing no patience for the bustle of the markets, reached out with his hand. Aisha

Aisha's Green Fountain and Shoemaker

brought her guard's arm down. "Not today, young man. I must visit my shoemaker." Aisha directed the boy's attention to another patron who might be more receptive.

Inside the next shop, her favorite shoemaker sat cross-legged in the middle of the raised floor. Wearing baggy pantaloons, he attended to the needs of his lone customer.

"I can't decide." The Turkish woman, sitting sideways on the ledge facing the street, slipped on a new shoe. Nearby, a well-dressed boy stood and watched his mother.

The arrival of Aisha caught the eye of her favorite shoemaker. His beard neatly trimmed, the greying shoemaker rose to his feet. "Sister of the Sultan, an unexpected pleasure to see you this morning."

"Go, please finish with your customer," Aisha said.

"I cannot presume—" The Turkish woman motioned for her young son, bundled warm, to come to her.

"No, do not let me interrupt."

"Very well." The customer slipped the other shoe on her petite foot.

Aisha leaned over and spoke to the young boy, "How old are you?"

The boy glanced at his mother and answered, "Almost five."

Aisha touched the boy's cheek. "You have a handsome young man."

"Thank you." The mother turned to the shoemaker. "This feels better."

"And the color?" the shoemaker asked.

"I like it. Can I wear them?"

"Certainly."

While the customer stood in her new shoes and completed her transaction with the shoemaker, Aisha and Filiz perused his varied selection. Low-cut shoes, arranged by shape and size, lined the shelves. Ankle-high boots, tied to cords, dangled from the ceiling.

With the departure of the customer and her son, Aisha asked, "Have you met Filiz?"

The shoemaker glanced down. "No, but I recognize the workmanship on your feet."

"From the shoemaker across the way." Filiz asked, "How did you know?"

"My shoemaker is best," Aisha interjected. "He always finishes his work on time."

"Did you see the fountain she built for me?" The shoemaker pointed to its green marble base. "And the water is sweet."

Another nearby fountain was well-known for its bitter taste.

"Filiz, every pair of shoes he has made for me has been crafted to perfection," Aisha said.

"You are too kind," the shoemaker said, "but I am just a loyal servant. As you may know, the shoemakers are the most loyal of all of the guilds."

"How so?" Filiz asked.

"In the time of Suleiman, the *Janissaries* refused to eat their soup, so the sultan swore he would disband them with the help of the shoemakers."

"What did the shoemakers do?"

"Forty thousand assembled from all four quarters of *Stamboul*. In front of the palace, the fully armed shoemakers shouted, 'Allah! Allah!' Sultan Suleiman welcomed their faithfulness. He asked for and granted their petitions."

"Petitions?"

"Their apprentices—if strong and able—were allowed to join the *janissaries*. In public processions, Turkish musicians would be allowed to join the shoemakers, because previously the musicians could only march with a colonel of the *janissaries*, the one responsible for collecting the *devshirme*."

"The tribute?"

"Yes, the *devshirme* are the young boys taken from Christian families every seven years to be groomed as *janissaries*."

"And what happened to the rebellious *janissaries*?" Aisha asked.

"Their appetite returned, and they devoured their soup." Her shoemaker asked, "What brings you to the market today? A pair of shoes for your friend?"

"No, Filiz is well-taken care of, but I wish to reward Dilara, an *odalisque* who has helped me." Aisha reached for and brought out the tracing of Dilara's foot. "Do you think you can make a pair for her?"

"I will do my best, but what style?"

"We like that one, the blue pair over there."

"I have the material." The shoemaker accepted the tracing. "And will start after midday prayers." He looked at the Green Fountain, where he and his neighbors would wash before praying toward Mecca.

"Yes, I must get back to my palace." Aisha started to leave, wishing to continue her conversation with her English slave.

"I will have the shoes ready within a week."

"Thank you." She turned to her guard. "We must go."

"Your driver has moved the carriage closer."

"*Excellente!*" Aisha told Filiz before turning back to her shoemaker. "Thank you again."

Aisha and Filiz walked up the narrow street, north to the edge of the Shoemaker Bazaar. As soon as they seated themselves inside the waiting carriage, it surged forward. It skirted the Bookseller Market and passed the *Cemberlitas Hamami*, the Turkish baths by the Column of Constantine. These newly built baths had separate entrances for both men and women.

Her ox-drawn carriage veered right and, as it reached the Hippodrome, the first call for midday prayer rang out. *Muezzins*, standing on the balconies of the minarets of Hagia Sophia Mosque, cried out again. The carriage hurried across the Atmeiden to the opening gates of her Palace of Ibrahim *Pasha*. Aisha would soon see her *Capitano*, her English slave.

Chapter 37 — Captain Francisco *del* Arco

"Things are now come to that extremity, that if my good sister [Queen Elizabeth of England] help me not and that speedily, I cannot maintain myself any longer against so mighty an enemy [Cardinal Albert of Austria], but must, rather than perish willfully, having no other means to do otherwise, seek a truce of the Spaniard, tho' utterly against my liking."
King Henry IV to English Ambassador Sir Anthony Mildmay
St. Germain-en-Laye, Ile de France, 29th April 1597

Salon, Palace of Ibrahim *Pasha*, *Rajab AH* 1011 (Late Dec. *AD* 1602)

AISHA MOTIONED FOR Filiz, her French translator friend, to sit down on thick, padded cushions. Claiming she might catch a chill, Aisha sent word to her mother that she could not accompany her to the grave of her father. The mausoleum of Sultan Murad III stood by the Hagia Sophia. The light drizzle had begun when they exited the Grand Bazaar. It turned into a steady rain. It sloshed against the long windowpanes of her comfortable salon.

"Shall I close the curtains?" An attendant reached up.

"Wait!" Aisha rose to inspect a small pool of water and turned to the main door. "Overseer, this leak must be fixed."

"Right away, My Lady." The tall Black eunuch asked, "Will you want to relocate to the Great Hall?" The Great Hall overlooked the Second Courtyard. "I could double the guard."

"I do not think we need to worry about the *capitano* escaping."

"Not for your slave, for the *sipahis*. You must have heard them on the *At-meydani*." The horse square butted against the outer walls of her palace.

"They were all huddled around the fires when we arrived from the Shoemaker Bazaar. Besides, when have the *sipahis* rebelled? In the past, only the *janissaries* have ever revolted."

"Very well."

"Go, and bring me the *capitano*."

Nothing could dissuade Aisha from finding out more about her slave.

"As you wish." The Overseer bowed, and with the eunuch's departure, the attendant pulled the drapes.

Other attendants lit more candles that had been brought from the candle shop assigned for Aisha's benefit. The room brightened late this dreary morning. Filiz told Aisha, "Last time, the *shish kebab* you served Dilara and me tasted so good."

"The *capitano* raved about it, too."

The large Black eunuch soon returned with Captain John Smith. "Are you certain you do not want to keep the slave bound?"

"That will not be necessary." Aisha motioned for the eunuch to untie him.

Another Black eunuch whispered to the Overseer, "She treats him like a guest."

Aisha gestured for *Capitano* John Smith to sit and dismissed the Overseer. "Not a word to my mother. That will be all." As servants brought coffee, Aisha asked, "Where were we?"

"I did not get to thank you for the *shish kebab*," Captain John Smith said. "Marinated and so moist, not at all like the fare we usually eat."

"The life of a recruit must be hard."

"That spring, many English soldiers worried about getting paid. Some officers had to sell their own plates."

"And you?"

"I did not worry," John said. "God provides for His servants."

"What happened to Gabrielle *de* Estrees?" Filiz asked in French. "Did the partisans in Paris throw her over the bridge?"

"*Non*, the Mistress of King Henry IV escaped."

"Tell us more about how Captain Joseph Duxbury recruited you," Aisha requested.

"Nearly six years ago, Captain Duxbury and I learned that Captain Francisco *del* Arco had returned from Amiens to Brussels in Brabant, a province of the Spanish Netherlands."

Aula Magna, **Coudenberg Palace, Brussels, Brabant, Mid-March** *AD* **1597**

SHORTLY AFTER THE capture of Amiens in Picardy, Sergeant Francisco *del* Arco and a small escort rode north to Brussels in Brabant. At the top of

296

Coudenberg hill, he entered through the main gate, stopping inside the inner courtyard of the palace. He dismounted in front of *Aula Magna*, the Great Hall.

Inside, Cardinal Albert of Austria remained seated in the large chair at the head of the hall. "Sergeant *del* Arco, we were waiting for news."

Sergeant *del* Arco told the Cardinal and the governing council, "Governor Hernán Tello de Portocarrero thought it best I personally deliver the news."

Members of the council remained seated on the rows of benches. Each had his own cushion.

"Early Sunday morning, fourteen of my soldiers and I brought our wagon filled with wood to Amiens. When several of my men disguised as peasants spilt a few sacks of nuts and apples, unsuspecting guards rushed to help." Sergeant *del* Arco related further details of how he led the assault at the Gate of Montrescu. "I overpowered the Captain of the guard. Even though the portcullis slammed onto the back of wagon, the gate could not close. The rest of your army advanced. With drums sounding as if in a parade, we captured the town."

"The losses?" Cardinal Albert asked.

"The French lost a hundred men, mainly on the ramparts."

"And us?"

"We lost only three men. And the arrears of all of the soldiers have been paid from the plunder."

"Such good news!" I must tell my uncle King Philip II and send a message with the first ship leaving Dunkirk for Spain. And for your heroic efforts? You deserve a pension of 300 ducats for life." The Cardinal glanced at the Count of Bucquoy and the other officers before turning back. "And a promotion."

"Promotion?" Sergeant *del* Arco asked.

"When you return to Amiens, you shall hold the rank of Captain."

"Such an honor. Governor Hernán Tello *de* Portocarrero will need more supplies to counter any siege, but Marshall de Biron has already disrupted the link with Doullens."

"So soon?"

"The Marshall attacked wagons leaving Amiens." The Cardinal turned to the Count of Bucquoy, who held his helmet beneath his arm. "Take your regiment to Arras. We must keep supply lines open." He turned to his Albanian cavalry commander, Nicolo Basta. "Where is Juan *de* Guzman?"

The Spanish officer stepped forward. "Here."

"Take five companies of horse to Cambrai, prepare to enter Amiens."

"Governor Tello needs an engineer," Francisco del Arco added.

"I know a Spaniard, the best."

Main Hall, Coudenberg Palace, Brussels, Late March *AD* 1597

INSIDE COUDENBERG PALACE, Cardinal Albert, working at his desk, set down his pen. Behind him, in the Tiltyard below, two knights practiced jousting. Soon, a messenger, appearing at the door, removed his hat. The Cardinal folded the letter and, as soon as his secretary poured warm wax on the fold, sealed it with his signet. He waved the messenger forward. "You may approach."

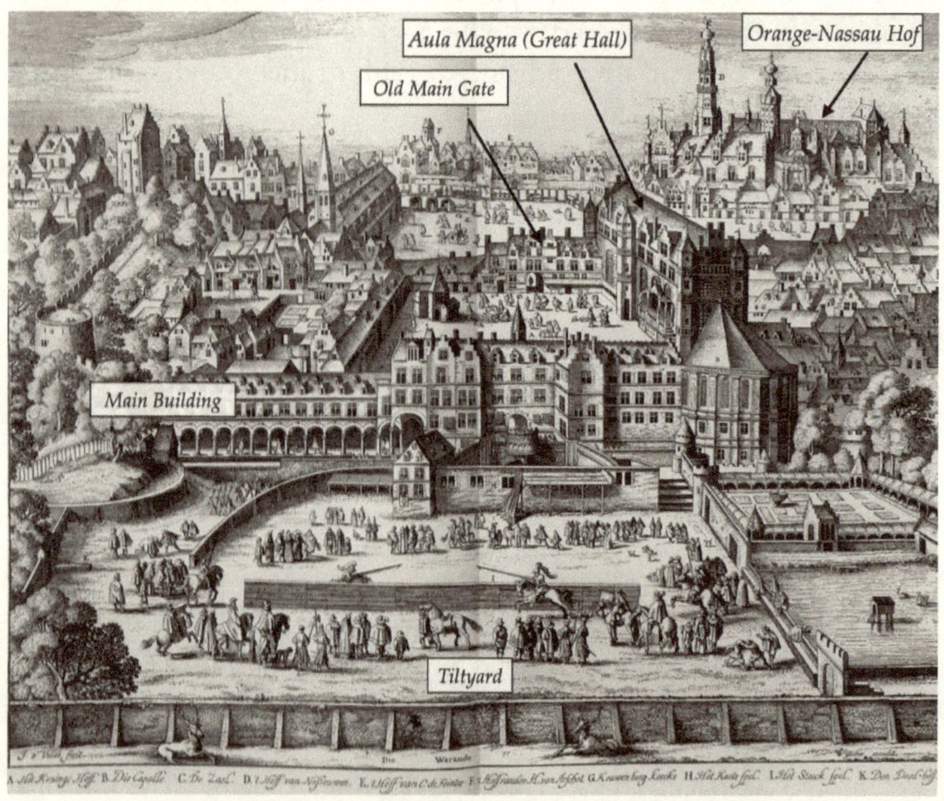

Coudenberg Palace, Brussels circa 1590

The messenger rushed forward with a letter in his hand. "From the Papal Legate in Paris."

298

"Continue."

The Cardinal's secretary unsealed the letter.

"The Legate is upset," the secretary summarized. "He wants to know why we attacked Amiens, when the King of Spain had promised a cessation of arms."

"I will tell him." Cardinal Albert picked up his pen and dipped it into the ink well. "It was King Henry IV who proclaimed war against his master. If he repents at length and finds himself weakened, he must first acknowledge that he is overmatched."

"And after the King of France does that?" his secretary asked.

"Spain will become more content and allow him to negotiate reasonable conditions for a just peace."

"I agree," the Secretary said. "We have other news. Marshall de Biron attempted to capture Doullens, but the garrison fought back."

"Is the Count of Bucquoy at Arras?" the Cardinal asked.

"No, he's brought his infantry to Doullens, along with Juan de Guzman."

Cardinal Albert remembered hearing about the Battle at the Heath of Tielen. During that battle in January, Juan *de* Guzman and thirty of his lancers returned to the heath. They almost captured Count Maurice before being pushed back by the English foot soldiers.

"Governor Tello tells the siege has begun in earnest," the secretary said. "King Henry has set up three strong forts in an arch."

"Was our Spanish engineer able to enter?" Cardinal Albert asked.

"Along with an artilleryman and four other horsemen, but every day it becomes more difficult to send reinforcements."

"We must send Juan *de* Guzman to help Governor Tello and the Marquis *de* Montenegro."

Countryside, North of Amiens, Picardy, France, 14th April AD 1597

AT DAYBREAK ON the 14th of April, a French scout reported to Sir John Aldrich and Captain Joseph Duxbury, "The Spanish plan to enter Amiens tonight."

A second scout galloped toward them. "Commander Juan *de* Guzman and five companies of horse."

John Smith spied the companies trotting south. "Three companies of lancers and two armed with arquebuses."

"Signal the alarm!"

Fires were lit, drums pounded to alert the "Thunderbolt" Marshall de Biron, encamped closer to Amiens.

As the Spanish riders approached Amiens from the north, Sir John Aldrich led his three hundred English soldiers ahead. The English pikemen and musketeers marched to the top of a knoll. Sixty more Frenchmen armed with arquebuses moved alongside the English, already poised to charge and to fire.

"We cannot confront champion horse with only our foot soldiers." Sir John Aldrich held his men back. Earlier, he had received written orders from the Queen's council to avoid taking undue risk and not to advance before the French. The Spanish horsemen passed below the knoll.

Within sight of the Gate of Montrescu, Commander Guzman signaled, and his five cornets sounded, alerting Governor Hernán Tello inside Amiens. His five companies quickened to a fast trot. He headed directly to the ditch between the Hermitage and the outer bastion protecting the northern gate of Amiens.

Hermitage, Abbey of Mary Magdalene, North of Amiens

WHEN MARSHALL *DE* Biron arrived with several hundred French pikemen at the Hermitage by the Abbey of Mary Magdalene, soldiers had already raised mounds of dirt. The Marshall and the first forty or fifty French soldiers charged down the sloped walls toward the ditch in front of a pointed bastion. This ravelin helped to protect the Gate of Montrescu, but in the ditch or *fosso*, the French pikemen blocked the advance of the Spanish and Italian horse.

Commander Guzman's horsemen fired their arquebuses, and French carbines fired back. Spanish riders lowered their lances and charged up the dry ditch between the Hermitage and the slanted walls in front of the Gate. More French pikemen swarmed into the *fosso*.

The first company of Spanish riders abandoned their lances and drew their swords. The gate of the ravelin in front of the main gate opened, but more French pikemen swept down from the mounds in front of the Hermitage.

From the top of the ravelin, Irish and Spanish musketeers fired, while below, the fighting intensified. French fighters became entangled in close combat with the Spanish and their allies. Irish pikemen of Lieutenant Colonel Thomas Bostock charged out of the Gate of Montrescu. A Spanish captain led his pikemen past the bastion.

French fighters turned around. Fighting in the counterattack, shots rang out and horses fell. Blood oozed onto the ground as the first Spanish horsemen escaped through the opened gate and into the occupied town. From the far side, Swiss pikemen, allies of the French, joined the fray. They fought pike to pike, clashing against both the Irish and Spanish. More than one limb was severed, abandoned on the blood-soaked terrain.

A Spanish captain, gravely wounded, was carried away. An Irish captain died, too. Within minutes, by the time the English reached the ditch, the skirmish had ended.

Dead bodies, both horses and men, littered the ground. Most of the Spanish lancers and other horsemen had escaped through the gate. Its portcullis shut.

Captain Duxbury stood next to Sir Aldrich. "Amiens has been strengthened."

"By nearly four hundred more horsemen."

Chapter 38 — Velvet Siege Begins

The courage of the defendants [Spaniards inside Amiens] was no less fierce and resolute, who, being careful not to pass by any opportunity for interrupting the works, sallied every hour— sometimes on horseback and sometimes on foot. By making the whole [French] Camp stand to their arms, they did by very long skirmishes keep the works at a stay, doing mischief sometimes in one place and often in another.
<u>The History of the Civil Wars of France, The Fifteenth Book</u>
Translated from the Italian of Henrico Caterino Davila by D.E.A.

Longpres-les-Amiens, Picardy, France, 15ᵗʰ April AD 1597

"YOUR ENGLISH RECRUITS should have stopped the Spanish cavalry," Charles *de* Gontaut, duc *de* Biron, found Sir Thomas Baskerville at *Longpres-les-Amiens* the following day. The French Marshall dismounted his horse and took off his gloves.

"Even the best foot soldiers cannot stop champion horsemen," Sir John Aldrich said.

"No more succors must be allowed into Amiens." Marshall de Biron ordered, "We begin our siege of Amiens here, at Longpres."

"We will build a half-moon," English General Baskerville directed. His second-in-command, Sir Aldrich, divied up the task.

"You should have seen it," John Smith told one of the English soldiers. "The fighting was intense."

"No more talking," Captain Joseph Duxbury gestured to a rock. After John lifted the heavy object up and carried it more than a dozen steps, Duxbury pointed. "Drop it here."

While John struggled to position it, another English soldier poured dirt from a gunny sack. Hours passed, and one side of the first fort at *Longpres-les-Amiens* slowly took shape.

By the next afternoon, after the first half-moon fort was formed, Captain Joseph Duxbury told his company, "The Marshall wants trenches."

"Where?" John asked.

"Extended all the way to the Hermitage."

"But that's more than a mile away," one soldier said.

"We don't have enough men," another added.

"English soldiers don't complain." Captain Duxbury handed that soldier a shovel. John picked up a spade.

English soldiers dug all day, not stopping until late evening.

~ ~ ~

HOURS AFTER DARK, noisy French families rushed across the pontoon bridge.

"Who goes there?" the sentinel asked.

"We've been kicked out of our villa," a French youth said. "They burn our homes."

"Who?"

"The Spaniards." The youth pointed east. "Near the Abbey of St. John."

In the distance, a fire glowed, brightening the night sky. One tree lit up like a torch. The fire grew rapidly, spreading from the banks of the Somme to the south, from slanted bastions of Amiens and its fortified walls to the outskirts of Longpres.

More French youths crossed the bridge. Families—men, women, and children—streamed out of the suburbs. Some headed toward Picquigny and Abbeville, while other families headed south toward Beauvais and Paris.

"Tello's burning all of the suburbs," John told his captain.

"We had no time to save anything," the French youth said.

By morning, most of the flames had died down. Only burnt timbers and crossbeams remained. More than fifteen hundred houses, mansions, and villas had burned.

"The Spanish have burnt our homes," the French youth told Captain Duxbury. "We want to help."

"John Smith, escort these young men to Marshall *de* Biron."

Hermitage, Madeleine Abbey, Amiens, Picardy, France, 18 April *AD* 1597

AT THE HERMITAGE before the Abbey of Madeleine, Captain Duxbury and John found the Marshall. "These French youths want to help."

"I cannot pay much."

"They burnt our homes."

"We need seven forts between here and Longpres, and just as many betwixt here and Camon."

"Take cover!" a sentinel yelled.

Culverins and cannons placed atop the scarp in front of the Gate of Montrescu pounded the Hermitage. Rocks and debris spattered. French youths and allied soldiers covered their heads. The French monarch's own cannons were being used against him.

When the firing diminished, Biron ordered, "Raise these works higher."

~ ~ ~

SEVERAL DAYS LATER, John escorted more French youths to the French commander at the Hermitage. While conversing, a French nobleman arrived, dismounted, and reported, "The King has returned to Paris."

"Has he been able to find money for the army?" Marshall *de* Biron asked.

"His Majesty says his finance minister has a plan, but I can report to you that the King is not happy. When the reports of the four hundred horsemen entering Amiens reached his ear, the King spoke openly."

"What did he say?" Marshall *de* Biron asked.

"Where I am not in person, things go with little fortune. Or much negligence!"

"Does he not give me some credit for his former victories?" The Marshall huffed and turned to the French youths. "Pioneers, we must finish the trenches! I will show the King how a siege is done!"

French pioneers joined the soldiers, digging throughout the day and into the night. Trenches deepened, and the siege works slowly heightened.

Longpre-les-Amiens, Picardy, France, 12th May *AD* 1597

ABOUT A MONTH after Juan *de* Guzman brought 400 cavalrymen and a Spanish engineer into Amiens, Marshall de Biron and Sir Baskerville entered the two newly built half-moon forts at *Longpre-les-Amiens*.

Sir John Aldrich found Captain Duxbury. "Your men have worked hard, but we need to move to bigger tasks. We will turn Longpres over to the French."

Marshall *de* Biron motioned to his new Commander of the Artillery, who approached. "*Monsieur* St. Luc."

John remembered seeing the French general at the citadel in Montreuil near Calais before the Spanish had captured Amiens.

"We must plant three cannons to dissuade Cardinal Albert from crossing here." *Monsieur* Francois de St. Luc motioned.

"Enough watching." Captain Duxbury turned to his men. "Break camp!"

"Where are we going?" John asked.

"Upriver, to join the other English forces at Camon."

Within an hour, the whole English company had gathered its belongings.

By noon, Duxbury's company had reached the Hermitage, opposite the Gate of Montrescu.

Alarms sounded.

"Take cover!" Duxbury yelled.

Culverins and small cannons fired from the Spanish ravelin.

French workers took shelter, scurrying down the trenches. French and English soldiers rushed to their arms.

Minutes later, the barrage subsided. While John and the other English soldiers cleared the debris, Biron ordered, "Raise the works higher."

French soldiers sheathed their swords. French pioneers grabbed spades and shovels and returned to the trenches.

With the debris cleared, Duxbury's company hiked a mile further upriver.

Camon, Picardy, 12th May *AD* 1597

WHEN DUXBURY'S COMPANY arrived at Camon, John saw that the work at its half-moon fort had not yet been completed. Not waiting to set up camp, Captain Duxbury ordered, "Start working."

"There are only two more hours of daylight," a soldier, a little older than John, said.

"No complaining."

John and the others set down their gear. Just like they had done downstream at *Longpres-les-Amiens*, the English used picks, shovels, and spades.

When dusk approached, they had not stopped for even five minutes.

While they worked, a line of dejected French citizens approached the pontoon bridge spanning the Somme. Two monks, wearing their long robes with heads lowered, followed them.

As soon as the first refugees crossed, work ceased.

"Ce qu'il s'est passe?" Captain Joseph Duxbury asked.

"Pestilence has spread in Amiens," one Frenchman responded.

"Tello has kicked the weakest out," another added.

Two young women helped a much older man sit down. "Our grandfather."

"Some Spanish soldiers have died, too. They have lost a hundred on the walls, but many more because of sickness."

While talking, French sentinels guarding the bridge pointed. "The Bishop of Amiens?"

"Governor Tello kicked the bishop out, too," the monk said. "Many of us tried to help King Henry capture the Gate of Noyon, but we failed." That gate faced west, toward the town of Noyon, where Jean Calvin once lived and preached the Reformation.

"When Governor Tello found out, he kicked the Bishop, along with us, out," the second monk said.

"Vous? The monks of St. Augustine?" John asked in French.

"If we did not belong to the cloth, Tello would have killed us all," the monk said. "Yet some of our brethren remain imprisoned."

"What do you mean?"

"Tello claimed the bishop and the Augustinian monks had aided the traitors at the Gate of Noyon."

"Traitors?"

"Nine Frenchmen inside Amiens were executed."

"For treason?"

"When Tello conquered, they had sworn allegiance to the Crown of Spain."

"My sick grandfather?" the older of two sisters asked.

"Rest tonight," Captain Duxbury said. "Tomorrow, we'll put him on a wagon. You can take him to Picquigny. There's a doctor there."

"And the bishop?"

"I want to meet with Marshall de Biron."

French guards accompanied the important cleric.

Somme Riverbanks, Gate of Montrescu (West), 24th May *AD* 1597

IN THE FORTY days since the siege works began, nearly four thousand French pioneers had joined the effort.

Captain Francisco *del* Arco led his men, undetected, along the river banks. Traversing gullies, his soldiers moved into position, hiding in the woods. Two other companies hid nearby.

Captain *del* Arco peered across the river. "We must slow their progress. Cardinal Albert knows our predicament, but needs time to raise the relief army."

"Will King Philip II be able to help?" one Walloon soldier asked.

"Since he repudiated all debts, the financiers have refused to help."

"Did we need to burn all of the suburbs?"

Across the Somme, timbers and crossbeams stood, tarnished, burnt remnants of former riches. Beautiful villas were gone.

"A miserable necessity."

"And today?"

"This enemy siege must be stopped."

Captain *del* Arco glimpsed the action from upriver. Governor Hernán Tello *de* Portocarrero and three hundred horsemen sallied out of the gate. Gray dust rose as the Spanish horsemen rode through the charred ruins of the Abbey of St John and attacked the French lines. Three hundred foot soldiers, both musketeers and pikemen, followed the Spanish governor.

Much closer, on the Artois side of the Somme, the Gate of Montrescu opened and the Neapolitan Girolamo Caraffa, the *Marquis de* Montenegro, appeared. At the head of three hundred lancers and *arquebusiers* on horseback, he charged past the hidden soldiers. Riding hard between the river and newly built trenches, the *Marquis* moved toward *Longpre-les-Amiens* with its two half-moon forts and three cannons.

In the intense skirmish, less than a mile away, the *Marquis* assaulted the French defenders. Before they could capture the three cannons, several hundred French light horse galloped and engaged the *Marquis*. Meanwhile, Marshall *de* Biron, with more heavily armed riders, trotted towards the pass where Captain *del* Arco remained, still hidden.

"The Marshall wants to cut the *Marquis* off." Captain *del* Arco drew his sword and signaled. His musketeers fired. Pikemen swarmed out of the woods, charging the French cavalry with their very sharp, hooked pikes.

The Marshall turned and fought, drawing his sword and raising it high. Though Spanish and Walloon pikemen pulled down many French riders, Biron's horsemen gained the advantage. French riders with carbines fired. Hardened swords swung down, clashing against long battle axes.

"Le Marquis!" Captain *del* Arco yelled.

Galloping quickly, after being dislodged from *Longpres*, Montenegro attacked Biron's flank. Spanish riders lowered their lances and charged the French rear. Riders and horses fell, blood gushed, soaking the ground.

Captain *del* Arco moved closer to the enemy commander. He wanted to take the Marshall prisoner. His infantry reengaged the French cavalry. The skirmish turned sharp, even bloodier than before.

More French cavalry, the reserve, charged. Arriving from the Hermitage, they joined the battle, already two hours long.

The Marquis of Montenegro signaled to Captain *del* Arco. Marching ahead of the Marquis, *del* Arco and two other Spanish captains retired to Amiens.

French horsemen refused to pursue and also retired. With the sun setting, the dead, both French and Spanish, would be buried the next day.

Inside Amiens, Governor Hernán Tello *de* Portocarrero seemed very pleased. "We disrupted their siege-works." He turned to a trusted officer. "I want to parley."

Chapter 39 — Talks Abruptly End

"Do you believe, then," answered [Monsieur Francois d'Espinay de] Saint Luc, "that Marshal Biron is to be taken by a sack of nuts?" This raillery disconcerted the phlegm of the Spaniard, and put an end to an interview . . .

Memoirs of Henry the Great, Vol. II

The Artillery was commanded by Monsieur de Saint Luc, who, excited by his own genius . . . busied himself with infinite industry in all occasions, in which the Swiss and the English were always more ready and more diligent than all the rest; for the French Infantry, except the Regiment of Picardy and that of Navarre, was all made up of new men, and such were not accustomed to toils and labors, and to lie in the field . . .

History of the Civil Wars of France, The 15th Book
By Henrico Davila, Translated from the Italian

Hermitage, Mary Madeleine Abbey, Amiens, Picardy, 26th May *AD* 1597

TWO DAYS FOLLOWING *Marquis* de Montenegro's attack, Captain Joseph Duxbury and his young recruit, John Smith, rode past the half-moon fort.

"Marshall *de* Biron wants these four cannons delivered to the Hermitage by noon," Captain Duxbury said. His English company guarded a convoy from Abbeville.

When the convoy reached the pass between Longpre and Amiens, the only sounds were the squeaks from cannon carriages and trotting horses. All talking stopped.

Gravediggers buried more fallen soldiers, as well as horses. Fresh graves numbered in the scores.

John spurred his horse and caught up with his captain. "More died than I expected."

"Biron was almost captured, but he's undeterred."

When they reached the Hermitage, French cavalry rode north to patrol. Inside, *Monsieur* Francois de Luc, the new Grand Master of the

French Artillery, met the convoy and inspected his four new cannons. "*Excellente*. These will be of great service."

John remembered the previous animosity that the French General had shown at Duxbury's visit to Montreuil. Some of that hostility dissipated.

While the inspection continued, a flag of truce was raised above the Hermitage. A Spanish messenger entered, and allied officers congregated in the center of the citadel. The messenger told Marshall *de* Biron, "Governor Tello wants to parley, to negotiate."

The Marshall glanced in the direction of the fresh graves and pondered. "We accept." He motioned to General St. Luc. "Governor Tello wants to parley."

"I knew Tello when he was Governor at Doullens." St. Luc accompanied the messenger out of the Hermitage.

With the suspension of arms, Captain Duxbury and John climbed to the top of the walls of the Hermitage. Along with French musketeers, they watched St. Luc cross the ditch and enter through the Gate of Montrescu into Amiens.

On the other side of the Somme, the twin towers and steeple of the Cathedral rose above the walls.

Hotel *de* Ville, Amiens, Picardy, France 26 May *AD* 1597

GLANCING UP AT the belfry, *Monsieur* Francois de Saint Luc entered the Hotel de Ville of Amiens. Inside the comfortable chamber, the commander of the French artillery accepted Governor Tello's invitation to sit down.

"Something to drink?" the short Governor asked.

"*Non, merci.*"

Tello waved the servant away and sat down. His feet did not quite reach the floor.

The French general leaned forward. "The Marshall knows of and respects your courage, but you must realize a reversal of fortune may one day ruin it."

"Certainly, my reputation is no match compared to the Marshall's."

"If you surrender Amiens, you will be allowed to leave on most generous terms. The lives of your brave men will be spared."

"*Au contraire!* Since the Marshall has moved so close to my front door, I plan to make him my prisoner."

"*Pardon!*" St. Luc glared down at the Governor. "Do you believe the Marshall can be taken with a sack full of nuts?"

"Enough!" Tello, flushed in the face, huffed. He slid off the chair. "Take your leave."

When Monsieur St. Luc crossed market square, he noticed the Spanish possessed amble ammunition, as well as a plentiful store of corn and grain. But having heard reports of a meat shortage, they must have been true. Down a side street, a horse was being butchered.

"No longer needed," the messenger said. "Some riders died two days ago, but the cavalrymen refuse to eat it, only infantry."

"Sick and infirm?" St. Luc asked when he saw citizens sent south out of the Gate of Beauvais.

"For their own good, but Tello has set up a hospital at the Monastery of St. Augustine," the messenger said.

"Behind the Cathedral?"

"*Oui*, next to the Gate of Noyon."

The Hermitage, Amiens, Picardy, Late May *AD* 1597

INSIDE THE HERMITAGE, Monsieur Francois de St. Luc finished his story about the meeting. "Governor Tello was not pleased."

"And neither was Francisco del Arco, the 'Captain of Nuts?' Marshall de Biron asked, smiling at the four gentlemen officers comprising his suite. "Perhaps we should give the governor a foretaste of what is in store for him. Lower the flag of truce."

"Where do you want the four cannons from Abbeville to go?"

"Reposition them to the very front."

As soon as soldiers dragged them up to the bastion closest to the counterscarp, *Monsieur* St. Luc ordered, "Fire!"

The battering of Amiens began.

Tello, using the king's captured cannons, fired back.

Hermitage, Abbey de Madeleine, Amiens, 7ᵗʰ June *AD* 1597

ARRIVING BACK FROM their patrol of the rolling countryside of Picardy, Captain Joseph Duxbury and his company of English recruits spied royal flags.

"King Henry has returned?" young John Smith asked.

The entourage of the French Monarch swept through the greening meadows north of Amiens. Moving quickly, with flags waving, King Henry IV passed the last of the seven small forts and headed toward the Hermitage.

"After nearly two months." Captain Duxbury spurred his horse and led his company into the Hermitage. Inside, Duxbury brought his horse company to a halt. "Not everyone seems pleased with the King's return."

The King had already dismounted.

"What do you mean?" John asked.

"Look."

"Marshall *de* Biron?"

"The Marshall must have remembered the King's chide."

John recalled, "After Juan *de* Guzman and four hundred Spanish lancers entered Amiens?"

"*Oui.* He was so unhappy at the negligence that the King said that things only went well when he was present."

"But the men love Marshall *de* Biron?" John protested.

"Not only the English, but also the French."

While other soldiers helped take care of the horses, John accompanied his Captain past the ruins of the Abbey. The roof of the church had been blown off, but the arches remained.

Marshall *de* Biron bowed to the King. "If Your Majesty had not returned so quickly, we would have finished digging the trenches."

The King looked at each wall. "Such good work. When I left, the Hermitage was barely a fort. But now? I have a citadel."

"I see you have not arrived alone," Biron said.

"I brought no army."

"I speak about *Madame la Marquise.*"

Sitting sidesaddle, Gabrielle raised her spring hat, her blonde hair flowing over her shoulders. A courtier aided the once more, thin-waisted woman, and she dismounted.

John leaned toward his Captain. "Will the colonels be pleased with women in the camp?"

Captain Duxbury gestured his doubts.

"Gabrielle, the King's true prosperity and good fortune," Biron spoke loudly.

Gabrielle d'Estrées smiled coyly.

King Henry IV motioned for Sir Thomas Baskerville and the other officers to gather closer around him. "Let it be known, I shall not leave the army until Amiens falls." The King paused and turned toward the occupied town. "I will restore this city to France and establish my crown." He gestured across the Somme. "Or lose Amiens and my life!"

Sir Baskerville coughed. "Will *His Most Christian Majesty* take command of the army?" Sir Baskerville used on the King Henry's recognized titles.

"*Non,* all shall remain as before," King Henry IV answered. "*Le Maréchal* will command all matters *militaire.*"

Officers and soldiers, both French and English, nodded and smiled at each other.

The King set up his tent behind the Hermitage in the ruins of the Abbey of Madeleine. His mistress set up her tent next to his. Behind a thick arch, workers pounded stakes, then tied the lines taut. Courtiers and counsellors set up tents further back. Several physicians attended to both the sick and the wounded in the expanding hospital. Apothecaries crushed drugs and mixed medicines.

After the meeting, Sir John Aldrich approached the English general. "Sir Baskerville, you are in pain."

Sir Baskerville grimaced and grabbed his side. "Sir Aldrich, you are the fittest and worthiest man."

"Doctors!"

Riverie Castle, Somme Riverbanks, Towards Camon, 15th June *AD* 1597

A WEEK AFTER the King's return to Amiens, a summer wind kicked up. A windmill turned next to the small Castle of the Rivierie, where the English regiment was headquartered. Within sight of French cavalry stationed at the half-moon fort near Camon, John asked his Captain, "How is our general doing?"

"After falling ill, Sir Baskerville was taken to the hospital at Picquigny. If our general does not survive, his two-month-old son will be under the care of the captains."

"Including you?"

"All of us. When his son Hannibal Baskerville was born at St. Valerie in April, all of his colonels and captains were made godfathers."

"A tradition of sons born to generals in the field?"

"A noble one."

Sir John Aldrich, appearing with many more English soldiers, dismounted. "We must complete these trenches; the approaches to Amiens must be closed."

"Sir Baskerville?" Captain Duxbury asked.

"Haven't you heard? Our general died yesterday at Picquigny."

"His mind was sharp, his valor strong."

"Yes, though his nobility was unquestioned, his body suffered much pain."

"Will Sir Baskerville be buried here in France?" John asked.

"His body is already on its way back to London, perhaps St. Paul's Cathedral." Sir Aldrich added, "But I have some good news."

"We could use some," Captain Duxbury said.

"Our Queen has agreed to send all of the four thousand men promised in the treaty, the Triple Alliance among England, France, and the United States of the Netherlands."

"Amiens can be fully surrounded and invested," Duxbury said.

"Some soldiers will join the regiment that has stopped the bands of Spanish and Walloon soldiers, who had passed the river and marched through the woods. And the King has advanced some monies for the pay and has promised to settle all accounts when Baron de Rosny arrives."

The digging resumed, noisily into the night.

Hermitage, Madeleine Abbey, Amiens, Picardy, 21st June *AD* 1597

ON THE LONGEST day of the year, clouds thickened above the countryside of Picardy in northern France.

"Hurry," Captain Duxbury pointed at the ramparts protecting the Gate of Montrescu. "Marshall de Biron wants us ready to breach the walls. We need more *saucissons*."

John Smith picked up and pulled open the neck of an empty leather sack. Another soldier scooped up gunpowder and poured it into the opening. As soon as the sack was filled, John secured it, tying it in a tight knot. Like butchers stuffing pork into sausage skins, the soldiers filled more *saucissons*, stacking the leather sacks neatly, side by side.

Evening blackened into night, so under starless skies, John and the other English soldiers slung the heavy *saucissons* over their shoulders. Duxbury's company moved quickly and quietly along the Somme river banks, towards ramparts extending out from the Gate of Montrescu. On the far side of the ramparts, a French company had been commanded to do the same.

Across the river behind the city's walls, torches flickered and illuminated the facade of Amiens Cathedral. Its two square towers stood like sentinels, one taller than the other.

Much closer, on the near side of the river, the English edged below the steep walls of the rampart. Captain Duxbury motioned for his company to halt. Above, only a few yards away, Irish guards patrolled the walls, dotted with torches. One stopped and peered into the darkness before moving on.

During the sentinel's departure, the English soldiers stepped into the shallow moat, only two or three feet deep. They waded the length and steeped, like tealeaves in a pot. Reaching a dry corner, the soaked soldiers stacked their sacks chest-high.

Above, another sentinel walked the walls, and the English soldiers quickly hid. When the guard, dressed in an Irish uniform and likely under the command of Lieutenant Colonel Thomas Bostock, resumed his patrol, Duxbury pointed out the places where the *saucissons* should be placed. John and the other English soldiers planted them against the wall.

Further downriver, on the other side of the ramparts, French charges fired, lighting up the sky.

Captain Joseph Duxbury commanded. "Light them!"

John lit the short fuse and ran back around the corner. The *saucissons* exploded, rocks flew high. Part of the wall shattered, its facade slipped down.

English soldiers rushed the moat, overcame the dust, and reached the wall.

"A breach?" Captain Joseph Duxbury yelled.

"No!" John examined the damage. "Only the facing."

"Plant more *saucissons*!" Duxbury grabbed a sack.

When another soldier brought the gunpowder, he told John, "Mines or petards would be better."

As John lit the fuse, shots rang out from above.

"Take cover!"

John zig-zagged to the other side of the moat, directly beneath the firing guards. A bullet struck John's compatriot, who grabbed his wounded arm. John fired his *arquebus* up at the guard, who fell forward and flipped, splashing into the moat.

The *saucisson* exploded, and debris flew. John protected his head and helped his friend around the corner.

More Irish and Spanish musketeers appeared above. Shots were fired at the English, who lacked cover. Fleeing behind the gunpowder sacks, the English soldiers aimed their firearms.

"The powder!" Captain Duxbury yelled.

"Take it?"

More Irish muskets were discharged. Bullets ricocheted above the powder. When a spark landed on one of the leather sacks, Duxbury signaled, "Retreat."

"The *saucissons*?"

"Abandon them."

With the fires fading, the English soldiers fled into the dark. The gunfire diminished and ended.

The next morning, John looked below the ramparts. Irish soldiers picked up the abandoned sacks and dragged them inside.

Captain Duxbury pointed to the top of the walls. "They've increased their guard."

"Spaniards and Walloons."

Chapter 40 — Maximilien *de* Bethune

In such circumstances all that a young man can do is to improve his morals, if he cannot his genius; for even the hurry and confusion of arms offer excellent schools of virtue and politeness to him that is desirous of profiting by them: but miserable, and that during his whole life, is he who engages in a profession so fatal to youth, without the having strength or inclination to resist bad examples . . .

The Council of the Finances, accustomed to rejoice in the calamity of the people, were soon comforted under these new subsidies, provided they might pass through their hands.

The King [Henry IV] replied, that the person he was resolved to employ should be invested with his authority, and that, with regard to the other qualities, he pitched upon me (I was present at this discourse) as the most industrious and most prudent amongst them, although the youngest.

Memoirs of the Duke of Sully, Book I and Book IX
Maximilien de Béthune, Baron de Rosny [Later, Duke of Sully]
Translated from French by Charlotte Lennox

English Headquarters, Chateau *de* Camon, Picardy, Late June *AD* 1597

TWO FRENCH NOBLEMEN arrived at the English Headquarters near the Chateau de Camon several days later. Sir John Aldrich said, "I see Baron de Rosny and *Seigneur de* Villeroy have arrived. The King must have been successful on his second trip to Paris."

"Didn't the King vow to stay at Amiens?" Captain Joseph Duxbury asked.

"Nobles refused to lend the monies promised, so the King returned to Paris last week." Sir John Aldrich added, "Captain Duxbury, come and receive your pay."

While the new English commander sent runners to bring his other officers, Sir Aldrich met the French nobleman, "Baron de Rosny, you are becoming very popular with both captains and soldiers."

"Let me meet your captains," Maximilien de Béthune requested.

"This is Captain Joseph Duxbury," Sir John Aldrich said.

"The King insisted you should be paid as soon as possible," the Baron said. Born at the Chateau of Rosny-sur-Seine, he appeared to be in his mid-thirties.

"The King has not returned with you?" Captain Duxbury asked.

Baron *de* Rosny took off his hat, revealing his receding hairline.

Maximilien de Bethune, Baron de Rosny

"His Majesty should arrive at Amiens within days. He is delayed at Monceaux."

"The estate of *Madame la Marquise*?"

"*Oui*, with his mistress," Max-imilien *de* Béthune agreed. While waiting for the other captains, Maximilien *de* Béthune explained the reasons for the delay. "Let me explain what has happened over the last few months. Upon his first return to Paris in April, the King met his council at the Archbishop's Palace."

Palace of the Archbishop, Notre Dame Cathedral, Paris, April *AD* 1597

AMPLY GUARDED BY Swiss soldiers carrying long halberds, the royal carriage crossed the parvis, the large square in front of Notre Dame Cathedral. As morning shadows lifted, they entered the adjacent gates of the Palace of the Archbishop of Paris. *His Most Christian Majesty* stepped out of his carriage and acknowledged the Archbishop.

"The Council awaits your presence," the Archbishop said.

They walked together into the chamber; all rose to acknowledge the King of France and Navarre. They bowed as he walked by and when all settled onto their chairs, the Archbishop reconvened the expanded Council of Finance.

King Henry IV rose to his feet. "Spanish cavalrymen have already destroyed the granaries between Artois and Amiens. With the capture of Amiens, our loss is great. If Cardinal Albert destroys the fields between Amiens and Paris, Paris will be a frontier town. Last year, when the plague

318

swept through Paris, you gave alms. This year, my army besieges Amiens and needs to be paid. I ask for alms for them." King Henry IV paused and beckoned. "Enterprises of this kind are always difficult, so my noble friends and financiers, what advice do you give me?" His Most Christian Majesty sat down.

A financier stood up. "New levies must be made."

"The financiers should lend the money," a nobleman countered.

"No, no, we need higher taxes."

Another financier suggested, "We can sell the offices of justice." The debate grew louder.

"No, the judges would not be able to collect what is owed."

"New imposts must be made on ships traveling the rivers."

"No, higher taxes on the rich merchants in the city."

"Yes, Parisians do not pay their fair share!"

"Their merchants already pay too much!"

Like a terrible tempest, the tumult intensified. Nobles and financiers glared at each other. The rancor quickly resumed, one faction opposing another, one side countering the other—like a cyclone spinning in disorder.

As the tumult reached its apex, the King stood up and calmed the gathering. "I do not have much experience in finance, but here is what I propose." The King pulled out a paper that Maximilien *de* Béthune, Baron de Rosny, had drawn out for him. "We will borrow from the cities and the wealthiest persons in France twelve hundred thousand livres, but that will be repaid within two years with interest, by levying a tax of fifteen sous on salt. In addition, we will augment the office of justices with the establishment of the third one. This new justice will sit every third year." The King finished the seven-point plan.

With stunned expressions, none in the whole council spoke one word.

"I take your silence to mean unanimous consent." The King added, "This Council is dismissed."

As the King exited the chambers, he smiled at the unknown author of the proposal. His army would soon be paid, he thought.

Chateau *de* St. Germain-en-Laye, Overlooking the Seine, May *AD* 1597

ABOUT TWENTY MILES outside Paris, at the garden palace of *St. Germain-en-Laye*, the King took an afternoon stroll across the large square between the two chateaus at St Germain-en-Laye. The chapel of *Château Vieux,* or the old castle, had been built by Saint Louis, but the *Château Neuf,* or new castle, was of recent vintage. Garden terraces extended all the way down to the Seine. Since leaving Paris, his doctors had continued the treatment for passing gravel. Every day, the physicians drew a few ounces of blood from the King's arm.

"Henri *de* Lorraine, the Duke of Bar, is here," his private secretary told the King. The King smiled at the son of the Duke of Lorraine. "My servant will show you the gardens, while I talk to Catherine."

"Bring my sister."

Accompanied by a lady-in-waiting, Catherine *de* Bourbon arrived from the *Château Vieux* and entered the King's chambers inside the *Château Neuf.*

After she kissed her brother, the King stepped back. "It is settled."

"But brother?" Catherine *de* Bourbon objected.

"Your marriage is for the good of France."

"But Henri *de* Lorraine is Catholic."

"That did not bother you when you wanted to marry your cousin, the Count of Soissons."

"That was different."

"How?"

"I loved him."

"What about the Duke of Montpensier? You did not complain that he was Catholic when I mentioned him in Rouen?"

"He is a Prince of the Blood."

"It is for the good of France. You might even become Catholic."

"Brother!" Catherine could not hide her disappointment; tears slid down her cheeks. "I will never abandon the Reformed Faith of our mother."

A few minutes later, after the weeping subsided, the Duke of Bar entered the chambers. After exchanging pleasantries, the King asked the Duke, "With regard to the matter of religion?"

Henri *de* Lorraine glanced at Catherine. "Madame's Reformed faith presents no obstacle with me, or my father."

After the Duke escorted Catherine to the gardens, Gabrielle entered from the adjoining room.

"See if you can persuade my sister," the King asked his mistress.

"Your sister loves you very much. She will see to your needs. I know how much you want to be allied with the Duke of Lorraine."

320

"And he with us. When his son marries my sister, our houses will be aligned." The King looked outside. "I would so much like to walk through the lower gardens. Perhaps after my treatment."

~ ~ ~

LESS THAN A fortnight later, while the King worked at his desk, his secretary entered his chambers. "My sister?"

"Last Sunday, upon her return to Paris, your sister again worshiped with those of the Reformed Religion."

"I am not surprised," King Henry IV said.

"Your Catholic subjects heard her singing psalms."

"Catherine wanted to show she would not abjure her Christian Faith."

"But we received other news from the Constable."

"Regarding the edicts?" King Henry IV asked.

"The Parliament in Paris refuses to register them. They object to the appointment of the third man to the offices of justice, the one approved unanimously by your council."

The King rose. "Parliament must register it, my army must be paid, and I must return to Amiens, to the siege."

La Chambre Dorée, Palais de Justice, Ile de la Cite, **Paris, 20 May** *AD* **1597**

LEAVING LOUVRE PALACE, the King's carriage soon crossed the *Pont au Change* across the right branch of the Seine. It turned into the *Palais de Justice*, the former home of Saint Louis, King Henry's noble ancestor. In the courtyard, the King exited the carriage and entered *La Chambre Dorée*, where the Parliament of Paris always met.

As soon as the King entered the plush chamber, the parliamentarians took their seats in a circle. Beneath a high ceiling covered in gilt, the King strolled to the center of the gathering:

"*Messieurs*, it is with extreme regret that I appear in parliament for the first time on my present mission. It would have been far more agreeable for me to hold a *lit de justice* to admonish you on your duties, but I am compelled to rebuke you for your procrastination, obstinacy, and disobedience. You have endangered the state, but my zeal for the rescue of the realm brings me here. My Chancellor will declare to you my royal will and intention."

The King sat down, not on a throne, for there was none, but on five raised cushions.

"Having heard his Royal will, the plan is proposed. With no objection," the Chancellor declared. "The edict registered! This Parliament is dismissed."

The King rose again, and the howls of protest quieted.

As he exited, the King told the Chancellor, "If those of the Reformed Religion join us, our army will be large enough to finish the siege."

Châtellerault, On the Vienne River, France, 16th June *AD* 1597

DUC DE THOUARS, Claude *de la* Tremoille, entered the large assembly room. Three years earlier, the King had made the *Duc de* Thouars a peer, one of only twelve in all of France. Inside, scores of members of the Reformed Religion had gathered in the hall at Châtellerault. Those noblemen who had gathered early at the *Chateau de* Saumur at the end of March had refused the king's summons. They had not come to His Most Christian Majesty's aid when Amiens was first conquered by a sack of nuts.

"This assembly is called to order!" the secretary proclaimed.

Besides the noblemen who had gathered at Saumur, each province sent a minister of the Reformed Religion and a representative of the Third Estate. King Henry IV had urged a larger assembly in order to persuade its leaders.

"Who shall preside over our assembly?"

"I nominate the *Duc de* Thouars!" one important nobleman shouted.

All eyes turned towards Claude *de la* Tremoille, and shortly thereafter, they gave their approval.

"We shall hear from the Governor of Saumur," the *Duc de* Thouars said. Though he had been raised Catholic, he had publicly accepted the Reformed Faith after his sister did.

"The King has given his consent for our assembly and wishes us to join him at Amiens for the good of France," Philippe *de* Duplessis Mornay, the Governor of the Saumur, said.

Eleven years earlier, Philippe *de* Mornay had taken two ships from La Rochelle to Guernsey at the behest of Claude's younger sister, Charlotte Catherine *de* La Trémoille, who was only seventeen at the time. Claude and Henri *de* Bourbon, Prince of Conde, had sought the aid of the Queen, but were unsuccessful and rotting in a state of despair on the island in the middle of the channel. During their absence, Charlotte Catherine had courageously defended her brother's castle at Taillebourg from attack.

A year after Prince of Conde married Charlotte Catherine in 1586, he again accepted the Reformed Faith, but when the Prince died, she was accused of his murder—even though, afterwards, she gave birth to his son. When King Henry IV acceded to the throne, Charlotte Catherine *de* La Trémoille was freed, and the boy was acknowledged as a Prince of the Blood. If King Henry IV did not father a legitimate heir, her son, Henri II *de* Bourbon, would become King of France.

"But what security does the King grant us?" one member of the Third Estate asked.

"If we send our fighting men to Amiens, who will protect us from the Roman Catholics who want our lands?" another asked.

"We are forced to pay tithes to Rome and cannot support our own clergy."

Ministers of the Reformed Christian Faith totaled nearly one-third of the assembly.

"The King must give us some satisfaction."

The opposition grew stronger, exceeding that seen in late March at Chateau *de* Saumur.

"We should give the King some concession," Duplessis Mornay said.

"Not until our demands are met!"

With debate at a standstill, the meeting at Châtellerault would continue for days. His mind on other matters, Claude *de* Tremoille penned a letter to Charlotte *de* Nassau, the daughter of the late William of Nassau, better known as William *the Silent*. He wished to marry this sister of Maurice of Nassau-Orange. In the meantime, the *Duc de* Thouars wanted to raise an army at nearby Poitou: in case the mood of the Assembly changed, he either aid the king at Amiens or openly rebel against him.

Louvre Castle, Paris, Late June *AD* 1597

"IT IS WITH regret that I had to return to Paris a second time," King Henry IV said, "but my army must be paid." He scanned the members of the Council of Finance inside the Louvre. Windows overlooked the inner courtyard of the small palace.

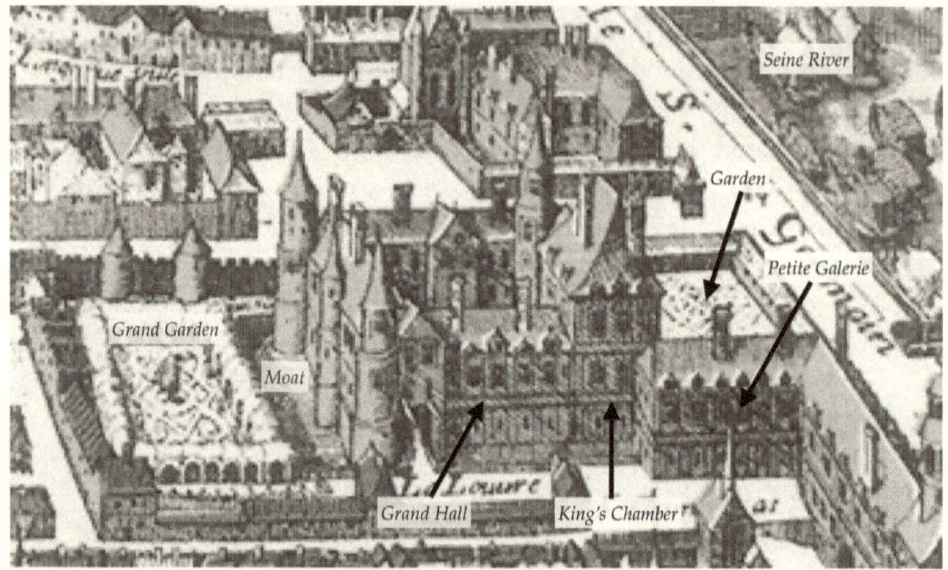

The Louvre Palace in 1615

"Yes, but with everything settled and the new imposts approved, we will be able do much," Nicolas *de* Harlay, *Seigneur de* Sancy said.

"As long as the monies go through our hands," another member added, "as before."

"I have other ideas," King Henry IV said.

"Yes, tax monies must go through our hands," *Seigneur de* Sancy said. "We have the most experience." He previously had chaired the Council of Finance.

"We must weed out corruption," the King said.

"We do not take offense," *Seigneur* Sancy said, "but whether alms are given to the people or monies paid to the army, it makes no sense unless it goes through our hands."

"I have decided," the King declared. "Everything will go through the hands of Baron *de* Rosny."

"But he's the youngest," *Seigneur de* Sancy countered. "He has no experience."

Though he was indeed younger than any other member of the Council of Finance, he was not inexperienced. When he was but eleven years of age, his father took him to Vendome and presented the youth to Jeanne d'Albret, the Queen of Navarre, and to her son, Prince Henry. The young boy knelt on the ground on one knee and confirmed his desire to serve. Prince Henry immediately told him to rise and commended the zeal that the family had always shown to his family. Henry promised to protect the young boy.

Negotiations for peace were concluded with Catherine *de* Medici. When her husband, King Henry II, seemed destined to die from injuries suffered in a jousting match, she sent his one-time mistress, who was twenty years older than Henry, away. She forced Diane de Poitiers to retire to Anet. Always fit and healthy, Diane first met Henry when he was seventeen and the Dauphin—the presumed successor to the French throne. On the day his opponent's lance shattered and splinted into his eye, King Henry II carried the colors of his mistress Diane, and not his wife Catherine. Ever since the jousting accident in 1559, the Queen Mother—perhaps mimicking the techniques of the former mistress—maintained vast influence over her children. Her three sons would become kings of France in succession, and the Queen Mother would occupy a whole wing of the Louvre for a quarter of a century.

The marriage between the Huguenot Prince and the Catholic Princess Marguerite, the sister of Charles IX, was arranged for the summer of 1572. Prince Henry of Navarre took his page Maximilien *de* Bethune to Paris, where the boy stayed with his governor, St. Julian, while studying languages at the College of Burgundy. Two months before the wedding, the Queen of Navarre, after receiving perfumed gloves from an Italian tied to the Queen Mother, unexpectedly died. Prince Henry became King Henry III of Navarre and married Marguerite in front of Notre Dame Cathedral in August of 1572. But the happiness did not last a week.

The Huguenot Admiral *de* Coligny was shot, and while recovering, a few days later, he was stabbed, thrown out the window, and beheaded in the presence of the Duke of Guise. Bells tolling signaled the beginning of the Saint Bartholomew's Day Massacre. When the boy's governor and valet went out to see the cause of the commotion, they were neither seen nor heard from again. The landlord of the building came in, pale and white, saying he had agreed to go to Mass. Maximilien did not think it proper to follow him, so, donning a scholar's gown and taking a prayer book, he headed for the College of Burgundy. Blood flowed in the streets as Huguenots, both young and old, were dragged out of their abodes. "Kill! Kill!" the mobs shouted. "Massacre the Huguenots!"

Though they stopped him several times, the murderers did not molest the youth and let him go when they saw the prayer book under his arm. He slipped a few coins to the guard at the college in order to see the headmaster. Inside, two Sicilian vespers said, "Not even infants at the breast shall be spared." But the principal led the boy away and locked him in a chamber. On the third day, Maximilien was freed. King Charles IX, plagued and torn between his body and his soul, kept a promise to his Huguenot surgeon that he would never force his doctor to change his religion.

Maximilien's father, by staying in the outer suburbs, had escaped the slaughter. The Baron *de* Rosny wrote and urged his son to stay with King Henry of Navarre, who was under strong guard at the Louvre. Since the boy could no longer study languages at the college, King Henry assigned a man named Chretien to teach him history and mathematics. Cretien tutored him in the same manner as the King had been tutored before. Yet the king's mother, who oversaw the prince's education, was perhaps even stricter with her son. She made him sleep on hay.

"Baron *de* Rosny is most trustworthy and most honest." The King glanced towards the man who had handled his financial affairs for a decade and a half. The baron recently had augmented that trust. Recently, when Monsieur and Madam Fervaques had asked Maximilien's permission for her son, Guy, the Count of Laval, to marry his daughter, Marguerite de Bethune, Rosny declined to answer. Instead, Baron *de* Rosny told the Fervaques to ask the King directly. When they did ask, the King approved of the proposal, telling Rosny, 'I believe it would be most advantageous to all.'

Earlier, the King's sister, Princess Catherine *de* Bourbon, had suggested to the Dowager Princess of Rohan and Maximilien's wife, Rachel, that her son, Henri II *de* Rohan, marry Marguerite. After his father died, Henri II *de* Rohan, like Maximilien before him, had joined the King's suite. However, King Henry IV was upset by the young Rohan's behavior. Since his Majesty had not been consulted, he objected to the agreement amongst the three women—the two princesses and Rachel de Bethune. The marriage to Guy, Count of Laval, would be consummated when Marguerite came of age—roughly a decade later.

"He's not even Catholic," another member said.

"My decision is final; Rosny is in charge of all."

After the meeting, *Seigneur de* Sancy approached the King. "Your Majesty, I see my services are not needed in Paris."

"Very well, you can join me at the siege and command a regiment of the Swiss."

English Headquarters, Camon, Picardy, Late June *AD* 1597

WHILE THE BARON de Rosny, who had inherited his title from his father, finished his story concerning the happenings in Paris, the rest of the English captains arrived.

Nicholas de Neuville, *Seigneur de* Villeroy, distributed all of the back pay to the quartermasters.

"I must return to Paris." Baron de Rosny, fully dressed in armor, mounted his horse.

After escaping from Paris at the age of sixteen, the strong and vigorous Rosny learned to shoot and fight. One Catholic officer, who served the King of Navarre, once told Rosny that he was so young, "the milk is not out of your nose."

"I am strong enough to draw blood out of yours with my sword," Rosny responded. Perhaps surprisingly, a Huguenot officer came to the aid of the Catholic, while his Catholic rival and other friends stood by Rosny. The ruckus grew louder; the verbal melee ended before physical blows landed.

Fully trained in arms, Rosny exposed himself to danger in a number of skirmishes, but he soon found himself better suited to engineering and other endeavors. At age twenty, he began to adeptly manage the finances of the Kingdom of Navarre. King Henry brought him to Pau, where his sister resided. Catherine *de* Bourbon introduced Rosny to the life of a courtier—a life fully propounded by the Italian Baldassare Castiglione. She taught young Rosny how to dance. The king, meanwhile, kept company with Catherine's governess, Madam *de* Tignonville.

Young John Smith watched Rosny, accompanied by a strong guard, cross the pontoon bridge over the Somme. When King Henry IV heard that Rosny inspected the *de* Luc's feats of engineering in the forward trenches, he became upset. If the trenches were suddenly attacked, the king might lose his most able minister. He needed to ensure his safety.

"Do not stand there and stare," Captain Duxbury said. "We have much work to do."

Smith and the other recruits grabbed their shovels and spades. Other recruits used picks and joined them. Resuming their efforts, they worked ever faster, piling mounds higher. They dug their trenches deeper and longer—ever closer to the outer walls of Amiens.

Chapter 41 — Building a Platform

By this misfortune, and the diseases which increased, the ardor of the Defendants was something cooled, insomuch that [Marshall de] Biron had conveniency to plant eleven great Pieces of battery in the Hermitage; which scouring the field, hindred them from sallying out of the Counterscarp, and sheltered those that began to work at the Trenches .

History of the Civil Wars of France, The 15th Book
By Henrico Davila, Translated from Italian

Hermitage, Abbey of Madeleine, Amiens, Picardy, 29th June *AD* 1597

CAPTAIN DUXBURY ACCOMPANIED the new English General, Sir John Aldrich, to the Hermitage and met the Marshall of France, Baron *de* Biron, who informed. "A new regiment from Champagne, our army has grown to nearly twelve thousand men. More soldiers are expected, part of the King's plan."

Captain Joseph Duxbury viewed the Champagne regiment. "How so?"

"Each region is responsible for raising and supporting its own regiment. Besides those from Champagne, regiments are being raised in the Isle of Paris, about Orleans, and throughout Normandy."

"And those of Reformed Religion?"

"With the King's permission, they returned to their homes. With greater authority and in larger numbers, assembled anew at Chatellerault. The King looks forward to their support, but they still delay."

Gunshots rang out, and Captain Duxbury and young John Smith rushed to the wall.

"The Marquis *de* Montenegro!" Duxbury pointed at the Italian cavalry commander from Naples.

Four companies poured out of the Gate of Montrescu. Half went one way, and half the other way. The horsemen charged and attacked the Hermitage.

Marshall *de* Biron rallied his troops and John rushed down from the wall. With the Marquis still attacking, the Count of Auvergne with the French light horse counterattacked. They pushed the Marquis back out of the Hermitage and into the dry ditch. As the French light horse pursued, both Irish and Italian foot sallied from the far wall. Supported by cannon fire, they forced the French horse back, then retired back inside the outer walls of Amiens.

The skirmish ended as quickly as it had begun, so Captain Joseph Duxbury surveyed the damage.

"How many died?" Marshall *de* Biron asked.

"I count about two hundred, your new recruits from Champagne."

"The enemy?"

"They lost ten."

"That cannot stand," Marshall *de* Biron said, "I have a plan. Sir Aldrich, one of your regiments must be held in reserve."

The English general turned and ordered, "Captain Duxbury, ready your men!"

Ruins, St. John Church, West of Amiens, Picardy, 30th June *AD* 1597

HIDDEN BY TREES, shrubs, and bushes at the burnt-out suburbs of Amiens, Marshall *de* Biron patiently waited. As the sky lightened, he viewed several of the two hundred French soldiers, who had remained hidden in the blackened remains of the Abbey of Saint John all night. Behind the Marshall, several hundred French riders, fully armed with carbines and arquebuses, kept their horses quiet.

Across the river, at the Hermitage, all was silent.

An hour after dawn, the gate to the suburbs opened. A train of Spanish riders rushed out. Biron motioned for his riders to mount. They did so—quietly and stealthily.

After the first Spanish riders rode through the abbey, trotting toward trenches surrounding the city, the two hundred French pikemen attacked. Shots were fired. The French cavalry charged.

Unable to retreat, the Spanish horse fought hard. Several hundred more Spanish infantry sallied out of the city, reaching the abbey and fighting ferociously.

The English regiment, held in reserve, marched up and pushed back the Spanish infantry all the way to the counterscarp by the gate. In close combat, the English slowly outgunned, overpowered, and overwhelmed the Spanish. Total victory was within their grasp.

Cannonballs then exploded in their midst. Still, the English pressed closer to the city, but Spanish musketeers unleashed a terrible volley.

Artillery once more fired round after round. Musketeers fired volley after volley, giving cover to the retreating Spaniards who retired through the gate. The two-hour skirmish finally ended—a fight some later swore lasted much longer.

English Headquarters, Camon, Amiens, Picardy, 30th June *AD* 1597

ABOUT NOON ON the last day of June, two distant cannons fired in rapid succession. John Smith climbed the short wall of the English headquarters at Camon and peered towards Amiens, the source of the sound. In front of the Gate of Montrescu, cannon smoke dissipated above the newly built parapet tower. Seconds later, a cloud of dust rose from the ground. As the cloud of dust grew larger, the sound of pounding hooves drew closer and boomed louder.

"Captain!" John yelled.

Duxbury rushed to the wall, saw the cloud, and turned. "Soldiers! Grab your pikes!"

Drums sounded the alarm, and English soldiers dropped their tools. They rushed from the trenches to their assigned positions.

As the cloud began to settle, John recognized the flag of Captain *del Arco*. His infantrymen advanced along the river in the direction of the mill, protected by a redoubt. A second Spanish infantry company marched, double-time.

Inside the English headquarters, soldiers scurried for their weapons. Some formed a line, but before they could prepare to receive the charge, the first Spanish horsemen circled around the side and lowered their lances. They swept through the English companies. No longer able to fall into order, the English fell back. The second company of Spanish riders raised their arquebuses. They fired their single-shot firearms at point-blank range. Scores of English soldiers died in the attacking wave.

From the walls, English muskets fired, but the enemy horsemen were too close, their armor too thick. Duxbury motioned for Smith and a handful of other English pikemen to stand firm. They raised their long pikes and charged the horsemen.

The Spanish rider drew his sword, but John ducked. The English soldier swept his pike around and pulled the rider down, and another.

The other English soldiers followed Captain Duxbury forward. Spanish arquebuses did not have time to reload, so they raised their swords. Pikes clashed against the falling swords, steel clanged against steel.

Spanish lancers discarded their lances and drew their second weapons. Swords, maces, and spikes flailed as the riders turned and spurred their horses anew. English musketeers blunted the flying riders, first with raised muskets, later with swords. The skirmish grew hotter, and sparks flew. Swords clashed and clanged; the metal vibrated in their hands.

The remaining English soldiers retreated to the exit. At the nearby mill, Spanish infantry overwhelmed the French in the redoubt. The Swiss in the trenches under Sancy likewise retired until French riders from Camon appeared.

Two more English companies regathered, regaining their strength. They reentered the headquarters in an effort to reclaim it. The Spanish sally, having done its damage, wound down. The footmen of Captain *del* Arco began their retreat; the Spanish horse provided their cover.

The Spanish commander, Juan *de* Guzman was the last to leave. Halfway back to Amiens, he, along with ten of his horsemen, found himself cut off. Two hundred French cuirassiers swooped before the Hermitage and attacked them. They surrounded the Spanish commander and captured his fine horse.

Seeing their commander bound, the Spaniards halted their retreat. Artillery fired from the walls in front of the Gate, stopping the French advance. A Spanish lieutenant led his men and as he was about to free Juan de Guzman, one of the French captors drew his pistol and executed his prisoner.

French horsemen pushed the Spaniards back once more. But the Spanish unleashed their artillery, more furiously than before. Cannonballs exploded in the ditch, causing more blood to flow.

At four in the afternoon, with nearly six hundred French dead, a truce was called by Marshall de Biron and Governor Portocarrero.

As soldiers retrieved the dead and tended the wounded, the King of France arrived back at Amiens. He had been absent nearly ten days, first in Paris, but lately at the Chateau of Monceaux, where his mistress Gabrielle planned to remodel her estate.

"Whose horse is this?" King Henry IV asked.

"Juan *de* Guzman," a French colonel said.

"The Spaniard who brought the relief?"

"Yes, your Highness?"

"Was he thrown into the ditch?"

"No, Juan *de* Guzman is dead, along with two of our soldiers—the ones who guarded him."

"Escort his body back to Amiens, so that Governor Hernán Tello *de* Portocarrero can receive it with honor."

As the King's command was carried forward and the corpse returned to the Spanish, the King arrived at the Hermitage. "Count St. Luc, we will build the platform you suggested."

"That should stop the sallies out of the Gate of Amiens," Marshall de Biron said.

"My thoughts exactly," the King echoed. "Twelve cannons should do."

"I already have them here," Count Saint Luc said.

~ ~ ~

THREE DAYS LATER, the platform had been raised high behind the forward walls. The pounding of the bastions and wall before the Gate of Montrescu began.

As buildings burned behind them, the enemy artillery could not silence the French cannons. In the summer heat, disease spread inside Amiens, and the daily Spanish sallies halted. The siege tightened, but rumors of peace spread.

Ladies who had escaped Amiens received passports to reenter the city. When they exited, John noticed they wore more jewelry.

"Governor Tello allowed diversions," Captain Duxbury said.

"And the French women?" John asked.

"They retrieved jewels hidden in their ransacked homes."

"But they joined with the diversions?"

"Yes, before leaving in the morning." Duxbury added, "I doubt if Cardinal Albert will be pleased."

John helped his friend, whose arm had been hit in the *fosse*, or ditch, onto a cart. The arm had turned green and needed to see a surgeon."

"I am lucky," his friend said.

"How so?" John asked.

"Who has ever heard of a hospital at a siege?"

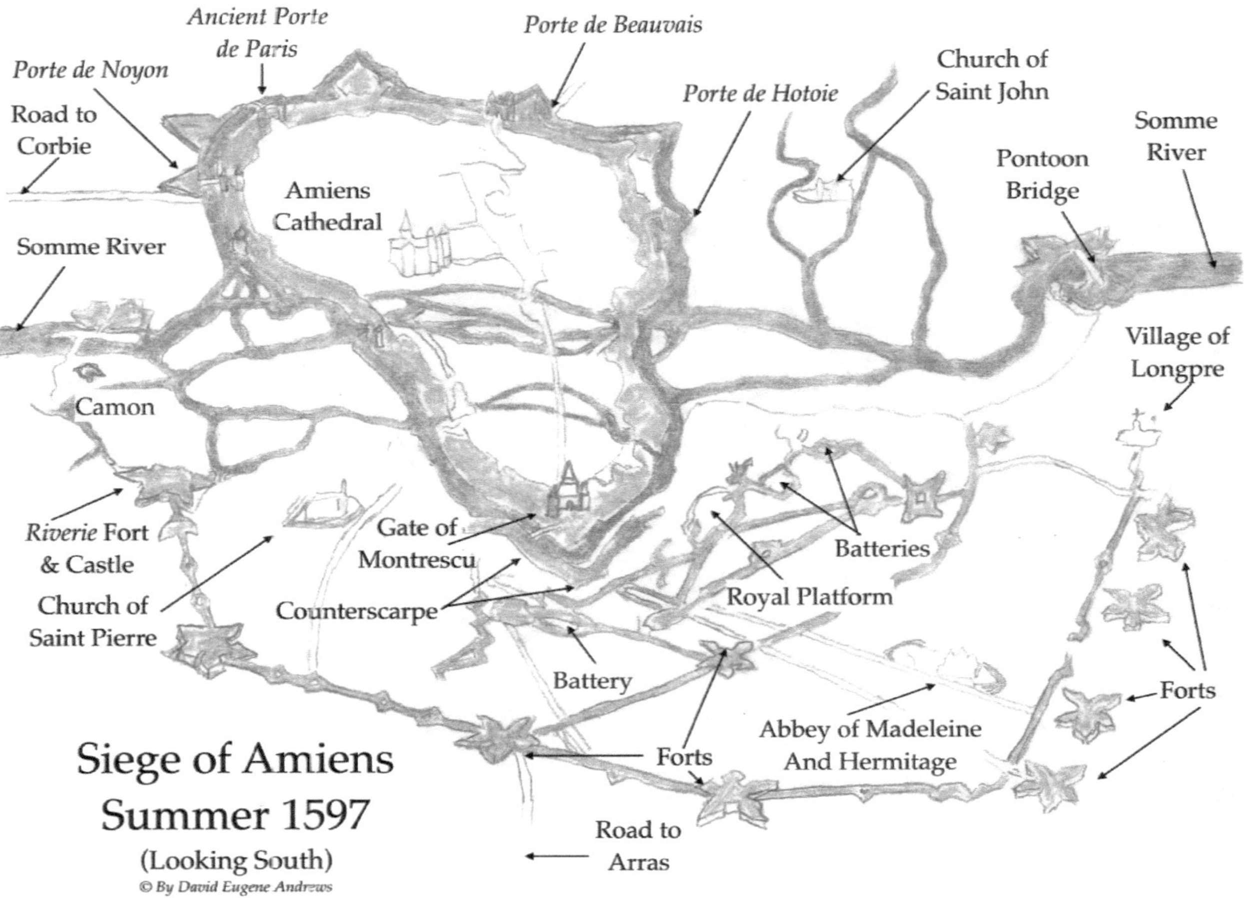

Siege of Amiens
Summer 1597
(Looking South)

© By David Eugene Andrews

On the way to the Chateau *de* Picquigny, where Maximilien *de* Bethune, Baron *de* Rosny, had established the second of two hospitals, he started to pass a young French soldier in pain.

"Are you going to the hospital?" John asked.

"Yes, my arm. A bullet is lodged next to a bone."

"Your name?"

"Armand from here in Picardy, and yours?"

"John, John Smith, from Lincolnshire in England. Is it true what they say about the men of Picardy, that you would never desert your post?"

"We vowed to be killed rather than ever abandon our position."

Second Hospital, Chateau *de* Picquigny, Picardy

WHILE LEAVING THE hospital at Picquigny, John Smith saw a Franciscan prelate surrounded by a few priests. John asked Armand, now with a bandaged arm, "Do you know who that is?"

"Buonaventura Caltagirone, the General of the Franciscans. Pope Clement VIII sent the Sicilian to pursue peace, but King Henry doesn't want anyone to know about the negotiations."

"But you revealed the secret?"

"We should not fall into trickery," the young French soldier said. "We are winning the siege."

John agreed, for trenches linked the outer forts surrounding Amiens. Relief from Brussels would be difficult. "Your arm?"

"My fighting arm is good."

"I can accompany you back to the siege."

"I need to find the captain of my company from Picardy."

Chapter 42 — Arrival of the King's Mistress

D'Aubigne relates, that is was commonly said at that time, that Henry IV had brought Paris with him before Amiens, to show the abundance that reigned in his camp. He likewise brought his mistress to Picquigny, at which the Marshall de Biron and other general officers murmured very much . . .
Cited in Memoirs of Maximilian de Bethune, Duke of Sully, Vol. II, Book IX
Translated from the French by Charlotte Lennox

By this misfortune, and the diseases, which increased, the ardor of the Defendants was something cooled, insomuch that Biron had conveniency to plant eleven great Pieces of Battery in the Hermitage; which scouring the fields, hindred them from sallying out of the Counterscarp, and sheltered those than began to work at the Trenches . . .
History of the Civil Wars of France, The 15th Book
By Henrico Davila, Translated from Italian by D.E.A.

Hermitage, Abbey of Madeleine, Amiens, Picardy, Summer *AD* 1597

BEYOND ENEMY MUSKET range, the Marshall of France, Charles de Gontaut, Baron *de* Biron, and several of his retinue of experienced officers set up their camp in front of the Hermitage. To their eastern side, a strong fort containing the regiment of Navarre blocked the main road to Doullens. Beyond the counterscarp and a ditch, the two spires of the Cathedral of Amiens rose above the walls.

Though the roof of the Abbey had been destroyed earlier in the siege, the king kept his headquarters aft of it. On the far side of the abbey where he had set up his camp, King Henry IV finished another letter. Though he was not in his palace, he kept writing, calling for more assistance from the nobles of France.

The King looked up and waved his nobles forward. "If my enemies had not divulged the secret negotiations with the Franciscan General, I might have been able to negotiate a surrender of Amiens."

"So we must continue the siege." Charles *de* Lorraine, Prince of Joinville and 4th Duke of Guise, had a narrow beard and long, curly hair.

He had become Prince of Joinville due to the most unfortunate of circumstances. Thirty-five years earlier, an assassin named Jean *de* Poltrot pretended to be a deserter from the Huguenot cause and murdered his grandfather, Francois *de* Lorraine, 2nd *Duc de* Guise. Caught and tortured, the assassin implicated Admiral Gaspard *de* Coligny and the other Huguenot leaders at Orleans. But Admiral Coligny adamantly disavowed and refuted all charges that he had been involved in such a despicable act outside the field of battle. The assassin later recanted before he was to be punished, to be drawn and quartered.

Nevertheless, Charles's father, Henry *de* Lorraine, 3rd Duke of Guise, and his uncle, Cardinal Francois, the Archbishop of Reims, blamed Coligny. Ten years later, Huguenots were invited to Paris for the marriage of King Henry of Navarre to Marguerite *de* Valois, known as Queen Margot. During the week following the ceremony, shots were fired from property owned by the Preceptor of the House of Guise in Paris, wounding Admiral *de* Coligny. Later that week, Coligny was stabbed and thrown out of his window. The Duke of Guise was present when Gaspard *de* Coligny was beheaded. Strung with ropes around his ankles, Gaspard's headless body was hung at the Gibbets—an open building set on a hilltop outside the walls of Paris.

On Saint Bartholomew's Day, during the night of the 24th of August 1572, thousands of Huguenots were dragged from their homes. Mobs yelled, "Kill! Kill them all!" in an episode orchestrated by Henry *de* Lorraine, the leader of the Catholic League, and Catherine *de* Medici, the Queen Mother. King Charles IX used a carbine that night, and within days, issued a decree forbidding the "Religion." In the Kingdom of France, a total of 70,000 Huguenots lost their lives over several weeks. The wickedness exhibited during those days shocked all Protestant nations, most particularly that of England, ruled by her Virgin Queen Elizabeth.

About fifteen years later, the War of the Three Henrys erupted. Henry *de* Lorraine, 3rd Duke of Guise, could not accept that King Henry of Navarre would become the future king of France, so he marched on Paris and captured the city from King Henry III. This reigning French monarch first fled to Chartres before retreating to Château *de* Blois. King Henry III signed a treaty, but shortly thereafter, when Henry *de* Lorraine visited the king at the Blois, this duke was assassinated. The next day, Christmas Eve, the 24th of December 1588, his brother, Cardinal Francois *de* Lorraine was likewise assassinated, this time by the Forty-Five, the royal guards of King

Henry III. In August of the following year, King Henry III suffered the same fate: a friar named Jacques Clément fatally stabbed King Henry III.

Before King Henry IV entered Paris in 1594, Charles *de* Lorraine, the Prince of Joinville, declared his support for him. Soon afterwards, the King, who had agreed to partake of the Mass, rewarded Charles *de* Lorraine by appointing him Governor of Provence in southern France. At Marseille, Charles de Lorraine, the Prince of Joinville and Fourth Duke of Guise, conquered one of the last holdouts of the Catholic League. The Duke of Epernon, too, submitted to the king. Bringing his men, the Duke of Epernon, dressed in full armor, agreed to join the siege.

"Yes. We could mount a frontal assault and conquer the gate," King Henry IV said. "But it would cost many lives."

"We must retake Amiens," Count Saint Pol said. The former governor of Amiens had barely escaped when the Spanish first captured the town. Though his wife was allowed to join him, she had to pay a ransom for her possessions.

"I have lost so many soldiers during these Wars of Religion," King Henry IV said. "I do not wish to lose more."

Charles *de* Valois, the illegitimate son of King Charles IX and his mistress Marie Touchet, approached. After the death of Charles IX, Marie Touchet married Charles Balzac d'Entragues and bore him two daughters, including Henriette, who had reached the marriageable age of 18. The young women remained at their chateau near Fontainebleau, southwest of Paris. Charles held the title of Count of Auvergne. "What is our plan?"

"We will dig trenches to the walls."

"Sap and plant mines?"

"Under the protection of our cannon. We will build a Royal Platform for ten or twelve pieces."

Royal Battery Platform, The Hermitage, Amiens, France, 8ᵗʰ July *AD* 1597

UNDER THE CAREFUL watch of *Monsieur* Francois *de* St. Luc, the Grand Master of the Artillery, cannoneers raised the angle of their weapons. French artillerymen, with the assistance of several English soldiers, redirected their aim toward the Parapet Tower, still standing in front of the Gate of Montrescu.

When the vigilant *Monsieur* St. Luc signaled, Captain Joseph Duxbury acknowledged and had the short fuse ignited. Accompanied by ear-deafening bangs, cannonballs flew over the ditch and the enemy ramparts. The barrage hit the tower, already half-demolished by a week of pounding. The dust settled.

Cannon, circa 1684

John Smith lifted another cannonball and grunted when it rolled down the cannon barrel. "What happened to the rumors of peace?"

"King Henry IV wanted peace, but Marshall *de* Biron told him that his army held the advantage. Delays and stalling tactics would only give Cardinal Albert of Austria time to raise a relief army, so the Sicilian General of the *Cordeliers* was sent back from Picquigny to Brussels."

After another round of destruction, the French General appeared pleased. "That should silence Spanish artillery."

In the rolling field between the Hermitage and the ramparts of Amiens, French pioneers inched their trenches forward. The two trenches, extending out from two redoubts, were less than halfway across. When these reached the enemy's bastion, mines would be sprung, crumbling the wall. When allied soldiers surmounted these walls, the Gate of Montrescu, the key to Amiens, could be captured.

As Captain Duxbury led his handful of English soldiers through the narrow passageway from the sturdy structure holding the French battery, John viewed the Abbey of Madeleine at the back side of the Hermitage. He noticed flags had been planted at the tent next to the King's. "*Madame la Marquise* is back in camp?"

"The King's mistress arrives now." Duxbury pointed at a group of riders. Adorned with a large necklace, Gabrielle dismounted. Diamonds sparkled in the bright summer sun.

"I thought Gabrielle sold her jewels for 50,000?"

"She did, but the King paid off the loans and retrieved all of them," Captain Duxbury said, "but that is not all the King did."

"What else?"

"King Henry bought the estates of Beaufort and gave them to Gabrielle. He raised it to a Duchy, so now the King expects all of his nobles to give her proper respect."

Under the watchful eye of the King, French noblemen kissed her extended hand. Each greeted her—not by her old title of *Madame la Marquise*, but by her new one. The Parliament of Paris registered it.

"*Madame la Duchesse*." Charles de Valois, Count d'Auvergne, kissed her hand.

Marshall de Biron did not appear pleased at the return of the King's mistress to the camp. Due to the disruption caused by her presence, she and her court would not stay—not even one day. The Marshall had most strenuously objected.

"Will Gabrielle become Queen?" John asked.

"Perhaps. All that is needed is for Queen Margot to ask the Pope to grant her a divorce, and Gabrielle will be able to marry the King. Their son Cesar could then be declared legitimate and become the *dauphin*—the heir apparent to the throne."

With two ladies-in-waiting attending her to every need, Gabrielle entered her tent. Along with pennants of the Duchy of Beaufort, flags with the *fleur-de-lis*, the triangular symbol of the French crown, waved overhead.

When officers gathered around the King, he told them, "We will not recklessly assault the Gate of Montrescu."

"How then?" a nobleman asked.

"By mining and sapping."

"But the danger increases as we get closer," the French general said.

"The trenches must be completed," the King declared. "For every six feet a soldier or pioneer digs, his pay is increased to 30 *sous*."

Twenty *sous* made a *livre* or pound.

"The regiment of Picardy volunteers to join the pioneers."

John recognized two of the captains. "They were at Doullons."

"Brave men, but their ladders were too short."

~ ~ ~

THAT EVENING, JOHN watched from atop new English trenches extending west from the Royal Platform toward the banks above the small village of Saint Maurice in the direction of Picquigny.

Captain Duxbury identified the forts built in a semi-circle north of the Somme. "On this side of the Hermitage, the Constable and the Duke of Epernon are quartered in those two forts. Furthest away, the Duke of Mayenne had overall command of the cavalry, so he is quartered at that fort in the distance."

"Not far from the *vivandiers*."

The *vivandiers* and merchants, many of whom followed the camp from Paris, provided fine fare and other sundry items to soldiers. Flags and banners from the bread, the fish, and other guilds flew in front of tents inside the outer line. At least one merchant brought his wife, who picked up a small, yapping poodle and carried it in her arms.

"And that fort closer to the Hermitage?"

"The Prince of Joinville occupies it."

Now, reaching within 200 paces of the Counterscarp in front of Amiens, the work in the trenches did not stop.

Chapter 43 — Unmatched Fury

*It was the Seventeenth day of July, upon the point of noon, when the Governor,
by a Cannon Shot, gave sign to fall on . . .*

*All captains dead upon the place, they routed and dissipated the whole Tertia,
which they chased flying to the very Redoubts of the Hermitage; in which place,
both the Fugitives and the Enemies fell so impetuously into the Regiment of
Champagne that was upon the guard, that it also being disordered, plainly took
flight, running to get themselves in order at the Alarm-place at their back . . .*
<u>History of the Civil Wars of France, 15th Book</u>
by Henrico Davila, translated from Italian

Northern Ramparts, Amiens, Picardy, Morning, Sunday, 17 July *AD* 1597

ATOP THE NORTHERN ramparts of Amiens, Captain Francisco *del* Arco
and Captain Diego Durango studied the fields across the Somme. Amidst
the tightening siege, French cannon remained silent this hour, but, for
nearly two weeks, those artillery pieces had blasted the outer fortifications.
Even though two stone ravelins—triangular-shaped bastions—added by
the Gate of Montrescu still stood, a newly built parapet tower had been
reduced to rubble. Behind the gate towards the cathedral, raised sheets of
cloth concealed the movement of both soldiers and horses as they crossed
the bridge.

"We must capture or destroy those dozen cannon," Governor Tello
had told his Council of War the previous afternoon. "The pioneers of
Picardy have not been intimidated by our sallies. Tomorrow's operation
will be overseen by our Sergeant-Major Andres Ortiz."

Beyond the forward trenches, redoubts with high walls protected
the royal platform with eleven cannon. A second, strengthened platform
held four.

"Today, we must halt the relentless pounding," Sergeant-Major Ortiz told the gathered officers. "Our cannon here on the ramparts can do limited damage."

"Their trenches lengthen every day." Captain Francisco del Arco viewed more dirt flying in the air. The trenches zigzagged ever closer to the outer wall, beyond the reach of Spanish ordinance. French engineers had used trigonometry to limit exposure to the destruction from the captured cannon. "And the regiment from Picardy has joined the pioneers."

"France's most veteran soldiers," Captain Durango said.

"Our plan is simple," Sergeant-Major Oritz said. "Captain Durango, your company of Walloon musketeers and Irish pikemen will attack the trenches to the left." He turned to the officer who had captured the Gate of Montrescu four months earlier. "Captain *del* Arco, your company of 150 men will attack the trenches to the right." He repeated the words of Governor Tello, "Our ultimate objective is to capture or destroy the royal cannon."

The Sergeant Major turned to two Irish captains. "You will second Captain Durango."

"Our three hundred pikemen will join the fight."

Shoulder to shoulder, those Irishmen likewise stood in the *fosse*.

"And the rearguard will be led by Carlo de Sangro."

"My eighty-five men have trained for months."

Carrying long halberds, the rearguard stood on a bridge leading from the center of Amiens.

"And the horses?" Captain del Arco asked.

"Captain Ruggiero Taccone and Francisco Fonte will back the infantry."

Each captain had one hundred riders under his command.

"And to keep the other French soldiers at bay, Captain Simone Latre will sally his horsemen from the *Porte de* Beauvais."

On the southern side of Amiens, the Spanish engineer sent from Brussels had constructed a large ravelin between the old Gate of Paris and the *Porte* de Beauvais.

"We will scour the field and keep the enemy on the defensive." Captain Latre had his company prepared to mount at Market Square in the center of the town.

"If needed, my horsemen will likewise ride through the countryside," the *Marquis de* Montenegro said. "And, when necessary, we will be ready to reinforce our attack."

Sergeant-Major Andres Ortiz stepped toward a forward cannon. "At the signal of this cannon, you shall charge out of the gates."

"My men are ready." Captains del Arco and the other captains descended the stairs to join a total of eight hundred men.

Fosse, Counterscarp, Gate of Montrescu, Late Morn, 17th July *AD* 1597

PACKED LIKE SAILORS in the belly of a ship, Spanish soldiers under the command of Captain del Argo awaited the signal in the *fosse*—the ditch behind the counterscarp. Not far away, Captain Diego Durango waited with other soldiers, all armed and ready to charge from the trench. Del Arco would lead his men to attack the right side.

Nearer to the gate of Montrescu, unmounted horsemen kept their stallions quiet. The wait for the signal would be short.

Above, with Governor Tello looking on and with the sun directly behind them, Sergeant Major Andres Ortiz pointed. The cannoneer lit the short fuse. The single cannon shot boomed. Dirt seeped through cracks, and the echo reverberated in the ditch below.

Two gates in the counterscarp walls swung open wide. Nothing stood in the way of the trenches straight ahead.

English Trenches, Chateau and Fort *Riviere*, Noon

YOUNG JOHN SMITH heard the distant sound of the single cannon shot. Stretching his neck out of the trench, he spied a plume of black smoke rising from above the walls of Amiens, but it slowly dissipated. When a second cannon shot did not follow, he slid back down into the trench. "They must be testing their cannon."

Normally, the enemy cannon fired one shot after another.

"Perhaps a misfire." Another young recruit finished chewing on some fish and bread. They had purchased the items from merchants and *vivandiers*, who sold sundry items to the soldiers. "Time for a siesta."

"Are you Spanish?" John Smith kept his hand on his pike.

"Recruits!" Captain Joseph Duxbury slapped the shoulder of the recruit who had just closed his eyes. "Be alert."

Scattered gunshots and distant screams broke the midday lull.

"Ready your muskets!" Captain Duxbury commanded.

"Grab your pikes!" another English captain yelled.

Forward Trenches of Picardy, North of the Somme, Amiens

UNMATCHED FURY ACCOMPANIED the regiment of Italians and Walloons under Captain Diego Durango exiting the Counterscarp. Quickly crossing the field, they swept into the French trenches. Captain Diego Durango discharged his single-shot pistol and drew his sword.

His men ran past him and ferociously attacked the first trench. Some discharged muskets into the shocked Frenchman. While they reloaded their weapons, scores of other soldiers charged ahead, jabbing the tips of their swords into defenseless bellies. Up and down nearby trenches, the fighters cleared paths, leaving fallen men in pools of blood. Other Spanish soldiers surmounted mounds, firing their reloaded guns at point-blank range. More French fighters died in this initial onslaught.

The Spanish soldiers of Captain Francisco *del* Arco were no less fierce. His company swooped into the trenches below the royal battery of the French king. The unsuspecting veterans of Picardy were busy finishing their mid-day meal when the attack commenced. Three Picardy captains roused their men as the Walloons and Italians slaughtered those fighting with only picks and shovels. Others countered with broad swords and sharp shafts. One captain confronted the advancing onslaught by aiming at Captain *del* Arco, but he met his end with the tip of a sword, slain in the back.

Irish pikemen joined the sortie, exiting beyond the counterscarp to second the two Spanish captains leading the charge. Those Irish soldiers overthrew more trenches. Just as sailors might be thrown overboard in tumultuous waves, more Frenchmen died: they perished in a sea of blood.

The midsummer sun beat down as Captain *del* Arco advanced his troops in a horrendous slaughter, trench by trench. Seeing them inching ever closer to the platform and the French cannon, a second Picardy captain roused his men. But it was too late for him, for he met the same fate as the first captain—*del* Arco bested him with his sword. Minutes later, a third Picardy captain dropped dead when a Spanish lieutenant overpowered him.

Behind them, closer to the walls of Amiens, horsemen spurred their steeds. The two companies of horse exited the Gate of Montrescu. One headed in the direction of Picquigny, putting those soldiers to the West on the defensive. The other company galloped eastward, toward Corbie, probing for weakness in the English trenches by their headquarters at the *Chateau Riverie.*

English Trenches, Amiens

CAPTAIN JOSEPH DUXBURY ordered, "Fire!"

His cord already lit, John Smith pulled the trigger. The ball from his arquebus hit the armored chest of the Spanish horsemen, but the stunned enemy rider did not fall—his plate armor was too thick. As Smith began to reload, another horseman stopped directly above him.

Duxbury slammed John's face against the near wall. The shot ricocheted off a rock, missing him by inches. Both reached for pikes to pull down the rider, but with weapons, it was all in vain. The enemy horseman had spurred forward in search of his next victim.

The riders continued their probing attacks, hitting the English company in the next trench just as hard.

"Stand guard!" Captain Duxbury ordered. "They will return!"

Champagne Trenches, Amiens, Early Afternoon

UNABLE TO STOP the advances of Durango and del Arco, the remaining veterans of Picardy abandoned their forward position. Beating a hasty retreat, they jumped into trenches manned by the regiment of Champagne, but to no avail. Walloon musketeers picked off some of the fleeing Frenchmen, while Italian and *arquebusiers* and pikemen pursued them on foot.

Spanish soldiers likewise joined the fray, pursuing the French companies with an angry vengeance in a war their sovereigns had declared. They slew some of the newcomers of Champagne and panicked the remainder. With the Irish pikemen on their heels, the French bolted backward, running past the platforms, towards forts even further away.

Captain Durango circled closer from the other side, overpowering a company of Swiss, part of the Sancy's regiment. Entrances at the redoubt stood clear.

Nothing stood in the way of Captain *del* Arco. "Capture the cannon!"

The French cannon would soon be his.

Chapter 44 — Victory or Death

In so great a tumult and flight, the Spanish commanders, valiantly followed by their men, [who] having filled the Trenches with slaughter, came up to the mouth of the Redoubts of the Hermitage, which would have been quitted, and by consequence lost, if the Marshall de Biron, with four Gentlemen of his own, and with Captain Francesco Benzi, a Florentine, with some few other Soldiers that followed him, taking up Pikes, had not exposed himself to the violence of the Enemy . . .

The Marshall de Biron all in sweat and blood, with the right side of his hair all burnt, still caused many signs to be given of his danger. Wherefore, the King [Henry IV] himself, not having a more reasonable remedy, alighted from his horse, and, taking a Pike in his hand, with those Gentlemen that were about him, ran desperately to defend his Cannon . . .

There grew so hot a conflict as had the appearance of a very great Battle.

<u>History of the Civil Wars of France, 15th Book</u>
by Henrico Davila, translated from Italian

Royal Batteries, Amiens, Picardy, France, 17th July *AD* 1597

FACIAL SCARS TESTIFIED to the battles Marshall *de* Biron had won, but he could not halt the fleeing regiment from Champagne. "We cannot lose our cannon!" His black eyes flashed. "Take up pikes!" Four gentlemen of his suite grabbed pikes and rushed past the cannon.

Several entered down one passageway and blocked the narrow entrance. Marshall *de* Biron entered the other passageway. The Marshall swooped his pike into the body of the first attacker and disemboweled the guts of a second one.

The clash of weapons grew louder as Captain Francesco Benzi, the Florentine ally, and a handful of other French soldiers fought valiantly. The first Spaniards who entered the passageway did not survive. One fell to the swipe of a pike, while the guts of another spilt to the ground.

The next Spanish attacker, likewise, was killed, yet the clash of weapons grew louder. Iron met iron, and the Spaniard blocked every blow. Five more stood behind him, determined as the first.

"We can't hold out much longer!" the Marshall shouted.

To his west, the captains of Champagne had abandoned their last attempts at rallying the few remaining recruits. Captain Diego Durango waved some of the 300 Irish pikemen forward. They attacked the one narrow entrance defended by two or three gentlemen of Biron's suite.

~ ~ ~

FROM THE EAST, Spanish soldiers sustained their attack and attempted to gain a second entrance to the platform. Despite the progress, Captain *del* Arco knew that taking the Hermitage would not be easy. Yet the big guns were within his reach, and he could turn them on the Abbey. Captain *del* Arco pushed ever closer to the platform. Only a few defenders stood between the battery and him.

French Fort, Hermitage

PRINCE OF JOINVILLE, Charles de Lorraine, seeing the desperate extremity facing Marshall *de* Biron, rallied the men stationed at the nearest fort. Swarming out like hornets protecting a hive, one hundred fighters flew towards the battery under attack. Before the mouths of the redoubt, they stung the Spanish fighters, who recoiled back.

Yet just as they began to get the advantage, the third wave of fighters exited the *fosse* through the *Cerrada* of the Counterscarp. Eighty men-at-arms, toting long halberds, hurried past the blood-soaked trenches, filled with nearly five hundred fallen men of Picardy. When they reached the entrance of the redoubts, they attacked the Swiss reinforcements, pushing them back. But the Prince of Joinville would not relent. The combat grew evermore intense.

English Trenches, Chateau *Riverie*

CAPTAIN JOSEPH DUXBURY urged his English recruits forward. Advancing from their positions on the east, John Smith and well-trained soldiers of this one-hundred-plus-man company began engaging the Spaniards of Captain *del* Arco. On the opposite or western side of the batteries, other English captains likewise advanced their companies from newer English trenches toward the Italians and Walloons of Diego Durango.

No longer a mere skirmish, the battle entered its second hour—the clashes of swords and pikes did not lessen along both edges of the widening conflict.

Two more companies of Spanish riders galloped out and scoured the field. They put the English trenches on the defensive for the second time.

Battery Platform, Second Hour

IRISH PIKEMEN PRESSED their advantage forward, pushing Marshall de Biron back, out of the passageway onto the platform itself. His few guards swung their pikes, engaging each Spanish soldier, mere feet from the cannon. A Walloon appeared and aimed his loaded arquebus at the head of Captain Benzi, his Florentine ally. The Marshall leapt and forced the weapon down, but the match was lit, and the flash pan ignited.

The Marshall slammed his eyes shut as flames touched his face. He felt the whole side of his black beard burn—clear to his cheek. The awful smell of singed hair filled the air. When he opened his lids, he found the gunman himself was already thrown to the ground. One of his noble friends ended that life with the tip of a pike.

Though the shot the gunman fired pierced neither head nor heart of the Florentine captain, it dealt a crippling blow. Captain Francesco Benzi held his knee in agony.

The noose around the platform tightened further. Looking past the wounded captain, Marshall de Biron saw no reinforcements coming to his aid—not a single company or squad came running to help.

If help did not arrive within a minute, the cannon and his life would be lost.

Battery Platform

"VICTORY OR DEATH!" King Henry IV declared from atop his horse. Like the Roman General Julius Caesar, who voiced a similar phrase when he conquered Gaul, the French monarch exclaimed and repeated the Latin phrase, *"Aut vincere aut mori! VICTORY OR DEATH!"*

Holding the reins of his stallion in front of the Hermitage, the King of France and Navarre had previously vowed, *I will either recover Amiens or I will lose my life and my crown.* He caught the eye of Marshall *de* Biron.

Clearly, the life of the Marshall hung in the balance—just like it did two years earlier at the Battle of Fontaine-Française. The Marshall and his troop of horse had advanced too far into enemy territory on June 5th, 1595, and found themselves surrounded. Riding without his helmet, the King charged and saved the Baron de Biron's life. When confronted by his advisors for risking his own life, the King told them that if he had not rescued him, the Marshall would have never let his Majesty live it down, 'as long as the Marshall lived.'

The danger faced by the Marshall was imminent and great. Though this time King Henry IV wore his helmet, he did not have his cavalry about him. Not even his closest advisors were stationed around the warrior King of Navarre.

His steed bucked and neighed, as though it would charge, but the passageway was too small for any horse, and certainly for this large stallion owned by the King. *No other remedy,* he thought to himself. The King alighted from his horse and onto the ground. He grabbed an abandoned pike and sprinted like he was a decade younger.

Inside the platform, the warrior King swung his pike and protected his own—the royal cannon. His youngest courtier, Henri II de Rohan, drew his sword and followed him.

Behind them, by the Heritage, more noblemen carrying pointed shafts rallied behind their sovereign. "Victory or death!"

Count d'Auverge and Count Saint Pol joined the fray that day.

During the third hour, the tide began to turn. The King watched the Prince of Joinville redouble his efforts. As the afternoon heat bore down, the Catholic prince slowly began to beat back the Spanish fighters of Captain *del* Arco. When, unexpectedly, the *'Captain of Nuts'* stepped back.

Middle Trenches

THE SOUND OF pounding hoofs and loud neighs stormed past the forward trenches. Accompanied by the sound of loud gunfire, thirty fully-armored *cuirassiers* swept past the Spanish captain. These thirty Spanish horsemen plowed straight ahead towards the Prince of Joinville and his reinforcements.

With the French forces divided into two, the passageway leading to the battery once more was cleared of obstacles. Both Captain Durango and Captain *del* Arco renewed their attack on.

"Push forward!" Captain *del* Arco ordered his men.

The great battle entered its fourth hour. Seven hundred of the French and their allies had already lost their lives.

Battery Platform

HIS MOST CHRISTIAN Majesty lost sight of the Prince of Joinville. Only King Henry IV, Marshall de Biron, and a handful of French noblemen protected the royal cannon. The king had always refused to be beholden to any foreign power. He risked his life once more to keep Spain from threatening his kingdom.

Likewise, fighting like a common soldier, the French general, Marshall *de* Biron, swung his long pike. An endless stream of Spanish soldiers threatened to overtake them.

The English fighters of Captain Duxbury, meanwhile, renewed their advance toward the center of the battlefield. They clashed in hand-to-hand combat in the trenches now occupied by the Spaniards and their allies.

The tiring battle had entered a stalemate when the distant sound of pounding hooves overtook the sound of clashing swords.

"It is the Duke of Mayenne." Young John Smith observed the Duke riding in front of the colors of Navarre.

"And the whole cavalry!" Captain Duxbury pointed to English ensigns advancing in a strong square.

The sight of five or six hundred enemy riders halted the attack on the battery. Captain Durango and Captain *del* Arco led a hasty retreat of their men. They reached the covering fire of the Counterscarp and escaped through the open door to the *fosse*. From the northern ramparts of Amiens, Spanish artillery rained down on the advancing French cavalry, so the Duke of Mayenne and his riders finally ended the pursuit.

Further away, at the mouths of the redoubts of the platform, King Henry IV called out and sought the Prince of Joinville. He searched for his friend and called out again. "Prince of Joinville!"

When Charles de Lorraine finally appeared, his face and arm were covered in blood.

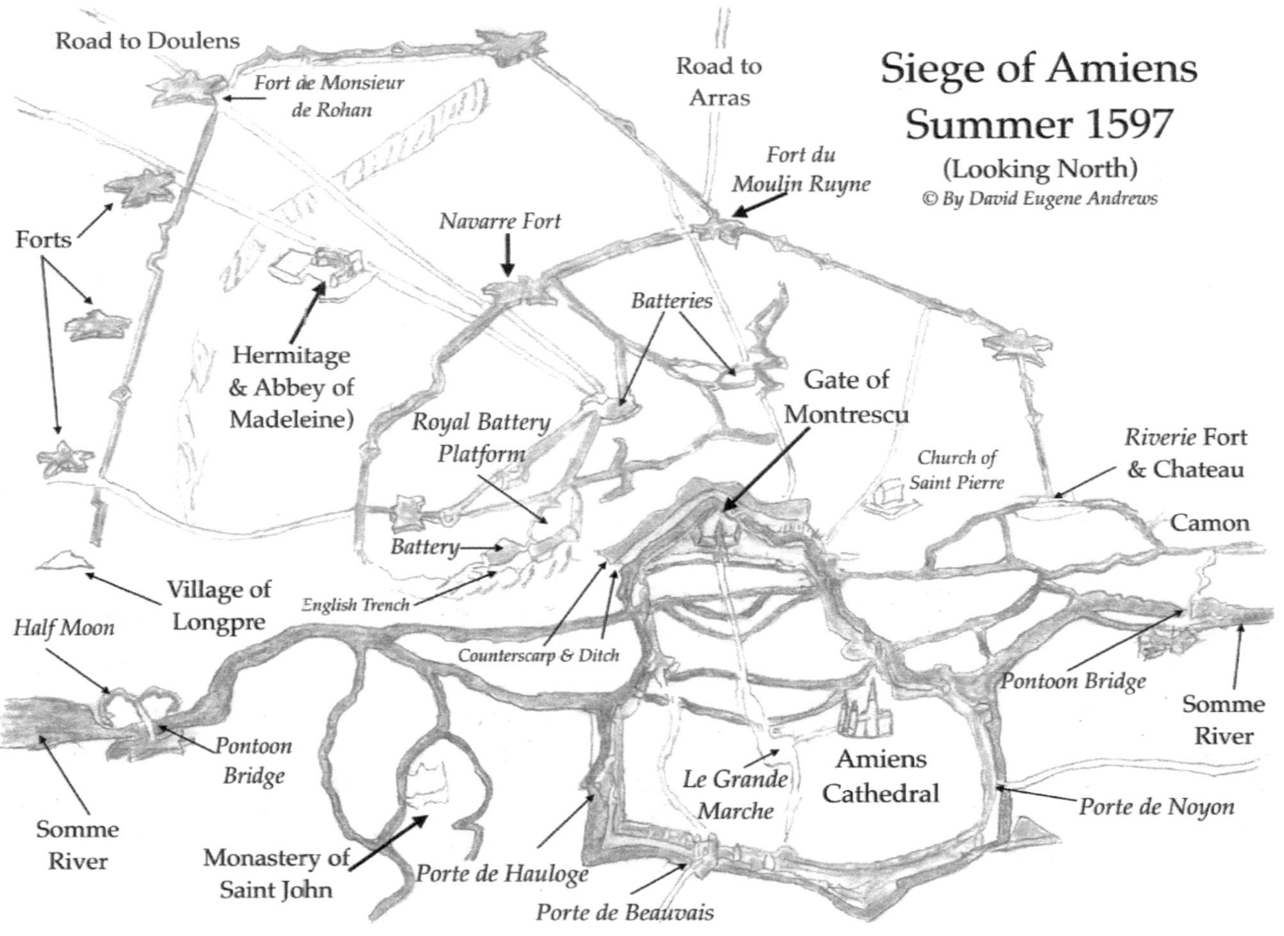

Siege of Amiens
Summer 1597
(Looking North)
© By David Eugene Andrews
Road to Doulens
Fort de Monsieur de Rohan
Road to Arras
Fort du Moulin Ruyne
Forts
Navarre Fort
Batteries
Gate of Montrescu
Riverie Fort & Chateau
Camon
Hermitage & Abbey of Madeleine)
Royal Battery Platform
Church of Saint Pierre
Battery
English Trench
Counterscarp & Ditch
Village of Longpre
Half Moon
Pontoon Bridge
Le Grande Marche
Amiens Cathedral
Pontoon Bridge
Somme River
Somme River
Monastery of Saint John
Porte de Hauloge
Porte de Beauvais
Porte de Noyon

From the platform behind him, the wounded Florentine Captain limped towards them.

"Your knee?" Marshall de Biron asked.

"Not shattered."

Elsewhere, across the wide battlefield and inside the deep trenches, French, Swiss, and English bodies littered the ground.

Monastery of Saint Augustine, Inside Amiens, Evening, 17 July *AD* 1597

INSIDE AMIENS THAT evening, Governor Hernán Tello *de* Portocarrero and Captain Francisco *del* Arco walked past the Cathedral of Amiens to visit their wounded soldiers.

"How many men did we lose?" the Governor asked.

"Seventy," Captain del Arco said.

"And the French?"

"Nearly nine hundred."

At the hospital inside the Monastery of St. Augustine, a Spanish doctor bandaged a wound. Tossing the extra wrapping aside, he pointed out patients suffering from the widening pestilence infecting the town. "Along with the summer heat, sickness has spread to the healthy, and we run low on medicine."

"Do what you can." The short governor turned to Captain *del* Arco. "We must stand strong until Cardinal Albert arrives with the relief army."

"We have little beef and no mutton," Captain *del* Arco said.

"Our storehouses have plenty of grain."

"Those citizens?" Captain *del* Arco pointed to several leaning against the pillars of the cloister.

"Send the weakest ones away." Governor Hernán Tello *de* Portocarrero then turned and dictated a short message to a Franciscan priest. "When you reach Brussels, tell Cardinal Albert our predicament."

After the priest exited through the Gate of Noyon, the Governor gathered members of his Council of War on the dark ramparts. "We cannot hold out forever."

"Queen Elizabeth sends 2,000 more English soldiers." The Marquis de Montenegro peered north, where campfires marked the forts. "Cardinal Albert needs an army of 20,000 to end this siege."

"And our soldiers?"

"Build a palisade beyond the counterscarp."

FILIZ FINISHED TRANSLATING the account of the battle that had lasted well into the afternoon. The sweet scent remained strong, but the tall, thin candles were gone—only a stub remained. A servant lit a new one before extinguishing the dying flame. The new erect one once more brightened the far side of the room.

"More coffee?" Aisha asked. The demi-cups steamed hot.

Captain John Smith put his hand up. "That will not be necessary."

Aisha waved the servant away before turning back to John. "King Henry IV could have been killed?"

"Both King Henry IV and Marshall de Biron fought bravely to protect the platform and the cannon. That was the second time the King had saved the Marshall's life. The king's valor in the open field was renowned, and now also at a siege. His actions endeared him to the whole camp."

"And the English?"

"All remarked about the intrepidness the English showed that day."

"And Paris?" Aisha asked. "They brought Paris to the camp?"

"Yes. Guilds from Paris set up tents behind the king's. The fish guild even sold fresh fish. And some nobles came for treatment in the two hospitals Baron *de* Rosny had set up."

"But Gabrielle d'Estrées?" Aisha asked. "Where did she stay?"

"*La Duchesse* Beaufort retired to the *Chateau de* Monceaux. Even in the midst of this French and Spanish war, she approved plans to augment its splendor."

"And you, *Capitano* John Smith?"

"I first engaged in close, hand-to-hand combat against the Spanish. I first learned to fight at Amiens in Picardy in France."

Chapter 45 — Mining and Sapping

"There will be a great scandal about it in this Kingdom [France], if I undertake to transport it [a large piece of the head of John the Baptist] out of the country, but I will try to contrive it as your Majesty [King Philip II] desires."
Cardinal Albert of Austria to King Philip II of Spain

Covered Way, Gate of Montrescu, Amiens, Picardy, 1ˢᵗ August *AD* 1597

IN THE TWO weeks since their assault on the battery on the Hermitage, Spanish and Walloon soldiers planted numerous brass-tipped poles. Under the cover of their artillery, Captain *del* Arco had built wooden palisades on the ramparts, blocking the easiest path not only to the doors, but also to the casemates, the vaulted gun emplacements. Although the Spanish fired their cannons, they reduced the number of their sallies: they could not stop the French trenches—drawing ever closer to their ramparts.

"Will our palisades stop the French?" one of his men asked in the early morning. The night guard had gone to the walls near the Cathedral to rest, for the French did not press Amiens on all sides.

"No, but they should delay French attacks long enough for the Cardinal and the Relief Army to arrive."

"But the trenches have almost reached us."

"Yes, they are at our door and will undermine our foundations by sapping." Captain *del* Arco nodded. "We must open up their trenches, make ready the Petards."

The next morning, his soldiers filled metal buckets with gunpowder. When the morning guard changed at the Hermitage, Captain Francisco *del* Arco sent his men out to plant the bombs and light the fuses. As soon as the men returned for cover, two petards exploded.

Captain *del* Arco led scores of soldiers out of the Covered Way, through an opening in the palisades, and attacked the French trench, pushing the shocked French soldiers back.

The shock, however, did not last: the French recovered quickly and drove the Spanish back. After extending their trenches several more feet, they resealed them again, but not for long.

~ ~ ~

THAT EVENING, THE French opened the end of the trenches. French soldiers climbed the slanted face of the bulwark and broke through the wooden palisade. Atop the rampart, they overcame the retreating Spaniards. As they waved for more French to join them, the Spanish commander of the artillery signaled.

A huge countermine exploded, throwing the forty Frenchmen into the air. Like an acrobat performing in the courts of Madrid, one French soldier soared straight up, more than eight pike lengths high. As the Frenchman struck the ground and before the debris settled, Captain Francisco *del* Arco led his men out of the Covered Way and retook the ramparts. His musketeers fired at the French retreating to their trenches, but the top of the bulwark had been destroyed.

That same day, the Grand Master of the French Artillery began building a second gallery at the end of the left trench, in the ditch adjacent to the ramparts. While the large battery of the Hermitage with its twelve cannons inflicted damage and provided protection, the eight new French cannons pounded the Spanish ramparts, both day and night.

Whenever the pounding slowed, the French attacked with their fireworks: they used *saucissons*, sacks filled with gunpowder, to light *fougades*, their land mines.With every French foray, Captain Francisco *del* Arco sent reinforcements and stayed the assaults. He needed to delay the capture of his casemates. Like himself, his men would rather die an honorable death than give one more yard to the French.

Outside Camon, Picardy, France, Mid-August *AD* 1597

AS CAPTAIN JOSEPH Duxbury and his company patrolled the French countryside, the clouds darkened. The wind kicked up, and distant thunder rolled closer. As they reached the top of a knoll to take shelter, the clouds burst open. By the time they had gathered beneath a grove of chestnut trees, the afternoon torrent had drenched the men.

Shaking off excess water, John Smith heard a twig break above. "Who's there?" He wondered who was hiding in the tree and grabbed his sword.

Chattering louder than the rustle of leaves, two squirrels did not seem to welcome their new visitors. They darted from branch to branch. Duxbury chuckled as John sheathed his sword. "It's better than being unprepared."

Minutes later, after the storm clouds had largely passed, one of the bushy-tailed rodents scurried headfirst down the trunk. It ignored John and his Captain, snatched a fallen nut, and scampered off with the small chestnut in its mouth.

The summer storm ended as quickly as it began; the rain tapered off. The mist, however, lingered on. As the sun broke through the puffy clouds, a full rainbow formed. Beneath it, an English rider galloped across the dampened countryside.

"Captain Duxbury?" The messenger saluted. "Maximilien *de* Bethune, Baron *de* Rosny, has returned."

"With the pay?" Captain Joseph Duxbury asked.

The English messenger nodded. "Rosny await you."

Captain Duxbury signaled for his company to assemble. "That's three months in a row." As they headed back to the English headquarters, he told John. "I have never seen an army paid better than this."

At the English Headquarters at Camon, Baron *de* Rosny and the Count of Villeroy finished distributing the full month's pay.

"When will we attack the Spanish?" one of the soldiers asked the new English General.

"The War Council meets at the Hermitage," Sir John Aldrich said. "Captain Duxbury, you will accompany me."

Captain Duxbury motioned for John to ride with them.

Over the past few weeks, the outer trenches, both upriver and downriver from the Hermitage, had deepened. They extended for miles. Each of the seven upriver forts was now fully manned, as more English and French arrived every week. Downriver, the new regiment from Normandy lodged at Longpre. The King, impressed by the bravery and valor of his young courtier, assigned the important fort guarding the road to Doullens behind the Hermitage to *Monsieur* Henri II *de* Rohan.

General Aldrich, Captain Duxbury, and the English recruit reached the enlarged French encampment. Countless tents had been set up behind the Hermitage and the Abbey of Mary Magdalene.

"Like Paris itself," young John Smith said.

"Ever since the guilds arrived from Paris and crossed the Somme with their ensigns flying, the camp has lacked nothing."

John recognized the banners of the corn, bread, fruit, and herb Guilds. The butchers and fishmongers, likewise, had separate tents. Individual taverns, cabarets and houses of cuisines had enlarged tents. Flags and banners waved in the breeze.

"More women at the Camp?" John asked. "It's almost too festive."

"Yes, the King's Mistress has also arrived back in camp. and Marshall *de* Biron is not happy." Duxbury pointed to the Marshall escorting the King past the cabaret. "Biron believes the women are a distraction and may cause another calamity."

"Like what happened in Flanders."

Minutes later, the women exited the tents. Guards escorted away in the direction whence they came—Paris.

While the King returned to his tent inside the Abbey, the Marshall met Captain Duxbury. "Only Gabrielle and her immediate court will remain."

Captain Joseph Duxbury seemed to understand. "My men want to know when we will assault the ramparts."

"Tell your men to be patient," Marshall *de* Biron said. "Our batteries pummel the ramparts, but the King does not want to recklessly assault and lose more nobles, especially since the Calvinists have refused to come."

"I thought the Calvinists convened a new assembly with new authority from the provinces."

"They did, at Chatellerault, nearer to Poitiers than Tours. And at first, La Tremoille even raised some troops in the King's name in Poitou."

"But?"

"The delegates arrived and instead of bending to the King's will, they became even more demanding, especially after hearing about the bad treatment that Catholic partisans in Burgundy gave to the widow of a Calvinist doctor."

"What happened?" John asked.

"After the good doctor died in Tonnerre last April, his wife asked the Administrator to allow his body to be buried in the graveyard at the hospital. Its Administrator agreed, but when the Dean of the Catholic parish heard about it, he objected. The widow and some friends attempted to avoid any scandal by burying the doctor's body at night. Before they could lower the coffin, a handful of monks and a small mob intervened.

They threatened violence and prevented the burial, so instead of the hospital, the widow decided to bury her husband's body at an estate she partially owned."

"So the doctor was buried?"

"Not at that estate. The mob, upset with the new decision, broke into her house and dragged the corpse to the Marketplace. They placed cards in one of his hands and dice in the other. The next morning, the Catholic partisans dragged the body and had peasants bury it in a dunghill. Even though they didn't even place it into a coffin, they went back to the widow and demanded she pay them for their troubles."

"And she refused?"

"They threatened to unearth her deceased husband's body and feed it to the dogs."

"Is there no justice?" John asked.

"Not unless the King intervenes." Captain Jospeh Duxbury paused. "Those of the Reformed Religion are even more adamant than they were at Saumur. Unless they receive an irrevocable edict, they will not come here, to Amiens."

"Will they succeed?"

"Unlikely, but it could be worse."

"How so?" John asked.

"Some in the Assembly want to take up arms against the King and establish a separate Protestant Kingdom. They have talked to the Catholic Duke of Mercoeur in Nantes, hoping for a peace with Brittany."

"And the Duke?"

"When Spain could not pay them, the garrison in Blavet, an important port in southern Brittany, mutinied. So, the Duke of Mercoeur considers the offer."

Sir John Aldrich approached. "Captain Duxbury, ready your men! When we take the ramparts, nothing will stand between the Gate of Montrescu and us!"

Chapter 46 — Mussels and Oysters

The Oyster-Fisher (Istridiajian) are 800 men, with 300 shops. They throw iron rakes into the sea with which they draw out oysters, shells, sea-chestnuts, and different sorts of such delicacies, which they sell to their wine-drinking brethren. The sort of oysters called lakoz are very strengthening; some eat them roasted in the fire on iron pans. If eaten quickly they are like swallowing a yellow slime, but they strengthen extremely, and therefore wholesome to men who wish to please their wives, in short it is a delicacy of debauchees.

The pilaf, made with shell-fish and pure oil, called midia-pilaf is also a delicious dish.
<u>*Narratives of Travel in the 17th Century*</u> *by Evliya Celebi*
Translated from the Turkish by Joseph von Hammer

Salon, Palace of Ibrahim *Pasha*, *Rajab AH* 1011, Late December *AD* 1602

"THE MEAL IS served." The Overseer opened the door, and servants brought in platters of appetizers for Aisha and her guests, women of her court, and her slave, the English recruit, *Capitano* John Smith.

"What is it?" John asked.

"Fresh mussels and oysters, battered and simmered in olive oil," Aisha said. "I saw them at the Fish Market when I was waiting for Filiz."

Filiz tasted the previously shucked yellow shellfish. "These are so delicious."

Before they had finished eating the *mezes*, servants brought in rice pilaf, mixed with carrots and peas. John accepted the serving with both hands. "You are such a good chef."

"Is it as good as the food from Paris?" Aisha wondered aloud.

"You mean when they set up boutiques and tents outside the French camp at Amiens?" John asked.

"*Si.*"

Filiz translated the Italian into French, "*Oui.*"

"And this?" John asked.

"*Imam Bayildi,*" Aisha said.

Filiz translated the Turkish into French, "The Imam Fainted."

"I do not understand," John said.

"Taste it."

"'Tis so good."

Aisha was pleased that John liked it so much. "I thought you would enjoy it."

"What is it?"

"It is made with eggplant," Aisha said.

Filiz translated eggplant into French, *"Aubergine."*

"Cooked in olive oil, the eggplant is stuffed with onions, garlic, and tomatoes."

"But why is it called 'The *Imam* Fainted'?"

"The prayer leader fainted when he tasted it."

John chuckled, "Because it was so good?"

"Or so expensive." Filiz glanced at Aisha.

"John, I am glad that you like it." The Sister of the Sultan turned to the kitchen help. "You may leave now."

"Can we return?"

"When your work is done."

"Thank you, Lady Aisha."

"Overseer, that will be all."

"As you wish."

Aisha and her guests settled comfortably back on the cushions, returning to their conversation anew, when seconds later, the Overseer returned through the same door he had just exited. "The *Valide Sultana* has arrived in the First Courtyard."

Aisha knew her mother did not like her spending so much time with her new slave, but she had nothing to hide. She straightened herself and turned to her maid servant. "Is my hair in place?"

"You look as lovely as ever."

Aisha turned back to the main door of her salon. "Mother, what an unexpected visit. You remember Filiz?"

"Aisha, do you always have guests?"

"Filiz is my friend," Aisha answered.

Safiye *Valide Sultana* stared at *Capitano* John Smith. "Daughter, I must talk to you about something important."

"Please, Mother." Aisha motioned. "Have a seat."

"Not in front of your slave."

"Very well." Aisha turned to John. "*Capitano*, the Overseer must take you back to your quarters now."

John glanced at the *Valide Sultana*. "Capisco."

Aisha understood, too, for she did not want to upset her mother. As Filiz prepared to leave, John walked in front of the Overseer and out the side door. Aisha thanked her French translator and escorted her to the main door. "Do not worry, Filiz," Aisha said. "I will send for you as soon as I can."

"I'll be waiting."

Aisha turned to her servants. "Bring refreshments for my mother."

"That will not be necessary." Safiye *Valide Sultana* pointed to the discarded oyster shells. Servants had not yet returned disposed of them.

Aisha directed two house servants to take away the empty platters and returned her attention to her mother. "What is so important?"

"I received a letter from the Grand Vizier."

"From Belgrade? Is he well?"

"Yes, very well. He said he wrote to you, too."

"He did? I did not receive one."

"I must have received mine first. Your betrothed has organized the frontier. He has assigned Pécs in Hungary and Pozega in Slavonia as the winter quarters for our friend *Ghazi* Giray II and his two sons."

Chapter 47 — Styrian Border Raids

Bishop's Castle, Pécs, Buda *Vilayet*, Hungary, Late December *AD* 1602

INSIDE BISHOP'S PALACE, the *Sanjak* of Pécs entertained *Ghazi* Giray II, whose warriors remained encamped outside the town's wall. At the behest of the Khan of the Crimean-Tartars, his two sons had journeyed from their assigned camp at Pozega, a long day's ride across the Drava River in Slavonia, the land of the southern Slavs. Though the *Sanjak* of Pozega had written and complained about *Kalga* Tohktamysh and *Nur-eddin* Sefer Giray's raids on his *timars*, that was not the reason *Ghazi* Giray II had summoned his two sons.

Finished with the appetizers and the first course, *Ghazi* Giray II addressed the *sanjak,* "Tell my sons your request."

"The *Sanjak* of Kanizsa has written me." The *Sanjak* of Pécs remained seated cross-legged on the floor. "His Turkish garrison needs to be resupplied before winter sets in."

"Cannot the Grand Vizier help?" *Kalga* Tohktamysh asked.

"No, he is in Belgrade, too far away."

"So you need our help?" *Kalga* Tohktamysh picked up a leg of lamb.

"We cannot supply him with Tartar horses," the younger son, *Nur-eddin* Sefer, added.

"No, but you can help gather supplies," the *Sanjak* of Pécs said.

"From Pozega?" *Kalga* Tohktamysh chomped into the meat.

"No, from lands around Szigetvar, further up the Drava River Val—." The *sanjak* stopped when he heard his name.

"Sanjak!" A messenger stood at the double doors of the large reception room.

Ghazi Giray II recognized the important messenger, who held a short truncheon in his hand. He had seen the *chiaus,* or usher, at the citadel of Belgrade. A symbol of authority as well as a weapon, the silver truncheon had a knob at one end.

"This cannot wait?" the *Sanjak* of Pécs asked.

"I am afraid that it cannot; the Grand Vizier told me not to delay." The *chiaus* apologized for the interruption. "He received complaints."

"From the *Sanjak* of Pozega?" *Ghazi* Giray II asked. He was not happy.

"You heard?" The *chiaus* handed the Crimean Khan a letter marked with the imperial seal. "Your two sons must stop raiding the *timars* assigned to the Turks."

"The Sultan promised we would receive our rewards," *Kalga* Tohktamysh, the Khan's eldest son, interjected.

Ghazi Giray II raised his hand and calmed down his sons. He broke the imperial seal and read the letter.

"And what did the Grand Vizier say?" the *sanjak* asked.

"Turkish *timars* in Slavonia, as well as in Hungary, are not to be pillaged and plundered, but left alone."

"But what about our reward?" *Kalga* Tokhtamish asked.

Ghazi Giray II did not disapprove of his son's fighting spirit. He had named his eldest son after his warrior ancestor who had fought against Tamerlane, and promoted him to be his *kalga,* the presumed successor to the Crimean-Tartar throne. He noted that the demeanor of his two sons remained severe. "The order from my friend, the Grand Vizier, is clear. We shall not raid the Turkish *timars.*"

"For now, you can help resupply the *Sanjak* of Kanizsa," the *Sanjak* of Pécs suggested.

"And later?" *Kalga* Tohktamysh asked.

"The border lands in Hungary beyond Kanizsa, towards Styria, have not been assigned," *Ghazi* Giray II informed. "You may gather what the Sultan and the Grand Vizier promised us."

"Very well, Father," *Kalga* Tohktamysh said. "We'll take our liberty to raid the borders of Hungary and Styria."

Szigetvar, Ottoman Hungary

Kalga Tohktamysh Giray and his younger brother *Nur-eddin* Sefer Giray, having sent for their warriors from Pozega, stopped outside Szigetvar, the next fortified town up the Drava River Valley. A bridge led to the *var* or castle portion of the town. Three of the walled sections of Szigetvar were likewise built on islands, but separated from the castle by deep moats.

When the Tartar warriors stopped at a rich *timar* nestled in the woods, they purloined both grain and animals. The Turkish owner protested when Tohktamysh commandeered carts and wagons, forcing Christian peasants to work.

"These spoils are not for us," *Kalga* Tohktamysh said, "but for the Turkish garrison at Kanizsa."

"You will return the peasants and wagons?" the *sipahi* asked. Like other *sipahis* in Hungary and Slavonia, at the end of the fighting season, they were released to return to their *timars* and work their lands.

"You have our word."

Beyond Szigetvar, the well-traveled road cut through thick forests and rounded rolling hills. Other Tartar warriors brought more carts and joined the train, now more than one hundred wagons long.

Kanizsa, Ottoman Hungary

TWENTY THOUSAND STRONG, the Crimean-Tartar army reached Kanizsa and set up their camp of yurts and tents in vast clearings not far from the river. Like Szigetvar, water completely surrounded Kanizsa, but unlike other fortresses they had seen in Hungary, Kanizsa appeared stronger. Outer triangular bastions, based upon and built using the modern Italian design, extended from five corners into the swamplands.

The two Tartar brothers crossed a bridge through one bastion and rode across a second bridge. The long wagon train and its escorts followed. Inside the town, as the Christian farmers, pressed into service by the Tartars, began to unload the supplies, the *Sanjak* of Kanizsa greeted the two brothers. "Thank you for your help."

Kalga Tohktamysh and *Nur-eddin* Sefer Giray dismounted. "This fortress appears stronger than others."

"It is." The *Sanjak* of Kanizsa pointed to a group of musketeers. "With the help of some French musketeer from Pappa, Hasan *the Addicted* captured this fortress several years ago, but only after a powder magazine exploded."

"French musketeers?" *Nur-eddin* Sefer asked. His title, *Nur-eddin*, meant 'Light of Religion.'

"Yes. For more than a year, the Holy Roman Empire did not pay three thousand Frenchmen, so they kicked their leaders out of Pappa and mutinied. When they still were not paid, they sent messages to Grand Vizier *Damat* Ibrahim *Pasha*. If the Sultan would pay their back wages, the French musketeers offered to surrender Pappa to the Ottomans,"

"So the Grand Vizier certainly agreed?" *Nur-eddin* Sefer asked.

"Yes, before Pappa could be surrendered and we could enter the town, the Germans and Hungarians attacked the French, killing many and making a spectacle of others."

"But that regiment of Frenchmen?"

"Part of the twelve hundred French musketeers who were paid joined the Ottoman. Their captain even became a Muslim."

When the peasants finished unloading, *Kalga* Tohktamysh pointed. "We could use the wagons."

"Take them," the *Sanjak* of Kanizsa said. "And I can provide you with a scout to show you the way into Styria."

~ ~ ~

THE NEXT AFTERNOON, as the Tartar warriors rode *en masse* through thick forests, *Kalga* Tohktamysh observed, "No sign of the enemy."

"Most of their army has already retired for the winter," the Turkish scout informed. "And they seem weaker than last year, when the armies of the Holy Roman Empire under Archduke Ferdinand besieged Kanizsa. They fought hard, but a winter blizzard broke their siege. We followed the retreating Christian soldiers for miles, killing thousands even as others froze to death. After the snow melted, we retrieved their abandoned equipment and supplies well into early spring."

After traveling about thirty miles, they set up camp by a stream. "The enemy's strongest garrison is at Kormend, further north, on the Raab River."

"I lost many brave warriors while fighting Transylvanian Christians in Wallachia last month," *Kalga* Tohktamysh said.

"So, you do not want to attack?"

"Not their strongest garrison."

The next morning, the Tartar army broke camp and headed west, toward the Styrian border.

When a scout sent two days earlier met the army, he reported, "We are lucky."

"How so?" *Kalga* Tohktamysh asked.

"It must be the first market day after their Christmas holiday. Farmers are already going into town on the other side of those wooded hills."

Feldbach, Styria, Inner Austria, Holy Roman Empire.

ATOP HIS CHESTNUT red Mongolian stallion, *Kalga* Tohktamysh Giray raised his great sword and signaled thousands of Tartar warriors. His warriors, with their quivers full and their bows ready, advanced out of the woods. As they swarmed onto the fallow fields in their black sheepskin garb, birds scattered high.

Crimean-Tartar Warrior

The town of Feldbach on the upper Raab River was directly ahead. A lone tower rose above the town's wall, but the large market itself was unprotected. It lay directly ahead, outside the weak fortifications.

Seeing the market was full of patrons and merchants, his warriors galloped hard. Before the townspeople had time to react, the Tartars attacked. Warning bells rang, but it was too late. The market town on the upper Raab River, just inside the border of Styria, part of inner Austria, was under attack.

A few musket shots rang out from the tower and along the tall walls, but the attack was a complete surprise. Men, women, and children running across the field were easily captured. Two men mounted horses and forded the river, heading to a mountain castle in the distance, but those heading upriver were cut off by his brother, *Nur-redin* Sefer Giray. Those warriors also followed peasants fleeing into the woods.

Some escaped into the walled town before the strong gates were closed. Scores of other citizens pounded at Market Gate, but the townsmen would not open it.

Market stands were torn down and buildings burned. Any man who resisted was killed. Musket shots from the town walls were countered by Tartar arrows, many deadly accurate. More fiery arrows arched over the walls. Inside, buildings and huts burned.

Within an hour, the raid was over.

"If we ride further to the northwest and cross into the next valley, we will reach Graz, the fortified capital of Styria," the scout reported.

"We will not attack Archduke Ferdinand directly," *Kalga* Tohktamysh said. "We will go back toward Hungary." His warriors put the younger children and their mothers into wagons, but the chained men and women were marched across the fields.

"What about those young women? For the imperial harem?"

"First spoils go to my father," *Kalga* Tohktamysh said. "Deliver the first four hundred to Pécs." Wagons veered south.

The scout pointed to an island fortress directly in front of them. "Ober-Lymbach, the Hungarians call *Fesol-Lyndva.* Upper-Lnydva marks the border of Styria and Hungary."

Fesol-Lyndva (Ober-Lymbach), Raab River, Hungary-Styria Border

CANNONS SHELLS EXPLODED in the narrowing Raab River Valley on the border of Styria and Hungary. Several Tartar warriors fell from the blasts, but when the cannons of *Fesol-Lyndva,* called Ober-Lymbach, became silent, *Kalga* Tohktamysh Giray signaled his warriors. They followed him at a gallop.

Another round of shells exploded on the ground. A few more of his warriors fell behind him. Still riding fast, other Tartar warriors unleashed their arrows toward the castle walls.

Safely out of enemy cannon and musket range in the open Hungarian fields to the east, *Kalga* Tohktamysh halted his warriors and waited for his brother *Nur-redin* Sefer Giray to follow.

"A year and one-half ago, after the victory of Hasan *the Addicted* at Kanizsa, we almost captured Ober-Limbach," the Turkish scout informed. "We had surrounded the castle on both sides of the river, but the enemy broke our siege on a Thursday night, just before our sabbath."

"How so?" *Kalga* Tohktamysh asked.

"While we besieged Ober-Lymbach from both sides of the river, an army of musketeers from the Holy Roman Empire circled around us and fired at our backs from these open fields. We turned around and bravely pushed forward to meet the threat from advancing volley fire. As we went to confront the enemy musketeers, defenders sallied out of the island castle and crossed the bridge. By the time we reached the musketeers, their army had disappeared. Those from the castle sallied and dislodged the remaining men in the trenches. Another enemy army attacked on the other side of the Raab. We lost thousands."

As soon as the younger brother of *Kalga* Tohktamysh caught up with him, *Nur-reddin* Sefer complained, "We should punish them for firing at us and killing our warriors."

"We do not have artillery," *Kalga* Tohktamysh said. "We do not attack Ober-Lymbach today."

"Then where?"

"Further up the Raab River Valley." *Kalga* Toktamysh led the Tartar warriors east, across the plains towards Eisbenburg. "And we have help." Marching to the sound of a small kettle drum, an *oda* of 300 Ottoman soldiers carried muskets on their shoulders. "*Janissaries.*"

Later, after circling north, *Kalga* Tohktamysh Giray sat atop his horse. Safely beyond musket range, he viewed the fortified walls of a strong Hungarian fortress. "Brother Sefer, Kormend is too strong to attack directly. Take the *janissaries* go further north, downriver."

"To Sarvar?" *Nur-eddin* Sefer Giray asked.

"Yes, and in the morning, attack them, keep them occupied."

"And you?"

"There are many villages between the Raab River and Pappa."

Sárvár, Raab River Valley, Upper Hungary

FIERCE TARTAR WARRIORS steadied their horses and readied their bows. *Nur-eddin* Sefer Giray gave the signal for his left flank to attack.

Without warning, the first wave of riders charged toward the fortified town of Sárvár embanked on the Raab River, between Kormend and the Danube. Peasants rushed for protection, but to little avail: warriors blocked all avenues of escape.

A second wave of warriors followed the first. Unleashing arrows by the thousands, the skies darkened. The riders swarmed toward the town's main gate.

Other warriors galloped along the river, where women, both young and old, stopped washing their clothes. Their primal screams alarmed those on the far banks, but those on the near bank were swooped up, one by one.

With the field of battle cleared, the *janissaries* marched forward. They drew closer and fired a volley at the town walls. When the enemy muskets unexpectedly stopped firing, they brought two cannons forward.

Enemy muskets resumed fire. Enemy cannon shells exploded, dotting the field. The *janissaries*, out of cannon range, halted their advance.

Chapter 48 — Beautiful Bursa

The emporium of silk, the ancient capital of this country (Bithynia) . . .

He [Osman, Founder of the Ottoman Empire] sent his son Orhan with Sheikh Haji Begtash, who renewed the siege, and built two great towers, one at the side of the hot baths (Kaplica), and the other on the side of the head fountain, which took seven months to complete . . .

Haji Betash instituted the new militia called Yen-cheri [Janissary]

The lower town was fortified in the time of Mehmet III, Conqueror of Eger [AD 1596], against the Anatolian rebels Kara Yaziji [Scrivano or Black Scribe], Kalehnder-Oghli, Deli Hasan [Hasan the Fool] and Jennet-Oghli, but it is not very strong, it extends from east to west, to the foot of Mount Olympus . . .

The inhabitants being fair, the air good, the water full of holiness, contribute altogether, to render Bursa one of the most delicious spots on earth.
<u>Narrative of Travels in Europe, Asia, and Africa in the 17th Century, Vol. II</u> by Evliya Efendi
Translated from the Turkish by Joseph Von Hammer

Cekirge Kaplica [Hot Springs], Bursa, Anatolia, Late December *AD* 1602

THE *KETHUDA*, DEPUTY to the *Sanjak* of Bursa, rose from the outdoor pool, part of the hot springs of Cekirge. Named for grasshoppers heard on summer evenings, Cekirge had two separate bathhouses—one for men and one for women. On the far side of the rocky pool and the bathhouse, a fully covered noblewoman exited her ox-drawn carriage—most likely aiming to meet her friends inside the bathhouse for women.

Not wanting to catch a chill as he stepped out the hot water into the cold air, the *Ketuda* quickly wrapped a towel around his waist. He entered an old domed building—the bathhouse for men. Inside, a few Turkish men soaked in baths as hot as the pool outside; the same sulphur springs found at the foothill of Mount Olympus fed both pools.

In one adjoining room, newly arrived guests washed their heads with water before stepping into the common pool.

In another room, the *Kethuda* quickly dressed.

"Your skin looks better." His servant held his silk robe. "The scabs are gone."

"The waters here are good." The *Kethuda* donned his turban. "But I did not want to stay too long. The *Celali* Rebellion is near."

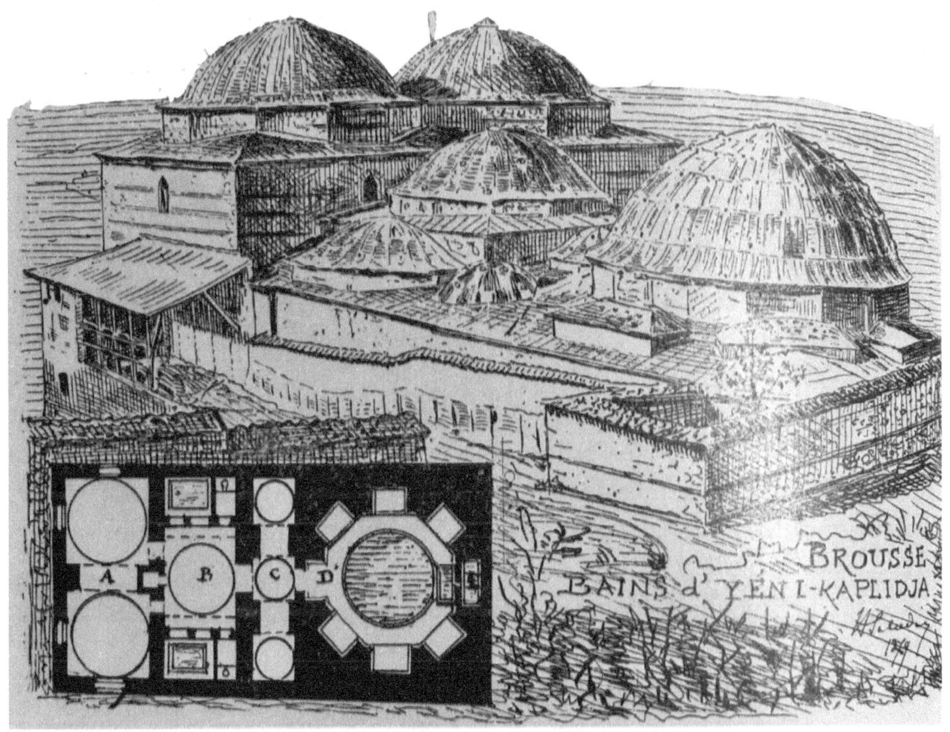

Baths of Bursa, Built 1553

"Will we now return to Bursa?" The trusted servant accompanied the *Kethuda* outside.

"No, we must go to the silk mill and meet the overseer. Yesterday, he was supposed to go to the Silk Khan."

The *Kethuda* and his servant mounted their horses and, as they exited the compound, a leper begged at the side of the road. With lumpy and discolored skin, he had neither eyebrows nor eyelashes.

"His breath can be contagious?" the servant asked.

"Perhaps not, but we will not get any closer." The *Kethuda* ignored the leper and pointed towards a nearby suburb. "The quarters for leprosy are always outside the town walls."

"But they want to bathe in the pool?"

"If the leper bathes daily in the hot springs and drinks its water for forty days, he may be cured."

"And the guest house?" The servant pointed back to a third building.

"Families from across the Ottoman Empire bring their sick family members and stay for a few days."

As the pair of riders headed down the hill, a line of camels, horses, and mules slowly approached from the southwest. "It has been two weeks since the last caravan arrived," the *Kethuda* said.

"From Smyrna?" The servant referred to the thriving port of Izmir on the Aegean Coast. Besides the Turks, both Jews and Christians, including recently arrived Englishmen of the Levant Company, populated that port city.

"And Magnesia," the *Kethuda* added. "The caravan would have gone over the long wooden causeway and stone bridge before entering that important town, where the Sultan and his older sister Aisha were born."

"Someone rumored that Prince Mahmud would be appointed Governor of Magnesia, like his father, Mehmet III, and grandfather Murad III."

"The Rebellion has made that appointment too dangerous for the Sultan's son."

"But it can be dangerous in *Stamboul*, too."

"You are right, young man," the *Kethuda* replied, somewhat surprised. "*Valide Sultana* Safiye prefers to keep a close watch on all of her grandsons and their mothers."

The pair of riders reached the main road and slowed behind a cart carrying a single large stone. The *Kethuda* could not read its Greek inscription.

"From Troy?" the servant asked. Ruins from that ancient city were further east.

"Perhaps. The stone will be used in a palace, perhaps for one of the *pashas* living in *Stamboul*."

The cart passed between rows of mulberry trees and turned north. The stone would be loaded at the port of Mudanya and shipped across the Sea of Marmara to *Stamboul*.

Silk Farm, Bursa Plain, Northwest Anatolia, Ottoman Empire

THE *KETHUDA* DUCKED beneath a mulberry tree, and the two men halted at a large shed in the middle of the field. Owned by a *vakif*—a foundation approved by the Sultan— revenues from the land and the mill supported that *kethuda*.

Surprised that the overseer did not meet him outside, the *Kethuda* dismounted and entered the building.

Inside the mill, a worker took a mulberry branch and placed it on a bed filled with green worms. In the next bed, more worms fed on the green mulberry leaves, already half-devoured. At a third bed, some worms, turning white, spun cocoons.

"Originally, all silk came from China." The *kethuda* led his servant to the other side of the room, where moths emerged from their cocoons and laid eggs. "Bursa was at the end of the Silk Road, but, under penalty of death, making silk was always kept a secret by the Chinese. Later, the Persians discovered the secret and transported eggs inside hollowed canes. The Byzantines, who had their capital at Bursa before the Ottomans conquered it, also learned the secret. Other tiny eggs were kept warm in dung and brought here."

"But how is silk made?" the servant asked.

"Look."

Young women retrieved empty cocoons from simmering water. They unravelled and stretched the thin silk strands from the cocoon. Once finished, they placed the thin piece, the size of a handkerchief, to the side.

"After Tamerlane disrupted the silk trade from China, the Persians supplied the factories and artisans of Bursa with raw silk from farms on the Caspian Sea via Tabriz."

"But Sultan Murad III's wars with Persia stopped that trade?" the servant asked.

"Yes, the courts in Europe and *Stamboul* still wanted silk, so now, these mills produce the raw silk for both dyers and clothiers."

When the *Kethuda* reached the corner where bolts of silk would be stacked, he turned. "Where is our raw silk?"

"Your overseer took the silk to Bursa an hour ago," the woman said.

"We stayed too long at the baths."

The two men went outside and once more remounted their horses. Several miles away, beyond the row of mulberry trees, stood Bursa, the first capital of the Ottoman Empire. All of the early sultans had built royal mosques, expanding the neighborhoods to both the east and the west. Royal and other important mosques anchored seven main neighborhoods, but more than one hundred mosques could be found in the other populated areas. Sunni Muslims had immigrated to Bursa from towns throughout Anatolia. Quarters for Armenians and Greeks each numbered less than a dozen. And none of these separate quarters were inside the grounds of the Upper Castle—the rectangular fortress overlooking the lower town.

Beyond the castle, forests of chestnut and fir trees blanketed the sharply rising slopes of Mount Olympus, or the Mountain of Monks. Named after Mount Olympus in Greece and for the Greek Monks who frequented it, this peak had many high pastures. Shepherds, who had gained the right to graze their sheep, in anticipation of winter, had previously brought down their flocks to the plains below.

Higher up, by the tree line, a large lake fed bountiful streams filled with tasty trout and long eels, but that lake had already begun to freeze over. Fresh snow already topped the mountain peak. Beginning in early summer, several hundred workers under the Head Iceman would harvest the iced rivulets and streams. Taken down the mountain in carts, the ice would be used to cool drinks called sherbet, not only in the palace and better inns of Bursa, but also in the palaces and khans of *Stamboul.*

Hot Springs Gate, Bursa

BY THE TIME the *Kethuda* and his servant arrived at the high stone walls of Bursa, the caravan from Smyrna had reached *Kaplica* Gate. Unable to pass, they waited for the camels to enter the fortress gate leading from the hot springs.

A Greek priest and his parishioner approached. "Sire, I have the tax demanded."

"I am not the tax collector," the *kethuda* said.

"But you were there when the collector demand the *kharaj.*" The priest referred to the extra tax that the *Qur'an* required of *dhimmis*—Christians and Jews, the two named peoples of the Book.

"Yes, yes, I remember, but you must pay the double tax yourself."

"We do not want to wait until next week, and Christians are unwelcome at the Upper Castle." The Greek handed over a coin.

The *Kethuda* examined the old coin. "What is this?"

"I know it is from the time Bursa was the capital of Bithynia."

"But the depiction?"

"It shows when Ajax killed himself at the foot of Mount Olympus after he fled from Troy. The coinage is pure."

"I'll take it." The *kethuda* put it into his purse. "But if there's a problem—"

"There will be no problem."

"As the Greek priest and parishioner climbed up the side of the lower foothills of Mount Olympus, only two more camels remained in front of both of them.

"Before Bursa was conquered from the Greeks," the *kethuda* said, "Orhan built a tower outside this gate."

"His father attempted to conquer Bursa, didn't he?" the servant asked.

"Osman, the founder of the Ottoman Empire, besieged this city three times, but Bursa would not fall," the *Kethuda* said. "About two hundred years before his reign, the Seljuks, the nomadic Turkish tribe, migrated from Central Asia to Asia Minor."

"So it was his son, Orhan, who won the city?"

"Yes, his father Osman had married a daughter of a sheikh, a direct descendant of the Prophet Mohammed, and she gave birth to Orhan. Years later, immediately after his father died from gout, Orhan conquered Bursa."

"How?"

"Orhan and Sheikh Haji Begtash spent seven months building two towers. One here, in front of Fortress Gate, and the other at the Gate of the Head Fountain, at the far end of the double walls of the Upper Castle."

"Sheikh Haji Begtash?"

"Revered as a saint, Haji Begtash of Khorassan founded seven hundred dervish convents, both in and around Bursa, and throughout the empire. He also founded the *janissaries*."

"The new army?"

Ghazi Sultan Osman, Founder, Ottoman Empire

"Haji Begtash took boys like you—the brightest and most able. Gathered as a tribute from the conquered Christian families of Bursa, the young boys were converted to Islam. Called *kuls* or slaves, most of those boys were groomed to be soldiers."

"*Janissaries.* And you?"

"Like them, I was taken young, but, like you, I am better with words and numbers than with arms and fighting," the *Kethuda* said. "After Orhan conquered Bursa, he appointed his brother First Vizier, the Bearer of the Burden." The *Kethuda* gestured toward several *janissaries* looking down from the top of the old Byzantine wall—never torn down, it still stood. "The son of Orhan, Sultan Murad I, gave the *janissaries* their *U'skufa* caps embroidered with gold."

After the two passed through the stone archway, they headed down to the lower town. Mirroring the rectangular shape of the Upper Castle, fortified walls now surrounded the lower town. Over the last few years, as the newest *Celali* Rebellion had spread through Anatolia, the *Sanjak* of Bursa had built the low walls. Its longest side extended east to west and protected brick-faced houses, open markets, and two-story khans from an unlikely attack.

The two passed the Chicken Market and the Fish Market, where vendors sold fresh carp, trout, and eels. They again caught up with the remnants of the caravan. Most of its travelers had entered the safety of the two-story Rice Khan. Other travelers would retire at one of the other 50 khans, both inside and outside the city walls. A few agents would go directly to the respective owners to deliver their goods.

As they turned down the main thoroughfare, the *kethuda* recognized one of the travelers. He knew that the jeweler would deliver his precious gems to the Jewelers Market beyond the main *Bedesten*. That domed bazaar, even larger than the Old *Bedesten* in *Stamboul*, stood up the street, just beyond the Silk Khan.

Silk Khan, Bursa

INSIDE THE SHADED courtyard of the Silk Khan, the *kethuda* and his able servant dismounted and handed the reins over to the attendant. "Take care of them."

"I'll house them in the halls." The attendant led the two steeds through the porticos of the two-story structure.

The *kethuda* and his servant made their way across the large courtyard. They jostled through the crowds, bumping against men dressed in turbans, who had just exited the small mosque built at its center.

Walking beneath the lower porticos on the far side, the *kethuda* and his servant passed a kitchen where cooks flayed trout and eels for their guests. They entered a large room crowded with silk merchants. Brokers weighed different kinds of silk: some of it processed and some raw; some of it colored and some pure white. One broker removed a blot of processed silk from a large scale and announced the price.

"That price is too low," the silk merchant said.

"The price is fixed," the broker replied.

"Pay the tax," an official seated at the tax table said.

"Ever since the Grand Vizier, Hasan *the Fruiterer,* cut the coin," the silk merchant complained, "monies are not worth much."

The *Kethuda* did not like hearing the hassles of bartering. "Pay the tax, we have business to attend to."

"We'll take the tax in silk." The tax official grabbed his share and stacked the silk behind him.

The silk merchant shook his head, shrugged his shoulders, and walked away.

The broker looked at the merchant standing at the head of the line. "Next!"

As that silk merchant moved his product to the scale, the *kethuda* turned. "Overseer!"

"I heard you were here, " the Overseer of the Silk Mill said. "I've finished my business. Here are the ledgers for the raw silk."

"Excellent."

Just then, a gardener from the Upper Castle entered. "The *Sanjak* must see you at once."

The *Kethuda,* his servant, and the escort immediately departed and headed up the street, past the *Ulu Cami,* the Grand Mosque with its two minarets and twenty domes. They crossed the grounds of the Upper Castle, surrounded by high walls. Not much larger than the Hippodrome of *Stamboul,* the well-protected castle had sixty-seven towers and a total of five gates. To the east, a covered bridge spanned a narrow valley and a stream. To the south, the double walls fronted a deep ravine. On the other side, the fountainhead was the source of the city's water supply. Beyond the forests, snow-topped Mount Olympus.

THE *KETHUDA* WAITED AT the palace entrance. When the *Sanjak* of Bursa motioned for him to approach, he bowed. "You called for me?"

"Yes, be seated."

"Coffee?"

"No, thank you."

"Fresh from Ottoman Yemen, delivered by the caravan from Smyrna."

"Very well." The *Kethuda* accepted the cup. "The gardener said it was urgent."

"We must ensure that the *Janissaries* are paid." The *Sanjak* glanced at the Head Tax Official.

"Is that our responsibility?" the *Kethuda* asked.

"Everyone must do his part."

"The raw silk from our mill has been delivered to the Silk Khan. As soon as it is sold, we will get our share." The *Kethuda* turned to the Head Taxman and pulled out the coin the Greek priest had given him. "That reminds me, here is the balance of the tax you went to collect last week."

The Tax Officer examined the old coin and told his assistant, "Mark it down."

Exiting the Old Palace building, the *Kethuda* and his servant stopped by the fountain in front of the Mosque of Orhan *Ghazi* with its single minaret.

"Is it true about the large drum hanging from the ceiling?" the servant asked.

"Yes," the *Kethuda* said. "Carried on the back of a camel, that drum last sounded when Orhan conquered Bursa."

"Around the time the Ottoman Empire was founded nearly 300 years ago."

"Yes." The *Kethuda* turned when he heard horses crossing the paved stones of the Upper Castle grounds. Several *sipahi* riders quickly dismounted.

The Mullah and the *Sanjak* of Bursa both appeared. "What is it?"

The *sipahi* rider knelt and rose. "The rebels near us."

"What about Khosru *Pasha?*" the *Sanjak* asked.

"Many of his men abandoned him and fled to Divas. The eunuch general himself retired to Diyarbakir. When the rebels marched west, Hafiz Ahmad *Pasha* shut himself inside Kutahya."

"And the rebels of *Deli* Hasan?"

"His Tartar allies are less than five miles away!"

"Sound the alarm!"

Trumpets blasted, and drums pounded. *Janissaries* carrying long muskets and quivers full of arrows rushed to the high walls of the castle and the low walls encircling the town below.

As citizens scurried across the paved square, the *Sanjak* turned to the *Kethuda*. "Come with me."

Inside the palace, the *Sanjak* quickly penned a note and addressed it to the Chief White Eunuch. Instead of using wax like Christian kings and nobles, he sealed it with ink. "Take this to Gazanfer *Agha.*

The *Kethuda* accepted the rolled-up scroll. "It will be dark soon."

"Horses are ready—go at once."

Near the fountain of Orhan *Ghazi*, the *Kethuda* and his servant mounted fresh rides. They exited *Kaplica* Gate and made their way down the hill to the plains.

As the winter sun set, they urged their horses north, past the Mulberry plantations, toward the port of Mudanya on the coast of the Sea of Marmara.

Chapter 49 — Bribes and Corruption

The Sultan [Murad III], who squandered large sums on the musicians, the parasites, and buffoons, by whom he loved to be surrounded, was often personally in need of money, and at last stooped to the degradation of taking part of the bribes, which petitioners for office gave to his courtiers. One of his principal favorites was Schemsi Pasha, who traced his pedigree up to a branch of those Seljukian princes, whom the House of Othman [Osman] had superseded in the East. The historian [Mustafa] Ali . . . relates that one day he himself was in that favorite's apartments, when Schemsi came thither from the Sultan's presence, and said with a joyous air to one of his domestics, "At last I have avenged my house on the House of Othman. For, if the Ottoman dynasty caused our downfall, I have now made it prepare [for] its own."

"Who has that been done?" cried the old domestic, gravely.

"I have done it," said Schemsi, "by persuading the Sultan to share in the sale of his own favors. It is true I placed a tempting bait before him; 40,000 ducats make no trifling sum. Henceforth, the Sultan will himself set the example of corruption; and corruption will destroy the empire."
<u>History of the Ottoman Turks</u> *by Sir Edward S. Creasy*

Coffeeshop, *Stamboul, Rajab AH* 1011, Late December *AD* 1602

GUZELCE MAHMUD *PASHA,* the newly appointed commander of Ottoman forces for Anatolia, welcomed the *sipahi* leader from Belgrade to sit down. "Some coffee, Osman *Bey?*"

Poiraz Osman *Bey* could not refuse. He joined the turbaned Ottoman official, sitting cross-legged on thick Persian carpets.

The shop owner and his servant quickly returned, bringing a low table and setting a plate of appetizers on it. They served dark Turkish coffee in *demi* cups.

"You may now leave us alone," Guzelce Mahmud *Pasha* told his friend, the shop owner.

The owner and his servant bowed and quickly departed, closing a beaded curtain behind them. Guzelce Mahmud *Pasha* picked up the amber tip of a flexible tube. He took a long drag from his *nargile*, the Turkish water pipe.

Poiraz Osman *Bey* nibbled on the appetizer. "You asked me to wait on you?" He sipped his steaming hot coffee.

"I know you enjoyed our last meal together." Guzelce Mahmud *Pasha* reminded him of the splendid feast of the previous week.

"Yes, it was most satisfying."

"Things have progressed further since that time. We must know your intentions." Gulzelce Mahmud *Pasha* took another drag. The water pipe percolated.

Poiraz Osman *Bey* squirmed. "I think I will smoke, too." Readjusting his position, he reached for and grabbed a second, flexible tube and inhaled.

Tobacco smoke soon filled the room.

"We must know what side you are on."

Nargile

"The Grand Vizier is my friend."

"What are your sentiments?"

Poiraz Osman *Bey* inhaled, but did not answer.

"The Grand Vizier is in Belgrade." Guzelce Mahmud *Pasha* looked directly into the *sipahi* leader's eyes. "Osman *Bey*, we have concocted this great measure. Not taking a decisive share in it is not wise. Besides, we have 30,000 *ducats* at our disposal."

"I hesitate to conspire." Poiraz Osman *Bey* wondered whether *it was safe?*

Guzelce Mahmud *Pasha* set down the amber tip and the tube. "Don't make yourself obnoxious: it's not safe to oppose the general voice."

Poiraz Osman *Bey* downed the rest of his coffee, all the way to the black grounds.

Home of Sun'Ullah *Effendi*, Stamboul

THE NEPHEW OF the former Grand Mufti Sun'Ullah *Effendi* met Guzelce Mahmud *Pasha* and Poiraz Osman *Bey*. "My uncle was expecting you."

When they entered the next room, Guzelce Mahmud *Pasha* bowed and kissed the hem of the former Grand Mufti's garment. "*Salam*, Sun'ullah *Effendi*. I have brought someone who agreed to hear you."

"Poiraz Osman *Bey*, I have learned so much about you," Sun'Ullah *Effendi* said.

"*Salam*, Sun'Ullah *Effendi*." Like most Turks, Poiraz Osman Bey held great respect and reference for members of the ulema and other religious authorities. "I have heard much about your wisdom."

"My nephew and Guzelce Mahmud *Pasha* have expressed much confidence in you."

"Thank you for your kind words." Poiraz Osman *Bey* bowed and stepped backwards.

Outside the room, the nephew of Sun'Ullah *Effendi* told the *sipahi* leader from Belgrade, "Osman *Bey*, we do not undertake these endeavors lightly." He pointed to sacks of coins stacked in a side room. "Everything has aligned with our plan."

"I am beginning to understand."

"Poiraz Osman *Bey*," Guzelce Mahmud *Pasha* interjected, "We must see some other officials."

"Who?" Poiraz Osman *Bey* asked.

"The two military judges who sit on the Divan."

One of those military judges decided the most important judicial matters for Anatolia or Turkey in Asia, while the other decided the judicial matters for Rumelia, Turkey in Europe.

Streets of *Stamboul*

POIRAZ OSMAN *BEY* understood the implications of the thirty thousand *ducats* at the disposal of the conspirators. For years, positions on the Divan had been obtained only after monies had been paid.

"Let me explain how things work," Guzelce Mahmud *Pasha* said. Avoiding the deep rut in the middle, they walked down a broad street. "Do you think I shall be appointed Deputy Grand Vizier, the *Kaimakam* of *Stamboul*, without monies being paid?"

"No," Poiraz Osman *Bey* answered. He vaguely remembered hearing the story of how bribery and corruption entered the empire during the reign of the previous sultan. Murad III had a great need for enormous sums to pay the musicians and entertainers who constantly amused him.

"Didn't it begin with Schemsi *Pasha*, a direct descendant of the Seljuk princes of the East?"

"Yes, Schemsi *Pasha* blamed the Ottomans for the fall of the Seljuk Empire, so he tempted Sultan Murad III with forty thousand ducats."

"No trifling sum."

"Yes, when the Sultan Murad III decided to sell his favors, Schemsi *Pasha* obliged."

Office of the Military Judge, *Stamboul*

ENTERING THE OFFICE of the Military Judge from Rumelia, Poiraz Osman *Bey* instantly understood how widespread their conspiracy had spread. Like the Military Judge of Anatolia, the Judge of Rumelia held one of the most important seats in the Imperial Divan. For years, the Sultan had stayed secluded inside the Imperial Harem, trusting the Chief White Eunuch Gazanfer *Agha* and letting the Divan debate the most important matters of state.

After meeting with the second Military Judge, Poiraz Osman *Bey* fully committed himself to the conspiracy: he would never turn back.

Chapter 50 — Admiral, Count, & Cardinal

Along with the arrival of the Admiral of Aragon to Brussels, who returned from his journey to Germany and Poland at the beginning of July, news came that Regiments of Germans and 4,000 Italians under Don Alfonso d'Avalos were marching . . . already in the Duchy of Luxembourg.

Guerras de Estados Baxos by Carlos Coloma
Translated from Spanish by D.E.A.

Moreover, it is certain that Cardinal Albert has arrived here with his army, that the old Count of Mansfeld [Peter Ernst I von Mansfeld-Vorderort] commands in the rank of Marshall of the Camp, and that they approach us . . . Because I defend and fight a just cause, I promise that God will give me the victory, if we come together; but to do so with more surety, it is necessary for you to advance all of the forces of horse and foot that I have mandated . . .

King Henry IV to the Ministers of his Council
From the Camp by Amiens, 25ᵗʰ of August 1597
Translated from French by D.E.A.

Salon, Palace of Ibrahim *Pasha*, *Rajab AH* 1011, Late December *AD* 1602

WISHING TO KNOW what her future held, Aisha, Sister of the Sultan, leafed through a book she often perused on her gilt bookstand. Her Overseer entered her salon and announced, "The French translator Filiz arrives."

Aisha closed the book, turned to the door, and greeted her friend. "I am so glad you made it here so quickly."

Filiz looked about the bright room. "Your mother?"

"I sent a messenger to the New Palace telling her I planned to rest today."

"Do you expect her later?" Filiz sat down on one of the cushioned benches.

"No. I told her not to worry." Aisha motioned for the Overseer to bring her slave. "I will visit the graves tomorrow."

Minutes later, the Overseer escorted her English slave into the Salon. When John Smith settled onto an adjoining cushion and after pleasantries were exchanged, Aisha asked her slave, *"Capitano,* what happened next at the Siege of Amiens?"

The French translator Filiz reiterated the question in French.

"One morning, five summers ago, in the year 1597, English and French soldiers crowded into trenches," John Smith began anew. "Not far from the Gate of Montrescu."

Ramparts, Amiens, Picardy, France, 24th of August *AD* 1597

CAPTAIN JOSEPH DUXBURY, John Smith, and the whole English regiment manned the crowded trench. A second battery of eight cannons had been raised in the ditch against the ramparts and, like the one in front of the other trench, pounded Spanish positions.

On August 24th, trumpets sounded. John and the other English recruits stormed out of the trenches. Not to be outdone, French soldiers from the other trench stormed the far side and up the side of the ramparts, too. Before nightfall, the fighting intensified, and they captured both ramparts.

Early the next morning, the Spanish pounded their drums. They counterattacked and beat back the English, as well as the French.

Later that same day, however, with French batteries raised higher and inched closer, the Spanish positions were pounded anew. As night fell, the English and French stormed again and reconquered what they had lost only hours earlier. The new regiment from Cambray occupied the French section.

When dawn broke on the 26th, John peered from the ramparts. In front of the Gate of Montrescu, Spanish soldiers emptied wheelbarrows filled with rocks. Other soldiers, one after another, emptied sacks and baskets filled with dirt.

"That half-moon wasn't there last week."

"We must cross a new ditch to reach it," Captain Joseph Duxbury said. "But we have learned that King Philip II wants the Head of John the Baptist from Amiens Cathedral."

"How did his head end up there?" Smith gestured to the Cathedral across the Somme.

"When King Herod married his brother's wife, John the Baptist told the King it was unlawful to do so. The King's new wife, Herodias, wanted the Prophet arrested, but Herod initially refused."

"What happened?"

"One night, the daughter of Herodias danced before the King. Herod was so pleased with her performance that he promised the daughter that he would give her anything she wanted, up to half of his kingdom."

"What did she want?" Smith asked.

"Having conferred with her mother, the daughter demanded the head of John the Baptist in a charger."

"So John the Baptist was killed?"

"Beheaded. Years after the body was buried, tradition holds that John the Baptist's head was taken to Constantinople, where it remained for nearly one thousand years."

"But how did it get to Amiens?"

"Almost four hundred years ago, during the Fourth Crusade in AD 1204, Constantinople was sacked. A French knight brought the head of John the Baptist to Amiens, and the Cathedral was built to hold it."

"But now?"

"King Philip II wants the relic taken to Spain and —"

"Men!" Sir John Aldrich, the new English General, interrupted the conversation. "Cardinal Albert approaches Douai."

"So near?" Captain Duxbury asked.

"Yes, along with the Admiral of Aragon."

"The Admiral was in Prague."

"Yes, but his year-long journey to the Holy Roman Empire has ended. He has returned with thousands of German soldiers."

"So many?"

"But there is more. *Don* Alfonso d'Avalos has crossed the Alps from Milan on the Spanish Road. He brings his *tercio*, more than three thousand veteran Italian soldiers. Cardinal Albert's army grows to twenty thousand strong."

Captain Duxbury grimaced with apparent concern for his English recruits. "Tell us what you know."

"A month ago, the Admiral of Aragon arrived in Brussels."

Coudenburg Palace, Brussels, the Lowlands, Early July *AD* 1597

IN THE PAVED Courtyard of Coudenburg Palace, Francisco *de* Mendoza, the Admiral of Aragon, bowed to Cardinal Albert, the Governor of the Seventeen Provinces of the Netherlands. When the Admiral rose, the Cardinal grabbed the forearms of his most trusted advisor. "So good to see you."

"A whole year has passed by." The former *Mayordomo Mayor*, the Head of the Cardinal's household, responded. They walked side by side into the Palace and up the wide staircase. "Your brother, the Emperor, as well as the Bohemian Parliament in Prague, appreciate all of the support you gave last winter."

Francisco de Mendoza, Admiral of Aragon

"For sending Giorgio Basta to command their army?" Cardinal Albert asked. "After Sultan Mehmet III's victory over the armies of the Holy Roman Empire at the Battle of Mezo-Keresztes last autumn, it is the least I could do."

"I have no doubt that Basta will be successful," the Admiral of Aragon said.

"Nor do I."

"According to instructions that King Philip gave me, I have arranged for his son, Prince Philip of Spain, to marry Margaret of Austria."

"Excellent, though it has been many years since I was in Austria." Cardinal Albert remembered his young cousin, the sister of the Archduke of Inner Austria. "And Margaret? What is her reaction?"

"Margaret looks forward to becoming the future Queen of Spain. Though young, she is very devout in her Catholic faith, and her mother is pleased."

"I must admit that I, too, look forward to getting married."

"Yes. How is *Infanta* Isabella?"

"She writes often, saying she takes care of her father, the King." The former Cardinal of Toledo sat down and motioned for the Admiral of Aragon to do likewise.

The Admiral of Aragon leaned forward. "I heard about the disaster at the Heath of Tielen."

"Our cavalry was chased off the field by Captain General Maurice."

"It should not have happened."

"It would not have occurred if you were in charge. *Tielenheide* was a devastating loss, especially with the death of the Count of Varax. However, with the capture of Amiens, we have been more than compensated."

"Will we be able to hold on to Amiens?"

"Not without help. Though I understand why King Philip renounced all debts last November, the Fuggers and the merchants have refused to lend us money."

"But our cause is more important than mere money."

"Amiens is besieged, hard-pressed on all sides. Governor Porto-carrero defends with vigor, but King Henry has blocked the approaches from the north with fourteen forts. And now he digs two more trenches toward the walls."

"What about peace? The Papal Legate?"

"King Henry has refused to accept the Legate's suggestion for an extended truce."

"And Brittany?" the Admiral of Aragon asked. "Can Philippe Emmanuel *de* Lorraine, the Duke of Mercoeur, renew his attacks?"

"Ever since King Henry caught two French messengers and executed them for treason in April, we have had little success," Cardinal Albert said. "In April, young Samuel *de* Champlain, who supports King Henry, was promoted to Captain in Quimper. And the Duke of Mercoeur almost lost Dinan in May."

"Near St. Malo? How?"

"Several of the Duke's former pages almost captured the Castle of Dinan. The traitorous Lieutenant would certainly have turned it over to King Henry IV if the Duke's Governor had not returned and restored order."

"So the Duke cannot assist us?"

"Very little." Cardinal Albert paused. "Without a miracle, I do not know how long Governor Hernán Tello *de* Portocarrero can hold on to Amiens."

"I have brought German regiments," the Admiral of Aragon said. "And *Don* Alfonso d'Avalos has recruited more than three thousand Italians from Milan. His *tercio* marches over the Alps even as we speak."

"The rumors are true." The Cardinal stood up. "Such good news!" He opened the door to the adjoining room.

Members of the War Council, including Peter Ernst, the Count of Mansfeld, rose in the Council Chambers. Mansfeld, who had fought in the Spanish Netherlands for many years, appeared younger than his eighty years. The Cardinal proclaimed, "Gentlemen, the Admiral brings great news. I want to introduce the new General of the Light Cavalry of the Lowlands."

"Such an honor." The Admiral received the congratulations.

Douai, Border of Flanders and Artois, 25th August *AD* 1597

DELAYED FOR WEEKS by the need to raise more monies and secure more supplies, the Admiral, the Cardinal, and the Count departed Brussels on the 22nd of August. Three days later, they reached the outskirts of Douai, a fortified town on the border of Flanders and Artois. While the Admiral rode on horseback, the Cardinal and the Count traveled in separate litters, wheelless carriages. Two pairs of mules carried each litter aloft, on pairs of poles.

The Commissary of the Army, Colonel Juan Contreras, accompanied the growing train of troops, as well as wagons and carts full of supplies. "The bulk of the army has already arrived at Arleux," the Colonel informed the Cardinal. "Four thousand Spanish veterans were the first to arrive."

In the heat of summer, the shortage of soldiers had evaporated. Besides the Spanish, three thousand Italian soldiers of *Don* Alfonso d'Avalos had joined the encampment at Arleux, a village to the south of Douai, halfway to Cambrai. The Count of Sultz, whose forces had been decimated at the Battle of *Tielenheide,* saw his regiment revived, growing with the recent German arrivals from the Holy Roman Empire and now totaling roughly six thousand strong. Troops in the Irish, Walloon, and Burgundy regiments together amounted to nearly seven thousand men. The veteran army now totaled twenty thousand.

Trained and drilled, these footmen more than equalled the size and quality of the French army, flushed with new recruits. In addition to the footmen and fifteen hundred Light Horsemen commanded by the Admiral of Aragon, the Cardinal had nearly one thousand knights, the *gens d'armes*. These knights from the feudal estates of both Spain and Belgium carried lances, plus second weapons of their own choosing. Both these riders and their horses wore full armor. No one doubted their skills and abilities to face down French riders of equal numbers.

Spanish and Italian officers from the encampment soon gathered inside the fortified walls of Douai. Cardinal Albert wanted to convene the War Council to consider all options, including an attack on the French town of San Quentin at the source of the Somme. While waiting for the rest of his principal commanders to arrive, the Cardinal reminisced about walking the corridors of *San Lorenzo d'Escorial* Palace with his future bride, *Infanta* Isabella, before King Philip II had appointed him to be Governor of the Lowlands.

Several paintings in the *Salas de Batallas* flashed across his mind. Those paintings depicted Philip's victories over French forces at San Quentin on the Feast Day of San Lorenzo, 40 years earlier. In honor of that victory, His Most Catholic Majesty had named his austere palace outside Madrid after the Saint. Though San Quentin had returned to French hands in the intervening years, an attack on it might force King Henry to abandon his siege of Amiens.

"Should we besiege San Quentin?" the Cardinal asked.

"This army is as fine an army as I've ever commanded," the old Count of Mansfeld said. "We have so many veterans."

"As well as younger men, strong and able," the Admiral of Aragon added.

"I look around and see able commanders, such as Luis *de* Villar," the Count of Mansfeld said.

"And don't forget *Don* Alfonso d'Avalos with his *tercio* from Italy," the Admiral of Aragon added.

"And *Don* Luis Velasco."

"Colonel Claude *la* Barlotte and Count *de* Buscouy, both able Walloons."

Cardinal Albert noted all present. "But back to the question. Should we besiege San Quentin?"

"Neither Peronne, nor San Quentin," the Count of Mansfeld said. "Remember, we lost Paris and Rouen because we delayed."

"We must act now," Colonel Claude *la* Barlotte said.

"Governor Tello must be rewarded; his men should not be punished for their bravery. If we throw relief into Amiens, we can defend it until winter. The King would have to abandon the siege."

"Very well," Cardinal Albert said. "His Most Catholic Majesty has also asked us to retrieve a large relic from Amiens Cathedral."

"The skull of John the Baptist, from King Herod's time?" the Admiral of Aragon asked.

"Yes," Cardinal Albert said. "I promised King Philip to remove it from France and transport it to Madrid."

"That would certainly cause a scandal," Count Mansfeld advised.

"Among the French, perhaps." Cardinal Albert nodded. "But we first need to break through King Henry's lines. What is the situation?"

"King Henry has built the Hermitage, a citadel in front of the Gate of Montrescu. His trenches are well-guarded and extend for miles, but the other side of the town is not besieged."

"How should we deliver the relief?"

"We will need to cross the Somme," the Count of Mansfeld said.

"Boats are ready, a pontoon bridge can be built, quickly and easily," Colonel Claude *la* Barlotte added.

"But below or above the city?" Cardinal Albert inquired.

"If we cross the Somme above, at Camon, the Gate of Noyon is unprotected."

"Downriver at Longpre might be better," another officer suggested.

The Cardinal turned to the Admiral of Aragon, "We must find the best path."

The Admiral of Aragon turned. "Colonel Contreras, take four hundred horse and go to Doullens."

"I will go, too." The Albanian cavalry officer, Nicolo Basta, volunteered. His bravery mirrored the valor of his cousin Giorgio Basta, who had gone to Prague.

"We must find weakness in King Henry's defenses," Cardinal Albert said.

"We will."

English Headquarters, Camon, Picardy, Evening, 29ᵗʰ August *AD* 1597

IN THE EARLY evening on the 29th of August, Marshall *de* Biron rode to the English camp. "Captain Duxbury, your riders!"

"Marshall?" Captain Duxbury looked up.

Biron pointed to King Henry. Roughly one hundred of his nobles rode alongside their King, east toward Querrieu. "The Vanguard of the Cardinal's army probes our line. We must join the King and meet the Spanish horse."

Captain Duxbury turned to his men. "You heard the Marshall. Men, mount up!"

John Smith and the other fifty English soldiers of Duxbury's company quickly saddled their horses. Minutes later, with night approaching, they followed the King.

As dusk ended, they encamped below a knoll near Querrieu.

Querrieu, Picardy, 29th August 1597

EARLY THE NEXT morning, about half of the horsemen were sent away, along different routes. When the King and his nobles rode to the top of the knoll, the Marshall with some French riders, as well as Captain Duxbury's company, followed.

Spanish riders emerged from the woods, so the King signaled; his cornet sounded. The Nobles lowered their visors, raised their weapons, and charged down the hill.

The stunned Spaniards turned their horses: fear swept over the riders' faces. Some pulled their swords, others hastily retreated. Like a pride of lions pursuing their prey, the King and his men ferociously attacked the enemy.

Suffering a deadly loss of nearly one hundred in the initial fray, the Spanish riders retreated across a river. Some scattered to the woods. Most galloped up the road alongside the Miramount, a tributary of the Somme.

King Henry did not relent. He pursued the Spaniards and Walloons for more than fifteen miles. They reached Hainaut Province and the outskirts of Baubame.

The Hermitage, Amiens, 29th August *AD* 1597

THAT SAME NIGHT, the King returned to the Hermitage in triumph. His Mistress Gabrielle d'Estrées, greeted him with open arms and a kiss. Others looked at the two captured cornets. Spanish prisoners were taken away.

"When we heard that four hundred horsemen were paying a visit, we rode to meet them," the King explained, and the gathering grew.

"As soon as his Majesty saw enemy scouts west of the woods of Querreiu, the King led the attack," Marshall *de* Biron reported.

"We charged the superior force, quickly gaining the advantage," the King said.

"The prisoners tell us they thought our whole army was there," Marshall *de* Biron said. "We pursued them to within three miles of Bapaume, killed three hundred, and captured two cornets."

"An excellent victory!" King Henry IV exclaimed. "But we must now press our siege and conquer Amiens before Cardinal Albert regroups and counterattacks." He turned to the Duke of Mayenne, whom he left in charge of the siege. "We must capture the Gate of Montrescu."

Minutes later, *Monsieur* St. Luc moved six of his cannons closer to the Spanish half-moon, the new bastion adjacent to the gate. While French miners and sappers brought gunpowder into the dry ditch below the enemy ramparts, the French General of the Artillery signaled. His barrage resumed, pounding the Spanish fortifications from both sides.

Chapter 51 — More Dangerous Thoughts

English Encampment, Amiens, Picardy, France, 30th August AD 1597

THE SHORT NIGHT abruptly ended when John Smith awoke with a start. Cold water seeped up his leg. With his pants drenched and his boots soaked, John reached for his weapon. He swung his legs around and stepped into inches of water, lapping against his bedroll. Above, not a single cloud dotted the brightening sky. The last morning star still shone over the horizon. Water dripped from his sword as he stood and wondered aloud, "What happened?"

"Soldiers!" Captain Joseph Duxbury roused his men. "Move your horses, get the baggage!" He pointed to the Somme, the river was backing up from Amiens. "Higher ground!"

Small animals rushed from the brush, scurried over grassy knolls, and into forests further upstream.

At the English Headquarters at Camon, Sir John Aldrich rushed from his tent. "Move the powder."

"Too late."

The gunpowder sacks had opened. Gray powder floated atop the rising waters, surmounting a small dike. Like soldiers storming a fort, the water breached the barrier and flooded the field.

After the soldiers retrieved as much baggage as they could, a few wagons floated away, toward the middle of the river. While most of the camp resettled on higher ground, Duxbury led his company to the Hermitage. "Our turn to man the walls."

At the forward ramparts, John saw the Spanish had not stopped working. In addition to the new Half-Moon in front of the Gate of Montrescu, they had built two more Half-Moons on either side.

"Will they ever give up?" John asked.

"Not as long as they have hope," Captain Duxbury pointed to the ditches in front of the Half-Moons. The deep ditches were no longer dry, but filled to the brim.

"The water?"

"That's why the Spanish Governor built dams, to back up the river. The water must be eight feet deep."

"How can we storm the Half-Moons?" John asked. "The saucissons and mines have been swept away."

"It only delays us," Captain Joseph Duxbury said. "Moats can be drained or filled."

Behind them, *Monsieur* St. Luc increased the number of cannons from six to thirty-four. He moved them closer and raised them higher. Redirecting their aim over the moat, the pounding resumed, more intense than ever. It provided protection to English and French soldiers in two new trenches. Using spades and shovels, the soldiers carried the dirt forward. Heavy rocks were thrown into the moat; wooden planks and ladders were held in reserve.

Amiens, Picardy, France, 4th September *AD* 1597

AFTER POUNDING THE three Half-Moon forts for nearly a week, King Henry advanced to the front. He gave orders to his Master General of the Artillery to attack.

With the English on his left and the French on his right, *Monsieur* St. Luc signaled for the pounding to halt.

"Charge!" the able general commanded.

Spilling out of the trench, Captain Duxbury and his English company charged the middle Half-Moon. They pushed forward, across the wooden planks, up the side. When the soldiers reached the top, the enemy, led by Captain *del* Arco, resisted with pikes, pistols, and swords.

John raised the ladder and started climbing. At the top, he blocked a blow. He ignored the vibrations and blocked another. He recognized the short Spanish Governor urging his men out of the Gate. The enemy rushed to defend their precarious position.

Spanish musketeers knelt and took aim. Two of John's friends fell backward. John climbed another step and blocked another blow.

"Fall back!" Duxbury yelled.

As John retreated and English muskets provided cover, John spied the Spanish governor grabbing his left side and falling to the ground.

John retreated. "Governor Tello was shot."

"Are you certain?" Captain Joseph Duxbury asked.

"I know what I saw."

The Hermitage, Amiens, France, 6th September AD 1597

TWO DAYS LATER, several hundred more French citizens departed Amiens via the gates facing Paris and Noyon. Several of them, who had all served their Spanish occupiers, crossed the Somme and were brought to the King inside the Hermitage.

"Amiens runs low on food, and many soldiers are sick," the citizen reported to the gathering of officers and men.

"What about the Governor?" King Henry asked.

"Governor Hernán Tello *de* Portocarrero is dead, buried at the Cathedral. The captains elected the *Marquis de* Montenegro, Jerome Caraffa, to replace him."

"The leader of their cavalry?"

"Yes." The citizen signaled.

"What about the Half-Moons?"

"They didn't trust us beyond the marketplace, but we heard the Marquis has sent his horsemen, whether Lancers or Cuirassiers, to the front. They know the Cardinal is on his way and trust God that He will deliver them."

Amiens, France, 8th September *AD* 1597

FOUR DAYS AFTER the Spanish Governor had been shot, *Monsieur* St. Luc urged both French and English soldiers forward. Two trenches edged closer to the Half-Moons on either side of the Gate. The Marshall *de* Biron took command of the English regiment, hundreds strong.

As they advanced, sporadic enemy gunfire hindered their progress, but not John and his fellow soldiers. Enemy muskets fired. Before they could reload, the English soldiers stood and dug through the mud. Some of the water had been drained, and it was now waist-high.

"Captain Duxbury!" Marshall *de* Biron pointed to the wall.

A Spanish gunner fired, and John turned. "*Monsieur* Saint Luc!"

"He's hit!" The Marshall ran to the General.

Other artillerymen gathered around their well-respected leader. When French noblemen carried *Monsieur* Saint Luc's body back into the Hermitage, the King appeared extremely saddened.

"I've lost a great general, an able noble, a true friend." The King shook his head.

After the body of Francois d'Espinay *de* Saint Luc was laid to rest, the Marshall and the Duke of Mayenne told the King, "A new Grand Master of the Artillery must be found."

Hermitage, Amiens, France, 9th September *AD* 1597

A FEW DAYS later, John Smith accompanied Captain Duxbury to the Hermitage. For the fourth month in a row, Baron *de* Rosny had arrived with more than a million *ecus* to pay the army.

"The King wants to appoint the Baron as the new head of the artillery," Captain Joseph Duxbury said.

"But?" John asked.

"*Madame la Duchesse* wants the King to appoint her father."

"As General of the Artillery?" John asked. "Isn't he old?"

"Yes, but the Mistress threatened, if the King did not listen to her, to become a nun."

"But what about the Baron *de* Rosny?"

"Gabrielle's father is old, and the King does not want the Baron to risk his life. He needs Baron's advice and also to ensure that monies arrive from Paris."

When they reached the tents of the Abbey of Mary Magdalene, the Baron distributed the pay. John pointed the fields outside. "More cavalry?"

"Finally." Baron *de* Rosny smiled. "Calvinists from Poitou."

"Their Assembly at Chatellerault?" Captain Joseph Duxbury asked.

"Most of the Calvinist leaders did not want to join the siege, but I wrote to *Monsieur* Claude *la* Tremouille to relent, to stay his demands."

"How?" John asked.

"I told them not to force the King to issue an edict granting the freedom to practice their Reformed Religion now, while His Most Christian Majesty is under duress. It would give the strong Catholic factions reason to reverse the edict at a future time."

"So they heeded your advice?"

"After receiving the pleadings from *Stadholder* Maurice van Nassau-Orange and the United Provinces of the Netherlands and your Queen Elizabeth."

Half-Moon, Gate of Montrescu, Amiens, 12th September *AD* 1597

SEVERAL DAYS LATER, the cannon smoke had not dissipated; the debris had not yet settled. English and French soldiers again charged the Half-Moon bastions. Wooden planks wobbled as John and the other soldiers crossed the moat. The walls, though steep, had been partially breached.

French soldiers charged one side, and the English stormed the other side of the narrow passageways. For hours, the defenders showered the attacker with rocks and stones. The gates were blocked, the Spanish undeterred. Scores of bodies rolled back into the shallow moat. Hour after hour, English and French captains sent waves of men, but to no avail. Progress could not be made.

In the afternoon, about two, trumpets and drums sounded. The assault was called off. More rocks were hurled down, and a musket shot struck a retreating soldier. Cannonballs from enemy culverins blasted to John's left. He veered right. His risky retreat was hazardous and unsafe. Out of breath, John barely escaped with his life.

When he reached the Hermitage and sat down, John heard violins playing and minstrels singing. Spanish and Irish soldiers on the ravelin lined up.

"They're mocking us," John said.

"And the French." Captain Duxbury picked up his sword. "We need to put a stop to it."

Marshall *de* Biron met the recovering English. "We face more perilous threats."

"More dangerous than this?" John asked.

"The Admiral of Aragon, the Count of Mansfield, and Cardinal Albert of Austria approach. Their Relief Army of twenty thousand marches: it crosses the Authie. The Regiments of Swiss and French from Picardy will continue the siege."

As the Duke of Mayenne approached the King, Captain Duxbury asked Marshall *de* Biron, "And us?"

"Retrieve your horses, we ride."

Captain Duxbury headed toward the waiting English riders, and the King prepared to mount his horse. Before he could, the Duke of Mayenne reached him. "You must stop!"

"What is it?" the King asked.

"You risk disaster."

"How so?"

"Those who tell you to meet the Cardinal know not the quality of the enemy as I do."

"Our horse is the best," the Marshall, primed for battle, interjected.

"You underestimate the Cardinal," the Duke of Mayenne said. "His veteran army is battle-tested."

King Henry IV motioned. "Continue."

"To venture with only your horse against such a potent old army puts yourself in danger of a sinister accident. To leave your infantry alone risks certain loss. After all the toil and labor to fortify them, your trenches would be lost; all would be lost. Your Kingdom is set upon one single point of a dyke."

"What should be done?" King Henry IV asked.

"We have come to take Amiens. Our minds must be focused on that end. Keep the army secure in the forts. Make the Cardinal decide to assault us and drive us from here."

"The enemy will pass the Somme and relieve the besieged."

"Let your Majesty set his heart at rest, for the enemy will neither pass the Somme, nor force these trenches."

The expression on Marshall *de* Biron's face sourced.

Chapter 52 — Relief Army Advances

Douai, Spanish Netherlands, Early September *AD* 1597

THE ADMIRAL OF Aragon, the Count of Mansfeld, and the rest of the Council of War listened to Commissary General Juan Contreras finish his report to Cardinal Albert.

"King Henry commanded his French Cavalry in person," *Don* Contreras, the third-ranking cavalry officer of the army, concluded. "I did not want to risk combat. We had to retreat—"

"Untrue!" A Spanish Captain interrupted. "King Henry was alone; he had no support. Because of your hasty retreat, we lost two or three cornets. We should have taken a stand."

"Our success was in doubt. I thought the whole French cavalry was behind the King."

"You thought wrong; it was a disgrace."

"You impugn my honor?"

"You may have lost your honor, but my lancers lost their lives. It was a cowardly retreat."

"A coward?" The Commissary General threw down his gloves.

"Gentlemen, gentlemen!" Cardinal Albert intervened before his Spanish Captain could accept the challenge. He could not afford to see his officers killing each other. "You will both have opportunities to prove your mettle. The Day of Battle will show who is bravest and most faithful to his duty."

Commissary General Contreras picked up his gloves. Both officers stepped back. Fuming in silence, they glared at each other.

The Admiral of Aragon stated firmly, "Not all was lost in the retreat."

"What do you mean?" Cardinal Albert asked.

"While Contreras retreated to Baupame, these two captains surveyed the whole of the French defenses."

The first captain stepped up. "Because they did not consider us a threat, the French ignored us."

"We saw it all, from the English headquarters at Camon near Corbie to the Hermitage in front of the Gate of Montrescu. That star-shaped Citadel is stronger than the city's fortified walls."

"Their weakest defenses are down the Somme River at Longpres-*les*-Amiens."

Arras, Province of Artois, Spanish Lowlands, 5th September 1597

A DAY AFTER Cardinal Albert joined the Count of Bucquoy at the fortified city of Arras, the Cardinal called his officers together. Nearly six months earlier, at the end of March, the Count had repelled an assault by French and English troops, led by Marshall *de* Biron. The Cardinal was pleased that the Count's strong regiment of Walloons would join his army.

Inside the citadel, the Cardinal spoke, "Gaspard Zapena, you shall be Lieutenant to *Don* Gaston Spinola and Camp Master General Mansfeld."

"As soon as the rest of the victuals arrive, we will march," the Count of Mansfeld said. "The boats for crossing the Somme are almost ready."

"No sign of the King of France advancing towards us," the Admiral of Aragon reported. "But on the Rhine River, *Stadholder* Maurice leads his Dutch army against Rheinberg."

"The Dutch rebels take advantage of us," Philip-William, the Prince of Orange. said. "Should we send more of the army to fight my younger brother?"

"No," Cardinal Albert said. "We must bring relief to Amiens."

Outside Doullens, Artois, Spanish Lowlands, 12th September AD 1597

ABOUT A WEEK later, the army had relocated to the banks of the Authie River outside Doullens. Cardinal Albert readied his final preparations at his tent.

While quartermasters distributed victuals to each soldier, a scout dismounted. "Governor Hernán Tello *de* Portocarrero has died."

"Are you certain?" the Cardinal asked.

"Three hundred French servants were expelled, no longer needed. Amiens is in dire straits. The captains have elected the *Marquis de* Montenegro to take his place."

The Cardinal scanned the Spanish encampment. With his relief army at full strength, he knew he had to act and pointed to the river. "We must cross."

The Admiral of Aragon led the Light Cavalry across. Regiment by regiment, the army of 20,000 foot soldiers followed.

~ ~ ~

TWO DAYS LATER, the last of the baggage forded the Authie, and a week's worth of victuals was distributed.

Like an armada sailing over rising swells, the Spanish army rolled over small hills. Under fair skies, Cardinal Albert pulled back the curtains of his litter. Raised aloft on poles connected to four mules, his wheelless litter gently rocked back and forth. He moved steadily south, toward Amiens. His personal guard, armed with firearms and swords, rode close to his side.

Two horse regiments flanked the army of four large squares, each thousands strong. Companies of fully armored Men-at-Arms rode on one side, while the Admiral of Aragon and his Light Cavalry protected the other. After putting them in order, the Admiral galloped toward the Cardinal, in front of the Vanguard of Luis *de* Villar.

Marching in a large square, the 4,000 veteran soldiers of the Vanguard kept pace. Both Spanish and Italian company banners flew in the midst of the forest of pikes and muskets. Behind the Vanguard, the old Count of Mansfeld occupied a second litter. Similar to the one the Cardinal used, the Count's litter was open and carried by mules.

Two Spanish commanders, Carlos Coloma and Lodovico Velasco, led the two center squares—the *Battalia*. The Walloons of Count *de* Bucquoy marched with them. On either side of the double-sized *Battalia*, hundreds of horsemen trotted, carrying firearms, pistols, and arquebuses, loaded and ready.

Tied together with great chains of iron, countless carts and wagons rolled forward, one after another. Twenty-five of the large wagons doubled as boats, so the army could cross the Seine. Towards the center, near nobles on horseback, other horses pulled cannons, both medium and small. The Rearguard, thousands strong, followed all.

Pleased with both the size and quality of his forces, the Cardinal noted several companies of French and English Light Cavalry riding in the distance.

Northern Picardy, France, 14ᵗʰ September *AD* 1597

THE FRENCH SCOUT finished reporting everything he had learned about the disposition of the Cardinal and his army.

"Excellent work." The general of the French Light Cavalry mounted his horse. Several French companies shadowed every movement of the enemy army.

"Will we engage?" Captain Duxbury, already mounted, asked. His company of horse had joined the French when they had left the Hermitage at the King's request.

"For now, we watch and observe." The General pulled his horse around. "We must keep track of the Cardinal's progress."

John Smith urged his horse next to his captain and, at Duxbury's direction, counted the number of cornets flying with the enemy horse. He noted the number of company banners in each square, as well as the size, type, and quality of enemy cannons and culverins. Whenever a cannon stuck on a rock or a wheel dislodged from a wagon, enemy colonels waved the rest of their regiment forward.

The two litters holding Cardinal Albert and the Count of Mansfeld gently rocked. The mules carrying the carriages aloft rarely stopped.

That evening, standing on the opposite bank of the Domart, the small tributary of the Nievre and the Somme rivers, John Smith watched the Spanish army set up camp.

After the Cardinal climbed out of his litter at the *Abbaye de Berteaucourt* outside the village of Domart, the French General of the Light Cavalry told Duxbury and his other Captains, "It is clear that the Spanish will attack French trenches from the northeast."

"I agree," Duxbury echoed. "Cardinal Albert realizes he has no choice if he wants to throw relief into Amiens."

"King Henry must be told." The French General pulled his horse around, spurred it, and led the Light Cavalry back toward Amiens.

After traveling several miles, the French general stationed a company of riders at a bluff near Vignacourt before leading the rest of the French Light Horse back to Amiens, ten miles further.

Hermitage, Outside Amiens, Post-Midnight, 15ᵗʰ September *AD* 1597

ALONG WITH CAPTAIN Duxbury and his company of English horse, the French Light Horse reached the Hermitage shortly after midnight. The French General and the other officers found King Henry still awake when John and the riders dismounted and informed him where the Relief Army would likely attack. Around midnight, after patrolling for nearly two days, the French Light Horse returned to the Hermitage. "The Cardinal is at the Abbey of Berteaucourt outside Domart."

"Perhaps I should have taken the offer of the General of the Franciscans."

"What offer?"

"Cardinal Albert said he would abandon Amiens if I would turn it over to the Papal Legate." The King pondered. "I refused, and now the Cardinal has found the means to attack."

After two successive days of constant patrolling, the tired English and French horsemen went to their quarters. John Smith felt relieved when Captain Duxbury ordered his company to rest.

~ ~ ~

AT DAYBREAK ON the 15th of September, the sound of pounding hooves awakened John. His overnight rest seemed very short.

King Henry mounted his stallion. "Sound the alarm!"

Trumpets blasted, drums sounded. The allied army roused.

As the Cavalry, both French and English, saddled and mounted their horse, the King sent his mistress, Gabrielle d'Estrées, southeast. Along with her entourage, Gabrielle rode away from the Hermitage and toward Corbie. Soon out of harm's way, she would be safe at her father's estate. The *Chateau de Coeuvres-et Valsery* was more than fifty miles away, far from the field of battle in the opposite direction.

With his whole cavalry summoned, Henry led them west to the fields north of the village of Saint Sauveur in Picardy. Sitting atop his horse, John Smith raised his visor; his heart pounded. The seventeen-year-old from Lincolnshire, England, viewed the Cardinal's Relief Army, more than twenty thousand strong. His heart raced faster.

Chapter 53 — King Henry IV & the Cardinal

Our place is so advantageous as that we may both hold the town assieged [besieged] and give the Cardinal [Albert of Austria] battle, whose tardivity in relieving and forces now gathered together, is of us much derided and nothing esteemed, and the rather for that we see that they will not fight in any ways they avoid it.

Thus hoping for good success for all our actions here, which is not too much desired of the French themselves, beseech the Almighty send you a happy return.
[Captain] William Lylle to the Earl of Essex
The Camp before Amiens, August 1597

North of Saint Sauveur & Somme River, Picardy, France, 15th Sept. 1597

JUST AFTER NOON on the 15th of September, King Henry IV of France and his whole cavalry found the Cardinal Albert and the Spanish Army of twenty thousand.

The English Recruit John Smith scanned the field. "Twenty-five wagons flank the far side. Has the order of the Spanish army changed?"

Captain Joseph Duxbury nodded and replied, "The Spanish General Carlos Coloma no longer leads the Rearguard, but the Vanguard."

"And the *Battalia?*"

"The regiments *Don* Luis *de* Velasco and *Don* Alfonso d'Avala."

Following its overnight rest at Domart, the Cardinal's Relief Army had resumed its slow, steady march.

"They dare not attack the Hermitage," John said.

"They must first push us from their way," Captain Duxbury said.

Avoiding direct confrontation at Amiens, the Spanish army had marched towards Picquigny, miles downriver. Its castle, the *Chateau de Picquigny*, commanded the Somme from a hill on the far bank.

In the distance, the litter of Cardinal Albert and the rest of his army halted. Horses brought pieces of artillery forward. Cannon blasts broke the midday bliss. The shots fell far short of the French cavalry, standing in squadrons of fifty, in battle formation.

"The Cardinal alerts the *Marquis de* Montenegro," Captain Joseph Duxbury said. "He wants Montenegro and his Spanish soldiers to sally out of Amiens when the Relief Army attacks."

At the center front of the French horsemen, a White Cross flew in the breeze. Below the Flag of France, the gallant French monarch, dressed in full armor, knelt, his hat in hand.

When His Most Christian Majesty stood, he raised both hands high and prayed aloud, "Lord! Today, if you resolve to punish me as my sins deserve, here is my head. I offer it up to thy justice. Spare not the guilty, but oh, God! In thy mercy, pity this poor kingdom. Let not the flock suffer for the faults of its shepherd."

~ ~ ~

ONLY A FEW thousand horsemen, French and English, Catholic and Protestant, blocked the enemy's path, but the enemy did not ride toward the King, the French horse, or the Hermitage.

The enemy army resumed its slow trek toward the Chateau *de* Picquigny, more than five miles downriver from Amiens. Most of the French and English cavalry maintained its distance, but when a Spanish company probed the field, a French horse company skirmished with the Spanish, first on one side, and then on the other. A Neapolitan Captain of Lancers was captured.

As the Captain was interrogated, the Count of Bucquoy, drawing a thousand Walloons from the *Battalia*, marched hard toward the village of Saint Sauveur. The Count brought twenty-five large wagons down to the water's edge, a mile upriver from Picquigny and nearly as far from Longpres, below a sharp turn of the river.

John pointed. "The Count?"

The wagons doubled as boats.

"He builds a pontoon bridge," Captain Joseph Duxbury said.

The Count's men tied the boats together, side by side. As soon as they finished the pontoon bridge, the thousand choice infantrymen rushed to the other side.

On the distant shore, Walloon musketeers fired at French archers, who defended a strong tower. Further in the distance, the firefight spread to a churchyard, dislodging the three hundred French fighters defending it.

After the Walloons entrenched themselves on the far bank, the Count *de* Bucquoy probed and tested, first in one place and then another. Walloon pikemen and musketeers advanced on the far side of the Somme, back toward Longpres and the suburbs of Amiens.

"Can't we help?" John asked.

"Stay in order," Duxbury insisted. "The King sends French reinforcements over the bridge at Longpres."

Several companies of French Light Horse, plus Lord *de* Vic's regiment, advanced to intercept the Count and the Walloons. They engaged the Walloon regiment of the far shore of the Somme. French musketeers fired their weapons and reloaded. Pikemen pushed the Count of Bucquoy back toward the tower and the church.

The King's heavy horse remained in good order between the Hermitage and the Cardinal.

The huge Relief Army slowed its pace toward Saint Sauveur when John spied the Admiral of Aragon raise his sword. His Light Horse, more than one thousand strong, flew and charged the Half-Moon fort that the English helped to build during the Spring. If the Spanish captured the fort and the bridge at *Longpre-les-Amiens*, they would be able to throw thousands of soldiers into Amiens.

The French trenches, though miles long, were thinly manned, not quite as strong as they had seemed. Far from the trenches of Longpre, the French heavy cavalry, *Cuirassiers* and *Carabiniers*, along with John Smith and the rest of the English cavalry, watched the attack unfold.

"They'll capture Longpre!" Marshall *de* Biron yelled.

The size and fury of the attack by the Admiral's Flying Squadrons frightened the French infantry. In droves, they abandoned their positions and ran out of the trenches. Some fled towards Amiens, but most skirted along the banks of the Somme towards Saint Sauveur and Picquigny.

"Victory!" the Spaniards yelled. "Victory!" The Light Horse drew closer. *"Battalia! Battalia!"*

The battle was almost won before it had begun.

"They halted their advance!" The King pointed.

The Cardinal sent neither the rest of his Vanguard nor his *Battalia* forward.

The calm did not last.

The King turned to his deputy commander of the artillery.

"All cannons, fire!" the deputy yelled. Messengers signaled and relayed the command to the forts.

Sporadic fire from French artillery resumed, and the barrage intensified. French cannons fired round after round, first from one fort, then the next, and a third. Black smoke enveloped the field.

The thickening haze obscured the enemy's vision. The Cardinal certainly could no longer tell whether French soldiers were still abandoning the trenches.

John saw enemy officers gathering in the distance, beyond the haze. French cannons bombarded the enemy with more shots. Even after Duxbury retired, the seven strong forts between Longpre and the Hermitage fired ceaselessly, forcing the Spanish Light Horse to regroup. King Henry redeployed the French and English horse.

"Follow me!" the Marshall led the Vanguard of his horse into the smoke-filled field. Cannons from the forts and the Half-Moon at Longpre provided cover.

Company by company, the *Cuirassiers* and *Carabiniers* lined up before the trenches. Smith and the other English riders joined the French, and Duxbury positioned his men next to a fort.

When Marshall *de* Biron galloped after the fleeing infantry, Duxbury pointed. "The Marshall shows the error of their ways."

While all of the King's horse stood in battle formation, the French infantry slowly returned to Longpre. Whenever Spanish riders ventured too close, cannons inflicted great harm.

For the remainder of the day, the Spanish held back their attack. As evening turned to darkness, the Spanish retired to their camp, less than a mile away.

That night, the Duke of Mayenne brought hundreds of soldiers to Longpre. In the darkness, they worked tirelessly on the trenches, fortifying positions on both sides of the river. Around midnight, the Spanish Light Horse probed, but the attack was unsuccessful.

Outside Amiens, Picardy, France, 16th September *AD* 1597

BY THE NEXT morning, *Monsieur* St. Vic had entrenched his companies across the river. The Duke of Mayenne reinforced French forts on both sides of the bridge of Longpre. Cannons were readied, munitions replenished.

Augmented by the *Corps de Garde,* the French infantry showed renewed courage. The final gaps in the trenches were closed; the works built even higher.

With his cavalry standing strong, King Henry IV motioned seven culverins forward, planting the small cannons on a little ridge. With the cannons overlooking the battlefield, the King signaled.

Shells struck the Cardinal's wheelless carriage, killing two of his mules. The remaining mules screamed and scattered. Other shots hit the Cardinal's personal guard. His cavalry dispersed in different directions.

Dressed in full armor except for his hat, Cardinal Albert quickly mounted his horse. He rallied his guard beyond cannon range and urged a response.

Spanish cannoneers moved six cannons forward, but their shells fell short, exploding harmlessly below the French stationed on much higher ground.

The Admiral of Aragon and his Light Cavalry once more ventured toward Longpres, where French cannons resumed their barrage, more deadly than the day before.

On the other side of the battlefield, closer to the Hermitage, French and English horse companies faced a more deadly threat. Poised for battle, fully-armored Spanish Lancers lined up side-by-side.

"Do Spanish lancers always ride alongside one another?" John asked.

"A matter of honor," Captain Joseph Duxbury said. "The *Gens-de-Armes* are noblemen from feudal estates. The Flemish and Burgundian noblemen cannot ride behind another of equal rank."

French nobles, however, did not use lances. Though clothed in armor to their knees, the French *Cuirassiers* carried long pistols, and instead of riding side by side, they rode in companies of forty or fifty. The French moved into position, in rows of six to eight men wide and in ranks nearly as deep.

Though not covered with armor as fully as the *Cuirassiers,* the *Arquebusiers à cheval* likewise fought on horseback. Most also could fight on foot. Unlike heavy cavalry, both rider and steed of the Light Horse were lightly armored. Riding fast horses, the Light Horse often scouted enemy sites or reinforced weaker positions under attack.

Hundreds of yards away, the Spanish lancers advanced at a trot. French and English horses matched the challenge, advancing at the same pace.

410

Spanish lancers galloped and lowered their long lances. The French and English riders charged, raised, and aimed their firearms. The two armies clashed. Lances met armor, bullets hit metal.

Scores of French soldiers fell in the first wave, while the Spanish suffered little, trotting back to the far side of the field.

Minutes later, the Spanish, Burgundy, and Flemish Lancers formed a single line again. Taking new lances from their pages, they again trotted and galloped.

Outnumbering the Spanish, both the French and English squadrons again trotted to meet the threat. The lowered lances hit their mark. French and English bullets hit the heavy armor. Once more, scores of English and French riders were on the ground; some dead, many wounded.

While the Spanish returned to their lines to get new lances, the French King galloped to the front of his cavalry. He directed the French and English companies to extend their lines. "Do not stick so close together!"

Several companies, including Duxbury's English company, moved beyond the end of the Spanish lines.

As the Spanish lancers charged again, fewer Frenchmen blocked their path. As they charged past Duxbury's company, Duxbury wheeled around. John and the other English riders charged the back of the Spanish Lancers.

The Spanish Lancers dislodged many French riders, but the Lancers faced a more ominous threat. Feet away, the first row of French and English carbines hit their backs. As soon as they fired and sped away, the second row aimed and fired.

John fired his weapon and hit a lancer in the elbow.

The Spanish cornets sounded, and the enemy Lancers trotted away.

The French and English horsemen returned to their lines. In battle formation, their horses breathed heavily, standing steady in front of infantry-filled trenches.

Chapter 54 — Right of Conquest

Which marvelous form of retreating, while so great and so numerous squadrons of the Enemy's Horse covered the field on all sides, drew from the King's [Henry IV's] own mouth: 'That no other soldiers in the world could do so much; and that if he had had that infantry joined with his cavalry, he would would dare to undertake a war against the world'.

The Marquis of Montenegro being at the head of them in a soldier-like gallantry, upon a brave horse, with a truncheon in his hand; and being come to the place where the King [Henry IV] and the whole army in battalia expected him, laying aside his truncheon, alighted and kissed the King's knee, and said, (so loud that he was heard by the bystanders): 'That he delivered up that place into the hands of a Soldier-King [King Henry IV of France], since it had not pleased the King his Master [Philip II of Spain] to be relieved by Soldier-Commanders'.

<u>The History of the Civil Wars of France, the 15th Book</u>
by Henrico Davila, Translated from Italian by D.E.A.

The King made his entry into Amiens at four o'clock on the same afternoon, and proceeded to the cathedral, where a Te Deum was chanted. . . The town, however, as Montenegro said, was now Henry's by Right of Conquest; and the people [citizens of Amiens] were compelled to submit.

<u>History of the Reign of Henry IV, King of France and Navarre</u>
by Martha Walker Freer

Vignacourt Mountain, Picardy, France, Late Evening, 16th Sept. *AD* 1597

LATE THAT EVENING, Cardinal Albert realized the results of the indecisive skirmishes: the Spanish Army was in no better position to throw relief into Amiens than it had been at the beginning of the day. Longpres-les-Amiens was better protected, so Cardinal Albert called his War Council to deliberate.

After servants added more wood to a nearby fire, the last council members arrived. Torches brightened faces.

"What are our options?" Cardinal Albert of Austria asked.

"We've never seen trenches so deep," the old Count of Mansfeld said.

"Or walls so high," a Camp Master added.

"Even if we capture Longpre and the bridge across the Somme, our success is not guaranteed," the old Count said.

"What do you mean?" Cardinal Albert asked.

"The Countryside is wasted, our horses will suffer."

The Cardinal glanced at the countless campfires of his army. The horses were calm that evening, but the grass was very short, the outlying fields untended. Countless raids and skirmishes through the spring and summer had trampled much of the countryside.

"The fields are barren," the Admiral of Aragon said. "Even if we throw relief into Amiens, we may not be able to sustain the army."

"Even as we speak, thousands of Huguenots join the King," another Spaniard advised. "The risk is too great. Scouts report more towns and cities flock to the King."

"So we all agree?" Cardinal Albert asked.

"The *Marquis de* Montenegro will be disappointed," the Admiral of Aragon said.

"Send the Baggage ahead," Cardinal Albert ordered, "to the Abbey of Berteaucourt by Domart."

Three hours before dawn, the first wagons and cannons departed Vignacourt.

French Camp, Picardy, France, 17th September 1597

AT DAYBREAK, JOHN Smith tended to his horse at the French camp outside Amiens. French scouts galloped in with the news. "The Cardinal is leaving."

Already fully armored, King Henry mounted his steed and led his cavalry, including Captain Duxbury's company, north.

By the time the French and English horse reached Vignacourt, the whole Spanish army was on the move. The King sent his horse to attack, but every time they did, the Spanish Light Horse turned and engaged.

Spanish drums and trumpets sounded. The Spanish pikemen stopped, turned, and formed a wedge like a Half-Moon. They shook their pikes and threatened the charging horsemen, who disengaged. Slowly, the Spanish squares—Vanguard, *Battalia*, and Rearguard—trudged away.

English riders circled and attacked the flank of the *Battalia*. When the Spanish countered with volleys from hundreds of their musketeers, Duxbury pulled his horse around. John Smith and the rest of the English riders returned to the French King.

Again and again the French charged, but when about forty French horsemen died, the King called off his attack.

At the sound of the drum, the enemy resumed its retreat, marching faster until it reached the banks of the Domart.

As the Spanish foot soldiers followed the cannons at the water's edge, Captain Duxbury, John Smith, and the other English riders joined the French charge on the Spanish Rearguard. As quickly as they attacked, Spanish riders flew and intercepted them.

As Spanish musketeers planted their rests, aimed, and fired, the pikemen soldiers of the Spanish Rearguard held firm. Once more, they shook their rattling pikes at the charging horsemen. As more Spanish horsemen interceded, both the *Battalia* and the Spanish Rearguard crossed the river.

When Duxbury and the French returned, King Henry told his officers in a strong tone, "If I had those foot soldiers along with my cavalry, I could conquer the world."

Domart River, Picardy, 18th September *AD* 1597

AFTER KING HENRY IV sent part of his cavalry back to Amiens the following morning, the Cardinal resumed his retreat. With fewer men at their side, the King and the Marshall, along with the French and English horsemen, kept their distance. By that afternoon, the Spanish Relief Army had crossed the Authie River, near the fortified town of Doullens. Satisfied that the Cardinal would not return, the King halted his pursuit.

Gate of Montrescu, Amiens, France, 19th September *AD* 1597

UPON HIS RETURN to Amiens, the King proclaimed to the Duke of Mayenne, "The Cardinal came in like a captain, but went out like a priest."

The Duke of Mayenne chuckled. "You have won a great victory."

As more French reinforcements arrived from other parts of France, Captain Duxbury put his men back into the trenches.

"Are we going to attack?" John looked at the Gate of Montrescu.

"No." Captain Duxbury gestured to a trumpeter approaching the Gate. "The King sends his Herald to the Spanish governor."

The messenger waited for the Gate to open, and when it did, guards escorted him to see the *Marquis de* Montenegro.

An hour or so later, when the Herald returned, the King asked, "Did the *Marquis* accept our honorable terms?"

"He has, along with all of his commanders," the herald said, "but the *Marquis* wants to send a Captain to receive the Cardinal's permission to surrender."

"We do not need more bloodshed. I do not wish to see any more gallant soldiers die."

An hour later, the Captain of the Spanish Artillery, Federico Paciotto, stopped at the Hermitage before going onto the city of Arras, where the Cardinal had retired.

~ ~ ~

SEVERAL DAYS LATER, Captain Joseph Duxbury told John, "The King has agreed that all prisoners would be exchanged, instead of ransomed."

While John cleaned his weapon, two French soldiers, wearing helmets, came to the Hermitage. "We captured this Spaniard during an earlier skirmish."

When the two soldiers took off their helmets, one of them had short hair, but the other's hair was much longer.

John realized the soldiers weren't male, but female. She let her hair fall to her shoulders. "Women?" John blurted. He recognized the two sisters. "I've seen you before."

"*Oui, Monsieur,*" the pretty one said.

John remembered seeing them earlier during the summer. They had been expelled from Amiens, along with their grandfather. "Your grandfather?" John asked.

"*Notre Grand Pere est mort à Picquigny,*" the older sister said.

"I am sorry for your loss."

"After his death, we took up arms." The pretty one fluffed her flowing hair.

"We fight for liberty."

"Like men?" John asked.

The older sister gestured 'no.' "Like Joan d'Arc."

Later that afternoon, the Spanish captain returned from Arras. "Cardinal Albert has agreed to the terms of surrender."

"All of them?"

"He was already prepared to turn Amiens over to the Papal Legate."

The Citadel of the Hermitage, Amiens, 25th September *AD* 1597

TO THE SOUND of a trumpet and at the beat of a drum, the *Marquis de* Montenegro carried a truncheon in his hand. Riding atop a horse, he led the Spanish, Irish, and Flemish defenders out of the Gate of Beauvais at about ten o'clock the following morning, the 25th of September.

With their colors flying and all their arms, the *Battalia* of eighteen hundred foot and four hundred horsemen crossed the bridge at Longpres and paraded past the large citadel known as the Hermitage.

After traveling nearly a mile and escorted by Marshall *de* Biron, the *Marquis* reached King Henry IV, who sat atop his richly adorned horse. Donning a white hat and dressed in royal armor, the King was surrounded by forty French riders, his personal guard. The French nobles, who for months had stood by the King, did not leave his side. More than a thousand Swiss infantry, pikes and muskets in hand, remained at attention as the *Marquis* alighted from his horse.

The *Marquis* kissed the knee of the French monarch. "It has not pleased the King my Master to be relieved by Soldier Commanders, so I deliver Amiens into your hands, a true soldier-king." The *Marquis's* personal entourage of one hundred thirty horsemen and more than one hundred chosen musketeers watched.

"It should satisfy you to know that you have defended Amiens as a good soldier," King Henry IV responded. "Now you have restored it into the hands of the lawful King with the honor of a valiant soldier."

The Marquis rose and after one hundred sixty wagons carrying baggage and the wounded trekked north, he introduced his officers, "*Capitano* Francisco *del* Arco."

"Yes," the King said. "You are the one, who captured of the Gate of Montrescu six months ago. You defended the ravelin and the Gate with much bravery. I could use a captain of your ability."

"I serve the King of Spain and will serve his daughter and her new husband, after *Infanta* Isabella marries Cardinal Albert."

"I hope we will have peace by the time she arrives."

"That is for Cardinal Albert and others to decide."

After Captain *del* Arco and the rest of the Spanish infantry and horse departed, the Constable entered Amiens.

In the town square, within sight of Amiens Cathedral, where the King had allowed the body of Governor Hernán Tello *de* Portocarrero to remain entombed, Marshall *de* Biron and other officers waited for the French King to enter.

"I appoint *Monsieur de* Vic to be the new Governor of Amiens," King Henry IV declared.

"Not Count St. Pol?" John whispered to his captain.

"Amiens rightfully belongs to King Henry," Captain Joseph Duxbury said.

"But isn't Amiens a free town?" John remembered hearing about the town's refusal to garrison the Swiss regiment.

"Before the siege, it was free," Captain Joseph Duxbury replied. "But Amiens now belongs to the French Crown."

"So it is a royal city?"

"By 'Right of Conquest.'"

"What happens now?"

"With the citadel guarding the northern approach to Amiens, the King will advance to Arras."

"And us?" John Smith asked.

"Most English will go to Montreuil, towards the coast. Reports say the Admiral of Aragon leads one third of the Spanish army, including the *tercio* of *Don* Luis *de* Velasco." Captain Joseph Duxbury added, "Tonight, however, we rest."

The full moon edged above the horizon.

Chapter 55 - Aisha Reacts and Filiz Departs

I enclose a letter from Ercole Remussati, son of Colonel Leone, who has been a month now at the Siege of Amiens.

I am glad to see such persons there, for they can learn more at this siege than in ten years elsewhere. The siege and assault are one of the most remarkable feats of arms of our day, since the Siege of Antwerp.

Piero Duodo, Venetian Ambassador in France
Letter to the Doge and Senate, Paris, 30th August 1597
Translated from Italian by D.E.A.

Salon, Ibrahim *Pasha* Palace, *Rajab AH* 1011 [December *AD* 1602]

"KING HENRY IV claimed Amiens?" Aisha asked.

"The King claimed it for the French Crown," John replied. "When a King conquers a place, he obtains the right to keep it."

"The right of conquest?"

"Yes, the refusal of Amiens to let King Henry garrison Swiss soldiers cost them their liberty. Amiens was no longer a free city: the French monarch claimed the city as his own."

"You fought in such a long siege," Aisha said.

"I learned much at the Velvet Siege of Amiens," John replied, "but the year was not over."

"You and Captain Duxbury did not stay in France?"

"No, we heard that the Dutch needed our help. The *Stadholder* Maurice had taken Rheinberg and was besieging Groenlo."

"Sieges take so long."

"Some take months, like the siege at Amiens," John said. "Other sieges can take years. But others are much shorter in time, lasting only a few weeks, or even a few days."

"Aisha, Sister of the Sultan." A servant pointed to a pair of tall candles flickering. Drips of hardened wax marked the sides. "Shall I replace them?"

Aisha looked at the beautiful mosaics adorning the opaque white walls. She noticed that most of her shorter candles had dimmed. Their lights, blinking in wide pools of soft wax, painted shifting shadows. Outside her salon, the bright midday sun had long departed. Lanterns in the loggia surrounding her garden courtyard had already been lit. "I did not realize it was so late."

Filiz grabbed her scarf. "I really must return to my house."

"I didn't mean to keep you so long." Aisha reached out to her French translator. "Thank you so very much for coming."

"Last time, I rushed away so quickly that I forgot to thank you for the eggplant."

"*The Imam Fainted?*" John asked.

The English slave must have understood the Turkish word, referring to the dish prepared with olive oil.

Filiz turned to John, "*Oui.*"

"Will you be returning?" John asked.

"If Aisha needs my help again."

"Perhaps." Aisha escorted her friend to the door of her salon and found her Overseer waiting. "You may take my slave back to his quarters."

"*Au revoir,*" John said as he was led away.

"*Au revoir,*" Filiz replied.

As the two women walked the cloistered walkways and reached the First Courtyard, Aisha asked, "What do you think?"

"About John?"

"Yes, yes."

"John is handsome."

"And his story?"

"As a new recruit, he learned much from Captain Duxbury," Filiz added, "And his French accent is remarkably good for an Englishman."

"Thank you again for coming."

"Your hospitality is unmatched." Filiz added, "And what about John?"

"If he returns to the Lowlands, I will bring the Dutch *odalisque* Dilara back to translate."

"Your secrets are safe with me." Filiz bade her friend '*adieu.*'

Chapter 56 — Sultan's Winter Quarters

*At your entrance into this hall [paved with a checker-work of black and white marble],
you see two doors, one on the right hand, the other on the left. That on the left hand
conducts to a flower garden; and the other is the door of a chamber, into which the Grand
Seignior [Sultan] comes, sometimes in the Winter-Season. This Chamber is one of the
most sumptuous of any in the Seraglio [Palace]. Its arched roof is divided into a great
number of little cells, triangle-wise, distinguish'd by two little filets of gold, with a green
streak in the midst, and out of every angle, there juts somewhat like the bottom of a lamp,
excellently well-gilt.*
"A New and Exact Relation of the Grand Seignior's Seraglio"
By J.B. Tavernier, Baron of Aubonne. Translated from the French.

*The Sultan's Quarter boasts no more than three Great Rooms, but those so splendid, and
beyond imagination, stately and convenient, that one, who never saw them, cannot
comprehend the twentieth part of the amazing excellences.*

*The roofs are arch'd, and set thick with glittering spires and balls of crystal, rim'd about
with gold and azure, whence in many places hang great golden globes, adorn'd with
diamonds of surprising luster, all the sides richly flagg'd in separate panels with white,
black, grey, blue, green, and other color'd marble, 'twixt every one of which runs one of
gold or silver, reaching like the rest from top to bottom . . .*
A Full and Just Account of the Present State of the Ottoman Empire by Aaron Hill

Winter Quarters, Sultan's Apartment, New Palace, Late Dec. *AD* 1602

COMFORTABLY SEATED AMONGST a bevy of embroidered cushions,
Sultan Mehmet III partook of the delectable fare, his second meal of the
day. The soft bread, still warm from the largest kitchen of the Second
Courtyard, melted in his mouth. He reached for the platter of seasoned
lamb and grabbed a piece with his fingers. He had no need for a knife, for
the lamb had already been cut into bite-sized morsels. His jeweled dagger
remained tucked in his sash. He recognized his most trusted and closest
advisor, "Gazanfer *Agha*?"

The *Kapi-Agha* or Chief White Eunuch, who also held the title of *Haz-Oda Bashi or* the Chief of the Chamber, was the only person allowed to touch the Sultan's person. The *Haz-Oda Bashi* oversaw the forty *ich-oglans* destined to become *pashas* or the great men of the Ottoman Empire, but every single one of those forty ranked lower than the four White eunuchs closest to the Sultan's person. The Chief White Eunuch stepped closer to the raised platform, now within an arm's reach of the Sultan's side. "The Cup Bearer told me fresh snow fell on Mount Olympus last week."

"Yes, I saw it yesterday on my afternoon walk," Sultan Mehmet III remembered.

"Packed snow from Bursa arrived this morning in the kitchens, and the Cup Bearer—"

"Yes," the Sultan interrupted, "sherbet would be nice after my late afternoon meal."

Every day during the seven years since returning from the campaign on the European frontier, the Sultan normally ate six times—twice in the morning, twice in the afternoon, and twice in the evening.

"I shall inform the Cup Bearer."

No longer famished and content with his meal, the Sultan signaled for trusted pages of the *Kilar*, the Cup-Bearer's Office, that he was finished and extended his right hand. One page brought some soap and another a basin of warm water to wash in. As he finished drying his hands, another trusted page removed the cloth of Spanish leather spread over his lap, making sure not to touch the sultan.

"Perhaps a new poem this afternoon?" Sultan Mehmet III asked the Chief White Eunuch.

"Yes, my brother-in-law Ali *Agha* has a new poem he would like to read."

Like most officials in the empire, Ali *Agha* had been promoted from the ranks of the *ich-oglans*, the pages trained in the Third Courtyard.

"Good, I look forward to it." The Sultan glanced at the *Chaznadar Bashi*, the Chief Intendant or Steward of the Treasury, standing on the opposite side.

"I shall be most pleased to listen, too." This Treasurer was responsible for the jewels of the Crown and other wealth belonging to the Sultan's person. He would normally accede to the *Haz-Oda Bashi*, the first of four eunuchs attached to the Sultan's person. If anything ever happened to the Chief White Eunuch, the *Haz-Oda Bashi* would normally succeed him, but Gazanfer *Agha* inherited that important position from his brother, who had died from the aftermath of his voluntary castration many years earlier.

Though the early morning had been cool, this spacious room in his winter quarters was quite warm. Thirsty, the Sultan turned to Gazanfer *Agha* and voiced his desire for drinking water, *"Su."*

Without speaking, the Chief White Eunuch signed to a waiting page standing at the door and assigned to the *Haz-Oda. Su.*

All knew the routine. The page standing at the entrance of the *Haz-Oda,* the Fourth Chamber, would signal the two pages guarding the entrance of the *Kilar,* the Cup-Bearer's office, where all of the drinks of the Sultan were prepared. One of these two pages would find the *Kilar Bashi* and cry out *"Su!"* The other of these two pages would approach the door of the *Haz-Oda,* the highest and most select of the four chambers of *Ich-oglans,* where the most senior of the forty pages acts as the Treasurer of Petty Enjoyments. He would always pay the second page of the *Kilar* ten sequins.

Attended by a train of one hundred pages, the *Kilar Bashi,* with great ceremony, would carry the great cup of gold to the door of the *Haz-Oda.* Filled with the approved water, this golden cup had been placed on a golden tray, two feet in diameter and embellished with precious stones both within and without. The *Kilar Bashi* oversaw not only the trusted pages within his office, but this White eunuch also oversaw others—the hundreds of the cooks who worked in the kitchens, and the hundreds of confectioners who prepared the countless sweets in the rooms built above them. He would carry the golden tray above his head, and two pages of the *Kilar* helped him, supporting his arms and guiding his steps down the gallery of black and white checkered marble leading to the Sultan's Winter Quarters.

The Sultan turned towards the door and saw the *Kilar Bashi* holding the tray and cup of gold above his head. Two pages stepped forward and relieved the two pages of the Kilar, who stayed outside. With the help of these two new pages, the *Kilar Bashi,* the third-ranking White eunuch attached to the Sultan's person, lowered the large tray. The *Kilar-Bashi* offered the Sultan the golden cup filled with water.

As soon as thirst was quenched, Osman *Kizlar Agha,* the Chief Black Eunuch, appeared at the door. "The *Valide Sultana* wishes to see you."

Knowing his mother would present one of the *odalisques* to him, like she had the week before, Sultan Mehmet III glanced at the raised bed in the far corner. "Yes, I wish to see her, too."

"She awaits you in the Dance and Music Room."

"I shall give notice." Sultan Mehmet III unlocked his folded legs and swung them over the riser before rocking to his feet. He sauntered across the carpeted floors and opened the back window. Beyond a large flower garden, at the highest point of the palace, water flowed from the huge bubbling fountain. The two rivers rushing from the fountain flowed in opposite directions and separated the Sultan's quarters from the Apartment of the Women. White eunuchs guarded the Sultan's side of the two drawbridges, and Black eunuchs guarded the far side, the Imperial Harem of five hundred women.

"Helvett, Gel-iyorum!" Sultan Mehmet III announced to the Black eunuch guards. "Make ready, I am coming!"

Chapter 57 — Dance and Music Room

Dormitory, Imperial Harem, 17 Rajab *AH* 1011 (31ˢᵗ Dec. *AD* 1602)

FROM THE GROUND floor to the open balconies above, the Imperial Harem bustled with movement. Hundreds of beautiful *odalisques* rose from their luxurious sofas, for in mere minutes. thirty of them would be chosen to entertain Sultan Mehmet III.

"*Hevlett!*" Two *Aghas*, the Black eunuchs in charge of the Greater and Lesser Chambers, spread the news. "Make ready!"

Odalisques on all three floors of the three-hundred-foot-long dormitory hastened to make themselves presentable, but in one of the dens on the middle floor of the *Büyük Oda* or Greater Chamber, the Dutch Translator Dilara stared out the latticed windows. In the Music and Dance Room, directly across the interior courtyard, the lessons must have already stopped, for a stream of women headed towards the dormitory. Dilara stepped away and moved past four beds to urge the newest *odalisque* to hurry. "Get dressed, don't be slow. The Sultan is coming."

"Our *kadun* said I would not be chosen." The Bulgarian girl with long legs pointed to the older matron on the other side of the room. Their *kadun* prodded the *odalisques* on the other side of the den. During the daytime, the *kadun* kept a vigilant watch over her brood of virgins and reported on their progress and temperament directly to the *Kahia Kadun,* the Mother of Maids. During the night, the *kadun* reclined on the bed set in the middle of the ten or fifteen *odalisques*. Like the other *kaduns* assigned to each room of virgins, this trusted matron ensured no untoward, Gomorrah-like behavior ever occurred. Tapered candles stayed lit until dawn, when the *odalisques* were always roused from their slumber. Together they faced Mecca, bowed and prayed, the first of five times every day.

"It often takes two or three years to be fully trained," Dilara said. Most of the *odalisques* in the dormitory had to work themselves up, step by step, before they would be chosen. First assigned to the food pantry, to the bath boilers, or the harem treasury, the *odalisques* entered the Greater and Lesser Chambers. Later, they would sharpen their skills—some learned to sew or embroider, while others learned to dance, sing, or play a musical instrument. "Nevertheless, you must get ready."

"How can I perfect my dance so soon?" the Bulgarian girl asked. "The Black eunuchs still must teach me to properly sing and dance."

"Perhaps you will not be chosen today." Dilara pulled out a deep drawer. "But the Sultan has already seen your beauty."

"Only once, when I first arrived." The Bulgarian girl slipped out of her attire. "I miss running and playing."

"No one ever returns to their parents." Dilara lifted out a smooth silk dress from her drawer. "Here, wear your silk outfit. The *Kadun Kahia* sometimes receives special requests."

The *odalisques*—all daughters taken from Christian parents and sent by powerful Ottoman *pashas* or the Crimean-Tartar *Khan*—received two robes of serge and one of silk every year.

"And I miss my brothers."

"Perhaps one of the Black eunuchs can send a message to them," Dilara said. "We can find out whether they are being trained as *Janissaries* in the First Courtyard, both here and in the Palace of Ibrahim *Pasha*."

"You can find out?" The Bulgarian girl smoothed her soft dress. "Why are you so kind to me?"

"When Aisha, Sister of Sultan, found out the Grand Vizier presented you to the Imperial Harem, she asked the *Kadun Kahia* for you to be placed near me."

"Is that why I have been assigned here in this room?"

Their *kadun* moved around one of thick vertical beams from the other side of the room. "If you must know, Aisha, Sister of the Sultan, has known me since her youth and had the Chief Black Eunuch arrange it." She motioned for the two *odalisques* to hurry. Like all the others, they busied themselves beautifying and perfuming.

"Ladies, are you ready?" The *Kadun Kahia* or Mother of Maids stood in the doorway. Meticulously dressed, she delicately held two narrow sticks with her fingers.

Dilara's *kadun* immediately lined up the dozen young women assigned to her den for inspection in front of their beds.

The *Kadun Kahia* did not bother entering. "I believe the Sultan would like to hear Dilara sing."

"Me?" Dilara was surprised because she was almost twenty-five years old, nearly beyond the age when Turks thought women were at their best. Her *kadun* must have recommended her to the *Kadun Kahia*. The Mother of Maids had coached Dilara and select *odalisques* in the finer points of pleasing the Sultan. If anything went amiss, the Sultan's Mother would blame her.

The *Kadun Kahia* tapped her waist-high stick on the floor. "Dilara, come with me."

With barely a chance to glance back at the Bulgarian girl, Dilara followed the *Kadun Kahia* out the door, joining other *odalisques* on the middle floor balcony. The *Kadun Kahia* tapped the wooden floor with the three-foot-long stick she held in each hand. She went room to room and selected the final *odalisques* to be presented. The twelve women from this floor headed towards the stairs at the very end of the dormitory.

On the other side of the wide opening, a dozen *odalisques* likewise moved graciously along the upper balcony in the same direction. Above, yellow candles flickered in the crystal chandeliers hanging from the open

426

ceiling. Below, a pair of Black eunuchs guided six more *odalisques* toward the far end. Instead of walking on wooden planks like the two galleries above, those six *odalisques* glided across large copper tiles—polished gilt, shining brightly, like burnished gold.

Dilara knew exactly what it meant to be selected to entertain the Sultan. If, perchance, the Sultan selected one of the thirty to bed, and if that *odalisque* of his affection birthed a son, she would become a *haseki* or favorite. She would live in her own apartment near the *Valide Sultana,* and after receiving jewels and a crown, she could select her court. If her son were the eldest at the time of the Sultan's passing, that boy would become the new Sultan, and as the *Valide Sultana,* she would rule the Imperial Harem.

Even though the Sultan had three living sons, another older son had already passed away. There was a chance that if an *odalisque* were chosen, she would give birth to a son; and if he were the eldest at the time of the previous sultan's death, she would become the new *Valide Sultana,* the Mother of the Sultan.

This glimmer of hope kept many young *odalisques* in line.

Baths, *Valide Sultana's* Quarters, Imperial Harem

"HAS YOUR DAUGHTER contacted the family of her new Bohemian slave?" *Haseki* Halime asked inside the private baths of the *Valide Sultana.*

"You should not be concerned whether my daughter receives a ransom or not," Safiye *Valide Sultana* said. The Mother of the Sultan did not appreciate the inquisitiveness of the mother of Prince Mahmud, the presumed successor to the Ottoman throne.

"I did not mean to offend you," *Haseki* Halime responded.

A Black maid scrubbed the back of the Sultan's Mother, who remained seated next to one of the elegant fountains attached to the spotless walls, built of white marble. The dome overhead provided plenty of light.

"Gently, I am not as young as I once was."

"Yes, *Valide Sultana.*" The maid turned the gilt faucet off after rinsing her back with a softer sponge.

Normally, Safiye *Valide Sultana* would sit and converse for a longer stay. That was not her purpose today. Unhappy with all of the jealous intrigues of the *hasekis,* the *Valide Sultana* decided to introduce new *odalisques* to her son.

"We can't join you?" the second *Haseki* asked.

"Not today." Safiye *Valide Sultana* retrieved her clothes. "Stay, relax, enjoy your bath."

Safiye *Valide Sultana* met Abdul Rezak *Agha* at the door. In the hierarchy of the Imperial Harem, only the Chief Black Eunuch ranked higher than the *Agha* of the *Valide Sultana*.

Accompanied by two other Black eunuchs, the *Agha* of the *Valide Sultana* escorted the Sultan's Mother through a mirrored Assembly room often used by the Sultan to meet and converse with his Favorites. "Your daughter wishes to speak to you."

"Today?" Safiye *Valide Sultana* asked.

"Aisha has already arrived."

Prayer Room, Chamber of Audience, *Valide Sultana's* Quarters

AISHA, WAITING INSIDE her mother's prayer room, looked through the cracked shutters. Supported by marble columns, the prayer room extended to the very tip of the palace. Beyond the tall Cypress trees and the outer palace walls, sailing ships plied the Sea of Marmara, and beyond the sea was Anatolia, Asia Minor. Like her brother, she had been born in the town of Magnesia across the water. Down below to her left, the Column of Goths stood in the middle of the garden, while closer to her right, a small minaret stood just out the window. Whenever the Black eunuch muezzin issued the call for prayer, her devout mother responded. Whether in private, or at one of the mosques, Safiye *Valide Sultana* insisted on setting an example—always praying the required five times each day.

Column of Goths below Imperial Harem, circa 1840

Aisha walked past the doors leading to her mother's apartment and stopped at the other end of the Prayer Room. She viewed the large quadrangle through the latticed shutter. On the left, the dormitory housing the *odalisques* ran the whole length of the inner courtyard; on the right another building, just as long and also three stories tall, lodged five hundred Black eunuchs. The Dance and Music Room occupied a portion of that building near its center.

Fountains and flowers, hedges and greens, paths and trees graced the whole courtyard, clear to its far end. A winding colonnade of red and white marble terminated the square, the largest of the twenty-four courtyards of the Imperial Harem.

When Aisha heard the door to the Chamber of Audience open, she walked to the side of the Prayer Room. Peeking through the wood shutters, Aisha saw the Chief Black Eunuch greet her mother and the *Agha* of the *Valide Sultana*. Aisha remembered the names of the other two Black eunuchs accompanying them. Narcissus and Hyacinth joined the other Black eunuchs stationed in the chamber. All Black eunuchs would be called by similar names—like Rose or Lilly or some other delicate flower, in keeping with the atmosphere and decorum of the Imperial Harem. Large porcelain vases, matching the everyday dishes used by her mother, graced the nooks and crannies of the chamber.

Aisha descended the crimson stairs, just as her mother stepped onto a raised platform. "Aisha, it is so kind of you to grace us with your presence." Her mother settled into her cushioned chair overlooking the Chamber of Audience—the center of power inside the Imperial Harem, if not, indeed, the whole Ottoman Empire. Two years earlier, instead of sending an ambassador to the *Sublime Porte* to negotiate a treaty, the King of Persia received assurances and consequently arranged for a Persian virgin to enter the Imperial Harem.

"My palace has taken all my time," Aisha spoke just above a whisper. She sat down in a crimson chair garnished with gold. The other chair on the opposite side of her mother remained empty.

"You must learn to do better. I had expected you to join me in the *bagni* this morning." Her mother used the Italian word for baths, for *Italiano* was the *lingua franca* of the inner palace.

"I was not feeling well this morning," Aisha responded in Italian, "so I rested."

Seated high on the platform, her mother glanced down at the *Agha* of the *Valide Sultana*. "Maybe I should send for my physician to call on you."

Any physician allowed into the harem was always blindfolded and never allowed to see any of the women. The only part of the woman's body he could touch was the wrist, in order to take the pulse. Whether a White eunuch or another doctor, he would then prescribe the remedy, usually some sweet elixir to drink.

"That will not be necessary," Aisha responded, "but that is not the reason for my visit."

"You need a reason to visit your mother?"

"I need to bring Dilara back to my palace."

"Taking an *odalisque* out of the Imperial Harem is unheard of."

"You allowed it last week. Besides, who else can translate Dutch, especially when I need her?" Aisha could tell her mother was upset. "The *capitano* fought for Holland, and the Dutch are rich."

All had heard how the Dutch had broken the Portuguese monopoly of the Spice Trade by sailing around Africa.

"Rich or not, taking an *odalisque* out of the Imperial Harem and bringing her back causes problems."

"Rumors and jealousies," the *Agha* of *Valide Sultana* said. "The *Kaduns* report that many *odalisques* are upset."

Aisha turned to the door and saw that *Kadun Kahia* had arrived with the thirty *odalisques* chosen to see her brother.

Two older dwarfs, little stout men with small swords, kept the line straight, and when finished with their task, they jumped up onto a nearby sofa. Those holdovers from her late husband, Murad III's time, had kept him amused for hours. He used to throw the little men up into the air and watch them fall into pools of water. The thirty young women, lined up in rows, all bowed, as they had been taught and trained.

"Rise, *odalisques*," the Chief Black Eunuch commanded.

Dilara and the others rose from their deep obeisance of respect. Looking at one of the massive mirrors mounted on the walls, Aisha caught the eye of the Dutch Translator standing in the middle row.

The *Valide Sultana* rose from her chair and descended the crimson stairs. "*Kizlar Agha* Osman, bring my son to the Dance and Music Room."

"As you wish." The Chief Black Eunuch exited the Chamber, through the courtyard, past the large buildings housing the harem boilers and baths.

The Sultan's Mother began her examination of the beauties of the harem. When she reached the Dutch translator, she halted. "Dilara, I do not think I will present you to my son today."

"You do not?" Dilara asked.

"No, I have decided that it would be best if you go."

"I am going?" Dilara asked. "My things?"

"Hyacinth will make certain you receive them at the Old Palace." Safiye *Valide Sultana* motioned for that Black Eunuch to escort Dilara away.

Aisha interrupted, "Mother, may I speak to you?"

"Not now, we must be settled before your brother arrives."

Safiye *Valide Sultana* and the *Kadun Kahia*, along with twenty-nine *odalisques* and their escorts, departed to go down the corridor to the Music and Dance Room.

As a Black eunuch escorted Dilara, Aisha stopped them. "Hyacinth, I would like to say a few words to my friend."

Marble Walkway, Sultan's Quarters, New Palace

ON THE MARBLE walkway leading from his Winter Quarters, Sultan Mehmet III looked forward to spending the rest of the morning with the women of the Imperial Harem. Strolling alongside his friend, Chief White Eunuch Gazanfer *Agha,* the Sultan plodded toward the first arch standing in the midst of the garden. The Sultan wanted to stop and smell the jasmine flowers that adorned the wooden archway, but those white blossoms were gone, retreating until spring.

On the other side of the arc, the marble walkway split into two semi-circular paths. Each path led to a drawbridge over one of the two rivers that separated the Sultan's Quarters from the Imperial Harem. The Sultan's Master of the Waterworks ensured that the water always flowed to the two rivers from their source at the top of the first hill of *Stamboul.* At the highest point of the New Palace, water flowed from a robust, gurgling fountain, directly ahead. The two hundred men under the waterworks maintained nearly one thousand fountains, both here in the interior part of the New Palace and along the exterior pathways. The interior garden extended from wall to wall, the whole width of the New Palace. Sultan Mehmet III did not doubt that he lived in a veritable paradise, the most commodious place on earth.

The Sultan and the Chief White Eunuch veered down the right walkway. As the bearded sultan moved forward, he touched the waist-high banister to maintain his balance. Gold balls topped the spires all along the curved banisters leading to the drawbridge. Flowers and trees dotted the well-groomed gardens on the other side of the waist-high rail. The flower gardens in this part of the palace were maintained solely by eunuchs—White ones of this side of the river and Black eunuchs on the other side of the river, bordered by a row of hedges on each side.

The Sultan slowed by the White eunuch guards stationed on this side of the drawbridge. Of all the White eunuchs, the Chief White Eunuch alone could accompany the Sultan into the Imperial Harem. He rarely followed, but when he did, he always stayed at the door, in the corridor. No other man could cross the river into the Imperial Harem without being seen: the water was too swift and the Black eunuchs on the far side of the drawbridge too strong. Certain death would follow an attempt by any man, White eunuch, or wandering gardener.

As the Sultan stepped to the center of the drawbridge, the Chief White Eunuch asked. "Shall I wait for you here?"

"No need to wait," Sultan Mehmet III said. "It may be hours before I return."

"Then I shall attend to other business."

"Yes, do that. My mother awaits me." The Sultan glanced down at the swift water flowing from the gurgling fountain. It splashed against the strong iron grates in the garden walls. After passing through the exterior garden, the small river flowed through the lower, outer walls and emptied into the sea.

Armed Black eunuch guards stood at the ready on the other side of the drawbridge. Within seconds, a hundred more Black eunuchs could rush from their respective stations and mow down unwanted intruders with hatchets and scimitars. The Black *Agha* of the Harem Gate, in charge of all of the Black eunuch guards, greeted the Sultan. "At your command."

The Sultan quickened his pace down the semi-circular path, now circling left. Except for the winding gallery that extended clear across the whole width of the Palace, in most respects this flower garden mirrored the one on the other side of the river. Coming from both drawbridges, the paths joined in front of a second archway—built in the same fashion as the first one, only more beautiful. The *Agha* of the Gate went no further, but on the other side of the Archway, the Chief Black Eunuch met him on the marble walkway. "Most eminent master, your mother awaits you in the Dance and Music Room. Are you ready?"

"Yes, Osman *Kizlar Agha,* let us go together." The Sultan looked forward to selecting an *odalisque* to spend the evening with. They walked toward the winding gallery and turned left, past the red and white columns, toward the three-story dormitory housing the Black eunuchs. Ever since Suleiman *the Lawgiver* had seen a gelded stallion mount a mare in the field, all of the Black eunuchs had been castrated, clean to the lower belly.

"Have you seen the *odalisques*?" Sultan Mehmet III asked.

"All thirty of them."

Dance and Music Room, New Palace, *Stamboul,* Late December 1602

BEAUTIFUL *ODALISQUES* DROPPED to their knees and bowed to Sultan Mehmet III, as he entered the Chamber of Repose, the Dance and Music Room.

"Rise," the Sultan's Mother commanded.

The Sultan, drawing closer to his mother, affectionately kissed several of the *odalisques* on their cheeks. He kept coins and jewels in his pocket to give to any *odalisque* who garnered his attraction. Flowery fragrances from Egypt adorned their bodies; loose strands of hair were meticulously placed in order.

"Some of the new girls are very talented." Safiye *Valide Sultana,* surrounded by pillows, remained seated. In earlier times, her daughter Aisha would have been seated cross-legged at her feet.

"I look forward to seeing them perform." Sultan Mehmet III sat down in a cushioned chair exactly like his mother's. The Chief Black Eunuch, standing tall, moved within earshot of both the Sultan and his mother.

Just like the Prayer Room of the *Valide Sultana,* this section of the Dance and Music Room was supported by columns. It overlooked a terraced courtyard, and beyond the forested slopes and pretty fountains, the lines and masts of ships anchored in the harbor could be seen. The busy suburb of Pera stood on the opposite shore.

Several musicians, holding stringed instruments, sat down on the cushioned seats below the tall windows, while other *odalisques* sat beneath the mirrors lining the two sidewalls. One door led to the quarters of the Black eunuchs, and the other one opened to the Apartments of his mother and his sultanas. The last wall overlooked the inner quadrangle—the shuttered windows of the Greater and Lesser Chambers could be seen across the way.

For the next two hours, the *odalisques* vied for the Sultan's attention, but even if one were chosen, she would never marry the Sultan. Ever since the time when Sultan Suleiman *the Magnificent* had married Roxlena the Ukrainian, every Sultan had refused to give any of his favorites the *kabin* — the dowry needed formalize a Muslim marriage. Like his father, Sultan Murad III, who had refused to marry Safiye, Sultan Mehmet III had done the same: for if he did marry any of his concubines, Sultan Mehmet III thought and feared he would die young.

Kadun Kahia organized the ladies inside the Dance and Music Room. The crowns of their heads were capped with gold cloth; a string of pearls, often with jewels, hung between their breasts, and smaller jewels adorned many of their ears. The musicians seated by the windows tuned their stringed instruments. The lute had a wide belly and a narrow neck. As one musician brought a flute to her lips, five other *odalisques* moved to the center of the room.

The music began, and the girls started their dance.

The short *odalisque* in the middle kicked up her leg.

"The oldest *odalisque* already shows much promise," the *Valide Agha* said. "She has learned to dance and can play a stringed instru-ment. She also has a good ear for the Persian tongue."

Musician, Dancer, & Governess in Imperial Harem

"A poetic language," the Sultan's mother whispered to the Mother of Maids. "If she continues to excel, perhaps my son will make this *odalisque* his concubine."

"But she looks so young," the *Kadun Kahia* said.

"Perhaps you're right."

434

The music softened, and the song soon ended. The Sultan's mother waved for the five dancers to exit.

Another four dancers moved to the center, and the music began anew. Slowly at first, the dancers moved to the rhythm.

When the music stopped, Safiye *Valide Sultana* noticed her son wore a worried expression on his face. "What is it, son?" she asked.

"I am not sure."

Two Circassian women displayed their needlework.

After more dancing, singing, reading, and music, the Sultan chose the first *odalisque*, the short one who had kicked up her leg. Instead of dropping his white handkerchief, letting her catch it, and returning immediately to his quarters, Sultan Mehmet III motioned for her to follow him. The Sultan, along with his chosen *odalisque*, headed in the direction of the Terrace of the Favorites, where the Sultan's favorites relaxed when the weather warmed. The Terrace overlooked a pool and the vast gardens of the lower palace.

For nearly one hour, the Sultan stayed and conversed privately by one of the fountains. When the pair returned, all of the other *odalisques* surrounded the chosen one and congratulated her.

The clock ticked, its pendulum swinging back and forth. Sultan Mehmet III, escorted by the Chief Black Eunuch, exited the Dance and Music Room. As his slippers clicked down the hallway back to his Winter Quarters, the *Kahia Kadun* told the other *odalisques*, "The chosen girl must be helped."

"Prepare her bath," the Sultan's Mother ordered.

Chapter 58 — Clockmaker's Letter

Thus, several odas of this corps receive nothing from the Public Treasury; and those that are paid pretending to be timarians [Timar landholders] like their comrades, always take part with the latter. They wanted to have the treasures of the mosques opened to them; but the Mufti, and the Kizlar Agha [Osman], the Chief of the Black Eunuchs, who by his place has the management of all the royal mosques, strongly opposed the demands of this mutinous soldiery.

One of their chiefs, called Houssain [Hasan Khalifeh], stirred up all those that were at Constantinople, crying they were the only victims of so many disorders; that, whilst all the revolted Pashas were seizing on the ruin of the empire, and maintaining their comrades in plenteousness at Bursa, Erzurum, and Sivas, they alone were starving at Constantinople, because they had not the spirit to demand what belonged to them. These seditious cries soon assembled those that had reason to complain.

The janissaries did not engage in this quarrel; but they saw with a secret pleasure this corp, generally more quiet than theirs, on the point of a revolt, and perplexing their chiefs.

<u>History of the Turkish or Ottoman Empire</u>
by Vincent Mignot; Translated from the French by A. Hawkins, Esq.

Imperial Gate, New Palace, 17 Rajab *AH* 1011 (31st Dec. *AD* 1602)

HUNDREDS OF ANGRY *sipahi* riders, armed with lances and swords, exited their encampment on the *Atmeidan* or Hippodrome, and trotted their horses past the Hagia Sophia Mosque. They swarmed below the outer walls of the New Palace and stopped in front of the Imperial Gate. "We demand to see the Imperial Council."

"What is your purpose?" *Capigi Bashi* Hasan asked. The Head of the Gate commanded fifty *capigis*, the guards of the gates. They all carried swords at their side, but some of them carried long sticks in their hands. Several carried two-foot firearms over their shoulders.

"Have you not heard?" Poiraz Osman *Bey* countered. "*Deli* Hasan and his army of rebels have besieged Kutahya."

"The news came last evening." *Capigi Bashi* Hasan relented, allowing them to enter the Courtyard of the *Janissaries*. Beneath the far porticos, Prince Mahmud, the Sultan's eldest son, conversed with the *acemi-oglans*, the *janissary* cadets.

Acemi-Oglan (Novice Youths)

Inside this first courtyard, the *sipahi* riders all dismounted. Some tied their horses to a tree in front of the hospital. But others tied their horses to a rail next to a Byzantine chapel repurposed as an armory. Poiraz Osman *Bey*, Katib Jemazi, Hasan Khalifeh, and the other *sipahi* leaders dismounted by the horse fountain. All knew that only the Sultan could ride horseback beyond the Gate of Greeting.

"Horses are not beasts of burden." Poiraz Osman *Bey* pointed at the four horses pulling the white carriage of the *Valide Sultana* through the First Courtyard of the Palace. "They should be ridden."

The curtains of the white carriage were drawn shut.

"The Queen Mother does what she wants," Katib Jemazi said.

At the Gate of Greeting leading into the Second Courtyard, Poiraz Osman *Bey* repeated his demand to see the Imperial Council.

"I do not see you on our list," the *Capigi Bashi* of the Gate of Greeting said. Like the first gate, this *Capigi Bashi* had fifty porters under his command.

"Do you dare defy the *sipahis?*"

Scores of *sipahis*, still armed with lance and sword, pressed closer as the *Bostangi Bashi* Ferhad *Agha* rode his small pony past the *acemi-oglans* and reached the Gate. The *Bostangi Bashi* had ten thousand gardeners under his command, not only inside the walls of the New Palace, but also in the nearby summer palaces frequented by the Sultan and his Favorites. Though he was not brought up as one of the forty *ich-oglans* of the inner courtyard, the Chief Gardener had much influence within the palace. He had direct access to the Sultan. Whenever Sultan Mehmet III requested the Royal Barge, Ferhad *Agha* commanded the helm. For hours, the Sultan sat next to him as they relaxed on the water.

"I have talked to *Kaimakam*, Hasan *the Clockmaker*. The Divan may have time to listen to your petition later this morning."

Divan, Second Courtyard, New Palace, *Stamboul*

DEPUTY GRAND VIZIER, Hasan *the Clockmaker*, chaired the Imperial Council or Divan meeting. Besides the military judge of Anatolia, the Divan also included Abdul-Miamin Mustafa *Effendi*, the *cazi* or military judge of Rumelia. Fourth Vizier, Hasan *the Addicted*, and Ali *Agha*, the *Agha* of the *Janissaries*, both took their seats. The *Kaimakam*, Hasan *the Clockmaker*, convened the Divan four days each week—Saturday through Tuesday. On this, the last day of their work week, the *Divan* considered matters both great and small.

The *Divan* listened to an appeal from a merchant who had been cheated in one of the bazaars. A small commotion garnered their attention. The *Kaimakam* recognized a member of the *sipahi* delegation being escorted from the Gate of Greeting across the well-groomed courtyard.

"I suggest we postpone the decision on this matter until next week," *Kaimakam*, Hasan *the Clockmaker*, told the merchant.

"But—"

The seven viziers, one by one, acceded to his judgement.

"We have other matters to attend to," Hasan *the Clockmaker* said.

When the *sipahi* leaders reached the building, one of its leaders demanded, "We must be heard."

"There are other people and cases before you."

"Not today!"

Kaimakam, Hasan *the Clockmaker*, conferred with an assistant and motioned for the *sipahis* to sit. "The Imperial Council must first hear the report ."

The *sipahi* leaders sat cross-legged on the carpeted floor. The Chief Gardener Ferhad *Agha* brought forward the messenger, who had arrived late the night before. To one side of the open building with its sloped roofs, scribes seated at low tables busily prepared their notes. Off to the other side, partially obscured by a post, *Kizlar Agha* Osman, the Chief Black Eunuch, watched. In front of the post, the Grand Mufti and a member of the ulema council of religious leaders listened.

438

Standing in front of the *chiaus* or messenger, the Chief Gardener interrupted the meeting. A wooden ball topped the staff, a symbol of Ottoman authority that turbaned *chiauses* always carried.

"What is so important, *Bostangi Bashi* Ferhad?" the Deputy Grand Vizier asked.

"A report from Hafiz Ahmed *Pasha* in Anatolia."

"My orders from the Governor of Kütahya are to deliver this message directly to the Deputy Grand Vizier." The *chiaus* handed over the sealed letter.

The *Kaimakam* perused the letter before delivering the bad news. "After the soldiers of the Khosru *Pasha* abandoned him, the eunuch general and his remnant retired to Diyarbakir. Hasan *the Fool* and the rebels have advanced West. Their army besieges Kütahya."

Knowing the Chief White Eunuch had insisted on the appointment of the eunuch Khosru *Pasha* as commander, Hasan *the Clockmaker* told the Chief Gardener, "The *Kapi Agha* must hear the bad news."

While the Chief Gardener headed across the courtyard to the Gate of Felicity, Guzelce Mahmud *Pasha* spoke up. "In the days since I replaced Khosru *Pasha* as *Beylerbey* of Diyarbakir, I have not received the support I need." The new commander of Ottoman forces in Asia stared at the *Agha* of the *Janissaries*.

"What do you mean?" Hasan *the Addicted,* the hero of the Ottoman capture of Kanizsa in Hungary, asked. The Fourth Vizier once led the *Janissaries*.

"Ali *Agha* has not provided even one *orta* to the campaign." The new Governor of Diyarbakir, serious and solemn, continued to peer at the *Agha* of the *Janissaries*.

"My *junissaries* only recently arrived back from the European frontier," the *Agha* of the *Janissaries* said.

As the messenger from Anatolia expounded on the movements of *Deli* Hasan and the rebels, council members questioned the ominous news. With the Chief White Eunuch now in attendance and the *sipahi* leaders listening at the back of the Divan, the messenger hinted at the intensifying dissatisfaction. "The *sipahis* who accompanied me lost their *timars.*"

"By Kütahya?" Hasan *the Clockmaker* asked.

"The rebels are strong."

"Winter approaches," Guzelce Mahmud *Pasha* said, "but steps must be taken."

"The *sipahi* leader Poiraz Osman *Bey* wishes to speak."

"Let him speak," one of the two military judges said.

"Many of my *sipahis* recently returned from the European frontier." The *sipahi* leader moved to the front of the Council. "The horsemen of the *Porte* have received their pay, but the *sipahis* of the *timars* have not."

"There is no precedent for the Imperial Treasury to pay the *sipahis*." The Deputy Grand Vizier recognized the Treasurer-General, the first of the three *tefterdars* who controlled the public treasury. The public treasury was kept in four chambers inside the Third Courtyard.

"Monies have not been allocated for that," the *tefterdar* for the Fourth Chamber said. This *tefterdar* had one of the keys to the chamber, while the Grand Vizier normally held the other. Since the Grand Vizier *Yemisci* Hasan *Pasha* stayed in Belgrade, the Deputy Grand Vizier held the second key to that Fourth Chamber.

"What about the lost *sipahi* pay?" Hasan Khalifeh, another *sipahi* leader, asked.

"Reports from the Treasurers must be received," *Kaimakam* Hasan *the Clockmaker* said. The Fourth Chamber of the Treasury would only be accessed on one of the days that the Divan met. Monies from trade flowed into the Imperial treasury, but the normal tributes from Transylvania, Wallachia, Moldavia, and the Holy Roman Empire had been curtailed by the Long War, already lasting nearly a decade. When *pashas* were dismissed and killed by mutes for malfeasance, their wealth would revert to the treasury, but few had been killed in recent years. Monies from Egypt, however, still flowed into *Stamboul*.

"The mosques have monies." The *sipahi* leaders looked at the Grand Mufti.

From behind the post, the Chief Black Eunuch, who besides the Imperial Harem oversaw all of the Royal Mosques, stepped forward. "Under no circumstance can you raid the mosques."

"Hasan Khalifeh," Hasan *the Clockmaker* concluded, "you must await the report of the *Tefterdars*. "

"Hasan *the Fool* and the *pashas* revel in plenty, but my *sipahis* grow hungry," Poiraz Osman *Bey* said. "Only because we do not have the spirit to demand what is ours."

"This is the fourth and final day of the court. You must wait until the Divan reconvenes next week."

"More *timars* have been lost outside Kütahya."

"Yes, we have heard the report, but for now, you are dismissed."

The disgruntled *sipahi* leaders stomped toward the First Courtyard.

With the discussion over, the Chief Black Eunuch exited the Divan in the direction of the Queen's Gate. Everyone knew that he would take the Golden Way back to the Imperial Harem and inform the Sultan's Mother.

The *Kaimakam,* Hasan *the Clockmaker,* turned back to the council. "Something must be done."

The military judges and most members of the Imperial Council followed the disgruntled *sipahis* toward the First Courtyard, while the Deputy Grand Vizier accompanied the Chief White Eunuch in the opposite direction. "We must tell the Sultan."

"We cannot anger him," Gazanfer *Agha* said.

"I must protest," Hasan *the Clockmaker* insisted. "This pot of unrest may boil over. The Sultan must be informed."

"Do not tell him. The Sultan's Mother and I will handle this."

"I need a letter."

Hall of Audience, 3rd Courtyard, New Palace, Tuesday, 31ˢᵗ Dec. *AD* 1602

THE CHIEF BLACK Eunuch brought the Sultan's Mother into the Hall of Audience, the Throne Room inside the Third Courtyard. The throne itself was covered by a cloth to protect it from the elements, unlike several weeks earlier, when the new and old Italian ambassadors were introduced to the Sultan. Held by two guards at their elbows, they bowed to Sultan Mehmet III and kissed the hem of his garment before backing away.

"*Kizlar Agha* Osman has told me about the *sipahi* demands," Safiye *Valide Sultana* told the Chief White Eunuch and *Kaimakam* Hasan *the Clockmaker.* Her son, the Sultan, conversed with an *odalisque* on a terrace overlooking the outer garden.

"The *Valide Sultana* does not want to upset her son," the Chief Black Eunuch said.

"It is my responsibility to inform the Sultan," Hasan *the Clockmaker* retorted.

"That cannot be done." Gazanfer *Agha* stood firm.

"I need a letter."

"Very well." The Chief White Eunuch sat down at a low table and dipped a pen into the ink well. As soon as Gazanfer *Agha* finished the letter and *Kizlar Agha* Osman signed it, Hasan *the Clockmaker* tucked it inside his robe.

Chapter 59 — Rebellion Reaches Bursa

This evil encounter [in Ankara in the summer of 1602] of these new [Ottoman] captains even at the first entrance into their charges given them, by the subjects themselves, increased the rebels' courage, so that they being in number forty thousand, under the leading of one of the Tartar Khan his brethren, besieged Bursa a great and rich city, being the storehouse of the warlike provisions of Asia, and the place whereunto the Turks' customs, taxes and subsidies of Asia were brought, and there kept. These men after certain days bestowed in the siege, and great resistance made by the besieged, at length by force carried the place, slew the inhabitants, and sacked the city. Which exploit gracing their fortune with honor and booty increased also their power and reputation, so that redoubled on all sides, and increased with courage and spoils, Mehmet [III] dismayed . . .
General History of the Turks, Second Edition (1610) by Richard Knolles

[The rebels] wanted to hazard and advanced their designs to their advantage. With courage in arms, they came to within a three-day journey of Constantinople [Stamboul] .

. .

L'Histoire de la Decadence de L'Empire Grec et Establissement de Celvy des Turcs, Vol I, Book 17 by Chalcondile, Athenien, & Artus Thomas. Translated from French by D.E.A.

East of Bursa, Anatolia, Wednesday, 18 Rajab *AH* 1011 (1ˢᵗ Jan. *AD* 1603)

WISPS OF CLOUDS encircled the snow-capped peak of Mount Olympus, the sublime mountain rising above Bursa in northwest Asia Minor. Early in the cool morning, Turkish herdsmen brought down their remaining flocks from the higher plateaus.

Atop a knoll a mile east of the first Ottoman capital, the three estranged half-brothers of the Crimean-Tartar Khan *Ghazi* Giray II viewed the imperial city. Shaped in the form of a rectangle, the longest side of Bursa extended from east to west.

"Salamet, should we give Bursa a chance to pay?" Shahin Giray asked his older brother. The walls surrounding the lower neighborhoods were low. Minarets of numerous mosques pointed skyward, but the old

442

citadel stood hidden above the rich town.   "Like Hasan *the Fool* gave those in Ankara?" Salamet Giray asked. Ankara had paid the rebels three hundred thousand ducats to avoid being sacked. "No, that is not our way."

Hundreds of Crimean-Tartar warriors crested the hill.

Salamet Giray told his youngest brother, "Mohammed, take your warriors and seize the flocks." Centuries earlier, when the Greeks ruled Byzantium, the Ottomans received the right to graze their herds on the eastern slopes of Mount Olympus.

"And the cattle?" Mohammed Giray asked.

"Take them, too."

Dressed in black sheepskin, the Crimean Tartars had augmented the rebel forces of Hasan *the Fool*, but now the brothers took the lead. Their horses had shaggy hair and strong legs, good for climbing the steppes of the Ukraine, the border area above their native Crimea. While Hasan *the Fool* and his fighters besieged Kutahya, slightly more than a day's journey to the south, the bulk of the rebel army of forty thousand men had joined the three brothers, poised to attack Bursa, the cradle of the Ottoman Empire. Orhan *Ghazi* had conquered the city and, in the Christian year 1335, made it his first Ottoman capital.

Bursa and Mount Olympus from the Plain and Abdal Koprusu (Bridge built 1669)

The youngest brother, Mohammed, Giray urged his horsemen up the path at the base of Mount Olympus. Dogs barked as his Turkish allies chased the shepherds away and rounded up the flocks of bleating sheep. While the Turkish riders ate mutton, the Tartar warriors preferred horse meat. One warrior carried a horse leg across his saddle.

The two older brothers spied a caravan leaving one of the khans. Tartar Gate, the eastern gate of the lower town, was wide open.

The whole rebel army began to gallop.

Green Mosque, Upper Citadel, Bursa

HAVING FINISHED HIS morning prayers, the *Sanjak* of Bursa conversed with a Dervish monk outside *Yesil Cami*, the Green Mosque. Named for its bright, blue-green tiles, the Green Mosque, with its double domes and single minaret, rose above the castle walls of the upper town.

"I have a bad feeling," the Dervish said. Dervish divines, supported by the Ottoman sultans since they first conquered Bursa, received visions in their twirling dances. No other city, except perhaps Baghdad, was as devout as Bursa. Known for keeping traditions, Bursa was also well-known for its Muslim scholars expounding on the meaning of verses in the *Qur'an*.

"How so?" The *Sanjak* of Bursa knew the Dervish Monk had come from one of the many Dervish schools dotting Mount Olympus, previously known as Monk Mountain because Greek Orthodox clergy had so often frequented the place. Some of their monasteries had been taken over by the favored Dervish, so some Turks called the snowcapped mountain *Uludağ*, meaning the Sublime Mountain.

"I do not know," the Dervish monk said, "just a feeling."

The pleasant sound of the fountain was interrupted. Two *chiauses* sprinted across the stone courtyard. "Rebels!" The faster *chiaus* pointed east. "Tartar rebels!"

"Sound the alarm!" The *Sanjak* of Bursa signaled.

The message relayed, a trumpet blasted.

"Shut the gates. Bring my armor."

Kettle drums pounded, and the sound reverberated across the marble square. *Janissaries* with lit cords carried their long muskets and rushed two by two up the high castle walls.

Another *Janissary orta* exited the long barracks. With quivers full of arrows, the foot soldiers hurried out of the citadel, making their way down into the lower town.

In the square towers punctuating the fortified walls, cannoneers primed their weapons.

"More powder!"

Still without his armor, the *Sanjak* of Bursa rushed to the eastern walls. Beyond the large ravine, hundreds of rebel riders made their way up the foothills. In the distance toward Izmir, ancient Nicea, black smoke rose from mulberry farms. Leaving the *timars* to burn, thousands of Tartars and rebels swarmed toward Tartar Gate, nearing the lower town walls.

"Whoever thought the rebels would be so audacious?" the *Sanjak* of Bursa asked. The Chief White Eunuch had advanced him due to his administrative abilities, rather than for his military prowess or training.

"We did not expect the rebel army to venture this far," a *kethuda* answered, "especially so late in the season."

"I should not have sent the other *ortas* away." The *Sanjak* of Bursa had sent more than one *Janissary* company away. His skeleton force of six thousand gardener-guards and *janissaries* now faced an army more than twice its size.

Below, camels grunted. The caravan drivers drove them back into the city with sticks.

"Shut the Tartar Gate!" the *Sanjak* of Bursa yelled.

Tartar arrows blackened the sky, and muskets fired back.

Gate of the Tartars, Lower Town, Bursa, Anatolia, Ottoman Empire

TARTAR ARROWS ARCHED over the lower town walls. As the earth exploded with cannon fire before them, the first wave of Tartar warriors resumed their gallop. Behind them, more horsemen unleashed their arrows. For the second time, the morning sky blackened, and Ottoman defenders raised their round shields.

The thick iron doors of Tartar Gate swung shut before the trailing camels at the end of the long caravan could reenter. Scores of arrows hit the beasts, and horrendous grunts could be heard above pounding hoofs. Some keeled over like ships whipped by waves onto their poor drivers, already slumped motionless, dead on the ground. For all the men and beasts locked outside the gate, there would be no escape. All would suffer the same fate.

Undeterred by the closing of Tartar Gate, another slew of arrows once more darkened the morning sky. Salamet Giray led his thousands of men along the northern walls. Tartar arrows countered the sporadic musket fire. His warriors rode hard, circumventing the lower town and probing the length for weakness. Some of the towers were not well-manned and showed no visible cannon.

Salamet ordered a thousand of his warriors to circle around a large grove of trees. They would provide cover to rebel woodsmen whom he had already assigned to construct makeshift ladders.

Filehdar Gate leading to the vast plains of the North and West remained open. Several turbaned riders exited the gate and rode hard northward.

"They'll reach Mudanya and catch a ship," his Lieutenant said. "Should we pursue them before they cast off and tell the Sultan?"

"Let them spread the news. Terror will strike their hearts." Salamet Giray turned and pointed at Filehdar Gate, its double iron doors still open. "Attack!"

When his warriors charged, Ottoman defenders shut them and sealed them tight.

"Surrender!" Salamet Giray yelled, "Save your lives!"

When the Tartar leader received no response, he resumed his assault. From the plains below, he saw Ottoman cannons firing at his youngest brother from the stronger towers of the upper citadel. Within an hour, the whole town was surrounded.

As the woodsmen constructed their ladders, Salamet Giray took some of his warriors to raid and pillage the surrounding *timars*—all the way to the stone bridge over the Nilufer River.

Exploring part of the fruitful plain, Salamet Giray stopped at a mulberry farm and entered a shed. "Where are the jewels?"

Silk worms ate the mulberry leaves. Women cowered in the corner.

"We have none," the Turkish overseer responded. "Just raw silk."

His men turned over chests and took bolts of raw silk. After they loaded it onto a cart taken from another farm, Salamet Giray gave the order, "Burn it all."

As the shed and the houses burned, Salamet Giray rejoined the siege.

"The ladders are finished," his lieutenant reported. "Should we wait until morning?"

"No."

Under the protection of Tartar arrows, Turkish fighters and Tartar warriors brought the newly made ladders to the low walls. Hot oil and rocks were thrown down upon the attackers, but his brave warriors continued their assault. More warriors scaled the ladders and rushed along the top of the northern walls.

By nightfall, Filehdar Gate had been captured. The iron gates were swung open, and thousands of Tartar warriors galloped past a large bazaar on the main street through the town. Some attacked the silk khans, while the rest attacked Tartar Gate from the inside.

As soon as it was open, many of the *janissaries* escaped to the Upper Citadel. The Tartar warriors of the middle brother Shahin Giray joined the attack. They pillaged and plundered the lower town, breaking down the iron gates of the rich khans. Others looted the wood and brick houses even as guards fired down from the high walls of the Upper Citadel. Fully occupied, the lower town was looted deep into the night.

Fountainhead, Upper Bursa, Asia Minor

THE NEXT MORNING, Salamet Giray and Shahin Giray, riding up the sloping foothills, joined their youngest brother Mohammed, not far from the fountainhead of Bursa, on a promontory overlooking the upper citadel. The large castle, roughly ten thousand paces around, had sixty-seven towers and five gates. They stayed out of musket and cannon range. Behind them, clouds rolled in from the west, enveloping the snow-capped peak.

Because of their great height, three sides of the fortress could not be scaled. The fourth wall by the mountainside had a spring. Further downstream stood the mills of the town. The stream in the ravine could barely power the mills.

Opposite this fourth side, across the ravine, *Janissaries* hurried along the top of the double stone-walls of the upper citadel. When Tartar warriors drew too close, they fired their muskets from the crenelated walls. Likewise, Ottoman cannoneers fired from the citadel's square towers. The treasures and tributes of Anatolia were kept inside the palace that once housed the first Ottoman sultans.

To their right, along the eastern side of Bursa, a single merchant bridge spanned a second ravine and a free-flowing stream. The last vendors of the wooden span had abandoned their shops atop the bridge, the iron gates on both ends bolted shut. Crossing the narrow bridge over the somewhat deeper ravine would bring little hope of success. The citadel gate appeared too strong.

"The Ottomans conquered Bursa by building towers," a disaffected *sipahi* informed. His horse was adorned with jewels taken from an earlier conquest.

"We have no time for towers," Salamet Giray said. "Fill the ravine."

"Yes," his brothers agreed. "We can fill it up and scale the walls."

The dismounted riders carried rocks and stones, casting them down into the ditch below. Even as it began to sprinkle, woodsmen cut down the taller trees. Some carpenters made planks and used them as levers to dislodge boulders. Other woodworkers prepared longer ladders to scale the high wall. By nightfall, the work slowed as dirt turned into mud. The sprinkles had turned into a steady rain.

By the third day, the rain turned stormy, and the stream in the ravine began to rise behind the rocky dam. With the advent of winter, the water spilled over the top. For every rock added, cold water carried another stone away.

"It is not worth it," Shahin Giray told his older brother.

"It will be weeks, if not months, before we would conquer."

"If the weather does not improve, we must go." Salamet Giray, accepting his younger brother's advice, sent scores of carts, already loaded, in the direction of Kutahya, where Hasan *the Fool* besieged another fortress.

Later that day, the cold rain turned to sleet, and the three Tartar brothers turned back. Thousands of Tartar warriors and enriched rebels trekked toward the southeast.

"In the spring, we return with Hasan *the Fool?*"

"Yes, next spring."

Chapter 60 — Safiye *Valide Sultana's* Court

Among all the passions, which rule the affections of Princes, Love (as the most powerful) triumphs more over great men than all the rest together, for they obtain no victories, but to increase its glory: covetousness heaps up to furnish the charges, ambition aspires to make it great. So we see the most powerful princes after they had subdued all other passions, were vanquished by love. Alexander laid the honor of so many victories in Persia at the feet of his captive Roxana. Caesar being in Alexandria, submitted all his triumphs to the beauty of Cleopatra, who afterward was friend to Anthony. And the Turkish monarchies make subject unto the allurements of their Sultanas, the glory and luster of the sovereign power, whereby they are Masters of the best parts of the World . . .

For the Prince [Sultan] being inclined to women, he is the Mercurio of his affections: the other inferior Black Eunuchs pass many times to the Grand Seigneur's Serrail [Sultan's Quarter], to carry the secrets of the Sultanas in sum . . . to the Kapi-Agha [Chief White Eunuch], who presents it to the Emperor: their Office honors them with this privilege above the White Eunuchs, which serve the Prince, who never enter into the Women's lodging, neither do they see them.

The Black [Eunuchs] go not out of the Serrail [Imperial Harem] without the leave of the Sultana Queen, Mother to the eldest of the Sultan's children. There are five hundred of these Black men, from the age of twelve years to five-and-twenty, and at the most thirty . .

The General History of the Serrail, and of the Court of the Grand Seigneur, Emperor of the Turks By Michael Gaudier.
Translated out of the French in 1630 by Edward Grimestone, Sergeant of Arms

Drawbridge, Imperial Harem, New Palace, Thurs., 2nd January *AD* 1603

A BLACK EUNUCH accompanied Aisha, Sister of the Sultan, across the drawbridge over the river that separated the Imperial Harem from the rest of the New Palace. Two more Black eunuchs joined her as she strolled through the center of the Greater and Lesser Chambers of the woman's dormitory. They walked around the fountain, while above them, curious *odalisques* leaned on the wooden rails of the upper two floors and peered down.

"Are you feeling better, Aisha?" One of the older matrons assigned to watch over the *odalisques* joined Aisha's growing entourage. "We heard you were sick."

"Yes, I feel much better. Thank you for your concern." Aisha stopped for a moment. "How is the newest *odalisque?*"

Either the Khan of the Crimean-Tartars or a powerful *pasha*, such as her betrothed, *Yemisci* Hasan *Pasha*, presented most *odalisques* to the Imperial Harem.

"The Bulgarian girl your Grand Vizier sent? She is bright. I doubt if she will remain in the kitchen for very long."

Aisha recollected about the intrigues that often occupied the lives of both the *odalisques* and the *hasekis*, the mothers of her brother's children. All of the older matrons had once been *odalisques,* and she considered many of them to be close friends. "Tell her that her two brothers are doing well."

"I shall."

Aisha did not want to get too involved, so she resumed her walk. She knew that if she delayed any longer, her mother might become upset at her absence.

When she reached her mother's chamber, the door was open. Aisha sensed the mood. It was sober and solemn. The Chief Black and Chief White Eunuchs were seated in the two chairs on either side, at the bottom of the carpeted stairs.

Her mother, seated in her throne above, caught her daughter's eyes.

Chamber of the Sultan's Mother, Imperial Harem, New Palace

"AISHA, ARE YOU feeling better?" Safiye *Valide Sultana* asked.

"Well enough to join you in the baths." Aisha passed between the Chief Black Eunuch and the Chief White Eunuch. Though White eunuchs were never allowed into the Imperial Harem, the Chief White Eunuch was the lone exception. Aisha climbed the carpeted stairs and took a seat on one of the thick cushions behind her mother.

Her mother turned to her and, in an unusually subdued voice, spoke, "What have you found out about the ransom monies?"

"Nothing yet, but John has decided to sail to Scotland to become a courtier for King James VI, the cousin of Queen Elizabeth."

"Yes, my friend." Her mother and Queen Elizabeth had exchanged numerous letters over the years.

"King James will become King of England when Queen Elizabeth dies," Aisha informed.

"Let us not speak of death." The Sultan's Mother dismissed most of her court, including the two *hasekis,* who had given birth to her three grandsons. "My daughter and I shall soon join you in the baths." She looked down the stairs. "Osman *Kizlar Agha,* inform my son that I shall be indisposed for the next few hours."

"As you wish." The Chief Black Eunuch began to rise when two Black eunuchs entered the chamber. The first one handed him a message. "It is for the Chief White Eunuch." He gave the unopened letter to Gazanfer *Agha.*

"What is it?" Safiye *Valide Sultana* asked. "The Governor of Kutayha?"

Upon the opening of the letter, Aisha could tell the Chief White Eunuch was upset. Though the Sister of the Sultan did not normally involve herself in the affairs of state, the turmoil in the *Atmeidan* or Hippodrome outside her palace was impossible to ignore. At last word, *Deli* Hasan *Pasha* still besieged the hilltop fortress of Kutahya.

The Chief White Eunuch tilted his head up and raised his eyebrows, gesturing 'no.'

"What is it then?"

Her mother's impatience showed on her face.

"The three Tartar brothers have attacked Bursa. The lower town has been sacked, and the Upper Citadel besieged."

"Are you certain? Bursa? The safest town in Anatolia?"

"There is no doubt," both *chiauses* confirmed. "Here is the letter from the *sanjak.*"

"Send for Ali *Agha* of the Janissaries and the Deputy Grand Vizier," Safiye *Valide Sultana* ordered. "We shall meet you in the Third Courtyard."

"The bath?" Aisha asked.

"Not today, and if you see your brother, say nothing."

Chief White Eunuch Apartment, Third Courtyard, New (Topkapi) Palace

SAFIYE *VALIDE SULTANA* convened the urgent meeting in the chambers of the Chief White Eunuch. Besides Gazanfer *Agha* and his brother-in-law Ali *Agha,* who led the *Janissaries, Kaimakam Saatçi* Hasan *Pasha* also attended the informal meeting. Sitting next to the Chief Black Eunuch, Safiye *Valide Sultana* told the messenger, "Let us hear the news."

"Tartar warriors pursued me, as I rode hard out of Bursa," the *chiaus* from Bursa reported, "but they turned back after I crossed over the stone bridge."

"The city was surrounded?" the Chief White Eunuch asked.

"Many khans and *timars* were burning."

"The *sipahis* will be upset," *Saatçi* Hasan *Pasha* said. The *Kaimakam* or Deputy Grand Vizier had the duty of running the Ottoman Empire, while the Grand Vizier remained away in Belgrade. Four days a week, *Saatchi* Hasan or Hasan *the Clockmaker* chaired the Imperial Council. This public Divan considered grievances, but would not reconvene until Saturday, the first day of the Muslim week.

"Can we send more *janissaries* to Bursa?" Hasan *the Clockmaker* asked.

"The fighting season has been long," Ali *Agha* reported. "Many of our *ortas* fighting in Wallachia and Europe suffered losses. Though the returning *janissaries* were paid, those companies are not at full strength. The *ortas* must be reconstituted."

"Something must be done," Safiye *Valide Sultana* affirmed.

"We must inform Guzelce Mahmud *Pasha* of the rebellion's headway." The Chief White Eunuch spoke of the *sipahi* leader recently assigned to lead Ottoman forces in Asia Minor. Known to be a close confidant of Sun'Ullah *Effendi*, he was not in the palace when the meeting was called.

"Gazanfer *Agha*, our *ortas* conduct drills every day," Ali *Agha* addressed his brother-in-law.

"When I convene the Divan on Saturday, we will address the advance of Hasan *the Fool* into Kutahya and Bursa," Hasan *the Clockmaker* promised. The Chief White Eunuch had given him a letter telling him not to tell the Sultan of the rebels' progress.

"We cannot wait any longer." Safiye *Valide Sultana* rose and headed to the door.

The Chief Black Eunuch accompanied her across the Third Courtyard, deeper into the inner palace. "Will you inform your son?"

"When the time is right."

Chapter 61 — Castle of the Seven Towers

In consequence of some malicious instigation of the soldiery, Saatçi Hasan Pasha [Hasan the Clockmaker] was removed from the Kaimakam-ship, and Guzelce Mahmud Pasha was appointed in his stead. These changes took place on the 20th of Rajab [Friday, January 3, 1603]. Ali Agha, Agha of the Janissaries, was also deposed and his office conferred on Deli Ferhad Agha, a Bostanji Bashi [Chief Gardener]. Saatçi Pasha was conducted to the [Castle of the] Seven Towers.

Annals of the Turkish Empire, Vol. I, by Mustafa Naima
Translated from the Turkish by Charles Fraser

Upon the last of the seven hills are yet to be seen the ancient building of a fort strengthened with seven towers in the midst of the situation; the Turks call it a Giedicula [Yedikule], that is to say, the Fort of the Seven Towers . . . Two hundred and fifty soldiers are in guard, commanded by a Captain who hath the charge, who may not go forth without the leave of the Grand Vizier . . .

The first Turkish Emperor, which posses't Constantinople, lodged their treasure in these towers: The one was full of ingots and coined gold; two of them contained the silver that was coined and in ingots; another had diverse arms and ornaments for soldiers, and the caparisons for horses, enriched with gold, silver and precious stones; the fifth served for ancient arms, medals, and other precious remainders of antiquity; the sixth contained the engines for war; and the seventh, the rolls and records of the Empire . . .

The General History of the Serrail and of the Court of the Grand Seigneur,
Emperor of the Turks, the First Book by Michel Baudier.
Translated from the French by Edward Grimestone (1635)

Hagia Sophia, *Stamboul*, Friday 20 *Rajab* AH 1011 [3ʳᵈ Jan. *AD* 1603]

THOUSANDS UPON THOUSANDS of *sipahis*, praying on their rugs and mats, bowed towards Mecca. These displaced *sipahis* could not attend the weekly service inside Hagia Sophia due to their vast numbers. Instead, they remained on the vast fields of the *Atmeidan*, the old Hippodrome, within sight of the mosque. Others, however, did attend the Friday service. Accompanied by important *sipahi* leaders, Guzelce Mahmud *Pasha* and

Poiraz Osman *Bey* entered the former Christian church, joining *sipahi* riders and city dwellers inside. Beneath the high dome, large windows and countless candles illuminated the morning gathering.

Salat or Ritual Prayers inside Hagia Sophia, circa AD 1840

The *sipahi* leader examined the section reserved for the Sultan, but it was empty. Sultan Mehmet III oftentimes did not attend this weekly service, preferring instead to worship Allah at one of the small mosques inside the New Palace. The ulema, however, was present. Those religious leaders, all with full and greying beards, sat in their place of prominence to one side.

The former Grand Mufti Sun'Ullah *Effendi* climbed the stairs of the marble minbar, the Muslim pulpit. Speaking to the thousands seated in rows and sections, he confirmed the rumors—*Deli* Hasan *Pasha* and his rebel army had advanced beyond the Vilayet, or Province of Karamania, to the fortress city of Kütahya. Furthermore, he told the worshippers that three Tartar brothers had attacked the royal city of Bursa, a mere three-day march from Scutari, the Asian suburb of *Stamboul*.

When the Muslim prelate finished his sermon, the congregants spilled from the mosque onto the streets. The *sipahi* riders and their leaders returned to the fields of the *Atmeidan*. The news of the disorder spread quickly and, within minutes, the noise emanating from the Hippodrome reached a fevered pitch.

A figure of a woman appeared at the balcony of the Palace of Ibrahim *Pasha* before disappearing behind the curtain. Aisha, Sister of the Sultan, had been promised in marriage to the Grand Vizier. The contract had been signed, the *kabin* paid, and the Grand Vizier would move into that palace after *Yemisci* Hasan *Pasha* returned from Belgrade. Poiraz Osman *Bey*, whom the Grand Vizier had promoted to lead the *sipahis* in Hungary, knew that would not happen soon. In the meantime, the *sipahi* leaders agreed. "Changes must take place."

"Yes, as agreed, the Chief White Eunuch's protege, Ali *Agha*, must be replaced," Guzelce Mahmud *Pasha* said. All knew that the eunuch Gazanfer *Agha* had arranged the marriage of Ali *Agha* to his sister Beatrice, who had immigrated from Venice a decade earlier.

"A new *Agha* of the Janissaries must be found."

"Deputy Grand Vizier, Hasan *the Clockmaker* must be held accountable for the disasters in Anatolia."

"We can wait no longer."

The leaders, including Katib Jemazi, Hasan Khalifeh, and other principals of the conspiracy to overthrow the Ottoman leadership, mounted their horses. With lances in hand and flags waving, they moved through the vast encampment. Leaving their horses to the attendants, other *sipahis* followed their turbaned leaders, moving *en masse* past the Hagia Sophia.

First Courtyard, New Palace, Friday Afternoon, 20th *Rajab AH* 1011

HUNDREDS OF ANGRY *sipahis* moved through the Imperial Gate, past the fifty gardener-guards and the *Kapuji-Bashi*, the captain of the gate. The *sipahi* leaders dismounted and tied their stallions by the Horse Fountain. Well-armed—yet on foot—their followers crossed the Courtyard of the *Janissaries* after them and soon reached the Gate of Greeting with its two parapet towers.

"We demand to see *Saatçi* Hasan *Pasha*," Poiraz Osman *Bey* told a second *Kapuji-Bashi*, the commander of the fifty gardener-guards of the Gate of Greeting.

"The Deputy Grand Vizier will not convene the Divan until tomorrow." Chief Gardener *Deli* Ferhad *Agha* stepped in front of the *Kapuji-Bashi*. *Deli* Ferhad *Agha* oversaw all of the Palace Grounds, including the outer gates. Unlike the *pashas* and *aghas* promoted from the forty *ich-oglans* groomed in the Third Courtyard, the Chief Gardener had been raised from the ranks of the *acemi-oglans,* the *janissary* cadets.

The *sipahi* leader glanced back at the *sipahis* behind him. From the hospital on the one side to the barracks of the *janissary* cadets on the other, more and more *sipahis* crowded into the First Courtyard. "Our demands cannot wait."

"I will talk to you." Hasan *the Clockmaker* appeared alongside Ali *Agha* at the Gate of Greeting. Ali *Agha* wore his customary, tall, plumed hat.

"*Kaimakam Saatçi* Hasan *Pasha,* you must answer to the people."

"I have done nothing wrong." The Deputy Grand Vizier attempted to calm the crowd, but to no avail.

"All of Anatolia is threatened," Guzelce Mahmud *Pasha* countered. He had recently been appointed to lead the army in Anatolia.

"But the turmoil is not my fault," Hasan *the Clockmaker* protested.

"You appointed the failed commanders," Guzelce Mahmud *Pasha* countered. "*Deli* Hasan *Pasha* has taken Ankara and now besieges Kütahya. Even Bursa is threatened."

"What do you want me to do?" Hasan *the Clockmaker* asked.

"Some *sipahis* want your head," Poiraz Osman *Bey* said.

"Assuage the anger of our men," Guzelce Mahmud *Pasha* gestured to more than five thousand men standing behind him.

Hasan *the Clockmaker* turned to the Chief Gardener. "*Deli* Ferhad *Agha,* take me to the Castle of the Seven Towers."

"Your seal?" Poiraz Osman *Bey* asked.

"I resign in favor of Guzelce Mahmud *Pasha.*" Hasan *the Clockmaker* gave the new commander of Ottoman forces in Asia the Imperial Seal.

Guzelce Mahmud *Pasha* accepted the seal and told *Deli* Ferhad *Agha,* "*Bostangi Bashi,* have your men escort *Saatçi* Hasan *Pasha* to the Seven Towers." He turned to the *Agha* of the *Janissaries.* "Ali *Agha?*"

"I shall resign, too." Ali *Agha* peered at his brother-in-law, Gazanfer *Agha,* who stood at the opposite end of the Second Courtyard. The beardless *Kapi Agha* remained with his white eunuch guards in the Gate of Felicity, the entrance to the Third Courtyard and the inner palace.

"*Deli* Ferhad *Agha,*" the new *Kaimakam,* Guzelce Mahmud *Pasha,* proclaimed, "you are now appointed *Agha* of the *Janissaries.*"

Castle of the Seven Towers, Saturday, 21 Rajab *AH* 1011 [Jan. 4, *AD* 1603]

LOCATED AT GOLDEN Gate, the western entrance to *Stamboul*, the Castle of the Seven Towers overlooked the Sea of Marmara. Ships entering from the White or Mediterranean Sea sailed past its walls. Previously, the castle held the treasures of the Ottoman Empire. Sultan Selim II, however, spent much of those riches on the navy, used to build the Ottoman galleys both before and after their defeat at the Battle of Lepanto on the Ionian Sea. His son, Sultan Murad III, transferred the remaining treasures to the New Palace. Ever since, the Seven Towers had been used as a prison for great men, not yet sentenced to death. The less-than-luxurious accommodations proved not uncomfortable.

Castle of the Seven Towers, Stamboul, Ottoman Empire, circa 1840

Hasan *the Clockmaker* knew that he had no choice but to resign. He clearly saw that the only way to avoid more turmoil was to appease the *sipahis*. "Captain, any word?"

"About your fate?" The Captain of the Guard answered, " No. Today's Divan has been postponed. The *sipahis* demand that the Sultan approve and appoint a new Grand Mufti."

Chapter 62 - Grand Mufti Sun'Ullah *Effendi*

They wanted to have the treasures of the mosques opened to them; but the [old] Mufti [Mohammed Effendi], and the Kizlar Agha [Osman], the Chief of the Black Eunuchs, who by his place has the management of all the royal mosques, strongly opposed the demands of this mutinous soldiery. . . One of their chiefs, call Houssain [Hasan Khalifeh], stirred up all those that were at Constantinople, crying they were the only victims of so many disorders; that, whilst all the revolted Pasha [Hasan the Fool] were seizing on the ruin of the empire, and maintaining their comrades in plenteousness at Bursa, Erzerum, and Siwas, they alone were starving at Constantinople, because they had not the spirit to demand what belonged to them. These seditious cries soon assembled those that had reason to complain.

<u>History of the Turkish or Ottoman Empire</u>
By Vincent Mignot. Translated from the French by A. Hawkins

These relaxations of the war in Europe and these disasters in Asia exasperated the patriotism of the sipahis in Constantinople [Stamboul] . . . The Title which the Grand Signor [Sultan] gives unto the [Grand] Mufti, when he writes to him is: "To the Esad, who art the Wisest of the Wise, instructed in all Knowledge, the most Excellent of the Excellent, abstaining from things Unlawful, the Spring of Virtue, and True Science, Heir of the Prophetic and Apostolic Doctrines, Resolver of the Problems of Faith, Revealer of the Orthodox Articles, Key of the Treasures of Truth, the Light to Doubtful Allegories, strengthened with the grace of the Supreme Assister, and Legislator of Mankind. May the Most-High God perpetuate thy Virtues."

History of the Present State of the Ottoman Empire, Book II
By Sir Paul Ricaut, Late Consul at Smyrna, London, 1686

Palace of Ibrahim *Pasha*, Sunday, 22 Rajab *AH* 1011 [5ᵗʰ January *AD* 1603]

SITTING COMFORTABLY UPON a cushion inside her salon, Aisha, Sister of the Sultan, addressed to her Black eunuch, "Overseer, have you heard anything more about the dismissal of the *Agha* of the *Janissaries?*"

"Ali *Agha* has already vacated the Palace of the *Agha* of the *Janissaries* and moved in with his wife, Beatrice."

"At the palace assigned to her by her brother?"

"Yes, your Highness. More than one hundred slaves attend to their every need."

"I knew Gazanfer *Agha* would take care of his sister," Aisha said, "but what about her youngest son?"

"The Venetian boy continues his training in the Third Courtyard."

Aisha finished writing a small note at her desk. "Here, give this to the messenger and him deliver this to her. I want her to know of my concern for her."

"There's a path from heart to heart."

"That is a true saying," Aisha said. "But what is wrong?"

"The *sipahis* outside our walls grow angrier every day," the Overseer said. "Many support Sun'Ullah *Effendi* and demand that your brother, the Sultan, appoint him to be Grand Mufti again."

"Sun'Ullah *Effendi* insisted that *Yemisci* Hasan *Pasha* immediately depart to the European frontier when he was promoted to become Grand Vizier."

"Yes, your betrothed did not like him and arranged for him to be removed as Grand Mufti."

"But now Sun'Ullah *Effendi* is back?"

"Perhaps. I will work and gather more news for you."

Grand Mufti - circa 1590

Divan, New Palace, Sunday, 22 Rajab *AH* 1011 [5th Jan. *AD* 1603]

THE MILITARY JUDGE of Rumelia, seated to the left of the new Deputy Grand Vizier or *Kaimakam,* addressed the Imperial Council under the

Divan in the Second Courtyard of the New Palace. "Cannot monies be found to pay the *sipahis* who have lost their *timars*?"

"You wish to pay them from the Royal Treasury?" *Kaimakam,* Guzelce Mahmud *Pasha,* turned to the royal treasurers on Sunday, the second day of the Islamic workweek.

"Expenses have not stopped," the Chief *Defterdar,* the Treasurer, reported. "As required, we sent monies to Belgrade to pay for the army. Each *janissary* received his allotment before returning to *Stamboul.*"

"Ali *Agha* had brought back many *ortas* with him." Ferhad *Agha,* the former Chief Gardener, said. The newly appointed *Agha* of the *Janissaries* now wore a full turban with a large feather. "They expect to be paid."

"And they will be. But revenues have dropped, the harvest was bad," the Second *Defterdar* added.

"This is not our only problem?" Guzelce Mahmud *Pasha* asked.

The Chief Black Eunuch Osman *Agha* stepped out of the shadows, from behind a pillar not far from the Queen's Gate and Golden Way to the Imperial Harem. "There is something else, is there not?"

"With so many people fleeing into the city, the warehouses are depleted."

"We must not run out of grain."

"No bread?" Worry swept over the new Deputy Grand Vizier, who turned back to *Agha* of the *Janissaries.* "What do the *janissaries* think of the *sipahi* demands?"

"The commanders tell me the troops are as upset as the *sipahis.* The losses in Wallachia and in Hungary, at Buda and Pest, were far greater than expected. More than a few want the Sultan to return to the field. They prefer a Sultan who personally leads his army."

Sultan's Quarters, New Palace, *Stamboul*

SULTAN MEHMET III, ensconced in his study, relaxed comfortably in his chair. He turned to the Chief White Eunuch, who always stood by his side. "Gazanfer *Agha,* I would very much like to hear another story."

"Ah, I know the perfect one." The Chief White Eunuch perused the bound manuscripts and found one placed flat on the middle bookshelf. "Here it is. Yes, from the *History of Forty Viziers.*"

"Go on." The Sultan picked up the amber end of the tube connected to the *nargile,* the Turkish water pipe. A trusted servant lit the fresh tobacco. The Chief White Eunuch gestured for a reader, one of the forty *ich-oglans* from the Third Courtyard, to approach.

The young scholar picked up the book and began, "From the *Trial of the Three Sons*:

'There was of old time in the palace of the world a great king, such that the world was under his rule. He had lived enjoying sovereignty for a hundred and twenty years in the palace of the world, and had grown old. He knew that in the near future he would be given to drink the potion of death. And the king had three moon-faced sons and likewise three able and skillful viziers.'"

Gazanfer *Agha* motioned to the *ich-oglan* to stop and asked the Sultan. "Shall we continue?"

Sultan Mehmet III finished another long drag of tobacco and exhaled the smoke. "Yes, Gazanfer *Agha*. I like this story."

For many minutes, the young scholar continued to expound the long story, written when the Persian influence on Ottoman culture was greater. Eventually, the Sultan waved for the *ich-oglan* to stop. "I think that is enough for today."

"Your next meal should be ready soon," Gazanfer *Agha* looked to the door and saw that the Chief Black Eunuch had arrived from the Divan in the Second Courtyard. "Before you partake of your meal, the new *Kaimakam* Guzelce Mahmud *Pasha* wishes for you to confirm a new appointment."

"For?" Sultan Mehmet III rocked forward.

"The *Sheikh ul-Islam*." Osman *Kizlar Agha* had met with Safiye *Valide Sultana* earlier in the day, before stopping at the Divan.

"Do you approve?" Sultan Mehmet III asked.

"Both of us do." The Chief Black Eunuch, responsible for the administration of all of the Imperial Mosques, stood taller than their friend, Gazanfer *Agha*.

"All it needs is your *tugra*." Gazanfer *Agha* referred to the calligraphic monogram, the Sultan's personal signature.

"As you wish." Sultan Mehmet III steadied himself at a desk before picking up the pen. He added fancy loops characterizing his *tugra*. "And this?" He accepted a second piece of paper.

"More changes in the council," Gazanfer *Agha* said. "The *Kadi* of Anatolia has resigned, so the *Kadi* of Rumelia will take his place, and the judge from Cairo will take his place."

"If you think it is best."

"Yes." Gazanfer *Agha* needed to appease the new *Kaimakam* Guzelce Mahmud *Pasha,* as well as the other *sipahis.* Safiye *Valide Sultana,* Osman *Kizlar Agha,* and Gazanfer *Agha* all agreed that it would be unwise to upset the Sultan with bad reports.

As soon as the Sultan finished signing, the Chief White Eunuch retrieved the orders.

"I'm famished," Sultan Mehmet III said.

"The Cup Bearer has been informed. Your meal is ready."

Divan, New Palace

"IT IS OFFICIAL," *Kaimakam* Guzelce Mahmud *Pasha* informed the Imperial Council. "The old Grand Mufti Mohammed *Effendi* shall no longer maintains his office." He turned to the gray-bearded prelate, whose nephew stood by his side."Sun'Ullah *Effendi,* you are the new *Sheikh ul-Islam.*"

"The dire state of the empire must be addressed," the new Grand Mufti said. "A General Assembly may be required."

Gate of Felicity, New Palace

LATE THAT NIGHT, Chief White Eunuch Gazanfer *Agha* placed a letter in the palm of a *Kapuji Bashi,* a captain of the outer palace gate. "For Grand Vizier *Yemisci* Hasan *Pasha,*" the beardless eunuch told one of his most trusted men.

"You do not want a *chiaux* to carry it?" The *Kapuji Bashi* spoke about utilizing one of the royal messengers, a sergeant-at-arms who carried cudgels—short staffs with silver knobs.

"Not this message." The Chief White Eunuch would normally have one of royal *chiauxes* deliver orders, but this message was far too important.

"The *sipahis* protest every day, who will take my charge?"

"Do not worry about your gardener-guards. Your lieutenant is capable and shall take your charge at the gate." The Chief White Eunuch motioned to the shadows of the Gate of Justice, Majesty, and Felicity.

The Third Treasurer stepped out of a nook and handed the *Kapuji Bashi* a small bag of coins. "For your journey, to cover your costs at the *caravan-serais.*"

The road to Belgrade, more than five hundred miles away, went through Edirne in Rumelia and Sophia in Bulgaria. Officials and merchants always stayed at the *caravan-serais* dotting the main roads of the Ottoman Empire. After leaving *Stamboul* through the Gate of Edirne, the journey would take many days.

"What shall I say when I get to Belgrade?"

"Tell the Grand Vizier that Sun'Ullah *Effendi* has become Grand Mufti again," Gazanfer *Agha* said. "This letter from Safiye *Valide Sultana* herself will explain everything. We know the new Grand Mufti does not like her."

The *Kapuji Bashi* put on his overcoat, for the shortened days of winter were at hand. "I shall leave before dawn."

"Your horse is waiting." The Chief White Eunuch watched the *Kapuji Bashi* hurry across the quiet Second Courtyard toward the Gate of Greeting. "Do not delay."

Chapter 63 — Not for Justice, but Necessity

While [Grand Vizier Yemisci Hasan Pasha] was to marry a sister [Aisha] of the Sultan,
twenty-five-thousand-armed Sipahis and Janissaries presented themselves at the Gates of
the Divan . . .

Storia dell' Impero Ottomano, Vol. II
Compiled by Dal. Cav. Compagnoni & Translated from the Italian by D.E.A.

These heads, said the sipahis, were to expiate the corruptions of the seraglio, and the
baneful counsels given to the Sultan by his favorites. The Empire could be regenerated
but in the blood of its corrupters . . . . But Osman the Kizlar Agha [Chief Black Eunuch]
and Gazanfer Chief of the White Eunuchs, more odious because they were more dear to
their master and to his mother sacrificed with tears by [Sultan] Mehmet [III], delivered
their heads though innocent to the sabers of the sipahis. The Sultan was compelled to
attend the execution, to salute the troops before the corpses, as if to thank them for the
crime, and devour his shame and sorrow in the secrecy of his harem.

History of Turkey, Vol. III by A. de Lamartine
Translated from the French by Appleton & Co.

New Palace, *Stamboul*, Monday, 23 Rajab *AH* 1011 (6th Jan. *AD* 1603)

BELOW THE MINARETS of the Hagia Sophia and the outer wall of the
New Palace, *Sipahi* leaders on horseback pressed through throngs of their
dismounted compatriots. A *khet-khoda,* an officer of the court, exited the
Imperial Gate. Riding in the opposite direction toward the Gate of Edirne,
he trotted past the *sipahi* leaders.

Poiraz Osman *Bey*, Katib Jezami. and Hasan *Khalifel* reached the
Imperial Gate with its fifty *bostangis,* the gardener-guards. The new *Kapuji
Bashi,* or captain of the gate, waved them through. At the far end of the
First Courtyard, not far from the famous *Janissary* Tree, the *sipahi* leaders
dismounted by the Horse Fountain. More and more of their men—all on
foot but well-armed and ready to fight—arrived behind them. This
massive wave joined the hundreds of *sipahis* already inside. The First

Courtyard of the New Palace, the home of Sultan Mehmet III, was as packed as the streets outside.

The Gate of Greeting, with its side niches, stood before them. Its heavy iron doors were nearly shut tight, open but a crack. The pair of parapet towers bracketed both sides of the gate. A dozen archers, stationed in its windows, looked down.

Brash as brass, the leaders told *Kapuji Bashi* Hasan *Agha,* "We demand audience!"

"For what reason?" The Captain of the Gate stood firm. His regular guard of fifty *bostangis,* or gardener-guards, had been augmented with fifty more.

Poiraz Osman *Bey* glanced back at the *sipahis* armed with round shields and sharp swords. "We wish to prostrate ourselves before the Sultan."

"Audiences must be arranged far in advance." The *Kapuji Bashi* perused his list. "None have been scheduled this week."

It was already Monday morning, the third of the four days of the public workweek of the Divan, when matters both great and small were settled.

"You dare to defy us?" Poiraz Osman *Bey* glanced back. One hundred *bostangis* and the dozen or more archers were no match for his legion of angry *sipahis.* Though dismounted, the seven or eight thousand veteran fighters remained fully armed. With their lances upright, their swords sheathed, and their shields at their side, the grim-faced veteran fighters stood in ranks. Facing the Gate of Greeting, all remained wholly dedicated to assisting their determined leaders.

Behind them, outside the Imperial Gate, more than twice that number seconded those inside. Nearly twenty thousand more *sipahis,* both on horseback and on foot, crowded the streets about the Hagia Sophia. Hundreds of them had been assigned to guard each and every gate of the New Palace. The vast fortress, three miles in circumference, was now a prison. There would be no escape.

Their just demands would be met. The bad administration and misuse of power had caused their *timars* to be lost; the *sipahis* would need to be compensated. But the Chief Black Eunuch, *Kizlar Agha* Osman, had refused to open the royal mosques.

The *Kapuji Bashi* slipped into the Second Courtyard to confer with members of the Divan. When time passed and no one responded, the patience of the *sipahis* came to an abrupt end.

"If this Gate of Greeting is not instantly opened," the *sipahi* leader yelled, "we will burn down this whole *seraglio!*"

"Wait for our answer!" *Kapuji Bashi* Hasan *Agha* came back. "Two of your leaders may enter."

"No," Poiraz Osman *Bey* conferred with the other *sipahis*. "We will not go in with less than thirty men."

"No arms are allowed inside."

"Agreed." Poiraz Osman *Bey* and the others put down their swords, shields, and lances. Beneath their cloaks, the fifteen *sipahi* leaders kept their daggers hidden. The somber *janissaries* likewise entered.

"*Kaimakam* Guzelce Mahmud *Pasha* and Grand Mufti Sun'Ullah *Effendi* will convince the Sultan to call a General Assembly, but first the new Deputy Grand Vizier wants the Imperial Council to hear the justness of the complaints."

The General Assembly would not meet under the sloped roofs of the Divan on the left side of the Courtyard. Instead, servants lined up two dozen chairs at the far end of the yard, in front of the Gate of Justice, Majesty, and Felicity. Low tables were prepared for the scribes and notaries.

Castle of the Seven Towers, *Stamboul*, Monday morning

HASAN *THE CLOCKMAKER*, the former Deputy Grand Vizier, stared at galleys and sailing ships plying the choppy waters. Winds constantly shifted between Asia and Europe, between the Black Sea and the Mediterranean. Beyond the Sea of Marmara and the northern shores of Anatolia, clearing skies revealed the snowcapped peak of Mount Olympus rising in the far distance. At its foot, the royal city of Bursa had recently been attacked and plundered by the Tartar rebels of the notorious Hasan *the Fool*.

"*Saatçi* Hasan *Pasha*." A guard roused him, breaking his reflection. "You are needed."

"How so?" Hasan *the Clockmaker* turned from the barred window. It had been three days since he had voluntarily surrendered and taken to the Castle of the Seven Towers. The accommodations of his cell, though not luxurious, were comfortable enough. Other high-ranking officials had been detained in the room over the past decade.

"A General Assembly will be called, and the Imperial Council demands your presence."

466

Armed guards escorted Hasan *the Clockmaker* from the Castle of the Towers and brought him to the *Atmeidan*, now largely devoid of the *sipahis* who had made that vast field their temporary encampment. Their horses, however, remained. Some grazed below the walls of the Palace of Ibrahim *Pasha*, the residence of the Sister of the Sultan. Young attendants watched them, making sure they would not wander away.

Hasan *the Clockmaker*, though unshackled, would not attempt to run away from the handful of guards. The *chiauxes* were too fast. There would be no escape. Besides, Hasan *the Clockmaker* was willing to accept his fate.

They soon reached the far end of the *Atmeidan*, where vast crowds of both *sipahis* and citizens streamed towards the New Palace, past the minarets of Hagia Sophia.

"Make way!" the *Chiaux Bashi*, the captain of the guard, yelled. Like ships cutting through troubled seas, the guards and their prisoner sailed through the growing crowds. As soon as Hasan *the Clockmaker* and the guards passed through, the angry *sipahis* filled the backwash. There was barely room to move.

The prisoner passed through the Imperial Gate. The *chiauxes* escorted him through the angry assembly packed inside the First Courtyard. These *sipahis* seemed even angrier than those outside. For the prisoner and his escorts pressing through the grim-faced horsemen, the progress toward the Gate of Greeting was slow and painful. Their sneers and jeers removed all doubt. Hasan *the Clockmaker's* life was at stake.

Gate of Justice, Majesty, and Felicity, Second Courtyard, New Palace

"THE OTTOMAN EMPIRE has been neglected," Poiraz Osman *Bey* addressed *Kaimakam* Guzelce Mahmud *Pasha* and the expanded Imperial Council in front of the Gate of Justice, Majesty, and Felicity. "While we were in Europe recovering the former Hungarian Royal Capital Szekesfehervar, *Deli* Hasan *Pasha* and his rebel army progressed unopposed in Asia and Anatolia. To this very day, the rebels remain strengthened and hidden in the lairs." While they were in Hungary, the Grand Vizier *Yemisci* Hasan *Pasha* had promoted Poiraz Osman *Bey*, but now his loyalties had switched. He had wholeheartedly joined the conspiracy.

The *sipahi* leader pointed at Hasan *the Clockmaker*, advancing from the Gate of Greeting through the center of the Second Courtyard. *Janissaries* stood beneath the porticos near the kitchens on one side of the Courtyard.

On the other side, beyond the Executioner's Fountain, a few young *acemi-oglans* stood beneath the Divan. Its clock tower rose above an angled roof. "The manner in which you confronted the rebels has led the empire down a path of ruin!"

Hasan *the Clockmaker* passed between the two delegations of *janissary* and *sipahi* leaders. Comprised of fifteen each, the thirty leaders sat cross-legged in rows on the grassy grounds.

Gate of Felicity (Entrance to Third Courtyard), New Palace

Hasan *the Clockmaker* reached the front of the assembly. Besides *Kaimakam* Guzelce Mahmud *Pasha*, those seated in front of the Gate included the two *Cadi-liskers* or Military Judges of Rumelia and Anatolia, the new *Agha* of the *Janissaries* Ferhad *Agha*, and the Fourth Vizier Hasan *the Addicted*. Except for the Grand Vizier away in Belgrade, all of the regular members of the Imperial Council took their seats.

But this General Assembly was much larger than the regular Divan: All priests of the Law and other members of the *ulema* readied themselves to hear the charges and complaints. The whole *ulema* or religious leadership attended. In the midst of all these respected authorities of Islamic law, the somber Grand Mufti, the *Sheikh ul-Islam* Sun'Ullah *Effendi*, sat most prominently.

Hasan *the Clockmaker* turned to face his accusers. "I pray that you question me with all humility. I ask for mercy on my innocence. I have not

468

failed in my duty." He looked into the eyes of the *sipahi* leader. "If shedding my blood is useful for the Ottoman state, you need not kill me." He spoke so all could hear. "I willingly die!"

Poiraz Osman *Bey* motioned for Hasan *the Clockmaker* to stop. "At this moment. this assembly does not require your blood." He caught the eye of Grand Mufti Sun'Ullah *Effendi* before starting once more. "We only ask that you justify the reasons for the disorders. If you do so, we do hope you will not die."

The *sipahi* delegation gestured its agreement.

"During the year the government has been put into my hands, I have done my duty." Hasan *the Clockmaker* said, "But if my death will be useful to the empire, you must know that the *Valide Sultana* and the *Kapi-Agha* will still be near his person."

The former Deputy Grand Vizier spoke of the Sultan's Mother and the Chief White Eunuch.

"Then—" Poiraz Osman *Bey* interrupted."We demand to see the Emperor!"

The two delegations—both *sipahis* and *janissaries*—assented.

The Chief White Eunuch escorted the new *Sheikh ul-Islam* Sun'Ullah *Effendi* and the new *Kaimakam* Guzelce Mahmud *Pasha* to the Sultan's quarters. They needed to convince Sultan Mehmet III to listen to the complaints of the *janissaries* and *sipahis*.

~ ~ ~

FOUR WHITE EUNUCHS carried the Ottoman throne from the Third Courtyard, centering it in front of the Gate of Justice, Majesty, and Felicity. They removed its protective covering at the very end of the Second Courtyard, revealing the red velvet and the fine workmanship of its arms.

Minutes later, Sultan Mehmet III, along with the Chief White Eunuch, arrived from the Inner Palace. He left his most trusted aide, Gazanfer *Agha,* standing in the shadows of the Gate. The Ottoman Monarch stepped up and seated himself on the throne. In the corner of the Second Courtyard to Sultan's right, between the Divan and the Gate of Felicity, deaf mutes awaited to execute any order he might give.

For the first time in many years, the Ottoman monarch had agreed to the General Assembly. He knew that the *janissaries* could be unbearable—numerous times over the years, they had caused tumult, ravaging the city whenever their demands had not been met. When the

Sultan first entered the city after his father's death, he distributed many coins to the *janissaries* and raised their pay. This General Assembly, however, was different. For he had been informed that the *sipahis*, more than the *janissaries*, were the ones who had demanded the General Assembly. Reluctantly, he agreed to listen to their arguments. He had to reduce the likelihood of seditious riots that could blanket the bazaars and overrun the markets of *Stamboul*.

Sultan Mehmet III signaled to the new Deputy Grand Vizier, *Kaimakam* Guzelce Mahmud *Pasha*, that he was ready. Behind him, Chief White Eunuch Gazanfer *Agha* listened.

The new Deputy Grand Vizier remained seated to the Sultan's left, the highest place of honor. "You may speak, Hasan Khalifel."

"Our very great and very fortunate Emperor." The *sipahi* leader stood up and began speaking in measured tones. "Your *sipahis* and *janissaries*, all of whom are your obedient slaves, are full of compassion, but we are pained at the sight of the loss of the estates of your Highness." The *sipahi* leader spoke loudly and clearly, "Our desire is for you to know the causes, so the remedy can be applied. May Allah grant that the cure will be big enough."

The Sultan signaled for the *sipahi* leader to proceed.

"The rebels, led by Hasan *the Fool*, have overthrown towns and captured vast territories. We believe the progress he has obtained has been concealed from you," Hasan Khalifel stated. "That is why we have assembled here today: to disclose the boldness that the rebel—so far from his home—has taken and to reveal where he can be found."

Hasan Khalifel turned to the *Sipahi* Secretary *Katib Jezami*.

"This past week, the rebel army attacked and plundered Bursa— only a short four or five days' march from *Stamboul*," *Katib Jezami* reported. "Even now, his army remains only seven or eight days away. He winters at Afyon-Kara-Hissar, the Black Castle fortress."

The *sipahi* leader Hasan Khalifel stepped forward again. "Both in general and in particular, we desire—we want to know—the total of all that has been manifested unto you. In short, will you take care of the government of this monarchy? Are you satisfied with everything that has transpired? Or are you taking part in it?" Returning to the front of the *sipahi* delegation, Hasan Khalifel finished his complaint.

The two delegations, both *sipahi and janissary*, stared grim-faced at the Ottoman monarch. No one said a word. Only the sound of water from the executioner's fountain could be heard.

470

SULTAN MEHMET III, much offended at what was just uttered, leaned back in his throne. Clenching his teeth, the Ottoman monarch attempted to maintain his composure. "Your words and your manners are most improper."

The Sultan glanced at the thousands of *sipahis* congregated in the First Courtyard on the other side of the Gate of Greeting. He addressed the thirty *sipahi* and *janissary* leaders still seated before him, "You ought to serve as an example of obedience to the rest of the subjects of the Empire. It is true I have not been advised of what has been happening, but I promise you I will remedy the situation. I will make it right."

The *Kaimakam* Guzelce Mahmud *Pasha* called forth the former Deputy Grand Vizier back to the center of the Assembly. "Hasan *the Clockmaker*, why have you failed in your duty? Why have you failed to report to His Majesty about the Asiatic rebellion of Hasan *the Fool?*"

Hasan *the Clockmaker* shifted from foot to foot. "I never shirked my responsibilities, nor failed in my duty." He glanced to the shadows of the gate behind the throne, where Chief White Eunuch Gazanfer *Agha* listened in silence. "But the *Kapi Agha* restrained and hindered me from doing so. Gazanfer *Agha* always implored me, saying, 'There's no need to upset his Highness.'"

"Is this true?" the *Kaimakam* Guzelce Mahmud *Pasha* asked.

"I have proof." Hasan *the Clockmaker* pulled a piece of paper from his pocket. "In the presence of Safiye *Valide Sultana* and *Kizlar Agha* Osman, Gazanfer *Agha* signed this letter."

A guard took the letter and handed it to the *Kaimakam,* Guzelce Mahmud *Pasha,* who, after he examined it, proclaimed. "I recognize the mark." He looked to the new Grand Mufti, the ulema, and the military judges, before turning to the other members of the Divan. He proceeded to turn the letter over to the Sultan to examine, but the Sultan waved him off.

"Hasan *the Clockmaker*," *Kaimakam* Guzelce Mahmud *Pasha* said, "You are not required to deliver your head. You are free to go."

Hasan *the Clockmaker* received the news with relief, and instead of waiting to hear what would transpire next, he hurried toward the Gate of Greeting. Two close friends of his joined him as he passed the Divan, where he had ruled for more than a year.

"We must hear from the Sultan's Mother, the Chief Black Eunuch, and the Chief White," the *sipahi* leader suggested.

As soon as the *Kaimakam* and the Sultan agreed, White eunuchs were sent to relay the message to the Imperial Harem. While they waited for the Chief Black Eunuch and the Sultan's Mother to appear, the *sipahi* leader said, "There are others who had a duty." He looked at the Fourth Vizier, Hasan *the Addicted,* seated next to the new *Agha* of the *Janissaries,* Ferhad *Agha.* "*Teryacki* Hasan *Pasha,* I have questions."

The Fourth Vizier moved to the front of the General Assembly.

"You knew about the progress of the rebels in Asia and the infidels in Europe. And you did not inform the Sultan?"

"No."

"Where is your letter?"

"I have none."

Two strong guards escorted the accused to the round Executioner's Fountain. Kneeling with his head forced down, Hasan *the Addicted* prepared to die. The executioner raised his sword, framing it to swiftly strike.

"Halt!" The delegation of fifteen *Janissary* leaders rose to their feet in unison. They had remained silent throughout the assembly.

Guzelce Mahmud *Pasha* motioned for the executioner to stop and turned to the *Janissary* leaders. "For what reason?"

"The hero of Kanizsa was raised a *janissary,* one of our own," a *Janissary* leader answered. "We cannot condone this execution of *Tiryacki* Hasan *Pasha.*"

An *orta* of Janissaries standing beneath the porticos on one side of the Courtyard joined the rising noise. "Spare him."

Sultan Mehmet III, seeing the rising tumult, waved off the executioner, who put away his sword.

Hasan *the Addicted,* breathing deeply, rose and walked away.

Arriving from the Imperial Harem, the Sultan's Mother and the Chief Black Eunuch joined the Chief White Eunuch at the front of the General Assembly.

"The *Kapi-Agha* hides the truth from your Highness," Hasan Khalifel proclaimed. "The rebels triumph in Asia and the infidels in Europe. His lavish spending on the palace empties your treasury. The greedy *Kapi-Agha* appropriates the public treasury for his personal use. The empire languishes as if it were dead."

Both delegations of *sipahis* and *janissaries* gestured their assent.

"Where is the glory of our army? Hunger, poverty, and shame have supplanted our victories," Hasan Khalifel faced the three standing. "These disorders must not be allowed go unpunished. Give us the heads of these corrupters. The *Valide Sultana* and the two *Aghas* must pay. Only their blood can purge the corruption!"

The whole assembly murmured its concurrence.

Sultan Mehmet III motioned for his subjects to stay calm. "For any caprice that may have been done, I will carefully consider the punishment. But I cannot condone their immediate execution." The overweight Sultan looked to the Imperial Council and then to the ulema before addressing the two delegations, "The charges and the merits must first be weighed, then justice will be done. Anyone who deserves to die shall be executed." The Sultan pointed to Prince Mahmud standing near an *orta* of young *janissaries* under the porticos beyond the nine imperial kitchens. "Even if my own son Mahmud is found culpable in the cause, I shall not hesitate. I will kill him. Justice will be done."

"You did not kill your nineteen brothers for justice, but for the necessity of the state," Hasan Khalifel retorted. "This empire must be purged by blood. All who bear responsibility must offer their heads!"

Sultan Mehmet III felt trapped and peered at the *ulema*, the respected priests of Islamic law. Grand Mufti Sun'Ullah *Effendi* did not move; the restored *Sheikh ul-Islam* did not flinch.

"Whether they are innocent or not does not matter," Hasan Khalifel looked at the seasoned *sipahis* ready to rise. "You must act. For if you fail to meet our demands and to chastise those who are responsible, we shall do it ourselves."

There was no doubt in the Sultan's mind that his reign was on the precipice, but Mehmet III refused the indignity of granting the death of his mother. "The *Valide Sultana* cannot be killed. Do you expect me to condone the killing of my own mother?"

Hasan Khalifel conversed with the other leaders seated in the front row and returned. "You must send her away."

"Away?"

"Relegate her to some place far away, like the Palace of Edirne."

The second capital of the Ottoman Empire was days away, further north in Rumelia.

Safiye *Valide Sultana* huffed and motioned for *Kizlar Agha* Osman to join her, but he was stopped.

"We have not yet decided the Chief Black Eunuch's fate," Hasan Khalifeh said.

Sent away, the Sultan's Mother did not stay to watch, returning through the Gate of Justice, Majesty, and Felicity to pack her belongings inside the Imperial Harem.

"*Kizlar Agha* Osman. You did not do your duty!"

Two guards grabbed the Chief Black Eunuch by the arms and dragged him to the Executioner's Fountain. With one swift stroke, the executioner cut off the eunuch's crown. His beardless head rolled onto the flat ground. The executioner wiped clean his blade. Remaining solemn yet determined, those in the assembly neither cheered nor cried.

"I ask for the head of the *Kapi Agha*." Hasan Khalifel turned to the Chief White Eunuch. "Will you voluntarily give it up?"

"I shall not!" Gazanfer *Agha* cried in a high-pitched voice. "What sin have I committed? Do I deserve death for governing?" He rushed to the foot of the Sultan and wrapped his arms around his master's legs.

A member of the *janissary* delegation jumped up from the front row. He pried the Chief White Eunuch from the Sultan's leg. He snatched him away, dragging him to the Executioner's Fountain. The executioner raised his glistening sword anew. The beardless head of the Chief White Eunuch rolled to the ground next to the other one. Two pairs of lifeless eyes remained open—blank to the sky. The decapitated heads of the Chief Black and White eunuchs lay side by side.

"What about the three Imperial *Defterdars*?"

"The Treasurers do not deserve death," the Sultan rasped.

"Very well," the *sipahi* leader agreed, "but they must go."

Sultan Mehmet III concealed his anger, yet relieved the three top *Defterdars*. New royal treasurers would account for the wealth of the Chief Black and Chief White Eunuchs, whose riches would return to the general treasury.

Though his two closest friends and advisers were no more, Safiye *Valide Sultana* and the House of Osman had survived. Aggrieved at the loss of his favorites, Sultan Mehmet III slowly rose from his throne and disappeared through the Gate of Felicity. The disgraced monarch retreated to his private quarters to wallow in his shame and sorrow.

Scarcely speaking another word, the whole assembly dispersed. The *sipahis* returned to their encampment at the Atmeidan.

Chapter 64 — Safe Inside her Palace

Palace of Ibrahim *Pasha*, Tuesday, 24 *Rajab AH* 1011 (7th Jan. *AD* 1603)

BEATRICE, THE VENETIAN sister of the late Chief White Eunuch, wiped away tears. "New treasurers came to my palace to take an accounting. They spent all morning taking an inventory of what Gazanfer *Agha* owned."

"Your brother loved you much." Aisha attempted to comfort the older Venetian woman and handed her a silk handkerchief.

Beatrice sniffled as another tear rolled down her cheek. "I know you wanted me to help translate John's Italian, but I cannot."

"Do not worry, Beatrice."

"I just don't understand why. Why did Gazanfer have to die?" Beatrice added, "I am also worried about my son. Will the *sipahis* go after him next?"

"I will ask my mother to help him."

"But the *Valide Sultana* has to leave. Even now, your mother packs to go to Edirne."

"She has yet to vacate the New Palace." Aisha touched her friend's hand. "My brother loves me as much as your brother loved you."

Beatrice sobbed, tears streaming once more. "I must go home." She retrieved her shawl and, after final goodbyes, went to find her husband.

~ ~ ~

AROUND MID-DAY, WITH only her maids in attendance, Aisha called to the Overseer, "Bring my English slave."

Seated comfortably on her cushioned sofa in her well-lit Salon, the Turkish noblewoman, ignoring the subdued turmoil outside, greeted her well-mannered captive. "*Buongiorno, Capitano.*"

"*Buongiorno,* Aisha, Sister of the Sultan." John deparated from her Black eunuch and took the offered seat. "Your friends?"

"Neither Dilara nor Filiz could make it today." Aisha turned to her Overseer. "Have the chef prepare stuffed green peppers."

"As you wish." The Overseer bowed, walked backwards, and withdrew from the room.

Aisha told John in Italian, "I know you will like the peppers that will be served to us." The dolma would be made with lamb, dill, and parsley.

"You treat me so kindly." Like a well-trained soldier, John sat perfectly straight.

Aisha brushed off the compliment. "Was that all that happened in France?"

"For that year. After Cardinal Albert retired through Flanders, peace between France and Spain would soon be at hand."

Glossary
Glossary of Terms

Acemi-Oglan   'Novice boys' who served in the under offices of the New Palace. Taken from the *devshirme* and trained in a craft or a trade, many later became *janissaries*.

Agha (Aga)   Leader or general; chief; master; commander as in *Agha* of the *Janissaries*.

AD   *Anno Domino.* Year of the Lord: Jesus Christ of Nazareth was born in Bethlehem.

AH   Latin *Anno Higra,* signifying the year of the Pilgrimage, referring to the Prophet Mohammed's flight from Mecca to Medina in AD 622.

Allah   'The God' in Arabic. Name of God among those who profess the Muslim faith.

Arc de Triumph   Ceremonial archway, often temporary, erected for celebrations or parades.

Bandolier   Shoulder belt worn by musketeers. Touch-box charges of gunpowder attached.

Bagnos   'Baths' in Italian.

Bash Kadin   Chief Lady of the Imperial Harem.

Bastion   Part of a fortification that allows a defender to fire in several directions.

Battalia   Middle or main regiment of a marching army.

Bedesten   'Market' in Turkish. In *Stamboul,* pillars supported two covered markets: the Old *Bedesten* (now the center of the Grand Bazaar) and the New *Bedesten* (or *Sandal),* where slaves were sold. Female slaves were also sold at the Avret Bazaar.

Bohemian   Besides persons from the Kingdom of Bohemia, also used to identify Gypsies or *Roma.* (Later referred to artists and writers maintaining relaxed social standards).

Bey (Beg)   Turkish Governor (usually of a city); equivalent of 'Lord.'

Beylerbey (Beglerbeg)   Governor of governors; head of an Ottoman province, i.e. *Beylerbey* of Cairo.

Bey-Ogli   Son of a governor. Title given (in 1602) to the son of the Crimean-Tartar Khan.

Bostangi Bashi   Chief Gardener. He oversees both the gardeners and the guards in the New Palace   and reports directly to the Chief White Eunuch.

Buraya gel   'Come here' in Turkish.

Caliph   'Successor' to Mohammed. One of the titles of the Ottoman Sultan, acquired after the Ottomans conquered the Mamluk Dynasty in Egypt in AD 1524.

Caliphate   Territory controlled by the Caliph.

| **Camet** | Cloth. |

Capitano 'Captain' in Italian.

Caravanserai Caravan 'Palace.' Khan or inn where travelers stay with their camels or horses.

Catholic League One of three groups vying for power in France in the late 1500s. Supported by King Philip II of Spain, the Duke of Guise led the Catholic League against the French *Huguenots* and the French royal families, first Valois, then Bourbons.

Cautionary A town held as collateral until a debt has been paid in full.

Cavus Sergeant or messenger in the Ottoman Empire.

Celali Rebellions Name of a rebel fighting against the Ottoman government in the early 16th century. After his death, term used to describe the ongoing Anatolian rebellions.

Chiaus (Chiaux) An Ottoman messenger(s) who carries a truncheon with a knob at one end.

Coat of Arms An emblem granted by a prince or monarch to knights showing valor in battle; Also granted to nobles, guilds and other organizations.

Concubine A woman who lives with a man as if she were his lawful wife.

Cornet Trumpet. Also name used for company of horsemen, similar to flag for footmen.

Cossacks Name of an independent people from either the Dnieper River toward Poland or the Don River towards Moscow, who raided Turkish lands in boats, or fought against the Crimean Tartars on horseback with bows, arrows, and firearms.

Council of Nicaea Convened by Emperor Constantine in the town of Nicaea (present-day Iznik) in *AD* 325. More than 300 Christian bishops rejected Arianism, unanimously agreeing to the Nicene Creed, confirming God the Father and Jesus the Son are One.

Council of Trent Convened in Trento, Italy by Catholic Church in the middle of the 16th Century: a key to the Counter-Reformation that also reaffirmed the Nicene Creed.

Crenelated Square or cubed battlements characterizing the tops of fortified walls.

Crimean-Tartars Ottoman Empire's most loyal allies. Descendants of one branch of the Mongols of Genghis Khan, the Crimean-Tartars converted to Islam and brought upwards to 100,000 warriors to the battlefield at the request of the Ottoman Sultan.

Cuirassiers Cavalrymen equipped with cuirass—plated or metal (not earlier leather) armor.

Damat 'Bridegroom' in Turkish. Title given to someone marrying into the Ottoman royal family, i.e. *Damat* Ibrahim *Pasha*, the first husband of Aisha, Sister of the Sultan.

Deli Turkish word meaning "Fool." A type of brave Turkish fighter who attached feathered wings to his helmet or shoulders. Name of rebel leader Hasan Pasha.

Defterdar Ottoman Treasurer. From the Persian *Defter*, meaning account and *Dar*, to keep.

Dervish Muslim sect known for its swirling dances.

Devshirme	Refers to boys between the ages of nine and twelve taken from their Christian parents in Ottoman Europe, collected as tribute to the Sultan.
Dhimmi	Non-Muslim.
Dragoman	Translator in the Ottoman Empire.
Ducat	Official Venetian coin widely used in the Mediterranean from 1300s to 1700s.
Eighty Years War	Dutch War of Independence from Spain: began in 1568 and lasted until 1648.
Eski	'Old' in Turkish.
Eski Serai	The Old Palace in *Stamboul. Serai*, meaning palace, is of Persian origin.
Eunuchs	Castrated while young, boy eunuchs did not grow facial hair during puberty. White eunuchs served in the Sultan's household, Black eunuchs in his Harem.
Firaris	'Runaways' from the Battle of (Mezo-)Keresztes (1596) joined *Deli* Hasan's rebels.
Fatwa (fetva)	An official decree or point of law signed by a mufti or *kadi*.
Fougades	French land mines placed to blow up stones and sections of walls.
French Wars of Religion	A series of eight conflicts between the Catholic League (supported by Spain) and French Huguenots (Calvinists) from 1562 to 1598, ending with Edict of Nantes.
Galley	A ship, often with sails, but mainly manned by slaves pulling oars in calm seas.
Geneva Bible	Main English Bible translation used in England and Scotland during late 1500s.
Ghilman	Young recruit who serve the Sultan (or serve the 'True Believers' in heaven).
Ghazi	Meaning warrior (*Jihadist*).
Grand Mufti	Leading religious authority (*Sheikh ul-Islam)* of the Ottoman Empire.
Haddith	Traditions of Islam, not part of the *Qur'an.*
Hajduk	Free-spirited Hungarian fighter. Hajduks considered bandits by Ottoman Turks.
Hajj	Pilgrimage to Mecca (one of the five pillars of Sunni Islam).
Half-moon	A type of fortification, built in the shape of a semi-circle.
Hamam	Turkish bathhouse.
Harem	Meaning 'Hidden' or forbidden. Term describes private quarters for women.
Hanseatic League	Merchant league controlling trade in Northern Europe and Baltic Sea during the Middle Ages and the early Renaissance period.
Hevlet	Yelled by Black Eunuchs to warn that the Sultan and his harem were coming.
Haseki	Mother of an Ottoman Prince.

Hijab	Veil or head-covering worn by Muslim women.
Horsetail	Used as a standard inside Ottoman Empire, horsetails usually attached atop a pole about eight feet long. The Sultan's standard had four horsetails while the Grand Vizier three; and important *Pashas* two. A *sanjak* carried a standard of one.
Hussars	Horsemen from Poland who wore feathered wings on their arms and backs.
Ich-Oglans	'Interior Youths.' Forty select *devshirme* were raised and trained in the Third Courtyard of the New Palace, destined to take over the great Ottoman offices.
Imam	Muslim priest.
In flagrante delicto	In the commission of the act from the Latin. Literally, 'blazing offense/crime.'
Indentured	Servant bound by contract for a term of years: if broken, servant bound for life.
Iznik	Ancient Nicaea; Anatolian town outside Bursa renowned for its ceramic tiles.
Janissary	*Yeniceri meaning* 'New Army,' the foot soldiers of the Ottoman Empire; started during the reign of Sultan Orhan through the collection of the *devshirme*.
Jesuits	Society of Jesus: Roman Catholic religious order founded by Ignatius Loyola.
Ghaza (Jihad)	Meaning 'struggle,' divided into Greater and Lesser *Ghaza (Jihad)*.
Ghazi	Warrior. Title given to Sultan Mehmet III after gaining a victory in Hungary.
Ka'bah	Name of altar in Mecca originally claimed to be built by Abraham.
Kabin	Like a dowry, but paid by the man to formalize an Ottoman marriage contract.
Kadi (Cazi)	Ottoman Judge.
Kadin	'Lady/woman' in Turkish. Also, consort of the sultan, having her own quarters.
Kadun Kahia	'Mother of Maids.' Responsible for all *odalisques* inside Imperial Harem.
Kadun	Older matron assigned to watch over the chambers of the Imperial Harem.
Kaimakam	Governor of *Stamboul*, or Deputy Grand Vizier who ruled the Empire while the Grand Vizier is leading the Ottoman army on the European frontier.
Kalga	'He remains.' If the Crimean-Tartar Khan died, the *Kalga* would remain.
Kapi Agha	'Captain of the Gate' of the Seraglio or New Palace; the Chief White Eunuch.
Kapigi (Kapuji)	'Gatekeeper.' In the New (Topkapi) Palace in *Stamboul*.
Kapigi-Bashi	Title of the Head gatekeeper in each of the outer gates of the New Palace.
Kapikullen	Door servant.

Khan   Compound or large home, usually with a large courtyard in the center; Also a title meaning leader, such as Khan of the Crimean-Tartars.

Kira   'Lady' from the Greek. Title of Jewish woman with access to Imperial Harem.

Kizlar(Kislar) Agha 'Master of girls' of the Imperial Harem. Chief Black Eunuch, *pasha* of three tails.

Knight's Templar Military order charged with protecting Christian pilgrims going to Jerusalem from the early 1100s to 1312. Also called the Order of Solomon's Temple.

Köle (kul)   Slave in Turkish.

Kulliye   'Complex' often consisting of a hospital, *medrese*, and a mosque.

League   A measure of land distance of roughly 3 miles. Secondly, a political association.

Legate a Latere   Personal ambassador of the Pope, usually assigned to a specific mission.

Long War   Fought between Ottoman Turkey and the Holy Roman Empire, 1592 to 1607.

Man-of-War   Sailing ship outfitted for battle, often escorted Merchantmen.

Medrese (Madrasa) Islamic school.

Merchantman   Ship carrying goods, often in convoys to the East or West Indies.

Mezes   Turkish appetizers.

Minaret   Cylindrical tower outside a mosque where muezzins issue call for prayer.

Minbar   Pulpit used by an imam inside a mosque.

Misericordia   From the Latin miser 'to pity' & cor meaning 'heart.' To avoid suffering, badly wounded soldiers might cry out '*Misericordia!*' asking 'mercy' meaning death.

Muezzin   Prayer callers.

Muslim   Follower of the Prophet Mohammed and the Islamic religion.

Nargile   Turkish water-pipe.

Nureddin   'Light of the faith.' Third in rank of the Crimean Tartars, behind the *Kalga.*

Oda   Chamber or school.

Odalisque   Virgins in the Imperial Harem.

Orthodox   Refers to the Eastern Christian Church after its split with the Roman Catholics.

Orta   A *janissary* battalion or regiment.

Qibla   Direction of Mecca.

Padishah   Sultan. From the Persian

Palanka	Ottoman fort or palisade reinforced by mortar.
Papal Nuncio	Permanent ambassador or emissary of the Pope.
Pasha (Basha)	A *"pasha* of two tails (horsetails)" denotes an important Ottoman official.
Patriarch	In a role similar to the Pope, the Patriarch of Constantinople led the Greek Orthodox Christians within the Ottoman Empire.
Pinnace	A small boat, usually with sails, used to shuttle between larger ships in a fleet.
Poop Deck	High deck behind the wheel on a ship, located towards the stern.
Qur'an	Koran. Chief book of Islam, written in Arabic.
Ravelin	Pointed bastion.
Rearguard	Last of three regiments (see Vanguard and *Battalia*) in a marching army.
Republiek	'Republic' in Dutch.
Reformation	Effort to "reform" Roman Catholic Church begun by the German Martin Luther and continued by the Frenchman John Calvin, and later by Scotsman John Knox.
Renegade	A person who abandons his upbringing. Used to describe those who abandoned the Christian faith and became Muslim, whether by force or persuasion.
Saatci	'Clockmaker' in Turkish.
Salic Law	French monarchy law whereby only male heirs can reign as king.
Sanjak	Ottoman leader of important towns, such as the Sanjak of Pecs in Ottoman Hungary. Each sanjak provided armed sipahis from timars in time of war.
Saray or Seraglio	From the Persian, meaning 'Palace.'
saucisson	Sack filled with gunpowder used at the Siege of Amiens.
Scimitar	Curved sword.
2nd Spanish Armada	After Sack of Cadiz (1595) by English & Dutch forces, Philip II sent his armada. The first fleet had been destroyed in 1588 in the English Channel
Segban	Paid fighter. Three hundred *segban* joined the Black Scribe rebels in Syria.
Shahadah	One of the five pillars of Sunni Islam: "There is no god but Allah, and Mohammed is his Prophet."
Sharia	Strict Islamic law.
Shia Islam	One of two major divisions in Islam. These followers, called Shiites, believe that Ali, a nephew of and early successor to Mohammed, is the true Caliph.
Shish Kebab	Turkish for 'skewer' and 'roasted.'

| **Skiff** | Small, flat-bottom boat. |

Sipahi — Turkish horsemen provided by leaseholders of Timariots or Ziamets.

Slaag — 'Battle' or 'Fight' in Dutch.

Standard — Symbol of Authority, normally flags on a pole.

Sof — Woven cloth.

Sphendome — rounded portion of a stadium, like the Hippodrome in ancient Constantinople.

Sublime Porte — Originally inside the New Palace, name of the gate before the Ottoman throne.

Sultana — Female member of Ottoman royal family.

Sunni Islam — Orthodox followers of Islam; Ottoman Turks and most Arabs follow the Sunni tradition and its Five Pillars. By contrast, most Persians are Shiites.

Tartaria — Land of the Tartars/Mongols. Greater Tartaria included vast tracts of Siberia, from Muscovy to China. Petite Tartaria included the steppe of Southern Ukraine.

Tartars — A tribe originally conquered by and assimilated into the Mongol Empire. The Tartars (Mongols) had many sub-tribes including the Crimean-Tartars.

Tercio — Spanish fighting unit—consists of 3,000 pikemen, musketeers, & swordsmen.

Ternayki — 'Addicted' in Turkish.

Tiltyard — Jousting yard with a long rail in the middle of it; i.e., *The white knight charges with his sharp lance and tilts at his foe.*

Timar — Non-inheritable feudal Turkish land-holding; the leaseholder is required to
(Timariot) provide and equip at least one *sipahi* rider to the Sultan.

Top-Kapi — 'Cannon Gate.' Gate of the New (Topkapi) Palace in *Stamboul* at Seraglio Point.

Touch-box — Small cylindrical containers holding a single charge of gunpowder.

Trinity (Triune) — Orthodox Christian belief that God the Father, God the Son, and God the Holy Spirit are one God, Three-in-One. Defining, essential tenet of Christianity.

Triple Alliance — Treaty amongst England, France, & Seven Provinces of the United Netherlands.

Ulema — Muslim scholar that helped to define and determine Islamic law.

Vakif (Waqf) — Islamic charitable foundation.

Valide Sultana — The Sultan's Mother, the most powerful woman in the Ottoman Empire.

Valens Aqueduct — Built by the Roman Emperor Valens, the aqueduct carried fresh water to cisterns within Constantinople/*Stamboul*.

Vanguard — Lead regiment or battalion of a marching army.

Var	'Castle' or 'fortress' in Hungarian.
Vero, nihil verius	'Nothing is truer than the truth.' Family motto of the Veres of England.
Vizier *Azem*	First Vizier or Grand Vizier.
Vilayet (Eyalet)	'Province' in the Ottoman Empire.
Voivode	Title of the leader of Moldavia or Wallachia, or other countries in Slavic Europe.
Walloons	A French speaking people of the Lowlands (present-day Belgium).
Ventre-saint-gris	*'The womb of Holy Christ.'* Gascon phrase spoken by King Henry IV. Perhaps a phrase of exasperation, invoking Saint Gris—supposed patron saint of drinkers.
Yemisci	Fruiterer; worker who tends and trims fruit trees. Title of Aisha's betrothed.
Yurt	Movable huts of the Crimean-Tartars
Ziamet	Larger *timar* or land holding. Leaseholders of *ziamets* were required to provide five or more *sipahi* horsemen to the Sultan during the fighting season.

Glossary of People

Nicolaes van der Aa   Personal Guard Captain of Captain-General Maurice of Nassau-Orange.

Abdul Halim (*Kara Yazici*)   Rebel leader in Anatolia. Known as *Kara Yazici* or '*Scrivano,*' meaning 'Black Scribe.' Died in 1602; succeeded by his brother *Deli* Hasan.

Abdul-Miamin Mustafa   *Kadi [Cazi]* of Rumelia, one of two military judges seated in the Divan in 1602, who became the *Kadi* of Anatolia by early 1603.

Abdur-Rezak *Agha*   Black eunuch in Imperial Harem in 1603, assigned to Sultan's Mother.

Baron d'Achicourt   Commander of 1ˢᵗ Walloon Regiment under Count of Varax at Battle of Tielenheide in 1597.

Prince Ahmet   2nd eldest son of Sultan Mehmet III. Son of Handun *Sultana,* 2nd *haseki*.

Aisha   Owner of Captain John Smith in late 1602 and early 1603. Daughter of Sultan Murad III & Safiye *Valide Sultana*. Sister of Sultan Mehmet III. Widow of *Damat* Ibrahim *Pasha* and betrothed to Grand Vizier *Yemisci* (Fruiterer) Hasan *Pasha*. The name Aisha originally derives from the child bride of the prophet Mohammed. (Charatza Tragabigzanda.)

Albert of Austria   Cardinal and former Archbishop of Toledo. Appointed Governor General of the Netherlands. Nephew of King Philip II of Spain and promised in marriage to the King's daughter, Albert's first cousin, *Infanta* Isabella Clara Eugenia.

Sir John Aldrich   English officer at the Siege of Amiens in France.

Alessandro *de* Medici   Cardinal from Florence; The *Legate de Latere* sent to Paris by Pope Clement VIII to negotiate peace between King Henry IV of France and King Philip II of Spain.

Ali *Agha*   Protege of Gazanfer *Agha*, the Chief White Eunuch. After marrying the Chief White Eunuch's sister, Beatrice, Ali rose to become *Agha* of the *Janissaries*.

Duke of Aumale   Charles of Guise. Member of Catholic League in Picardy fighting against King Henry IV, who later served the archdukes in Brussels.

Duke of Bar   Henri II de Lorraine. Second son of Charles, Duke of Lorraine. Arranged to be married to Catherine *de* Bourbon, sister of King Henry IV.

Sir Thomas Baskerville   Colonel of English forces fighting for King Henry IV in France in 1597.

Giorgio Basta   Able Albanian Catholic officer who fought for the Spanish and Albert of Austria in the Lowlands and later for Holy Roman Emperor Rudolph II in Transylvania.

Nicolo Basta   Brother of Giorgio Basta, a Catholic commander of horsemen in the Lowlands.

Sigismund Bathory	Appointed Prince of Moldavia, Transylvania, and Wallachia by Emperor Rudolph II. Captain John Smith fought for Prince Bathory in Transylvania in 1602.
La **Balvena**	*Seigneur*. Assigned to the Count *de La Fera*. Cardinal Albert of Austria sent *la* Balvena negotiate with King Henry IV.
Claude *la* **Barlotte**	Catholic Colonel of 2nd Walloon regiment at Tielenheide. Officer for Cardinal Albert in Lowlands.
Marcellus Bax	Commander of a cavalry unit for Captain-General Maurice van Nassau-Orange.
Beatrice Michael	Venetian sister of Chief White Eunuch Gazanfer *Agha*. She fled her failed second (Fatima Hatun)marriage in Venice and had it annulled in *Stamboul*. After converting to Islam, took the name of Fatima Hatun and married Ali, who later became *Agha* of the *Janissaries*. Assigned to a palace by her brother, she owns 100 or more slaves.
Peregrine Bertie	Friend of John Smith. Younger son of Lord Peregrine Willoughby
Robert Bertie	Friend of John Smith. Older son of Lord Willoughby. Robert fought and knighted at Cadiz in 1596.
Thomas Bostock	Lieutenant Colonel of the Irish regiment at the Amiens.
Catherine *de* **Bourbon**	Reformed Church (Huguenot) member. Sister of King Henry IV. Married Henri II de Lorraine in 1598.
Buonaventura	Sicilian General of the *Cordeliers*, a Catholic religious order, part of the Calatagirona Franciscans.
Kira **Chacun**	Rich Jewish woman allowed access into Imperial Harem circa 1600-03.
Charles II	Former Archduke of Styria, part of Inner Austria. (d. 1590)
Charles V	Holy Roman Emperor. Born in Brussels, Charles abdicated his throne, leaving the Holy Roman Empire to his brother, Ferdinand; the Lowlands, Spain, and New Spain went to his son Philip II.
Charles *van der* **Noot**	Vanguard leader on march to Turnhout; in the Rearguard at Battle of Tielenheide in late January 1597.
Cigala Zade Sinan	*Pasha*. Former Grand Vizier of the Ottoman Empire.
Paul Choart *de* **Buzenval**	French Ambassador of French King Henry IV to the Seven United Provinces of the Netherlands at The Hague.
Jean (John) Calvin	Following in the footsteps of the German Protestant Martin Luther, Calvin, born in Noyon, France, authored *The Institutes of Religion* detailing Reformed Christian doctrine and published in Geneva.
Clement VIII	Pope of the Roman Catholic Church from 1592 to 1603.

Carlos Coloma	Spanish commander at Siege of Amiens in 1597. Wrote *Historia*.
Cristobal *de* **Moura**	Chief Domestic Minister to King Philip II of Spain.
Jeronimo Dentice	Sergeant Major of Catholic forces under the Count of Varax in early 1597. Dentice held direct command of the Neopolitan *tercio* of the Marquis of Trevico.
Robert Devereaux	Earl of Essex. Secretary to Queen Elizabeth.
Dilara	Dutch translator, an *odalisque* of the Imperial Harem. Friend of Aisha.
Henry Docwra	Captain of a company of English footmen under Sir Francis Vere. Later commanded an English regiment in Northern Ireland.
Joseph Duxbury	English Captain who recruited John Smith in Rouen to fight with the English army in France and the Netherlands against the Spanish and their allies.
Queen Elizabeth	Daughter of King Henry VIII and his second wife, Anne Boleyn. Sir Walter Raleigh claimed Virginia and named it after his virgin Queen.
Duke of Epernon	Jean-Louis de Nogaret. Catholic duke, who held Provence in southern France, but submitted to King Henry IV in 1596.
Ernst of Mansfield	Young Catholic Lieutenant to Count of Sultz at Turnhout in 1597.
George Everard	Count of Solms. German commander in service of the United Provinces.
Esperanza Malchi	Former Jewish *Kira* who communicated with Queen Elizabeth for Safiye *Valide Sultana*. Esperanza Malchi amassed wealth and was later killed.
Fatima	Younger sister of Aisha and wife of Khalil *Pasha*.
Ferdinand II	Archduke of Inner Austria (1590-1637). Later, Holy Roman Emperor (1619-1637).
Ferhad *Agha*	*Bostangi Bashi,* Chief Gardener after 1600. Responsible for the New Palace gaurds, grounds, and Sultan's yacht, under Chief White Eunuch.
Filiz	French translator, friend of Aisha.
Francisco *de* **Mendoza**	Admiral of Aragon. High Steward, Head of Household for Albert of Austria. Important military leader.
Francois *ler* **d'Espinay**	*Seigneur de* Luc. Commander of citadel at Montreuil in Northwest France. Appointed Grand Master of the Artillery at Amiens.
Frederik Henry	Younger brother of Maurice of Nassau-Orange. Studied at Leiden.
Gabrielle d'Estrees	*Madame la Marquise de* Monceaux. Mistress of King Henry IV. Mother of two children — their son Cesar and their daughter Catherine-Henriette.

Gazanfer *Agha*
Kapi-Agha, Chief White Eunuch after 1581. Son of a Venetian official, Gazanfe and his siblings were captured at sea. Gazanfer served Selim II, and became Master of the Turban under Murad III. He established a *medresse* next toAqueduct of Valens in 1595, during reign of Sultan Mehmet III.

Ghazi **Giray II**
Warrior Khan of the Crimean Tartars whose nickname *'Bora'* means storm.

Handan *Sultana*
Second *Haseki*. Mother of Prince Ahmet, Sultan Mehmet III's second eldest son.

Mohammed Giray
Former *Kalga* of the Crimean Tartars. Half-brother of *Ghazi* Giray, joined Celali rebellion in Anatolia.

Sahin Giray
Half-brother of *Ghazi* Giray II. Joined Cecali rebellion.

Salamet Giray
Half brother of *Ghazi* Giray II. Joined Cecali Rebellion of *Deli* Hasan *Pasha* in Anatolia.

Savigne *de* **Rosne**
Marshal. Led Spanish attack of Calais; died in Spanish siege of Hulst.

Sefer Giray
Nureddin of the Crimean Tartars. Second Son of *Ghazi* Giray II.

Toktamish Giray
Kalga of the Crimean Tartars. Eldest son of *Ghazi* Giray II.

Lewis(Louis) Gunther
Of Nassau, Cousin of *Stadholder* Maurice of Nassau. Commander of Dutch forces at the Sack of Cadiz in 1596.

Guzelce Mahmud *Pasha*
Sipahi ally. After failure of the eunuch general, Guzelce was appointed by the Imperial Divan to counter *"Deli"* Hasan and the "Cecali" rebellion in Anatolia. Later promoted to *Kaimakam*.

Juan *de* **Guzman**
Spanish cavalry commander for Cardinal Albert at Tielenheide & outside Amiens

Hafiz Ahmed *Pasha*
Governor of Kutahya in Anatolia when it was besieged by *Deli* Hasan *Pasha*.

Haseki **Handun** *Sultana*
Consort to Sultan Mehmet III. Mother of Prince Ahmed.

Richard Hakluyt
Compiled *Principal Navigations, Voyages, & Discoveries of the English Nation*.

Haseki **Halime** *Sultana*
Consort of Sultan Mehmet III. Mother to his eldest living son, Prince Mahmud.

Deli **Hasan** *Pasha*
Hasan *the Fool*. Successor to his brother *Scrivano*, opposed to Ottoman throne.

Hasan Khalifeh
Sipahi leader in *Stamboul*.

Kapuji-Bashi **Hasan**
Head gatekeeper of the Imperial Gate, outer gate of the New Palace.

Saatci **Hasan** *Pasha*	Hasan *the Clockmaker. Kaimakam* in *Stamboul,* Deputy Grand Vizier in 1602. Imprisoned in Castle of Seven Towers before escape to Trebizond.
Tiryaki **Hasan** *Pasha*	Hasan *the Addicted. Fourth Vizier.* Former Agha of the Janissaries. Responsible for Ottoman capture of Kanizsa in 1600, so life spared.
Yemisci **Hasan** *Pasha*	Hasan *the Fruiterer.* The *Vizier Azem,* Grand Vizier of the Ottoman Empire. After the death of *Damat* Ibrahim Pasha, he was engaged to Aisha, Sister of the Sultan. He purchased Captain John Smith at Axiopolis on the lower Danube, late 1602.
Henry IV	Known as Henri *le Grand* (the Great) of House of Bourbon. King of France, also warrior King Henry III of Navarre. Father of Louis XIII.
Hocazade Mehmed	*Effendi.* Grand Mufti from August 1601 to January 1603.
Philip of Hohenlohe	Cavalry Commander, United Provinces of the Netherlands.
House of Bourbon	Name of the royal family of France, starting with King Henry IV.
House of Carafa	Neapolitan noble family.
House of Fuggers	Influential family of German merchants and bankers, allies of the Habsburg.
House of Habsburg	Important dynastic family, providing many of whom served as Emperors of the Holy Roman Empire. Since 1282, the House of Hapsburg provided dukes of in Austria and Styria. Its influence lasted until 1914 when a Serbian nationalist assassinated Archduke Franz Ferdinand in Sarajevo, Bosnia, starting World War I.
House of Lorraine	Ruling family of the independent territory of Lorraine (now France).
House of Medici	Important Italian banking, political, and religious family from Florence.
House of Plantagenet	Royal family of England from 1145 to 1485.
House of Tudor	Royal family of England from 1485 to death of Queen Elizabeth in 1603.
House of Valois	Royal family of France from 1328 to 1589 when King Henry III died.
Huguenots	'Vow Fellows.' Name Catholics called those in France who followed the 'Religion' or Calvinist doctrine. More accurately called Reformed church.
David Hume of Godscroft	Scotsman who met John Smith in Paris and gave him letters of preference to his Scottish friends at the Court of King James VI of Scotland. Notto be confused with David Hume, the Scottish philosopher of the 18th century.
Damat **Ibrahim** *Pasha*	Aisha's first husband who died in 1601; not to be confused with Ibrahim *Pasha,* Grand Vizier of Suleiman *the Magnificent,* who built the Palace of Ibrahim *Pasha*

Infanta Isabella   Daughter of King Philip II of Spain. Promised in marriage to her cousin, Cardinal Albert of Austria. Her full name is *Infanta* Isabella Clara Eugenia.

King James VI, Scotland   Later (1603), King James I of England. In Paris, David Hume of Godcroft gave letters of introduction to young John Smith to take to Scotland. Later, King James I united Scotland and England into Great Britain. Believer in "Divine Rights of Kings" & unhappy with margin notes in the Geneva Bible, James 'authorized' new version, insisting on 'bishops.'

Juan *de* **Idiaquez**   Foreign Minister of King Philip II of Spain.

Katib Jemazi   Important *Sipahi* leader.

Khalil *Pasha*   Former governor of *Stamboul*. Married to Fatima, the younger sister of Aisha.

Khosru *Pasha*   White eunuch. *Beylerbey*, the Governor General of Diyarbakir Province

Henry Lello   English Ambassador to the Sublime Porte from 1597 to 1607.

Marguerite *de* **Valois**   Queen of France. Her husband King Henry IV kept her isolated at the Chateau d'Usson in the south of France while he sought to have their marriage annulled.

Prince Mahmud   Eldest son of Sultan Mehmet III and his *Haseki Sultana* Halime.

Margaret of Austria   Betrothed to Prince Philip, son of King Philip II of Spain.

Marguerite *de* **Bethune**   Young daughter (b. 1595) of Maximilien de Bethune and wife, Rachel.

Marguerite *de* **Valois**   Queen of France. Known as *La Reine* Margot.

Marquis *de* **Montenegro**   Girolamo Carafa. Fought under the Governor Tello at the siege of Amiens. The Neapolitan nobleman led five hundred horseman.

Mathias of Austria   Habsburg Archduke of Inner Austria (1593-1608). Later, Holy Roman Emperor.

Maurice of Nassau-Orange   *Stadholder* in Lowlands. 'His Excellency' was Captain General of the Seven United Provinces of the Netherlands and commanded their army in the field.

Maximilian   Archduke of Further Austria. Member of Habsburg family. Younger brother of Holy Roman Emperor Rudolph II and Cardinal Albert.

Maximilien *de* **Bethune**   Baron *de* Rosny (later Duke of Sully). Advisor & confidant of King Henry IV. A member of the "Reformed" church & responsible for financial reforms in France. Father of Marguerite *de* Bethune by his second wife, Rachel de Cochefilet

Sultan Mehmet III   Ottoman Empire ruler, from 1595 to 1603. Son of Murad III and Safiye *Valide Sultana*. Brother of Aisha.

Nicolas *de* Harlay   see *Seigneur de* Sancy.

Philippe de Mornay   *Seigneur du* Plessis-Marle. Important Huguenot nobleman.

Sultan Murad III   Father of Aisha & Mehmet III. Ottoman Empire ruler who died in January 1595.

Sir Alexander Murray   Commander of the Scottish regiment fighting with the United Provinces

Mustafa *Agha*   A lieutenant to Grand Vizier Hasan *the Fruiterer*. Fought beside *Ghazi Giray* II. Collects provisions in Bosnia and Buda in early 1603.

Nicholas *de* Neuville   *Seigneur de* Villeroy. French nobleman responsible for pay at Amiens.

Sir Edward Norreys   English governor at Ostend.

Nur Banu   *Woman of Splendor*. Venetian Mother of Sultan Murad III, grandmother of Aisha.

Johan van Olden-Barnevelt   Land's Advocate of Holland and West Friesland, a very important ruling position.

Osman *Kizlar Agha*   *Daru's-sa'ade agasi*. Chief Black Eunuch Osman. Oversaw Imperial Harem plus all imperial mosques.

Nicholas Parker   Captain of English horsemen at Battle of Tielenheide Brabant early 1597.

Philip II   King of Spain and obedient Lowlands, and New Spain. Also King of Portugal; son of Holy Roman Emperor Charles V.

Philippe Emmanuel   Duke of Mercoeur, Member of Catholic League and ruler of Brittany in Northwestern France. Full name was Philippe Emmanuel *de Lorraine*.

Philibert *de* Rye   Count de Varax. General of the Artillery for Cardinal Albert. General of Spanish forces at Turnhout & Tielenheide in 1597. Brother of the Marquis of Varambon.

Philip William   Prince of Orange. After his father, Prince William of Orange, was assassinated, Philip William was kidnapped & raised Catholic; also, half-brother of Maurice of Nassau-Orange.

Poiraz Osman *Bey*   *Sipahi* leader promoted by the Grand Vizier Hasan *the Fruiterer* and who, after the fighting season in 1602, returned from Belgrade and joined the conspiracy.

Catherine *de* Parthenay   Dowager Duchess of Rohan. Intelligent and pious Huguenot. Mother of Henri II *de* Rohan (Later, Duke of Rohan) and Anne *de* Rohan.

Count St. Pol   Francois III d'Orleans Longueville. French Governor of Amiens when it fell by deceit in April 1597

Jean Richardot   President of the Privy Council of Cardinal Albert in Brussels

Henri II *de* **Rohan**	Young courtier of King Henry IV. Later, *Duc de* Rohan (1603-1638) and prominent Huguenot defender at la Rochelle.
Savigne *de* **Rosne**	Marshall of Catholic forces, the *Maestro de Campo* General of Cardinal Albert of Austria.
Roxlena	*Hurrem Haseki Sultana.* Great Grandmother of Aisha. Originally from Ukraine, she married to Sultan Suleiman *the Magnificent.*
Rudolph II	Emperor of the Holy Roman Empire, who moved its capital from Vienna to Prague, Bohemia. Rudolph was also King of Bohemia and King of Hungary.
Seigneur de **Sancy**	Nicolas *de* Harlay. Former French ambassador to the Sublime Porte in Constantinople. One of King Henry IV's closest advisors in charge of finances before the king replaced him with Baron de Rosny (Maximilian de Bethune).
Scrivano	Meaning 'Black Scribe." See *Kara Yazici* Abdul Halim.
Safiye *Valide Sultana*	Powerful and influential mother of Aisha and Sultan Mehmet III.
Sekul Murish	Former Prince of Turtzfeld, an independent kingdom in the mountainous border of Transylvania & Wallachia. Saw Grand Vizier Hasan *the Fruiterer* in Belgrade.
Sultan Selim II	Called "The Sot." Father of Murad III, Grandfather of Mehmet III and his sister, Aisha.
Thomas Sendall	Merchant of King's Lynn. John Smith worked as an indentured servant
Captain John Smith	Born in Louth, Lincolnshire, England *circa* 1580. In late 1602, sorely wounded while fighting for the Holy Roman Empire, John was sold into slavery at Axiopolis on the lower Danube, and sent to Aisha, Sister of the Sultan, so she could ransom him. Five years later, Captain John Smith was later elected at Jamestown as the first Colonial Governor of Virginia and, in 1616, became Admiral of New England. In years before George Washington, Smith was referred to as "Father of America."
Karl Ludwig, Count Sultz	Leader of the German regiment at the Battle of Tielenheide in 1597.
Sun'Ullah *Effendi*	Former Grand Mufti (1600 to August 1601), the *Sheikh ul-Islam,* who insisted Grand Vizier Hasan *the Fruiterer* lead the Ottoman Army in its fight against the Holy Roman Empire. Sunni religious leader of the plot against the Chief White and Chief Black eunuchs in early 1603.
Sir Robert Sydney	English Governor of the 'cautionary' town of Flushing (Vlissingen) in Zeeland.
Claude de la Tremoille	Powerful Calvinist (Huguenot). Ally of King Henry IV of France.
Marquis de **Trevico**	Former Commander of Italian *tercio* for Cardinal Albert, who returned to Naples in 1596.

Count of Varax   Philibert de Rye. General of Artillery at capture of Calais in 1596 for
                              Cardinal Albert. Overall commander of Spanish forces at Turnout & the
                              Heath of Tielen, Brabant in early 1597.

Sir Francis Vere   Lord Marshall of the English expedition to Cadiz in 1596; With rank of
                              Colonel, commander of Queen Elizabeth's English forces in Lowlands.

Captain Horace Vere   Younger brother of Sir Francis Vere. Captain of a company stationed in
                              Breda, the Lowlands

Seigneur de **Villeroy**   Nicolas *de* Neufville. French Foreign Minster for King Henry IV.

Lord Willoughby   Peregrine Bertie. Famous English soldier, who knighted Sir Francis Vere
                              at Bergen op Zoom. Former employer of George Smith, the father of
                              John Smith; his two sons, Robert and Peregrine Bertie, were boyhood
                              friends of John.

Etmekji Zadeh   Treasurer for the Ottoman Grand Vizier Hasan *the Fruiterer* in Belgrade.

<h1 align="center">Glossary of Places</h1>

Alcazar	A Spanish royal palace, located in Toledo, Castile, Spain.
Aleppo	Town in northern Syria controlled by the Ottoman Turks.
Amiens	Gateway to Paris on Somme River, Picardy. 'Velvet Siege' site in 1597.
Anatolia	Main Province in Asia Minor, Turkey in Asia.
At-Meidan	Turkish for 'Hippodrome,' ancient 'horse' stadium in Constantinople.
Chateau **d'Aumale**	In Aumale, a town between Rouen, Normandy and Amiens, Picardy.
Axiopolis	Old Roman fort on the lower Danube, near present-day Cernavodă, Romania. Captain John Smith was sold into slavery here in late 1602.
Bakhchysarai	Palace on the Crimean Peninsula. Capital of the Crimean-Tartars.
Baranya *Palanka*	A square palisade in the *Villayet* of Buda, Ottoman Hungary.
Barbary	Northern Coast of Africa on Mediterranean; part of Ottoman Empire.
Belgrade	City on Middle Danube. Grand Vizier Hasan *the Fruiterer* resided there.
Bies Bos	Inland waterway fed by Rhine & Maas rivers, by Brabant & Holland.
Black Sea	Forms the northern coast of Asia Minor and the southern coast of present-day Ukraine and Russia. Crimean Peninsula extends out into it.
Bergen op Zoom	Fortified town in the Lowlands.
Bohemia, Kingdom of	In central Europe with capital at Prague—known as Czech Republic.
Bosphorus Strait	Connects Black Sea to Sea of Marmara; separates Europe from Asia.
Brabant	Province in the Lowlands, located in present-day Belgium.
Breda	Fortified town in the Lowlands.
Brittany	Duchy in northwestern France.
Brussels	Capital of the Obedient (Catholic) Provinces of the Netherlands.
Buda	Important Hungarian town and fort on the Danube. Pest, located on the opposite bank, was a separate town, but now recognized as Budapest.
Bursa	First capital of Ottoman Empire in northwestern Anatolia in Asia Minor.
Byzantium	Earlier name of Constantinople, present day Istanbul.
Cadiz	Port west of Gibraltar, Southern Spain. English sacked Cadiz in 1596.

Calais	French city on the English Channel. Captured by Spaniards in 1596.
Column of Constantine	Located inside Constantinople. Called 'Burnt Column' — result of fires.
Constantinople	Also called *Stamboul* meaning city. Present day Istanbul, Turkey.
Coudenberg Palace	In Brussels. The seat of Albert of Austria.
Crotoy	French town opposite St. Valery at the mouth of Somme River.
Crimea	Peninsulaon northern part of Black Sea. Old home of Crimean-Tartars.
Damascus	Town in Syria controlled by the Ottoman Turks
Danube River	Flows west to east from Alps to Black Sea. Europe's 2nd longest river.
d'el Escorial Lorenzo	Stark palace built by King Philip II outside Madrid. Its full name is San d'el Escorial, since King Philip II won a battle on Saint Lawrence Day.
Divan	Meeting place of Ottoman Council inside second Courtyard of the New Palace; (2) name of that Imperial Council; & (3) raised cushion platform.
Diyarbakir	Important Ottoman seat near the Euphrates assigned to eunuch Khosru *Pasha*
Drava River	Tributary of the Danube.
Edirne	Second Capital of the Ottoman Empire, Called Adrianople in honor of Roman Emperor Hadrian, builder of Hadrian Wall in northern England.
Edirnekapi	Gate leading to Edirne in old Theodosian land walls of Constantinople.
Eski Serai	The "Old Palace," where concubines of the deceased sultan were sent to live out their days. Located where the University of Istanbul stands.
Esztergom	Fort upriver from Buda overlooking the Danube.
Geertruidenberg	Rendezvous location for United Provinces before march to Turnhout.
Golkonda	Kingdom in eastern India. Many 'white' eunuchs who served in the Third Courtyard of the New Palace came from this kingdom.
Gorinchem	Town in the Lowlands.
Groningen	Hanseatic trading town in northeastern part of the Netherlands.
Hagia Sophia (*Ayasofya*)	The famous Byzantine Christian church built by Emperor Justinian around 537 and turned into the main imperial mosque after the Ottoman conquest in 1453.
Hungary	Kingdom in central Europe. Royal Capital of Székesfehérvár captured by Ottoman Turks in 1543. Site of most battles and skirmishes during Long War (1591-1606).

Holy Roman Empire   Fashioned after the ancient Roman Empire, but comprised largely of Christian (both Catholic and Protestant) German states who elected Emperor Rudolph II.

Hulst   Town north of Calais, Marshall Savigne *de* Rosne killed here in 1596.

Ibrahim *Pasha* Palace   The Palace of Aisha, Sister of the Sultan, facing the Hippodrome. Parts of it are still existent, housing the Museum of Turkish and Islamic Arts. Constructed by Ibrahim *Pasha*, Grand Vizier of Suleiman *the Magnificent*.

Iznik   Town in Anatolia, famous for its tiles. Formerly known as Nicaea.

Kaffa (Caffa)   Important Ottoman slave town in Crimea. Present-day Feodosiya.

Kale-Megdan   Upper castle of Belgrade. Seat of Ottoman power in Europe..

(Nagy)Kanizsa   Strong Hungarian fort near Styrian border. Captured by *Damat* Hasan *Pasha* & Ottoman Turks in 1600. Besieged by Holy Roman Empire, 1601.

Karaman (Karamania)   *Villayet* in southern part of Asia Minor. Governed by a *beylerbey*.

King's Lynn   Lynn, formerly Bishop's Lynn. Town in Norfolk County, England.

Kutahya   Important mountaintop town in Asia Minor, where *Beylerbey* of Anatolia resided.

le Havre de Grace   Town at the mouth of the Seine River in northwestern France.

Louth   Town in Lincolnshire, England where John Smith went to school.

The Louvre   Royal palace in Paris. Now a famous museum.

Magnesia   (Magnolia or Manisa). Birthplace of Aisha in western Asia Minor.

Marmara   Sea between *Stamboul* & Asia Minor, derived from island by same name.

Mezo-Keresztes   Battle site in northern Hungary between Sultan Mehmet III & the Holy Roman Empire in October 1596, resulting in an Ottoman victory.

Mohacs   Battle site between Sultan Suleiman and Hungarian King Louis II.

Gate of Monstrescut   Main gate of Amiens on Somme River. Captured by Spanish by deceit.

Montrieul   In northwest France. Citadel under command of French General St. Luc.

Naples (Italy)   Known as Neapolitans. Ruled by a Spanish viceroy from early 1500s.

Navarre   Independent kingdom in Southern France, near Spain. Pau in Bearn is its capital.

Oslijek   On the lower Drava River in Hungary. Location on the long Suleiman Bridge.

| **The Netherlands** | Meaning Lowlands; Seventeen Provinces, once controlled by Spain. During the Eighty Years War, seven Provinces, including Holland, rebelled, while ten remained "obedient" to Brussels and to Spain. |

New Palace — Now known as Topkapi Palace—derived from *Top-Kapi*, Cannon-Gate.

Normandy — William *the Conqueror* invaded England from this Northwest French region in 1066.

Ober-Limbaugh — Fortified town on an island in the Raab River, on the border of Hungary & Styria.

Oosterhout — Small town in Brabant south of Geertruidenberg.

Ostend — On the coast of Flanders. Site of a long siege starting in 1601. Per Anna Simoni, "Spaniards assailed the unassailable and the Dutch defended the indefensible."

Ottoman Empire — Began in *AD* 1299 & lasted until 1922, when Ataturk founded Republic of Turkey.

Pau — Capital of the Kingdom of Navarre. (Southern France)

Pecs — City of 'Five Churches' in Hungary, or, in Latin, **Quinque Ecclesias.** Crimean-Tartar Khan, *Ghazi* Giray II, wintered here in 1602/1603.

Pest — Located on the left bank of the Danube opposite Buda. Now part of Budapest.

Picardy — Region in northwestern France.

Pont au Change — Bridge of Change. Over the Seine in Paris.

Pont au Meunier — Bridge of Millers, downstream from the *Pont au Change* in Paris, but s wept away a few days before Christmas in 1596.

Pozega — Seat of a *sanjak* in Slavonia assigned to the two sons of *Ghazi* Giray II in winter of 1602/03.

Ravels — Small town near Turnhout in Brabant.

Rez — Village in Mountains of Dukagjini, Albania. Birthplace of Safiye *Valide Sultana.*

Ridderzaal — Knight's Hall at The Hague, Holland.

Rouen — City on the Seine River in northwestern France.

Rumelia — Originally called Thrace, later, Land of the Romans / Turkey in Europe.

St. Valery-sur-Somme — Fishing town at mouth of Somme River in France.

Sava River — Tributary of the Danube that empties into Belgrade.

Sehzade Camii	The Prince's Mosque, located near the Valens Aqueduct in *Stamboul*.
Stamboul	Ottoman name for Constantinople, present-day Istanbul, Turkey.
Szekesfehervar	Royal capital of Hungary, conquered by the Ottoman Turks in 1543.
Szigetvar	Town and fort in Hungary, not far from Pecs and Kanizsa.
Tielenheide	Heath of Teilen in Brabant. Location of the Battle of Tielenheide in 1597 between forces of Captain General Maurice and the Count of Varax. Major Dutch victory with capture of 38 flags and a coronet.
Timber Gate	*Odun Kapi* or Woodgate. In seawall of *Stamboul*. Imperial candle workshop site.
Palace *de* **Tuilleries**	Adjacent to the Louvre, known for its gardens. Built by Catherine *de* Medici, Residence of Princess Catherine *de* Bourbon. Burned down in by the Paris Commune in the late 1800s.
Turnout	Small town in Brabant, where forces of Cardinal Albert gathered in early 1597 before Battle of Tielenheide.
Transylvania	Northern province of present-day Romania.
Chateau **d'Usson**	Castle In southern France, where King Henry IV kept his estranged wife, Queen Margot, under guard.
Republic of Venice	An independent entity until the 1800s. Their governing council elected a *Doge*.
Wallachia	Ottoman Tributary. Southern province of present day Romania.
Willemstad	Named for William the Silent, the river port stood in Northern Brabant.
Hotel *de* **Zamet**	Owned in Paris by Italian financier Sebastien Zamet. Site of masquerade in February 1597.

Acknowledgements

The author wishes to thank Gothenburg Konstmuseum for granting permission to use a copy of Henry IV of France at the Siege of Amiens in 1597 by Peter Paul Rubens as artwork on the book cover.

About the Author

Author & Storyteller David Eugene Andrews at Tuileries Gardens, Paris, France

DAVID EUGENE ANDREWS loves languages and has studied German, Chinese, Italian, French, and Dutch. His travels have taken him to the Far East, the Middle East, and Europe. He earned two degrees in International Affairs, including a Master's Degree from Columbia University in New York City, where he specialized in International Economics. He has edited and published numerous international economic forecasts for Fortune 500 companies.

Following the fall of Saigon, he worked at a Vietnamese refugee camp, setting up English as a Second Language classes across the state of Washington. While in Oregon, he co-chaired an International Affairs Symposium on the Middle East and the Oil Crisis. The first time he saw the Great Pyramids of Egypt, he rode horseback over the dunes with a friend. At the height of the Cold War, an AP photographer captured him bearing an American flag, shaking hands with a Russian holding a Soviet flag. USA Today featured Andrews, a former ski instructor at Mt. Hood in Oregon, on its front page during its coverage of the Opening Ceremonies at the 1984 Winter Olympics in Sarajevo, Bosnia.